After taking
taught Mod
worked with
ran a booksh
been writing full time. She lives in Oxford.

ELIZABETH JAMES

Claudia and Amy

HarperCollins*Publishers*

HarperCollins*Publishers*
77–85 Fulham Palace Road,
Hammersmith, London W6 8JB

This paperback edition 1997

3 5 7 9 8 6 4 2

First published in Great Britain by
HarperCollins*Publishers* 1996

Copyright © Elizabeth James 1996

The Author asserts the moral right to
be identified as the author of this work

ISBN 0 00 647978 2

Set in Ehrhardt

Printed and bound in Great Britain by
Caledonian International Book Manufacturing Ltd, Glasgow

To Sid, Deejay, Cathy,
Matt, Kath, Stevie and Laurie
with love and pride

Part One

Chapter One

'Who's she?'

Noel Campion turned to his friend Matthew Kilvert. He indicated a young woman who'd just entered the Kilverts' long, parquet-floored billiard room. It was nine o'clock. In three hours' time 1918 would draw to a close.

Matthew glanced across at the newcomer and frowned, seeming to search his memory. 'I *think* it's the vicar's daughter. Haven't seen her since before . . . If it *is* her she's grown up rather pretty.'

'Yes. That's little Amy Winter.' Matthew's wife, Phyllis, confirmed.

Discreetly, from where he sat with Matthew and Phyllis, Noel continued to observe her. She stood talking to Lavinia, one of Matthew's self-assured younger sisters.

The vicar's daughter – she couldn't be more than eighteen, Noel reckoned – had an appropriately demure look, and wore an unflattering, obviously home-made dress in worn brown velvet, probably cut down from some garment of her mother's. The scooped-out neckline was edged with a lace collar the colour of weak tea. Noel guessed the trimming to be a family heirloom which, over the years, had adorned a succession of dowdy frocks.

But above the gloomy ensemble the girl's cheeks and her grey eyes shone as if from a walk in the freezing December air and her blonde hair curled in graceful, artless tendrils. Her full lips, curved in an attentive, social smile, had an unconscious sensuousness about them. Her features combined to produce the impression of a ravishing, fragile and very English prettiness. He watched her with private interest.

'I'm not sure I can take the speeches that are going to be cranked

3

out at midnight,' Matthew stated suddenly, vehemently. 'Pontificating old buffers who'd cack their breeches in real life if a shell landed within a ten-mile radius . . .'

Phyllis winced at her husband's language, but the homecoming heroes were still permitted a certain leeway. It was less than two months since the armistice had been signed.

Coldly Matthew's eyes followed the portly figure of his father crossing the room to join Lavinia and the vicar's girl. 'Glorious new era, I can just hear it, of sugar and spice and all things nice for God's chosen people – bucketfuls of jingoistic claptrap vomiting out in great smug, rolling waves. The war *they* started and sent other poor idiots out to die in.'

'Leave it, Matt.' His friend's unrelenting resentment produced a deep weariness in Noel, for all he agreed with most of what he said. Last night he'd witnessed a snarling brawl blow up out of nothing between Matthew and his father. Two days earlier Noel had fled his own home, unable to cope with the sentimental talk of 'our dead boys'. But it was the same wherever you went.

During the month or so since he'd been home from France, Noel had felt chilled by a bleak and bleary indifference to everything. And then, from time to time, the inertia would erupt into sudden anger, exploding like boiling lava from some subterranean volcanic tension.

'. . . Would have thought you'd be ecstatic at being with your nearest and dearest at long last. We've been simply dying to have you all home for Christmas and now you seem so grouchy and quarrelsome . . .' Phyllis's round, pleasant face was screwed into an expression of simpering reproach. No, that was churlish. Unfair. She was a nice woman. But Noel felt too apathetic to respond to her teasing.

'We're brutes, Phyll.' The attempt at badinage was tired and hollow.

Sometimes Noel had the impression that he was looking out on a world that had nothing to do with him, some setting from a Hogarth cartoon, peopled with grinning grotesques. Now, at the Kilverts' New Year party, the feeling invaded him again. The faces in the room repelled him, looked greedy, self-indulgent, callous. And, unbidden, images of men in his division drifted into his head. Young faces,

4

taut, hard, not social masks. His mind flashed a picture, flaring like the dazzle of a tracer-shell. A skewed head, distorted mouth, wild, sightless eyes. The boy Walters, suspended in a vile ooze of mud and excrement. Bone-white, hollow-eyed, shockingly beautiful as an angel of death. Noel held his breath, willed the image to recede.

He gazed across at the girl Amy. Talking gravely and attentively to Lavinia and her father, Arthur Kilvert, she appeared to be playing her part in the social game. And yet it seemed to Noel that she was going through the motions in some way. He fancied he saw a scepticism in her grey eyes, a holding back. And, perversely, his mind linked her young face with the shadowy visions of dead soldiers that haunted him.

Touching Matthew's arm, Noel said, 'Introduce me to the vicar's daughter.'

Amy had never felt comfortable at the Kilverts'. The invitations they issued were more like summonses. Throughout her childhood – at irregular intervals, and always at very short notice – she'd been sent for to provide stopgap entertainment for the Kilvert girls, Lavinia and Charlie.

The Kilvert family's call always sent Margaret, Amy's mother, into a frenzy of anxiety. In an instant Amy would be ordered to stop whatever she was doing. She would be washed and brushed with brutal thoroughness and made to change into a dress that never normally saw the light of day except on high days and holidays. And even then Margaret would straighten her collar and pull at her skirt, dab at her hair with moistened fingers, as if she were still vaguely dissatisfied with her daughter's appearance.

Then Amy would walk resentfully to the other end of the village and up the long, wide, gravelled drive towards the towering three-gabled silhouette of Beech House, feeling small and exposed, imagining every window held a pair of scornful eyes. She didn't really think Charlie and Lavinia wanted to play with her and she certainly didn't want to play with them. They were noisy, boisterous girls and Margaret had impressed on her that she wasn't their equal. They

5

were the squire's children. Nowadays a lot of people thought the word 'squire' a bit of a joke, but Margaret wasn't one of them.

Amy was embarrassed by the fact that Mrs Kilvert would talk about her, just as if she wasn't there, to any visitor who happened to be present.

'Most of the Crofton village children are impossible. But Amy's really quite presentable – the vicar's sprog, you know.'

There'd been an afternoon when Amy was about ten, when she, Lavinia and Charlie were skipping, getting on quite well in fact. The Kilvert parents had had guests for lunch and were showing them round the garden. It seemed to Amy that the grown-ups were rather red in the face and laughing a lot. Someone asked who she was and Mrs Kilvert explained.

'Pretty kid,' a man said and stared at her, stared really hard, making Amy feel so self-conscious that her legs wouldn't obey her and she stopped skipping and just stood there, wishing the ground would swallow her up.

'She's a dear!'

'Oh, Amy's a sweetheart,' the Kilvert parents had chorused with a fulsomeness that was absolutely out of character. Amy knew their raptures to be false, and they knew she knew. But they didn't care. All they were interested in was putting on a show of niceness for their guests. And Amy could only blush and look a fool.

Now she was seventeen, Amy was better at keeping her poise. She took the Kilverts with a pinch of salt. Life as vicar's daughter in the tightly knit Cotswold village of Crofton entailed a multitude of obligations. The Kilverts were just one among many. To be fair, they treated her affably, though Amy wasn't blind to their self-congratulatory, 'hobnobbing-with-the-lower-orders' heartiness – an impersonal joviality that Margaret defined reverently as 'breeding'.

After all these years her mother became as agitated as ever when Amy was summoned to Beech House, fussing over her clothes and her hair. Amy let her fuss. It was easier that way. Margaret had fretted and chivvied before she came out to the party tonight.

'Don't forget to hold your Dorothy bag over that worn patch in your skirt.'

'Won't you wear my silk rose in your hair, Amy?'

'Give me your left shoe. I'll dab a bit of black ink over that scuff mark.'

Privately Amy was perplexed. Why was Margaret so het up? Did she think Amy would let them down? The Kilverts, surely, knew her well enough after all these years. Or did she perhaps harbour the secret hope that her daughter might meet some suitable young man? Amy was under no illusions. The Kilverts invited her to make up the numbers, to make themselves feel democratic, part of the fabric of village life. Lavinia and Charlie and most of the women there would be wearing new, slim, fashionable dresses in silky materials and heartening colours. In her old-fashioned, made-over velvet Amy would look like a poor relation.

She'd run into Charlie the day before in Crofton High Street. Charlie was rushing as usual, climbing into the back of one of the Kilvert family motors while a chauffeur held the door.

'See you tomorrow, Amy.' Charlie looked flushed and charming in a low-brimmed dark blue hat and a matching coat worn dashingly loose and open. 'It won't be just the usual crowd. Matthew's asked one of his war chums. He's staying with us now. He's awfully good-looking.' The chauffeur slammed the door and Charlie waved vaguely as they pulled away.

The news made little impact. Charlie never seemed to recall that her 'usual crowd' was not Amy's. Amy doubted she'd be able to distinguish Matthew's awfully good-looking friend from anyone else.

But tonight it was impossible not to be cheered by the festive atmosphere of the Kilverts' spacious billiard room. Electric lights glowed inside red and amber lanterns. A ten-foot Christmas tree shone silver in the far corner and a quartet of musicians played tunes that everyone knew. The men in evening dress formed a sombre background, against which the silks and satins of the women's dresses glowed bright as jewels. The scene struck her forcibly as a positive incarnation of the brave new dawn of peace everyone was talking about.

The first person she bumped into was Lavinia, plump and peachy in pale pink silk, a beaded bandeau in her upswept brown hair.

7

'I'm admiring your decorations,' Amy said.

'They *do* look lovely, don't they? Actually we've been slaving like Trojans all day to set up the lighting.' A wry smile. 'You can't trust the servants with anything electrical.' Dramatically Lavinia laid one small, soft hand to the complicated ruching that covered her breasts. 'Quite frankly I'm exhausted as it is. I'm sure I must look a wreck. Honestly, Amy, this is the fourth do I've been to in five days. I just can't stand the pace!' A pause. 'Have you been madly busy over Christmas?'

'Well, there was the candlelit supper two nights ago . . .' Amy began drily.

'Oh yes! We so much wanted to put in an appearance . . . Only there were so many other . . .'

Amy murmured reassurance. 'It didn't matter, doesn't matter . . .'

The candlelit supper was an annual event, in which the poor of Crofton were treated to a seasonal meal by their better-off neighbours. And, yet again, Amy found herself cornered into one of *those* conversations with the Kilvert girls – exchanges in which she figured as the vicarage prig and Lavinia or Charlie expressed voluble and insincere regrets at having been unable to play their part in whatever charitable activities had just taken place. The underlying implication being that Amy had nothing better to do with her time, while their lives brimmed over with invitations and fun. It was true. Those were their respective roles. But Amy couldn't help wishing that the obvious need not be restated every single time they met.

'Lavinia keeping you entertained is she, young lady?' Arthur Kilvert joined them, sweating and genial.

'Absolutely.' Amy smiled at him. Then, by way of conversation, she remarked, 'You must be so happy and relieved to have Matthew home safe and sound.'

Lavinia pouted. 'Except that he's a shocking old grouch.'

'Lavinia!' Arthur remonstrated. He turned to Amy. 'The boy's frightfully tired. He's exhausted. And it's hardly surprising.'

Amy could see Matthew across the room, sitting with his wife, Phyllis, and a tall, fair man. She hardly knew Lavinia's older brother. He'd always been away at school, at university, in the army.

8

She had just one memory of him and it was years old. Amy recalled standing by the tennis court with Charlie and Lavinia, watching him play with a friend. All at once there was a cry, 'Get out of the way!' and his solid young man's bulk had hurtled towards them, chasing a difficult ball. They scattered. He missed and yelled, 'Buzz off, you sprogs!' Amy had been quietly impressed with his sweating and panting, his casual rudeness.

Out of nowhere the memory came back to her, as she chatted stiltedly to Lavinia and Arthur Kilvert. Then suddenly Matthew was standing in front of her, with his broad, blunt features and crisp, cropped hair. He was bending towards her, greeting her as if they were old friends.

'How are you, Amy? So good to see you after . . . I can't imagine how many years. May I introduce Noel Campion, a comrade-in-arms . . . Noel – Amy Winter.'

Behind him stood the tall man she'd glimpsed from across the room. He stepped forward and took her hand. To Amy there seemed something grave and sincere in his smile that immediately set him apart from the Kilverts.

At eleven o'clock a buffet supper was served and Noel managed to isolate himself with Amy in two rattan chairs he found in the conservatory, carried through and placed next to the Christmas tree, some distance away from any of the Kilvert clan. He was half surprised by his own energy and enterprise in contriving to be alone with the young woman. He would have thought the effort beyond him.

The meal was lavish, with potted venison and hare, roast pheasant, smoked duck, a variety of salads and sharp relishes, fancy breads and rolls, along with glasses of a full-bodied Bordeaux.

'You'd never think there'd been a war,' Amy marvelled. She ate with appetite, balancing the plate on her knees, but didn't touch the wine, Noel noticed.

'You've had shortages then?' he asked, for something to say.

'You don't want to hear my civilian bleatings.' She was quoting Matthew, who'd been holding forth scornfully on the peevish self-pity

9

of the stay-at-homes over the minor inconveniences they'd had to suffer.

He smiled. 'Yes I do.'

'I mean we haven't gone hungry exactly. It's just –' a quick, enchanting smile – 'you can get awfully tired of split-pea soup.'

'So I imagine.' Noel had detected signs of defensiveness when Amy talked to the Kilverts. He had the impression that she felt more at ease with him, more able to be herself. Why this should be he couldn't tell, but the thought pleased him.

At the same time he felt rather at a loss, foolishly out of practice in the art of social flirtation, or even ordinary, everyday conversation.

'You did war work, I suppose?' How dreary he sounded.

'Oh lots. My father's the Vicar of Crofton, so you can guess . . . Bazaars, bottling fruit, bandage-rolling and the like. Oh, and I've knitted more than my fair share of khaki socks, I can tell you.'

Noel laughed. The reply delighted him. The girl seemed exotic to him with her candid self-mockery, the way her thoughts and moods showed in her eyes, in the quirk of her lips.

He was twenty-seven. Only nine or ten years older than she. But he felt that aeons separated him from such lightness of heart. He could no longer recapture a sense of himself in the time before his life became hedged about by anger and fear that hardened little by little into a numb deadness of spirit. A deadness that wasn't just a shell round something warm and living, but coldness and inertia through and through.

'I'm not asking you about your experiences. I hope you understand,' Amy said suddenly. Her grey eyes looked searchingly into his. 'I read a long piece in the newspaper the other day that said you shouldn't press . . . You should wait for the men back from the front to tell you what they want. When they feel ready, that is.'

It was as if she'd read his mind. He was disconcerted by her sudden seriousness. 'Certainly, I'd rather not . . . I appreciate your thought . . .' And simultaneously he was invaded by a sharp sense of the absurdity of the exchange – the tactfulness of this *child*, his own startled, stammered acknowledgement.

'What will you do now you're back to normal life?'

'I write. I'm a journalist. I've got the offer of a job from *Witness* magazine.'

He expected the name to mean nothing, but her face brightened. 'Really? I see that sometimes. Mr Bessell, the headmaster, passes it on to us. My mother disapproves, though. Too free-thinking. She tries to throw it away as soon as my father's read it. But most of the time I beat her to it.'

Noel was surprised and intrigued. He reproached himself for assuming that this girl's life was wholly rural, wholly pastoral, all of a piece. *Witness*'s readership was largely liberal and politically informed, comparatively avant-garde.

'Your father doesn't disapprove, though?'

'No, he's quite broad-minded. Too much so for some people.'

This hint of wider-ranging interests lent piquancy to her almost ethereal prettiness. As he looked at her Noel felt cloddish and unworthy, like Caliban casting covetous eyes on some fair creature from another world. With the bloom of her skin, the touching childish softness of her hair, her smiling yet diffident eagerness, she was so perfect, so unspoiled. She seemed not flesh and blood, but something more flawless and enduring. Noel knew from experience that flesh and blood were ugly and vulnerable, rotted and stank. He was filled with the abrupt and ineradicable conviction that this girl – with her youth, grace and kindness – was the one person in all the world who could melt the thick-ribbed ice in his soul.

Chapter Two

Ever since Amy could remember, a large, gilt-framed photograph of her mother had stood in the small parlour next to the kitchen where, from the age of four, she used to do her piano practice. It showed Margaret as she'd looked aged nineteen, shortly before her wedding to Edward Winter.

In the picture Margaret had on a plain, dark dress with a high neck and long, narrow sleeves. At her throat was a delicate crucifix on a chain, which she still wore. She was unsmiling, her face inclined slightly forward and to one side, while her eyes gazed straight at the camera, wide and untroubled. Small shadows at the corners of her mouth lent a wistfulness to her expression. Her pale hair, brushed back from the forehead, had a sideways sweep which softened the severity of the style. In her simplicity Margaret was beautiful, immaculate.

Amy had stared at the photograph so often and for so long that every line, every nuance of light and shade, were imprinted on her brain for ever. As a young child, when she read stories of female saints, it was this image of her mother that came to mind.

And even now, when her view of Margaret was considerably more realistic, when she knew the disappointments and rancours that writhed beneath her parents' relationship, Amy could still look at that picture and imagine how Edward, as an unworldly curate, might have been dazzled by this vision of alluring purity.

Edward and Margaret had married at the turn of the century. Edward was just back from Rhodesia, where he'd spent five years teaching in a small, remote missionary school. He loved the heat and colour of Africa and would have stayed there but, approaching his mid-thirties, he began to dream of a wife and family.

He returned to England and became curate of a church in Gloucester. Margaret White was a young parishioner who lived with her widowed mother and made ends meet by giving piano lessons. Shortly after the wedding Edward was made vicar of the church of St Michael in nearby Crofton. Amy, their first child, was born the next year. A square, sturdy house of honey-coloured stone served as vicarage and the Winter family home.

Crofton had been Amy's world for all of her seventeen years. The Norman church of St Michael lay at the village's northernmost tip, set in a damp green hollow studded with rows of gravestones mottled turquoise and ochre with lichen. To the south stood Beech House with its pastures and deciduous woodlands. Two large farms occupied the eastern and western outskirts. The village High Street and tributaries were a jumble of houses, cottages and shops all built in the same mellow stone as the vicarage. On bright days in winter the bricks seemed to glow with sharp mustard-yellow tints, which faded in summer to a warm, soft amber.

As a child Amy loved the ducks on the pond by the green, the plaster pig in the butcher's window with its striped apron and roguish eyes. Best of all was the heroic inn-sign for the George and Dragon. She used to be in love with pallid, noble St George until the sign was repainted and his lips became too pink, his eyes too blue and bright.

In those days she took the village for granted in the same way as she took her parents for granted, and her three younger brothers and her grandmother, who lived with them. This place, these people were her life.

Then, one night when she was nine, Amy woke to hear Edward and Margaret arguing in the passage outside the room she shared with three-year-old Phillip, her youngest brother.

'Are you mad? The whole day with that drunken sot!' Margaret's voice had the high, furious pitch that Amy dreaded when it was directed at herself.

'The man was dying.' There was a hard hostility in Edward's tone.

'Twelve whole hours. Give me strength!'

'He was dying in that filthy shack. I was the only person in the world –'

13

'The Lucases were waiting for you! From midday until four. You told them you'd be there. Don't tell me you couldn't have found someone to sit with old Gaskin!' She spoke the name with venomous contempt.

'There are things more important than the whims of a local land-owner. You astound me with your callousness. This was comfort for a dying man, Margaret.'

'So saintly, so perfectly pleased with yourself. And meanwhile I have to make lame excuses to the Lucases' housekeeper and she looks at me as if I'm something the cat brought in.' Margaret's accusations took on a kind of overwrought rhythm. 'These people are important to you and you spend the day with that tramp. I don't suppose he even knew who you were by then. You're just a fool and a self-righteous fool at that!'

'That's enough!' Edward silenced her with threatening finality. It sounded like the voice of God.

Amy was scared and shocked by this evidence of antagonism between her mother and father. She believed grown-ups all liked each other, agreed with each other, that they all thought the same way.

If anything she sided with Margaret. The Lucases were important people. That was one of the facts of life. And yet nearly every day Edward told them that everyone was equal, no one was any better than anyone else. But old Gaskin was horrible. He smelled. His coat was streaked with dirt and he had a wet, pink tongue like a dog's and there was snot in his beard. Secretly Amy had a feeling of guilty relief that he was dead and she wouldn't have to walk past him outside the George and Dragon any more.

But the scene she'd overheard – curled in the blind warmth of her bed, with little Phillip breathing peacefully beside her – turned everything on its head. Until then Amy had never questioned the premise that her parents were two-in-one, indivisible. If that was a lie, who knew what else might prove to be untrue. She began to look at people more closely and think about what they said.

Margaret loomed largest in her world, so most of all Amy examined her mother. She started to notice things she didn't like. The memory of Margaret's private taunting of her husband was disturbingly at odds with the image she presented the world of forbearing self-sacrifice. 'Duty' was her favourite word, pronounced with a special quick, nervous, yet oddly gloating smile: the same smile that flickered when she turned down any mild pleasure – a walk in the woods with Edward and the children, an after-lunch cup of tea in the garden in the sun – in favour of carrying out some joyless parish chore.

It was the same when her mother imposed these obligations on others. On a day, say, when Amy was asked to tea with her friend Nancy Bessell, Margaret might give that small, elusive smile before replying, 'No, it won't be possible, Amy. I need you to help me get the vestry ready for this evening's bible class.'

Nancy Bessell was the daughter of Leonard Bessell, headmaster of Crofton Elementary School. She and Amy were in the same class. Margaret considered the family sufficiently exalted for Amy to be allowed to stay to tea on occasion, home chores permitting. Right from her first visit to the Bessells, Amy was astounded by their free-and-easy ways.

She remembered sitting at the table in the comfy, untidy parlour, rather shy that first time, with Nancy, Mrs Bessell, and Nancy's two brothers, Curly and Davey.

'Oh, Ma,' Curly had groaned, 'not another of your rubbery bread puddings.'

Amy held her breath at the lese-majesty.

'You could use it to mend boots with,' little Davey chirped.

'Want your ears boxed, my lad?' Mrs Bessell was tall and beaky with a toothy smile. She raised her fists threateningly, but Amy could see she didn't really regard the boys' remarks as cheek, more as a cosy, well-worn joke they were all a part of.

'I'd better warn you, Amy,' Nancy's mother grinned across the table, 'I'm not a great one for cooking or anything like that.' She held up a slice of the infamous bread pudding. 'This would probably bounce if you dropped it on the floor.'

Amy listened, shocked and intrigued by the novelty of the confession.

'To be quite honest,' Mrs Bessell went on, 'I'm just an out-and-out

15

bookworm. On a sunny day I'll think, blow the house, and I'll go and sit in the garden with a cup of tea, a round of beef sandwiches and a lovely fat novel.'

Over the years the Bessell house had become Amy's second home. After a visit there she was always struck by the atmosphere of . . . caution that reigned in the vicarage, and by her own mother's need to appear faultless. In the Winter household, if the potatoes were undercooked, no one said anything. There was an instinctive conspiracy of silence. Margaret must not be undermined.

When Amy was a child the grown-up she most trusted was Grandma White, Margaret's mother. She was a small, slight woman with a young complexion, who wore her greying hair in long, thin plaits that wound round her head like a crown. Grandma looked always the same, dressed in black, bandbox neat. Amy knew her grandmother would always listen to what she had to say, would never hurt her feelings.

But even as a young child it was clear to her that her Grandma wasn't as important as Edward or Margaret. She didn't have the same say in the running of the family, even the running of her own life.

'Mother, could you see to the vegetables,' Margaret would say in the same cool, commanding voice as she used to Amy herself. It didn't matter if, just at that very moment, Grandma was playing beggar-my-neighbour with the children.

'Certainly, dear.' She would jump up with docile haste, leaving the game unfinished.

To Amy her grandmother seemed terribly old. At the same time she had a funny feeling that the friendship between them was almost furtive, like the solidarity between two children who are powerless in the hands of omnipotent adults.

When Amy was ten or so Grandma fell ill and lay in bed coughing for a long time, perhaps even more than a year. Amy wasn't sure.

'Sit with Grandma' became one of the children's chores. Amy didn't mind doing it. The room was clean and warm and Amy could read. Grandma smiled wanly at her from time to time and Amy knew she liked her being there.

Then one day, when she came home from school, Grandma had died. Amy was allowed to see her, lying where she always had, but still and white, her mouth half open, skin sunk against the bones of her face. Amy stared, awe-struck. Two days later, in history lesson, it dawned on her that she would never see Grandma again. She laid her head on the desk and couldn't stop crying.

But everything carried on. After a bit you almost forgot that it hadn't always been just Edward, Margaret and the children. It was as if deep water had closed over Grandma's life, Amy thought, leaving no trace.

From the age of eight each of the three Winter boys – Andrew, Eric and Phillip – was sent away to an academically reputable Anglican boarding school in Gloucester. Their education was funded by a charity set up to cater for the sons of clergymen. Daughters were not provided for and, since the Winters were not well off, Amy attended the local village school.

She felt no resentment over the uneven treatment. If anything, Amy was relieved not to be removed from everything and everyone she knew. Margaret considered most of the village children too common for her daughter to visit in their homes, but during school hours Amy reckoned that what the eye didn't see . . . She felt free to play with anyone she pleased, though lanky, ringleted Nancy Bessell remained her best friend. But Margaret would have had hysterics if she'd known that the sweetheart Amy had chosen for herself – and who remained so throughout her schooldays – was Paul Oates, sixth child of the feckless, notorious Oates family of poachers and scroungers.

Paul was a tall, skinny boy with a narrow face and dark hair that hung in his knowing, black eyes and gave him a sort of squinty smile. Amy loved that smile – so secretive and alert, so unconsciously, perfectly devastating. His clothes were old and shabby but he wore them with what she could later define as natural elegance. At the time she just thought he looked nicer than the good boys in their Eton collars and flannel knickers.

17

She knew, of course, that all right-thinking people regarded the Oateses with distaste. It was one of those accepted facts that gave the more virtuous villagers something in common, something to talk about, along with the weather and the price of coal.

The Oateses were a big family, far too big for the ramshackle cottage they lived in on the edge of Arthur Kilvert's woodland – 'just handy for them to help themselves to his deer and pheasant,' people sniggered.

Ida Oates was a self-assured, sharp-tongued woman – a breeding machine, the local gossips termed her. She generally had her latest brat slung slantwise across her body, swaddled in a dirty red knitted shawl. Her glossy black hair was forever coming loose and hanging down her back in a slatternly tangle. Her comings and goings were observed by the men of Crofton with furtive, unacknowledged fascination.

Jesse Oates boasted the same thick black hair as his wife. He was tall and strong, had no regular employment, but people hired him by the day when they wanted some rough digging done, recommended him to their neighbours if a path or a wall needed repairing.

'He's cheap. Only keep an eye on him and don't leave anything lying around.'

From the day they could walk the Oates children were taught all the illicit skills they needed for survival – poaching and scrumping, opportunistic pilfering, the knack of being in the right place at the right time in order to peddle some ill-gotten prize to the very person who happened to need it.

The qualities that made the Oates tribe the scourge of the adult community rendered them glamorous and desirable in the eyes of their fellow pupils. Amy was highly honoured to be claimed by Paul as his partner in country dancing lessons, and pursued by him when a game of kiss-chase was mooted in the playground.

Amy and Paul would exchange kisses in the little bindweed-festooned alley behind the smelly toilet huts. And once she held up her skirt while he pulled down her drawers, but straight away she got scared in case anyone saw them and told Margaret, and she never let him do that again.

18

Amy remembered sitting in that same alley all through one long dinner playtime on a sultry July day, with her back against the crumbling brickwork of the girls' toilets, arms circling her knees. Nancy was there too and a boy called Hubert Green, and all three of them listened enthralled while Paul Oates told them how babies were made. The bricks were cool against her back, her face and legs baked. A low, excited incredulity knotted her stomach as Paul proceeded with his matter-of-fact explanation.

'My big sister's up the spout,' was his laconic parting shot. The phrase and his tone of voice stayed with Amy for the rest of her life.

She loved him with all her heart, but in the street with Margaret, or anyone who might tell, Amy had to ignore him. The crass hypocrisy of it made her smoulder inwardly with resentment and shame, but Paul seemed to understand and not to mind.

All through school they were a pair, their relationship recognized by their fellows. But after they left everything changed. Amy was home-bound, forced to help her mother with household tasks and parish obligations. She was never alone. She and Paul drifted apart and after a while she heard he'd taken up with Bridget Hodge, who was pasty-faced and dumpy, not worthy of him at all. But she was said to be fast, so that must be what he saw in her.

'Your Pa looks like someone out of the Bible,' Paul had mocked once.

'No he doesn't!'

Amy hated it when anyone pointed out that her family were holy, different in some way. But secretly she'd always thought Edward resembled John the Baptist – tall, sinewy, bearded, hollow-cheeked. His hair was rough and curly and looked wild if he didn't have it cut often enough. There was a swarthiness to his skin, as if the African sun had marked him for ever. His brown eyes could be distant and other-worldly, but when he preached they held those of his listeners with disconcerting intensity.

Until Amy was fourteen and left school, she and Edward merely coexisted. To her he was a remote figure who wore a black cassock

19

and was constantly preoccupied with weighty, worthy matters, like birth and death, the comforting of the bereaved, the counselling of the distressed. He left the running of the house and the family entirely to Margaret and never interfered.

But, her schooldays over, Edward stepped in. It was as if he'd suddenly woken up to the discrepancy between Amy's education and that of the boys, grasped the unfairness of it. Actively he resisted Margaret's plans to make Amy's life a facsimile of her own, a round of domestic and parochial minutiae – until such time as a suitable husband came on the scene.

'You must *never* stop learning, Amy,' Edward urged now. 'Not even when you're old and grey.'

He began to lend her books and newspapers and the copies of *Witness* magazine that Leonard Bessell passed on to him. And he made it quite clear that all this was vital, not some optional frippery to be crowded out by jam-making and visiting the sick.

Amy was delighted by this novel turn of events, thrilled to have Edward on her side. Her father's endorsement, his interest in her, lent reading an aura of magic. She devoured the books and periodicals he offered and discussed them with him, feeling adult and important. It was a two-way process. Amy could see that Edward derived genuine, unlooked-for pleasure from this new companionship with his eldest child. The knowledge made her glow.

Margaret was furious. The children – and especially Amy – had always been her unchallenged province. Now, abruptly, here was her husband poking his nose in, encouraging the child in some typically useless and time-wasting course of action.

'What on earth is the good of it?' Amy could picture Margaret's face above the supper table – just a few days after Edward had first made his decree – flushed, hostile, her voice high and hectoring. 'The girl will marry. There are a hundred more useful things she could be learning!'

'Amy's got a brain. She's got intelligence. It should be encouraged for its own sake. Expediency, Margaret, is not the sole yardstick.' Always Edward exuded moral superiority, absolute certainty. He remained master in his own house.

The dispute added a fresh dimension to the continuing battle between the two of them. At home, if not elsewhere, their differences were out in the open now, no longer a hushed secret from the children, to be aired only after they were safely tucked up in their beds. Even eight-year-old Phillip, shortly to join his brothers at boarding school, had a wordless understanding of the situation.

Margaret considered Edward idealistic, unrealistic, a kind of saintly fool. Someone who wilfully neglected to cultivate the sort of people who could do him good and spent far too much time sorting out the problems of ineffectual nobodies who took advantage of his conscientious nature. A man who would never amount to anything in the real world.

As for Edward, he was profoundly disillusioned with the sweet, devout beauty he thought he'd married. She had turned out to be a remorseless snob who would roll over like a performing dog for anyone with money or land, but – though she carried out her duties as vicar's wife coolly and punctiliously – had not the faintest interest in the poor and the powerless.

More than ever, after she left school, Amy found she needed to escape to the easy-going Bessell household. Nancy lived in an elongated two-storey cottage by the green which, in autumn, was bright with the orange berries of a pyracantha bush that grew up the façade as high as the eaves.

'I'm off to see Nancy.'

Each time the words were a gauntlet she threw at Margaret's feet. Since she'd started reading newspapers and topical magazines Amy had come across the notion of women's rights. Margaret turned red with anger if the girl so much as mentioned the phrase and Amy knew that she was trapped – like a goldfish in a bowl – in her preordained role as vicar's daughter. Deciding when and how often to visit her friends seemed a small enough freedom to claim. Margaret made scenes though, tried to squash the slight rebellion. But on this issue Amy was not going to back down.

Ellen Bessell's kitchen was large, cosy and untidy, the chaotic heart of the house. There were plants on the windowsills, piles of books on the big Welsh dresser, Nancy's bold watercolours on the walls –

since leaving school her friend had enrolled in painting classes in Gloucester. An atmosphere of warmth engulfed Amy as soon as she entered the back door.

'Come in! Come in, dear. How lovely to see you.' Mrs Bessell's welcome never disappointed. In her friend's house Amy felt whole-heartedly accepted.

Tea would be brewed and Ellen, Nancy and Amy would chat round the kitchen table, gossip and laughter shading into concern at the latest news from the war. Sometimes Curly and Davey would be there, good-naturedly teasing and provoking. Always Amy felt heartened by the atmosphere of tolerance and affection.

Now she'd started to go there more often, it began to dawn on Amy that Edward, too, regarded the Bessells' house as a refuge. Often she would hear his voice in Leonard Bessell's study, then her father might come into the kitchen to say hallo. Amy was always struck by how easy and smiley he looked, far more so than he ever did in his own home.

The war produced further tensions at the vicarage. Edward had not been impressed by the euphoric patriotism that greeted the onset of hostilities. He could find no righteous justification for the slaughter. And, by the time she'd read a succession of oblique hints in *Witness* magazine – outright allegations would have been ruthlessly censored – as to the incompetence and corruption rife among the top brass, Amy agreed with him unreservedly.

Margaret was appalled. The Kilverts and the Lucases had sent sons to the front – she made no mention of the humbler village lads who'd volunteered. Alan Lucas had died at Mons.

'What gives *you*, Edward, the right to belittle his sacrifice?'

As always, in argument, Margaret was immediately choleric while Edward retained a majestic certainty.

'That's not what I'm doing at all,' he explained with ostentatious patience. 'I'm saying that his sacrifice is for no good cause. Can you not see the difference?'

But, for once, Edward showed some caution. His liberal views were already unpopular with the local landowners. He knew it was more than his position was worth to preach pacifism from the pulpit.

At the same time he declined to hold God-on-our-side thanksgiving services to mark the Allies' all-too-rare successes.

By the same token Amy was sucked into a maelstrom of patriotic bustling. Margaret thrived on the heightened atmosphere, organizing a plethora of fund-raising bazaars, sewing and knitting circles, seeing in these activities a fresh means of ingratiating herself with the local bigwigs. Amy played her allotted part, feeling helpless, a hypocrite, cornered into constant mimicry of someone she was not.

In 1917 Margaret became pregnant. Amy was amazed and rather repelled. As far as she could see her parents spent their parallel lives in a state of closed neutrality, punctuated by squalls of hostility and anger. She would never have dreamed that they still made love. The incongruity of it puzzled and haunted her for weeks.

'You'll have to take things more quietly for a time, dear,' Edward advised with awkward solicitude, as if he were out of practice.

'Yes, I know.' Amy was enchanted by the artless smile with which Margaret repaid him. She was so used to her mother's rancour.

And from early summer Margaret was as good as her word, renouncing her frenzied round of war work, staying home a great deal, sitting in the sun unpicking the boys' outgrown pullovers to knit up into baby clothes – all but khaki wool was in short supply – seeming calm and contented. Mrs Bracken, who helped mornings in the house, was happy to work additional hours. She was a widow with two sons away in the army. She liked to fill her time and the extra cash was more than welcome.

Abruptly Margaret seemed to lose all interest in her Dorcas Society, pledged to compete with the neighbouring villages in producing mountains of socks, mittens, mufflers and balaclava helmets for the men at the front. She appeared to lose interest in everything except a dazed, soft-eyed contemplation of her own changing body and of the child to be born.

As a result Amy found, quite suddenly, that she had more freedom than ever before. As long as she put in a token appearance at the society from time to time, Margaret was content for her to pass the time reading and playing tennis and taking walks with Nancy. She even spent a whole glorious, sunlit, carefree week with the Bessell family in a rented cottage in the Forest of Dean. Margaret seemed only too glad for her to go, as if Amy's very presence at home was an interruption to her peaceful trance.

Arriving back from the short holiday, Amy let herself in via the unlatched front entrance. The air was cool in the long, narrow hall that ran the length of the house to a back door, which stood open, revealing a rectangle of the vicarage garden.

It was early evening. Amy saw that her parents were sitting together on the lawn behind the house. Silently she gazed at them. Margaret reclined, passive and madonna-like in a wicker chair, hands in her lap below the ballooning belly, her light hair drawn straight back from her forehead and caught in a classic knot behind. Edward's chair was close to hers. He leaned forward, took hold of one of her hands, and they sat for a moment in wordless communication.

Framed in the doorway, they appeared frozen, a tableau – not so much Margaret and Edward as fecund woman, protective man. Amy was strangely impressed. She tiptoed to the kitchen, poured herself a glass of water. Then strolled into the garden as if she had just arrived.

'It's me. I'm back.'

The baby, a girl, was born in November. She was christened Emily. Margaret adored the child, luxuriated in caring for her. She indulged herself, staying late in bed in the mornings, suckling Emily as she leaned back against a pile of pillows, hair hanging in a plait over one shoulder. As the child nursed, Margaret murmured to her, an infinity of love in her voice.

'Dear little Emily. She's such a *good* girl.'

One morning Amy was with her in the bedroom, discussing what groceries Margaret needed from the village. Edward was on his way out and came to say goodbye, stooping and kissing his wife gently on the forehead. And it seemed to Amy that, with this new child, they had rediscovered – at least temporarily – some kindness from

24

an earlier era of their marriage. Margaret smiled up at him, then looked down at the baby, her face shining and transfixed. Amy felt a rush of tenderness for her mother mixed with a sharp, unlooked for stab of jealousy, which softened into an unspecified sense of sadness and regret.

Chapter Three

When, on the first day of the first peacetime New Year, Noel Campion asked if he could call and see her, Amy was surprised and not surprised, both at the same time. His pretext was to lend her a rather damning book on the war by H. G. Wells that both she and Edward had been wanting to read for ages.

Objectively speaking, Amy marvelled that any friend of the Kilverts should be sufficiently bothered to want to lend her anything. And yet, last night at the party, a sixth sense had discerned that Mr Campion singled her out in some way. It had been as if neither he nor she belonged at this clannish, county gathering, as if they had more to say to one another than to anyone else.

Edward was out when Mr Campion called in the early afternoon. Margaret and Emily were upstairs. Amy answered the door.

'Good afternoon, Miss Winter.' He gave a nod that was respectful, rather formal. In the frosty light he appeared pale. His eyes – grey like her own – looked very sharp and clear. Not yet demobilized, Noel Campion wore uniform with a khaki greatcoat, from the pocket of which he drew out a blue volume. 'I've called with the book I promised.' He held it out to her, the gesture slightly awkward, almost shy.

'That's very kind.' Amy felt abashed that this tall, correct man was calling on her account. 'Won't you come in for a moment, Mr Campion?'

'Thank you. I'd like to.'

Some spirit of perversity made Amy ignore the empty best room, ever scoured, polished and ready for guests. Instead she showed Mr Campion into the living room, where the boys – home for the Christmas season – were sprawled round the table doing their holiday homework. The choice was instinctive, a small rebellion, she supposed, against the fuss Margaret would have made over the arrival of such a distinguished visitor. As far as Amy was concerned, this friend of the Kilverts must take them as they were or not at all.

She introduced the boys and went to tell Margaret they had a caller. When she returned Mr Campion was helping Eric with some maths. The boys seemed impressed with him and had assumed the boarding school airs they generally laid aside a day or so after arriving home.

The five of them exchanged pleasantries for a while, on neutral topics like the boys' schooling and how long Campion was staying in the area. The Winter children found themselves – not unpleasantly – in awe of the new arrival. He was older than they and yet still young. He was handsome, well-built, well-spoken. His uniform bore witness to an unknown world of action and danger. Yet he talked to them as an equal, ignoring these advantages. They were charmed. The conversation was halting but conducted with great goodwill on all sides.

Suddenly Margaret came into the room and was introduced. She'd changed her dress, brushed her hair, laid Emily down to rest. Her cheeks were pink and she radiated a bright tension.

'Has no one offered you any refreshment? Amy, I'm surprised at you! Mr Campion, do come into the other room and stay for a cup of tea.'

Her fluster broke the spell, dissipated the fragile atmosphere of well-intentioned give and take.

'A kind offer, Mrs Winter . . . but I'm afraid I must be going.' Mr Campion seemed to retreat, as if the social skills involved in drinking tea with Margaret would be beyond him.

Amy never knew whether it was planned or sheer chance but, as Noel Campion was taking his leave, Margaret clapped one hand to her mouth.

'I've a letter needs posting. Amy dear, you couldn't walk with Mr Campion as far as the letter box?'

He seemed pleased but slightly at a loss as they walked together down towards the High Street. It was cold and sunny. Frost still lay in the hollows under hedges and in the shade of walls.

'You're much outnumbered by brothers,' he remarked. 'Do you find that hard?'

'Not really. I'm here and they're away at school most of the time. And once they've been there for a few terms they change. They're a bit like strangers. We're sort of . . . polite, where we used to fight and scuffle.'

He looked down at her. 'That sounds rather sad.'

'Lots of things are sad. But you get used to them and you stop noticing.'

'That's true,' murmuring agreement as if to himself, and giving Amy a wry glance as if he found her comment unexpected and illuminating. Again she thought how very clear and light his eyes looked in the chill sunshine.

They walked on in silence for a little while. Then Noel Campion said, in a sudden rush, 'Miss Winter, I so much enjoyed talking to you last night. I may not have the chance to be alone with you again so I'm going to be rather forward . . .' His steps had slowed and now he came to a halt, turning to face her. 'I'd like to call on you again. Perhaps we could become friends . . . Would that be possible?'

Amy was nonplussed. He seemed so grown-up, so far removed from her world. Could she really believe that this adult, with his unconscious authority and *savoir-faire* would want to be friends with her? She was seventeen. Her world was so narrow. She did what her parents told her and had seldom been further afield than Gloucester.

She stared at him dumbly, then stammered, 'Well, certainly . . . If you wanted to visit . . .'

'I've not met anyone, for so long, who interested . . . attracted me as you do,' he told her with an outspoken fervour that struck her, paradoxically, as totally self-possessed.

To her embarrassment, Amy felt herself blushing. 'It's kind of you . . .'

'I *may* call on you again?'

She was filled with elation, confusion. 'Oh yes.'

* * *

'The very best type of Englishman.'

During the months of their courtship this phrase haunted Amy. It was a description she'd read in a newspaper once – goodness knows when and said about Lord knows who – and it had stuck. The very best type of Englishman. That was what Noel seemed to her.

Everyone said how handsome he was. Amy didn't think that exactly. He didn't make her catch her breath the way Paul Oates still did when she glimpsed him in the street. But Noel was someone you noticed. She was proud to walk down the road with him. There was a reliable solidity to his physical presence. Amy felt that, if she tripped, he would be fast enough and strong enough to catch her before she fell.

Noel had thick, fairish hair – she thought of it as 'manly' hair. It stood away from his scalp with a kind of wiriness before settling into the plain, side-parted style he wore. Sometimes he looked pale but more often there was a healthy, though never florid, ruddiness to his complexion. His skull was long, the features regular – eyes grey, brows and lashes neither too light nor too dark, nose straight, lips fine and rather firmly set.

In repose there was something stern, even bitter, about his expression that contradicted the public school homogeneity of his looks. There were lines of strain round his lips and eyes. Twin furrows ran from his nose to the corners of his mouth. This harshness secretly intrigued Amy, making her think of Mr Rochester and his buried demons. Though he wasn't the type to parade his griefs, it was plain to Amy that the war had scarred him badly. There were times when he seemed to withdraw and become a remote and flinty stranger, as if musing on some hellish inner landscape. Then the moment would pass. The edge of dourness made his smile, when it came, that much more gratifying.

People in Crofton appeared to think more highly of Amy now she was known to be keeping company with this distinguished young ex-officer who worked in London and came up regularly to see her. Even her own family – the boys and Margaret anyway, not Edward – seemed to look at her through fresh, more appreciative eyes. Amy

29

was dubious about this new esteem. There was no real reason for it. She was just the same as she'd always been.

Even so, she couldn't help being amused by a conversation she had with Charlie Kilvert in the High Street in late February.

'I hear Noel's coming up to see you again this weekend,' Charlie remarked casually after they'd exchanged bland comments about the weather.

'Yes, he'll be arriving Saturday lunchtime. Staying with your brother, I believe.'

'You're a dark horse, Amy, and no mistake.' Beneath the brim of her blue hat there was an odd expression on Charlie's round pink and white face, half accusing, half admiring. 'Noel never stops telling Matthew how bright and beautiful, wise and wonderful you are . . . I'm sure the village never realized what a jewel we had in our midst.'

Aiming for lightness of tone, Charlie couldn't keep a note of envious pique out of her voice. Amy savoured a moment of malicious and thoroughly unholy pleasure.

Yet Amy herself remained dazed and unbelieving at the turn events had taken. One moment her life was out of kilter – she was bored and ill-at-ease, forced to play a role her heart wasn't in, and from which there seemed no prospect of escape. Then suddenly, fast as turning a page, her days were lit up by the presence of an ardent and desirable suitor whose intentions seemed quite breathtakingly honourable.

The very best type of Englishman. The description continued to drift through her brain and, for all her delight and dazzlement, it trailed an elusive aura of menace. What was she, Amy Winter, doing with someone of that description? In the lone small hours of the morning she would feel ordinary and unworthy and could only trust blindly in Noel's declarations of love and admiration.

Little by little, as the months passed, Amy compiled some sort of a picture of Noel's background and past life. She seized on every fragment he let fall, fitting each new piece into the rudimentary jigsaw. Some things he told her she might have expected, other elements came as a surprise.

She was astounded, for instance, to find that he had been born in Denver, Colorado, that his mother was American.

'But you're so English,' she marvelled. Immediately the exclamation struck her as fatuous. So was she English. So was everyone she knew.

Noel, though, seemed to find sense in the remark. 'Sadly, you've hit the nail on the head.'

He'd loved his mother and she'd died when he was sixteen. 'I was devastated, but I was away at school at the time. The done thing was to flaunt a stiff upper lip and I did. I've always felt I belittled her by not mourning properly . . . She was like you – gentle.'

Amy let that comment pass. She didn't think of herself as gentle – not from choice. But it seemed petty to quibble. And she was honoured, anyway, that he had thoughts about her at all.

Their time alone was rationed. Margaret kept an alert and dutiful eye on the couple. Edward liked to chat to Noel about books and politics. Matthew and Phyllis Kilvert entertained them to dinner. Their courtship was conventionally public. Talk was general and largely confined to neutral topics. But one afternoon in March Noel and Amy found themselves alone together in the Winter family living room. Grey and black clouds raced outside the window. Rain gusted against the panes, while a fire glowed in the open grate.

Amy began to ask Noel about his family. In their cosy isolation he became expansive, his conversation more personal than she had ever known it.

Apparently his parents had met in Lausanne while his mother, Kitty, was touring Europe in the manner of wealthy young Americans. Noel's father, Ralph, a doctor, fifteen years her senior, was on a walking holiday with a friend. Kitty was enormously impressed by him.

'Only it seems to me, looking back, that she was never at home in England,' Noel mused. 'My father has a rigid side to his character. He's a stickler for form and doing the right thing . . . He wore my mother down.'

31

Kitty bore three children. Noel had a brother, Thomas, eight years older than himself, a sister, Carrie, ten years his junior. On each occasion his mother had insisted on returning to her family in Denver to give birth.

'When Carrie was born I went with her and stayed out there for nearly a year. I loved it. Colorado's the most beautiful . . .' Noel was silent for a moment, staring into the fire, then he added, 'Without my father's dead hand on her, Mother became quite different – open and lively. Teasing. Playful. It was a revelation to me.'

Kitty's younger brother had taken him riding and camping in the Rockies. Noel couldn't remember ever being as happy as on those trips.

'I swore I'd go back there to live when I grew up. For fully two years afterwards I *dreamed* of Colorado.'

But the dream had faded. Reality – his father's reality – seeped into his bones and hardened there.

'I wanted to be like Mother's family – straightforward, genial and easy-going.' Noel spread his hands with a deprecating, wry, endearing smile. 'But after she died I lost touch with their world . . . I can't help knowing that I'm more like my father, whether I like it or not.'

Ralph had become eminent in his profession, a sought-after specialist in skin disorders. Eventually he'd had a practice in Harley Street. The family home was in the Avon Valley but, for some years, the Campions rented a house in Marylebone too. Ralph would have liked his sons to follow in his footsteps. He had his own inflexible notions on what constituted success.

'He was harder on my older brother than on me – when Thomas was twenty the two of them literally came to blows. My brother left the house. He left the country and took an agricultural job in South Africa. Father relented then – sent him an advance on his inheritance, enough to buy a farm.' Noel compressed his lips. 'It's quite probable none of us will ever see Thomas again.'

At school Noel excelled at Modern Languages. His father considered that a lowly branch of knowledge and ignored the prizes he won, the scholarship to Cambridge. Still Ralph suffered his son to read German and French at university, paid for him to spend some months in Paris and Berlin – financially he was never mean.

'Then the war came along, I suppose,' Amy prompted.

She heard the scrape of the front door opening, Margaret's voice in the hall outside and Emily's light, fluting tones. Amy cursed inwardly. So much for their brief hour of intimacy – though Noel would probably have clammed up about the war anyway.

Abruptly her mother opened the living-room door. She looked beautiful, flushed with the outdoors, dewy with the damp air.

'Oh!' Margaret started. 'Good afternoon, Noel.' She was ill-at-ease with her daughter's exalted suitor, and turned to Amy. 'You've let the coals burn terribly low.'

'My fault.' Good-naturedly Noel reached for the coal and the fire irons, began stoking and repairing the fire.

'So where's your father now?' Amy asked him, to fill the awkward silence that had fallen.

'Retired.' Noel glanced up briefly from his task. His manner had changed, become light and social. 'He lives in our house near Stratford and terrorizes my little sister. Apart from that he's quite the country gentleman.'

One Sunday in May the two of them set out together for a ramble to the nearby village of Painswick.

Noel had asked Edward's permission for him and Amy to be allowed to go hiking unchaperoned. After due warnings and admonitions, his request had been granted: there was no doubt that Edward considered Noel as fine and trustworthy as did everyone else.

It was a perfect green and gold May morning. They carried rucksacks with them containing their sandwiches. Noel looked uncharacteristically informal in soft old grey-black corduroys and a sports jacket. Amy had borrowed an outgrown pair of her brother Eric's walking boots. With them she wore her favourite old school straw hat and a summer dress she liked – off-the-peg rather than home-made for once – in a cream open-weave material which bloused stylishly over a narrow, plaited leather belt.

33

Their route led through Arthur Kilvert's wood, permissible so long as ramblers kept to the designated paths. Amy felt happy and exhilarated, sloughing off the self-consciousness that sometimes hedged her about when she was with Noel, the need to live up to him, to try and be clever. On this spring morning she was content merely to chat about everything and nothing. Noel responded to her mood, becoming light-hearted and playful. So often there was something restrained about him, as if he harboured private preoccupations.

As they skirted a small clearing a figure became visible in the middle distance between the slim, vertical ranks of the tree trunks, the fresh young foliage.

Casually Noel nodded. 'Someone over there.'

As they approached Amy saw that the figure was that of a young man. Paul Oates, she realized. His skin looked white and translucent in the slanting greenish light of the wood. He stood immobile as they drew near, with a watchful, even, she fancied, a guilty look in his brown eyes, as if he might have his own reasons for being in the wood.

But he smiled as Amy came towards him, staring at her steadily, appraisingly, his hair in his eyes as of old. ''Lo, Amy.'

'Hello, Paul.' She sounded cagey. They both did.

He transferred his unabashed gaze to Noel. 'Nice day for it.'

He was as heartstoppingly beautiful as ever. 'We're going for a walk,' Amy explained unnecessarily.

'Enjoy it, won't you?' Was she imagining a muted insolence in his tone, a veiled *double entendre* in his words?

When he was out of earshot, Noel asked, 'Who was that?'

'A boy who used to be in my class. Called Paul.' Then, on a sudden, imprudent impulse, 'He was my sweetheart.' She tried to sound flippant and sophisticated, but it didn't work.

Noel turned sharply to look at her, but made no comment. He'd been to Rugby, of course. His experiences would have been altogether different.

'We all had sweethearts.' Amy hastened to reassure him that it didn't mean anything. But perhaps she sounded as if she had a guilty conscience.

'Really?' His smile was thin, uncomprehending. But quite soon he appeared to forget about the conversation – the sun was so glorious, the sky so blue, the air so soft and fresh.

From the wood they struck out across meadowland, where grazing cattle watched them pass. They took a breather by a narrow little stream that bordered one of the fields. Noel reclined on one elbow, gazing idly at the sparkling water, the multi-coloured pebbles that formed the bed of the stream.

As he lay there, Amy watched him covertly. He seemed to withdraw abruptly into his own musings. It came to her how unknowable he was, how uncompromisingly separate and self-contained. A stranger, if the truth were told. Could she really tell herself she loved him?

Sometimes Amy suspected that she was simply swept along by a whole atmosphere. By the wonder of his turning her unsatisfactory life around and the way other people seemed suddenly to envy and think well of her. Perhaps what she felt was just awe for his natural authority and distinction, coupled with gratitude for his noticing her at all. Then again perhaps what everyone agreed to call love was merely that – a mosaic of these random, mundane elements and not some deep, pure, burning secret.

She glanced at him again. Lying there, lost in thought, he exuded a kind of lonely austerity.

Impulsively Amy blurted, 'Sometimes you look as if you'd got a secret sorrow.'

He turned to face her, surprised out of his private reverie.

'What makes you think that?' His smile was tenderly amused, as if a child had said something perceptive.

'You seem so severe and sad.'

'I'm sorry if I was distant. I'm aware I go off into a brown study at times. It's . . .' hesitating as if he were embarrassed to continue. 'Pictures come into my head, Amy. Memories from back in France, Belgium and . . . There was a boy, your age I'd say, kind and beautiful as an angel, lying broken in the mud like a cheap toy . . . I can't seem to forget some of the things . . .' Noel shrugged his shoulders. 'I don't have nightmares, it isn't that, but . . . it's as if everything I

35

saw and experienced is buried deep in my bones, right in the very core and marrow. And that's what's real. Conversation and smiling and laughter is false. It's all just so much acting.'

He spoke with reluctance as if confessing to weakness. Amy was filled with quiet pride that this grown man had confided in her. Determined, too, that she would not back away from the challenge, but give him all the reassurance she was able.

She took his hand. It had always been Noel who made such moves. 'You could talk about it to me. Might that help . . . Noel.' She still found it hard to use his name.

'Dearest Amy.' He smiled. 'You *are* a little angel. I'm touched, more so than I can say. Only there were awful things. It would be unforgivable if I were to describe –'

'I'm not as fragile as you seem to imagine.' She spoke with an edge of impatience, piqued by his dismissal of her desire to be of use and by his sentimental view of her. 'When you live in the country, you . . . Well, *I've* seen animals slaughtered and I've not looked away. I've always thought it would be dishonest to do so.'

Noel ignored this remark as if he didn't know how to respond to it. But he tightened the grip of his hand in Amy's and addressed her earnestly.

'You *do* help, Amy, whether you know it or not, just by being who you are. Times when I feel dead inside, I think of you and . . . unfailingly . . . I can grasp, really understand, why life is good and should be lived . . .'

Extended full-length and leaning on one elbow, Noel pulled her down so they were lying face to face. Amy was mesmerized. The sun burned pleasurably into her limbs and the grass had a sweet, elusive scent of hay and Noel was so close. She had never shared a moment of such intimacy with him.

The look on his face was naked, almost pleading. 'Amy, don't laugh if I tell you that for me you're the embodiment of youth and happiness . . . But it isn't just that. You've got a kind of wisdom all your own. Ideas that are yours and no one else's. I notice that all the time – it's as if you're teaching me to see in quite a different way.'

She stared at him entranced, like a child listening to a story. Noel moved yet closer and laid his lips to hers, blocking out the sun. He kissed her gently, softly at first, and then with increasing fervour, caressing her arms and shoulders, chastely, but with a passionate tenderness.

And Amy was lifted on an answering swell of emotion. Tears welled behind her eyes and the doubts that had troubled her earlier about her feelings for him were not so much dispelled as forgotten.

'I love you,' she said for the first time.

Painswick was delightful, with its little hilly streets and silvery church spire but to Amy and Noel it seemed insubstantial, a stage backcloth to their fierce absorption in one another. They toured dutifully, filing away the required impressions to report back to Edward and Margaret, but the intensity of their embrace by the stream overwhelmed the outside world, claiming all of their visceral energy and attention.

They almost forgot to eat and were on their way out of the village before it occurred to them that their rucksacks should, by now, be light and empty. They looked at one another and laughed, charmed that this most basic of functions had been overlooked in the magic of their mutual preoccupation.

On this side the village was bordered by fields containing rows of neat, pruned fruit trees. They were in bloom, a mass of pink and white blossom, as profuse yet ordered as in a Japanese print. And, placed conveniently opposite, was a bench with a plaque dedicating it 'To the memory of Henrietta Minns, who loved and laboured in these orchards.'

'Take a seat, Amy.' Noel dusted off the bench with the sleeve of his jacket. 'I'm sure Henrietta wouldn't mind.' His earlier light-heartedness had returned.

They sat and ate their sandwiches and feasted their eyes on the view.

Out of the blue Noel said, 'So he was your sweetheart, that boy in the wood.'

Startled, Amy glanced at him, but read amusement and indulgence

37

in his eyes, and a flicker of something else – an eagerness, a curiosity that was deeper and keener than his teasing smile suggested.

'Oh.' A shrug, gently dismissive. 'Years ago.'

'I wouldn't mind betting he was in the Kilverts' wood on some nefarious mission.'

A little later he asked, 'What did your mother make of your choice? Of sweetheart, I mean.'

'She'd have died. But she never knew. I was freer at school. She couldn't monitor *everything* I got up to.'

'And what *did* you get up to?' His bonhomie had an awkward ring.

'Nothing much. We used to kiss sometimes. Behind the outhouses.'

'Did you now?' She glimpsed that look in his eye again. A sharp speculativeness that showed through his efforts to sound casual.

The feel of those times invaded her now, unexpectedly. Amy said musingly, 'He was a bad boy and I was a good girl. We were born to those roles . . . just because of the families we came from. It could have been the other way round. It's hard for children to be anything but what they're meant to be.'

'Would you have liked to be something else? Some*one* else?'

Amy folded the muslin cloth her sandwiches had been wrapped in and replaced it in her rucksack. 'I just wanted to be anonymous.' She smiled at Noel. 'Because my father was vicar people expected me to be good and nice and helpful. They had an idea of me that was nothing to do with me. If I didn't live up to it, I was told I'd let my parents down. But I never asked to be thought of like that in the first place.'

She buckled the rucksack and looked out across the orchard. The sky above it was azure with its full mellow afternoon glory. Amy leaned back on the bench, stretching her arms above her head. 'I used to dream about running away to somewhere where nobody knew who I was and I could just be me.'

'You don't dream that any more?' He looked nice with his fair hair ruffled, his skin warmed by the sun, a wry, sympathetic look on his face.

'Of course not. It's a kid's dream. Where would I go?'

'Come to London. Marry me.'

38

She gazed at him, incredulous – though he had been courting her for almost half a year and she'd daydreamed this moment many times. Noel Campion was proposing to her. Somehow the prospect had always seemed too fairy-tale a climax ever to come true in her humdrum life. Amy clasped her hands, looked doubtfully at him.

'What do you say . . . my little Amy?' He pronounced the endearment with a sudden shyness that she found charming.

For an instant that pinprick of hesitation returned. Did she really love Noel as she should, as people did in books, passionately, without doubt or reservation? But the wavering thought was enveloped by a surge of gladness and exhilaration, golden and giddy, to which she surrendered recklessly.

He was waiting for her reply, his grey eyes earnest and nakedly vulnerable.

Amy leaned forward and placed a soft kiss on his smooth, firm mouth. 'Dearest Noel. I say yes.'

Chapter Four

It was a balmy May evening six months after the end of the war, when Joachim Werner crossed Berlin's Henriettenplatz on his way home to Grunewald. A couple of miles to go yet. Joachim strolled, taking his time. After a business meeting in town the walk was a positive pleasure, and Erna, his wife, would be pleased. She'd been lecturing him recently about getting more exercise.

Though Joachim considered himself trim enough for his forty-five years. Karl Kraus, the client he'd lunched with, had been an obscene porker of a man who spent the meal boasting about the young mistresses he was able to treat himself to. Poor cows. What a fate. Girls who were desperate to earn some money any way they could in this risky, precarious post-war world. A few years ago he'd have condemned them out of hand. But times were damned difficult and he was slower to judge.

His nostrils caught the faint, elusive drift of cigar-smoke. That spicy tobacco-scent on warm summer air always stirred in him a vague, indefinable erotic ache. He no longer tried to recollect why. If it was connected with some episode in his past, Joachim had long ago forgotten what. And yet, again, unfailingly, the aroma worked its nostalgic spell.

Above the brouhaha of the street – the chatter, the clip-clop of a horse's hooves, the rumble of a motor – he became aware of another, more exotic sound – that of a female voice raised in song. It stole up on him, a song he knew, that every German knew.

> *Die Luft ist kühl, und es dunkelt,*
> *Und ruhig fliesst der Rhein . . .*

The legend of the Lorelei. Hearing the slow, spiralling melody in this incongruous setting, Joachim was moved by the beauty of a tune he'd taken for granted ever since he could remember. The voice was young and strong and true.

He glanced in the direction from which the sound came. On the north-west side of the square stood a large, cuboid, grey apartment building, with pompous colonnades set into its façade and a bas-relief of shields and scrolls. The ground floor, though, was used as a café. It had plate-glass windows and a green awning. The Silbernagel it was called, Joachim recalled. It looked solid and unpretentious. He had never been inside.

His eyes scanned the pavement and picked out a figure in black, looking small and alone, but singing gamely. An upturned black hat lay on the pavement beside her. He smiled, amused by the young woman's dogged perseverance, and felt in his trouser pocket for some change.

Joachim stood for a while at a distance, waiting for her to finish the song. Then he approached and tossed a few pfennigs into the street singer's hat. Other people had also made donations, he noticed.

With a small bow, he addressed her. 'Thank you, Fräulein. That was charming.'

Then he frowned. The woman's features seemed familiar, but he couldn't place . . .

'Herr Werner!'

The voice triggered his memory. 'Claudia!' Immediately he was seized by doubt. 'Is it?'

She laughed. 'Yes, it's me . . . I'm embarrassed.'

'You look . . . You're so thin.'

'Times aren't easy.'

Claudia Farnholz. The name returned to him. She was the daughter of a former neighbour, Friedrich Farnholz. The families used to have friends in common, attended some of the same social gatherings. But Farnholz had gone bust in the war and committed suicide some two years ago. It had caused quite a stir at the time. Joachim had heard from former neighbours that Claudia was living in a rented room, not too far away from him. Apparently she'd worked in a munitions factory

41

for a time. But he hadn't come across her for some years now.

She'd changed, become womanly, but shockingly thin and shabby compared to the plump, prettily dressed child he remembered.

'Have you eaten?' Joachim winced inwardly. What on earth had made him come out with that question above all others? The comparison, presumably, between her look of deprivation and his own comfortably full stomach.

Claudia looked bemused, but smilingly so. She shook her head. 'Not today. Not yet.'

'Miss Farnholz, would you allow me to buy you a meal?'

The interior of the Silbernagel was cool and dark. Old-fashioned, with a bare floor and basic wooden tables. Discreetly Joachim avoided the seats by the window. A passing acquaintance might see him with a young woman and jump to the wrong conclusion. He led Claudia to a table for two in a far corner.

He ordered a bottle of Rhine wine. Since the onset of war prices had risen steadily and scandalously, but Joachim was philosophical. He could afford it. If you didn't pay, you didn't get.

'White sausage on the menu today. And lentils. There's no choice. Will that do for you, Miss Farnholz?'

She looked at him with good-humoured cynicism. 'I'm so hungry, I could eat pigswill.'

He raised his eyebrows, slightly shocked by her outspokenness, but also a little excited. The war had changed many things. Even well-brought-up girls, even his own daughters, were sometimes bolder than Erna thought quite right.

'*Prost*, Miss Farnholz.' He raised his glass.

She reciprocated, smiling, took a sip of the chill liquid and sighed. 'Nectar. Pure nectar.'

Joachim looked about him. The clientele of the Silbernagel was predominantly male, though with a sprinkling of wives and girl-friends. Clerks, in the main, and other petty white-collar workers, relishing a well-earned beer. A pleasant atmosphere. No rowdiness. That, in itself, was rare enough nowadays.

He was nervous about conversing with Miss Farnholz. There seemed a positive minefield of subjects she might prefer him to avoid. Her father's death, for instance, not to mention her own obviously straitened circumstances, the fact that he'd come across her singing in the street to earn a few pfennigs.

But Claudia brought that particular matter up herself, grinning at him across the table and declaring frankly, 'I was dreading anyone I knew seeing me out there . . . Only I'd earned nothing today. I went out after a job and it fell through. I chased a few more red herrings, but there was nothing doing. And I couldn't bear the thought of going home empty-handed.'

'What was this job you were after?'

She grimaced. 'Some silly advertising stunt. I did it yesterday. There's a soft drink called Dulciana . . .' She rolled her eyes expressively ceilingwards. 'We girls had to dress up in green frocks and each carry a letter spelling out the name and walk up and down the Ku'damm . . .'

Joachim laughed incredulously.

'Don't.' She smiled. 'You feel such an idiot. But there's money in it. Not much, though.'

'What about today?'

'When I got there they'd given my A to somebody else – some little girlfriend of the organizer's . . .' Claudia pulled a droll, forlorn face. 'The competition's cutthroat, even for something as stupid as that.'

Joachim was amused. He was beginning to feel more at ease. The dough-faced waiter brought Claudia's plate of anaemic sausages flanked by a watery, yellowish gruel of lentils.

'Heaven!' She flashed a grateful glance at Joachim. 'This is so kind of you.'

He watched as she ate. It was clear the young woman was trying not to wolf the food down, but to eat in an acceptably casual manner.

Claudia had an odd face. Not pretty at all, but definitely arresting. She was olive-skinned with dark hair that showed reddish glints and was cut in a thick, uncompromising fringe that ended just above straight, emphatic eyebrows. Her eyes were dark too, and slightly protuberant, the sockets cleanly etched with no spare flesh beneath them. But it was her mouth you noticed. It was wide and humorous, giving her a knowing, irreverent air that seemed at odds with her youth and what he knew of her upbringing, and which he found rather disturbing.

Claudia wore a black blouse and skirt, and it came to Joachim with a shock of remembrance that of course the girl's mother had died as well, in childbirth, early in the war. By that time he and Erna were moving in different circles and the news had not really touched him. In any case it seemed that Claudia had taken all these disasters in her stride. Children were resilient and Joachim was relieved. He could not have coped with misery.

'Come across any meat in those sausages yet?' he asked like a jovial uncle.

Claudia shrugged. 'I'm not probing too deeply. They're filling. I don't ask for more.'

The skin of her forearms and neck, and across her collarbones, was tender and young. A golden, tawny colour. He allowed himself to imagine her naked body, slight and smooth and angular. An adolescent's body.

'How old are you, Miss Farnholz?' It was a personal question, but the wine was glowing pleasantly in his veins. And anyway he was certain that Claudia was indifferent to such niceties.

'Eighteen next month,' she answered through a mouthful of sausage, seeming incurious as to why he'd asked. He didn't really know himself.

A long-suspended memory surfaced in his mind. An interminable summer afternoon at Willy Körner's house. The Körners had a young cousin staying, a pallid, humourless girl who was going in for teaching. She'd taken charge of the children, got them organized into staging an entertainment for the adults. The show had gone on and on and, after each turn, they all had to clap and coo fulsomely over the youngsters' talent.

Claudia had sung some chirpy little song about a family of robins. She must have been ten or eleven at the time, wore a pink dress and ribbons in her hair, was plump and confident as you please, her voice pure and rather strident. She'd brought the house down. Wryly

Joachim had admired her nerve, but Erna pronounced her an awful little show-off.

She'd been a cherished child, the apple of her parents' eye. The three of them seemed to radiate *joie de vivre*. Claudia, Friedrich and Lotte – that was the mother's name. She'd been an attractive woman, he remembered, with the same golden skin as her daughter. And now both parents were dead, leaving the child to fend for herself.

He would have liked to mention the robin song to Claudia. It might have amused her. But, Joachim decided, better not. Better leave them undisturbed, those memories of better days.

Claudia felt profoundly at peace, with the starchy meal lining her stomach, the wine producing counteracting sensations of giddiness and light-headedness. She had been careful to eat slowly. The last time she had a square meal she'd bolted it and felt ill afterwards rather than comfortably full.

Leaning back on the rustic chair with its cut-out fretwork hearts, she smiled at her benefactor. 'Herr Werner, you've done a good deed.'

The comment appeared to please him. He ducked his head momentarily, a stiff, rather shy gesture. 'My pleasure, Fräulein.'

Werner ordered another bottle of wine from the lugubrious waiter. Then, as an afterthought, he called for a cigar. Claudia was surprised. The meal over, she expected them to go their separate ways.

Two bottles of wine. The man's largesse impressed her. Not everyone, it seemed, was on the breadline.

'You've kept your head above water, then, in these exciting times.'

'I manage.' People were cagey nowadays, Claudia thought, about admitting to solvency.

'You must be one of those dastardly profiteers everyone's talking about.'

She'd meant it as a joke, but saw a hurt look in his eye and felt mean. He'd been kind to her.

Defensively he explained, 'I just happened to be in the right line of business. Kopisch and Werner. We manufacture woollen garments.

45

We had contracts continuously throughout the war. But I assure you, I'm no millionaire.'

'I was only teasing, Herr Werner.'

The wine arrived, along with two clean glasses. Werner tasted and approved. He lit the slim black cigar the waiter had brought and relaxed against the back-rest of his chair as if settling down to a further leisurely stage of their conversation.

'You're living with your little brother and an aunt, so the Brandts told me – is that right?'

'Yes, we rent a room from Frau Kästner. Her husband was killed, you know.'

'Yes, I'd heard.'

The two of them began to chat about people they might have in common and what had become of them. Claudia experienced a sense of unreality. She hadn't seen Herr Werner since ... well, before Mutti died, she was sure. To her he'd always been a grown-up, a member of a separate species. Now he was just another person, perfectly approachable, not absolutely sure of himself.

Actually, as middle-aged men went, he wasn't bad-looking. Quite slim for his medium height. Balding a bit, but nice eyes and nice lips. A clipped pepper-and-salt beard and tidy, arched brows lent his face definition. And he was well-groomed, with a starched shirt and a dark suit.

'And how is your wife?' she asked politely. Claudia recalled Frau Werner as not a bad sort, quite smiling and gracious, inclined to blush.

'Erna's pretty well, thank you.'

'And your daughters? You have two, don't you?' She remembered them as giggly. A bit younger than herself. They'd all been together in a sort of pantomime at the Körners' once.

'The girls are growing. Erna worries sometimes that they're a bit wild. Your generation has come up through such cruel times.'

'I suppose so.'

Abruptly, almost convulsively, Joachim Werner reached across the table and closed one hand over Claudia's wrist. The warm pressure of it was unexpectedly comforting.

'I'd like to say . . . Claudia . . . that I sympathize . . . I do so feel for you. Losing your parents so young and in so short a space . . .' His well-shaped hazel eyes were intense, a touch fevered, his face flushed with the wine. 'I hope you don't find it too painful, my mentioning . . .'

His obvious emotion sparked a response in Claudia. She saw herself from his viewpoint – an orphan whose warm, safe world had been snatched away. And simultaneously an image of Mutti flashed into her mind, smiling over one shoulder, tender, careless and happy. Involuntary tears pricked behind her eyes. Claudia cursed herself – she'd learned not to cry. She stared fixedly at the wall behind Joachim Werner, not trusting herself to speak.

A wave of dizzying lust swept over Joachim as he gazed at the young woman. She resembled a crestfallen child, her eyes bright with tears, the playful assurance of her earlier behaviour quite dashed.

'Claudia, I'm sorry . . . I shouldn't have . . .' His voice was thick. He cleared his throat.

With her free hand she made a small, deprecating gesture, shaking her head and lowering her eyes. Joachim couldn't take his eyes off her wide, mobile mouth, twisted now and tremulous, exciting him unbearably.

In his imagination he saw the canny smile of porcine Karl Kraus, and heard his fly, confidential tones. 'I tell you, Joachim, if you've got a bit of spare cash these days you can pick and choose among the women.' The words played like an insinuating refrain in his head, no matter how hard he wished them away.

Joachim was a faithful husband, a family man. Erna was pretty and good-tempered. He'd always congratulated himself on that. But in recent years they'd become companions rather than lovers. They knew each other through and through, and when they did make love it was – not perfunctory exactly, but wholly to the point. The shortest route to mutual satisfaction. After which they turned over and went to sleep, torpid and physically at peace like domestic animals.

Sometimes Joachim had the anguished certainty that never again would he experience the chancy, excessive, out-of-his-depth feelings he recalled from his youth, when he'd flirted with machinists and shop-girls, before he married Erna.

Hedwig especially, with her compact little body and brazen eyes. He'd been both devastated and relieved when she threw him over for some Neanderthal brute of a soldier.

Joachim couldn't remember when he'd last been alone with a young woman. It could be years before he was again. And he wasn't getting any younger. He had a place they could go to as well.

'Fräulein Claudia, I've got a small apartment not far away in the Duisburgerstrasse.' With the wine he was in a reckless, all-or-nothing mood. 'Perhaps I could offer you a coffee before we say goodbye.'

The coffee was delicious. It was *real* coffee, fresh and rich and dark. Claudia hadn't tasted anything so good for years. She couldn't imagine where Herr Werner had procured it. And afterwards he produced a tall, thin bottle of colourless raspberry liqueur and two small, ornate Bohemian glasses.

'My parents used to drink this,' Claudia marvelled. 'Every Sunday after lunch. It was a ritual. I could never understand why, if it was made of raspberries, it wasn't red.'

She'd got over her attack of the miseries. It was nice here. The apartment was filled with good, solid Biedermeier furniture, regularly cleaned and polished by the caretaker's wife. Claudia relaxed in an unctuous maroon velvet armchair and Werner sat opposite in another. Ranged on the windowsill, a row of healthy-looking plants stood silhouetted against the darkening sky. A fire had been laid in the grate and Herr Werner had set a match to it, not so much for warmth as for cosiness – *Gemütlichkeit* – as he said with a smile.

'I could get used to this comfort.' The liqueur burned luxuriously in her veins. She hadn't felt so full and warm for months. 'Frau Kästner's rooms are going to seem even gloomier by contrast.'

Herr Werner had originally rented the flat in his student days – 'It was a lot more spartan then, I can tell you.' Since that time he'd simply kept it on, though he and his family lived in a large house out in Grunewald. The rent was reasonable and the premises useful for all manner of purposes – as a *pied-à-terre* for relatives up from the country, a meeting place for business associates, somewhere convenient for him and Erna to sleep after a night at the theatre or the opera. Claudia couldn't help wondering if he ever brought women here. It seemed a perfect love nest.

In fact, when he suggested their taking coffee in his apartment, her first thought was that perhaps he intended to try to seduce her. Immediately Claudia rejected the notion as unworthy and wildly improbable. He was a comfortable family man, and full of fatherly concern over her orphan status.

But now, again, as he sat across from her, chatting with an oddly unfocused and preoccupied air while gazing at her with shy, speculative insistency, she returned to her first intuition.

As she sipped her liqueur and responded to the threads of his conversation, her brain was engaged in the unreal and quite separate activity of pondering the idea of being seduced, wondering how she felt about it. It was a measure of the exigency of her present life that Claudia's first coherent thought was that Herr Werner would probably give her money. Perhaps even quite a lot of it. Or some coffee. Tante Agathe would go mad with joy if she brought some of that home, no matter how she'd come by it.

And then it occurred to her that she'd be selling her virginity for this – the money or the coffee – and to mild-mannered, middle-aged Herr Werner. There was something darkly comic in the thought. Out in the suburbs, among the secure and prosperous middle-class families the Farnholzes had frequented in the old days, virginity was traditionally acknowledged to be a matchless treasure – as well as an inestimable bargaining commodity – not to be given away without the due return of a solid marriage.

But Claudia had always found it difficult to believe that she owned something so sacred and so valuable. It would amuse her, be almost a relief, and certainly more in tune with the times, to get rid of it on the cheap.

Her choice was made, but Werner seemed woefully indecisive.

49

They might well sit here all night if she didn't take matters into her own hands.

'Could I have a refill, Herr Werner?' Claudia held out her glass with a flirtatious smile.

'Of course, Fräulein Claudia.' He jumped up with nervous alacrity, picking the elegant bottle up from the table.

As he poured her drink, she gazed at him, her head a little to one side, with what she hoped was a subtly brazen come-hither look. His hands were trembling.

Claudia stood up and gently removed the bottle from his grasp, placing it and her glass on the table at her side. Then she stood before him in an attitude she imagined to be passive yet inviting, arms by her sides, staring earnestly into his eyes.

'Claudia.' He took the hint, grasping her left wrist and pulling her close. 'Little Claudia.' His hand cradled her head, laying it against his shoulder as if he were comforting a child.

'Look what I've got, Tante Agathe!' Triumphantly Claudia waved the paper bag she was carrying. She made a sound like a flourish of trumpets. 'Can you believe this? Real coffee!'

She got in quickly before her aunt could launch into a reproachful tirade about how worried she'd been. The ploy paid off. The miraculous word, coffee, diverted Tante Agathe's attention momentarily from the fact that Claudia had been out all night.

'Dear God, Claudia, where on earth did you find that?'

Claudia had her story ready. She would pretend that she'd got the job yesterday and that this had been a perk. Far-fetched indeed, but she didn't think Tante Agathe would enquire too closely.

'They asked us to work late last night and Herr Schlammer who's in charge of hiring and firing – he's up to his neck in the black market – he promised us all half a kilo if we . . .' Claudia gave her aunt a kiss, and put on the contrite expression Tante Agathe found irresistible – she was already beginning to smile. 'I'm sorry if you were anxious, but I thought it was worth it. I stayed over with one of the other girls, and I couldn't let you know . . .'

She placed two marks on the table. Joachim had given her a fair bit more, but that would remain a secret for the time being. Her aunt wasn't stupid.

'You're a good girl, Mausi.' Agathe used her childhood pet name and shook her head with a mixture of disapproval and admiration. 'But it's wrong that you're having to grow up so fast . . .'

'Where's Rudi?' Claudia asked quickly, in an attempt to head off the gloomy meditations on the breakdown of society which would inevitably come next.

'Your little brother's down with Frau Kästner. She offered to save him a couple of slices of bread.'

'Tant' Agathe.'

'What is it, Mausi?'

'Let's make ourselves a cup of coffee right now. I want to drink mine in the garden. It's such a beautiful morning.'

However sombre her rooms, Frau Kästner couldn't keep the sun out of her garden. Claudia sat on the grass with her back against the gnarled trunk of a purple lilac, hoping her aunt wouldn't look out and be scandalized and wail that the grass was damp and she'd catch pneumonia.

It was a good moment, with the morning sun flooding her upturned face, the scent of the lilac, the heartening, roasted warmth of the coffee. She needed to be alone to let her impressions of the previous night turn and tumble in her head, and then settle.

'Child. Claudia, child.'

In her mind she could hear the voice of Herr Werner – or Joachim, as he'd instructed her to call him – hoarse with tenderness but also a racking urgency that startled and amazed her in this buttoned-up contemporary of her parents.

Repeatedly he called her child, with husky sentimentality, while his fingers probed the crevices of her body, or he forced his entry into her with the hard baton of flesh. Mostly she'd felt detached, observing the experience with wondering interest, but once she lost control, thrashed and cried out with the convulsive, powerful sensations that swept through her.

She was embarrassed afterwards, but Joachim had been ecstatic,

51

kissing her over and over and covering her body with his as if he wanted to become one flesh with her, murmuring yet again, 'Dearest, dearest child.'

Claudia couldn't say how she felt about it. The interlude had been unique, repellent and addictive both at the same time. She could feel a tingling tension in the pit of her stomach right now, thinking about it.

He offered her money in the morning. 'Don't be insulted, Claudia. But you *are* hard up and I can help. Don't feel cheapened.' She hadn't responded to that, but took the money with modest gratitude.

'Could I ask a favour?' she said haltingly, then broke down in ladylike confusion.

'Don't be shy, dear,' Joachim urged gently.

'I was wondering . . . Could I have some of that coffee? It's not for me, only Tante Agathe does love it so, and most people never see such a thing from one year's end . . .'

He'd been surprised, then effusive – 'Why of course, Claudia!' – and given her a generous bagful.

'Could we meet again, child?'

'Yes, Joachim.' As if butter wouldn't melt . . . Same time next week, they agreed.

'Claudia!' Four-year-old Rudi came down the small flight of stairs from Frau Kästner's kitchen. He was barefoot, his dark hair tousled, and he held a stale-looking piece of bread in one hand. 'Where were you last night?' he asked crossly.

His only pair of shoes were far too small for him, Claudia mused. With the rest of Joachim's money she could buy him some new ones. Agathe would be suspicious as to how her niece had laid hands on that much cash. Not to worry, she'd think up some story.

'Child!' Tant' Agathe called from an upstairs window. 'That grass must be damp. You'll catch your death!' Claudia wondered how she was going to hide her blood-stained drawers. Life got complicated once you started having secrets.

Chapter Five

Claudia could remember singing and dancing for her mother, Lotte, one day. She must have been three or four and made her performance up as she went along, crooning a formless melody, waving her little arms and legs at random, while Lotte sat curled in a leather wing chair, wearing a blue and white dress, knees drawn up, resting one cheek on her curved hand, watching and smiling.

Lotte's smile was heaven. Not a big, curving clown's grin, but something peaceful and slow-burning, wise and good-natured, that came from deep within and shone through in her eyes.

Claudia danced on and on, basking in the warmth of that smile, until Mutti opened her arms and said, 'Come, Mausi,' and cuddled her, murmuring, 'What a clever little actress.' Claudia had never forgotten the infinite tenderness of Lotte's tone.

She had photographs of her mother, but was terrified of losing touch with the essence of Lotte, her smile and her voice. Claudia rationed herself, getting out the photos not more than once a month, so they didn't become stale and meaningless.

Lotte had been lovely, with skin the colour of apricots, long, languorous brown eyes and dark, lustrous curls. She was plump, and her plumpness seemed a further perfection. But it was her inner loveliness that made her special, the gentle, unruffled, amused glow that everyone responded to.

Friedrich, her father, was quite different, very tall and thin and pale, with fine, straight hair, prominent cheekbones, and large, luminous eyes. In photographs, it seemed to Claudia now, that his expression was sad, even haunted, except in those where he relaxed in the company of his wife and daughter.

Even as a young child she understood that Friedrich was

desperately, nakedly in love with her mother. When Lotte reached out, in her slow, smiling fashion, to touch his cheek, he would gaze at her like a boy, a terrible gladness in his eyes.

He called their house Mailied – May Song – after a love poem by Goethe and sometimes, in a skittish mood, he would recite it dramatically to Lotte. Claudia hated it when he did, pummelling him with her small fists and shouting at him to stop. Laughingly Friedrich played up to her childish fury, enunciating the ode with outrageous, hammy fervour and holding her flailing wrists at arm's length. She could see now that it had been rivalry. Both of them adored Lotte and competed for her love. As a young child Claudia sometimes fantasized her father dying, herself living alone with Mutti, never needing to feel jealous or left out.

At the same time, she *did* love Friedrich, found his pale, grave face endlessly fascinating, was charmed by the way his dreamy, absent expression metamorphosed into a smile of great sweetness when he talked to her, like sunlight emerging from behind a cloud. Her father explained things to her as if she were an adult, and always seemed to have time.

Apart from family, the household consisted of two young maids called Resi and Grete – who'd been plucked from an orphanage in Hamburg which specialized in turning out skilled domestic servants – and Otto, a lanky Berliner with a tough, crooked smile. He fulfilled a variety of roles, from maintenance man, through jobbing gardener, to part-time chauffeur. All had been chosen by Lotte for their youth and cheerfulness.

'I couldn't bear my daughter to grow up surrounded by crabby old servants the way Friedrich and I did,' Claudia had heard her telling friends and neighbours. 'A child has the right to be happy at home.'

Claudia regarded them rather as indulgent young aunts and uncles who made her laugh, taught her popular songs and slang, looked after her in a rough-and-ready fashion when they had to – Lotte wouldn't have a nanny in the house.

They lived in the leafy, lake-studded suburb of Grunewald. Their house overlooked the Hundekehlesee, one of the network of lakes that ringed the city, and had a long sweep of garden that ran right down to the water's edge, to a clump of weeping willows, a small boathouse and a jetty.

On summer evenings Friedrich would take them rowing. To the end of her life Claudia recalled the breathless, unearthly peace of those outings, with their small boat gliding across the smooth, silent water that reflected the colours of the sunset. She liked to gaze back at their house with neutral eyes, as if it belonged to someone else, but exulting quietly in the security and familiarity of ownership.

Mailied was, in effect, a glorified, white-painted chalet, spacious but homely, not grand like some of the villas that ringed the lake. It was three storeys high and all the windows were flanked by tidy, varnished shutters. A decorative wooden balcony ran right round the first floor of the building and, at ground level, a verandah, festooned with roses, clematis and jasmine, looked out towards the lake. What Claudia liked best were the two carved horses' heads that adorned the apex of the steeply pitched roof, one facing east, the other west. They were two-dimensional, like a child's hobby horse, with pricked-up ears and stiff, curving manes and, in Claudia's view, they made the house special.

Inside it was light and airy. Lotte favoured white-painted walls and plain furniture, though Claudia realized later that their tables and chairs, chests and cupboards were handmade by celebrated craftsmen, their value belying the simplicity of their design.

In comparison, the house of friends and relatives seemed formal, dark and stuffy and Claudia was confirmed in her childhood conviction that her own home, her own family were the yardstick by which all others should be judged.

The firm, Stephan Farnholz, based in Hamburg, imported exotic fabrics, carpets and knick-knacks from the orient to embellish the homes of the well-to-do bourgeoisie. During the eighties and nineties trade flourished and, in the early years of the century, the decision was made to open a branch and a retail outlet in Berlin's busy Tauentzienstrasse. Though the import side of the business retained the solid Farnholz name, the shop – after a deal of soul-searching – was called Bagatelle to appeal to the more frivolous clientele of Berlin. It fell on Friedrich, as son and heir, to establish the new enterprise.

Friedrich's father had always run the firm on liberal and paternalistic lines. Employees who showed flair and application were promoted and given responsibility. Two of these trusties were found homes in Berlin and dispatched to help and advise Friedrich in his undertaking.

In particular, a long-serving retainer called Herr Hassreiter, an elderly martinet with a tiny nutcracker face and gold pince-nez, knew everything there was to know about the business and Friedrich relied on him heavily.

'Herr Hassreiter will see to it,' was his breezy evasion whenever he wanted to avoid getting bogged down in the tedious nuts and bolts of pricing and accounting.

To the extent that, when Claudia, aged six, was urged to practise her letters and numbers, she retorted cheekily, 'Herr Hassreiter will see to it.' Friedrich and Lotte were enchanted by her precocious wit and the phrase passed into family legend.

Friedrich enjoyed all the vaguely artistic aspects of his work – selecting and arranging rich fabrics, rugs and unusual pottery for the shop, or planning eye-catching advertising ploys – but the day-to-day running of the business bored him profoundly. It had always gone smoothly and satisfactorily and he assumed it always would. He regarded days spent in the office, consultation trips to Hamburg, as interruptions to his real life.

Some mornings, as he left, Friedrich and Lotte would perform a private pantomime, a kind of operatic farewell scene, with Lotte, in her ivory silk dressing gown from Bagatelle, hanging on her husband's arm and begging him to stay, while Friedrich, in his dark suit and starched white shirt, would edge with melodramatic reluctance towards the door.

'Don't be so silly!' The clowning bothered Claudia. She didn't understand it.

'Don't you like it? It's Verdi.' Friedrich was laughing, but the laughter was between himself and Lotte, and excluded her. She always hated that.

Her father tended the business as little as he was able. He used to joke about the Teutonic work ethic and how it seemed to have passed him by completely.

He and Lotte were perfectly happy to spend whole days pottering with their respective hobbies. Lotte loved to look after the garden and do the odd little tapestries she designed herself, like bright, colourful doodles. Friedrich enjoyed sketching and playing the piano. He told Claudia once he would have liked to be a musician.

'Why didn't you then, Papi?' She'd learned to have scant respect for Friedrich's line of work.

'Grandpa Stephan wouldn't let me,' he replied, with that look in his eyes that meant he was teasing in a grown-up way she couldn't understand. Then he gave a short, dry laugh. 'And anyway, if you don't try, you don't have to fail.'

To round off these leisurely days, Friedrich, Lotte and Claudia would often drive out to the Kleine Brücke restaurant on the shores of the Wannsee and eat dinner out of doors on a balcony overlooking the water while a string quintet played Strauss waltzes. Between them, over the season, they managed to try out every one of the thirty flavours of ice cream that were the speciality of the restaurant. Propped on a cushion across from her parents, the three of them laughing at absurd family jokes, Claudia felt supremely happy, blissfully secure.

At six years old Claudia started school and regarded it rather as Friedrich regarded work, as a necessity imposed by society that had really nothing much to do with her. It wasn't unpleasant. She mastered her lessons without difficulty, didn't mind her teacher, Fräulein Hoffmann – though her face was too narrow and her nostrils too wide – enjoyed playing in the adjacent field with the other children. But it all seemed somehow monochrome and insubstantial compared to the highly coloured pleasure of her home life.

For her seventh birthday treat Claudia was taken to the Palast

Theater to see a variety show, a series of turns ranging from clowns and comedians to magicians and performing dogs. She was transported by the brightly lit rectangle framed by gold-and-maroon velvet curtains, within which everyone was pinker, more smiley and more strikingly dressed than in real life.

She was particularly taken by a comedian called Bruno Sperling. He wore a big checked suit and had eyebrows painted on his forehead like black rooftops and looked at the audience over one shoulder with a sly, simple-minded grin. Claudia caught Lotte and Friedrich exchanging dubious glances above her head as she laughed delightedly at the rude things he said, just like the boys at school.

But her favourite was Alma Albrecht, who had thick, curly red hair and a dress fit for a princess, with shiny sequins, iridescent like pearls, but which stopped short halfway down her thighs to reveal pink tights and dainty pink shoes whose laces crisscrossed right up to her knees. She sang like an angel in a sweet, soulful voice and did a slow balletic dance, then was joined by a chorus of ladies in white bloomers, and began belting out a cheerful, raucous song in Berlinese dialect, followed by a rowdy, frenetic cancan.

For days Claudia relived the woman's performance in a kind of dazzlement, trying out steps on her own and for Lotte, who whooped and called 'Hoppla!' when she kicked up her legs.

'Would you like to be a dancer, Mausi?'

Claudia nodded. She could imagine nothing more glorious than to wear a short, pearly frock and stand in the spotlight – out of breath, smiling impishly and fanning herself with one hand – as Alma Albrecht had done, while below, in the warm, dark auditorium, complete strangers erupted into a frenzy of stamping, clapping and cheering.

'You never know.' Lotte pulled the wry, funny face that seemed to say, I understand exactly how you feel.

A few days later Claudia was taken to the Bernhard Dancing Academy in the Königsallee. It was housed on the ground floor of a typically massive Berlin apartment block. She and Lotte were shown into a long, high, echoing room, with elaborately moulded ceilings and mirrors on all the walls, in order to sit in on a ballet lesson for ten- and eleven-year-old girls.

They were supervised by Frau Marianne Bernhard, a slim, dark woman in her late twenties, whose black, centrally-parted hair was partially hidden under a bold mauve-and-black scarf tied gypsy-wise. Her athletic body appeared to advantage in an austere black uniform, consisting of a sleeveless, belted tunic and tights. She carried a cane, with which she emphasized her orders and rapped out rhythms on the bare parquet floor. In one corner a self-effacing young male pianist sat at an upright piano, starting and stopping the music as required.

The pupils were attired like their teacher, though their tunics were pale grey. Their hair was drawn back and secured under black chenille nets. At Frau Bernhard's command they struck a continuing succession of graceful poses. Her instructions were issued in ringing tones and in a baffling jargon that Claudia found highly impressive. But she was particularly intrigued by the faces of the young dancers – their remoteness and haughtiness, their utter seriousness.

None of this bore much resemblance to Alma Albrecht's boisterous capering, but it had a ritual and a powerful magic of its own that caught Claudia's imagination.

Halfway through the lesson the class took a break and Lotte conversed with Marianne Bernhard and her small, lithe husband, Hugo. Claudia paid them no attention. She had eyes only for the young pupils, standing chatting in a variety of negligent, stylish dancers' attitudes. Some balanced on the points of their toes, others stood hands on hips, one knee out-thrust. A girl with slanting brown eyes straightened her right leg against a bar on the wall and laid her forehead flat against it. A golden-haired child bent to adjust the ribbons on both shoes, pointing each toe in turn. All displayed a similar graceful self-absorption as if they shared membership of some rare and exclusive cult. Claudia felt she'd glimpsed an enviable and mysterious new world. She longed to be initiated.

At Bernhard's Academy Claudia discovered a new sphere that rivalled that of her own home in excitement and satisfaction. She revelled in the sense of belonging to this fresh and exotic milieu, of being an insider. It was bliss to wear her tunic and tights, the severe yet dramatic hairnet, to lace on her satin shoes. She loved to watch her reflection in the mirror pointing its toes and raising its arms, fingers elegantly curved, just like a real dancer.

She was in awe of Frau Bernhard – who had to be addressed as Madame – with her autocratic, black-ringed eyes, high-bridged nose and plum-red mouth, her succession of bright, patterned headscarves. When taking her classes, Madame never used the special, honeyed talking-to-children tone that Fräulein Hoffmann, Claudia's school-teacher, favoured, but retained the matter-of-fact harshness her voice possessed naturally. Neither did she make allowances for seven-year-olds. The simple movements she asked of them had to be as perfect as those executed by the older girls, with several certificates to their credit. At the same time she was fair, never personal or vindictive, inspiring worship rather than fear in her pampered young pupils from the suburbs.

Her husband, Hugo, was far more approachable, a small man with steel-rimmed spectacles, rough brown hair, a rueful, smiling face and an engaging giggle. His pupils called him simply Herr Bernhard, and he appeared to play second fiddle to his formidable wife, though later Claudia came to realize that it was Hugo who taught the top girls, the ones who showed promise and persisted beyond the level of mere childhood dancing classes.

Both the Bernhards had lean, flexible, whipcord bodies and moved, so Claudia thought, like a ferret she'd once seen running through long grass, in one fluid, sinuous, seemingly effortless motion.

At dancing class Claudia met Lili Klarmann, her childhood best friend. Lili was small with a pert little face, a turned-up nose and soft brown hair cut in a short bob that was unique among pupils of the Academy. In her regulation hairnet Lili looked a bedraggled sight, curls scraped back from her rounded forehead and locks of hair escaping wispily from between the black chenille threads. Some of the girls made fun of her and Lily pretended to ignore them, though Claudia could see she was hurt. Claudia always liked the way she looked, fluffy and cheeky like a baby bird.

It turned out that Lili lived only half a mile away in Grunewald so the two girls often travelled in together, in one or other family motor. They played together on Saturday afternoons, dressing up from a box of cast-off finery Lotte had put together, continuing their dancing-class activities to begin with, but gradually widening their scope, inventing a plethora of imaginative games. They were queens of their own secret country, explorers discovering a new island and camping on its shore in an improvised tent. They were horses, they were Hansel and Gretel, clinging and cowering, but going on to triumph over the wicked witch. Claudia had never met anyone like Lili, who could throw off reality, forget who she was, and lose herself so passionately in a world of fantasy. Afternoons spent with her new friend passed in a heightened blur.

'Lili's father's quite well known.' Lotte and Friedrich seemed impressed with the friendship.

'Claudia's quite chummy with the Klarmann child,' they told acquaintances.

Apparently Andreas Klarmann was a moderately well-known writer. They always played at Claudia's house because he mustn't be disturbed. But on some warm Saturday evenings the Klarmann parents strolled across to pick Lili up and stayed for a cup of coffee, or even some chilled wine, in the garden. Claudia noticed that in his company Lotte and Friedrich seemed flustered, almost nervous.

Eva Klarmann was young and looked a lot like her daughter, childlike and round-faced, with that same soft brown hair cut in the same daring bob. Andreas was older. Lotte said he was sophisticated and had an aristocratic face, but these words had little meaning for Claudia. She noticed his skin was beige-coloured and that he had dark bags below his eyes. He seemed friendly and miles away both at the same time, and smoked cigarettes with a tired and wonderfully elegant air.

Lili didn't go to school, but had her lessons at home with a governess. And on Saturday mornings a young actress friend of the Klarmanns arrived to give her elocution and singing lessons.

'Fräulein Böhm is with Max Reinhardt's company,' Claudia had heard Eva explaining to Lotte, and her mother had made admiring sounds.

About a year after the two girls had met, Eva Klarmann graciously

61

extended an invitation to Claudia to come and share in the Saturday morning classes.

'Would you like to?' Lotte asked. Adding encouragingly, 'It might be fun.' As ever, her manner was calm and caressing, but Claudia could see she was quite excited by the honour.

So once a week, for the next four or five years, Claudia joined Lili in the schoolroom tucked away at the top of the Klarmann house. It was a large room with sloping ceilings, surprisingly bare and spartan for the only child of a wealthy family. The floor was uncarpeted. The furniture consisted of an upright piano, a large, polished table and four chairs, a tall bookcase which held dull-looking tomes in leather bindings. An imposing globe on a stand – its continents and oceans meticulously hand-painted – provided the only splash of colour.

In her late twenties, Fräulein Böhm was voluptuously fat, with clear, creamy skin and wide, myopic chestnut eyes. She wore gathered skirts and patterned smocks, and spirally locks of red-brown hair escaped from her chignon to frame her large and rather beautiful face. Both speaking and singing the actress possessed a voice that was as vibrant, richly textured and pleasing as music played on a seasoned cello.

Fräulein Böhm devoted the first hour to speech, the second to singing. Their voices echoed in the hollow roof-void. The actress's bohemian air was deceptive. Her methods were rigorous and exhaustive, thoroughly Germanic. Though Claudia was tickled by the idea of sharing with Lili, she couldn't really call the lessons enjoyable.

But, as time passed, it began to dawn on her, when she heard the other children at school singing or reciting, that they were breathing in all the wrong places, and their voices sounded pinched and tinny. Claudia longed to correct them, and understood that she'd learned more than she realized, that it was a privilege really, quite a stroke of luck to have a teacher as eminent as the redoubtable Fräulein Böhm.

Lili's parents took them to the Deutsches Theater to see Maria Böhm, as the programme named her, in a production of *Romeo and Juliet*. Although their teacher was a young woman, she played the nurse, and stole the show with the busybody hint of a Saxon accent she used for the part and the way she got the audience on her side with a confidential smile that wasn't crude or overdone, but just right. Fräulein Böhm was *good*, Claudia thought, as she sat in the dark, listening to the familiar rich, rounded voice.

As they grew up, she and Lili shared an all-absorbing fantasy. Whenever they were together the two of them played at being actresses. They weren't concerned with technicalities – Fräulein Böhm took care of those. It was image that obsessed them.

Motoring into Bernhard's Academy they sat in dramatic poses, legs crossed, heads thrown back, gazing languidly at the world through lowered eyelids. And on Saturday afternoons they locked themselves in Claudia's bedroom, took turns at the triple dressing-table mirror and made up their faces with thinned-down colour from her paintbox.

Claudia felt scared and excited by how different they looked. Sort of seductive, to use one of Fräulein Böhm's favourite words. Lili was like a pretty, painted boy, with the short, buoyant curls surrounding her new face with the blue eyelids and cherry lips. Claudia loosened her hair and let it hang, crimped from her plaits, smudged her eye sockets with smoky violet, gave herself a crimson slash of a mouth. They laughed but were shocked and fascinated by their unfamiliar, alluring selves. The masks were washed off before they unlocked the door. A sure instinct told them their parents wouldn't approve.

'When we're actresses . . .'

They invoked the fantasy endlessly, imagining themselves famous and still friends, playing opposite Kurt Eulenburg, the actor they'd seen as *Romeo*, with his melancholy eyes and sweep of blond hair, having him somehow fall in love with them both. Though, alongside this dream, Claudia still pictured herself as wife and mother, staying home and running the house like Lotte. The contradiction didn't bother her. Being grown-up was a long way off.

Chapter Six

Right from the start 1914 was a portentous year. During the iron-grey, icy days of early January, Grandpa Stephan died of some kind of lung collapse. All his adult life he'd been addicted to strong cigars. The doctor looked no further for the cause.

His was the first death that touched Claudia directly. She'd somehow thought her own family immune. It made a solemn impression but she felt no real grief. Lotte only took her to Hamburg once a year, usually in winter. The house there was big and stuffy, crammed with furniture and ornaments. Friedrich's unmarried sister, Agathe, was nice, but Grandma and Grandpa seemed terribly stiff and old-fashioned and Claudia could never think of anything to say to them.

But his father's death put Friedrich in charge of the whole firm. In March he had to go and stay in Hamburg for three tedious weeks to sort things out. The prospect hung over him like a black cloud. The minutiae of the import business were an oppression to his soul.

'Poor darling.' Lotte embraced him protectively as he left. It was early morning. She was still in her pale silk dressing gown, dark undulating hair hanging on her shoulders. She smiled sleepily. 'You look as if you're going to your own execution.'

'I am.' There was no answering glint of laughter in Friedrich's eyes.

While he was away Lotte looked white and drawn. Twice Claudia heard her being sick. To her amazement it turned out that her mother was pregnant. Lotte was thirty-five, Claudia twelve – thirteen in June. It had never occurred to her that she would be anything but an only child. The baby was expected in November.

It was a little embarrassing when friends found out. Some of the girls she knew sniggered. The gap since Claudia was so large. And Lotte was special – youthful and still attractive – not one of those righteous Catholic matriarchs who produced a brat every year or so. No one took any notice of their fertility. Claudia herself was bemused. Why had it happened now? Why, after all these years?

Her mother's pregnancy was grim and debilitating. Spring was beautiful, flooded with bright, brash sunshine, but Lotte stayed indoors, neglecting her beloved garden, resting wanly on the angular Rosenheim chaise longue. Claudia couldn't remember her ever looking like this before – features thickened and waxen, hair limp, limbs sausagey and swollen. She had almost no appetite, retched uncontrollably whenever she did manage to eat, suffered with frequent headaches.

'This is so silly, Mausi.' Lotte appeared bewildered. Her health had never let her down. 'But it's early days. Soon I'll be back to my old self.'

Friedrich was concerned, but had his own worries. He was distant and withdrawn with the pressure of being responsible for the whole of the Farnholz business. In late April Herr Hassreiter died quite suddenly of a stroke. Without his mentor's testy, reassuring presence Friedrich felt quite terrifyingly exposed.

Sensing the atmosphere the maids, Resi and Grete, became unsettled and petty squabbles punctuated their normally equable relationship. Suddenly Mailied was not the charmed and sunny enclave it had always been for Claudia, her serenely self-contained home.

She remembered one soft May evening, Friedrich's beanpole figure seated at the grand piano, pounding out a Chopin polonaise with haggard ferocity, it seemed with a kind of despair.

Lotte was in bed. Claudia sat out on the verandah, staring through the blue dusk at the shiny, darkening water, and she was invaded by a feeling of anguish, envisaging, for the first time in her life, the possibility of ill fortune.

Her happiness depended on these two beings she'd thought changeless, whose careless invulnerability she had always taken for granted. Now it occurred to her that the bright bubble around them could be breached, and she was afraid.

As the year went on, Claudia began to notice that her parents' friends and neighbours talked about war a great deal, almost as if they wanted it to happen.

Even at the *Gymnasium* in the Friedrichsruherstrasse, where she was at school now, Fräulein Richter, the history teacher, who always seemed so dowdy and demure, spent half a lesson telling them how Germany was put upon by its neighbours and would someday teach them a lesson they wouldn't forget. Her face went red and her eyes grew quite wild. The girls were impressed. There was usually a lot of chatter in her classes but, that afternoon, Fräulein Richter kept her audience enthralled.

War fever was assimilated into the make-believe world Claudia inhabited with Lili. They played at being actresses with soldier-lovers, made veils out of an old black lace apron in Claudia's dressing-up box, and acted out passionate farewell scenes.

'Vati wouldn't be too pleased if he could hear me now,' Lili confided, with an adorable, quick, guilty smile. 'He's a pacifist.'

'What's that?'

'Someone who hates all fighting.'

'Lili's father's a pacifist,' Claudia told Friedrich.

'He'd better keep quiet about that,' her father replied. 'All decent Germans are just spoiling for a fray if only they can find a halfway plausible excuse.' He sounded cynical as if, in his heart, he sympathized with Andreas Klarmann.

At the end of June Archduke Franz Ferdinand of Austria was assassinated by a Serbian nationalist and Friedrich reckoned that might turn out to be the pretext they needed. Claudia couldn't imagine why. Austria and Serbia were miles away.

In early July the Farnholz family went on holiday to Norderney. The sun was brilliant and twinkled on water that reflected the azure of the sky. Propped on a bank of cushions, Lotte sunbathed among the sparkling white sand dunes. Husband and daughter rigged up makeshift screens to protect her from the wind. Her face took on some colour and she and Friedrich joked the way they used to. Claudia began to think that everything was coming right again.

When the fortnight was over, they arrived home to find a pile of mail waiting on the blond wood table in the vestibule. There was a letter for Lotte from Eva Klarmann. It appeared to be written in haste and informed Frau Doktor Farnholz that all future lessons with Fräulein Böhm were suspended. The Klarmann family had left Berlin to take up residence in Zurich.

'For good?' Claudia was stunned.

Lotte spread her hands, looking mystified. 'That's all it says.'

'It's obvious, isn't it?' Friedrich spoke with casual finality. 'It's the international situation . . . with him a pacifist.'

Claudia was baffled, then there came a glimmer of understanding. 'You don't mean that Serbian thing?'

Friedrich was adamant, but Claudia couldn't credit it. What had Serbia got to do with them? How on earth could something so entirely irrelevant take Lili away from her?

Her whole being protested. This just wasn't right. Darling Lili was her partner in a potent, exotic fantasy world they could enter at any time. They'd created it together in glorious earnest, rejecting by mutual consent the need for giggling and embarrassment. That would never be possible with anyone else. And now she was left behind with just drab reality. It was too sad. It wasn't enough. And how could Lili just melt away like that with no warning, without even writing?

'They'll have had to go quickly,' Friedrich comforted. 'And secretly. Herr Klarmann will be seen as a traitor now, you know.'

A traitor. Claudia pictured his poker face, his languid, enviable way with cigarettes, and preferred it to the over-eager businessman who'd shared their railway compartment on the way home and echoed Fräulein Richter's speech almost word for word, with the same heightened colour, the same hot look in his eyes.

Claudia grieved for the loss of her friend with a raw, private ache. At the same time it was impossible not to be distracted by outside events. Apparently Friedrich had been right in his improbable prediction and the Austrian assassination was going to produce fateful upheavals. As the days went by all sorts of ultimata were issued by countries the length and breadth of Europe. Even Russia was somehow involved. Claudia's grasp of the situation was vague but the feverish excitement was contagious.

By early August Germany was at war with several other nations. All the neighbours were euphoric and hung flags from their balconies to celebrate the initial successes of the German Army. Prudently Lotte hung a banner or two from the upstairs window. These days one had to be seen to be patriotic. There was a special charged feeling in the air. People stopped and talked to perfect strangers and everyone had something in common, everyone felt involved. The intoxication infected Claudia, she couldn't help it. But simultaneously her suspicion hardened that life wasn't safe or predictable any more.

At home the unsettled atmosphere returned. Friedrich jeered at the universal hysteria, but his business was hard hit by the onset of hostilities. The kind of fripperies his livelihood depended on were expendable at a time like this, and anyway, all available ships had been requisitioned for the war effort. Lotte, after her brief rally, had succumbed again to grey-faced lethargy.

'Everything'll be fine, I'm certain, once the baby's here,' she kept reassuring Claudia. 'But never again, Liebchen, never again.'

Tante Agathe arrived at the beginning of November, ready for Lotte's lying-in. She was down-to-earth and practical, not like Friedrich at all. It was good to have her there. She dispelled the scared feeling Claudia sometimes had that she and Lotte and Friedrich had been jinxed.

About a week after Agathe's arrival Claudia came home from school to find that her mother was in labour.

'Just get on with your homework, child, as if it were a normal day. Stay out of the way. There's nothing you can do.' Agathe pulled a droll face. 'Childbirth's no spectacle for a child of your age.' Friedrich's sister wasn't pretty but she had warm luminous eyes and a smile with nothing complicated behind it. You couldn't take offence at her plain speaking.

Claudia finished her mathematics and her French and ate some soup Grete made for her. The coming and going was distracting. She could hear the rumble of the doctor's voice through the ceiling. Every so often Agathe or a nurse would trip down the stairs and up again on some mysterious mission. Lotte was quiet, though occasionally she whimpered a little. The wait seemed interminable.

Claudia wandered into the darkened living room and jumped. Friedrich sat silent on the chaise longue, visible only in the shaft of light that fell across the floor from the doorway. In the dimness he looked white and strange, a wraith.

'*Na, Claudia.*' He held out one hand to her.

She sat with him for a while, but it seemed they had no comfort to offer one another. Both were focused on Lotte. She was the bridge between them. Without her soothing presence Claudia sensed a gulf that harked back to earliest childhood when they were rivals for her love.

'Papi, I'm going outside for a bit.'

'Don't catch cold.'

Claudia took an old sheepskin rug from the cupboard in the vestibule. Friedrich had always claimed it used to be wrapped round his parents' knees when he and Agathe were children and the family went for sleigh-rides across the frozen Elbe estuary.

She walked down to the jetty at the end of the garden. It was a still night, and icy cold. Wrapping herself in the sheepskin, Claudia sat down with her back against the boathouse wall. The lake looked black and shiny, the stars very clear. The aloneness was peaceful.

Lotte, Friedrich, Claudia. For the first time, consciously, she framed the thought that their triangular relationship was about to alter its dynamic for ever. Their threesome would be augmented by a new and real human being, who would burrow out a place among them, have the right to consideration, be as important, as . . . solid as any of them. A person. The notion was revolutionary. Until then, Claudia realized, the baby had been just an abstraction. She looked up at the vastness of the sky, feeling small but safe cocooned in her blanket, feeling eager for the change.

Claudia heard footsteps, but stayed where she was. It was Friedrich.

He stood for a moment, looking down at her. She didn't know how long she'd been there, couldn't tell what he was thinking.

He bent down and touched her shoulder. 'Come and see your brother.'

An old-fashioned oil-lamp burned in Lotte's bedroom – only the ground floor of the house had electricity. Her mother lay back on a big square bolster. Her dark hair was spread across a white pillowcase edged with the thick handmade lace that adorned most of the linen they'd brought with them from Hamburg. Her cheeks were flushed. In the soft light her eyes looked very black and bright, the sockets deeply shadowed.

'Darling, where have you been? I've been asking for you.' No other voice had that special lingering tenderness. 'Look at him.' She leaned a little sideways to peer into the muslin-draped crib by the bed. 'He's adorable. And he's got curly hair just like me.'

Claudia stared into the cradle. Above the knitted cotton blanket she saw a tiny face. The baby's eyes were closed. She thought he looked like a miniature Eskimo with his flat features and fine, dark hair. So this was the little creature who, simply by being born, had earned his place in the Farnholz family circle. She gazed at him with affectionate ambivalence.

'I've been thinking about the baby,' Claudia said. 'And how he's one of us.' She threw her arms round Lotte's neck, laid her head against her mother's shoulder. It felt as if some ordeal had been endured and they had survived. She began to sob, quietly, convulsively, a mixture of joy and tension released.

'Don't cry, Mausi.' Lotte stroked her hair. 'Everything's all right now. Don't cry, darling.'

Friedrich came in with four tulip-shaped glasses and a bottle that was almost as dark as the black, lacquered tray on which it stood. He opened the champagne with skittish flamboyance, making the cork pop and fly across the room, then filling the glasses with a sommelier's deft twist of the wrist.

Tante Agathe joined them and, in the flickering lamplight, they

70

drank to the new life. Claudia picked up the cork and slipped it into the pocket of her dress as a keepsake. Now her tears were done she was filled with a torpid happiness. Later, beneath her feather quilt, she slept the sleep of the just.

Next morning Claudia woke to a calm sense of pleasure. She sat up and swung her legs out of bed. Her first impulse was to go and see Lotte and her baby brother. Barefoot and still in her white flannel nightdress, she left her room. The landing outside was deserted, yet seemed pervaded by an atmosphere she couldn't place, as if something were not as it should be. Lotte's door stood ajar. Cautiously – her mother might be sleeping – Claudia peered into the room. The bed was empty, the crib gone.

She heard the click of Agathe's bedroom door at the far end of the hall. Over her high-necked nightgown her aunt wore an embroidered Chinese wrap.

'Claudia, you're awake.' Agathe's hair hung in two loose plaits over her shoulders. 'We let you sleep – you were dead to the world.'

Her aunt came and laid reassuring hands on Claudia's shoulders. 'You mustn't be frightened, dear. Only your mother's in hospital. During the night she had a fever. She was delirious. Your father drove her to the infirmary – he's still there. I'm looking after the child.'

Claudia struggled to make sense of Agathe's words, but they didn't tally with last night's gladness and relief.

'We'll know more when you come home from school,' her aunt continued. 'I expect Papi will take you to see her tonight. Get dressed and have your breakfast. Be sensible, Liebling.'

Claudia did what she was told. She wasn't worried, just disappointed that their new life would be postponed for a day or two. That evening Agathe said she wouldn't after all be allowed to go and see Lotte. The outside world, with its infections, must be kept at bay. Apparently even Friedrich was banished to a bench in a corridor.

'I'm so sorry, dear. Try not to be upset. It'll help everyone if you're sensible.'

For three days Claudia was sensible. She went to school and did her homework in the evenings. It was dull and oppressive, her life reduced to a long, unspecified wait, but she did her best to be patient. No one had time for her. Friedrich spent his days and nights at the hospital. Agathe was wrapped up in the unfamiliar minutiae of nurturing a baby, feeding the child endlessly – so it seemed to Claudia – from a sort of teated bottle.

On the fourth day she came home to find Agathe solemnly waiting.

'Come into Papi's study, child.' Her aunt was terse, impressive.

'What is it?'

Agathe closed the door and turned to face her. There was a look in her aunt's eye that frightened Claudia – a funnelled determination. As if she were preparing to plunge into deep, icy water.

'Dear, you've got to be very, very brave.'

Claudia's stomach lurched. Her whole being stiffened with an unthinkable suspicion. 'Why?'

'Your mother died this afternoon.'

When Claudia looked back on the years that followed Lotte's death, she pictured herself crawling blindly through a long, dark tunnel. Her life was defined by mental pain. The war was an irrelevance. She was just vaguely aware that, after the first exhilaration, events went less well and the people around her began to grumble, became cynical and went hungry. But this affected her only distantly, like a thunderstorm rumbling a long way off.

Body and soul were consumed in an agony of loss. Never again would anyone love her as Lotte had, with the same unconditional generosity, that combination of tolerance and passion, firmness and indulgence. No one else would ever have the same smile, tranquil yet playful, infinitely kind.

She would never see Lotte again. That was the bald fact, and Claudia was annihilated by it. Though in dreams and in moments of distraction she could forget briefly, then wake to reality and be forced to make the same lacerating discovery all over again. She was an automaton, attending school, coming home, eating, sleeping, but dead inside.

There was a photograph from that period, taken by Agathe on

Claudia's fourteenth birthday. It frightened her. She hid it between the pages of a book and couldn't bring herself to retrieve it until years later. Had she really looked like that? So painfully emaciated, with such staring, mistrustful, defeated eyes. Her hair was clumped and uncombed, carelessly caught back with a crinkled piece of ribbon, her mouth twisted as if with disgust.

If anything Friedrich was worse. Lotte had been his life. She'd filled his austere world with love and now that world was empty. Silent and withdrawn, he seemed a ghost in the house, but erupted at times into despairing, unreasoning fury. In particular Agathe's moist-eyed solicitude seemed to goad him. One evening at table his sister pressed him to finish up a nourishing vegetable soup she had cooked specially for him. Instead Friedrich rose wildly to his feet, dashing his bowl to the parquet floor, where it shattered, splattering the steaming fragments of turnip and carrot far and wide. As Claudia sat by, tense and miserable, hot, silent tears coursed down her cheeks, splashed and spread on the heavy blue Indian cotton cloth.

'He's not in his right mind,' Agathe explained sadly as she gathered up shards of china and shreds of scarce, precious vegetable from the floor. 'You must try to understand, darling. He's mad at the moment. Quite literally mad with grief.'

Claudia saw now that Friedrich was essentially a solitary man. Lotte had been his connection with the outside world. She'd fostered the small, hard seeds of sociability in him. Now it appeared that even his own daughter was nothing to him in the absence of the woman that bound them together. Claudia had sensed it the night Rudi was born. Without the warm, live presence of Lotte, she and Friedrich lived like strangers, shrinking from touch, avoiding being alone together.

It was Agathe who kept the stricken household going, bringing up Rudi, trying clumsily to comfort her distraught brother and niece. Friedrich's sister was well-meaning, a gallant, unexceptional middle-aged woman, doing her best against fearful odds. But hers was a thankless role. She lacked completely Lotte's magnetic glamour and neither Friedrich nor Claudia could forgive her for that.

She was in the nature of a blunt instrument, plodding doggedly

73

on through the jagged atmosphere of the Farnholz home and through starving war-time winters. And even if her nearest and dearest were in no state of mind to appreciate her courage, Agathe was admired by friends and neighbours for the way she'd stepped in and taken up the reins of domestic management.

One woman, particularly, a Frau Kästner, who lived just round the corner, became Agathe's close friend. In more carefree days the Farnholz family had regarded her as something of a joke. She was genteel and sentimental, a sturdy woman with watery pale blue eyes. Unguardedly Frau Kästner had let slip once that her husband's pet-name for her was *Seelchen*. Little soul. From that day it was impossible for Lotte and Claudia to catch sight of her upright, eminently respectable figure, her uncompromising brown felt hat like an upturned coal-scuttle, without being put in mind of the wildly incongruous endearment.

She was childless and her husband was away at the front. The two women were company for one another, pooling skills and resources to beat the war-time shortages, spending whole afternoons together unpicking long-discarded garments to remake into wearable clothes. Friedrich was in no condition to forage for food, but Frau Kästner was a renowned local worthy and had ways and means of obtaining little extras now and again. And she was generous in sharing her good fortune with her friend.

But Rudi was Agathe's real consolation. She was the only mother the boy had ever known. He was her child. As she did her homework Claudia would hear her aunt talking to him in the kitchen and could picture her brown eyes, soft with love.

'Frau Kästner's found you a little drop of milk, my dicky-bird, and your auntie's going to make you some lovely bread and milk . . .'

And Claudia knew the child was smiling at the familiarity of her voice and her face, and she pitied him for having to content himself with this substitute mother, for the fact that he would never know the rare creature who'd given birth to him.

One bright autumn day, just before her brother's second birthday, Claudia looked through the window and saw Agathe and Rudi in the garden, chasing a big red ball.

'Run, dicky-bird! Fast now!' Agathe was calling.

And for once, in spite of the iron in her soul, Claudia warmed to her aunt, touched by her unselfconscious grin, the way she threw dignity to the winds, holding up her war-shabby black skirt and taking tiny steps, so that Rudi's little legs could carry him way ahead of her.

He picked up the ball, turning to Agathe with a loud, triumphant, hiccupping laugh, and it struck Claudia, like a sudden, painful stab-wound, that his was the only laughter that was ever heard in her home.

One blustery afternoon in early March 1917 Claudia returned from school to find the maids looking after Rudi. Agathe had gone out.

Grete seethed with suppressed excitement. 'A policeman came. Your auntie went away with him . . . She didn't even stop to put her hat on.'

It was dark before Agathe returned. Entering the dimly lit vestibule in her worn brown coat, greying hair straggly with the wind, she looked suddenly old. Her face was set and ashen.

'Something's happened . . .'

Claudia experienced a chill of apprehension.

'It's Papi –' Agathe stopped short, her eyes stricken.

'What?' In the bare hall Claudia's voice rang sharp.

'I've just seen . . . his body . . .' The words jerked out. '. . . In the police morgue.'

Claudia stared. The information made no sense.

Her aunt continued brokenly, 'He was found in the woods . . . Old Hermann stumbled on him . . . Claudia, child . . . he shot himself . . .' Emotion choked her.

Blindly Claudia stepped forward, held Agathe to her, fierce and still, as if a show of calm strength could counter the older woman's distress. Simultaneously her brain struggled to encompass the monstrous reality behind her aunt's disjointed statement.

'Next to him they found Grandpa's revolver . . . the one he kept

in the velvet case ... Mausi, his face was ... smashed, gone ...'
The words broke through a sob.

'Sh-h-h, now ... Don't ...'

Claudia stroked Agathe's hair, while her horrified mind hallucinated the stark vision of a workman she'd seen once, fallen from a ladder, his brains and bright blood splashed across the grey cobbles, a picture buried and denied for years. Then an image of Friedrich rose up in her head, the way she'd seen him only that morning, grave-faced, his tall figure stooping to pick a spray of the white violets Lotte used to love, pinning them in his buttonhole with unhurried care. He'd looked so normal. And all the time ... She closed her eyes, overwhelmed by a graphic sense of Friedrich's desolation, his final, despairing resolution ...

Dully Agathe released herself from Claudia's grasp. 'Rudi mustn't see me like this. I'll go and tidy myself before ...' But reaching the stairs she collapsed, and gave way to a fit of cataclysmic weeping. It was as if, not merely the shock and grief of her brother's suicide, the memory of his mangled corpse, but all the rebuffs, all the discouragement she had suffered since Lotte's death, swept over her in a sudden, monstrous tidal wave.

Claudia was lost in the face of such blind, frenzied, overwhelming emotion from the woman who had been their rock for the last two and a half years. In times gone by she would have called a doctor, demanded a sleeping draught, but doctors were not available for such trivialities nowadays.

Her aunt's anguish was like some convulsive natural disaster absorbing all of Claudia's attention. She felt powerless, then remembered in a flash of inspiration that, locked away in the cellar, stood the remains of Friedrich's pre-war stock of fine brandy. Over a scrappy, hastily built wood fire she heated up the small, sacred cupful of milk Frau Kästner obtained for Rudi every so often. Into the precious liquid she poured a hefty measure of cognac. Begging and threatening, she managed to persuade Agathe to drink the mixture down and, within a few minutes, her aunt was helplessly sozzled.

With the help of the maids, Claudia half dragged, half carried her up the stairs and laid her on the bed, still fully dressed. She sat with Agathe, soothing and consoling, until her aunt began to snore, overcome by the merciful oblivion of a drunken sleep.

Rudi was scared and unsettled by the alarming change in his safe, loving protector.

'Come and have your supper, sparrow.' Claudia lifted him up. 'Auntie's sleeping. She'll be better tomorrow,' forcing herself to sound calm and unconcerned.

The maids were cooking potatoes and she took some for herself and Rudi. He was abashed and round-eyed with the novelty of being looked after by someone other than Agathe, and gratifyingly biddable, allowing himself to be fed and tucked up in bed.

Deliberately Claudia postponed her own confrontation with Friedrich's death until Rudi and Agathe were settled. Her brother lay now with his mouth a little open, one small, soft hand, fingers curled, visible above the white coverlet. He began to breathe quietly and regularly. She tiptoed out, went to her own room, undressed, then lay chilled and huddled under the feather quilt.

'Papi's dead.' She whispered the words to herself, but her mind could not encompass them.

In the darkness a picture came to mind of Friedrich the way he used to be, on one of the idle, blissful days he used to spend at home when she was young. He'd sketched a portrait of Lotte on a pad of cartridge paper and was holding it up to show his wife and child.

'Another masterpiece!' Friedrich was laughing but, across the years, Claudia had kept the memory of a look in his eye that had disturbed her then, though she didn't know why. It was a look of incredulity, even fear, that belied his smile, as if he'd known all the time that his contentment was fragile. It seemed then that a light shone out of him, a kind of watchful hope, as if he hadn't counted on happiness but miraculously it had been granted and he could never quite believe it.

Since Lotte's death the light had been doused. And Friedrich had never fought to rekindle it. It was as if the happiness had been lent and the bleakness that engulfed him was simply what, in his heart of hearts, he'd always expected from the world. He had accepted the inevitable.

Tears began to well from beneath Claudia's closed eyelids, and along with them came a feeling of passionate pity. She was crying, she realized, for Friedrich's life rather than his death.

In time she drifted into sleep. When she woke the sun was shining through cracks in the shutters. Claudia felt rested, restored. She was invaded with an energy she barely recognized. It had been years since she felt so ready to face the day. Half guiltily she perceived that the optimism had its roots in a sense, not of loss, but of relief.

'We're going to be poor,' Agathe kept repeating, over and over, in hushed, incredulous tones.

For the first time she and Claudia had been forced to come to grips with the Farnholz family finances. Both women had been brought up in the belief that men understood the managing of money. Also to assume that, since funds had always been plentiful, they always would be. On both counts they could not have been more wrong.

Friedrich was up to his ears in debt. The war had closed Bagatelle down and decimated the family import business. But, on top of that, it was clear that in the last years he had let everything drift. He owed thousands on costly oriental carpets, wall-hangings and porcelain; he owed on the unexpired lease of the shop, on freight charges, account-ants' and lawyers' costs, household bills, even on Claudia's school fees. The drawers of his handmade beechwood desk were stuffed with unopened envelopes.

Once or twice the conjecture flickered like a pale flame at the back of Claudia's mind that perhaps her father's suicide had a certain amount to do with the accumulating mountain of financial muddle and his own pathological inertia, and was not altogether the heart-rending *Liebestod* Agathe sighed over with such reverence.

'Herr Viertel says we have to sell Mailied.'

This was the message Claudia brought away with her from a meeting with Friedrich's lawyers. Herr Viertel was tall, white-haired and unsmiling, reminding her of the portrait of Bismarck that used to hang on the classroom wall when she first started school. He made his contempt for Friedrich's bungling abundantly plain.

Claudia felt protective of her father and couldn't imagine how it would feel to be as ponderous and infallible as Herr Viertel. Though Agathe was devastated by this latest development, some malign spirit in Claudia was titillated by the drama. It was like living in a novel. Money had never been quite real to her anyway, had never needed to be.

The extremity of their plight only served to heighten the vigour she had rediscovered. In the wake of her brother's death Agathe was tearful and tremulous, racked with guilt, however unjustified. Claudia took her place now as the family's driving force.

She turned sixteen in June and promptly left school. With the turbulence of her life it seemed irrelevant, even absurd, to spend time composing essays on Frederick the Great or translating Caesar's *Gallic Wars*. Agathe protested, but it was a token gesture. She understood perfectly well that her niece was a free agent now. Claudia was heartily glad to be done with her prim, black school overall with the stupid white collar you had to take off and wash every two days, when there was no soap to be had for love nor money.

In September 1917 the house and contents were sold by auction. They were bought by Herr Ackermann, a neighbour whom Friedrich used to like, a music publisher and, by all accounts, a shrewd businessman. With the war prices were at rock bottom.

'Jews.' Agathe spoke the word with an uncharacteristic sneer. 'Trust them to root out a bargain.'

'The only reason the house went to Herr Ackermann,' Claudia pointed out, 'was because he offered a higher price than the rest.' But Agathe wasn't interested in logic.

'Please, ladies, when you leave, take away any small mementoes that are particularly meaningful . . .' Herr Ackermann was the soul of chivalry.

Claudia was in no mood to pick over the bones of her childhood. She kept the family photograph albums and a framed portrait of Lotte that Friedrich had done. She couldn't wait to be rid of the whole lot. It was cleaner and simpler that way.

But Agathe was brazen, gathering up choice ornaments and silver bibelots, an expensive set of Lötz-Witwe iridescent glass goblets, making her selection with a self-righteous, put-upon air, while Herr Ackermann watched in stunned silence.

'Many thanks, Herr Ackermann . . .' As she took her leave Agathe gazed at him, steady-eyed, challenging him to challenge her.

They moved into two rooms on the top floor of Frau Kästner's house. Her husband had died in France. Claudia, Agathe and Rudi were her first lodgers, but there would be others. After Friedrich's debts were settled there was enough left over to pay a year's rent in advance and to hide a small, flat canvas bag of banknotes behind the portrait of Lotte. That and the ornaments were all that stood between them and destitution.

The rooms were gloomy, the furniture heavy but, lying in the big, hard, gingery-brown bed that first night, fingers laced behind her head, Claudia felt light and free. Once she'd thought herself financially secure, but that had been an illusion. Now she knew exactly where she stood.

Sleepily Claudia gazed into the unfamiliar chiaroscuro of her room, at the black hulking shape of the mahogany wardrobe, the paler shimmer of the curtained window. She would have to find work. That was what girls did in novels when they fell on straitened circumstances. She was a little hazy as to how you went about it, but she would learn. She'd do anything, Claudia thought drowsily, cleaning, factory work, whatever . . .

By and by she drifted into sleep and dreamed of Lili, and Fräulein Böhm of all people, whom she hadn't thought about for ages. In the morning, lying half awake, Claudia knew once and for all that what she'd really like was to be an actress. But that would have to wait until after the war.

Chapter Seven

Amy stood on tiptoe to brush her hair in the square, black-speckled mirror that stood on top of the conker-coloured chest of drawers. She looked all eyes, apprehensive, rather as if she were about to go in for an examination for which she was unprepared. Behind her stood a big brass bed covered with a faded pink paisley eiderdown.

A woman had come out from Morwenstow, apparently, to clean and tidy the cottage. It smelled of furniture polish, as if to testify to her diligence. She'd laid a fire in the grate, ready to light. Robert Beadle, Noel's best friend, had made the arrangements. He and Noel had spent a blissful month here on the Cornish coast in the summer of 1914. Before the deluge.

'It's a marvellous little hideaway,' Noel had enthused. 'The perfect place for a honeymoon. And in autumn there'll be no one there but the locals. Absolutely far-from-the-madding-crowd.'

Amy was disappointed, though she tried not to show it. Barring the smell of cabbage, Plough Cottage was depressingly like old Mr and Mrs Pugh's place in Crofton, and she'd never thought there was anything particularly marvellous about that.

'I imagined we'd stay at some swanky honeymoon hotel,' she had protested cautiously, way back in July, when he first came up with the idea. But she'd said it in a half-joking way. There were attitudes and assumptions in Noel's world that Amy didn't yet understand, and she didn't want to look an idiot.

But the Kilverts had visited London recently and Charlie talked about the Kilbracken Hotel where they'd stayed. Apparently it was all done out in a pinky-beige colour, had lamps that looked like glowing tulips and baskets of fruit in the bedrooms. And while you were out at the theatre or dining, the maids turned down a corner of the sheet and laid one perfect rose on your pillow. Amy was intrigued and thought the whole thing sounded rather jollier than a primitive, mildly chilly cottage. And Noel could afford it. He had a private income from his father on top of his salary as a journalist.

'When you go somewhere like that, then it comes home to you that the war really is over,' Charlie cooed.

'Yes, Charlie *would* swoon over that sort of flash,' Noel had commented scathingly, and that was that.

The woman from the village had left a mutton stew in a saucepan, which they heated over the fire, and Noel opened a bottle of champagne. Amy had never drunk wine in her life, apart from a sip or two at the wedding yesterday. It made her feel slightly dizzy, not quite in control. It was fun sitting in front of the fire and she took Noel's hand, thinking it would be nice to kiss and cuddle in the warm glow.

But he said rather stiffly, as if a decision had been taken, 'Why don't you go and get ready for bed, darling?' He called her darling now that they were man and wife. 'I'll come and join you in a little while.' She was sure it wasn't intentional, but there was a hoarse, hollow sound to his voice that made the assurance sound like a threat.

'All right.' The merest breath of displeasure in her tone. His suggestion, his whole manner, lacked warmth and dispelled the cosy feeling she'd had a moment earlier.

Now, upstairs in the white-washed bedroom, Amy climbed into the high brass bed. She wore one of the basic square-necked nightgowns Margaret had sewed for her trousseau from some cheap, unbleached cotton. A candle burned on the bedside table. The air struck cold although it was only September.

They had motored down from Crofton in Noel's father's little Austin. Last night, after the wedding, Noel had slept at Matthew Kilvert's, Amy in her own room for the last time. Momentarily she was seized by a wave of nostalgia for the familiarity of the vicarage, the safety of her own bed. But that was sheer cowardice and sentimentality. For months she'd been aching to leave.

As she sat and waited for Noel, Amy thought about the manual called *Conjugal Love* that Margaret had handed her, without comment, a few days earlier. The book had been utterly dispiriting, with its buff cardboard covers, the flimsy, yellowing pages. The contents combined a strangely prurient emphasis on personal hygiene with graphic line drawings of the reproductive organs, the whole thing awkwardly spiced with incongruous flights of high-toned romanticism. Amy shivered. It was enough to damp the ardour of even the most hot-blooded prospective bride.

She heard his footsteps on the stairs and landing, the click of the latch and Noel entered the bedroom. As always, after even the smallest of absences, she was dazzled anew by the fact that this tall, clever, handsome, indubitably distinguished, indubitably superior being had chosen her to love and to marry.

Sometimes, privately, she thought his complexion too pink and English but, in the candlelight, his skin was as matt and pale as she could wish, his eyes as deep and luminous. His white shirt was casually open at the neck and she was moved by this contrast to his formal, public self.

He stood by the door for a moment, gazing at her. 'You look lovely,' he said simply and fervently.

Noel came and sat on the edge of the bed. 'We're really alone, Amy. No relatives to humour, no obligations. It's just us.' She was elated by the gladness in his voice. He reached out and held her close. Amy let herself relax against the warmth and strength of his body. Enfolded by his arms and bathed in his tenderness, she savoured a moment of pure happiness.

He began to kiss her, lightly at first, then with greater insistence and urgency, shifting to lie alongside her on the bed, caressing her arms, then her breasts, murmuring endearments. Amy kissed him back, entranced by their closeness. Through the months of their engagement opportunities for kissing and touching had been almost non-existent.

'Wait, darling.' Gently Noel pulled away and sat up. His eyes looked fevered and heavy. With vigorous, impatient movements he stripped off his shirt. In the brief moment before he extinguished the candle she glimpsed his bare torso, taut and muscular. When he lay down beside her under the bed covers, he was naked.

83

'Beautiful Amy.' Their embrace was like a homecoming. She strained against him with the whole length of her body, heard him gasp as though awed.

He touched the thin cotton of her gown. 'Take this off, darling, won't you . . .'

Amy sat upright, gathering the material of her nightdress, and pulled it over her head, finding the gesture an exhilaration, a liberation.

They fell again into one another's arms and now, with her own skin, Amy could feel clearly all the textures of his, the hard elasticity of muscle, the wiriness of hair on chest, legs, in his groin. She was half incredulous with the intimacy of the embrace.

'God, I love you,' Noel breathed, pressing himself to her, running his fingers down the smooth curves of her back, buttocks, thighs, groaning with the pleasure of it. Wonderingly she caressed him back, enchanted by the living warmth of their flesh, this breathtaking licence for the merging of their bodies. For Amy each moment was new, perfect, sufficient to itself. She let herself be carried along, an explorer on this unfamiliar tide of love and desire.

For a time Noel fondled her greedily, seeming intoxicated by her body, as if he could never have enough. Then, little by little, Amy sensed his ardour change, somehow lessen, though he continued to touch and embrace. An edge of bewilderment clouded her happiness, but she trusted Noel, had put herself in his hands.

Suddenly, though, he pulled away, and said with a kind of anguish, 'It's no good.' He rolled on to his back and lay with one arm shielding his eyes.

Amy was chilled. 'What's the matter?' she whispered into the dark.

'It's no good,' he repeated in the same stricken tone.

She was totally at sea. 'What's no . . . ?'

'Amy, I can't. Do you understand?'

'No.' To her own ears the response sounded artless, childish. But, even as she spoke, there came a wisp of memory – a sultry day, the parched alley behind the girls' toilets, Paul Oates, her childhood sweetheart, explaining mysteriously '. . . see, they lie down together and the man gets horny . . .' The fragment merged with one of the stark diagrams in *Conjugal Love*. Intuitively her mind made a connection. 'Oh, I see . . . I think . . .' the words trailing off inconclusively.

He didn't respond, lay in silence, one arm – she could dimly see – still laid across his eyes. Amy was devastated by a sudden sense of isolation and disenchantment, a creeping fear she didn't understand.

After a long silence Noel sat up and swung his legs abruptly over the edge of the bed. He stood up. She heard the rustle of clothes.

'I'm going downstairs for a bit.' A careful, withdrawn neutrality in his tone. 'Why don't you try and sleep.'

Then he leaned across and gently touched her cheek. 'Amy, I can't tell you how sorry I am.' He sounded stiff and embarrassed. He sounded ashamed. Her splendid Noel ashamed. She couldn't begin to contemplate the thought. Amy was left alone in the big brass bed, staring sightlessly at the ceiling. She felt young and inadequate. She felt scared.

'I'll show you all the places Robert and I discovered,' Noel had promised before they came.

He was as good as his word. They scrambled along the cliffs of Morwenstow, visited the church, picnicked in sheltered smugglers' coves. They motored to Bude and Tintagel, walked miles across Bodmin Moor under the hot, mellow September sky, drank cider and ate huge meals in rustic pubs. It should have been paradise, but Noel's humiliation and self-disgust was always between them, a festering presence, tainting all their enjoyment.

He tried to make love to her again, several times. As she lay waiting, Amy began to see herself as a wall to be scaled, a castle to be stormed. Neither tenderness nor pleasure had any place in this activity. She wished he wouldn't try so hard, would simply lie and hold her, so they could talk, quiet, close, together. But Noel had the compulsion to attack, caressing her with fevered concentration, failing repeatedly in his objective, flinging himself away from her, his reactions becoming each time more despairing.

'Amy, darling, won't you touch me?' He guided her hand to his penis, demonstrated what he wanted her to do. She massaged the soft flesh for minutes on end, feeling nothing, just a dull hope. There was a response, a slight blooming, but it soon faded and they were left silent and disappointed.

'Is it my fault?' she asked hesitantly as they lay side by side after this latest frustration.

He answered with an impassioned denial. 'You're beautiful, glorious. God, any man would give years of his life to make love to a child . . . a woman like you . . . Can't you see? That's why I hate myself . . .' He choked on a sob. Amy felt her own tears welling. Gently she put her arms around him and for once he allowed himself to be comforted.

Often, during the ten days of their stay, Noel retreated into his own thoughts, was visibly wrestling with his own demons. She felt lonely and shut out, but hadn't the courage to initiate conversation on a subject that distressed him so.

One afternoon they lay in the sun in the long, whippy grass that grew on the clifftops, overlooking a sea that reflected the azure of the sky. After one such long silence Noel said softly, as if he were speaking his thoughts aloud, 'It's France, the war, the whole experience . . .' He turned to her with a glazed and brooding look in his eye. 'Can you understand, Amy? It affects everything, every single thing in my life.'

He shrugged and turned again to gaze at the hazy horizon, adding bleakly, 'It will pass, I'm sure. As the memories fade. If you can be patient, it will pass.'

Noel strode across the yellow-green moors in tepid, driving rain. This afternoon he'd left Amy reading by the fire. He couldn't just sit, though. He was driven to physical activity by the restlessness inside him, the heaviness, as if he could walk his despair into the ground.

Gratefully he breathed in the freshness of the air, the spicy, herby smells released by the sodden undergrowth. But he was haunted by a phantom – Amy and the way she'd looked when he left, half frowning, bewildered, as if she still couldn't grasp the blight that had fallen on her happiness. He shook his head to dispel the thought, instead summoning up another. Picturing a knife twisting in his own entrails, needing to focus on an image so violent it could outweigh the pain that was always there churning his guts.

Constantly Noel was ambushed by the memory of her that first night, when he'd lain naked beside her. She'd come to him so open and ardent, a beautiful child, a fantasy mixture of innocence and eagerness. But already that quality had gone. His failure had eradicated it. Now there was apprehension and uncertainty. His bungling had ruined something that should have been breathtaking, erotic, golden. He wanted to howl at the waste.

Wet hair clinging to his skull, he trudged doggedly up a featureless hillside. Perversely his brain conjured up fragmentary images of past lovers. Noel had never been a Don Juan, had never possessed the necessary ease of manner, but neither had he felt inadequate in any way.

There had been Enid, when he was a student at Cambridge, with her pale eyelashes and smooth-shiny white skin, a town girl who worshipped him and he'd been flattered at the time. Shy Etta in Berlin. Elspeth, the fast, modern sister of a fellow-journalist. Then Vera, down in Dorset where he trained before leaving for France.

At school one year there'd been a boy, Mark, but that was just experimentation, though it excited him for a while. In France, too, there'd been a lad in his division, Walters, a farm-labourer in real life. Nothing had happened, nothing would, just that Noel knew he could have been tempted. The youth had been as beautiful as . . . Amy. But, at the same time – early on in the war, in a lull between offensives – Noel had had an unlikely affair with a French woman, Gabrielle. She was dark and hairy, complacently obsessed with her own sexuality. There was attraction and dislike between them and he fucked her with a hostile violence that disconcerted him, though she seemed to like it, love it . . .

Compared to Amy these people were nothing, yet with Amy he'd failed. An angry shame rose up in his throat. Noel felt sick.

The warm rain made him think of Arras, the trenches, but then everything did. Sun and snow and mist. Mud and dry, cracked earth.

Meat in a butcher's window. A dead mouse rotting in a trap. The stink of urine in an alleyway. The stink of shit. The stink of his own body. Repeatedly his brain squirmed with disgust.

And images he tried to suppress would surface, starting low and insinuating like the stirrings of sexual desire, but rising up, taking over, flaunting themselves with a nightmare clarity as if back-lit by sheet lightning, even as he embraced the warm, lithe body of his wife.

The boy Walters, lying dead and still, half-buried in mud and sewage. A rat, the size of a dog, gnawing the face of a dead soldier with steady, blank, repetitive application, up and down, up and down, as if a man's face were meaningless as a hunk of stale bread. Two women lying dead in a cottage abandoned by the Germans, mother and daughter, skirts raised, legs parted, their genitals torn and bleeding, ripped by bayonets. Such images, these and many more, writhed through his head whenever he was roused from the deathly protective inertia that for months, years, had shielded him from feeling, so he hadn't wanted sex, or anything living and warm.

Now he wanted to escape the horror and build a world to his own design. Have a wife and children, friends, an intimate, everyday life full of small pleasures. And Amy fitted so perfectly into the dream, with her sweet smile and thoughtful eyes, her alluring young body. Noel longed to love and care for her, earn her respect. There were so many things he wanted to teach her. It was all so nearly within his grasp. But the demons pursued him, torturing his mind and blighting his body with a curse that cancelled out the fantasy at a single stroke.

Chapter Eight

Everything felt better when they got to London. There was so much more to think about. The flat Noel had found them was in St George's Square, Victoria, a short walk from the offices of *Witness* magazine in Buckingham Palace Road. It was on the first floor of a tall, grey-white building called Gresham House, with heraldic-looking stonework above the imposing front door. There were two bedrooms, one big and one small, a large sunny living room, a bathroom, a tiny, shiny modern kitchen. And electricity – back in Crofton her family only had gas.

Amy loved it immediately. 'It's so urban,' she marvelled, gazing out of the big living-room window at the traffic in the street below. Noel observed her pleasure with smiling, indulgent eyes.

The flat was furnished with all the necessities, but there was plenty of scope for them to impose their own personal taste. Noel encouraged her to go out and make purchases. 'I want you to feel at home, my darling. You must buy any fripperies you think will make the place more comfortable.'

He told her how to get to a shop called Liberty, a strange, tall, half-timbered building that was filled top to bottom with carpets, furniture, bed linens, table linens, fabrics, crockery, ornaments, all very stylish and unusual. Amy was dazzled but overwhelmed, and the prices struck her as downright immoral.

Noel pooh-poohed her scruples. 'You're a town mouse now. You must learn to forget your church mouse ways.'

He encouraged her to buy clothes as well. She was tempted. The post-war fashions appealed to her, with their fluid lines that skimmed the body, skirts that showed the leg to mid-calf, silky underwear, fine stockings and pretty shoes with louis heels. And Amy discovered jerseys, soft, practical garments, but which set off the figure in a subtle, easy manner. She bought several outfits that made her feel up-to-date, very London, but Margaret's upbringing was deeply ingrained. Real extravagance was beyond her scope.

'These clothes aren't just for you, you know.' Noel urged her to be less circumspect. 'They're a treat for me. I love to see you in smart new things. I'm proud of you, Amy.'

The idea crossed her mind that by encouraging her to spend Noel was somehow trying to compensate for his sexual shortcomings, but there seemed no point in dwelling on that.

As winter drew on they saw a lot of Robert Beadle, who lived not far away, in Ebury Street. He and Noel had been at Rugby and Cambridge together and were the best of friends. His war service behind him, Robert had been called to the bar. Robert was probably six foot three and lanky with it. He wore round, owlish glasses, which gave him an effete air, though behind them – Amy noticed only gradually – his features were expressive, cleanly modelled, even hand-some. He had brown eyes that were distant and shrewd, both at the same time, and full, mobile lips she found oddly watchable. His voice was intimidatingly plummy. Amy thought him rather bloodless-looking, but was won over by his obvious affection for Noel.

She was wary of him at first, but had to admit he was good company. Though patently sharp and clever, Robert had a taste for trivia. He would break off from an account of his day in court to flaunt a new shirt he was wearing and demand, 'Guess how much?' or discuss Gloria Swanson's latest hairstyle or relate the newest devel-opments in the tumultuous love-life of a suave, grey-haired, distinctly elderly colleague in chambers.

He had a female friend called Prudence who worked in women's magazines. Like Robert and Noel, she was in her late twenties – distressingly old for an unmarried woman according to Crofton lore – and presented herself rather amusingly as a hopeless neurotic, though Noel claimed this was just a pose.

Prudence was elegant in a wind-swept fashion, with a bird's nest of wavy, dark hair, prematurely streaked with grey. Her clothes were well cut and invariably sombre in colour, drawing attention to her face, which was made up in a way that would have scandalized Margaret. She was striking, with heavy eyebrows and a prominent nose, and had a habit of peering quizzically through half-closed lids at whomever she was addressing.

Amy had never met a woman who earned her living like a man. And Prudence wasn't pretty, but it didn't seem to matter. Robert and Noel obviously found her more than acceptable as she was.

'Are Robert and Prudence engaged?' she asked, after their first meeting.

Noel shook his head with a quirkish smile. 'No, Amy, they're lovers.'

She was taken aback. In Crofton such a woman would have been gazed at askance and socially snubbed. Here she seemed perfectly respected. But, after her initial shock, Amy found it exhilarating to have acquaintances who flouted convention, however discreetly.

They came by at least once and sometimes twice a week, bringing wine as their contribution to an improvised meal. Amy was tickled by the novelty of their dropping in on such an informal basis. Her parents never had visitors, apart from the troubled parishioners Edward saw alone in his study.

If she had enough warning, Amy might make the hotpot that had been Margaret's speciality. Personally she preferred to cook bacon, eggs and fried potatoes – they'd never had cheerful things like that half enough at home. But, if she was caught on the hop, Robert and Prudence were just as happy with bread and cheese eaten round the fire with a hearty Beaujolais, while the wind rattled the big living-room window and the sky outside turned from dark blue to black.

Sometimes the four of them went to the cinema together. To Amy it seemed the height of enviable urban depravity to be able simply to walk round the corner at any time and see Chaplin comedies, Pearl White adventures, biblical sagas with sultry black-eyed slave girls, Gloria Swanson, Theda Bara . . . Noel had a passion for Westerns because they reminded him of Colorado.

In those early months the friendship and the constant presence of Robert and Prudence meant a great deal to Amy, gave her a sense of belonging. Their evenings reminded her of the ease and warmth of the Bessells' kitchen in Crofton, with Nancy and her mother, only this was London and the company was sharper and more sophisticated.

The others teased her for being a kid, a vicar's daughter to boot, an innocent, and she learned to play up to the role they assigned her; it was fun, just as Prudence paraded her legendary neuroticism.

But she relished their discussions on politics and current affairs. Amy had more time than the others to read the newspapers, and she was able to back up her opinions with facts. Edward's egalitarian views had left more of a mark on her than she'd realized and she often clashed with Robert, who was far more reactionary in his thoughts on the unemployed, the housing shortage, German war reparations.

As the weeks passed Amy became less intimidated by the weight of Robert's age and experience, more willing to say bunkum to his more extreme ideas. Sometimes their arguments became quite heated, but both enjoyed a scrap. Their spirited antagonism became assimilated, a ritual ingredient of the group friendship.

But most of the time their talk was far more trivial and undemanding. Gossip and private jokes provided the staple fare as they drank coffee and stoked up the fire and shared out the last drops of whatever bottle Robert had brought, with scrupulous exactitude.

Amy loved to see Noel relax with the wine and the company. Often he'd lounge on the floor, an elbow propped against one of the big Liberty cushions she'd bought. In his shirtsleeves, and bandying repartee with Prudence or Robert, a cigarette between his fingers – he'd learned to smoke at the front and the habit persisted – Noel looked young and open, casually amused, like the carefree student he must have been before the war cast its oppressive shadow across his life.

'Robert, my lad, I don't know about you, but I'm for the apples and pears.'

This was Prudence's traditionally unsubtle hint that it was time to leave. It was usually around midnight when the couple tiptoed down the flight of stone stairs and out into the cold and dark, ready for the walk back to Ebury Street where they rented separate rooms.

Then Noel and Amy were left with the dying embers of the fire.

Bedtime held a tension always. Ritual chores lent a protective busyness.

'You see to the fire, Noel. I'll clear up these glasses and cups.'

'D'you want to use the bathroom first, darling?'

This was the hour when it was no longer possible to forget that they weren't a normal, happy pair of newlyweds, but that their marriage was undercut by a fatal flaw.

When at last they lay side by side between the linen sheets, in the solid walnut bed that had come from Noel's family home, he would reach for her.

'Come here, little Amy.' Underlying the husky tenderness of his voice was an uncertain, pleading note, and it hurt her to witness the laying low of his pride.

To be held was still a joy, to drift off to sleep in one another's arms. But Amy was always on the alert for signs that he wanted more. When he made the first tentative moves towards lovemaking, her heart would sink, she just couldn't help it.

Amy did whatever he asked, but it was hard to bring conviction to her love-play while continually anticipating failure. Though that, in itself, was bearable. What she couldn't take was his misery and self-reproach, her own powerlessness to help.

'If you can be patient,' he'd said. Amy tried. But the pattern of failure became ever more firmly established.

After a while Noel gave up all effort on his own account. 'Just let me give you pleasure.'

When, during the day, she thought about what he did, Amy became shivery and tense with a shamed excitement. He would play with her nipples, stroke between her parted thighs until she writhed with helpless pleasure, the sensations gathering and deepening until they were too intense to bear and resolved into racking shudders of release. And one night Noel's lips moved from her breasts, down across her abdomen and stomach until his head rested between her legs and he licked and teased her there until she cried out with the dark, forbidden joy of it, twisting in the throes of what she now knew was called an orgasm.

'God, I love you so much, Amy.'

93

After times like these Noel was feverish and glazed, laying his powerful body on hers, straining and writhing in an agony of excitement and frustration.

He liked her to wear filmy underwear and silk stockings, liked to touch and caress her before she was fully undressed. All this made her stomach knot with arousal. And yet she was uneasy. It all felt wrong to her, more than anything because of the one way nature of the transaction.

She felt manipulated, saw Noel as a voyeur. A eunuch. Deep down, in the lonely secret truthfulness of her heart, Amy despised his impotent lust, though she knew she wasn't being fair, it wasn't his fault. To compensate for the treachery of her thoughts she would hug and kiss him in passionate private atonement.

'What's this, Amy?' he would say, a glad light coming into his eyes.

In spite of everything, she was young and resilient. Waking in the morning to a new day, Amy felt optimistic, even happy. She'd rather be here than anywhere else. She'd rather be with Noel. Her memories of Crofton had become nightmarish to her, the restrictions, the mediocrity. Nothing on earth would make her go back.

Chapter Nine

One evening in the new year of 1920 Noel came home and told Amy that he had something important to discuss with her. Roland Delane, the editor and proprietor of *Witness* magazine had sent for him. He was thinking of opening up a new office in Berlin, as he had the previous year in Paris. Noel, with his knowledge of the German language, was the logical candidate for the enterprise. Delane sounded him out as to his reaction to the potential move.

Noel looked Amy in the eye. 'I said I couldn't possibly discuss it until I'd talked to you.'

She was caught off balance. After all, it was a mere matter of months since she'd left her home village to move to London. 'I'm not sure I know enough about what we'd be letting ourselves in for.'

'You're right to wonder.' With his ingrained honesty Noel would not sugar the pill. 'Berlin's not a particularly pleasant place at the moment, not like it used to be. There's poverty and there's a lot of unrest . . . You know as well as I.'

Amy was silent but her mind hummed, seeming to race ahead of structured thought. What Noel said about Berlin wasn't new to her. She read the papers. It was a volatile place, brutal by all accounts, nothing like London. Yet, oddly, that fact held an attraction of its own, a perverse and unfamiliar excitement.

During their courtship Amy had barely pictured Noel's working life. He had a very English aversion to talking shop in social gatherings. Occasionally she'd heard him mention to Edward that he'd interviewed such and such a politician and had been surprised and impressed. But, generally speaking, that side of his life was never quite real to her.

It became more so, naturally, after she arrived in London. His office was nearby and she met colleagues, became involved in his day-to-day activities and preoccupations. *Witness* ran a continuing campaign against the lack of provision made for returning soldiers, both on the employment and the housing front. Swimming upstream, against the current of popular opinion, the magazine voiced its disagreement with the harsh conditions laid down by the Allies against the defeated Germans. Even before that Noel had denounced, time and again, the callous food blockade maintained by the Allied powers for eight whole months after hostilities had ceased. No one could plead ignorance of the effect it had had on the starving, demoralized population and especially on the children.

Amy read, marked and digested the *Witness* editorials and formed a more or less accurate mental picture of Noel's working environment, an atmosphere in which he was thoroughly at home. His fragmented accounts of the day-to-day routine in Buckingham Palace Road had left her with a blurred impression of clubby editorial meetings, a lot of lunchtime socializing, a cosy interconnectedness – the way everyone there had been at school with everyone else's brothers, cousins, nephews, fathers, uncles . . . It sounded a closed, congenial and absolutely masculine world.

'You do realize, Amy, that you married the most eligible, the most promising young journalist in London?'

Prudence had fired the rhetorical question one night when Noel was speculating on his chances of obtaining an interview with Lady Astor who'd just been elected to Parliament, the first woman MP ever.

There was a note in her voice Amy couldn't define. It was difficult to tell whether she was being ironic, or whether she genuinely thought Amy took her good fortune too much for granted.

Drily Noel put in, 'Amy loved me when she thought I was just a humble woodcutter.'

* * *

Noel always maintained that Roland Delane – the editor of *Witness* – was the most genuinely open-minded person he had ever met. 'He's the sort of man who treats a dustman with the same respect and genuine consideration as he would . . . the Prime Minister. And it's not a pose.'

Apparently Delane had stood three times as a Liberal parliamentary candidate during the latter years of the previous century, failing each time to get elected. But he was in love with politics and decided, pragmatically, that political journalism was the next best thing to a career in Parliament. As second son of a wealthy Victorian engineering dynasty, he had the means to take his fate into his own hands.

Witness magazine reflected the outlook of its founder, taking a stance that was liberal and unbiased, progressive without being revolutionary for its own sake. For all the affable clubbiness of its management, the end result was not amateurish. New periodicals were ten-a-penny in both pre- and post-war London, most of them here today and gone tomorrow. But *Witness* had proved to have longevity. It had also acquired status. And its circulation continued to multiply.

'He's poured thousands into the magazine. It's his grand passion.' This was the popular word on Delane. But his approach paid off. He could afford the best people, diversify into social issues and the arts. The review's opinion was highly respected in the circles on which it concentrated. Among politicians, social reformers, writers, painters, musicians the magazine's verdict was taken increasingly into account.

The editor hailed originally from Manchester and made sure that his brainchild remained outward-looking, not arrogantly and incestuously preoccupied with the London scene. He employed good freelancers in the provinces and took their concerns seriously, with the result that *Witness* had readers among the liberal-minded in every corner of the British Isles.

It was as an undergraduate that Noel had first encountered Delane. At Cambridge he made a point of reading *Witness* each week. The review was a smaller, less established concern in those days. To buy it was to show evidence of free thinking, a willingness to question the status quo.

Noel contributed to various student magazines. Then one day, almost idly, he penned a wry analysis of the vaguely feudal institution of college servants – middle-aged family men, for the most part, engaged to cater to the needs of young puppies who were frequently rude and thoughtless. It was clear that some of the employees bristled with suppressed class resentment, while others seemed to acquiesce and even revel in their servitude to the arrogant young nobs in their charge. He was quite pleased with the way the article turned out and, on an impulse, he posted it off to *Witness*.

Almost by return he had a letter from Delane himself who seemed amused by the piece and proposed to publish it on the review's 'Free-For-All' page for the princely fee of half a guinea. The editor invited the young student to submit further examples of his work.

For the remainder of his time at Cambridge Noel continued to contribute intermittently to *Witness* and during part of one long vacation, he worked in Buckingham Palace Road as a sort of glorified office boy. After his finals Delane offered him a junior post on the magazine.

When he looked back on that year he'd spent in London before war broke out, Noel conjured up his younger self with a mixture of incredulity and affectionate contempt. How strong he'd felt, how joyous and sure. Clichés sprang to mind. The world had been his oyster. At the same time – as subsequent events proved – he'd been living in a fool's paradise. But, taken all in all, that period was probably the happiest of Noel's life.

Friends had been envious of his good fortune in landing a job on the magazine *par excellence*. Colleagues, in the main, had been congenial and helpful. His salary had been adequate and supplemented by an allowance from his father, in spite of the fact that his parent viewed *Witness* with distaste as a smart-aleck rag, too radical and too clever by half. Noel had a shabby, glorious small flat in Chelsea, and an attractive and rather racy girlfriend, Elspeth, the sister of Francis Ross, a fellow journalist on *Witness*.

There had been minor annoyances. As junior member of staff

the unenviable scissors-and-paste task of compiling the weekly news résumé fell to Noel. But, in consolation, the keen young newcomer had been entrusted with 'wages and working conditions' as his particular sphere of competence. He'd covered a dockers' strike, probed the exploitation of machinists in the East End, produced some vividly damning evidence. Noel attacked government policies with righteous, unassailable logic, his hedonistic 'young-man-on-the-make' persona redeemed by the corrective counterweight of a social conscience.

It had been the delicious lull before the storm.

If he survived the hostilities, his job would still be there. This much had been made clear to Noel. When he did come home a great deal had changed. During the war years *Witness* had consolidated its reputation for unbiased, courageous reporting and editorial comment. The publication had gained in maturity, was less the sole preserve of the avant-garde. After war-time restraints on production, the magazine was poised to expand.

And Noel had gained instant seniority. The cliché now was 'dead men's shoes'. Francis Ross and another promising contemporary, Chris Burningham, had been killed. The sound middle-aged men who'd kept the review going in the interim were four years older. Caleb Crawford, the puckish pre-war columnist, whose sparkling insights used to dazzle Noel, had become a garrulous, embarrassing drunk, tolerated by Delane only for old times' sake. Noel, with his single year's experience, was all that remained of the magazine's young blood.

His post-war dourness was perceived as hard-earned gravitas. The older men, without war records, instinctively deferred to him. He'd become austerely impressive, an excellent front man, imposing enough to interview the most exalted politician, though his interests still lay in the area of social issues rather than politics pure and simple.

For Noel his job had been a lifeline, the daily and weekly deadlines providing something external and immediate to focus on, punctuating the flat infinity of his desolation. He worked concentratedly, knowing himself to be lucky – the redundant, misfit ex-officer was becoming a recognized social type.

His output was well received and his reputation grew as a young journalist to reckon with. Privately Noel was amazed that the alienation that pervaded his whole life didn't scream from everything he wrote. Politicians appeared to him stale – with insincerity, repetition, tired fake indignation. Even the social injustice that used to exercise him seemed inevitable, something that had always been there and always would be. Human beings were not perfectible.

Elspeth was married now to a middle-aged Liberal politician and was quite the hostess. She gave Noel to understand that her marriage need make no difference to the way things had been between them. Her insinuating eyes and fuchsia-coloured smile hinted at unfathomable depths of erotic lasciviousness, and struck him as faintly ridiculous, an overwrought and misleading self-advertisement. No one could live up to *that* much promise. Back in those early post-war months the only thing that seemed untainted to Noel had been his mental image of lovely, quiet Amy Winter. The rest was mere sound and fury.

However much Amy and Noel tried to deny it to themselves, the prospect of a move to Berlin took possession of them. They were aware that the project was far from settled, a possibility and nothing more, yet somehow the mere idea altered everything, made their present way of life seem fluid and impermanent. It made them dream.

Amy bought a German grammar and began to teach herself the language, studying for several hours each day. It gave her a sense of purpose, filled a void she was beginning to perceive at the centre of her life. Up to now she'd pottered with cooking, soft furnishings, clothes. Her days had been pleasant but empty, revolving round Noel's return from work, the visits of Robert and Prudence.

Working her way through the little blue cloth-covered book, Amy could *see* the progress she was making, measure it in pages. It wasn't so hard – a lot of the words were like English. She went to her studies each morning with positive pleasure, and became thoroughly engrossed. Then afterwards there was the satisfying feeling that she had something concrete to show for the day.

'How's my studious little girl?' Noel teased when he came home each night. *'Wie geht's, kleine Studentin?'*

He was charmed by her initiative, seeing it as an earnest and touching attempt on Amy's part to support him in his career. In the evenings he helped her with pronunciation, rehearsed snatches of elementary conversation with her, warming to the role of school-master to her eager pupil.

Amy felt obscurely that her lessons had been appropriated, con-verted in Noel's perception to a kind of flirtatious game. All the same she liked the sense of a shared goal. It lent an element of comradeship to their marriage. But by March there was still no word from Roland Delane.

In the meantime there was an attempted right-wing coup in Berlin, foiled only by a general strike on the part of the workers. With fascination they followed the progress of the putsch in the news-papers. Amy was quietly elated at this confirmation that she and Noel would indeed be entering a chancy, unpredictable world. Fingers crossed. If everything turned out the way they hoped.

On the first day of April 1920 Roland Delane confirmed Noel's appointment. He left for Berlin two weeks later to find them some-where to live. Amy was to follow him at the beginning of May. Before that there was masses to do in the way of shopping, sorting, packing. By day Amy buzzed with nervous energy. At night she couldn't sleep for anticipation.

Chapter Ten

Joachim Werner raised himself on one elbow and gazed at the young woman lying next to him in the big, carved, oaken bed.

The white feather quilt was pushed down as far as her waist. How perfect she was with her slender arms and tawny skin, the small breasts as perky and pointed as springtime buds on a young sycamore twig. Claudia's wide mouth was pale, swollen a little from sleep. He marvelled at the tender skin of her closed eyelids with their faint mauve veining, delicate as a baby's. Her short, dark hair lay rumpled on the square, solid pillow. A few weeks ago she'd had it cut into a bobbed shape that went with the thick fringe she always wore.

'You look like a naughty little boy,' he'd told her when she first appeared with the new style.

In fact Claudia, with her arresting jolie laide features, looked quite stunning. But the transformation unsettled Joachim, accentuated the anxiety that was beginning to gnaw at him in her company. She looked so modern and chic, so absolutely sure of herself.

A couple of weeks ago Joachim had succumbed to vanity and introduced Claudia to a client of his, Karl Kraus, a complacent, gold-toothed tub of lard, who described himself, with a street-wise grin, as a dyed-in-the-wool Berliner.

Kraus was always bragging about the women he'd laid and Joachim had the sudden craven desire to prove ... What? That he too could be a smirking man of the world?

The two of them had got on famously. Kraus had trotted out his ribald Berlin wisecracks for the girl and she replied in kind, though afterwards Claudia pronounced him a lecherous little pillock.

'Sharp as knives, that kid,' Kraus commented cheerfully next time he and Joachim met. 'She's one too many for you.'

'Claudia knows which side her bread's buttered,' Joachim had retorted with feeble bravado.

'You mean you keep her in coffee and the odd new dress.' A brief, scornful exhalation of breath from between his front teeth. 'There's plenty'd be happy to do that. Steer her my way the day she gets tired of you.'

Kraus's taunts had touched Joachim on the raw. Claudia had bloomed in recent months. She was better fed, thanks to him, and better dressed. She'd become harder too, he thought, and her language sometimes shocked him. In the early days it had been possible for Joachim to see her as an orphan tragically stricken by the war, himself as a humane family friend, to read affection into their relationship.

But, as time passed he'd come to view their affair more and more as the world might. A good-looking girl and a comfortably off older man using one another. A commonplace situation, sordid in its realism. The thought was distasteful to him. There were times when he wished he'd never strayed from his blameless life with Erna, and he yearned to be rid of the compulsive, undignified lust.

Yet the thought of losing access to that slim, golden body was like death. Joachim was helplessly addicted to her long, coltish legs and flat belly, the narrow, boyish buttocks, the innocent-erotic way she walked about his bourgeois apartment naked and free as a kid on the beach.

He'd taken some photographs of her like that once. When he asked if he could she'd screwed up her face and looked at him with a flicker of . . . not contempt – it wasn't that – more as if the request was only what she would have expected.

Then she posed with mock-provocation on the velvet sofa he and Erna had chosen together years ago.

'Saucy enough for you?' she asked with a crooked smile.

These days Claudia was getting out and about more. He'd seen her from the apartment window a little while ago walking down the Duisburgerstrasse with an unknown female friend. The two of them together seemed to him typical of the brassy, free-and-easy – whorish, Joachim thought privately – young girls you saw everywhere in Berlin now. They were laughing together as they walked towards the flat, and Joachim was filled with the sudden cold suspicion that they were laughing about him. Then Claudia gave a casual little wave to her companion and sauntered across the road for her assignation with her middle-aged lover.

Claudia came to with the sensation of queasiness that was becoming all too familiar to her. If she lay still it sometimes passed. Her eyes opened to encounter Joachim's still, silent gaze. His patient adoration. She experienced a niggle of irritation. Her lover seemed to parade his devotion quite deliberately, as if it were a present she must be happy to receive.

Almost instantaneously Claudia readjusted her attitude. Irritation was a luxury she couldn't afford. The situation with Joachim was what it was, and God knows she and Agathe and Rudi depended on his generosity.

'You slept well, dearest?' he asked tenderly.

'Excellently, Joachim.' The smile she gave felt thin and unconvincing, but he appeared gratified.

The nausea in her belly persisted. If she could eat something . . . That usually helped.

Joachim reached for her, his right hand coming to rest lightly on her stomach. 'I mustn't linger today, Claudia. It's Erna's birthday tomorrow. I'm putting together a little celebration and there are final arrangements . . .'

'Don't let me keep you.'

That was another niggle. The way he talked about his wife with a reverent catch in his voice, almost a mental genuflection – as if she were some kind of a saint – when he'd been cheating on her for almost a year, regularly and with conspicuous enthusiasm.

'Don't be impatient, darling.' He enjoyed her moments of pique, interpreting them as jealousy. 'There's still time enough . . .'

He came closer, moved his hand languorously down to cup her pubic mound. Claudia caught a blast of sour early morning breath and, with her queasy stomach, almost gagged. She shifted her body quickly, then slowed the motion into one of pouting playfulness.

'I'm awfully hungry, Joachim. If you loved me you'd slip down to the corner shop and buy some rolls.'

Der Seeräuber – The Pirate – was a bar in the Wedding district, a cellar with an entrance to one side of a tobacconist's shop. The bar consisted of a single huge room with red electric lighting. Some lengths of fishing net, looped along the brick wall, a couple of skull-and-crossbones flags supplied the décor. Chairs and tables stood in jumbled circles round a small dance floor and a low dais at one end of the room. Every Thursday the management held a talent night.

Claudia had started going there secretly with a girl called Rosa, and Rosa's brother. Nobody else knew. She'd got talking to Rosa at an audition for film extras. Neither of them had been taken on. There were literally hundreds of young women chasing the few vacancies going, all at least as eager and pushy as Claudia herself.

She and Rosa walked together to the tram afterwards and swapped stories about all the jobs they'd been after. Both had acting ambitions, but the competition was almost as fierce for the waitressing and office work they chased too, in an effort to keep the wolf from the door.

'I got a day's work as a mannequin three weeks ago,' Claudia told her. 'They said they'd put me on their books and contact me when there was anything going, but . . .' She shrugged resignedly.

'Tell you what,' Rosa said. 'I go to this bar on Thursdays. It's a free-for-all – you get a chance to sing.' She grinned. 'They'll boo you off if you're no good. But if they like you there might be a few tips in it. Anyway, it's practice . . . And you never know, you might be spotted.'

Claudia had been several times since. Tonight, as she took her place with Rosa and Rosa's brother, Franz, at one of the tables close to the stage, the squeamishness in her stomach persisted. Joachim's warm, crusty bread hadn't helped that much.

'I'm in the money tonight,' she announced. 'Drinks are on me.'

Joachim had been in a sentimental and extra-generous mood that morning – something to do with his wife's birthday perhaps. Claudia had been able to hand over to Tante Agathe both money and almost a pound of butter, while keeping a little cash back for herself.

She lied to her aunt constantly. And – it had to be admitted – increasingly perfunctorily. Agathe must have at least some suspicion as to the manner in which Claudia came by the precious goodies. But a façade was maintained, however improbable, of sudden short-term jobs and employers up to their ears in the black market, of sleeping over at a girlfriend's. That way her aunt and their landlady, Frau Kästner, could rest easy in their consciences while still profiting from the wages of sin.

'There's schnapps tonight,' the waiter murmured surreptitiously. They were regulars.

'Three.' Claudia felt impulsive, though the *Seeräuber* was a place where you were permitted to sit all night in front of a single glass of flat beer.

She and Rosa always brought Franz along with them. He was big and tough. Two women on their own were fair game for men on the loose, and that wasn't why they were here.

The drinks came. Claudia raised her glass.

'*Prost.*' She took a sip. The warmth of the cheap spirit felt good in her acid stomach.

'*Prost, Kinder.*' Rosa smiled, showing her crooked front teeth.

It occurred to Claudia to wonder what Agathe would say if she walked in and discovered her niece on such breezy terms with these two decidedly proletarian Berliners. Claudia was ruefully convinced that her aunt would be less scandalized by her sexual liaison with Joachim Werner – at least he wore clean white shirts and came from leafy Grunewald rather than the slums of Moabit.

The three of them had got here early to bag a good place. On the dais the three-piece band was still tuning up – piano, trumpet and drums. Pale and etiolated, like cellar-plants which never saw the light of day, the musicians were working men who performed here simply for tips.

Now they struck up a dance tune with an American sound, lively and insinuating. Rosa Edelmann leaned back in her chair, crossed her legs, took a swig of her schnapps and listened with half-closed eyes.

'Heaven ... Music, a drink. Who needs more?' She was plump by post-war standards, with smooth skin the colour of milky tea and frizzy mousy-gold hair that framed her round and rather plain face like a blurred halo. Full-bodied, with sturdy, pear-shaped thighs, Rosa had a look of slatternly sensuality that some men found highly attractive.

Physically Franz Edelmann was her male counterpart – same pale buff complexion, light grey eyes, frizzy hair – but larger and more muscular. He'd been conscripted in the last months of the war and now formed part of the new army of the unemployed. The Edelmanns lived in two rooms, together with a bedridden, asthmatic mother. Mostly Rosa was the breadwinner. Lacking regular work, she slept with men for money or gifts. The situation was so commonplace nowadays as to be pretty well acceptable. But her ambition was to be a singer.

'Place is filling up,' Franz remarked, looking round.

The *Seeräuber* was something of a meeting place for the mildly raffish elements of Wedding and Moabit, its clientele mainly working-class and unpretentious. The first time she came Claudia had half expected one of the legendary dives Tante Agathe tutted over when she deplored the current state of society and harked back to the golden age of the Kaiser – the sort of bar where men danced in the arms of other men, kohl-eyed women embraced women, while the police looked on with Olympian indifference.

Instead she found working families, courting couples, a rough, good-humoured crowd out for a cheap good time. Thursdays were popular. By introducing an amateurs' night, the proprietors of the *Seeräuber* had turned a 'dead' evening into their most successful money-spinner.

Small groups were arriving thick and fast, the men in their everyday clothes, women more festive in make-up and shabby finery. As they took their places there was a deal of humorous banter with the waiters and with other regulars. Rosa and Franz called across to people they knew.

The band began to play a silly, catchy song called 'Happy in Berlin'. A few couples took the floor.

'Dance?' Franz offered casually. Claudia nodded, and they stepped up to the rather meagre area set aside for the purpose, close to the musicians.

There was a special style of dancing in places like these, Claudia thought. Very bouncy, very belly to belly, almost a parody. She grinned as she jigged with Franz, feeling better than she had all day.

'We'll have another glass of that schnapps,' she told him.

Rosa was dancing with a bull-necked young man. They were chatting animatedly.

'Who's he?'

Franz glanced in his sister's direction. 'No one really. She's known him all her life.'

He was a man of few words, apart from when the conversation touched on his grand passion, revolutionary politics. Then he would change dramatically, become flushed and touchingly voluble, Claudia thought, though she had scant interest in what he was actually saying.

The band played for half an hour or so, but everyone knew the dancing was just a curtain-raiser. Claudia and the Edelmanns were back in their seats with a second drink when the music stopped and, for a while, the only sound was the general hubbub of talk and laughter.

Then there was a sudden drum-roll. It was a signal. The conversation fell away and hush descended, happy and expectant. A small, agile man aged around sixty walked jauntily on to the dais.

'*Abend! Abend . . . Meine Damen and Herren!*' He grinned, raised his arms and was applauded.

Falke, the compere, was a character in the district, so Claudia had gathered. A sinewy man, but very slight in build who, improbably, had once been a boxer. His complexion was ruddy, face bony and alert, and surprisingly delicately modelled – sharp cheekbones tapering down to a narrow cleft chin, almond-shaped eyes, a shapely mouth. But the fineness of his look was belied by his foxy smile, a rasping, nasal voice, a bald and racy turn of phrase that delighted his audience. Falke wore a leather jacket and a white silk scarf round his neck, the ends left trailing.

This kind of free-for-all needed a sure hand at the helm and Falke, with his cheery menace, supplied it. He had bouncers planted among the clientele – any trouble, any dispute was swiftly nipped in the bud.

He saw to it that there was a mix of talent. Each Thursday fresh faces alternated with tried and true performers who'd proved their worth in previous weeks. Sadistically Falke liked to include one or two really bad new turns. The derision of the punters, their boos and catcalls, the consternation in the eyes of the victim, all these were part of the fun.

Tonight he opened proceedings by playing a sentimental card.

'Here's someone you all know, ladies and gentlemen. A lovely girl, pretty as a picture, voice like an angel ... I give you Granny Keller!'

Amid affectionate applause an old woman stepped up onto the rostrum. She radiated a still containment that was at odds with the general jollity. Her grey-white hair was drawn severely back from a pale, angular, wanly handsome face. Her grey dress was worn-looking and perfectly simple in style. Falke greeted her with a kiss on the cheek, and stood with one arm round her shoulder as he shushed the audience.

Then she began to sing. Her appearance invited goodwill, a suspension of the critical faculties, but no such indulgence was needed. Frau Keller's presence was calm and sure, her voice still strong, without reediness, but overlaid with an intriguing hoarseness that merely added to the impression she gave of resilience and stoic experience.

She sang a song called 'The soldier's woman' that Claudia knew slightly and which dated back to the Franco-Prussian war when Frau Keller must have been young. It had a stark and haunting melody, heartfelt lyrics. The atmosphere she engendered was potent, the silence dynamic and succeeded by a storm of applause.

'Phew.' Claudia was impressed by the woman's power and conviction.

'She's been a midwife in Moabit ever since I was a kid.' Rosa supplied a biographical footnote. 'Old battle-axe she is an' all.'

'Could have been a real singer.'

After each completed turn Falke's bouncers passed the hat. No one here was well off and there was genuinely no compulsion to give. But the few pfennigs here and there sometimes added up to something worth having and Granny Keller was seen as a worthy recipient.

Next in line came a new face. A large, a very large man, youngish, with pale, puffy flesh, the self-indulgent profile of a Roman emperor, a sweep of wavy brown hair. He wore a belted jacket and snuff-coloured corduroy trousers. As Falke announced him, he stood on the stage, hands on his broad hips, surveying the audience with an expression that seemed sneering, but was probably only a mask for his nervousness.

'How come he's so fat?' the taciturn Franz was moved to comment.

Hardly anyone had that much flesh to spare nowadays – only the legendary profiteers who ground the faces of the poor. Claudia couldn't help thinking his corpulence would tell against him.

His name was Nolde and he began to sing an improbable ditty about the love affair between a dog and a sow. Supposedly comic, it involved a deal of grunting and yapping and Nolde appeared to lose confidence in his act quite early on. But he ploughed on despairingly, the fixed grin on his lips increasingly at odds with the rising panic in his eyes.

'Poor bugger,' Rosa said, with a wry sideways smile.

Little eddies of unkind laughter began to ripple from the crowd, followed by muted whistles and boos. Nolde sang on like a plucky politician defying hecklers. The booing multiplied but he kept going.

Falke, the compere, walked up to the microphone and grinned at his audience. He turned to Nolde. 'I think they're trying to tell you something, friend.'

The performer ignored him and quavered on.

'Sod off!' Falke shouted through the microphone, to the hooting merriment of his public, and finally Nolde slunk from the stage.

As if to demonstrate how it was done, a regular named Lecki Bauer came on. Short and balding, with a face as lugubrious as a bloodhound's, he sang a song in Berlinese dialect about an adulterous wife whose excuses for her misdeeds became ever more crazily inventive as the song went on. Seemingly without trying, the droll, wide-eyed Bauer held the rowdy audience in the palm of his hand, and was rewarded with a resounding ovation.

'Time we had something tasty to look at,' Falke announced with a lustful leer.

Another newcomer took her chance. A blonde young woman with pretty, unformed features, a white dress and a silk rose in her hair. Her round blue eyes held a kind of pleading. Standing next to the grimacing Falke, she seemed to present herself passively for public inspection, as if only the audience's approbation could validate her existence. The approval came in the form of masculine cheers and whistles, and the young woman glowed demurely.

When the appreciative whooping died down she began to sing '*Das Veilchen*', a song Claudia had learned at school. Her voice was sweet and pure, but nigh on inaudible past the first row of tables.

After a few moments there were shuffles of impatience.

'Sing up!' came the brisk, but amiable advice from somewhere near the back.

The young woman's eyes widened. For a second no sound at all emerged from her mouth, though it still moved. Then the tiny, sweet soprano resumed, with added tremor.

The impatience grew.

'We can't hear!'

'Give up, Liebchen!' someone advised, and there were muffled giggles.

As she sang on, the trembling in her voice increased. A little later she came to a dead halt, standing in the spotlight, her eyes blank and stricken. Falke crossed the dais, coming to her rescue but, before he could reach her, she turned and ran from the stage.

'I'd die if that happened to me,' Claudia said.

'But it wouldn't,' Rosa replied. 'You'd never let it.'

Claudia drained her second glass of schnapps. It glowed hearteningly in her veins. She felt warm and relaxed. Mentally she checked on her sick stomach. It had receded far into the background. Sitting there bathed in wellbeing, Claudia was startled when Falke called her name.

'Your turn.' Franz nudged her.

Claudia experienced the familiar rush of terror and excitement. The first time she tried her luck at the *Seeräuber*, she'd almost passed out with fear – suppose she forgot the words, suppose they all booed and she had to beat an ignominious retreat. But even then she'd known that nothing in the world would stop her from having a go.

Since then the terror had lessened – marginally. They never *had* booed. Not so far. And tonight, coming after the blonde young woman, she was going to look competent, at the very least.

'Knock 'em dead,' Rosa said. 'I got some cash on me too – I'll buy you a drink for when you come off.'

Claudia rose to her feet. She was wearing a black dress Joachim had bought for her. It had a low, square neck that made her look as if she'd got a bit of bosom, and the skirt was daringly short. I wouldn't like you to go out in it, he said when he bought it, but wear it for me. It was a lovely dress, though she never had it on for more than half an hour before Joachim had eagerly stripped it off. Claudia touched her hair. The new style was like a disguise, making her feel like someone else, giving her confidence.

'. . . One of our new little pets,' Falke was announcing with a taut, insinuating grin.

She joined him on the dais. Her legs felt like faulty clockwork.

'A good-looker, I'll say . . .' Falke cast a stage leer in her direction. '. . . And a democrat, don't you know. A young lady from the smart side of town.'

He used the fact that she wasn't one of them as a two-edged weapon. If she succeeded it lent her a certain exotic appeal. If she failed, then the punters could indulge themselves by bringing her down a peg. Either way she was good business.

'So mind your manners, and welcome . . . Fräulein Claudia Farnholz!'

Claudia was surprised and warmed by the amicable buzz that greeted her, the good-natured applause.

She had talked to the musicians earlier about the songs she planned to perform – she was doing two and so was Rosa. The first was a ballad everyone knew, the second something a bit different. She'd had to hum it for them, but they were used to improvising and soon got the hang of the tune.

The first time she came here, she just sang, just aimed to get through it. But, during the following week, thoughts about the whole thing kept drifting through her head at odd times – lying in bed or walking into town in a futile search for some job that paid enough to make it worthwhile. And it came into her mind that it wasn't the singing that was really important to her. More the idea of projecting something – a mood – something singular and personal that belonged to her and nobody else. The song was just the vehicle.

As she stood on the stage, ready to go, Claudia felt scared again. Poised like a diver on a springboard, she wasn't quite sure what it was she wanted to put across. It was indefinable, an essence. Then again, whatever it was Lecki Bauer or Granny Keller had projected, you'd be hard put to it to describe in words.

Claudia glanced across at the musicians. 'Ready when you are,' she murmured.

The ebullient sound of the opening bars revived her spirits. She launched into a song called 'Hungry Kisses' that was popular that year, a 'poor-but-happy' song about a soldier home from the war. Everyone there knew it, and it had a bouncy, irresistible tune. If she performed it halfway decently, she couldn't go wrong. It was the sort of number people were inclined to sing with a brave, beatific smile, all about light heads and empty pockets, blissful nights of love.

It seemed to Claudia that life wasn't as easy as that and she tried to inject the lyrics with a certain wryness, a knowing cynicism, to make them a bit more complex.

It was a good song to try it with – the melody was strong enough to carry her through. But the audience seemed to respond to her interpretation anyway. They sang along on the chorus and erupted into enthusiastic applause at the end.

'More! More!'

'Bravo, Claudia!'

She was touched by the use of her name. It made her feel accepted.

Claudia was glad of the goodwill since she knew her choice of a second number was risky and could fail.

A little while ago she'd plucked up courage to go, on her own, to a cabaret called *Schall und Rauch* – Noise and Smoke. She'd been attracted by the name and the fact that it was run by Max Reinhardt, director of the company Fräulein Böhm – her old drama teacher – used to belong to. In fact she half hoped Fräulein Böhm might be there. Claudia desperately needed a contact who could put in a good word for her, give her a bit of an edge at one or other of the endless, fruitless auditions.

The smoky basement had been full of clever, eccentric people. On stage seasoned performers had sung topical, satirical songs that were greeted with bursts of hard laughter, spontaneous witticisms. Claudia didn't understand a quarter of what was going on, though she'd been both enchanted and intimidated by the rowdy, irreverent atmosphere.

Then a young woman – she only looked a kid – came on and did a weird little song about a girl who'd stolen money from her mother's employer, and now repented, but was too scared to own up, too ashamed to look at her own face in the mirror. Claudia had never heard anything quite like it, she'd been transported. The girl was such a waif, tragic and funny both at the same time, and sort of worldly-wise too. And she sang in a small, unemphatic voice, with no big, grand gestures and, in that huge noisy room, you could have heard a pin drop.

She brought the house down and had to perform the song all over again and Claudia found a pencil and an envelope in her handbag and wrote down as many of the words as she could, concentrating ferociously, so that afterwards she was able to fill in the gaps from memory.

'Claudia?' The long-faced, rather attractive pianist looked at her enquiringly and she nodded.

It was stealing, to be sure, but she was going to try and do that song herself. The performance would be different. She wasn't the same type as the kid from *Schall und Rauch*. And this was certainly a quite different venue.

As the pianist began to play the dark little melody, Claudia prayed for all she was worth. She could fall flat on her face. It could be a disaster. But if she managed to pull it off, how absolutely . . . satisfying it would be.

She could see people were confused when she first started singing. The thing was not to worry about that, or she would lose conviction. Putting a song across was a bit like having an argument, trying to impose your own view on everyone else.

The lyrics were in a sort of street-dialect and that came as a shock to this audience who saw her as coming from the other side of the tracks. In her mind she was a skinny street-kid, with tangled hair and holes in her shoes, precocious and uningratiating. The words were brilliant, just right, bald and understated, unemotional. She felt good singing them, they really worked and gradually she could see the circle of faces turning from puzzled to interested, even amused.

Almost all of her energy was concentrated on the act of shaping her performance, but a corner of her attention remained alert to the reactions of her shadowy public. From her place on stage, the crowded cellar looked strangely impressive – some painter's vision of hell – red-lit, with clustered black silhouettes and drifting spirals of cigarette smoke. From time to time one particular group or figure would catch her eye, offer up a brief, vivid tableau, then blend again into the whole.

Intermittently she was aware of Rosa and Franz, leaning towards her, listening intently, Rosa gripping her brother's forearm. In Claudia's empty place a glass of brandy awaited her exit from the stage. She saw a thin-faced man at a neighbouring table whisper something to the woman he was with. She nodded, then they both turned back to regard Claudia with a sort of companionable curiosity. From the corner of her eye she noticed Falke, smoking a cigar and observing her with silent, enigmatic absorption.

Three-quarters of the way through her number, Claudia had decided that at least it wasn't going to be a disaster. Nothing had shaken her confidence in the song. Barring accidents, she was home and dry. She sang the final verse with absolute conviction.

Then it was over, and there was a heartbeat of silence, after which the applause came. It wasn't as natural and full-blooded as the clapping and cheering that had greeted her ballad, but she hadn't expected to raise the rafters. It seemed to Claudia that there was an exploratory quality to the ovation, as if the audience were still examining its own reaction to the song, recognizing that she had tried something new.

'Thank you.' Claudia felt drained, but gratified. 'Thank you very much.'

She saw Rosa raise her hands above her head in a triumphal gesture and Franz give a slow, bemused smile.

Falke stepped up beside her and quipped, 'She's been coming here too long. She's beginning to sound like one of us.'

The witticism was a reference to the song's urban dialect. It could have been a jibe, but it wasn't, and the laughter that greeted it was good-natured.

'Drink up, girl. You look as if you need it,' Rosa said when Claudia got back to the table.

Her legs felt weak. She sat down and drained the glass of schnapps in a few long gulps. The burning glow of the neat spirits revived her.

'You *did* need it,' Franz grinned.

'What was that song?' Rosa asked, looking at Claudia with an odd expression on her smooth, rather heavy features, half disapproving, half admiring. 'I could never sing anything like that.'

'I heard it in a cabaret once.' Claudia was deliberately vague. 'I pinched it.'

Rosa gave a throaty laugh. 'It was good, though. Depressing.'

She would be going on last. Rosa was the current favourite of the *Seeräuber* regulars and Falke held her in reserve. Claudia loved to watch her. She was a natural – smiling, flirtatious, brisk, tough. And her voice was rich, strong and brassy.

None of the subsequent acts held Claudia's interest for long. No one was quite bad enough to be bad, or good enough to be exciting. A handsome tenor with a blond quiff caught Rosa's eye. She nudged Claudia and whispered that she wouldn't mind a late-night duet with him.

Claudia was trying to decide whether or not she felt the same, and whether the sickness in her stomach wasn't coming back, when someone tapped her on the shoulder. She turned her head.

A tall man stood behind her. He looked to be about forty. His pallid complexion and a tendency to jowliness were emphasized by dark, shiny, severely slicked-back hair.

'Fräulein Farnholz, would you allow me to say that I enjoyed your performance enormously?' His voice was smooth and pleasant, with the hint of a Viennese accent.

'Thanks.' Claudia felt caught on the hop. 'Thanks . . . I'm pleased.'

'You're very assured – and most original. You're an amateur?'

'Yes.' The collection for her had netted two marks and fourteen pfennigs. Did that compromise her amateur status? Claudia hardly thought so. 'Though I aspire to be a professional.'

'It's possible I could help you in that respect.' He passed her a small piece of white pasteboard. 'Come and see me.'

She looked at it stupidly.

'Fräulein Farnholz.' He bowed and was gone.

'He looked like a vampire,' Franz said.

In the gloomy, satanic light Claudia peered at the card. It said 'Georg Buresch, Theatrical Agent', with an address on the Budapest-erstrasse, near the Zoo. She pulled a face and showed the card to Franz and Rosa.

Rosa shrugged. 'You never know.'

But it was her moment to perform. Falke announced her with an exultant air, as if he were playing his trump card. By saving her till last he was assured that the punters would sit tight, buying drinks, right to the end of the show.

With a larger-than-life exuberance, Rosa bounced on to the dais. Without further ado she attacked her first number, an upbeat love song called 'Sun and Rain'. She showed no nervousness or hesitation. The message she gave out was that this stage was her element.

She came into her own now – sexy and approachable, her body sturdy and emphatically female – not remotely beautiful, but aware of her own worth. With her frizzy hair, cheap pink dress, darned stockings and worn-down shoes, Rosa was someone with whom people could identify. She seemed to embody both human fallibility and human optimism, convincing her audience for a while that nothing could get them down – not all the poverty and hunger of these post-war days, not all the uncertainty in the world.

'She's amazing, your sister,' Claudia said to Franz, and he smiled with a mixture of scepticism and pride.

But, increasingly, Claudia's attention was distracted from Rosa's triumphant routine. The queasiness in her stomach was returning with dizzying force. Maybe she should have steered clear of the schnapps. There was something dicky about it, a metallic aftertaste you had to try to ignore. And she'd drunk three chunky glasses.

'I don't feel too good,' she said, and got to her feet. Franz looked concerned but there was no time to reassure him.

Claudia lurched through the serried rows of tables and chairs towards the *Seeräuber*'s revolting privy. No one used it if they could possibly help it. The stink of urine hit her as she opened the door and the floor was awash. Three overflowing buckets stood side by side. She leaned over the closest one and retched violently. Then her whole system convulsed and she regurgitated the brandy, along with masticated pellets of the bread she'd eaten hours ago.

The racking spasms brought a kind of relief. From beyond the privy door Claudia heard the tumult of Rosa's ovation. But her mind was busy coping with a truth she'd denied and suppressed for days now. She was pregnant.

Chapter Eleven

❦❦❦❦❦

Claudia couldn't sleep. She'd lain awake for hours in the chilly room at the top of Frau Kästner's house, trying to come to grips with the bizarre notion that a baby was growing inside her, laying one hand experimentally on her hard, flat stomach, which felt exactly the same as it always had.

But the idea was still too abstract for her to concentrate on for long. And, as she shifted restlessly between the rough, unbleached sheets of Frau Kästner's big bed, Claudia's thoughts were ambushed by other, more trivial matters.

The taut, shrewd face of the compere, Falke, drifted into her mind.

'Do that song again another time, that weird one,' he'd instructed her. 'Do it again next week. People were caught off balance by it this evening, but they could get to like something like that, something dramatic. I reckon you could create a demand.' In the darkness Claudia relived the shock of pleasure Falke's verdict had given her.

After the *Seeräuber* closed Rosa and Franz had dragged her off to the room of some friend of Franz's. Claudia felt washed out. She'd much rather have gone straight to bed. But she was staying over at the Edelmanns', so she didn't have much choice but to tag along.

Rosa had persuaded the blond tenor to come with them as well. It was clear she had designs on him. The friend's room was bleak and uncomfortable. He only had two chairs and everyone ended up on the floor. Rosa was all over her young singer, so Claudia sat with Franz, listening glumly to one of his political diatribes.

He was rattling on about last month's putsch, claiming that the right-wing putschists should have been smashed. Instead the bastards were allowed to slink away to make trouble again in the future.

'Who was supposed to smash them?' the friend asked languidly.

Claudia had the impression he was less than delighted by their unannounced visit. He had a strange, rather interesting face, she thought sleepily – bony and cynical, with amused brown eyes. Though he was young, not much older than herself, she guessed.

'The left should've smashed them!' Franz replied sweepingly. 'We should organize. We're far too busy squabbling among ourselves.'

Claudia yawned. Jokingly Franz put his arm round her, laid her head on his broad shoulder. She stayed put. It was a relief to lean on him and doze, while he set out his plan of campaign.

The next thing she knew, Rosa was shaking her. 'Come on, Claudia. Wake up. We're off.'

'Not very lively, is she?' Johann, Franz's friend commented.

Still half asleep, Claudia made a rude gesture and told him to sod off, echoing Falke's terse instructions to the failed singer earlier that night. It made everyone laugh. She was supposed to be the classy one.

On the way home Rosa and the blond boy walked ahead with their arms round one another, singing.

Claudia and Franz trailed behind. Franz tried to kiss her.

'No.' She turned away. 'I'm sorry, Franz. I really am tired. Honestly I am.'

He was sweet, a gentleman, and perfectly amicable about her refusal.

An overpowering miasma of damp rot hung over the rickety staircase in the Edelmanns' lodgings. Their rooms were on the third floor, dark and poky. Rosa warned them to keep their voices down. Her mother was asleep in the room that also served as a kitchen.

The second room was divided by a skimpy green curtain on a wire, providing Franz and Rosa each with a token privacy. It was gone three in the morning. Rosa and her singer retired to bed. Franz insisted that Claudia take his sagging couch. He would doss down on the floor.

Soon he was snoring. Exhausted as she was, Claudia couldn't sleep. She lay tense, silently riveted by the whisperings and murmurings, the hoarse breathing, the creak of the bed from Rosa's side of the curtain. The muffled love-making was insidiously exciting. As she lay there listening, Claudia half regretted rebuffing Franz. He was nice and his body was large and warm. She toyed with the impulse to wake him up, invite him into his own bed. But discretion carried the day. Claudia suspected that Franz might turn out to be romantically inclined, when all she fancied was a quick, urgent screw.

And, anyway, Joachim had told her that if he ever found she'd slept with someone else, he'd drop her just like that. She *had* been faithful and she needed him now more than ever.

'Fräulein Claudia!' Frau Kästner's voice wafted from downstairs. 'There's a letter.'

'For me?' Correspondence was a rarity in Claudia's life.

Halfway through April Frau Kästner was still in her thick old winter dressing gown, hair hidden under a scarf like a Russian peasant.

'Nice stationery,' she remarked. 'Distinguished handwriting.' Curiosity lent her pale eyes a naked look.

Claudia went back upstairs to finish her coffee – the last of Joachim's most recent consignment. Agathe was preoccupied with an attempt to persuade Rudi to finish his bread, which was brittle and dry. 'Eat your crusts,' she cajoled, 'and you'll grow up to be a big, strong soldier.'

Claudia couldn't place the black gothic script on the envelope. Eagerly she slit the letter open with a knife and pulled out a single sheet of smooth, thick paper.

'My dear Claudia' – the writing was sprawling, erratic:

This has been the most appalling day of my life. I shall come straight to the point. Shortly before her birthday celebrations were due to begin, my dear wife, Erna, discovered certain photographs I had taken of you. Since then she has been prostrated with nervous debilitation and grief. I cannot forgive myself for causing her this anguish.

Under the circumstances, Claudia, it will be impossible for you and I ever to meet again. At present I cannot even bring myself to say that I have valued our relationship. It seems merely sordid and unworthy. If it lay within my power, I would cancel out the whole episode. I am sure you understand.

Yours, Joachim Werner.

Claudia sat staring blankly at the paper. It seemed to her that she could feel, physically feel, the blood draining from her face. But her expression remained neutral. She'd learned how to do that. The habit of lying had become ingrained. All the same, she was relieved that Agathe was occupied with her little brother.

Her first – irrelevant – thought was that she'd always had a bad feeling about those photographs. A premonition. Their mere existence had always seemed to her like a plot-device in a novel, a clue, a potential catalyst, which would one day precipitate disaster.

Casually she folded up the sheet of paper and got up from the table.

'What's the letter?' Agathe asked as she wiped Rudi's mouth.

'Another audition.' Claudia faked a wry grin. 'I shouldn't hold your breath.'

She crossed the room, needing to be alone. Closing the door behind her, Claudia reflected with a glint of black amusement, that Joachim's birthday surprise for his wife hadn't been quite what he intended.

The following week Agathe left for Hamburg, for her annual visit to her mother. Grandma Farnholz had never got over the suicide of her son, the loss of the family business. She was strange now, and being looked after by nuns. It was a duty-trip. Agathe said openly how pointless it was, what a waste of money. Grandma Farnholz no longer even recognized her own daughter.

'All the same, I wouldn't feel right if I didn't go,' Agathe said, with a moist gleam in her big, luminous eyes. Claudia felt a wave of love for her aunt and gave her a kiss on the cheek. Agathe looked pink and pleased.

To her niece's relief, she took Rudi with her. Claudia had plans of her own. She bought a whole bottle of the *Seeräuber*'s lethal schnapps and waited for Tuesday night when Frau Kästner visited a nephew in Wilmersdorf. As soon as she was gone, Claudia began heating bucketsful of water on her landlady's gas-range, humped them up to her own top floor room and filled the tin bath.

Rosa claimed to have brought about an abortion by sitting in a boiling hot bath and drinking a bottle of schnapps. Claudia had resolved to try it for herself. Without Joachim's money and support, she couldn't possibly allow this pregnancy to continue. She needed to provide for Rudi and Agathe. A big belly, a nursing infant, were unlikely to be assets in that undertaking.

Between her trips up and down stairs, the water in the bath cooled. Claudia was afraid she wouldn't be able to get it hot enough. But the final two bubbling bucketsful, added simultaneously, were enough to make the water as hot as she could possibly bear.

She stripped off, opened the bottle of schnapps and climbed gingerly into the steaming bath. It seemed scalding at first, but gradually her body got used to the temperature. The situation seemed unreal to Claudia – both the fact of her own pregnancy, and this clumsy attempt to terminate it – as if it were happening to someone else.

She took a swig from the bottle and pulled a face. After the other night the stuff seemed hateful. Never mind. It was medicine. She wasn't supposed to enjoy it.

Claudia found that, if she breathed through her mouth, she barely noticed the hard, metallic aftertaste. It took an effort to shut out the memory of the other night, herself doubled up and vomiting over a stinking pail in the *Seeräuber* privy. But that effort must be made. Otherwise she would simply throw up, here and now, before she'd swallowed enough of the brandy to have any effect.

The thing was to keep calm. She lay back awkwardly against the end surface of the bath and tried consciously to relax. In front of her stood the huge mahogany wardrobe Frau Kästner used for her sheets and towels. The doors and drawers were decorated with stiff, stylized carvings. Claudia focused on a pair of flowerpots blooming with angular flowers. Her mind traced the mosaic of circles, triangles and rectangles that made up the odd, ugly little decorations. Meanwhile she breathed deeply and took regular gulps from her bottle of brandy.

Quite soon she no longer needed to work at relaxing. Her legs seemed to float in the water, loose and languorous. Her hair was damp and tangled, face running with perspiration. She had to concentrate on keeping a tight grip on the bottle. Her arms and hands felt flaccid as waving waterweed, palms slippery with sweat.

Claudia felt her mouth hanging slackly, lids drooping over bleary eyes. Still she tippled doggedly at the schnapps, losing all awareness of the passing of time.

As it had the other night at the *Seeräuber*, nausea struck with dramatic finality. All at once there was a sour bubbling in her stomach, a violent paroxysm. Hastily, clumsily Claudia hauled herself into a sitting position, the three-quarters empty bottle slipping from her fingers. She seized one of the galvanized iron buckets just in time to catch the stream of vomit that erupted from her heaving guts.

After that she was helpless. There was nothing Claudia could do to combat the wave upon wave of sickness that convulsed her whole being, even after nothing remained for her stomach to reject. She had no idea how long she sat, leaning over the side of the bath, embracing the metal rim of the bucket, comatose and empty of thought.

Eventually, though, she managed to drag her slack limbs out of the luke-warm bath and crawl across the room to her bed, pull herself up, and collapse on to the hard, wide mattress, body still wet and dripping.

She slept on and on, waking occasionally to retch into the bucket, then falling again into insensibility. When she came round it was early evening the following day. The room stank of brandy, her throat hurt and her head throbbed with an intense and vibrant ache. Dully Claudia examined the sheet she was lying on. Not a trace of blood. She'd botched the abortion too.

She wrote to Joachim at his factory. A grown-up, civilized letter, saying that she quite understood his reasons for putting an end to their relationship. Only something had come up, she was expecting a baby. Claudia emphasized that she was making no claims on him, wanted an abortion in fact, because of her responsibilities to her little brother and her aunt. If Joachim could see his way clear to sending her, say, fifty marks – that should be sufficient – she would never contact him again.

Two days later she received a stiff reply, addressing her as Fräulein Farnholz. Joachim explained that he had no intention of forwarding money for the purpose mentioned, which was, in any case, against his religious principles. If she was, indeed, pregnant, he had absolutely no way of knowing whether or not he was the father. In view of the distress caused to his wife, he would be grateful if Fräulein Farnholz would refrain from contacting him again. If she did approach him he would have recourse to his lawyers.

Reading the letter, Claudia grew hot. She found herself literally trembling with mortification and rage. For a few mad hours she entertained the notion of turning up at Joachim's factory, heaving stones through the window, buttonholing his employees and letting them know what kind of a mean-minded bastard it was they worked for. She said as much to Rosa.

'Oh wonderful!' Rosa rolled her eyes with eloquent derision. 'Then he sends for the cops and you're carted off to chokey.'

'It'd be worth it.' But Claudia knew she wouldn't do it. She was powerless.

Tidying her room, ready for Tante Agathe's return, Claudia came across the card given her by the vampire-like theatrical agent. It lay half hidden by a pair of discarded stockings on the floor of her wardrobe. Since that night at the *Seeräuber* two weeks ago, she hadn't given the man a thought.

Was it worth going to see him? Claudia was cynical. This wasn't the first time some stranger had offered to advance her career. And here she was, still no further forward. Then again, why not? She had no better option. And if he could steer her towards some money, there was still ample time to procure an abortion.

Georg Buresch's office in the Budapesterstrasse did not inspire optimism. Not quite dirty, it was certainly scruffy. It seemed he lived there too. On a grey and white chaise longue lay a floral pillow and a rumpled blanket. And when Claudia arrived Buresch hastened to open the windows and let in some air, as if he felt the room might be stuffy or smelly, which it was.

He crossed to a cheap, functional desk, pulling on his jacket as he went, smoothing back the oily wings of his black hair. These actions appeared to symbolize the donning of his professional persona. In the light of day Claudia thought he looked seedy. And the pleasant, Viennese-inflected voice seemed to have something unctuous about it. There again, she was anxious and overwrought, and it could be her imagination.

She came straight to the point. 'The other night you said you might be able to help me.'

Buresch nodded non-committally.

'I need work. I really need money.' Claudia had decided in advance to be frank about the urgency of her situation. In the past she'd been cool with people, kept her pride, and it hadn't done her any good. 'If there's anything at all . . .'

'Things are slow at the moment . . .' He pulled a face, made a disparaging gesture with one hand. He seemed heartened by her evident need.

'If you can think of anything,' she persisted. 'I really don't know where to turn.'

'May I ask why you need money so much, Fräulein Farnholz?'

Claudia hesitated, then took the plunge. She'd come this far. Why stand on dignity? 'I'm pregnant and I need an abortion.'

'I see.' He was silent for some moments, but sat with his head cocked slightly to one side, as if to indicate thought, though his pale, puffy face remained impassive.

Finally he spoke. 'I'm not sure I . . . Fräulein Farnholz, I have a friend . . . an acquaintance. She's a trained nurse and scrupulous as regards hygiene . . .'

'Does she . . . ?'

'On occasion. She's a kind-hearted woman and, well, an accident like this can ruin a young woman's life. My friend does perform the operation you mentioned.'

Cautiously Claudia perked up. 'Could you introduce me . . . ? How much does she charge?'

'It's by no means certain. I believe she charges somewhere between thirty-five and forty marks.'

'I see.' Claudia shrugged. 'I'd have to earn it first anyway.'

Buresch was silent again, as if giving her time to reflect on her plight. Then he said, 'If you'll bear with me, I think I can suggest something.'

She glanced across at him, but it seemed he avoided meeting her eye, as if suddenly relinquishing the psychological advantage he had held until that moment. Head to one side, Buresch stared down at his desk and spoke in a confused, rambling fashion about shame and honour, and how many, many actresses had been forced to sacrifice their artistic integrity, just once, *in order*, he stressed, to regain control of their lives. The rigmarole made no sense to Claudia.

Politely she murmured, 'I'm not sure I understand what you're saying.'

He looked up suddenly and met her gaze. Now his eyes were brazen and level, matter-of-fact. There were beige shadows beneath them, the kind Claudia thought of as peculiarly Eastern European.

'Let me explain. I can arrange for my friend to take away your baby. I can arrange for you to earn sufficient money . . . I would like to take some photographs of you, now . . . Intimate photographs.' He paused and stared into her eyes as if to check that she understood what he was proposing, seemed satisfied, and carried on. 'The pictures will never be circulated in Berlin. My markets are in Prague and Vienna. So rest assured, Fräulein Farnholz, your friends will never see them.'

Claudia was dumbstruck and gazed at him like a rodent at a swaying cobra. Buresch had regained his sang-froid. He sat waiting calmly for her to make up her mind.

Her first reaction was a sinking feeling of inevitability. There were sure-fire ways, it seemed, for a woman to survive in this city, here and now. All she wanted was work, a decent job, but that ambition seemed peculiarly elusive. Claudia reflected ruefully that she'd already let Joachim photograph her nude, and no good had come of that. The thought of repeating the experience was profoundly ... depressing, humiliating. And Buresch was creepy.

'I don't know you. How do I know I can trust you?'

His shrug was positively debonair. 'You don't. But you can. I give you my word.' A pause. 'You need me, you know. And after this you need never do anything of the sort again.' He smiled, eyelids drooping in a sleazy fashion. 'Though it's easy money. A good-looking woman's always got it made.'

What choice had she? This could be her final chance.

He had pulled a suitcase full of lingerie out of a cupboard in the corner. 'You can wear some of these.'

Claudia wanted to laugh when he held up the garments. They must be years old, cheeky, *fin-de-siècle* underpinnings.

'How long have you had these?' she asked incredulously.

Buresch had been defensive. 'This is good stuff, real silk and satin. Punters like the look. Reminds them of their youth.'

Again, the clothes weren't dirty, but there was a musty smell about them, as if they'd been jumbled up in that suitcase for decades, bar the occasional outing. Claudia guessed she was by no means the first woman to pose on the shabby chaise longue in a satin corset and long, frilly drawers with the crotch part missing.

And once again she was invaded by a sense of unreality. The situation seemed bizarre rather than shameful or embarrassing. Buresch, with his camera, seemed merely a businessman trying earnestly to capture the images he thought his public would respond to. When it was over he told her to come back the next day at half-past four. His friend would be there. He repeated the instructions several times, as if to stress his good faith.

At intervals throughout the evening and the following day Claudia was invaded by an insidious, shivery feeling at the thought of the ordeal ahead. Would the operation by performed in the man's office, she wondered, on the same scuffed chaise longue on which she'd pouted and smouldered to Buresch's instructions? The thought had a black humour. Claudia shivered again. She was deeply dubious. Actually she was terrified.

Buresch's room was empty when she arrived the following afternoon, the door with its frosted glass panels banging in the through-draught from the open windows. Claudia stepped inside. It appeared that the office had been ransacked. Drawers had been pulled out of cabinets, their contents strewn on the threadbare carpet.

She knocked on the door across the landing. It was answered by a stocky man who looked like a wrestler. He wore a singlet and had a towel draped round his neck.

'Do you know what's happened to Herr Buresch?' Claudia asked anxiously.

The man shrugged, turning down the corners of his mouth. 'The police were here this morning. They seem to think he's done a runner. Don't ask me why.'

Claudia gazed at him, vacant, stricken. 'Will he be back?'

'Doubt it.' A mocking grin. 'Not if he knows what's good for him.'

'Oh . . . Thanks anyhow.' She turned away, started back down the stairs. Inside her came the first stirrings of a reaction that swelled into a nauseous wave of anguish, and craven relief.

Chapter Twelve

It was a sunny Sunday in May. Arms outstretched, Noel leaned luxuriously back in his wicker chair on the verandah of the house he'd found for them to rent in the uncommonly attractive suburb of Grunewald.

'This is the life.' Always, now, his moments of happiness were shot through with an ache of sadness and dread. But, on this glorious, golden morning, these emotions were further from his mind, more muffled than usual.

Amy looked up and smiled, then returned to the fat volume of *War and Peace* she was reading. Lately she had a real bee in her bonnet about improving herself, a thirst for making good the deficiencies in her education. Noel was touched by the earnestness of her endeavour, though, in his opinion, she was already far better read than most women, more keenly aware of what was going on in the world.

He looked about him with satisfaction. This really was the most beautiful place and, with the rate of exchange, quite ludicrously cheap. To his right a pink-tinged clematis frothed extravagantly along the white-painted wooden railings of the verandah. Later there would be roses and jasmine. At the far end of the garden a lake sparkled through willows arching their fresh young foliage towards the lapping water. There was a boathouse, a small jetty.

'We must get that little boat seen to,' he said. 'It'll be perfectly serviceable with some patching-up. Can you imagine, darling, rowing out on balmy summer evenings . . . ?'

'Heaven.' Amy smiled again, but her soft grey eyes were glazed. She was lost in her book.

The house was called Mailied. Noel had recognized it as the title of a poem by Goethe. He'd taken a volume from the shelf in the living room and showed it to Amy. The verse was simple, the language almost childlike. With only a little help Amy had been able to translate it. Her German really was coming along. He gazed at his wife, contemplating her many perfections.

'Won't you hate living among Germans so soon after fighting them?' his sister had asked when he and Amy had paid a last visit to Noel's parental home in the Avon Valley.

'But I don't hate them,' he'd replied, genuinely surprised that Carrie thought he might.

'Lots of people do,' Carrie replied stoutly. 'The majority, in fact.'

She was right, of course. Yet the idea of embracing the popular prejudice had never, ever occurred to Noel. He used to like Germany, he'd had good times there. The fact that governments had forced the men of their respective countries to fight one another changed nothing as far as he was concerned.

The prejudice worked both ways. Already, in Berlin, he'd been made aware of hostility towards himself. Most Germans saw themselves as the innocent victims of the aggression of jealous enemies. And the post-war food blockade, the swingeing reparations demanded by the Versailles Treaty had heightened their perception of the Allies' vindictiveness. The Germans felt humiliated. They'd been forced to give up huge tracts of – admittedly debatable – land. Their treasured army had been reduced to a paltry token force. Noel had been harangued in the street by a neat little man in his forties, shabby-genteel and clerkly-looking, incoherent with righteous anger. He'd been spat at by a vagrant with crazy eyes, wearing an iron cross on his filthy jacket.

But Noel had discovered, deep inside himself, a sense of affinity with the war-ravaged nation. He'd never admit to it out loud. The notion sounded self-deluding and sentimental. At home he felt cut off by his war experiences, he felt a freak. Over here – so much more visibly than in England – the war had laid people low, robbed them of their certainties, their self-respect. He experienced a private, passionate fellow-feeling for the maimed men he saw everywhere, for girls as young as thirteen murmuring indecent invitations to passing men.

There was a group of beggars he saw often on a corner of the Potsdamerplatz near his office in the Leipzigerstrasse, though sometimes the police moved them on and they had to disperse. In the main they were simply ragged and hopeless-looking, most had rotting gap-teeth or none at all. But one had had part of his upper lip blown away. A single brown tooth hung in his shrunken gum, giving him a terrifying, malevolent look until you saw the desperation in his eyes. Another man had his right leg missing, breeches pinned over the stump. He leaned on a pair of makeshift crutches.

Noel always gave them money when he passed. A few days ago the tall, cadaverous one had thrust it back at him with a hoarse insult against the English. Most simply took his offering with a poor grace.

But from the one-legged beggar he sensed a measure of tolerance, even goodwill. One day the man gestured that he'd like a cigarette. Noel gave him one and lit it for him.

With a kind of ecstasy the beggar took his first drag. Then he grinned, his leather face crinkling into amiable folds, so that Noel caught a glimpse of what he must have looked like before he came to this dehumanizing pass.

'War no good,' the man said in English.

'*Das stimmt*,' Noel agreed. He was moved by the small moment of contact.

'I'm hot.' Amy laid aside her book. 'Think I'll stroll down to the water.'

She bent to kiss the top of Noel's head as she passed. He caught her hand, laid his lips against the inside of her wrist. With a mixture of pleasure and pain he watched her walk down the long sweep of grass.

He loved her private stay-at-home look. Today she wore her soft curling hair in a long, pale plait that fell forward over her right shoulder. She had on an old summer dress in thin, cream-coloured cotton, beneath which her legs and feet were bare. He was mesmerized by the tender, sun-dazzled blue-whiteness of skin that was normally kept hidden. Noel longed to take her back to bed, but he stifled the urge; that kind of impulse was for couples whose sexuality was easy and confident.

Sometimes he was invaded by visions of his ethereal child-wife being savagely fucked by some rampant, anonymous male body. Then he closed his eyes and visualized a knife stabbing at his own guts, the way he'd pictured it before, conjuring up a pain so violent it could challenge the anguish of his thoughts.

Last night, in a dream, he had relived a forgotten incident from the war. Reconnoitring during a brief cease-fire, he'd stumbled on a shell hole filled with raw young recruits, all gassed, dead. Desperate for fresh air, Noel guessed, and in their inexperience imagining the danger past, they'd snatched their masks off too soon. And now they lay, in a ragged semi-circle, some hugging the earth, some clutching their throats, faces purplish, agonized, lips skinned and black.

In his dream, though, they'd risen from the hollowed-out bowl and, with ponderous movements – like so many dancing bears – they had chased after his wife. For all their clumsiness, Amy could not escape them. Her face was white and panicked. They'd seized her from behind, their hands fondling her breasts and reaching under her skirt.

She was sitting on the jetty now, motionless, in profile, her bare feet trailing in the water. He watched her with empty eyes.

The sun, burning into her back, contrasted pleasurably with the cool water lapping her toes. Across the twinkling surface of the lake she could see little white sailboats wheeling in the breeze. The sky was cloudless, a heavenly blue. Amy turned her head and gazed back at the house, a large white chalet, spacious yet friendly, and festooned with that marvellous clematis. Two rustic horses' heads adorned the steep roof. It was impossible not to be seduced.

And yet. She'd hoped for something more urban, something in the thick of things. She had spent nearly all of her life in picturesque rural seclusion. London had changed all that and she would have wished the change to continue.

'It's idyllic, Amy,' Noel had enthused. 'The loveliest place you ever saw.' How could she dampen such eagerness?

Then there was Frau Gast, the housekeeper. 'She's a nice, motherly woman,' Noel said. 'You'll be able to speak German together.'

Sometimes it amazed Amy how little her husband understood her. Ever since she could remember people had classified her as a pretty girl, a sweet young thing, dismissing inconvenient complexities. But with Noel she tried to be frank, to talk seriously, discuss things. Yet even he favoured his own preconceived, sentimental, two-dimensional image. When it suited him? No, that wasn't fair. His tunnel vision was not deliberate. Why, then, should he think she was the sort of person who wanted to live in a charming house in a pretty suburb, and practise her domestic German with a motherly housekeeper?

Apart from anything else, she didn't see Frau Gast as motherly. True, she was middle-aged, with a heavy bosom under her clean, floral overalls, wore her blonde-mousy hair in a haphazard bun. But, however much she smiled, her eyes made Amy think of a description she'd once read of the eyes of a great white shark – flat, devoid of animation, yet ever alert. Amy saw her noticing things and disapproving. It was clear she thought her young employer far too much of a bookworm. And she'd glanced at Amy's bare legs this morning, tightened her lips and, just perceptibly, shaken her head.

Frau Gast was an annoyance, but not more than that. Amy felt a new obstinacy in her heart, a determination. Little by little – like a featherless bird tapping its way out of an egg – she was going to break free from the mould of compliance she had been born and brought up to.

Chapter Thirteen

❦❦❦

She'd seen her three times now, on different days, passing the front of the house. A girl about her own age – at almost nineteen and married for more than eighteen months, Amy still found it hard to think of herself as a woman. On each occasion the stranger had looked up at the chalet with an interest that was far more than casual, before turning away, almost reluctantly, and walking on.

She was someone you noticed. Olive skin, dark hair that shone in the sun with reddish tints, a short, modern hairstyle, a wide mouth emphasized with red lip-balm. Each time she'd worn a wine-coloured dress and carried a black straw hat.

But, in a sense, the details of her appearance were irrelevant. It was her air that intrigued Amy, the self-assertive walk, the sharply humorous look in her brown eyes beneath the heavy fringe. The feeling she radiated – consciously it seemed – that she could look after herself. Amy admired that.

'Do you know who that is?' she asked Frau Gast.

'Why do you ask, Frau Campion?' The antipathy in the house-keeper's eyes went far beyond her habitual bland disapproval. 'What interest could *you* have in a painted creature like that?'

The girl came by again the following day, just as Amy had returned from her daily walk and was fitting her key into the front door lock. She stared at Amy and Amy stared back.

The stranger nodded as she passed and gave a sassy, amiable grin. '*Guten Tag.*'

Noel had rented a small suite of rooms in the Leipzigerstrasse – a largish office that looked out on the street, a washroom and lavatory, a modest bedroom. The rent was minimal, the place simple and functional. The caretaker's wife from downstairs took care of the cleaning, delighted to earn a little extra cash.

The suite was essentially a base from which Noel could operate. As yet he had no need of staff. Like most journalists he typed his own copy, or telephoned it through himself. But he needed a place where he could meet people and talk to them without interruption. The office was conveniently central and within easy walking distance of the bar at the Adlon Hotel where foreign correspondents habitually congregated to compare notes, a shifting, ad hoc club.

Noel stared out of his window at the street below, as he drank a cup of muddy coffee substitute from a nearby café – he'd developed a perverse taste for the muck, though he and Amy drank the real thing at home. He found himself endlessly drawn to this gazing, though the scene outside was drab and dispiriting. For all his advance research he had been unprepared for the privation and demoralization of this defeated city.

It wasn't solely the extremes that caught his attention – the maimed and hopeless beggars everywhere. It was the shabbiness and sallowness of almost everyone after years of malnutrition, the sparseness of the traffic in the streets, the shop windows displaying faded paper streamers because they had no goods to put on show.

Below his window a peasant woman sold spring cabbage from a handcart. In no time at all she'd shifted the whole lot. People were desperate for fresh vegetables – so much of Germany's produce was dispatched direct to France as part of the war reparation scheme. The Potsdamer Bahnhof was nearby. Each morning men and women arrived from the outlying country districts with their paltry wares – a few potatoes, onions, root vegetables – and sold them within minutes. But these luxuries were just a drop in the ocean.

He watched two women, arm in arm, heading towards him along the cobbled pavement. A mother and daughter, he guessed. The older woman, grey-haired and grey-faced, wore an almost caricatured expression of dull endurance, seemed the embodiment of a suffering proletarian from some poster by Käthe Kollwitz. Her daughter walked with an insolent swing of the hips. Her face was painted into an aggressive mask and she ogled passing men with eyes that were calculating and joyless. To Noel the couple encapsulated the two parallel styles of post-war Berlin womanhood – the downtrodden and the predatory.

For the umpteenth time he thanked his stars that he'd found a house for Amy out among the lakes. For all she talked about living at the hub of things, it went too deeply against the grain for him to expose her to all this ugliness.

But Noel found himself markedly stimulated by the tawdry unfamiliarity of his surroundings. He was half ashamed of his reaction. It wasn't compassion that moved him, if he were honest, but outright curiosity – an almost prurient feeling, like turning over a stone to contemplate the scurrying secret life beneath.

In a sense this was what he had hoped for. In London he'd felt himself a hollow hack, working from expediency rather than enthusiasm. Here the long-stifled green shoots of professional inquisitiveness were breaking through. He was intensely eager to know more about this new society. And again – as he drained the thick, black brew in his cup with an automatic grimace – there came that drift of empathy, diffuse as smoke, the shadowy sensation that he had something in common with the war-weary figures in the street below.

His workload here was not onerous. His brief was to produce a weekly newsletter. If something significant was going on, he would naturally write about that. Otherwise the subject matter was left to his discretion. And every month he would produce a longer, in-depth piece shedding light on some intriguing aspect of the new German republic for readers back home. It meant he could work the way he enjoyed, at an unhurried pace, polishing and rewriting as he went. Noel's contract didn't preclude him from contributing to other papers and journals, and he'd resolved to keep a diary of his time in Berlin, which could well be published later in book form – an on-the-spot view of a singular moment in history.

He was fascinated by what he'd gathered of the political situation. The democratic government seemed a compromise, voted in to appease the Allies, but too tame and toothless to arouse enthusiasm even among the moderates who supported them *faute de mieux*.

Passion was reserved for the extremists at both ends of the scale: the combative socialists who'd briefly seized power at the end of the war on the one hand, the monarchists and militarists on the other, hankering after the good old days and maintaining that Germany had been defeated not by her foes, but stabbed in the back by the Bolshevist enemy within.

All over Germany ex-soldiers had formed up into private armies – the *Freikorps* they called themselves until they were officially 'disbanded'. To Noel they seemed a dangerous crew and one which would repay investigation by an enterprising journalist. Last night in the Adlon bar he'd sniffed out a couple of likely leads. He resolved to follow them up without delay.

From her visit to Hamburg Tante Agathe had brought back a photograph of the Kaiser in an ornate gilded frame, salvaged from the Farnholz family home. He wore a helmet with an imperial eagle atop it, a moustache that spread across his cheeks like a double-headed hammer. His eyes were stern and judicial. Agathe hung the portrait above the table in her room where she, Rudi and Claudia took their meals.

Each morning, after creeping downstairs to the toilet to be furtively sick, Claudia found it unnerving to be faced with this judgemental figure as she sat down to her morning hunk of bread – coffeeless and butterless now that Joachim was no longer on the scene. But Agathe seemed to find the royal presence a comforting reminder of the days when you knew where you were, and what was what, when there was order and respect.

Currently she was up in arms about the Jew, Ackermann, lining his pockets by letting out her brother's home. And to foreigners, former enemies. For Agathe the situation typified the topsy-turvy new way of the world.

'That's how it is nowadays – it's the Jews, the profiteering fly-boys who rake in the shekels while, round the corner, people who never did any harm to anyone are stuck in two poky rooms living on dry bread, not knowing where their next meal is coming from.'

'The house hasn't done him much good so far,' Claudia commented. 'It's been standing empty for more than two years. About time he got some kind of a return on his investment ... The wife's very pretty,' she added as an afterthought. 'I've seen her out walking once or twice.'

She was intrigued by the blonde young Englishwoman. She seemed a romantic figure. So ravishing, yet something lonely about her. She'd smiled yesterday and remarked on the weather in attractive, halting German. It would be interesting to get to know her, perhaps see inside the house again. Quite apart from anything else, these well-to-do foreigners would most likely have access to decent food. It was always worth cultivating people like that. On the off chance.

Claudia had resigned herself to the fact that she wasn't going to have an abortion. She'd made her bid – three bids, in fact. And the fates had blocked each one. She'd stopped struggling, was drifting day to day. But sometimes at night fear of the future made her heart hammer, her stomach clench, and in the morning she could hardly bear to face her own reflection in the mirror, the staring panic in her eyes, hair wild and matted with sweat. Yet habit died hard. The moment she crossed the threshold of her room Claudia summoned up a breezy smile, a jaunty, indomitable demeanour.

'What would we do without you, Mausi, cheering us all up?' Agathe sighed frequently.

Claudia's best hope of employment lay in a bottle factory that was opening, not too far away, in Wilmersdorf. She'd put her name down and they'd told her to come back in three weeks' time. She still had several months' worth of work in her, Claudia reckoned. If anything she was getting skinnier. So far nothing showed at all.

Sooner or later, of course, she was going to have to break the news of her pregnancy to her aunt. Claudia wasn't looking forward to that. Agathe never liked to venture too far outside her own reassuring version of reality.

Chapter Fourteen

◆━◆━◆

As Amy made her way along the rose-walk in the park, a summer rain began to fall. All day the sky had been overcast, heavy and brooding. The downpour was a welcome relief. She breathed in the deeply familiar smell of dampened earth with its vague nostalgic reverberations.

In her long mackintosh Amy continued unhurriedly along the grassy alley bordered with pastel-coloured roses, which drooped and grew sodden, their petals dropping. A mother and two children ran for cover. Amy savoured the melancholy freshness of the almost empty park.

It was more peaceful here than at home. Frau Gast and the terrified young girl who helped her had both tied up their hair in dusters and, all day, they'd been cleaning windows and beating carpets with a ferocious, self-righteous concentration of energy. Frau Gast had gazed askance at Amy whenever she passed by, clearly considering her employer's struggles with dictionary and exercise book the height of futile self-indulgence.

She turned the corner onto the paved, yew-bordered path that led to the park exit. Her soles and heels clipped mutedly on the hard surface. After a while she realized that another pair of shoes was tapping along behind her own. Casually she glanced over her shoulder and saw her slight acquaintance, the girl who went by the house each day.

Amy slowed so that she could catch up.

'*So viel Regen,*' she remarked, summoning up a few lumbering German words on the spur of the moment – no time to construct anything more inspired. She'd been presented with an opportunity and Amy was determined to get talking to the girl – someone her own age and who looked amusing.

'Much rain,' the girl echoed laughingly in English, holding out her slim arms and looking up at the sky.

She was wearing her wine-red dress, with nothing over it. The material was soaked. The straw hat she had on was limp and dripping.

'*Sie sind so nass.*' Amy gestured concernedly towards the stranger's wet garments, but the girl shrugged with elegant indifference.

Side by side they walked through the imposing wrought-iron park gates. Amy indicated the direction in which she was going and the young woman fell into step beside her.

'*Ich gehe nach Hause,*' Amy said.

'*Moi aussi.*' Mischievously the girl added to the confusion by introducing yet a third language into their exchange.

As they walked Amy racked her brains for some way of prolonging the encounter.

'*Wollen Sie Kaffee trinken?*' she blurted, then felt foolish. The invitation sounded abrupt and premature.

'Now?' The young woman, too, seemed taken aback by the suddenness of the offer, but good-naturedly so.

Amy nodded emphatically.

The girl shrugged again, with her wide, accepting smile. 'Why not?'

Sitting on a sofa in what had once been her living room, Claudia felt somewhat dazed. Partly at the sheer fact of being a guest in her own childhood home and partly because of the ease with which she'd got here. She had expected to have to pass through several weeks at least of nods and smiles and comments on the weather – everyone knew how stiff and standoffish the English were. But it appeared that the young Englishwoman was as eager to become acquainted as she was.

Claudia wondered why, then decided the answer lay in nothing more complicated than a desire for entertainment. It must be grim here all day with just servants.

She'd glimpsed the housekeeper as they came through the hall, and classified her right away as one of those disapproving old cows, hellbent on making everyone else's life as dreary as her own, and all in the name of decency and hard work – the sort of person Lotte would never have had in the house. Claudia had to stifle a giggle at the housekeeper's expression when Frau Campion – they'd introduced themselves – ordered coffee to be made for this drowned rat brought in from off the streets.

She looked around her, recognizing very little of the furniture. Ackermann, Claudia presumed, had appropriated most of her parents' modern, hand-made furniture for his own use, along with the expensive, imported Bagatelle carpets and curtain fabrics.

The stuff he'd replaced it with was mass-produced but not unpleasant – a walnut table and secretaire, a sofa and chairs upholstered in nubbly jade-green wool, amber and green glass lampshades, attractive but run-of-the-mill. Claudia was glad it was changed. Quite suddenly she knew she would have burst into tears otherwise – she wouldn't have been able to stand it.

'Do you like this house?' she asked Frau Campion. For the time being they spoke English. Claudia had learned it at school for six years or more. She'd enjoyed speaking foreign languages even then. It was like acting.

'It's charming. My husband found it.' Claudia sensed something evasive in her response.

'You stay long?'

'I think so. We plan to.'

There was a knock on the door. Frau Gast entered with coffee and cups on a tray. Claudia recognized the cups. They'd been presented to Friedrich one Christmas by the staff of Bagatelle – sweet little things in thin white china with multicoloured butterflies round the rim. They were Claudia's favourites but Friedrich and Lotte rarely used them. It was poignant to see them in the indifferent hands of this uncongenial female.

The housekeeper's smile was thin as she set down the tray on a low table next to Frau Campion.

'*Danke schön, Frau Gast.*'

The older woman nodded, gave another strained smile, then darted a look at Claudia that spoke of dark misgiving. As she left the room her buxom figure was stiff with displeasure.

Claudia grinned, her good spirits restored. 'She doesn't like me, your maid.'

A quick, answering smile in Frau Campion's soft, grey eyes. 'I'm not sure she likes anyone very much.'

They laughed together with wary complicity.

The coffee was mellow and strong and there were little caraway seed cakes to go with it. Their conversation was halting but friendly and well-intentioned, an erratic mixture of German and English. Frau Campion talked about her husband and his work, very little about herself. She seemed more interested in finding out about Claudia.

Claudia made a point of stating that she was in need of work. You never knew. This apparently well-connected foreigner might get to hear of something.

Stretching the truth quite shamelessly, Claudia claimed to be an actress who'd done many small parts but found herself temporarily at a loose end.

'I would take any kind of work at this time,' she said. 'You see I have an aunt and a little brother to feed.' But she spoke lightly, as if her plight were mildly amusing, not pressing at all. Naked need was disconcerting and she didn't want to alienate her new acquaintance.

'My husband may hear of something. I'll certainly ask him.'

'That would be kind.' Claudia swallowed the last of her coffee. 'I should go, Frau Campion.'

'Will you come again, Fräulein Farnholz? I've really enjoyed your company.' Claudia sensed an intensity behind the request that went beyond mere social amiability.

She smiled. 'Yes. Happily.'

'Frau Campion, may I speak to you?'

'Yes, of course.' Amy looked up from her book.

Wholesome in a starched blue print overall, Frau Gast gave the pink, bridling smile Noel found motherly. But she was bursting with some kind of suppressed emotion.

'It's about Fräulein Farnholz who drank coffee with you the other day.'

'Oh yes?' So far Amy's German stretched to the conversation. But she was guarded. It was clear that, for some reason, Frau Gast had taken against the young woman.

'I'm listening.' Amy smiled in her turn, trying to elicit some warmth from the housekeeper, but Frau Gast's eyes remained blank as the sky.

She launched into a tirade which Amy couldn't follow but which – from the tone of her voice and the look on her face – was evidently critical.

'I don't understand. Speak more slowly please.' Amy quoted two of the earliest phrases in her German book. She reached for her dictionary, indicating that she could look up the hardest words as Frau Gast went along.

With an impatient gesture the housekeeper waved this offer away. 'That young woman is not good for you,' she enunciated loudly and clearly. 'Fräulein Farnholz is not good for you.'

'Why not?' Amy shrugged and shook her head, miming good-natured incomprehension.

'It would be better if I talked to Herr Campion. He will be able to translate.'

'Good idea.' Amy was relieved to be done with the conversation. By the time Noel came home she'd forgotten all about it.

But, after supper, when they were sitting on the verandah with their coffee, the housekeeper approached again. There was a portentous, pained look on her face as if she had an unpleasant but necessary duty to perform.

Amy clapped one hand to her forehead. 'It'd slipped my mind, Noel. Frau Gast wanted a word with you.' She smiled at her husband and the older woman, including them both in her goodwill. 'We tried to talk earlier but, frankly, my German wasn't up to it. We thought you might translate.'

'Frau Gast?' Noel had a pleasant, respectful way with servants which Amy approved. At the same time, with his height and his gravity, his severe good looks, there was no danger of anyone taking advantage.

For the second time that day Frau Gast presented her case with voluble passion. Noel questioned. She added fresh protestations. He listened with an attentive, judicious air. In Amy's eyes the dialogue between her husband and the housekeeper took on the displeasing aspect of two adults discussing what was best for a child in their care.

Finally Noel smiled at Frau Gast and courteously dismissed her, explaining, so Amy gathered, that he would talk the matter over with his wife in private. The housekeeper went back inside the house with reluctance, as if she felt she should have a stake in the ensuing conversation as well.

'What was all that about?' Amy asked when she was out of earshot.

Noel leaned down and placed his empty coffee cup on the floor by his chair. He looked up with a quizzical smile. 'She seems to think this new friend of yours isn't quite the thing.'

'What do you mean?' She was irritated by Noel's casual amusement and by his referring to Fräulein Farnholz as her friend, when he knew perfectly well she'd only been here once, was a simple acquaintance. It sounded superior, jocularly patronizing.

'There are rumours, it seems, about your Fräulein Farnholz.' A satirical note in Noel's voice. 'Apparently her morality isn't above suspicion. The story is she had an affair with a married chap, upset the fellow's wife . . .'

Amy recalled the housekeeper's avid busybody air and her annoyance increased. Coolly she remarked, 'I'm not sure we should be encouraging Frau Gast to repeat rumours.'

'Perhaps not . . .' Noel spread his hands as if the matter were unimportant. 'All the same, darling, perhaps you should give this Fräulein Farnholz a wider berth in future.'

'What are you saying?' She was incredulous. In an instant a hot anger had flooded her veins. 'That I should live my life according to the prejudices of Frau Gast?'

Her vehemence seemed to take him by surprise. He frowned defensively. 'Of course not! Only don't forget, Amy, she *is* a native. She understands the society here . . . And perhaps, as foreigners, we should be a bit cautious . . .'

Amy barely heard him. 'It's absolutely none of her business who I choose to . . .'

The force of her anger appeared to touch and amuse him. He smiled at her with a bemused, indulgent tenderness, as a parent might smile at the vehemence of a toddler throwing a tantrum. 'She's only trying to be helpful,' he remonstrated soothingly. 'After all, darling, you *are* an innocent abroad.'

'I'm amazed you take her interfering seriously even for a moment. And what if the girl has had an affair? That doesn't affect . . . What about Robert and Prudence? Our friends. Shall we be cutting them when we get back? I enjoyed my conversation with Fräulein Farnholz and I'll see her again whenever I want.'

Amy found herself almost incoherent with indignation. And yet, in a sense, the situation had a familiarity to it, almost an inevitability. All her life people had known what was best for her. She'd had to fight for her visits to Nancy. She'd had to cut Paul Oates in the street. As a child she'd complied. There had been no choice. But, as an adult, she would claim the right to choose her own friends.

'Of course, darling, if it means that much to you.' It was clear Noel thought her anger an overreaction.

Chapter Fifteen

The minor clash with Noel toppled Amy into a morass of discouragement, as if her subconscious self had simply been waiting for an excuse of this sort. True, she'd made her point about seeing Fräulein Farnholz as and when she pleased. But, perversely, from that point on, the determination she'd harboured about taking her life into her own hands had begun to crumble and slip through her fingers. Try as she might, Amy couldn't think herself back into her previous resolute state of mind. She felt out of her depth, powerless to change anything.

She and Noel were invited to a party at the Dahlem home of Art Krell, an American foreign correspondent, and his bright, attractive wife, Laura. Among the articulate, international guests Amy felt young and shy, overawed. She had a mental picture of herself – a tongue-tied country bumpkin in an incongruously fashionable and expensive gossamer dress, wearing a distant, ironic smile to disguise her helpless disarray.

At home the presence of Frau Gast was becoming increasingly oppressive to her. Her nerves felt jittery and exposed and she could barely stand the self-important clatter of the housekeeper's dusting and sweeping, the judgemental air she wore constantly, as much a part of her as the succession of crisp, flower-printed overalls. Amy felt overwrought, couldn't relax. It was as if Frau Gast were expanding, gaining in weight and power, while she herself became ever more shadowy and marginal, a stranger in a strange land, without friends or family to underpin her sense of who she was.

What wild self-delusion had led her to believe she could start a new life in this hostile, alien environment?

* * *

Amy sat working in a small, bright first-floor room she'd claimed as a study. Outside it was hot and humid. With a dictionary at her elbow she was attempting to decipher a leader in the *Berliner Tageblatt*. It was difficult and the self-imposed effort struck her today as absolutely pointless. She could feel the sweat in her hair and under her arms. The piece she was reading seemed an absurd and windy parody, a distillation of German pomposity. She was powerfully tempted to cross her arms on the table in front of her, lay her head on them and close her eyes, give up. But she forced herself to carry on.

Frau Gast knocked and entered. 'Can I ask you to move, Frau Campion? I need to clean the room.'

Her manner implied that the enquiry was merely for form's sake. She had no doubt but that Amy would spring up with an obliging smile and be gone.

A sharp irritation pierced the younger woman's boredom. Her reply came faster than thought. 'Come back in an hour, Frau Gast. I'm busy just at the moment.'

The measured coolness of her own voice took Amy by surprise, pleased her.

The housekeeper, too, appeared taken aback and flushed angrily. 'Very good, Frau Campion.' Her ill humour was made clear though her tone remained just acceptably polite.

Quite suddenly Amy was possessed by a clean, clear sense of annoyance at Frau Gast's constant ungracious presence, her taking for granted that her own bustling should take precedence over her employer's desire for peace and quiet. The exasperation refreshed her like a drink of cold water.

Behind the housekeeper's left shoulder she saw the blank, white face of the waiflike child who helped her. Frau Gast turned and muttered some curt, incomprehensible instruction to the girl, who rolled her eyes expressively heavenwards. She was a timid creature who would never have risked such a brazen gesture without the tacit connivance of the housekeeper.

'You've no objection, I take it?' Amy's voice was sharp. She'd just learned the apt phrase from her German book.

'No, Frau Campion.' The reply held a veiled insolence. The older woman turned away.

'Frau Gast!' Amy called. The housekeeper stopped in her tracks. 'Come in here and close the door.'

When she'd complied the two women faced one another mistrustfully. Amy wasn't really sure what it was she wanted to say. Only she was tired of Frau Gast's elusive provocation – never quite overt enough for her to reproach but sufficiently pronounced to unsettle the whole atmosphere of the house. She needed to confront the situation, if her German would stretch to such a thing.

'I think we ... don't understand each other well,' she began falteringly.

The housekeeper stood blank-faced, ungiving, waiting for her to continue.

'I think we are not fond of each other.'

'My work is satisfactory?' Frau Gast spoke slowly and clearly.

'Yes, but . . .' She was struggling, searching.

The older woman left her to flounder. The jaundiced sunshine from outside lit up her pale eyes, which seemed to Amy to gleam mockingly.

'You are not friendly. You don't smile. You are not polite.' Amy stammered on, aware that she was cutting a poor figure with the limited vocabulary at her disposal. Also that she was entering deep waters. 'We're not fond of each other,' she concluded lamely, for the second time.

'Tonight I'll talk to Herr Campion,' Frau Gast stated briskly and made as if to leave the room.

'No!' Amy was emphatic.

They stared at one another, openly hostile.

'This is not a matter for Herr Campion.' A crisp, remembered phrase came to Amy's aid. She added, less felicitously, 'This is *my* matter.'

'I don't think we can go further. Herr Campion will translate.'

'No,' Amy repeated stubbornly. She held up her much thumbed dictionary. '*We* will talk.'

Affronted and amazed, Frau Gast glowered. Her skin was suffused with an angry flush, a shiny film of perspiration. There was no attempt now to hide her spleen and Amy knew that she herself had gone too far to patch things up.

It came to her quite simply and suddenly that she could dismiss the housekeeper. It was within her power to be rid of this disagreeable presence within twenty-four hours if she so chose.

What she should do by rights, of course, was to give Frau Gast a warning, offer her another chance, allow her to mend her ways. But Amy couldn't face the rigmarole. She disliked the woman and, with the best will in the world, she knew it could never be otherwise.

The truth was, Amy admitted to herself, that she was ill-at-ease with servants. They belonged to Noel's world. More than likely Frau Gast's presumptions reflected a weakness in herself. But she'd no interest in a struggle for power. Far better to call a halt. Amy was decided. She would offer two months' salary in compensation. And then she would be free.

'I've been thinking, Frau Gast,' she said, and began to leaf through her dictionary for the words she would need.

Noel was angry with her. That was something quite new and rather upsetting. It had to happen some time, naturally. No two people could live side by side indefinitely without conflict. But she'd been lulled up to now by her husband's unequivocal support and admiration.

But suddenly she'd questioned his judgement and he was telling her she'd been absurd and hasty, that her dismissal of Frau Gast had been a childish whim – it wasn't too late to change her mind, pour oil on troubled waters. He kept his temper, but was seriously displeased. She felt a chill of fear.

All too easily Amy could visualize herself giving in and seeing the situation through his eyes. She *had* been uncharacteristically headstrong, was half abashed by the boldness of what she'd done.

At the same time she was filled with a low elation which could not be doused. It seemed she could, after all, be something other than the docile, amenable wife. The small act of self-assertion was a catalyst, restoring her mood of resolution, the determination that had been ebbing away. It was a beginning.

Calmly she tried to explain herself to Noel. 'In the way of things, I spend a lot of time here alone, with just the housekeeper for company, so it seems madness to employ someone I simply don't like . . .'

'It's not necessary to *like* the domestic help,' he exclaimed. Noel had lived with servants all his life and took them for granted. Though he treated them with consideration it was clear they barely impinged on his consciousness.

His genuine annoyance was unfamiliar to her. She observed the physical signs with disconcerted clarity – a hardness to his eyes, a set to his lips. The furrows that ran from his nose to the corners of his mouth looked harsh and deeply etched. This new aspect of her indulgent husband was shocking, unsettling. On the other hand it gave Amy something to resist, to push against and, in a sense, that helped.

He appealed coldly to her conscience, attempting to fan a sense of guilt. 'Frau Gast is a widow, a woman alone. It may not be so easy for her to find alternative employment. You know what things are like out here . . .'

The reminder had its effect but Amy refused to allow herself to weaken.

'I see that and I'm sorry. But we'll take on someone else and then we'll be providing that person with employment. I don't feel I owe Frau Gast priority – or the sacrifice of my own wellbeing.'

'Who will we take on? It's a bore, the process of separating the sheep from –'

'I'll see to it,' she said, sweeping his objections aside.

The bottle factory had recalled Claudia and she was due to start work on Monday, but the wages were pathetic, the hours long and the journey took almost an hour. Tante Agathe had had one of her turns the previous day and wept over the state of the world and what

Friedrich would say if he could see his daughter and sister come to such a pass.

And Rosa had been beaten up by some man she'd gone home with. Her face was purple and swollen, a mess. Franz was threatening to get some of his mates on to the bastard, but Rosa begged him not to – the man had some ugly connections. Best to leave well alone.

Claudia decided to go and visit Frau Campion, the young Englishwoman. She had a longing for some decent coffee, the atmosphere of calm and comfort that reigned in her childhood home.

It was a surprise when Frau Campion herself answered the door. Claudia was prepared for the harpy of a housekeeper to appear, looking down her broad, blunt nose.

'Fräulein Farnholz.' The young woman seemed genuinely delighted to see her. 'I was just thinking about you. I need your help.'

It was startling how pretty she was. Her beauty had an elusive, volatile quality that the memory couldn't retain, her grey eyes and dewy complexion changing with the play of her emotions. Confronting her again in the flesh, Claudia mentally caught her breath. Frau Campion wore a thin blue dress with embroidered panels, her soft pale hair hung in a loose plait. Today she seemed to radiate a suppressed excitement that made her cheeks pink and her eyes shine.

Claudia smiled. 'My help? What can I do?'

'Come with me.' In a sprightly fashion she led the way into the living room, towards the walnut secretaire, where an exercise book lay open. Frau Campion picked it up.

'I'd be grateful, Fräulein Farnholz, if you would read this over for me.' She spoke slowly, in English. 'It's important that the grammar is correct.'

'Of course.' Automatically Claudia took the book from the young Englishwoman's hand and glanced at the lines of flowing, forward-sloping writing striped with deletions and amendments.

It appeared to be an advertisement for a housekeeper. Running her eyes down the paragraph, Claudia mentally rejigged some of the phrases to make them sound more natural.

Then a thought occurred. 'But you have someone already – the lady I saw last time I was here.'

Frau Campion shook her head with slow, wry emphasis. 'She's gone.'

'She has left?'

'I dismissed her.' The words were simply spoken but Claudia seemed to discern a small gleam of pride in the young woman's eyes as if she could not quite believe her own daring.

'This goes in the newspaper then?' Claudia indicated the handwritten text.

'That's right.'

Turning back to the pencilled advertisement, Claudia frowned as she rearranged it in her head.

Then – with an inspired inevitability – an idea came to her. 'I could do this.' Eagerly she looked into Frau Campion's grey eyes. 'I am looking for work. I could be your housekeeper.'

Faster than words, images filled her brain. The house was so close to where she lived. There would be no journey. And the job couldn't be worse paid than the bottle factory. There might be food too, coffee, fruit, milk for Rudi.

'Won't you let me try?' Claudia offered her most winning smile.

Almost imperceptibly the young Englishwoman shook her head. She looked bewildered. 'But you're an actress. I couldn't ask you –'

'An actress with no work,' Claudia reminded her drily. 'With an aunt, a small brother.'

It seemed to her abruptly that this job should be hers by right. This was her house. It was fated. For a rash second she toyed with the idea of explaining this to Frau Campion. But there was a risk of being thought odd and unbalanced.

'Give me . . .' Her English failed her. 'I want to say, let me try. For one month. Then we can see.' Claudia laid one hand to her breast. The gesture struck her as old-fashioned, imploring. 'I would do well, you'll see.'

Dubiously the young Englishwoman wrinkled her brow. But

Claudia didn't miss the spark of interest her eyes betrayed as if, in spite of herself, she was attracted to the proposal. She must realize it would bypass the tedious necessity for advertising, interviewing.

'Just a month,' she urged.

Chapter Sixteen

Noel was uneasy about the new young housekeeper. It was so clear she wasn't really a servant, though he had to admit she worked hard and well. But he found her presence about the home disturbing. Instinctively he preferred domestics who blended into the background and Fräulein Farnholz, with her dashing short hairstyle, her vibrancy, was not someone you could easily ignore.

He felt uncomfortable having her wait on him at table and serve coffee on the terrace in the evenings. She was obviously a well-bred, educated young woman who'd fallen on hard times and it seemed ill-mannered to talk in front of her without including her in the conversation.

Left to himself, Noel would have dismissed her after the month's trial period on some pretext or other. He would have hired some pleasantly unobtrusive middle-aged woman – assuming she would prove more biddable than the 'motherly' Frau Gast – and settled into a comfortable, unruffled home routine.

But Amy appeared delighted with the new help. And, as she'd pointed out and he had in all conscience to agree, the servants affected her day-to-day wellbeing far more radically than they did his own.

Early on, when Amy first told him what she'd done, he had been shocked into anger, felt undermined. He hadn't expected this self-assertiveness from his dovelike wife. But he'd readjusted his thinking, come round to seeing her point of view and, on the whole, respecting her stand. This *was* after all her realm. It was right that she should have the final say.

But Noel couldn't altogether deny a spark of irritation – admittedly not unmixed with an amused tenderness – at his wife's erratic way with servants. To be sure it wasn't her fault. Margaret, Amy's mother, never had more than a daily woman to help, so her daughter had no model on which to base her behaviour. But it seemed to him that she'd been far too susceptible to the Gast woman's moods and now she was a great deal too friendly with Fräulein Farnholz – Noel had even heard them calling one another by their christian names. And Amy's German was improving with a rapidity he found revealing. It was clear they chattered much too much.

All the same, he'd thought last night at dinner how pretty and animated she looked, repeating some juicy piece of local gossip Fräulein Farnholz had told her about the government minister who lived in the handsome house with the imposing wrought-iron gates just along the lake from them. Amy seemed happier all round since the new housekeeper had joined them and that was reason enough for Noel to suppress his own misgivings. Bleakly he saw this indulgence as atoning in some small measure for his own mortifying failure as a lover.

'Here you are, *Spätzlein*, a dozen perfect potato dumplings.' Frau Kästner's watery blue eyes sparkled with the fun of the deception.

'My saviour.' Claudia planted a smacking kiss on her landlady's soft, wrinkled cheek. 'What would I do without you?' Frau Kästner turned pink with pleasure.

Taking breathless care, Claudia transferred the wrapped dumplings to her shopping-basket and made ready to saunter back to Mailied as casually as if she'd slipped out for a moment to shop. The whole household was ecstatic at Claudia's new job and hellbent on ensuring that she keep it. Feverishly Frau Kästner and Agathe attempted to compensate for her ignorance in domestic matters, pooling their own skills, plying her with household hints and advice.

With application and energy – and the help of Frau Gast's former skivvy – Claudia was confident she could keep the house shipshape. But cooking was not her strong point. She'd never needed to bother with it. Once upon a time there'd been the maids, since then her aunt and Frau Kästner. And, anyway, for years the only available food had been basic and monotonous.

Now, suddenly, she had choice ingredients to prepare, was expected to produce a palatable meal nearly every night. Agathe and Frau Kästner rallied round. It was a blessing they lived so close. Claudia could pop out, ostensibly to buy potatoes or post a letter, and collect some delicacy they'd prepared with the ingredients she supplied, so that all she needed to do was just pop it in the oven, then serve it up later with a modest smile.

'Don't forget to start the stew for tomorrow,' she reminded them hurriedly as she left. 'I did bring some onions, didn't I?'

'Don't worry, Mausi,' Agathe reassured her. 'There's even dill from the patch we planted in the garden. They'll be in heaven.'

'I'll take it in first thing in the morning.'

As she strolled back to her childhood home Claudia reflected wryly on the precarious way she was hanging on to the coat-tails of competence. Though, in her employers' presence, she was careful to radiate unruffled efficiency.

As Claudia had hoped there were perks in the shape of kitchen leftovers.

'Take what's left for your little brother, Claudia,' Amy told her most evenings and often there was enough for the others to have at least a taste. Rudi was wary of the meat she brought home and had to be coaxed to try it. He wasn't used to much other than the cheap, strange-tasting American bacon that flooded into the shops every so often.

Sometimes Amy would wrap up a chunk of cake for Rudi specially, or a packet of coffee for Agathe. Claudia suspected she ordered more groceries than necessary for this very purpose. Her young employer seemed only too aware of the food situation, almost a little guilty about it, as if she personally felt responsible for the post-war food blockade, the current shortages and exorbitant prices. Claudia made sure she took only what was offered. It would be stupid to become greedy and risk losing her job.

'What's she like?' Agathe was intensely curious about the blonde benefactress she'd glimpsed only from a distance.

'Nice . . . Bit of an innocent, though. You can see she's had it easy.'

The reply summed up Claudia's attitude to her employer, which combined liking and impatience.

She was constantly dazzled by Amy's beauty – the clear skin, perfect teeth, soft, healthy hair, the radiant smile. But aware that, in Germany, only the profiteers and the rich bastards had that look of health, the sweet temper that comes with regular food, the absence of anxiety. Claudia thought of the young woman as a sort of moral virgin, unacquainted with the harsher side of life, looked on her with a private sense of battle-scarred superiority.

At the same time, as an employer, Amy Campion was pretty well ideal – considerate and friendly, able to give orders in a way that didn't cause Claudia's hackles to rise. And, work apart, she had the clear impression that the young Englishwoman genuinely liked her.

The two of them were almost twins, they had discovered, both just nineteen, both born in June, though Claudia was a few days older. They chatted often during the day, once or twice even drank coffee together. Claudia was relieved. Even for the extra food she could not have borne some snob, for whom a servant was part of the wallpaper. This way she managed not to feel too demeaned by her position. A lot of the time in fact she rather enjoyed the job.

'I'm not so sure about the husband,' she told Agathe. 'He's more difficult. I'm not certain he likes having me in the house.'

If her post here were to founder, it would be because of Herr Campion. Though he was polite, even pleasant, towards her, she guessed he would have been happier with a more orthodox servant-type and tolerated her only for his wife's sake. Waiting on him, Claudia took pains to be deft, discreet, demure. Even so she sensed a lack of ease on his part.

Noel Campion interested her. At first meeting she had summed him up easily, superficially as an English gentleman, impressive enough on his own terms, but having no point of contact with herself. In passing she'd noticed that he was well built, well groomed and pleasing to look at. She liked his voice – deep and agreeably toned – admired the excellence of his German accent, was charmed by the remaining traces of a foreign intonation. But, over the weeks, she became intrigued by a self-containment she perceived in him. Claudia noticed an observant quality to his grey eyes, an unexpected harshness in the lines of his face that she found sexually attractive.

Claudia went home to sleep, generally after she'd served coffee to the Campions and made sure that Moni, the girl, had cleared away all the clean dinner things. One evening she was later than usual and, passing the open door to the verandah, saw Herr Campion out there on his own, smoking a cigarette, seemingly lost in thought. An empty brandy glass stood on the small table beside him. In the normal way, it was agreed, Claudia ignored after-dinner cups or glassware, left them for the following day.

For a silent second she watched him through the open glass door. Then some urge drew her out there towards him.

'May I take the glass?' She spoke from some obscure desire for communication. The words meant nothing.

He turned his head and looked at her. 'Thank you, Fräulein Farnholz.'

Disconcertingly Claudia sensed that her eyes were sending him some intense, wordless, erotic message and there seemed an answering susceptibility in his, an acceptance that, for a moment, there was something between them. She leaned forward to pick up the empty glass and it seemed that this action, too, had a languorous, suggestive significance. Then, suddenly self-conscious, she panicked, felt young, gauche and breathless, knew she was blushing, but managed to turn and go without tripping or dropping the glass she was carrying.

It was an odd and isolated moment. For it was clear to anyone with half an eye that Noel Campion was deeply in love with his wife. Even young Moni remarked on it, half jeering, half wistful. And there was something . . . decent and straight about her employer that told Claudia he was a one-woman man.

'*Es macht nichts.*' It doesn't matter. That was a phrase Claudia used often, with a tough sort of grin, an easy, accepting look in her brown eyes, the ghost of a shrug. Amy was privately impressed by the quick, intensely personal combination of speech, expression and body movement, which seemed to her to sum up her new housekeeper's resilient attitude to life.

It was clear to Amy that the young German was considerably better educated than herself. She could speak English with creditable fluency, had even laughingly quoted Shakespeare at her once – a play she'd studied at school. Amy gathered her family had been quite well off and she'd trained as an actress. But now – due to the war and the social chaos that had upended the lives of so many of her compatriots – Claudia was forced into domestic work in order to support her two dependants. Yet she faced this reversal with apparent courage and good humour.

Amy admired such toughness and, in a strange way, envied Claudia her misfortunes. In order to be plucky you needed something to face up to, you needed the opportunity to demonstrate your pluck. She herself had nothing quite so clear cut to confront.

Chapter Seventeen

Furtively Claudia examined herself in the gloomy cheval mirror on Frau Kästner's dark second-floor landing. She wore a green summer dress that used to be Lotte's. It hung, loose and full. Nothing showed, she decided. At least, not to the casual eye. Naked, Claudia was aware that her skinny midriff had taken on a more solid look, but that was all. As far as she knew Tante Agathe had never yet suspected her pregnancy, not even for a second.

Once or twice recently Claudia had experienced a slight flutter in her belly, quite a pleasant feeling in fact, as if the creature inside her – she couldn't picture it as a live human baby – had briefly flexed small fins or tested its gills in the quiet, dark waters in which it lay suspended.

It couldn't be long, though, a month at most, before her condition became obvious to all the world. Claudia dreaded the fits of weeping she could expect from her aunt, the self-reproach, the outpourings on the breakdown of decent society.

But worse than that was the dull recognition that, sooner or later, she must lose this post that had made so much difference to the welfare of them all. A job, also, that in many ways she rather enjoyed, with agreeable employers, the odd brush with an enlightened, vaguely glamorous international world – imagine doing such menial work in the household of some stolid Prussian bourgeois swine.

Noel Campion might actually decide to dismiss her on the spot – Claudia had an inkling this could be just the excuse he was looking for. Left to herself, Amy, who was kind-hearted, would probably keep her on for as long as she could. But the time would come when she was too huge and lumbering to do her work properly. She'd be an eyesore. Mentally Claudia shuddered.

And, once she'd had the kid, well, the job wasn't a welfare scheme. She could hardly expect them to make allowances for a brat.

That evening Herr Campion was out and his wife dined alone. Claudia took coffee to her out on the verandah as usual. Amy invited her to stay and drink a cup. Claudia sat down in one of the wicker chairs that used to belong to her parents and poured coffee into the familiar little butterfly cups. She had an impulse to tell Amy, but stifled it.

It seemed to Claudia that the young Englishwoman was freer and more animated when her husband wasn't around. Today Amy had been out with a red-headed woman called Laura Krell who visited the house with her husband from time to time.

Out of curiosity the two of them had been to see the so-called Dada Fair, a current cause célèbre. 'Laura said we should get in quickly before they close it down.'

'What was it like?'

'It was a protest against the war, I think. Ugly, but sort of powerful at the same time . . . There were paintings of war-cripples, shocking pictures. A figure of a soldier in German uniform hanging from the ceiling, and it had a pig's head . . . And signs everywhere saying things like "Art is Dead".'

'Did you like it?'

'Not like exactly. It wasn't something you could *like*. Exciting, though, in a dark sort of way. You wouldn't want to go to a Strauss operetta after that.' It was clear that angelic, romantic Amy had been intrigued by the perverse brutality of the images and Claudia was surprised.

Having drunk her coffee she made polite leaving noises.

'You don't have to go,' Amy said. 'I'd love you to stay if you've got time . . .' She added daringly, 'I could pour us both a brandy if you like.' She got to her feet. 'Should I?'

Claudia shrugged good-humouredly. 'As far as I'm concerned.'

While Amy was inside Claudia leaned back in the wicker chair contemplating the deeply familiar view spread out in front of her – lawn and shining water, the shrubs Lotte had planted, willows that trailed

into the lake. What she saw was so much a part of her growing-up –
imprinted into her very soul – that in a sense she hardly knew whether
her eyes were open or closed. There were differences of detail – in
the interim the willows had grown and the yellow rambling rose
Lotte was so fond of had become a huge thicket smothered in bloom.
When Amy returned Claudia continued to gaze out across the garden
landscape, almost as if she could see the ghosts of Friedrich and
Lotte, her own younger self, coming and going on the grass.

'It *is* lovely.' Amy placed the two glasses on the table between
them. 'I would have preferred to live in the centre, but this place
is . . .'

'It's my home.' The words slipped out, faster than thought. It was
too late for her to take them back. She turned to look at Amy. 'It's
true . . . I lived here.'

The Englishwoman stared at her. There was disbelief in her wide
grey eyes. 'What do you mean?'

Claudia shook her head. 'I didn't intend to say it. But now I have
. . . This house belonged to my father and mother. I lived here until
I was sixteen. When my father died it was sold to Herr Ackermann.'

Amy gazed at her, trying to come to terms with the information.
'You must hate working here. How can you do it?'

'It's a good job.' After a pause Claudia added, 'No, I don't hate it.'

In the warm summer evening they sat sipping their brandy and
talking and, after a while, Amy seemed to get used to the startling
information Claudia had sprung on her. The sky began to darken
though the evenings were long. The cognac warmed Claudia's insides,
made her feel calm and reckless. It was the right moment, she decided,
to come clean about her pregnancy.

'There's something else I have to tell you,' she said. Thanks to
the brandy and the leisurely conversation they were more at ease
with one another than ever before.

Amy gave a bemused grin. 'What now?'

'I must tell you I'm expecting a baby.' There, she'd done it. Come
what may.

'Oh.' As before there was silence while the words sank in. Then Amy pulled a quick, droll face, like a child. 'You're full of surprises tonight.'

'Yes.' Claudia gave her employer a long, level look. 'I don't know what you'll do about it.'

'Nothing for the time being. You'll stay, won't you? When will the child be born?'

'December. Or the end of November.'

'I see.'

Claudia waited for her to speak again, to ask about the father, the possibility of marriage, whatever.

Instead Amy said flatly, 'I can't have children.'

The statement was a bolt from the blue and Claudia felt wrong-footed. Her mind floundered for an acceptable response. Tact and sympathy seemed in order but she couldn't switch them on just like that.

Almost in self-defence Claudia replied, with cynical flippancy, 'I'd give you mine with pleasure.'

Amy gave a startled smile, her eyes widening. Claudia cursed her own clumsiness.

Noel still wasn't home when Amy went to bed. She lit a stump of candle so he could see to undress without putting on the light. In the darkened room she lay and watched its small, restless flame, feeling wakeful, unsettled by Claudia's revelations. Jumbled fragments of their conversation kept drifting through her mind, no matter how resolutely she tried to concentrate on sleep.

Amy still felt almost horrified to think that she was employing Claudia to perform domestic work in her own home. It was like something out of a melodrama. And she seemed so sanguine about the situation. Time and again Amy relived the casual shrug of her slim shoulders, the philosophical look on her face. 'I don't hate it.'

Still more uncomfortable was Amy's awareness of her own indiscretion. What muddled urge had impelled her to claim she couldn't have children? The words had been blurted, willy-nilly, in response to Claudia's bombshell about her pregnancy. It was as if the taboo that surrounded Noel's impotence, the secrecy, had led her to hint at the truth in this complicated way. But why mention it at all? She was trapped now in the lie.

'You can have mine with pleasure.'

Claudia's idle statement reverberated in her head. Amy knew it to be a brittle, half-embarrassed joke, yet after she'd said it the assertion seemed to hang in the air, with an inescapable logic for them both. But they hadn't mentioned it again.

Noel let himself into the house. It was almost two o'clock. He'd spent a most fruitful evening talking to a young German ex-army officer, by way of research for his extended piece about private armies, resistance to the republic. The young man – his name was Ulrich – had been in one of the *Freikorps* regiments that attempted to topple the government in March.

Ulrich looked about twenty-four, was tall, slim, dark-eyed, rather sensitive-looking. He worked, currently, as a professional dancing partner at the Eden Hotel. He'd come, by previous appointment, to Noel's office, but quite soon the German suggested they adjourn to a nearby bar. They'd spent the whole evening drinking inferior champagne while Ulrich expounded his *Weltanschauung*, becoming progressively drunker and more vehement.

He clearly enjoyed the sensation of being interviewed by a journalist, even an English one. In fact Ulrich appeared to take to Noel, as a fellow veteran, and they swapped war stories for a while.

Then the young German became confidential, going into frank detail about the perks of his job. It seemed that, in return for a little attention, a few compliments, a hint of romance, the rich, neglected wives of speculators and businessmen 'showered' him with gifts in good, solid, inflation-proof gold. Sometimes he didn't even need to go to the trouble of bedding them. He recounted this quite matter-of-fact, without conceit or man-of-the-world posturing.

As the evening wore on Ulrich got to talking his own brand of politics, which consisted largely of vituperation. The young ex-officer hastened to assure his new acquaintance that he had nothing against the English – respected them in fact as fine soldiers. His bitterness and loathing were reserved for the enemy within.

The targets of his rage were predictable – the communists, the craven, treacherous government, the Jews in general, whom he saw as being, on the one hand, capitalist exploiters, and simultaneously a revolutionary rabble spoiling to undermine the state. These were the flies in the ointment, the dung beetles who'd lost Germany the war. As he warmed drunkenly to his subject Ulrich's face took on a flushed heaviness.

'We've been humiliated,' he declared repeatedly. 'And for people like myself, Noel, only blood can cancel out the indignity.'

He had beautiful eyes, of a brown so deep and dark it verged on violet. Under normal circumstances their expression was courteous and caressing – Noel could imagine how they might charm his faded dancing partners. But now their look became hot and frantic, unnerving.

It was clear he saw no way out of his country's predicament but through a fresh build-up of military strength. For the present, though – with Germany's neighbours on the qui vive – that process would have to take place by stealth.

'Would you say it was a fact then,' Noel asked, 'this clandestine rearmament?'

With a small, tight smile. Ulrich met his gaze. 'Oh yes.'

After that he clammed up, as if he might have said too much, and began to tell Noel about his father who'd given all he had to the war effort – a stableful of horses, the family jewels – and lost everything with no hope of redress.

They shook hands cordially on parting. Noel decided he would walk home. It would take an hour or more but the night was warm and he fancied the air and the exercise. He was elated by his interview with Ulrich. Though the man's message had been ominous, even sinister, his pronouncements would make wonderful copy. Noel could remember being enthused like this about stories back before the war, during his first year in London. Since arriving here he was rediscovering the low, buzzing excitement that used to invade him when he knew he'd got something compelling to write about, knew he was going to hone and rework until he'd expressed it in a style that crackled with vitality and precision. Delane had been well pleased with the work he'd turned in so far.

His footsteps rang hollowly as he walked down the broad, tree-lined boulevard that led to Grunewald. Mentally Noel had already begun to compose phrases and sentences that would bring Ulrich vividly to life for readers who had no inkling of his world.

The house was silent as he let himself in. With amusement he noticed the cognac bottle out on the table in the living room. Recently Amy had discovered a taste for it and she often had a glass with him after dinner. He teased her about it sometimes and she retorted cheekily that she'd never touched even a single drop of alcohol before she married him. The truth was he liked her taking a nip. It made her playful, pink and lively, kittenish in bed, less bothered by his sexual shortcomings, more open to experimentation.

One of the benefits of Noel's new zest for his work was that it took his mind off brooding about his impotence. For hours at a time he quite simply forgot about it and went about his business, feeling like a normal man, whole and unimpaired.

Though in the end, inevitably, the consciousness and the pain returned. Now – when some of the raw anguish had dulled from his images of the war – he was haunted constantly during sex by an overwhelming consciousness of past failure, of failure upon failure, so that any chance of change was crippled at birth.

He could wait and wait for things to mend and not get any further forward. And Noel wondered how long before Amy became tired, or passionate to have a child, and left. The thought tormented him. She wouldn't do it lightly, he knew – his wife was staunch and loyal – but there were limits to everything.

'Do you mind me asking who the father is, Claudia? You never did say last night.' In the morning sun Amy and Claudia were weeding the patch of earth round the big yellow rose bush. Amy straightened up and looked levelly at her housekeeper. 'Tell me to mind my own business if you like.'

'Doesn't matter. He was a bourgeois. He looked after me, gave me things for Rudi.' She glanced at Amy with a glimmer of defiance. 'You don't know what it was like then. There was no food. Nothing.' A pause. 'Not that things are so much better now.'

'I'm not judging you.'

'The man went back to be a good husband,' Claudia said ironically. 'And he said it wasn't his child.'

'Have you made any plans?'

The young German smiled crookedly. 'I never make plans. If I do they go wrong.'

'Would you want to keep the baby?'

'I'm not really sure.' Claudia turned away, bent forward to sniff a full, perfect rose. 'My mother planted this bush,' she told Amy, who took the hint and dropped the subject.

The notion of the Campions adopting her baby began to prey on Claudia's mind. Although, before she'd made that smart remark the other night, the thought had never once occurred to her. It was as if the words themselves had brought the idea into being and now, as she went about her work, it unfolded in her mind, growing from a seed and gradually expanding, as all the implications and advantages of the plan presented themselves to her one by one.

The wealthy, likeable Campions would make ideal adoptive parents – the child would be secure and loved, well fed, well dressed and educated. And, so Claudia assumed, they would probably provide for her in some way, so that to an extent she'd be freed from her ever-pressing financial worries. Then perhaps she could leave Frau Kästner's and make an all-out effort to pursue her acting career, live an unfettered, bohemian young person's life.

Her mind raced away with the possibilities and Claudia regretted having sounded so lukewarm yesterday, when Amy seemed to be sounding her out. Pray God she would bring up the matter again.

* * *

On Sunday Noel and Amy went hiking. It was becoming a habit with them. Amy liked the feeling of strength in her legs, the way they gradually and relentlessly ate up the miles, loved to wander among the fir trees and the slender white birches of the Grunewald with the scent of sun-warmed conifer needles in her nostrils. It surprised Amy how pleasurable she found the physical activity, along with the delicious weariness that invaded her at the end of the day. Already they were contemplating the possibility of a walking tour in Bavaria, perhaps in October, which Noel could combine with a professional reconnoitre in the city of Munich, reputed to be the epicentre of Germany's fanatical nationalist movement.

At present, though, Amy had something else on her mind. Today's hike seemed an opportunity to broach the matter of Claudia's pregnancy, to probe Noel's reaction to the notion of adoption.

Since Claudia's revelation, Amy, herself, had been restless. The idea of having a child was something quite new, a question she'd pushed to the back of her mind as irrelevant under the circumstances, a thought to be suppressed in case it brought her pain. But Claudia's remark had caused her to strip away the cautious layers of denial. And Amy had come to understand that the desire for children was ingrained in her, as natural and instinctive as the desire for happiness.

She hadn't yet mentioned the possibility to Claudia. Unless Noel agreed there would be no point. But Amy felt, passionately, that there might never be another opportunity as good as this.

'I was talking to Claudia the other day . . .' she began, as they skirted a wide, tree-fringed meadow.

'And?'

'And apparently she's pregnant.'

'Poor kid. That's not going to be easy for her.'

She was encouraged by his wry sympathy, for Amy knew he thought she was too familiar with a young woman who, whatever her background, was engaged as a servant.

'She and her aunt are living hand-to-mouth as it is.'

Their path led over a stream, then back in among trees. Noel leaped across, then offered Amy his hand. She liked the solid resistance of sinew and muscle as he helped her. It pleased her to see him like this, in open-necked shirt and hiking boots, hair ruffled, skin tanned and dappled with the light and shade of the trees. She had a brief, vivid sense of the two of them as a couple.

But, returning to their conversation, Amy was far from sure of her ground. 'I was wondering if we could help Claudia in some way.'

'How, Amy?'

'Oh, I don't know . . .' She hesitated, then decided there was no evasive way of phrasing what she had to say. 'Noel, suppose we offered to adopt Claudia's child.'

At once she was braced for dismissal. To Noel the suggestion would be unheard of, an absurd novelty, bearing no relation to anything they had ever talked about before.

Sure enough, without a second's thought, he scoffed, 'Oh come on . . .' His tone held an easy, confident finality.

Amy refused to be rattled. Evenly she urged, 'It's a new thought, I know, a bit of a bolt from the blue, but don't just reject it out of hand.'

'It's a harebrained scheme.'

'Not so harebrained. People *do* adopt children, for whatever reason. The idea seems to me to have advantages for all concerned.'

'No, Amy. I refuse even to consider it.'

Claudia and Moni had Sundays off. When the Campions got back from their walk Amy made soup and cheese sandwiches, padding around barefoot and wearing a striped apron she found hanging behind the kitchen door. Noel watched her tenderly. In her white blouse and sailor collar she looked for all the world like a child playing at housekeeping. Her cheeks glowed with the day's exercise and unruly wisps of hair curled artlessly round her face.

But, as they sat companionably at the kitchen table, Amy jarred the atmosphere by bringing up the adoption thing again. 'Noel, while we're on our own I'd like us to talk again about Claudia and her baby.'

He was irritated and replied harshly, 'There's nothing to say. I've told you what I feel.'

'But you didn't think about it, not for a moment. You said no, just like that,' Amy protested, countering his brusqueness with a provoking air of calm.

A wave of anger swept through him because again she was questioning his decision. 'What the hell would I want with a Hun brat?' he sneered. Even as he said it Noel heard echoes in his own voice of his overbearing father.

'I don't see what nationality has to do with a baby,' Amy replied coolly and he felt angrier because she was right about that. And also because, with her quiet and control, she'd claimed the moral high ground for her outlandish proposal.

She returned to her theme with muted obstinacy. '*You* may not want a Hun brat, but there are two of us. Don't I even get taken into consideration?'

'You're asking too much.'

They went on to quarrel briefly, but bitterly. Amy stormed off to bed. But now, as he lay next to his sleeping wife, Noel was unhappy about his own role in the proceedings, his loss of temper. The truth was he'd been touched on the raw by Amy's talk of a child. It implied she saw his impotence as something long-term, even permanent, requiring a change of strategy, and not as some passing misfortune. Admittedly he was coming to perceive it that way himself. Yet his belief in Amy's belief had somehow buoyed him up.

She didn't know it, but in London Noel had been to see a doctor, a consultant who specialized in such things. He'd found the man deeply uncongenial, too friendly and full of brash optimism like a transatlantic salesman. He'd shown Noel several gadgets he claimed were foolproof, but which Noel could only see as turning the act of sex into some precarious mechanical achievement, a manoeuvre, farcical and devoid of passion. He was convinced they could only make his problem worse.

And anyway he would never dream of inflicting any such thing on Amy. He wanted her to desire him, experience ecstasy. Even suppose that, with perseverance, he managed penetration, the act would be a grotesque parody, a mockery of them both. Noel had left the consultation depressed and disillusioned. He preferred to leave things the way they were.

'There are two of us. Don't I even get taken into consideration?' Then, as now, his wife's words had given him pause. Though he hadn't showed it at the time.

He was surprised and angered by her persistence, at her not backing down. Though in theory he'd claim to be a champion of women's equality, Noel conceded that like most men he took it for granted the husband had the final say.

Quite properly Amy had pointed out that she had some rights in the matter, and Noel conceded to himself that he'd been hasty, selfish. She'd never ever reproached him for his sexual incapacity but, if he couldn't give her a child, would it not be monstrous of him to deny her one from somewhere else? And anyway, it occurred to him, if she had a baby to think of, there'd be less danger of her leaving. Perhaps the idea was worth looking into after all.

Chapter Eighteen

Claudia tried to think of it as a holiday, this protracted stay in a cottage in the North of England, surrounded by rounded grassy slopes, dense clumps of trees, and by sheep. Emerging from the front door of the house, she could see nothing to indicate that she was living in the twentieth century. It could be medieval times. Claudia marvelled at such isolation. Sometimes, in an odd way, she liked it. But often it seemed oppressive – the grass and the sky, just Amy for company, her own burgeoning belly, vibrating with the baby's thumps and kicks. The waiting.

But, when all this was over, she would be free. Agathe and Rudi would be taken care of – Noel Campion's financial offer had been more generous than expected, he was even making provision for Rudi's education. Finally it would be worth the emptiness and the endlessness of each passing day. Her own life would begin.

The cottage was called Kirk Head. To Claudia it looked grim from the outside with its rough grey stone walls, the roof that came down to within a couple of metres of the ground, like a long fringe over the eyes of the windows. But inside she was rather taken with the rustic flagged floors, the fireplace with its stone surround, the sofa and chairs covered in pale floral linen you could take off and wash. She liked the sloping ceilings of the two bedrooms and, in the single bed with its much-mended patchwork quilt, she slept a wonderful, deep, refreshing sleep.

Amy seemed perfectly contented, even happy. She had the right temperament for the blank, unstructured days they were living. She read for hours and went for long walks, cooked their meals on the old-fashioned kitchen range. They shared the chores now. Claudia was no longer a servant. Amy was excited. After all it was she who would have something to show for all this. She would have the baby.

Amy felt a sort of responsibility at keeping Claudia here, incarcerated in a strange land in total isolation. But these had been the conditions that Noel laid down. He wanted the child to be passed off as their own.

He had travelled to London to talk to Robert Beadle. Noel had been frank with his oldest friend about the whole situation. Robert was sympathetic and willing to help. He knew of a doctor in Yorkshire who'd secretly delivered a baby for the daughter of a colleague. The man was contacted and agreed to bring Claudia's child into the world, while certifying that Amy was the mother. Noel rented a cottage on the North Yorkshire Moors, a couple of miles from where the doctor lived. The two women would stay here until the baby was born.

As far as acquaintances in Berlin knew, Amy had gone home to wait for her confinement. She wasn't happy about the deception, but Noel had made concessions to her, and it seemed only fair that she should do the same.

Before she came to England, Claudia's pregnancy hadn't slowed her down, not a bit. After she'd stopped being sick she felt as active and skinny as ever. But when, at the beginning of August, she arrived at the cottage – although there were still four whole months to go before she produced, and only if they looked very hard could people guess at her condition – Claudia was conscious of a languor stealing over her. She felt beached, like a ship coming into dry dock for the winter. Nothing was expected of her until the child was born.

August and September were lovely golden months. Amy was always on the go, working at her German or exploring the country-side, but Claudia felt no urge to do anything but sit in the sun outside the cottage and dream of how it was going to be when she was back in Berlin, trim again, with money in her pocket. She dozed and ate and gazed incuriously at the landscape like some great fat cow.

Almost at once she began to put on weight, the way you were supposed to when you were expecting a baby. In this rural district at harvest time there was so much good food to be had. Dr Jarrold brought cheese and eggs from a nearby farm and told her she must eat plenty for the child's sake. There was fruit and soft white bread, freshly dug potatoes, bacon and mild-tasting English sausages.

One day Amy brought some small, mauve and white turnips home from the nearby village shop. Claudia threw up her hands and exclaimed in mock horror, 'Those I won't eat!'

She told Amy about one winter during the war when the only thing there had been to eat was turnips. 'We had turnip soup and turnip salad and turnip coffee. I tell you, Amy, people *smelled* of turnip – on their breath, in their sweat, when they . . .' She pulled a face and made a farting sound.

Amy laughed, contemplating the offending vegetables, heaped now on the kitchen table. 'Perhaps I can feed them to the sheep.'

Claudia allowed Amy to arrange a trip to Whitby on the bus one day. She went along meekly like a child being taken for a treat. The town was pretty with its steep, narrow streets and little boats, the silver shining sea and blue ethereal sky. She even struggled up a long flight of steps to a ruined abbey. Claudia thought it all picturesque, but gazed with passive eyes as if she'd landed on an alien planet, and made no attempt to make sense of anything. She wasn't here for sightseeing. She was a vessel, a container, her only emotions a dull endurance mingled with a sense of relief at anxieties laid to rest.

She was glad when Amy relinquished her feelings of unease at the monotony of their days and stopped trying to entertain her, offering books, urging her to explore. As winter drew closer, the cottage was warm and cosy. There was plenty of fuel for the fire in a byre that had once housed animals. In this tiny world Claudia wanted for nothing. Quite easily, she knew, she could have screamed at the narrowness of her confines, thrown things, smashed plates and cups. But she'd opted for dogged patience.

Almost imperceptibly she and Amy evolved their own method for living side by side with the minimum of chafing and irritation. They lived parallel lives. It was as if each followed her own inward rhythm, the one best suited to getting her through the months of waiting.

'We're like an old married couple,' Claudia marvelled as they sat by the fire one late October night, Amy reading as ever, while Claudia stared into the restless flames. 'We don't even need to talk.'

In Amy's mind Dr Jarrold brought the word 'abortionist' to mind, though – having no experience of the breed – she wasn't quite sure why. There was something evasive about him, so perhaps that was it. When he spoke the doctor looked sideways and at the ground, avoiding her eye. 'Hangdog' was another word that occurred in relation to him. At the same time he seemed a kindly, humane man, and Robert Beadle had vouched for his professional competence.

He was softly spoken, with grey-white curling hair, a straggly, grizzled beard and moustache, though his complexion was comparatively pink and youthful. On his visits to Kirk Head he wore a grey mackintosh that had seen better days, and a long, flecked black and white scarf, hanging loose. He had a motor-car, but generally visited them on an old bone-shaker of a bike. Claudia and Amy would watch his approach down the rutted farm track with a kind of stifled, hysterical suspense, expecting at every moment his flapping scarf to become entangled in the wheels of his cycle.

He and Claudia seemed to take to one another. Almost at once their smiles had a kind of complicity as if, on some wordless level, they understood each other. By the third visit they were on teasing terms. He called her Miss Claudia and she addressed him as Herr Doktor. She twitted him for his bike and his mac, for being a country doctor instead of sitting in a big smart office bilking rich patients and counting his money. She told him his hands were like cold codfish. Briefly Amy had been anxious that he might take offence, but he clearly enjoyed Claudia's insults and responded in kind, poking fun at her twiggy thinness at first, later at her gargantuan appetite for food and sleep.

With her sense of responsibility for Claudia, Amy was pleased and relieved that the two of them liked each other. In this situation

Jarrold's rather louche persona was an advantage. As an unwed mother and stranger in a strange land, Claudia would almost certainly have felt ill-at-ease with some austere pillar of the community bristling with professional integrity. Then again, Amy reminded herself ruefully, such a person would never have allowed himself to be bribed, never agreed to the deception in the first place.

Claudia went into labour on the last day of November. By eight in the evening there seemed no doubt that the process of birth had begun.

'I'll fetch Dr Jarrold.' Quickly Amy put on her coat and found a torch. She hurried down the dark farm track towards the lights of the village.

Jarrold came to the door himself. His breath, she noticed, smelled of beer. A nurse had been booked to bathe and look after Claudia and the baby. He phoned her to come to Kirk Head first thing in the morning. Then with Amy he set out on foot for the cottage. She hoped the walk would clear his head.

'I'm perfectly sober,' he told her, as if reading her mind.

From the entrance hall they could see through into the living room. Claudia was sitting by the fire, hands braced against her belly. She had changed into a white flannelette nightgown. Hearing them arrive, she turned sharply. Amy thought she looked a little scared.

'Right, Miss Claudia, you can get a move on now.' Jarrold entered the room, still wearing his mac and scarf.

Relief at his presence shone through Claudia's crooked smile. 'You'll take your coat off finally, I hope, Herr Doktor.'

'I'll light the fire in the bedroom.' Amy had laid it ready. Upstairs she set a match to the heap of paper, coal and wood in the small, black hearth.

As it flared the room was illuminated. Standing for a second by the door she contemplated the sloping ceiling, the plain rustic bed with its patchwork quilt, the rag rug on the floor, washstand, table, two rush-seated chairs. An unremarkable setting for something that was to change her life. She lit the oil-lamp that stood on the table and went downstairs.

The whirling pain ebbed away, gradually subsiding. Claudia muttered, '*Gott sei Dank.*'

The relief was unutterable. But it wouldn't last. She lay on her side in the narrow bed, knees drawn up, arms cradling her belly, embracing the absence of pain, but poised for the next contraction.

'That's settled then. When you're the toast of Berlin I'll come and see you.' Jarrold's soft voice rustled into the silence. 'I'll appear one evening at the stage door with a great swanky bouquet of red roses.'

Claudia half turned her head. She gave a wan smile. 'Lilies are better. I want lilies.'

'White ones?'

'Yes.'

'To go with your white Mercedes,' Amy put in. She had pulled her chair up close to the bed.

'You'll be there from the past as . . . *Erpresser.*'

'Blackmailer,' Amy supplied.

The doctor gave his sheepish, evasive grin. 'Shame, Miss Claudia. I'll be your humble admirer.'

Claudia smiled again, closing her eyes. How unlikely it was, the whole scene. What was she doing here? In England of all places, giving birth in a strange bed, with two strangers. Prattling foolishly, idly, between contractions. Almost cosy, with the lamplight and the shadows, the empty teacups, her muted, concerned companions.

From far off she felt the pain approaching again, like a sneak thief that got bolder and bolder, until she lost all control, gripping, crushing the hand Amy offered, and there was a roaring in her ears and she heard herself cursing and calling out for Lotte as the attack reached its howling climax. Then, blessedly, it lessened, slipped away, and was gone.

'Time's getting near,' Jarrold said. 'Turn on your back, Claudia. I'll take a look.'

'Should I go?' Diffidently Amy rose to her feet.

'No. Stay!' Claudia ordered roughly, affronted by the reticent good taste that was bred into the English girl, ingrained. But it wasn't just that. Obscurely she felt that her suffering deserved a witness. And anyway all this was for Amy's benefit. She couldn't just opt out when the fancy took her.

'If you're sure . . .'

'This is for you. It's your child.'

'I wasn't running away. Only I thought you'd –'

'I know. I know. But stay.'

Amy watched, awe-struck, as the top of a fuzzy black head strained from the cleft between Claudia's thighs.

'Push! Come on, push!' Jarrold exhorted.

He'd abandoned his whimsical, hangdog charm. Workmanlike, sleeves rolled, he squatted by the bed, badgering and bullying his patient on to greater efforts.

'Harder, girl. Harder!' Unceremoniously he pinned Claudia's knees back against her chest.

'Bastard!' she hissed at him as, body rigid, lips drawn back, she bore down with every last ounce of energy she could find. The effort forced from her a protracted, ugly, animal groan.

Amy saw the area of the baby's head expanding painfully. 'For God's sake, don't stop!' she urged fervently. 'You're so close, you can do it. You're so close!'

But Claudia subsided back into thankful passivity. '*Du lieber Gott*,' Amy heard her mutter, for no one but herself. '*Ich kann nicht mehr*.'

But a new contraction invaded her body, then another. And each time the head came that much closer to emerging. Amy felt that she – that all of them – had never wanted anything so much. Yet to achieve it she and Jarrold must stand by and witness this agony.

'Next one,' Jarrold said. 'Give it everything. Amy, you hold her legs.'

As the contraction bit, Amy fought to pin Claudia's legs back against her body, struggling against the muscular strength of the other woman and the force that possessed her.

'That's it. That's got it.'

Through her efforts Amy was aware of a firm lunge on the part of the doctor, a long, slithering movement, a mewling sound, and the child was born.

'You've done it,' she breathed, seeming to feel the same wild relief as Claudia herself, who fell back against the pillow with a cry of triumph, a fierce smile on her face.

'A girl. It's a girl.'

The tiny, vital body lay, blood-smeared, on the coverlet, alongside Claudia's hip. She glanced down at it and laid one hand on the child's stomach in a gesture of possession. Amy found she was weeping with the intensity of the process she had shared in. They were four now in the bedroom, the three adults joined by this small, pulsating life. The thought passed through her mind, too swift for words, that the child belonged to Claudia and if, even now, she claimed it, that would only be right.

The nurse had arrived half an hour or so earlier, was downstairs boiling water on the range. When Jarrold had finished tying and cutting the cord, he wrapped the small creature roughly in a square of sheeting and laid her in Claudia's arms.

She glanced down at the child she was cradling. Sweat matted the new mother's hair and shone on her skin. Her expression was unreadable. Then she looked up at Amy wearing the tough smile with which she chose to confront the world, and handed the baby to her.

'Take her. Here's your child. Take her.'

Chapter Nineteen

As he approached down the rough, dirt track that led to Kirk Head, Noel could see that the door of the cottage was open. It was a December day of watery sunshine. He was going to see his wife after a four-month separation. And a child whose existence as yet meant nothing to him.

For four months a framed, enlarged photograph of Amy had stood on his bedside table. It was a favourite of his. He'd caught her unawares and she looked serious and thoughtful, unselfconscious, sitting on the grass in the garden, arms clasping her drawn-up knees, chin lifted a little, pale hair caught loosely in a ribbon and hanging down her back the way he liked it. She wore an old, unpretentious summer dress and her feet were bare. She was exquisite. Hungrily he had contemplated the portrait last thing at night and in the mornings when he woke.

In the intervening months he'd been busy, lived a full and fascinating life. As well as his weekly newsletter, the *Freikorps* piece had been completed, published and received with lively interest. He'd paid a visit to Munich – the trip he and Amy had talked about making together – encountering the phenomenon of the NSDAP, a small and rowdy, but fiercely determined, anti-Semitic, nationalist party, whose simple and grandiose aim it was to bring down the Republic. He'd talked to and written about its largely thug-like members, finding himself intrigued and repelled. Delane had been enthusiastic about his coverage, instructing him to keep an alert eye on future developments.

But it hadn't been all work. He'd seen friends, gone to some raunchy nightclubs with Henry Bowen, a raffish fellow correspondent, and rather enjoyed himself, visited theatres with the Krells, flirted decorously with red-haired Laura.

And – little by little – the photograph by his bed had become less real to him. Did this grave and desirable woman really exist? He had letters from her protesting that she missed him and he wrote back with the same message. But Noel found it possible to visualize a day when, through prolonged absence, the photograph might become an icon, with no underlying life. He found an unexpected comfort in the thought. This must be how you got over a doomed love affair. If his greatest fear were to be realized and Amy ever left him, this was how he would, finally, survive – by filling his life to the brim with work and distractions. But now, in this unlikely setting, he was about to see her again. And Noel knew that – like Sleeping Beauty in reverse – her kiss would instantly rekindle all the rawness of his love for her.

When he was still thirty or so yards from the cottage, a figure emerged from the doorway and turned to gaze up the track. With a kind of incredulity his eyes met those of his wife.

He called her name and she raised her hands to her head, miming wonder and dazzlement, then began to walk towards him with jaunty steps. Amy wore a red jersey he'd not seen before, a black and white tweed skirt. Her calves were slim and shapely in dark stockings. Her hair hung in a single plait over one shoulder, while stray locks curled wispily round the hairline. Her face looked fresh and rosy, her grey eyes bright and, as she approached, she wore a broad smile. He was filled with wonder at her radiance, her familiarity.

'Is it really you?' Her voice was merry. She came to a halt in front of him, reaching up laughingly to grasp his shoulders, as if testing their solidity, then threw herself into his arms.

'Amy!' He embraced her fervently, kissing her soft lips, rediscovering the lithe feel of her. 'God, but it's so good to see you.'

His arms crushed her to him, while all the cold, cautious, defensive thoughts he had harboured about distraction and survival fell away in a moment. She was all he wanted.

'I've *missed* you.' Her voice was tender and happy. 'You can't believe what a quiet, blameless life I've been leading,' adding with sprightly reproach, 'while you've been gadding about.'

'Only killing time. *Murdering* time. Till I saw you again.' He meant it utterly.

'Come and see Vicki. She's the most adorable . . .' Amy tucked her arm through his and explained. 'I call her that – it seems to suit her. But I'm open to discussion.'

'Where is she?'

'The nurse is bathing her. I allow her to once in a while, to justify her existence. But mostly I can't bear not to do everything myself.'

The cottage door opened on to a small hall with a central staircase. Amy shooed him into a flagged kitchen on the left. 'Wait there. I'll bring her to you.'

She went into the other ground-floor room, pulling the door to behind her. After a brief, inaudible exchange, he heard his wife protesting to the invisible nurse, 'It doesn't matter. She's not going in for a baby show.'

A moment later Amy reappeared carrying the child. 'Mrs Bull's not finished with her. She wanted to put her pretty dress on, but I couldn't wait.'

The baby was dressed in a white woollen top and white drawers. Noel could see a small head, with a profusion of wispy dark hair, nestling into his wife's shoulder, tiny legs with turned-out feet kneeling against her breast, one pale, minuscule hand with soft, tapering fingers resting at the base of her neck.

'This is your daughter.' Amy turned the child to face him. He stood beside her, gazing down into the small, blank face, the closed eyes and questing, sucking mouth, like a sea anemone.

A new human being, scarcely a week old, and her life would be their shared responsibility. Her life would dictate to their lives. As Noel looked into the tiny face he experienced a hidden thrill of triumph and relief, sensing that – more surely than anything – this scrap of humanity had the power to bind Amy to him.

Claudia had a luxurious private room in the cliff-top nursing home in Scarborough that Robert Beadle had booked for her. The décor – to her mind – was stiflingly girly, with sprigged muslin curtains, a dressing table with a ruched skirt, a frilly bedspread in matching material. Her meals were brought on a tray prettified with a little vase of forced flowers that got in the way, seemed always in danger of overturning. The food was nourishing but dull and overcooked. Claudia longed for a salted herring, or even one of the rubbery, bread-filled, but spicy sausages Frau Kästner got under the counter from the local grocer who used to be a pupil of her late husband's.

The only thing that made her days bearable were the room's two large windows with their view of the rough, gunmetal sea, and the sky with its black and grey rolling clouds, its chill apricot sunsets. These and the daily visit from Dr Jarrold.

Though he came simply as a friend now. He'd fulfilled his function and been paid off. Claudia was currently in the care of the nursing home's doctor-in-residence, a gaunt, ivory-skinned individual, with fuzzy side whiskers and a permanent air of disapproval.

She appreciated Jarrold's bothering with her now he had nothing to gain from it, actually getting his precious motor-car out to come and visit. His ambiguous, shambling presence always made her grin. She noticed the anodyne nurse with the fixed smile looking askance at him and his moth-eaten beard, his none-too-appetizing overcoat.

They didn't have that much to say to each other, but it didn't matter. There seemed a kind of kinship between them, deep down, as if neither quite came up to society's professed standards. On and off Jarrold kept her entertained with anecdotes about his patients, his fantasy of appearing at the stage door one day when she was rich and famous.

One afternoon he asked, with his habitual oblique, rather shame-faced look, 'You don't regret anything, do you?'

She was startled, as if he'd read her mind. It had been with her all day – that moment when the baby's live little body lay alongside hers and she put out a hand to touch her. Just that moment, nothing more.

Dubiously she replied, 'I don't think so . . . In everything that you do there is good and bad.'

'True,' he agreed feelingly.

'I have done the best for her, but . . . I want to go home. It will be better when I go home.'

'Course it will, Miss Claudia.'

During the months at the cottage she had felt lazy and bovine. Now her energy was surging back. She was frustrated in this warm, pretty cell. Even Frau Kästner's gloomy, monumental house seemed desirable.

Claudia pictured Rudi's solemn black eyes and dark curls. She longed for Tante Agathe, who'd been a rock when it mattered. Calm and realistic over the planned adoption, laying aside her customary tears and lamentations. She longed for tawdry, familiar Berlin and the new life she was going to lead.

Jarrold had guessed right. She was having some regrets. But her passage was booked for 22 December. She would be home for Christmas. Everything would be fine once she was home.

Noel was amazed to find himself fascinated by the baby, endlessly absorbed in observing her. Touched by her small limbs, her fingers and toes, her tiny genitals. Proud of the warm colour of her skin, the lusty expansion of her ribcage, the surprising strength of her grip, her kicking.

He loved to watch her feed from the bottle, sucking at the milk with total, ferocious concentration, as if she were absorbing life itself. He was amused by the droop of her head, her small writhing movements, the way her little blank face suddenly seemed to break into a distant smile, or a look of comic anguish.

She was the first baby he'd really had anything to do with. Faintly he remembered his sister, Carrie, as an infant. But she'd been a figure like a doll, swaddled in frills and bonnets, briefly put on display by a nanny, then whisked away to be subjected to her mysterious baby routine.

Noel had imagined that his wife, too, would give her child over to some hired expert, but found he approved Amy's physical approach to baby Vicki, the way she loved to bath and feed her, play with her and cuddle her. And, unbelievably, he discovered that he enjoyed taking part in all these rituals himself, taking his turn to cradle her while her small mouth worked on the bottle, powdering her after a bath, sitting on the floor with her while she kicked her tiny legs languorously. He even changed her napkin once, when Amy was out shopping, but decided that wasn't really his forte.

With shame and incredulity he recalled spitting out the vicious epithet 'Hun brat'. How could he? The child was so perfect, so trusting. So dependent. Noel realized he had fallen head-over-heels in love.

During that Christmas and New Year spent in the cottage alone with Noel and Vicki, Amy was glowingly and consciously happy. She dismissed Mrs Bull, the nurse, with no hard feelings, paying her for the rest of the month, wanting to be alone with the people she loved, wanting to look after Vicki herself.

Never had she and Noel been so open with one another, so free and easy. In their shared enchantment with the baby they were, Amy thought, like two happy children with a marvellous new plaything. And in bed at night Noel caressed her body with an ardour that, for once, seemed unmixed with anguish, and she felt able to respond to him freely, with no fear of a sudden access of mortification and self-reproach.

Their Christmas was simple, with a small tree bought from a nearby farmer – for which Amy made paper decorations – a chicken she cooked herself, a bottle of red wine. In the afternoon they wrapped Vicki up warmly, improvising a sling from a crocheted blanket in which Noel could carry her, and set out on foot for a local beauty spot, a romantic, wooded valley with a waterfall that cascaded into the rocky riverbed below.

As she and Noel stood side by side watching the wild, foaming water, with Vicki sleepy and warm in the sling, Amy wished with all her heart that she could hang on to the moment, preserve it, bottle it, to be relived at will, so intensely aware she was of her own fierce happiness.

In the evening they sat by the fire and lit candles. Noel swore that

Vicki's eyes were focused on the flicker of the flames. They poured themselves brandy and drank a toast to their child and to Claudia.

'She'll be back home in Berlin by now,' Amy mused. 'I hope she's happy too. I do hope she's had no regrets.' To her the thought of giving up the perfect baby in her lap was inconceivable.

Noel was sanguine. 'It was her decision as much as ours.' He bent and kissed the top of Vicki's head.

Frequently – though, as Amy would have been the first to admit, not insistently enough to mar her pleasure – thoughts of Claudia drifted through her mind. All of them had agreed that, the day after the baby was born, Claudia would leave the cottage and be taken to a convenient nursing home to await her return to Germany. That way there would be less danger of her forming an attachment to the child. Claudia herself had been adamant about this.

Which didn't stop Amy from being troubled by a sense of guilt when Dr Jarrold lurched down the track in his motor to pick her up and Claudia emerged from the cottage wearing her shabby dark brown coat, leaving her new-born baby behind. It was as if, having served her purpose, she was to be hustled from the scene.

Though she attempted the jaunty grin that was second nature to her, Claudia had looked white and rather subdued in the cold winter light. Her wide mouth was unpainted for once, and this added to her air of vulnerability. Amy had felt a passionate pity for her, which she tried to hide under conventional cheery farewell remarks, wishes for a good journey and a happy homecoming, as she stowed Claudia's suitcase in the boot of the car.

'Miss Claudia,' Jarrold urged in his soft, homely voice, 'let's be moving, hey?'

The two women embraced. Claudia pulled Army close and held on to her. Was it simple emotion or did she feel she was drowning and needed a life raft?

'Claudia.' Amy wanted to say something meaningful, but what? There were tears in her eyes. 'I'll never forget . . . You know, don't you, how much this means to me?'

Claudia nodded. She was crying too. 'And we'll stay friends, won't we, when you come back to Berlin?'

Amy was moved and surprised. She thought Claudia wanted to forget the past, move on, find new friends. And she knew that Noel would prefer them to sever the connection at this point. But suddenly that idea seemed unthinkable, inhuman.

Releasing Claudia, Amy patted her shoulder, smiling through tears. 'Of course we'll stay friends.'

Part Two

Chapter Twenty

When in 1921 she first started running into Johnny Kröger Claudia thought him an arrogant little pissquick.

For one thing he'd been christened just plain Johann and she despised people who followed the modish practice of giving themselves American nicknames.

Neither was he handsome but, perversely, behaved as if he were. Johnny Kröger was skinny and young-looking, with a bony face, thick dirty-brown hair, an insolent grin and brown eyes that cut you mockingly down to size. They had mutual friends so he popped up every so often like a bad penny.

He designed some sets for a group she acted with once in a while – a people's theatre sort of setup, which meant you got no money but plenty of cachet. His backcloths consisted of spindly drawings of emaciated men on crutches, or with claw-like prosthetic hands, mutilated faces.

'Not more war cripples!' Adelheid, a fellow actress, had expostulated.

'Bit of a cliché, are they?' Kröger had enquired with smooth mock-concern. He flaunted his proletarian accent like a challenge. 'Too old hat, the war-wounded?' He'd given a careless shrug. 'As you please.'

Adelheid was a loud, argumentative woman, for whom Claudia had no great love. She thrived on confrontation, but Johnny's courteous sarcasm took the wind out of her sails. Temporarily he rose a notch in Claudia's estimation.

The play ran its course. The backcloths were much admired and Adelheid played a spunky, argumentative proletarian with great success. The people's theatre wasn't the place for subtlety. Claudia knew that she herself was merely adequate. This wasn't her sort of thing, though she liked the political credibility it conferred.

After the last night there was a party at someone's flat and her opinion of Kröger plummeted again when he made a crude and self-satisfied pass at her.

She was weaving her way through the crowd in the hall with a drink in her hand, when he came over to her in the crush. 'I've just worked out where I've met you before,' he told her. 'Ages ago. I knew I had. It's been bothering me.'

He was slightly drunk, wore a smile she saw as leering and seemed to have no doubt that she would be as interested in the conundrum as he.

'*I* don't remember,' Claudia replied rather coolly.

'You know a fellow called Franz Edelmann, don't you?'

'Vaguely. His sister Rosa's a friend of mine . . . Though I don't see as much of her as I used to.'

'You came to my room once. With Franz and Rosa and some other fellow. At some ungodly hour. You dozed off on Franz's shoulder.'

'Oh.' Claudia recalled the occasion. It was the night she'd been sick in the privy of the *Seeräuber* club and admitted to herself that she was pregnant. 'Yes, I remember.'

'Small world.' A satirical grin acknowledged the platitude, but seemed to signal that it was a necessary evil in order to keep her talking. She found she was being manoeuvred into a position against a wall, where there was little chance of escape. 'God, that Franz was such a bore with his arsehole political theories.'

'I think he's quite sweet.'

'Fancy him, do you?' Kröger asked with heavy provocation.

'Not particularly.' Claudia felt trapped in her corner.

'I saw Rosa in the street a couple of days later. She told me you sang at that place . . . The . . .' He appeared to expect her to supply the name, but she decided not to give him the satisfaction. 'I went there the next week to hear you.'

Claudia sipped her drink, making no comment.

'You were good.' He looked at her with an earnest expression on his odd, angular face and braced one hand against the wall beside her, imprisoning her more surely. 'It's all coming back to me. You sang some song you'd done the week before. By popular request.' He pronounced the words with smiling mockery. 'A cabaret thing. Blandine Ebinger used to perform it.'

She was surprised and impressed at his knowledge.

'You remember the one I mean?' He was determined to elicit a response from her.

'Yes.' Claudia softened, smiled. 'I scribbled the words down frantically on the back of an envelope. And I taught the tune to the band by humming it.' She pulled a wry face. 'It terrifies me now just thinking about it. Thank God they got it right.'

He grinned, sharing in the reminiscence. 'I wanted to talk to you afterwards and get to know you if I could. But you must have left at once and you never sang there again.'

She'd bought her bottle of schnapps and slunk home, waiting for an opportunity to try and abort her pregnancy, Claudia recalled.

'Why didn't you ever come back?'

She shrugged. 'Life moves on.'

Unconsciously his face assumed a look of . . . opportunism overlaid with sincerity, the look Claudia recognized as belonging to a man who is about to make his move. Absently, lightly, Kröger ran his fingers down her bare upper arm. 'You were lovely singing that song,' he told her. 'Sort of scared and brave at the same time, like a little girl.' His voice dropped to an insinuating murmur. 'So sexy . . . I tell you I got a massive hard on watching you that night . . .' His fingers caressed her arm again, speculatively.

She felt a kind of exasperation at his taking her for such a pushover as to be impressed by his clumsy, calculated dirty talk. At the same time, to her private chagrin, she found her body insidiously roused.

'That's all water under the bridge, Johann,' she said, enigmatically, meaninglessly.

Adelheid was passing by looking truculent in an incongruous flouncy green satin dress. She would do as a diversion.

'Adelheid!' Claudia called. 'I need a word with you.'

* * *

She didn't see Kröger again for another couple of months, then happened on him round at the flat of a male friend and occasional lover of hers called Peter Eisler. Peter, a dreamy, likeable character, did reviews for the *Vossische Zeitung* and tried to write screenplays in his spare time. The door to the apartment was open and Claudia could hear voices from the large room that served as living and sleeping quarters. She was thirsty and went through to the small partitioned-off kitchen to get a drink of water. Claudia was at home here. Peter's friends came and went as they pleased.

The talk was arty as usual and she recognized one of the voices as belonging to Johnny Kröger. Peter was arguing that Dadaism was finished. He was always discussing things like that as if they were vitally important. Claudia couldn't see that they mattered all that much and tried to keep his feet in touch with the ground.

The whoosh of the tap obscured their words for a moment and when she turned it off Kröger was speaking in intense, persuasive tones.

'. . . didn't know what had hit me – I didn't know anything at the time. I was just a printing apprentice. But there was the pig in uniform and that big painting by Grosz, *A Winter's Tale*. I didn't know what to make of it, but it spoke to something inside me so strongly and so deeply. I was knocked out.' He paused, then added, 'I heard someone say, "This is art," and someone else say it wasn't, and there was that notice saying, "Art is Dead", but none of that mattered . . . I just knew I wanted to be part of whatever it was.'

The declaration was followed by a moment of silence as if his listeners found themselves impressed. Either that or embarrassed. He must be talking about the exhibition Amy had seen, Claudia guessed, the summer she'd been working for the Campions. He sounded young and incoherent, painfully passionate, among his more sophisticated companions. And, in spite of her antipathy, she warmed to him.

She entered the room and said a general hallo. Kröger's greeting was good-natured and, if he recalled that she'd rebuffed his advances, it clearly didn't rankle.

Soon afterwards he said he had to meet someone and got up to go. On the way out he reached up to hook his fingers over the top of the doorframe and, with casual vitality, he pulled himself up to chin it. Claudia was charmed by the negligent grace of the movement. But then he was gone.

Kröger was notorious for having many lovers, but that wasn't unusual nowadays. Everyone she knew took sex casually and for granted, including Claudia herself. It was expected. Though Claudia knew how to take precautions now, had bought a rubber pessary from a shabby-looking shop in Spandau. She had no intention of jeopardizing her new freedom with another pregnancy.

She'd seen Johnny once or twice with a woman she knew slightly, a friend of Adelheid's. Her name was Luise Walther, and like Adelheid, she was a political activist. Claudia rather admired her looks. She seemed anaemic and was clearly undernourished, but managed to make both conditions appear chic, with a slash of lipstick, her short, thin hair pulled taut across her forehead in a stark and uncompromising style.

Calling on Adelheid one day to return a script she had borrowed, Claudia was surprised to see austere Luise slumped in a chair, looking awful, with big, red, tear-swollen eyes.

In the hallway, on her way out, Claudia whispered to Adelheid, 'What's the matter with her?'

'She's in love, the idiot.'

'What, her?' Luise was fanatic about female equality. It was strange to imagine her looking so cut up over a man. 'Who with?'

'That bastard of a Kröger.'

Claudia was meeting Adelheid and some other people later in a café in the Pragerplatz. Johnny Kröger was there, sitting at a table apart with Luise. She was crying in earnest. He had hold of her hand and was talking to her volubly and seriously. But there was something jumpy and impatient about the set of his body and Claudia could see he couldn't wait to have done with her vapours and be gone.

In '21 and '22 people had pulled long faces about inflation and asked where it could possibly end. In 1923 they had their answer. By

September a tram ticket cost four hundred thousand marks and hundred-thousand-mark notes could be picked up from the gutter, tossed there by beggars who knew them to be worthless.

Time and again Claudia thanked her stars that Rudi and Agathe had been made safe by Noel Campion's monthly cheque, made out in inflation-proof Sterling. There was food in the shops now – no need to resort to the black market – if only you possessed the astronomical sums necessary to pay for it. Rudi, nearly nine now, looked sturdy and healthy. Agathe had a new serenity.

Claudia had only herself to support. And in 1923 she was earning millions. So much money she didn't know where to put all the shiny, crackly, freshly printed notes – the sheer volume of them was a problem. But, if you knew what was good for you, you spent them at once, before their value swooped still further, as it inevitably did.

There was a weird atmosphere in the air. She noticed it all the time. A sort of suppressed hysteria. And an unspoken understanding that – under the circumstances – it was fine to be greedy, selfish, dishonest, lustful. Decency was a luxury few could afford. You boasted about your vices, not your virtues, grinning – as someone said – as if you'd swallowed vinegar. And you grabbed all the fun you could get.

One day in September Claudia ran into Johnny Kröger in the Tauentzienstrasse. Currently she had no work and was strolling idly in the early evening sunshine, debating with herself whether to make the trek out to Grunewald and beg a decent meal from Tante Agathe.

Johnny carried a bursting briefcase under his arm and explained that he'd just been paid for some hack illustrating work he'd done. 'I'm off to buy myself a smallish good time. Want to come and help me spend it?'

She hesitated.

He grinned, lifting his free hand in a cheery disclaiming gesture. 'I won't try anything, honest.'

She was seduced by his frank good nature. 'If you're sure. I warn you, I'm broke myself.'

Claudia fell into step beside him. As they crossed in front of the

Kaiser Wilhelm Memorial Church Johnny took a bundle of notes out from his briefcase and handed them to a syphilitic-looking beggar slumped against the frontage of the building. The man looked up sharply as if to thank him but Johnny walked on.

'That's my good deed out of the way,' he said dourly.

In front of them stood the Romanische Café, shabbily imposing, the self-conscious rendezvous of artists, actors, writers and other assorted bohemians. Claudia liked its cosy, pretentious, smoky atmosphere. 'Shall we pop in for a drink?'

Johnny pulled a face. '*Luftmenschen,*' he said scathingly. 'And anyway there's a couple of people I owe money to . . . I'd rather spend my wad on us.'

They veered off down the Kurfürstendamm and after a while turned left at a side street. Johnny led her through a doorway and down some dank stairs, away from the mellow evening light. Ahead of them was a second door, above which was spelled out in watery, mauve illuminated letters *Die Mandoline*.

The room they entered was dimly lit. There were tables and chairs and a sparse-looking bar at one end, a subterranean smell as if of mushroom compost. Three of the tables were occupied by shadowy couples.

Johnny steered her to a place by the wall. He must have sensed that she was less than impressed because he reassured her. 'We won't stay here very long. But it's a cheap joint to get some food inside you and get drunk.'

'We're getting drunk, are we?'

'Up to you. If you so desire.'

The owner, sallow and slick-haired, was called Gerold. He and Johnny seemed to know each other. Johnny ordered two 'specials' and champagne.

'Champagne?' She was startled.

He spread his hands with mock modesty. 'No job tonight?' he asked.

''Fraid not.'

'Not even at the people's theatre?' Pronouncing the words with satirical emphasis, a sly gleam in his brown eyes.

'Not even there. Actually I don't really fit in with Adelheid's set-up . . . They're all more serious than I.'

'They're full of shit.'

'I don't know . . . They mean well.'

'Where do they get "people's theatre" from? The only people that go there are tossers like themselves.'

'You work with them yourself on occasion.'

'I've got my reasons.' He paused and smiled. 'Not the money though, that's for sure.'

'I agree with their ideas completely. I mean I don't want to see kids starve while industrialists live high on the hog . . . But I've been to some of their meetings and –'

'They go round in ever-decreasing circles.'

Gerold arrived with the specials, which, disappointingly, turned out to be two plates of sausage and bread. He opened the champagne with a flourish and poured two glasses.

Claudia was hungry and took a big bite of sausage. 'It's *good*,' she exclaimed, surprised.

He looked pleased. 'They make it themselves. Don't ask me what's in it. But the end justifies the means.'

She washed it down with a swig of champagne. It had a strange, metallic taste. Claudia blinked. 'This is home-made too, I'll bet.'

Johnny grinned. 'Maybe. But it does the business.'

'Why's this place called The Mandolin?'

'Gerold strikes up when the mood takes him and serenades the ladies with Italian love-songs.'

She was diverted by the fantasy. Claudia discovered she was rather enjoying sitting here in this grim little cellar downing fake champagne. As Johnny said, it did the business. She felt loose-limbed and receptive. Euphoric enough to suspend her resistance to Kröger and find his company quirkish and amusing. To be intrigued by his alert, hungry face and speculate almost subconsciously how it would feel to kiss those full lips that looked dry and faintly scabbed, like a child's.

They went on to another club called *Der Nordpol*, which was a lot livelier, with a jazz band and a crowded dance floor. They jigged around for a bit, but it was impossible. Every couple of steps someone backed into you or trod on your heel.

It seemed more interesting, anyway, to sit and drink wine and talk about themselves. While they conversed Johnny doodled with a black pencil on the back of a price list that was propped on the table. After a while he pushed the rectangle of card across to Claudia. She peered at it in the muted amber light.

'Goodness.' She was faced with a flattering, stylized, but boldly executed portrait of herself. Claudia looked at him, impressed. 'So easy. How can you do that?'

He shrugged, face expressionless. 'It's one of my seduction techniques.'

Johnny claimed that, as a boy of fourteen, back in the Moabit tenement where he had been raised, he'd lost his virginity, seduced a young housewife who lived upstairs, by drawing a ravishing picture of her.

'Nowadays she's got five kids and she does the washing for the whole building. But she's still got that portrait framed on her wall. Memory of an afternoon's madness.'

'I sold my virginity for half a kilo of coffee.' Over the years Claudia had converted the experience into an amusing anecdote, and she told it now to Johnny, though leaving out the sequel of the unwanted pregnancy.

He was fascinated. When she'd finished he commented, 'That's what's so great about the way things are now. The randomness of everything, the unpredictability.'

'That's great?'

'Yes. It challenges people.' He was adamant. 'Take you . . . You'd have been a prosperous bourgeois waiting for a prosperous husband . . . You're a hundred times the person you would have been if everything had stayed the same.'

'What about you?'

'I'd have been a drunken, bullying printer like my dad.'

Claudia considered the proposition in dubious silence.

'What's your ambition, Claudia?' he asked. 'If you had your choice what sort of work would you do?'

She smiled and raised her hands. 'Honestly, I'm not that ambitious. I just like performing. I like the life. The make-believe. The freedom. I'll act in anything that comes up. I'm happy earning enough to live on with no responsibilities.'

'But you were so good that night at the *Seeräuber*.' He spoke musingly, as if to himself.

'It's a good song.'

'Yes.' He paused and took a breath, as if he were about to say something, then paused again. 'I've been wanting to say sorry. I was an arsehole that night . . . at Adelheid's.'

'That sounds to me like your second option.' Claudia laughed equably at what she saw as his crestfallen quasi-sincerity. 'First the full frontal attack, then the sensitive apology. What comes next?'

'Nothing.' he looked levelly at her, abandoning the persona he'd briefly adopted. 'There's plenty of women around.'

The appearance of a cabaret turn neutralized the edge of hostility that had arisen between them. A young woman appeared on the dais in front of the band. Claudia disliked her on sight. There was something smug and considered about her smile and her thick pink make-up. She had crinkly blonde hair brushed away from her forehead and wore a black dress with shoulder-straps, black gloves to the elbow, silk stockings and high-heeled shoes. Placidly the woman sang a couple of nondescript songs. Her performance was uninspired and rewarded with tepid applause.

Then, to the sensuous accompaniment of a tenor saxophone, she began to undress, dropping her gloves with a self-congratulatory air, lowering her shoulder-straps and smiling complacently at the men in the audience. Eventually the woman shed her dress to reveal a stocky white body, a shiny chemise. Claudia preferred the body to the woman herself. It was what it was, sturdy and female, serviceable, with no delusions of glamour.

As she wriggled out of her underpinnings, Claudia glanced at Johnny. He sat blank-faced, entirely absorbed in the process, oblivious to anything else. She was both offended and excited by his naked concentration. For a second or two the young woman stood triumphantly before them in shoes and silk stockings, before the stage was plunged into darkness.

Normal business resumed. Johnny summoned the waiter and handed over almost all the money he'd brought with him. Outside he swung the briefcase to show how light it was.

'I'll walk you home,' he said. They set off in the direction of Charlottenburg, and Claudia knew she would invite him to stay.

In her rented attic room with its posters and magazine cuttings on the walls, Johnny kissed her in a deliberate, almost speculative fashion. At the same time his fingers played insistently with her nipples, his groin pressing hard into hers – there was no doubt as to his arousal. But she had the impression that he preferred to keep control, while attempting to induce in her a state of feverish wanting.

Strangely she felt he would have liked it better if she had resisted him, that he would have respected her resistance. But intelligent women didn't do that nowadays, holding a man off in order to increase her value in his eyes. Such behaviour belonged to a different world, seemed the most arrant hypocrisy.

With the same seeming detachment, he pulled up her skirt, pushing one hand between her legs. She was wet with lust. Perversely, it was the very qualities that had repelled her in the first place – his odd, urchin looks, his arrogance and ungraciousness – that she found had a reverse side of attraction, compulsion.

'Come to bed,' she urged softly.

His body was wiry, his penis hard and erect. Peremptorily he turned her away from him, entering her immediately from behind. One hand brushed her breasts, descending to caress her sex. Ready as she was, Claudia came almost at once, and soon afterwards he was rocked by his own orgasm.

He lay alongside her then, pulling her tightly against him, pushing his face into her breasts like a child. Claudia was awed and rather scared by the strength of her response to him, but some self-protective instinct told her he mustn't know he was special.

'There's plenty of women around,' he had told her frankly that very evening, and she didn't want to end up a fool like Luise Walther.

After a while Johnny stirred and kissed her softly, brushing his fingers lightly across her warm, bed-softened skin. 'We'll take it more slowly this time,' he murmured.

Chapter Twenty-one

They met quite regularly after that, freewheeling friends and lovers who led their own busy lives and made no promises to one another, who had other friends and other lovers – that was understood. Or so it seemed on the surface.

But, for Claudia, Johnny Kröger had abruptly become the focus of her world. She could no longer imagine that time when she'd looked critically at him, seen him as ugly and uncongenial. She wasn't blind to his faults – far from it – but they fascinated her. His flaws and failings were more addictive than perfections could ever be.

But the knowledge remained secret. She told no one, least of all Johnny. Sometimes she wondered whether he suspected. But actions spoke louder than buried emotions. Claudia made no demands on him, took care to be sprightly and sceptical in his company – the way she was with everyone – cancelled appointments once in a while, marvelling sometimes at her own iron will.

What kept her in check was the spectre of Luise Walther, abject and tearful, a pain in the arse. If she ever became like that Johnny would avoid her and she wouldn't even have the portion of his affection that he casually offered her now.

Claudia was intensely curious about everything that related to him. During the time they spent together she constantly steered the conversation round to his family, his background, and Johnny was more than happy to talk.

She discovered with amazement that, like Amy, he was her twin – almost – born the same month, the same year. Johnny was the youngest of five brothers. As he'd mentioned that first night, his father, Stefan, was a printer. Kröger senior had never been short of work and, in the stable pre-war years, it should have been possible for the family to move on from the overcrowded warren they inhabited in working-class Moabit.

But there was something in Stefan that protested against bettering himself – a confused and passionate identity with his roots, an angry class-hatred, a hostile mistrust of *die Bonzen* – the nobs, the bosses, anyone in authority. And, apart from that, he was a drinker, considering it his inalienable right to extract from his pay-packet whatever he needed for the purpose, leaving the family to get by on the remainder.

He harboured obscure, simmering grievances, the conviction that somehow life had cheated him, that no one accorded him the respect and gratitude he deserved. And when he returned home drunk these obsessions came to the boil. He became a time bomb. The pettiest provocation on the part of his wife or his sons would trigger an explosion of vicious, snarling violence.

'I hate the bastard,' Johnny said whenever he mentioned his father. Stefan was far from well now. The booze was attacking his liver. 'He can die for all I care.'

On the other hand Johnny worshipped Ingeborg, his mother. The second time Claudia visited his room he'd opened a folder of artwork and pulled out a drawing he had done of her. It wasn't his usual spidery cartoon style, but a classic portrait, executed with love and infinite care.

It showed a woman with a broad-boned, slavic-looking face, her hair drawn back into a plain but graceful chignon. Her expression was one of patience and dignity, bringing to mind a moody poster that had haunted Claudia as a child – something to do with the exploitation of working women.

'It's a beautiful picture,' she told him, and glimpsed a touching and unexpected gleam of gratification in his cynical brown eyes.

Ingeborg had acted as a buffer between her husband and sons, a peacemaker, forever trying to defuse Stefan's outbursts of anger and protect her children from his blows. Attracting his brutality to herself in the process.

As Claudia got to know him better she became convinced that his mother had shaped Johnny's view of all females. What he admired in women were the qualities Ingeborg possessed – gentleness and patient self-sacrifice, a presumed sexual demureness.

In real life, though, he gravitated towards females who were liberated and modern, sexually accessible. He told Claudia once with a smile she saw as callous that he liked politically motivated women like Luise and Adelheid. 'They think it's their duty to sleep with guttersnipes like me.'

But Claudia came to realize that, at the same time and probably subconsciously, he despised them. They didn't conform to his ideal of chastity and self-denial. He took full advantage of their availability, but saw them as desiring and deserving humiliation.

On the surface her own relationship with him was affectionate, egalitarian, not complicated at all. But – on a deeper, wordless level – there was always something punishing in his lovemaking. She saw it as meaningful that the first time they'd had sex he'd turned her away from him, entered her from behind like an animal, as if needing to demean her and demonstrate his own dominance. In itself the act was not significant. But Claudia saw it as somehow defining his attitude. And, contrarily, it aroused in her a hot, half-reluctant excitement and she connived in his hostile fantasies.

He remembered his schooldays with dislike. His education had been basic, state-provided and had, so he claimed, nothing to do with anything. Johnny had been a nondescript pupil with a single talent – for drawing. He was more than capable of producing the meticulous, carefully shaded exercises demanded in class, but his tastes ran towards caricature.

He had been chastised any number of times for drawing cruel little portraits of his teachers, pointing up their physical defects with merciless spot-on accuracy.

'The old farts were impressed, though. They wouldn't have got so steamed up about them otherwise, would they?'

He left school as soon as he legally could and Stefan found a place for him as a printers' apprentice. It was wartime and all the able-bodied men – including three of Johnny's brothers – were away at the front.

At the works he met Alberich, an intense, consumptive-looking twenty-year-old with black eyes and a weedy black moustache. He was lame and so not eligible for military service. Alberich, too, had vague artistic leanings and once a week they went together to a local evening class, held in a long, bleak room above a café, and laboured over dark pencil studies of goose-fleshed nudes.

Afterwards they drank beer in the café and Alberich talked politics. He was a communist, though he hid the fact at work. The young printer railed against the injustices of society with a passion that was somehow sulky, and Johnny couldn't help thinking that he sounded a bit like Stefan, who preached revolution in the same way sometimes, though he'd never actually done anything about it.

But later their attention always turned to the free-and-easy young women who frequented the café. The wartime shortage of men made it easy for them to score, in spite of Alberich's limp and Johnny's youth, which he tried to disguise with an absurd gangsterish hat and a silky white scarf. And Johnny's mind began to form an incongruous, inconsequential association between drawing, sex and politics.

In the starving winter of 1917, when Johnny was sixteen, two of his brothers were killed at the front, within three weeks of one another. Ingeborg was prostrated by a devastating combination of malnutrition and grief. Stefan blamed the war on *die Bonzen* and Johnny saw that it was true. Young nobodies like his brothers had been dragged into the slaughter willy-nilly, and now they were dead. Suddenly the hot air Alberich talked made a kind of sense.

By the end of 1918 it seemed for a while as if the nobodies had seized control. The troops rose up against their officers. There was fighting in town. Lorry-loads of revolutionary soldiers and sailors cruised the streets. Red flags flew everywhere. Unbelievably the Kaiser fled to Holland. Johnny saw officer-types being roughed up and his heart was filled with vengeful joy. Christmas was coming. He and Alberich drank in tinsel-hung bars with revolutionary soldiers. Johnny was seventeen. Life was an adventure.

But by and by it all subsided. The moderates called in the loyal troops of the regular army, along with irregular *Freikorps* regiments to restore law and order. Karl Liebknecht and Red Rosa, the revolutionary activists, were murdered by *Freikorps* men in cold blood. The fun was over.

But the memory of those days stayed locked inside him. Life could be lawless and chaotic, it seemed, even in his familiar old streets. The knowledge scared some people, but it made Johnny feel restless. He grew impatient with the predictability of his own way of living.

Alberich had friends who were putting out a subversive little magazine called *Der Freibeuter* – scores of similar publications were mushrooming all over the city. Johnny did some illustrations for it, spidery little pictures of politicians and actors, copied from photographs, but comically exaggerated, like the caricatures he used to do of his teachers.

He started going to *Freibeuter* editorial meetings, usually held in cheap cafés. They were casual affairs, with friends and friends of friends dropping in at random, then wandering off again. He learned words like Dada and Expressionism, keeping quiet about the fact that he had only the vaguest idea as to what they meant. The *Freibeuter* people seemed to take it for granted that everybody was in the know. Some of them were women, of a type he'd never met before. They seemed clever and argumentative – they scared and attracted him.

One night he had a fight with Stefan and left home, moving in with Alberich until he found a cheap room in the Wedding area. He gave up his job. Plenty of the people he now knew seemed to live on fresh air. But Johnny was more practical than that, managing to find himself freelance illustrating jobs with advertising agencies and small publishers, inventing a miscellany of fake art-school qualifications to impress prospective employers.

He was still doing his caricatures for *Der Freibeuter*. Johnny began to understand that this odd, ephemeral skill he possessed was something he should play up. It made him interesting to the new people he was meeting. He became more conscious of the effects he could create in his drawings and started to look at other people's work, to compare. He went to exhibitions of painting and graphics. He was learning fast.

And he was gradually becoming absorbed into a fresh and desirable world. During his childhood no one had seriously questioned the straitjacket assumption that what everyone needed was a steady job and a family to support. However vicious and frustrated it made them – witness Stefan. But these friends he had begun to frequent, courtesy of Alberich, laughed at such tame certainties and Johnny knew he was born to laugh with them.

He revelled in the freedom of walking the streets and drinking in cafés at any hour of day, the edgy feeling of being paid in fits and starts, living high on the hog when you could, begging and borrowing when you were broke. The times, anyway, were chancy and that chanciness seemed to have entered everyone's blood. His new acquaintances were shabby, hungry as often as not, but full of talk, full of arty and political theories, sort of cynical and idealistic both at once. Posers most of them, of course, but lively and out for a good time.

Johnny discovered that the women he'd found so daunting at first were just as easy as the working girls he and Alberich used to fuck during the war. More so sometimes, because they were bolstered by principle – for these young bohemians sexual emancipation was part and parcel of their philosophy of life.

In a sense he was disappointed. Romantically he'd imagined having to do battle with all sorts of resistance, a host of moral scruples, before obtaining one of these prize specimens for himself. But it seemed that the majority of them were open to the most perfunctory of advances, even grateful for his casual lust.

Johnny never ceased to be amazed that women could read Goethe and Schiller and Karl Marx – it was more than he'd ever done – and write poems of their own, speak fervently or, more remarkable still, logically at some packed political jamboree. He marvelled too that he, Johnny Kröger, was permitted to sleep with a selection of these singular beings. And he loved to demonstrate – to himself and to them – that they could be reduced to the same abject, writhing lasciviousness as any pox-ridden local whore.

Sometimes, for his sins, they fell in love with him, and that boosted his morale a treat. But Johnny didn't think he'd ever fall in love himself. He was far too lacking in illusions.

Alberich became an all-out member of the KPD, the German Communist Party. Johnny rather regretted the development. It made his friend less fun, rather cagey at times, as if there were now certain things he was not at liberty to talk about.

Johnny was a communist by instinct – everything they said seemed to make sense. But he wasn't a joiner, preferring to keep his options open. Most of Alberich's spare time was taken up with party chores now and that kind of discipline didn't appeal to Johnny at all.

His friend took up with a personable female comrade called Anna. The two of them decided to live together. Anna was black-haired, with stern dark eyes, and she had Alberich where she wanted him. She sensed Johnny's disapproval of this state of affairs and an undercurrent of animosity sprang up between them, which they suppressed for Alberich's sake.

One cold, rainy evening Johnny called on the couple, only to find that Alberich was out on some political errand or other. Anna stood sullenly blocking the doorway to their apartment.

'Can't I come in?' he asked. 'It's a dog of a night out there.'

They sat for a while on two upright chairs, conversing awkwardly. But later – to their mutual surprise – they found themselves making love in the poky, mildewed bedroom. For Johnny it was an unexpectedly erotic experience. Anna had a lovely strong country girl's body, her very severity excited him enormously. And the encounter was spiced with the aphrodisiac scent of betrayal.

Afterwards, as they lay close and warm, she raised herself on one elbow and looked down into his face. The streetlights shining in from outside illuminated in chiaroscuro her white face, dark eyes and pleasingly rumpled black hair.

'I've been thinking about those drawings you do,' she told him.

He was almost more flattered by that statement than by the fact that she'd gone to bed with him. Anna was twenty-six, six years older than himself.

'What about them?'

'You could do something with them, you know. Put them to a political purpose.'

'Oh.' Johnny was mildly put out that even at this intimate moment her mind was on the cause. But her words stayed with him.

One day shortly afterwards he took a block of cartridge paper, black ink and a selection of pens and sat down at the table of his room in Wedding with the express purpose of producing a political cartoon.

You couldn't go wrong, he reckoned, contrasting a bloated profiteer, wearing an astrakhan coat and carrying a fat cigar, with a street beggar in big black spectacles which only partially hid his burned and mutilated features. Johnny drew the picture with enormous care and detail. It was one of his best.

Underneath he added a line from the sermon of a local pastor that had been much quoted in the press, to the effect that we all have our roles in life and should strive to fill them with gallantry and pride.

Johnny gazed dubiously at the finished product. Its message appeared to him pathetically obvious, glaringly unsophisticated. Then again that seemed to be no great drawback as far as cartoons were concerned. Or political theatre or cabaret for that matter. He signed it 'Johnny' and gave it to Heinz, the editor of *Der Freibeuter* the next morning.

Who seemed rather pleased with it. 'More of these, Kröger. Just the thing.'

The day it was published he took it to show Alberich and Anna. Alberich was delighted and patted his friend on the back. He was sorry Johnny wouldn't commit himself more wholeheartedly to the Party, but this showed he was thinking along the right lines.

He sat down at the kitchen table, holding the cartoon admiringly at arm's length.

Above his head Johnny looked at Anna. Her expression was approving and subtly flirtatious. He held her eye with silent insistence.

She shook and half turned her head, dismissing his gaze. 'It's excellent,' she said. 'You could make a name for yourself.'

*　　*　　*

Johnny thought she might be right and, because of that, he began to read the papers more closely, scouring them for ideas and incidents he could present in a cartoon form. His point of view was socialist, anti-war, anti-nationalist, anti-big business and its exploitation. There was nothing particularly original in all of that. Johnny knew the points he was making were dead obvious.

'*That* doesn't matter,' Anna claimed forcefully. 'The things that need saying, again and again, aren't complicated.'

But in Johnny's mind the politics remained a secondary consideration. For him the passion and pleasure lay in the act of drawing, which was a totally private process. He competed with himself, constantly refining his style so as to depict his characters with the maximum possible directness and clarity, but always with telling detail.

He collected faces, watching the men and women around him and committing their features to memory, cutting pictures from newspapers and magazines. The characters in his cartoons were not mere ciphers but based on the close observation of real individuals. His friends thought it amusing to be portrayed in his work as industrialists or prostitutes, affluent bourgeois matrons or monocled Junkers.

As time passed 'Johnny' cartoons became a minor cult and the circulation of *Der Freibeuter* increased. Johnny made contacts in other areas of the arts, did some book illustrations for a friend's slim volume of verse, designed backcloths for small avant-garde theatre groups.

Johnny was sceptical about people who thought they could change society and wary about being viewed as one of their number. At the same time he enjoyed his modest celebrity status and the political credibility his cartoons conferred on him.

By the time he got to know Claudia in 1923 he'd carved out a small niche for himself in an agreeable world. In a peculiar way he rather relished the crazy spiralling inflation. Everyone was in the same boat, and it was good to be reminded once in a while that life was chaotic, safety an illusion.

What he liked most about Claudia was the fact that she wasn't serious. Both of them vaguely believed in a fairer society, who didn't? The thought barely needed articulating.

But, like himself, Claudia was simply knocking on the door of a bohemian community that seemed desirable to her, with nothing to prove, no particular mission in mind beyond belonging and enjoying belonging. They were like two wilful toddlers exploring an enticing new kindergarten, dilettantes going to all the films and shows and exhibitions they could afford, looking out for fashionable new fads, frequenting a variety of friends and lovers, taking none of it too seriously.

She was attractive too with that wide, mischievous smile and slim golden body. He still had a vivid memory of watching her perform, way back, in that god-awful club with its leering compere. Claudia had stood there in the spotlight, so brave, so sweet and ironic, so alone, entrusting herself to the tender mercies of the Wedding workers who formed her audience, and bringing the gamble off. She'd been magic. Nowadays she wasted that special quality she had in walk-on parts in trashy films and ponderous revolutionary plays, when she should be performing on her own terms. But that wasn't so easy to do when you had to earn a crust.

Chapter Twenty-two

Claudia faced the camera as Bruno Berg lit a cigarette for her. Briefly the match flared, illuminating her face, palely powdered beneath the deep brim of her hat, eyelids heavily accentuated. She cupped one hand round Bruno's as she inhaled, lowering her lids when the cigarette caught, then lifting her eyes to his face and giving a small, dry half-smile, a brief nod.

'That's the one.' The director's voice rustled into the silence, flat and matter-of-fact.

Claudia relaxed. She was free to go. They were running late and at one point it had seemed they'd have to work far into the night. She had a nice little part as the girlfriend of a gangster. In the third reel she got caught in the crossfire and killed, but before that she had some excellent scenes. It wasn't badly paid either. Now – early in '24 – the mark had been stabilized and you knew what your money was worth. The knowledge could be sobering sometimes, but at least it was possible to plan ahead.

'Come for a drink,' Bruno suggested.

He was a new young hopeful, a star of the Hamburg theatre, whom UFA, the film company, were trying to launch. Claudia thought his performance rather original, thought he might make the grade. He had a boyish, slightly self-indulgent face which he used to good effect. The offer of a drink was tempting but she'd promised to meet Peter Eisler and she was already late.

'Can't. I've got to be off.'

'I'll drive you back into town,' he offered.

'If you twist my arm . . .'

He had a smart black Steyr two-seater. Claudia sat back and relished the comfort and effortlessness of her journey through the dark, wet streets. And Bruno pampered her further, with flattery.

'You ought to have the main part, you know, Claudia, in this picture. Meta's far too milk and water.'

'They always give the lead to the pretty one. But mine's a much better part.'

'Pretty!' He repeated the word contemptuously, glancing sideways at her, looking the perfect playboy with his wavy hair and paisley scarf. His youthful features had an intriguing soft depravity – which didn't necessarily mean that he was depraved. 'But you're such an absolutely contemporary type. You're the embodiment of "now".' His voice was smoothly sincere, wonderfully confidential.

She laughed. 'Aren't I just?'

Yet what he said put into words a consciousness Claudia possessed herself. The quiet yet effervescent conviction that this was her era, these were her years, and she mustn't for a moment forget it. She refused to spoil things by being ambitious and living for tomorrow. She had the life she wanted today.

'Meeting a lover?'

Claudia smiled and hesitated. 'Sort of.'

She did still sleep with him on occasion but Peter, with his book reviews and his dark, imaginative, unsuccessful screenplays, was more of a friend. A dear friend. He was tall, wore wire spectacles and had an engagingly sweet and sheepish smile. A mild man, but extraordinarily decisive and opinionated on matters cultural. Peter was just one of the people she mentally dubbed 'family' in her charmed and agreeable life.

'We're going to see some friends – I expect it'll turn into a party.' They were going to the flat of Anneliese de Groot, a strange and beautiful singer who looked like a handsome boy, rangy and elegant in the narrow black trousers she usually wore. Anneliese was dark-haired with a quiff that rose from her hairline and swept across her forehead with immaculate insouciance. Her voice was smokily smooth and the love songs she was currently performing at Rosa Valetti's new cabaret appealed equally to both sexes. Debonair and assertive on stage, in private life the singer was serious and vulnerable.

Claudia's spirits rose at the thought of the hours ahead. She'd felt a bit cut off recently with the irregular hours of filming. Tonight there would be friends she hadn't seen for some time. There would be beer and cheap wine and laughter and it would all go on until morning. And there was a good chance Johnny might be there.

'I feel a bit out of my depth here in Berlin,' Bruno confided with winsome diffidence. 'Everyone seems so confident and bold and sophisticated.'

'It's just self-defence really. A front,' Claudia replied without giving the matter much thought. She was wondering how her outfit would go down tonight. Against regulations she'd kept on her film costume, a black leather coat and high lizard-skin boots that made her look like a whore on the Tauentzienstrasse.

'I hardly know a soul . . .'

She guessed he was fishing and it was on the tip of her tongue to invite him to join her and Peter. Probably she would do so but, for some reason, Claudia hesitated.

They drove for a while in silence. Then Bruno asked casually, 'What do you think of Zeller?' He mentioned the director of the film they were working on.

'Fine. Though some of his ideas are a bit . . . well, sort of predictably pretentious.'

Bruno seemed encouraged by her reservations. 'A Jew. What d'you expect? UFA's riddled with them.'

There it was again. That thing that raised its head every so often. Claudia left Berg's statement to die away in her unreceptive silence. But it was disconcerting and mystifying the way it popped up as if, for some people, the idea of Jewishness was a sore, festering under the surface, when everything ought to be smooth and easy.

It took many forms, from Tante Agathe's sour prejudice to the quasi-scientific innuendo of a self-styled anthropologist she'd come across in a magazine a few weeks ago.

The indictments were as vague as they were confusing, sometimes equated with exploitation and financial sharp practice, sometimes with poverty and indiscriminate breeding, at other times with communist infiltration – a sort of catch-all smear campaign, very often with high-flown nationalistic overtones. Claudia had never really understood.

But she was glad she hadn't asked Bruno to the party. Peter was a Jew and so were many of the people who would be there tonight.

They were approaching the Tiergarten station. 'This is fine,' Claudia said. 'You can put me down anywhere here.'

Claudia went to see Amy once a month or so. She visited when Noel was not there, knowing that he was less than enthusiastic about his wife's continuing relationship with the natural mother of their adopted child. Amy, though, had remained stubbornly faithful to the pledge she'd made, three years ago now, in Yorkshire.

'Of course we'll stay friends.' Claudia could still visualize the English girl's face, smiling, but concerned. She herself had felt numb and dazed as she climbed into the waiting car, ready to drive off into the unknown, leaving her new-born child behind.

But now her friendship with Amy was a solid and uncomplicated pleasure, quite separate from the hurly-burly of her everyday life. She thought of her visits to Mailied as a refreshing dip in a clear, placid stream. Afterwards she felt calm and renewed, returning to her own shifting reality with the remembrance of a quieter, more traditional way of life.

She felt strengthened always by revisiting her childhood home. It reminded her of who she was. And it was good to talk to a friend with whom she felt not the slightest stirring of the rivalry that could creep willy-nilly into relationships with other actresses, women trying to make their way in the same small world as herself.

'Welcome, stranger!' Amy was always so pleased to see her. From the moment of arrival Claudia felt enveloped in her warmth.

Her friend had changed in the last years, seemed vibrantly happy, had shed the romantic loneliness that had first caught Claudia's imagination. She was still studious, but her studying was fitted in round everything else, had not the single-minded quality that used to make it appear a compensation for some perceived lack in her life.

She had her child and friends now. The household was lively and bustling. And the little servant-girl – timid, saucer-eyed Moni – had bloomed too. She'd taken on new responsibilities, was smilingly efficient and doted on Vicki.

Amy had more colour now and had filled out a smidgen, become more womanly. To Noel's personal chagrin she'd cut her long, pale hair into a light and curly chin-length bob, which made her look brighter and more modern, though in repose her grey eyes were still serious and her face had a delicate, virginal quality.

In conversation, though, she radiated playful contentment. It was pure pleasure to sit with her in the long, light living room, or on the verandah in the sun, drinking coffee and eating one of Moni's excellent fruit tarts, gossiping and watching little Vicki toddling back and forth across the garden that used to be Claudia's own.

Agathe and Frau Kästner insisted that she was wrong to stay in touch with her daughter. Cool reason told her the same. But the thought of never seeing Vicki, of severing all connection with her, was too cold and cruel to contemplate.

Always she carried pictures in her head of the child, pictures which superseded one another as Vicki grew. At first there had been the image of a sleeping baby, with her delicate beige-brown, slightly shiny eyelids and small, soft relaxed mouth, a vision of utter peace. Later she remembered watching Vicki, aged eight months or so, lying on her stomach in the garden on a red crocheted shawl. Claudia recalled how she'd turned to look over one shoulder, with her gentle, trusting baby's smile.

'Noel adores her,' Amy said often. This fact appeared to give her enormous happiness. She loved to see him playing with the child, making faces and funny noises, throwing gravity to the wind.

Claudia liked to imagine her daughter cherished, protected, made much of. Those early mental images were a source of undiluted joy, holding no down side of regret. It paralleled the pleasure she felt in Agathe and Rudi's new security, a serene consciousness of matters satisfactorily arranged, along with a fervent gratitude for her own consequent freedom.

Vicki began to walk. Her hair grew in delicate, wispy curls. She had large, luminous brown eyes like Agathe's, golden skin like

Claudia's own. She began to talk, her wide eyes seeming to focus inwards as she constructed chains of words, gravely eager to communicate her thoughts.

Claudia remembered a day when Vicki was nearly two. Amy had come to the door carrying the child on her hip.

'Who's this?' she asked Vicki as Claudia stepped inside.

Vicki gazed solemnly at her, then broke into a slow, radiant smile. 'It's Fräulein Claudia,' she said in her light, lisping tones.

The smile affected Claudia with the force of a revelation. For a vivid moment she glimpsed, in the two-year-old's animated face, the spirit of Lotte. She was overwhelmed by the brief vision and by the goodwill that flowed towards her from the child, unearned and undeserved.

From that day Claudia's mental images of her daughter no longer yielded the same clear pleasure. They had taken on the power to disturb. At times she caught herself wondering how it would have been if Vicki were still hers to raise and to love.

But Claudia was a realist. 'We'd be poor,' she told herself derisively. 'She'd be pale and undernourished. Rudi too. And I'd still be living with Tante Agathe and Frau Kästner, driven half mad by their infernal talk about the good old days ... Vicki would simply be a millstone round my neck.'

Cool reason was convinced, but a wistfulness remained.

Chapter Twenty-three

❖❖❖❖❖

Noel let himself into the house, trying to do so quietly. He liked to catch a glimpse of his wife and child before they saw him, to catch sight, just for a moment, of the way they looked when he was not there.

From the hall he heard Amy, dramatic, emphatic. '. . . I'll *huff* and I'll *puff* and I'll *blow* your house down!'

Vicki's voice was a squeaky, excited counterpoint. '. . . So he huffed and he puffed . . .'

Noel opened the door to the living room. For a split second he was able to savour the atmosphere of animated, unselfconscious harmony. Vicki sat in Amy's lamp, the set of her small body simultaneously relaxed and eager. Both were utterly engrossed in a storybook. The picture they made struck him, as ever, with its heart-stopping beauty. An image from a sentimental, hand-coloured postcard – the sort he would once have scathingly dismissed – but altered for him, deepened, by personal experience, personal significance, wonder. He belonged to these peerless beings and they to him.

Noel made his presence known. 'Little pigs, little pigs, let me come in . . .'

At once their faces turned towards him, smilingly reproachful. 'Noel don't *do* things like that!' Amy fanned herself, miming nervous debilitation.

'Daddy!' Vicki wriggled from Amy's knee and ran towards him in her slippers and red woollen dressing gown, adorably fresh and fragrant from her bath.

'How's my darling?' He swung her up to his level. She planted a kiss on his cheek with her soft, touchingly pursed lips.

Then he crossed to where Amy was sitting, bent and kissed her.

'How was the rabbi?' she asked. Today Noel had met with a Jewish community leader by way of research for a piece he'd embarked on about anti-Semitic attitudes in the new republic.

He pulled a face. 'Illuminating . . . Depressing. I'll tell you over dinner.'

'D'you want to carry on reading to Vicki? I'll go and see how Moni's getting on with the meal.'

'My angel.'

Each commonplace exchange resonated in his heart. Constantly he recognized his own good fortune. He was intimately involved with this beautiful, intelligent, loving woman. The minutiae of their lives were inextricably entwined.

And together they doted on their child. Noel manoeuvred himself into the easy chair, settling Vicki on his lap.

'Where were you up to in the story?' he asked her.

'House of sticks . . .' she began, then stopped short. 'No. Start again, Daddy.'

'From the beginning. You monster!'

'Please.' Her little face twisted with comic, pathetic, manipulative pleading.

At this point in their lives the Campions appeared blessed. It seemed to all their many acquaintances that nothing could go wrong for them, and all agreed that they deserved their good fortune. They were the nicest couple – bright, easy-going and unassuming, and so devoted to their delightful small daughter.

Noel had made of his Berlin posting an unequivocal success. *Witness* magazine was enormously enhanced by his chatty but penetrating newsletters, which sparkled with the personal fascination he still felt for his adopted environment. And readers were enlightened by his longer, analytical pieces about life in the young republic. As a much-read, much-quoted correspondent, Noel had gone some way towards toning down the vengeful attitude which many readers still harboured with regard to their former enemies.

'You've opened my eyes to the suffering these benighted folk have endured,' a woman reader wrote to tell him. 'And I'm beginning to see that they, as much as we, are victims of the self-aggrandizing presumption of a powerful minority.'

At the same time he wasn't blind to the dangers that twitched and writhed below the surface of precarious democracy, particularly from the militaristic nationalists who burned to restore Germany's lost 'honour' in the eyes of the world. The unforgiving harshness of the Allies, so Noel was convinced, only served to recruit further converts to their many clubs and organizations. It was pure self-interested good sense, he claimed, to stop treating the Germans as international pariahs. His logic convinced many, but also made him enemies in more hide-bound, jingoistic circles.

Noel's 'Diary of a Tenderfoot', covering the first two years of their stay in Berlin, had been published by Jasper Metcalfe, a thrusting young pacifist and internationalist, whose radical Atlas Press was attracting enormous interest in post-war London.

Metcalfe had a shock of red hair, wore a ginger corduroy jacket and a provocative red tie. He'd taken Noel to lunch and wooed him assiduously over pork pies and beer, the most exalted fare his social conscience would allow.

'You've got to keep on with this project,' he declared forcefully. 'With your "butter-wouldn't-melt" diary form, you're making points in the most readable and innocent fashion possible. And that's by far the best way to influence people . . .'

The second volume promised to be highly eventful, covering as it did the wild period of inflation, the stirrings of a new economic confidence with the stabilization of the mark, a bungled putsch in Munich by the uncouth, runtish, yet oddly charismatic leader of the NSDAP, a man called Adolf Hitler – by a fateful coincidence Noel had happened to be in that city at the time.

But it wasn't just professionally that the Campions prospered. Their air of happiness attracted many friends.

They were closest to Art and Laura Krell from Chicago. The couple were a few years older than Noel and their children went to boarding school in England. The two men had work in common, and Noel was drawn to Art's quiet cynicism, mingled with unexpected areas of a rugged, old-fashioned idealism, which made him think of his own relatives far off in Colorado.

Laura was smart and worldly, but affectionate and approachable. Amy felt able to ask her advice when she felt out of her depth socially. The two women lent each other books, and together they caught up with all the new films and exhibitions.

A crosscurrent of mutual attraction spiced their collective friendship, a small crackle of safe flirtation.

Laura claimed laughingly that Noel's English accent brought her out in goose bumps. Sometimes, when the four of them were dining together, she would gaze at him, sultry-lidded and breathe, 'Say that again, Noel.'

And he would take her hand with mock fervour and comply.

The relationship between Amy and Art was more muted. The simple truth was that, on some instinctive level, they liked one another enormously, shared a basic quiet seriousness which each recognized in the other. In discussions between the four of them opinions were generally polarized. Amy and Art versus Laura and Noel. The fact amused them, forming one of the entertaining peculiarities of their friendship.

The Campions had come to know their landlord, Gustav Ackermann, and his wife, Emma. They were warm, homely and cultured, happily absorbed in the upbringing of their articulate and gifted teenaged children. The whole family adored Vicki and she loved to visit their big, comfortable, unpretentious house, where she was indulged and entertained by adults and children alike.

They had their separate friends as well, of course. Noel had the journalistic cronies he drank with in the Adlon bar. Amy knew local women, mothers of children who were Vicki's playmates.

And, best of all, she had Claudia, with her wide, piratical smile and faintly disreputable air, a connection with a harder, less protected world which Amy was determined not to relinquish, though Noel thought she should.

'It's an impasse,' Amy told him. 'We'll never agree. And it's not just that Claudia is Vicki's mother. In some way you really rather disapprove of her . . .'

'Only as a friend of yours. She's so different from you.'

'Different from what you want to think I am,' she riposted sharply, though that issue came up less often now.

But, as Amy had said, the situation was an impasse. She continued to see Claudia, Noel continued to disapprove. Though, as time passed and their friendship brought no discernible disaster in its wake, it became a *fait accompli*. Noel and Amy rarely discussed it. For the sake of harmony they let sleeping dogs lie.

They had never yet succeeded in luring their parents out to Berlin – not even with promises of first-class travel, pre-paid – but for the younger members of the two families Mailied twinkled like a promised land. All Amy's brothers had visited more than once, as had Carrie, Noel's younger sister.

It was amusing for Noel and Amy to see themselves through the eyes of their siblings. They were viewed as glamorous expatriates, radiating an enviable cosmopolitan sophistication. With their new parenthood they seemed adult and mature. At the same time they were family, young and easy-going, approachable.

You could let off steam to them over the fogyish quirks of parents, confide crushes and love affairs, as well as ambitions and insecurities. You could turn to these wise and successful beings for advice, and know it would be up-to-date and realistic, not harking back to some antediluvian set of pre-war values.

Robert Beadle, Noel's oldest friend, came to stay, bringing Hester, his new young bride. Amy felt indignant that he'd ditched Prudence, whose wry humour she used to like, who'd been part of the small, charmed circle that had given her such comfort when she first arrived in London.

So perhaps it was prejudice that set her against dark, smooth-haired Hester, who struck her as smirky and shallow, far too interested in hairstyles, designer clothes and the snobbish little doings of the smart set as reported in society gossip magazines.

'Why on earth did he choose her?' Amy protested to Noel. 'Prudence was a hundred times nicer.'

'Prudence was no spring chicken,' Noel replied mildly.

'Is Robert?' Amy almost shouted.

She was shocked to hear Noel, whom she considered by and large to be the best and fairest of men, take it so for granted that his friend would prefer Hester's youthful prettiness to the dashing style and dry wit of his former lover.

But, by and large, the visit was a success. Robert was still good company and they shared some lively evenings with the Krells, sampled a little of Berlin's nightlife.

Robert was a trusted friend, the only one who knew the secret of Vicki's birth. He was unused to children and wary of them, but clearly thought Vicki an appealing member of the species. He seemed sincerely impressed with the life Noel and Amy had created for themselves and his admiration was like a mirror, reflecting back a pleasing self-image.

'Know what you remind me of?' he confided one day. 'The King and Queen of Camelot.'

They were sharing a pre-dinner drink on the verandah at the time. Amy's eyes focused idly on the horizon. It was dusk and the surface of the lake was darkening, but still studded with the red and white sails of small boats. The sky above was streaked gold and blue-green. She turned to glance at Noel relaxing with rangy elegance in a wicker chair with Vicki dozing on his lap. Her wispy hair was tousled with sleep, lips pouting a little, limbs soft and golden. Amy felt lazily content. The reference to Camelot was not impossibly far-fetched.

She smiled playfully at their tall, gangly friend. 'Robert, you always had a way with words.'

It was a curious and interesting fact, Amy was coming to realize, that however shiny and golden your happiness, however genuine, it was never the whole story. Human beings were never as simple as to be defined by a single, all-embracing emotion. In real life feelings lived alongside their opposites. Happiness co-existed with anxiety, with pockets of restlessness, even regret.

So it was that sometimes, in the early hours, warm and snug

between her freshly laundered sheets, with Noel breathing steadily beside her, she would be troubled by the thought of how tame her life was. Like everyone, Amy supposed she had wild instincts, an attraction towards danger, that conventional ways of living stifled and denied. She would think of Claudia, with her hand-to-mouth existence and shabby, eccentrically decorated room, her kaleidoscope of acting jobs, her shifting framework of lovers and friends. She, Amy, was cocooned and privileged. Claudia was in touch with the rawness and untidiness of life.

Then there was sex. They had adjusted to Noel's impotence, which showed no signs of recovery, the pattern if anything reinforced. They coped. Since Vicki's birth they were closer and found it easier to be free and open with each other. Noel gave her a lot of pleasure, her body was vibrant with it. And she was less dubious now about dressing up in shiny boots and skimpy underwear. In fact Amy liked the way she looked in the outfits Noel favoured, her peachy wholesomeness enhanced by lace and leather.

All the same there were times when she was eaten up by curiosity, burned to take part in a simple, urgent act of copulation, with no frills or accommodations. The fantasy was so basic, yet so inaccessible.

Noel claimed, as she did, that he'd never in his life been happier than he was now. Yet he clearly had his own tensions and temptations. He'd taken to meeting colleagues and interviewees in the racy nightclubs Henry Bowen had introduced him to. Places where the women danced naked and pretended to have sex on stage, even involving customers in their risqué shows. He made no secret of his visits and, if she asked, was happy to tell her what went on. Amy was unsettled by it, not quite sure what she thought.

'What's the attraction?' she asked.

He shrugged as if the answer were self-evident. 'It's nothing. It's all part of the Berlin scene.'

'Those women you gawp at,' she said to him once. 'They're all someone's precious daughter. Like Vicki.'

He gazed at her, startled, for a moment, then smiled with indulgent tenderness. 'Amy, you're far too . . . You're terribly sweet, you know.'

Chapter Twenty-four

'Your coffee, madame.'

Claudia opened her eyes, feeling tranquil and voluptuously rested. Sergei had come home with her last night. They'd made love pleasantly, unmemorably. But his body was warm and compact, just the right size and shape to interlock with her own, and she'd fallen into a wonderful, deep, refreshing sleep.

He was standing by the bed now, holding two thick white cups and saucers.

'You've been down to the café.' She smiled sleepily at him. 'The man's an angel ... Put mine over there on the table, won't you, darling?'

Sergei Rykov was a Russian, one of the many in Berlin. He painted, apparently, had an exhibition on somewhere and had offered to take her. They'd had nothing much to say to each other – his German wasn't that good and she spoke no Russian. They'd fallen back on sign language, platitudes and goodwill. But she liked his looks – rough dark hair streaked with grey, a broken nose, the sweetest smile – and his good nature, the air he had of being an indulged child, offering back to the world in general all the fondness that had been lavished on him.

Claudia swung her legs sideways over the edge of the bed and reached for a small heap of soft material that lay on the floor beside it. Her Indian shawl. She'd bought it a little while ago because it reminded her of Bagatelle, her father's shop, though Friedrich would never have sold anything so cheap and shoddy. But Claudia liked the strident pink and Prussian blue glowing against the dusty black of the background.

Deftly she wrapped the shawl round her body, passing the material

226

under her arms, above her breasts, crossing the ends over and knotting them, halter-style, at the back of her neck. The improvised dressing-gown never failed to produce a reaction.

'*Bellissima!*' Sergei exclaimed on cue. She twirled, smilingly, to show it off.

A knock came at the door. Claudia pulled a face. 'Who can that be?'

She crossed to the door, opened it a little, peered curiously round it.

'Expecting a rapist?' a flat voice said.

'Johnny!' Her heart leaped to see his odd, bony face and subversive eyes. 'Good to see you.' She kissed his cheek, masking the rawness of her response to him with a show of bland, generalized affection.

'I was in the area and . . .' He realized she was not alone.

'This is Sergei.' Claudia was not ill-pleased to be caught in exotic *déshabillé* entertaining a lover. It made her look adventurous and insouciant, exactly the image she wished to present to him.

'Sergei Rykov.' Johnny shook his hand, seeming rather impressed. 'I've seen your exhibition.'

Sergei looked boyishly gratified. 'You liked it?'

'On the whole . . .' Johnny flashed a charming, deprecating grin. 'But you're too influenced by Beckmann . . . You don't need to be.'

'I don't want to be.' Sergei shrugged, appearing not at all put out by the criticism. 'But he enters my dreams.'

'Let's sit down.' Claudia gestured towards a pile of cushions. She collected them and friends added to her collection. They formed the basis of a moveable décor with which she colonized any new room she rented.

Arranging them into a companionable circle, she smiled at Johnny. 'You can share my coffee if you like.'

Sergei had to go quite soon. Perhaps Johnny would stay and they could go back to bed.

'Like the dress,' he told her, a discreetly insistent look in his eyes, and she guessed he had the same idea.

They lounged and talked. Johnny smoked a cigarette. The two men seemed to take to one another. Johnny pulled out a copy of *Der*

Freibeuter to show them his latest cartoon. It turned out Sergei had seen some of his work and liked it.

Slowly Claudia drank her coffee, occasionally offering a sip to Johnny, sensing a pleasing electricity in the touch of their fingers as they passed the cup from one to another. Leaning on one elbow, she felt elated yet completely in control, diverted by the civilized titillation of the situation.

She was intimate with both these men. All three were aware of the fact and accepted it without jealousy or angst, with a sort of unruffled complicity. She was amused by the fact that both men appreciated one another's work as if, in some unspoken way, this raised her stock in the eyes of each.

Sergei was immensely appealing with his ugly, impish looks and sweet personality. But Johnny's amiable malice had entered her bloodstream like a virus. She watched him covertly as he sprawled and smoked, brown eyes narrowed, a sceptical smile on his lips, looking scruffy-elegant in a soft brown leather blouson he'd swiped from a nightclub a few weeks ago.

'Some drunken capitalist prick left it behind,' he'd explained. 'Marxist principle demanded I liberate the thing.' And his friends all laughed and approved.

Sergei shifted, sat forward, as if about to get to his feet and leave. They heard women's voices outside on the stairs. Another knock came at the door. It was Claudia's landlady, Frau Gerlach.

'There's a lady to see you, Fräulein Farnholz.' Something in her manner suggested that this visitor didn't belong with the normal riff-raff who came and went as they pleased.

'A lady?'

Frau Gerlach stood aside to reveal Amy, looking flushed, playful, ravishing.

'I hope you don't mind, Claudia. It suddenly seemed a good idea. I'm meeting Laura later.'

'Mind! Don't be silly.' Claudia embraced her in a spontaneous rush of affection. 'Come in and meet my friends.'

Amy's arrival altered the whole dynamic of the room. Before there had been muted sensuality, a certain air of gentle decadence. Amy brought in the bright cold air from outside, she brought radiance, and was the sudden focus of all attention, glowing with the outdoors and with the impulsiveness of her visit.

Fleetingly it occurred to Claudia that whereas she, Sergei and Johnny were flawed flesh and blood, Amy seemed made of some more perfect material, her eyes brilliant, skin unfeasibly smooth and luminous. Her hair, curling and clinging round her face, appeared to be spun from some unknown substance – pale, fine, silky, resilient.

Everything she wore was tactile, from the sinuous softness of her black and white wool two-piece to the diaphanous shimmer of silk stockings. Her underwear would be delicate, satiny, lacy. The luxury of her clothing was contradicted by the engaging eagerness of her manner. Amy radiated unassuming 'niceness'.

Sergei and Johnny seemed bemused by her. Sergei stammered a few polite, conventional German phrases, but he was leaving anyway.

'He looks rather sweet,' Amy said. 'His exhibition seems to have been well-received.' Nowadays her German was fluent and confident.

'Where's Amy going to sit?' Johnny asked dubiously.

She laughed. 'On the floor, of course, like everyone else.'

'I'll go down to the café and bring us all some more coffee,' he suggested. Claudia was surprised by this uncharacteristically helpful offer.

When he'd gone Amy took her hand. 'I love your new place.'

With her film money Claudia had rented a larger room in a smarter part of town near the Nollendorfplatz.

'It's so bohemian,' Amy marvelled. 'And that shawl you're wearing. You look devastating. I feel a dull old thing.' She was perfectly sincere.

With a nod of her head towards the door through which Johnny had recently exited, Amy commented, 'He seems interesting.' A glance of mischievous enquiry. 'Is he someone special?'

Claudia smiled dismissively. 'Oh no. Just a friend.'

She could have trusted Amy with the secret of her passion for Johnny. It couldn't have done any harm. She was discreet and anyway lived far removed from the circles Claudia frequented. But the habit of dissimulation was ingrained.

By the time Johnny came back with the coffee, they'd settled on the floor. Amy reclined decorously against a red embroidered cushion, her legs tucked modestly beneath her skirt. She asked Claudia about her work prospects.

'Another film,' Claudia reported with satisfaction. 'Another bad girl who gets her comeuppance. I'm acting with Bruno Berg again. He's definitely going places and he particularly asked for me.'

Teasingly Amy raised an eyebrow.

'There's nothing between us,' Claudia stated flatly. 'I can tell you that for free.'

'Don't you like him?'

Claudia hesitated. 'I admire his acting. He's brilliant on screen – sort of spoiled and shifty, but charmingly so, if you can imagine such a thing.' She pulled a face. 'But he's got his little obsessions. Hates Jews, hates communists. He's trying to fit in so he has to be a bit cagey about it. But you get the feeling that if he met a like-minded pal he'd really let rip.'

Johnny said little, she noticed. He'd lit himself another cigarette, sat back with ostentatious relaxation, his face a cool and enigmatic mask. But Claudia knew him well, and seemed to sense an aura of tension surrounding him, a low-burning excitement.

It came to her all at once that Amy – with her air of unavailability, the feeling she radiated of being a happy wife, a young mother, her playful but innocent charm – was exactly the kind of woman to impress him. And this was combined with an intriguing foreignness, a fresh and dazzling beauty. He *was* impressed. She could tell.

'What do *you* do in life, Johnny?' Amy asked, attempting to include him in the conversation.

'I doodle a bit with pen and ink,' he replied unhelpfully.

Claudia produced his cartoon. Amy admired it, asked him questions, tried to draw him out. He responded to her overtures in a satirical, subtly mocking fashion as if wishing to disconcert this prim young stranger. Claudia recognized a brattish desire to be perverse, to be noticed for it.

Amy looked at her watch. 'Time I was going.' She set down her cup and saucer. 'This has been so nice, Claudia. I love the room.

Would you mind if I came again? Moni enjoys having Vicki to herself once in a while. I'm much freer than I used to be.'

'Which way are you going?' Johnny asked quickly.

'I'm meeting a friend at the Galerie Blumenthal.'

'I'm going in that direction too. You don't object to my walking along with you?'

Amy smiled. 'Of course not.'

Like a vivacious automaton Claudia kissed them goodbye, waved them off down the stairs, told Amy to come back any time. Then she closed the door of her room. She shivered in the bright shawl which now seemed ridiculous to her. Before Amy burst in on them all, she just knew Johnny had been intending to stay.

Chapter Twenty-five

'I heard Rosa Edelmann on the radio yesterday.' Johnny addressed Claudia across the café table.

'Did you? Haven't heard anything of her for ages. We were quite chummy once.'

'She's resident singer with some band. Manfred something-or-other. All good tuneful, wholesome stuff.'

Claudia nodded. 'She'd be good at that.'

It was the first attempt at conversation Johnny had made since arriving at the Tänzerin Café in the Ku'damm. Now he was here Amy, too, was tongue-tied. He sat and smoked and the tension between the two of them was oppressive. It roared in her ears, making her feel faint with the effort of her false, feigned self-control. Didn't everybody notice?

There were five of them sitting on the terrace, while the May sun shone through their glasses of tart, chilled wine, beaming bright reflections on to the square of white paper that protected the table-cloth below. Apart from Claudia, Johnny and herself, there was a dark, thin young woman called Käthe and Claudia's friend, bespectacled Peter Eisler. Amy liked him a lot, not least because he knew and respected Noel's journalism.

'So glorious.' Claudia turned her face towards the sun. 'We could almost be in Paris.'

With her current period of prosperity, she looked chic in a pinafore dress over a black sweater, a black beret perched sideways on her short, dark hair, which glinted in the May light with reddish tints.

'Typical German,' Peter snorted. 'Always hankering after "abroad" as if it's inherently more glamorous. Berlin's a thousand times more –'

'Simmer down. I was only trying to provoke you.' Claudia smiled with comradely malice, her eyes closed, her face still tilted up towards the sun.

There was a feeling in the air that Berlin was beginning to come into her own again after the ravages of the war. There were pockets of prosperity, a new sharp sense of potential. And a sudden surprised realization by Berliners that all the scattered experiments – in film, architecture, music, whatever – that had sprung up like mushrooms out of the ruin and nihilism of the post-war years, added up to the most modern and adventurous culture in the whole of Europe. Admittedly it co-existed with unemployment, poverty and political unrest. But the optimism was there. However elusive and superficial, it couldn't be denied.

Amy, as a foreigner, felt it too. She was increasingly drawn to Claudia's set, saw her friend at least once a week. Noel was a little tight-lipped about it, but in all fairness couldn't complain. His work took him out often enough, evenings too. He could hardly begrudge her a social life of her own.

Laura was all in favour. 'Vicki's adorable and Noel's an angel. But you don't want to make the mistake of living through them. Push the boat out. These friends of yours sound fun.'

To her surprise, Amy found herself at ease and casually accepted in this raffish company, just one of a loosely shifting population. On that first visit to Claudia she'd felt embarrassingly overdressed. Since then she wore fair-isle sweaters, pleated skirts, brogue shoes, unobtrusive clothes, barring their superior quality.

In her quiet, intense fashion Käthe told her she *must* see the new play Piscator was staging at the Volksbühne. As it happened, Amy and Noel had already arranged to go with the Krells.

Peter showed her a poem he'd written, a cynical little piece – 'It's a lust-poem,' he explained. He was planning to set it to music with a friend. 'Maybe Claudia could sing it now she's making a bit of a name for herself.' He sounded endearingly vague about the project.

Last week Amy had met the notorious Bruno Berg. With her he'd been subdued and attentive, almost shy. She discovered that he, too, had a father in the church. As a child it had been drummed into him that he must never let his parent down. And, like Amy, he lived with the feeling that the eyes of his father's flock were eternally upon him.

'I expect that's why I took up acting,' he'd confided with his boyish, but louche and fascinating smile. A fallen choirboy, one critic described him.

He kept telling her how beautiful she was and Amy surprised herself by the easy self-possession with which she responded to his blandishments. Sometimes she had the impression that her lack of anxiety with these interesting friends of Claudia's had its roots in a sense of wild relief at the mere fact that they were not Johnny.

Everything changed when he came on the scene. The easiness vanished. Every word he uttered, every gesture he made seemed charged with a tense and predatory significance. He raised an eyebrow, he lit a cigarette, and it was subtly directed at her. She felt targeted like a rabbit caught in the headlamps of a car.

And, feveredly, it seemed to her that each of her own words and movements acknowledged the fact. She lifted the pretty, sparkly glass of wine to her lips and imagined that the gesture screamed with the consciousness of Johnny watching her.

'Peter, I hate you.' Claudia was laughing and pushing at Eisler's shoulder.

Amy had no idea what had made Claudia say it. The behaviour of her companions had suddenly become distant and mystifying. They were still sitting on a café terrace by a broad, sunlit boulevard and she was somewhere else entirely.

Sharply, covertly, her attention was riveted on Johnny. At first glance he seemed an unlikely candidate for such fixation, with his scruffy urban wiriness and pallor. His face, though expressive and animated, conformed to no known standard of good looks. At present he looked positively surly as he sat and smoked. Yet he exuded an irresistible sensual power. Was she the only one to see it?

He glanced towards her and his expression didn't change, though his gaze lingered momentarily. It was nothing, nothing at all. Yet between them lay the secret knowledge that he wanted her, was obsessed by her. The thought made her dizzy. She'd wanted danger and here it was. But it was impossible. She couldn't do that to Noel.

Peter Eisler had an acquaintance called Viktor who ran a nightclub-cum-cabaret in the Tauentzienstrasse. He agreed to allow Claudia to do a guest spot. She would perform two songs Peter had written and set to music with a friend. Her modest connection with the UFA film company was in her favour.

'You'll come, won't you,' Claudia asked Amy, 'and give me moral support?'

'I'd like to but . . .' She knew Noel would disapprove. Her visits to Claudia had so far been confined to the daylight hours, the sort of jaunt a young married woman could permit herself. But, closer to the time, she discovered that Noel would be in Munich on the night in question. Amy decided to go.

The club was called Bärbel after Viktor's wife, who roamed among the tables wearing black lipstick and acting the part of character-in-residence. Claudia would receive no money, but was promised free drinks in lieu – as many bottles of the cheapest house white as her party could consume.

Along with Peter, Sergei Rykov was supposed to be coming. But he dropped out at the last minute and Johnny dropped in. Amy was disconcerted. She hadn't expected him to be there. But with the wine and the muted lighting she felt camouflaged and cocooned, less like a specimen butterfly under a collector's spotlight. And the atmosphere between them was mellower than usual.

'I'm terrified,' Claudia said, as she left to go backstage. 'I want it to be *good*.'

'It will be,' Johnny assured her. 'This is the kind of thing you should have been doing all along.'

'That's why it's important to me.' She pulled a wry face. 'I'm better off when I don't give a damn.'

When Claudia appeared in front of the white curtain patterned with black cubist designs, Amy herself felt as nervous as a mother watching her child in a school play. Her friend wore a dark dress and, at Peter's urging, the tilted black beret she'd adopted recently.

'If it goes well the beret could be a kind of trademark.'

'And if it goes badly it could make me look like a pretentious idiot.' But she'd taken his advice.

Amy thought Claudia looked pale but heroic, more fragile than she did in reality. But her uncompromising belle-laide features were as arresting on stage as in life. With the tension she was experiencing on Claudia's behalf, the opening notes of the song seemed to resonate almost painfully through her own head.

The song was called 'First Love', the story of a young girl who loses her virginity to a happily married bourgeois 'for a kilo of coffee'. Later she becomes pregnant and the man denies his involvement, orders her to be off and not to distress his wife. She turns to a backstreet abortionist. This was the version of her story Claudia had told Peter and he'd made it into a song.

Claudia sang without pathos or histrionics, her impassive delivery serving to heighten the impact of the song. Occasionally, deliberately, she allowed the hard veneer to slip, revealing pain and betrayal, but only for a moment. Amy thought her performance was more like acting than singing. Claudia invested the words and the catchy, off-beat tune with the unmistakable conviction of experience survived.

'She's got it right,' Johnny whispered. 'I knew she would.'

Peter sat silent as she sang, his eyes inscrutable behind wire spectacles. The oblique lighting made his long, sensitive face look smooth and almost handsome.

Ruefully Claudia had once described to Amy what it had been like singing in *Der Seeräuber*, some years back, when she was still in her teens.

'They got confused if you sang anything peculiar or arty. You'd look out and see all these puzzled faces . . .'

The audience tonight was quite different. They recognized and appreciated experimentation, irony, alienation. From that point of view it should be easier to win them over. On the other hand they were more sophisticated, less easily impressed. But they greeted Claudia's performance with applause and approving murmurs.

The second number was jauntier – Peter's 'lust-song'. Claudia sang it brazenly as if surprised and amused at herself, hitting just the right balance between brashness and whimsicality. It was short, sweet and startling. The applause was prompt and enthusiastic.

'They're bound to ask her back,' Peter exulted. He looked dazed with relief.

On stage Claudia bowed with a catlike smile.

When Amy emerged from the ladies' lavatory she found Johnny standing waiting.

He grabbed her wrist. 'I've got to talk to you.'

'What about?'

In the gloomy red light of the dingy corridor a couple stood intimately entwined. The man's hand reached under the woman's skirt. She reacted with a muffled giggle.

Brutally Johnny turned his attention to them. 'Why don't you just lie down on the floor and have done with it?'

They gazed at him in comical outrage, began to stammer an inarticulate protest. But, clearly, they were intimidated by his glowering vehemence and retreated through the double swing doors that led to the nightclub proper.

'Tossers,' Johnny hissed.

Again he faced Amy. She thought he looked young and scared. But determined to act on some private decision.

'You know I'm mad about you,' he declared with sudden energy, but somehow without conviction, as if the words he'd planned to say held no meaning for him at the moment of emerging from his mouth.

Stupidly she stared at him, trying to arrange her thoughts.

'You know it, don't you?' he urged with an insistence that sounded more threatening than anything else.

'I know there's something going on between us. But I don't know what it is.'

'I'm in love with you.' This time he spoke with a very personal intensity. 'I think about you all the time. I dream about you.' She was mesmerized by his eyes, black and glittery, glowing with heightened, wine-induced fervour.

She panicked. 'I'm a married woman. Happily married.'

Even as she spoke Amy despised her own words. The statement was a cliché, evading the complexity of truth, a cowardly contrast to Johnny's reckless self-revelation.

He ignored it, continuing with single-minded sincerity, 'I've never felt like this about any woman in all my life.'

They gazed at one another in the eerie light. His breathing was hard, as if in the wake of physical effort. Amy was touched by the nakedness of his emotion. She experienced the abrupt and powerful impulse to reach out and pull him towards her, lay her lips to his. Simultaneously the deeply ingrained habits of circumspection and self-denial reasserted their stranglehold.

'Johnny, don't . . .' She shook her head, but knew there was confusion, contradiction in her eyes. 'Don't talk like that. Nothing can happen between us. It's impossible.'

Chapter Twenty-six

With smooth, stylish strokes Noel rowed his family across the lake in the little white-painted boat they'd recently bought. Vicki sat between his knees. He held her soft little hands on the oars as if she were in control of their progress.

'In – out, in – out,' they chanted in unison.

From her seat in the bow Amy marvelled, 'You're *speeding* us along, Vicki.'

Vicki smiled ecstatically at the pretence that it was her strength and skill that propelled them across the water. She was half triumphant at tricking her mother, half aware that Amy wasn't really deceived.

'Which one's our house, Vicki?' Noel asked.

She scanned the shoreline, then pointed to the familiar white chalet shape, the carved horses' heads on the roof.

'Yes, that's the one.'

The glassy surface of the lake gleamed with August evening sunshine, reflecting the pale blue of the sky and the small, pink-tinged clouds. There was silence but for the dipping and splashing of the oars, the creak of the boat.

Lulled by the peace and the leisurely movement, Amy's mind idled and, as happened so often recently, thoughts of Johnny rose up to fill the void. The images that flickered in her head – as she smiled at the antics of her husband and child – were not taken from life, but shimmering pictures on a screen.

Some days ago Claudia had taken her round to the room of her dark, intense friend Käthe.

'It's a film show. You'll recognize the actors . . .'

Käthe had rigged up a sheet to form a screen and she projected a couple of reels she'd shot herself at a picnic by the Wannsee with Claudia, Sergei, Johnny and others.

Johnny was the star of the picture, bare-chested and manic, with a scarf tied pirate-wise over his hair, clowning with the women, showing off, performing handstands and somersaults, smoking a cigar, grinning with his taut, lean jawline, staring into the lens with eyes that seemed black and opaque.

'How the camera loves him,' Claudia mocked.

'How he loves the camera,' Käthe corrected.

In the darkened room Amy watched with a private greed, feeling like a voyeur, both seduced and disturbed by this reflection of careless, confident high spirits, seeing something ruthless in his smiling charm. And she felt obscurely that, if Johnny loved her as much as he claimed, he'd no business to be having such a good time in her absence. Her stomach twisted with envy of the whole laughing, sun-tanned group, their insouciance and freedom.

'Looks enormous fun.' Some comment seemed called for but, to Amy's own ears, her voice sounded dry and hollow.

Thinking back, she felt ashamed. Envy was such an abject emotion. And, in any case, surely she was the enviable one. As if in confirmation, her eyes rested on elfin Vicki, so adorably comical in her padded life jacket, Noel in the carefree mood she loved best, with his broad, reliable shoulders and ruffled hair. At the same time Amy could not deny the fierce stab of desire she'd felt for the flaunting young man on the improvised screen.

In Claudia's circle she was surrounded by people enjoying casual affairs, seemingly without guilt or anxiety. And even Noel had his sorties to raunchy nightclubs, shrugged off as merely an amusing, exotic ingredient of the Berlin scene.

While – as if none of this existed or need affect her – she continued with her goody-two-shoes role as beatific wife and mother. There was truth in the role, but it wasn't the whole truth. A part of her was excited and elated by Johnny's pursuit. And her blood continued to crave the simple, basic act of sex, and she could have it so easily.

Sitting there in the bows of the boat, with a golden sun beginning to set over the lake, Amy experienced a sudden flash of inevitability.

Of course, sooner or later, she and Johnny would have an affair. Her instinctive self had known it for ages. Her conscious mind was finally catching up.

She shook her head, snapping out of the reverie. 'My turn to row, chaps,' she said.

Claudia lounged in the big, luxurious bathtub Käthe let her use occasionally, in spite of the disapproving looks of her fellow-tenants; in Claudia's own building the washing arrangements were grudging and spartan. She'd scented the water with sandalwood and washed her hair. Tonight she was seeing Johnny. But her pleasure in the ritual was marred by a heaviness of spirit she couldn't shake off.

When she'd arrived at Käthe's, with her towels and lotions, ready for the anticipated soak, her friend had been running that damned film yet again for yet another of her chums. She was immensely chuffed with her camera-tricks – the way she made people seem to vanish into thin air, leap backwards on to high walls and the like. Before retiring to the bathroom Claudia had lingered for a few minutes, watching Johnny cavort, smiling again at his antics, while her heart contracted with a fear that was becoming familiar to her.

Now, as she relaxed in the warm, perfumed water, her mind drifted back to the day, last week, when she'd invited Amy up to view Käthe's film show. Even now Claudia wasn't sure why she'd done it.

Of course she'd seen from the start that Johnny was highly intrigued by Amy. That, in itself, was bearable – Claudia had lived with his flirtations for as long as she'd known him. He was fickle, susceptible. And she was comforted by her vision of Amy as a contentedly faithful wife, a woman not subject to the same grubby temptations as the rest of humanity. The thought of her entertaining streetwise Johnny as a lover was laughable. Unthinkable.

And yet, for some perverse reason, Claudia had harboured the desire, even the need, to watch Amy watching Johnny, to spy on her reaction. She had observed her friend by the light that flickered from the improvised screen, and been disconcerted by the intensity of Amy's gaze.

'I ask you, what a ham!' Käthe had groaned, but Amy's laughter at her mockery was strained and false as if the image of Johnny aroused emotions in her that were far more powerful and private than mere bland amusement. Watching her, Claudia felt abruptly as if someone had walked across her grave.

Sunlight, filtered through the thin blue curtains, cast watery shadows on Claudia's bare limbs. Slowly she soaped her arms and her breasts, picturing herself and Johnny together in her soft, wide bed. As she did so, Claudia admitted to herself another motive for showing Amy the film – the vaguely malicious wish to demonstrate to her that Johnny and Käthe and Sergei, Claudia herself, and the others, formed a happily self-sufficient circle. Amy was an outsider. Willy-nilly a muffled hostility had begun to infiltrate the warm feelings Claudia had for her English friend.

'Claudia!' Käthe called through the keyhole. 'Have you died in there?'

'Just getting out!' Claudia lied.

She reached for Käthe's long-handled brush and began to scrub her back. The scratchiness was invigorating. Claudia ran some cold water into the bath and splashed it on her face and body. She felt better, more like herself. All this soul-searching was morbid. She was inventing shadowy terrors for herself, hallucinating like a child alone in the dark. Nothing had really changed. Had it?

It was the car Johnny noticed first. One of those neat, yellow three-seater Citroëns women often drove, and it was parked by the kerb outside Claudia's flat. Curious, he approached to inspect it. In the passenger seat sat a woman with a sleeping child in her lap. It was Amy.

'Hello,' he said softly, so as not to startle her.

She turned her head. Seeing him she broke into a sweet, spontaneous smile. Carefully, trying not to disturb the child, she opened the car door. It was a balmy August evening.

He squatted down to talk to her. 'So this is your little one.'

The child was dead to the world, a pretty creature with wispy curls. Something in the picture she and Amy made together stirred an echo in his mind – a photograph of Ingeborg, his mother, himself as an infant asleep in her arms.

'We've been to the zoo,' Amy said. 'With my friend Laura.' Glancing down at her daughter she added, 'The excitement's been a bit too much . . . Laura's popped up to see Claudia. I've got to cancel an arrangement for tomorrow . . . I didn't want to go up myself and wake Vicki.'

Her manner was calmly amicable as if the unexpectedness of their encounter made it possible to ignore all the unresolved tensions that spiked their relationship.

'She's beautiful.' For once he wanted to soothe and flatter rather than provoke.

'Yes, isn't she?' Amy's smile held nothing but simple goodwill. At that moment he was glad she'd refused his advances, showed herself worthier of respect than other women.

In the glow of a nearby streetlamp she looked all silvery – her skin, her hair and the pale summer dress she was wearing. He couldn't have enough of gazing at her beauty. Abruptly the idea of possessing it seemed a guttersnipe's dream of defiling something perfect and beyond his reach.

Claudia arched her body towards him as Johnny jerked with the spasms of his climax. She had reached her own orgasm minutes earlier, but to her this was as fulfilling – having him lost like this, calling her name, to experience vicariously the racking convulsions of his release.

Gradually the shuddering subsided and he lay damp and spent on her body, nuzzling his face into her neck, kissing the smoothness of her shoulder.

'I love you, Claudi,' he murmured. 'You know that, don't you?'

To Claudia it sounded like a declaration of affection, an admission that he could offer her that but nothing deeper.

'I know,' she said soothingly, as if to a child. And this, too, was shorthand, signifying that she accepted what he could give.

In the faint twilight that penetrated her curtains, Claudia ran her thumb down the side of his face, tracing the prominent cheekbones, the angular jaw. She could picture rather than see the dense brown hair hanging over his forehead in clumps.

They lay silent for a while, then he turned away from her as if preparing for sleep.

For some reason the animal indolence of the movement triggered in Claudia a sudden rush of anger and despair. She loved him, was good and brave and didn't make a nuisance of herself. He used her. She let him, and never rocked the boat. Accepting his tepid, sentimental assurances of love, letting him get away with everything on his own terms. And in return he . . .

'It's Amy you love,' she said brutally.

'Yes.' In the lethargic afterglow of sex he spoke as if it didn't matter.

She'd expected him to deny it and the pain of his confirmation knocked the breath out of her. She lay very still in the darkness, with the conviction that, if she moved, she would go whirling out of control, spiralling down into a bottomless black abyss.

Yet she'd known for months. She'd known. Even as she dismissed his interest in Amy as the usual flirtation. Just as long as Johnny said nothing, she'd been able to close her eyes, hold the pain in abeyance.

And all that time a fresh image of Amy had been developing inside her, like a photograph gradually darkening in its bath of chemicals. Now she released it like a genie from a lamp. That silver-blonde beauty and artless, affectionate smile masked danger and betrayal, like a perfect but poisonous flower.

'You'll never get to fuck her.' Claudia's tone was hard and contemptuous. 'Amy's a good girl.'

'We'll see,' he said, as if speaking from some secret knowledge.

Weeks ago Johnny had invited both Claudia and Amy to drop into the Valentin Theater during the day to see the backcloths he'd designed for a review that was being mounted in early September for the new winter season.

Apparently it was to be a frivolous affair, though staged by a young hopeful Johnny had got to know during his brief and abrasive stint with the 'people's theatre' crowd. Since then the man had gone on to more ambitious things.

'We'll be preaching to the converted here,' the young director had confided, 'so we won't be making any heavy political points.' The show was going to be fun.

In accordance with this brief Johnny had drawn a row of monster chorus girls, each one with her own individual character, high-kicking across the back of the stage. Their lifted legs could be made to move comically in time to the music. Both director and cast were enraptured with the result.

Amy, too, was charmed by the set, so playful and absurd, very much Johnny. Claudia hadn't arrived yet. She waited for a thoroughly entertaining hour or so, watching the actors rehearse, chatting to the stagehands, drinking dubious coffee from a cracked cup. But by midday Claudia had still not appeared.

'She must have been called to the studio unexpectedly.' Johnny seemed convinced that she wouldn't come.

'Maybe we should give her a little longer.'

'It's not worth it. She'd be here by now if . . . I'll go and see her later tonight.' With a satirical flourish, he offered Amy his arm. 'Let's go and walk in the sun.'

Smilingly she accepted. The theatre was near the river and soon they were strolling along the Reichstagsufer in crisp September sunshine. The water shone, its surface wrinkled with tiny, even, Canaletto-like waves. Barges glided and hooted. Amy and Johnny walked in and out of the long shadows of tall, handsome buildings.

'The air's so bracing in Berlin,' Amy said. 'I've heard it said people don't get hangovers here. And you can go to bed at three and be up by seven and never feel tired.'

'You never tried it?'

She laughed. 'I'm too clean-living.'

He glanced at her with amiable irony, but made no comment.

A couple of urchins waved to them from a passing boat. They waved back and Johnny shouted something incomprehensible in Berlin dialect. Standing next to him on the bank, wearing a new red dress Noel had urged her to buy, Amy felt like someone else.

'I've never seen you in red before,' Johnny commented, as if reading her thoughts. 'And lipstick, is it?'

'I put some on, and some powder. I'm too pale to wear red.' She could feel herself blushing.

'On the contrary,' he teased. 'You look rather healthy.'

It felt unreal to be alone with a man of her own age, to be flirted with. It was like playing truant, being offered delightful new possibilities for a day that had seemed mapped out in advance. It was like being a single girl – free and self-sufficient – the kind of single girl she'd never had the opportunity to be.

It was easy to be with Johnny today. His amusing side was on display, rather than the predatory, the perverse.

After a mile or so they drew level with an enticing terrace that overlooked the water. The Café Csokor.

'They do the best goulash here I've ever eaten,' Johnny enthused. 'May I invite you?'

Amy hesitated. Dining with a young man – an admirer at that – seemed far more of a commitment than a mere stroll in the sun.

'You like goulash?' he urged.

'I do . . .' She shrugged and smiled. 'Thank you. I'd like to.'

The sunshine was losing its sharpness, shading towards afternoon mellowness. The terrace was clean and unpretentious, with painted, peasanty-looking chairs and red cotton tablecloths. The clientele appeared to boast a representative of every country in Eastern Europe, either lunching or lingering over coffee in an atmosphere of unhurried enjoyment.

The goulash was rich and full-flavoured and Johnny had ordered a bottle of wine. He seemed perfectly at home here, was known to the waiters, joking with them in the tough, urban manner Amy still found rather daunting.

She had a sudden wry flashback to her rural vicarage childhood and marvelled at being at home in Berlin, dining with an up-and-coming cartoonist and theatre designer, eating spicy Hungarian food, watching the boats on the Spree.

'You look so happy,' Johnny said suddenly. 'Some women seem to think it's beneath their dignity to seem as if they were having fun.'

Amy gestured at her surroundings. 'I come from a tiny village. It's still like a dream sometimes to find myself here.' She felt not quite in control, as if the single glass of wine she'd drunk had gone straight to her head.

'I come from a rabbit warren in Moabit. I can't believe I'm sitting here with a modish English lady.' A crooked smile lent irony to his words. To her relief, he made no mention of love and desire. She was not in the right frame of mind to stand on dignity or take instant moral decisions.

As the meal drew towards its close, Johnny said, 'I live near here. We could take coffee at my place if you liked . . . You've never been there, have you?' he added disingenuously.

'No I never have.'

Now was the time to demur and claim she had appointments to keep. But she hadn't. And no one was expecting her. Amy decided to push the boundaries still further. She could have coffee with him. There was no harm in that. And she was intensely curious to see where he lived.

As they strolled toward the Kleiner Tiergarten, Amy was aware that she was being foolhardy. Barring Claudia perhaps, no one she knew – not even Laura – would condone this whim.

But a recklessness had invaded her. Righteous-living people, women especially, were hemmed in at every turn by small, senseless restrictions. And today she felt like defying all that, doing what *she* wanted. Her mind made a sudden connection. Walking arm in arm with Johnny was like wandering the streets with Paul Oates, her childhood sweetheart, something she'd longed and longed to do. But the modest ambition trailed an aura of madness, badness, sheer unthinkability. The mere request would have stirred up a whirlwind of hysteria.

Johnny retained the helpfully neutral disposition he'd worn all day, as if her decision were perfectly unremarkable.

'That's it.' He pointed to a handsome, solid, yellow-grey building with balconies that overlooked the park. 'Second floor.'

Vaguely Amy had expected a scruffy bachelor apartment, with an unmade bed, unwashed cups, piles of drawings everywhere. But Johnny's living room was tidy and modern, with a large table, a businesslike drawing-board, parquet flooring, a couple of Bauhaus-looking rugs, curtains hand-blocked with an abstract black and yellow design, shifting in a slight breeze from the long windows that led out on to a wrought-iron balcony.

'This is charming.'

'Don't sound so surprised.'

'Do I?' A smiling apology.

'I make good coffee too. My mother showed me how. I always take her a packet when I visit.'

He disappeared into a communal kitchen on the floor below. She heard the crank of a coffee-grinder. After a while he reappeared with a tray holding a coffeepot, cups, sugar, cream.

The coffee *was* excellent and they drank it sitting by the open window on two plain wooden chairs, looking out on tree-tops, blue sky and drifting white clouds. The conversation was desultory. A question mark hovered between them now as to the next step. What would happen when the coffee had been drunk? In spite of the illusion that had gripped her briefly the other day in the boat, Amy could not really believe she would do anything but take her leave and go.

Johnny stood up. He seemed restless. Amy drained her second cup. As he took it from her their eyes met.

'You're right,' he said. 'You *are* too pale to wear red. You ought to look like a scarlet woman, but it doesn't work . . . You're more of a vestal virgin . . .'

She gave a startled laugh.

Placing her cup on the table, he turned back to her. 'You're so . . . I'm stunned by you.' The words fell heavily into silence. Almost immediately he pulled a face, assumed a satirical look of distaste. 'Why. on earth does the fellow have to ruin a perfectly pleasant day with his embarrassing love-talk?'

'That's not what I think.' Amy got to her feet and crossed the room. Without the tough, defensive smile that usually protected him, Johnny seemed vulnerable. Her instinct was to comfort him. She kissed him on the mouth, innocently like a child. Some muffled intuition told her he would value that above a more erotic appeal.

'Amy . . .' His voice was hoarse with emotion, doubt.

He seemed dazed as he pulled her close, awkward, like a boy taking his first woman in his arms. He squeezed her, patted her shoulder, as if demonstrating affection rather than any sexual intent.

Then gravely, deliberately, as if a pact were being sealed, he kissed her on the lips. 'I love you,' he told her seriously.

She embraced him again, but didn't feel capable of replying in kind.

Gradually his kisses became more insistent, his gestures more intimate, but he proceeded slowly, always giving her the opportunity to resist. But, without ever having framed a conscious decision, Amy knew there was no turning back.

And anxiously, at the back of her mind, the thought hovered that he mustn't find out the truth about Noel. Her husband must be protected from the curiosity of strangers, she was adamant about that. Even with their restricted sexual play, Amy was no longer technically a virgin. But now it was imperative she show no hesitation or alarm, that she take the novelty of penetration in her stride.

Meanwhile she was perfectly at home with the preliminaries. Amy caressed him, coolly and deliberately at first, in full possession of her sang-froid. But Johnny's mounting passion affected her, like a titillating mirror-image at first, then with her own hot, gathering excitement. The feel of his penis hardening beneath her hand made her breathless with half-fearful anticipation.

'Come next door,' he murmured huskily.

Like a sleepwalker she went with him through a doorway into a small side-room that was almost filled by a big, old-fashioned bed, with a carved headboard, a worn and rustic-looking flowered eiderdown, quite different from the spare modernity next door. Johnny pulled curtains across the windows to shut out the sunshine. The muted light was intimate, private, suggestive.

His face had taken on a heavy, glazed look. She stood passively offering her body as, through her dress, his hands caressed her breasts, buttocks, brushed her pubic mound.

'Take this off.'

Blindly she unbuttoned the red dress, slipped it over her head. He growled softly, lustfully at the sight of her in lace-trimmed cami- sole and knickers, silk stockings to mid-thigh.

'Come and lie down.'

Sliding in beside her under the eiderdown, he wore only his own undergarments. He kissed her softly as his hands languorously explored her body, slipped between her legs, finding a way beneath the silk underwear. He caressed her as Noel did until she was weak and wet with arousal.

Smoothly he shrugged off the eiderdown, removed his clothes. His body was slighter than Noel's, wirier. She had never seen an erect penis. Dark and engorged it reared, half threatening, seemingly with a life of its own. Without more ado he kneeled astride her, probed with his fingers, pushed into her with the blunt baton of flesh. Ready as she was it took an effort and he gasped with the sensation of being so tightly enclosed.

His entrance completed, he braced himself for a moment above her, gazing down into her face as if contemplating some longed-for possession.

'I've got you.' His voice rustled into the silence, silky and almost malevolent.

Then, slowly and sensuously – as if willing her to share in the languor of each separate stroke – he began to thrust. As she moved with him, tentatively, experimentally, Amy was flooded by an incredulous and slowly mounting elation. So this was it, this was what it was like. The deep, visceral, probing rhythm stirred sensations that gathered and bloomed inside her and which – enhanced by the newness, the wondering excitement – found release in a sudden, startling orgasm.

'Christ.' He was awed by her response. And the rhythm of his movements changed, became faster and more forceful. She was trans- fixed by the rising tension she could sense in his body, the blind, convulsive violence of his thrusting, culminating in a climax that

emerging from the shadow of his wife, keen to try his luck with a sexual escapade or two.

'Mind you, there's something about the masculine one . . .'

Alberich was becoming an irritant with his wishful thinking, the remorseless way he insisted on assessing the potential of every woman he saw. Johnny bit his tongue. He'd been on the point of retorting that neither Claudia nor Anneliese would give the young communist, with his hungry eyes and weedy beard, the time of day.

One of the articles of faith Alberich had absorbed from his years in the KPD was the concept that sex was no more meaningful than a drink of water. He repeated this platitude *ad nauseam*. Once Johnny might have been inclined to agree with him, but nowadays he knew the adage to be so much shit.

'Come over here, darling . . .' Alberich was murmuring in silky tones. He'd turned his attention back to Claudia. He flashed Johnny a foolish, pissed grin, which Johnny ignored.

Under normal circumstances Alberich's tipsy desires might have amused him. He would have egged him on, got involved. But recently he'd no patience with such lumbering. Johnny felt his skin stretched tight, his nerves painfully exposed. The reason was Amy.

He'd never had emotions that he couldn't control, not since school-days when his temper used to get him into fights. But his obsession with Amy tossed him like a cork on a stormy sea – like a woman, he might once have said – from ecstasy to despair, via every shade of feeling in between.

He was hopelessly addicted to her elegant white body, her hair, her smell, her voice, her tender but unnervingly self-possessed smile. That smile tormented him, seeming to signal that she didn't need him, not really, that she would never really be his.

Slumped in the corner of Anneliese's settee, Johnny stared dully ahead of him, but it was the pictures in his head that were the compelling ones. Visions of Amy, as she might look tonight, in a black lace dress, at some cliquish journalists' thrash, squired by her tall, handsome, arrogant husband – Johnny had seen him once at the theatre. Distributing her precious smiles, flirting a little, untroubled by thoughts of what *he* might be doing. Johnny was just her lover, with his allotted space, simply one piece in the jigsaw that formed her life. While he *lived* for the intoxication of seeing her, holding her, plunging himself into her lithe little body.

'God, you're a bore tonight.' Alberich hauled himself up from the settee, and ambled off through the crowd in search of booze and a woman to seduce.

It wasn't that Johnny didn't fight his fixation, using ploys that had always worked in the past. He tried to unsettle Amy by dropping the names of other women. But it seemed she knew and accepted his philandering reputation and didn't expect him to change. Which was ironic because, ever since he'd started his affair with her, ever since he'd met her, in fact, Johnny had simply had no eyes for any other woman.

For his own peace of mind he tried to degrade the wide-eyed image he found so appealing and so unique. It was an illusion, he told himself. She liked to fuck as much as anyone, was as hot as any other woman. She sucked his cock, kneeled on all fours like a bitch in heat waiting to be served. This was the malign litany he repeated over and over inside his head.

But somehow his vision of Amy remained untouched by these attempts at denigration. After their lovemaking, she would wash, dress in her soft clothes, brush her childishly pale hair and turn to him with a smile as tender and touching as a virgin, her whole-someness restored in his eyes. And he would embrace her gratefully, smell the soap on her skin, kiss her unpainted mouth, enslaved as before by her clear grey eyes, her sincerity and sweetness.

Enslaved was not too strong a word. It scared him. Tonight he had drunk far too much in an effort to blot from his mind the sheer . . . abjectness of his situation. Adoring a woman who belonged to someone else. It ran diametrically counter to the image he'd carried of himself through all his adult life. As exploiter, never exploited. Heart-whole. Heart*less*.

Sometimes at night, to his shame, Johnny lay spreadeagled, pressing his body into the mattress as if it were a liferaft, marooned in endless black space, annihilated by the terror of losing Amy.

'Hello, stranger.' Claudia stood above him wearing her cowgirl outfit. In the festive, red-tinted lighting, her expression struck him as deliberately opaque as if, like his own, her thoughts were too private and painful to be revealed.

Strings of tiny red and silver lanterns crisscrossed the ceiling of the Krells' long living room. A tall, silver-hung Christmas tree stood in one corner. It was nearly midnight. Two maids were circulating with trays of tall champagne glasses, which shone and caught the light, reflected the lazy flickering of the fire.

'Champagne time, everybody,' Laura was calling, vivid and flustered with her red hair, high colour, hooked nose, rainbow-coloured dress. 'Has everyone got a glass?'

There was a general murmur of assent as the bronze and glass wall-clock began to strike.

Amy felt enfolded by the universal expectant warmth. Noel had his arm round her shoulder. Momentarily she leaned into him, catching the eye of Carrie, his sister, and smiling. Carrie stood hand in hand with Gerald, her young man. In a drift of pleasure Amy pictured Vicki, waving to them as they left for the party, wearing her red dressing gown and holding her Charlie Chaplin doll, standing in the doorway with Lise Ackermann, one of their landlord's likeable daughters.

Across the room her eyes picked out stocky Henry Bowen making some remark to Laura, something risqué most likely, from the look on her face. Roy Anderson, another of Noel's fellow correspondents, swigged unsteadily from a whisky bottle. Art Krell raised his glass to Amy in affectionate dumb show. Surrounded by faces she knew, Amy felt moved. It was good to have your own place in the world on New Year's Eve.

At the twelfth chime of the clock a hubbub of good wishes broke out, a round of hugging and toasting and champagne drinking.

'Carrie darling, happy 1925!' Amy embraced her sister-in-law.

'The ladies, I love 'em.' Broad and curly-haired, expansively drunk, Gerald enfolded them both in his robust arms. 'May you achieve everything your little hearts desire in the coming year.'

'Likewise I'm sure.' Amy kissed his rubicund cheek.

Then she was face to face with Noel's dear, familiar features. Amy embraced him with special tenderness. She loved him and was betraying him – the world would say – though her betrayal made her love and prize him more.

'Year Seven begins,' he said simply. It was the anniversary of their meeting. His eyes met hers with affection and trust. 'And I'm happier with you than I've ever been.'

'Happy New Year, my darling.' She hugged him, loving and knowing herself loved while, at the back of her mind, Johnny's irreverent eyes looked on, his passion for her enhancing everything she possessed, investing it all with a vibrant magic.

'My turn.' Laura appeared beside them, her chic, beaky face animated by the general euphoria.

Noel laid his two hands on her floaty chiffon shoulders. 'Got you, my proud beauty. Kiss me, woman.'

Chapter Twenty-eight

A scent of tobacco wafted in from outside. Beyond the drawn curtains of Johnny's room the sun was shining. Voices came and went, floating on the warm June air. While inside he lay silently with Amy in his arms. His body enclosed hers almost totally. Their warmth and sweat combined, smoothing her skin to unearthly softness. She was asleep, or almost, but he lived every moment of their intimacy. These hours with Amy were the focus of his week.

'Nearly four.' It occurred to him to lie, to keep her with him for longer. Soon she'd be gone and he would be left with waiting, his life suspended, while she lived hers elsewhere.

'I'll have to be going soon.' She linked her arms round his neck, snuggled her naked body closer into his, triggering a new flicker of arousal. He slid his hand across her belly and between her thighs.

'No.' She stopped him. 'There's no time.'

A hot rush of anger swept through him at the control she had over their time together. He was free, he had all the time in the world. She set limits. But deliberately he doused his annoyance. She would leave in any case, and he'd no desire to live out the long week ahead with bad blood between them.

After a while she slipped silently from bed. He watched as she set about resuming her public face, washing in a bowl patterned with roses and forget-me-nots that used to belong to his mother. In the filtered light Amy resembled a Bonnard nude. Lilac soap scented the room.

Watching this process was a visual and sensual feast, part of the ritual of their meetings. But increasingly his pleasure was tainted by a creeping sense of stalemate – together they were going nowhere and one day, some day, their relationship would just stop. And, after

Amy had gone home, the despondency would stay with him, and he would have to go out and be with other people, act the clown, or the wretchedness would colonize his soul.

'I could hate you so easily.' He spoke lightly, though inside a vehemence welled. 'Just a small shift in emphasis. That's all it would take.'

Pulling on her stockings, she gave him an amused, exasperated glance. 'What harm have I ever done you?'

'You do me harm every moment.' Again, a tone of amiable malice.

Amy shrugged with ironic impatience. They'd had all this out before. She had a child, was part of a family. That meant, if he couldn't accept her terms, she would be forced to break with him. There was no ambiguity in the situation.

Swiftly she pulled on a blue-green dress, slipped on her shoes, unhooked her straw hat from the peg behind the door. She crossed to the bed and kissed him gently, seriously, then kissed him again as if overcome by a private wave of tenderness.

'Look at you.' She stood up and gazed down at him, bare-chested above the coverlet. Her expression was both mocking and vulnerable. 'You're such a poisonous little . . . I do love you, Johnny.'

He was moved. She'd never permitted herself to say it before.

As she left Johnny's flat that afternoon and walked alone through the sunny alleys of the Kleiner Tiergarten, Amy's mind was free to return to the secret she had kept to herself for almost a week now, approaching it cautiously like a dangerous beast.

It was time to confront it. She would speak to Noel that very evening. Amy was dying inside. But resigned too, since it had to be done. She would say the words and they would change her world.

The sun shone on her bare arms. A breeze lifted her hair and ruffled her skirt. With it came the spicy, evocative scent of some Mediterranean shrub. Each small, separate pleasure was sharp and perfect. It felt like the golden age before the fall.

* * *

Amy was already in her night things when Noel came upstairs.

'I've got to talk to you, seriously,' she announced.

He found her earnestness touching and smiled. He turned and stood in front of the dressing table, arms folded, to demonstrate that she had his full attention. 'What's this all about?'

'It'll come as a shock,' she warned.

He smiled again, feeling like her father. 'Fire away.'

'I've been sleeping with someone. I'm expecting his baby.' His wife's tone was even, neither cowed nor defiant.

Behind her the open window showed a summer night sky. Amy sat on the bed, on the crochet linen coverlet, arms circling her knees. She looked steadily at him, waiting for his response. Noel stood there stupidly. What she said made no sense.

'I'll understand . . .' Amy was husky and cleared her throat. 'I'll understand if you want to leave me.'

Confronting him was the familiar loved image of his young wife. Grey eyes, pale hair above the girlish blue nightgown. His thoughts could not keep pace with the statements Amy was offering. She was in possession of some piece of knowledge which he, too, must try to come to grips with.

'How long has . . . ?' He groped after facts. Facts were something to hang on to.

'Since last September.'

He was still numbed. Yet there was incredulity. All that time. How could he not have suspected?

'Who is he?'

She shrugged. 'His name's Johann. He's one of Claudia's friends.'

Mention of Claudia produced a gut reaction. He'd always felt – obscurely – that she was trouble.

'Bloody Claudia.'

'What d'you mean?'

'I might have guessed she'd be involved somewhere.'

Amy stared. 'You think this is somehow Claudia's doing? If I'd broken with her . . .' She shook her head, sarcastic, unbelieving. 'You must think I'm . . . Noel, I make my own decisions.'

'How laudable.'

His icy hostility hung in the silence between them.

Amy inclined her head. 'I did wrong. Only . . .'

'Only what?'

'Only . . .' She hesitated. 'Look. I was curious. I wanted to know what it was like . . .'

In an instant her admission resurrected the old gnawing pain which recently had been all but dormant. Their happiness was so palpable he'd been half convinced that his impotence really didn't matter to her. That a child and family were all she needed. What a bloody fool.

'Curious!' He spat the word.

'Not just that. He was . . . He wanted me, he made it very clear, and . . .'

Noel guessed she'd been about to say that she wanted him, and the old goading, maddening images he'd smothered burst through the thin membrane of balance and sanity he had managed to impose, returning in full virulence. His wife's tender body impaled on a rod-like penis, her face twisted in anguished pleasure. The vision re-entered his bloodstream like a poison.

And the craven anxiety recurred. 'Did you tell him about me?'

'No.' Her answer came pat. He read contempt in her eyes. Real or imagined. Noel reflected that he could fabricate all the moral indignation in the world but the fact remained that, in the most visceral sense, he had failed her.

'I'm not trying to excuse myself.' Amy dropped her eyes for a moment, then looked searchingly at him. 'I just want to make it clear that it's you and Vicki who are the important ones to me. Being with Johann made me appreciate that. If anything it's made me love you better –'

Brutally Noel interrupted. 'Not that shit!'

He was invaded by a surge of murderous anger. He couldn't breathe. Noel bore down on his wife, sitting so demurely on the bed, with a confused need to rout her composure. He seized her by the shoulders and shook her, back and forth, back and forth. Then he slapped out at the angelic, treacherous face, sent Amy toppling backward, hitting her head against the wall. He experienced a savage satisfaction in the ungainly sprawl of her body.

But her dazed eyes focused suddenly on something behind him. He turned to see Vicki standing in the doorway. She was barefoot in her nightgown and carried her Chaplin doll. Her face was expressionless, her eyes huge.

Already Amy had struggled to her feet. Swiftly she crossed the room, stooped, and picked the child up in her arms. 'Come along, sweetheart. I'll take you back to bed.'

For days they hardly spoke. Noel couldn't bear to look at the smiling, innocent photographs of his wife on the walls and desk of his study. He was rarely at home. And Amy took Vicki to the zoo, to the fair, to the cinema to distract her, no doubt, from the memory of her loving father attacking her kind and gentle mother.

He was tortured by the notion that his candid child-wife – not that exactly, but something only a little removed – had it in her to collude with another man in sexual deception. The torment of that thought was beyond everything. Perhaps he might have borne it if she had wept and begged forgiveness, expiated her sin with humility and remorse. That, if he were honest, was what he would have expected. Then again, Amy had always claimed that the vision he had of her was sentimental and wrong. And finally the accusation began to make a glimmer of sense, since Amy remained subdued – but calm and gallingly unbowed – concentrating her attention on Vicki.

Meanwhile, in the solitude of his office in the Leipzigerstrasse, Noel continued with his analysis of the first two months in office of the new President of the Weimar Republic, the veteran soldier, von Hindenburg. Methodically he conducted telephone interviews with government officials, checked and cross-checked facts, while inside his pain smouldered and flickered and flared like a corrosive ulcer.

One night he arrived home late to find Amy still up and reading in the darkened living room, under the glow of a standard lamp. She looked up. He ignored her.

After some moments of silence she asked quietly, 'What's going to happen to us?'

'You tell me.'

'I'd like us to carry on.'

The look he gave her was closed and sceptical.

'We can, I think. I've hurt you and it'll be different. But there can still be love between us . . . And there's Vicki.'

'You'll get rid of that brat.' He nodded towards her belly.

Her reply was prompt and certain. 'No. I won't do that.'

'Then there's no point in even discussing . . .'

She stood up, shrugged her shoulders, and crossed to the door. 'At least give it some thought.'

Even later Noel summoned the energy to pour himself some gin. He drank it neat to ease the tension and misery that knotted his guts. The burning liquid seemed to scald away the bile that had clenched his stomach for more than a week, bringing a brutish relief. The green glass bottle stood near him on a low table and he poured himself another large slug of the spirit.

He had the illusion that he was sitting here alone in the small hours of the morning, having divorced Amy, that he was pouring booze down himself to still despair and loneliness rather than betrayal. It occurred to him that he could punish his wife by getting custody of their child. Amy was, after all, the guilty party. But, even at first glance, the revenge seemed shabby to him and, in his heart of hearts, he knew Vicki needed Amy more.

And he *would* be lonely. The loosening of his body prompted a dour mental honesty he hadn't allowed himself until then. What woman worth having would give time to a lover who couldn't get it up? Yet Amy knew the worst and was prepared to stay. Amy, who made all other women look earthbound and ordinary. Along with Vicki, his darling daughter.

Mechanically he lifted his glass, downing another large swallow of the healing gin, but grimacing now at the taste. It came to him that it would be so simple to pass this new brat off as his own . . .

Carefully Noel put down his glass, leaned back in his chair and closed his eyes, sitting boneless and vacant as a rag-doll in the pool of lamplight. What time was it? He couldn't move.

He heard the click of the door. Amy appeared in her nightdress, tousled and heavy-eyed. She sat down beside him, put her arms round his body, laid her head on his chest.

'I can't sleep. I need you. Come to bed.'

Chapter Twenty-nine

❮❮❮❯❯❯

Claudia sat on the terrace of the Café Josty, staring into a florid cup of hot chocolate, decorated with whorls of whipped cream. It was her breakfast. A note from Amy had brought her here, dragged her out of bed inconveniently early – she'd been up until well into the small hours. The note had been terse and scrawled, uninformative. Claudia was irritated.

And Amy was late. Claudia glanced disinterestedly at the mid-morning bustle of the Potsdamerplatz. Her friend's choice of rendez-vous was inexplicable. No one she knew ever came here.

Claudia had avoided Amy for some weeks and wasn't looking forward to seeing her now. The Englishwoman's beauty had come to provoke in her a kind of superstitious dread. As if, simply by being herself, Amy could have anything she wanted, airily, carelessly, taking from others without even noticing. Her friend's child, her friend's lover, both had been appropriated with the same wide-eyed charm.

Her rancour was irrational, Claudia knew that. She'd been only too pleased to have Vicki taken off her hands, she'd assured Amy that Johnny was nothing to her. So she had no logical cause for grievance. But resentment simmered and festered of its own accord and there was nothing she could do about it.

On the corner of the Leipzigerstrasse a slim, blonde figure alighted from a tram. She recognized the sea-green dress and matching straw hat as Amy's, watched her coming without the gladness she would once have felt. Amy entered through the arch that led to the terrace and looked about her. Claudia was struck by how drawn she looked, how tired and defeated. There were rings under her eyes, a blister at the corner of her mouth, a nerviness in her movements.

264

'What on earth's the matter?'

Amy sank into the chair opposite. 'Everything.' She made a deprecating gesture. 'Everything.'

A ray of unworthy hope lit up Claudia's curiosity. 'Something to do with Johnny?'

'Partly that. Claudia, I'd like a real drink. I need it.'

'Brandy?'

'Fine.'

She looked affectionately at Claudia. 'I'm so pleased to see you.' Reaching out and taking her hand across the table-top. 'It seems to have been ages.'

'It is ages.' Claudia reflected ruefully that it was easier to warm to a friend who was clearly down on her luck, than one dancing through her own blinkered and triumphant reality. 'Tell me all about it. How's Noel anyway?'

'He's in England, trying to arrange for a transfer back to London.'

'Oh.' A few moments earlier Claudia would have met this news with unmixed relief. But the situation was clearly more complicated than she had imagined. She ordered a brandy from a passing waiter, then turned back to Amy and waited for her explanation.

'This is secret.' Amy regarded her wearily. 'But I know I can trust you.'

'Yes.'

'I'm pregnant.'

'Whose child?'

Amy was adamant. 'Johnny's.'

'You're very sure.' The ghost of a smile.

'There's no doubt.' Amy had claimed she couldn't have children. But her manner discouraged further questioning.

Her brandy arrived. She lifted the glass, took a long, reflective sip and then another. The calming effect of the drink was visible, though Amy made no play of its effect. She replaced the almost empty glass on the table and gave a crooked smile.

'I don't want to go home,' she said. 'I've always thought of England as a judgemental place. I don't feel that here.'

Claudia grinned. 'You should live with my aunt and her landlady.'

'I know. I've been lucky in the people I've met. You and your friends . . . and Johnny.'

'Does he know about the child?'

'No, and I'm not going to tell him.' A pause. 'Quite understandably, Noel doesn't want me to communicate with him any more.'

'Poor Johnny.'

Amy responded gently, 'Poor Noel.'

'He's agreed to adopt the child?'

'Yes.'

'That might be difficult. Don't you think?'

'I've made it clear I'm not prepared to live as a penitent, forever atoning for my sins.' Amy's eyes were steady and she spoke with contained intensity. 'If he accepts the situation, it's because – under the circumstances – it's best for him as well. Not because he's magnanimous . . . But I think I owe it to him to go home. Away from Johnny, I suppose. Start a new chapter.'

Claudia was quietly impressed by Amy's hard-headed summary of the situation, but she had doubts. She'd seen how much Noel adored and trusted his wife. Could he really settle for something more tepid and compromised?

'Noel's done extraordinarily well here.' Amy turned her empty glass nervously between her fingers. 'I'm certain Delane will rush to offer him an advantageous new niche.' Her voice had a dying fall.

'I think I'll join you in a brandy,' Claudia decided suddenly.

Two more glasses were brought to their table. After a few sips Claudia felt a little odd. The spirits mingled uneasily in her stomach with the rich chocolate drink, and she was privately amused by a ripple of shocked interest in herself and Amy from a group of solid burghers at a neighbouring table.

With the brandy in her bloodstream she felt confiding. 'I'm almost pleased you're taking Vicki away. When I see her I feel far too much for her.'

'I'm glad there are some advantages in . . . But I'll keep in touch, and send you news and photographs.'

'You must. Really you must.'

'And we'll meet again some day. When all this has died down and we're proper, sensible grown-ups.'

'Yes. Except we'll never be sensible grown-ups.'

'I'm afraid I'm going to have to be.'

A silence. Claudia saw that there were tears in Amy's eyes. 'Please tell Johnny I had to go. Tell him I love him.' Her cheeks were wet now.

'I will.' She had a sudden urge to confide in Amy, to confess her own feelings for Johnny, but the words died on her lips.

'I do love Noel. He and Vicki are my life.' Amy wiped her eyes and tried to smile but it ended in a wan grimace. 'But Johnny was subversive. He was special. My timid venture outside the rules. And, God, I'll miss that.'

Amy's crestfallen tears touched Claudia's heart, calling forth as if at the touch of a button the old affectionate friendship. Her sympathy was quick and poignant and absolutely sincere. At the same time she was washed with a flood of relief at the thought that this invincible rival would shortly be gone.

Chapter Thirty

'Stay with me tonight.' Johnny was incapable of pleading, but Claudia recognized the black urgency behind his request.

She was vexed. There were things she had to do in the morning. It would be far more convenient for her to return home.

'Won't you, Claudi?'

Claudia hesitated. As usual she had dropped in to see how he was and to keep him company for a while, echoing the concern all his friends were feeling. She knew he was taking advantage, but understood the vastness and intensity of his desolation.

'All right. I'll stay . . . But this can't go on.' As ever, she found it impossible to refuse him. Johnny's disarray touched her in a way no one else's ever could.

Though he was depressing company. Once upon a time, when friends called, he'd delighted in brewing good coffee, regaling them with gossip, sceptical and humorous. Nowadays he sat, dirty and unshaven, on one of his modern, streamlined, uncomfortable chairs, smoking cigarette after cigarette, talking only desultorily, his remarks interspersed with long periods of sullen silence. Amy was never mentioned, but her presence filled the room like an angel of doom.

He'd done no work for weeks. He seemed in shock, vacant and apathetic. In company he ignored the conversations that buzzed around him. But it appeared to Claudia that he was locked in a never-ending internal dialogue with Amy, and with himself.

And there were times, like tonight, when he couldn't face the emptiness of being alone. She knew that he would lie in her arms, clenched and despairing, until eventually the warmth of her body lulled him into fitful semi-sleep.

There was no question of sex between them. If there had been,

Claudia hoped she'd have the strength of will to reject him. Her sense of self rebelled against the indignity of being used as a pacifier, a blatant substitute.

Johnny looked across at her. His eyes made her think of a drowning man. 'You're a pal,' he said bleakly. 'A woman, but a pal.'

'Gracious as ever,' she replied.

In the latter part of 1925 Claudia was having a certain success with her singing. Her stage personality – a waiflike yet knowing presence, cynical, sassy and direct – had been honed and refined. She sported her trademark black beret and dark, stark dresses. Though for certain numbers she found it effective to adopt a disguise – a cowgirl outfit, a man's suit. Peter Eisler had supplied her with further songs and, almost to her surprise, she'd even written a couple herself.

Claudia had gathered her own public, nothing huge, but the kind of audience she aspired to, sophisticated and discerning, people whose opinions she respected. On the strength of her following at Bärbel she was offered a number of appearances at the *Kabarett der Komiker* on the Kurfürstendamm, and her reviews were, on the whole, gratifyingly enthusiastic.

But Claudia was deeply disappointed that Johnny, who for years had pressed her to try her luck as a chanteuse, was now far too embroiled in his own suffering to rejoice in her good fortune.

In early December she ran into her old friend, Rosa Edelmann, opposite the Anhalter Bahnhof. She looked impressively prosperous in a modish monkey-fur coat, her frizzy hair blonder than it used to be and tamed into artificial curls.

Rosa was enjoying her own, far more mainstream success, singing with the Manfred Biene Orchestra and broadcasting on the radio every Thursday evening. Privately Claudia despised her material – sentimental tosh for drunks to sing along with, full of *Gemütlichkeit* and edelweiss. She doubted that Rosa, slum-kid that she was, had ever seen an edelweiss in her life. In her turn Rosa clearly had no time for Claudia's pretentious cult status.

All the same it was amusing to see her and reminisce ruefully

269

about talent nights at the *Seeräuber* and never having two pfennigs to rub together.

'How's Franz?' Claudia asked after Rosa's brother.

'He's working in Munich. Walks, talks and dreams politics.'

'Used to be a bit of a communist, didn't he?'

Rosa pulled a droll, pop-eyed face. 'Better not let *him* hear you say that. He hates the *Kozis* now. He's with those National . . . Can't remember the whole rigmarole. He worships that Hitler fellow.'

'Fancy.' Claudia was not particularly interested. She knew the name. Johnny had mentioned the man in terms of deep loathing, whereas Bruno Berg half approved of him, she seemed to recall, though in an amused and patronizing fashion. 'Got to rush. Good to see you, Rosa. Remember me to Franz.'

In February 1926 Claudia heard that Amy and Noel had a new baby daughter. They had christened her Grace.

By then Johnny had left Berlin. For Paris initially, but later – over months and even years – she received occasional cards from Nice, Rome, Madrid. He was living rough, Johnny said, paying his way by drawing caricatures. Later he wrote mysteriously that he'd met some generous friends. Claudia chose not to speculate. Johnny was nothing to do with her any more.

She was glad to shrug off the madness of her obsession with him. Claudia enjoyed the peace and pleasure of living on an even keel. She moved in with Sergei Rykov. They weren't in love, both agreed, but they were terribly fond of one another.

They rented a spacious flat, with a studio for Sergei, in a converted warehouse overlooking the Landwehrkanal. His sweet, equable nature seemed wrong for an artist, but his increasingly abstract paintings were well regarded. To the amusement of their friends they were featured as a couple in the popular illustrated *Querschnitt*.

'Two common or garden maggots transformed into the chic-est of butterflies by the magic wand of publicity,' Peter mocked.

'Hark at him.' Claudia grinned at Sergei. 'Isn't he just pulsating with envy!'

But Peter was prospering too. The songs he'd written had brought him to the attention of a film producer. The minor mogul had been smitten by one of the many neglected screenplays languishing in Peter's desk drawer and, after some frustrating delays, the project was going ahead. It would be a sound production and Claudia would sing a song over the opening credits and again later in a nightclub scene.

The job seemed to encapsulate her current enviable status. She'd been chosen particularly, because of a special quality that was perceived in her, for work of an original and avant-garde nature. No compromise involved. None of the drawbacks of unmanageable fame.

Bruno Berg was huge now. It was impossible to open a magazine without coming face to face with his handsome, soft, evasive features. In interviews he was becoming increasingly open about his nationalistic tendencies, the more so since the new proprietor of UFA films was the ultra-conservative millionaire, Alfred Hugenberg.

'For years,' Bruno declared frequently, 'love, honour and patriotism have been dirty words. But I detect the turning of the tide . . .'

Although Claudia found it hard to equate the professed old-fashioned decency of his views with the actor's taste in women. His present lover, Franziska, was a glossy, macabre creature with expensive tastes and no visible means of support. For publicity purposes she promenaded a young leopard on a chain and affected lipstick in a shade Claudia had always thought of as heart-attack purple.

She and Sergei spent an evening at Franziska's apartment once. She offered cocaine and became quite volatile, reciting poems by Rilke and George in an overwrought fashion. Bruno was clearly embarrassed though far too loyal to say anything.

His loyalty extended to Claudia too. Fixed in his mind was the sentimental conviction that, as a young actor arriving from the provinces, he'd been welcomed by Claudia, guided by her through the hostile and baffling urban maze. She was the only one, so he claimed, from among the ranks of the pretentious, egotistical, sneering artistes of Berlin to bother with him at all.

'I'll never forget your kindness to me, Claudi,' he confided,

271

moist-eyed, after a day's filming, when the star made it his habit to drink a democratic glass of beer with technicians and cast.

As far as Claudia was concerned the cherished memory was purest fantasy, but she didn't contradict him. Bruno Berg was a useful ally.

One evening in the autumn of 1928, at the Schiffbauerdamm Theatre, Claudia glimpsed Noel Campion edging his way between the seats towards his place four rows in front of her. From Amy's letters she knew that he still came to Berlin often. Both of them were there to see the hit show of the season, the Brecht–Weill version of *The Threepenny Opera*.

He looked older, she thought, his cheeks more lined and hollow, grey strands shining in his rough fair hair. It suited him, as if he were still growing into his looks. Noel must be veering towards his late thirties.

She arranged her face in an expression of eager amiability and willed him to look her way. He did glance across the rows of seats, as if scanning the auditorium for familiar faces. Claudia was half convinced that he saw her, but their eyes did not meet. He took his place and from then on gazed resolutely in the direction of the stage. She decided not to approach him.

Chapter Thirty-one

How long was it since she'd visited Tante Agathe? At least two months, Claudia reckoned. She'd been neglectful. Her aunt could be aggravating, but she had a good heart. And with Rudi away at school in Wilhelmshaven she often felt lonely.

Claudia shivered. Her feet were wet with slush and, in the freezing wind, even her wool coat was inadequate. On her way to catch the tram she passed the Tänzerin Café on the Kurfürstendamm. Cheerful, artificial light shone from its plate-glass frontage, the café's clientele appeared rosy and warm. Claudia used to frequent the Tänzerin and even now she rarely went there without encountering a sprinkling of acquaintances.

Agathe would have to wait a little longer. Claudia had a sudden longing for a hot drink, a one-mark *Frühstuck*. They would fortify her against the petty irritations of her aunt and Frau Kästner.

A blast of warmth hit her as she entered the café. What luxury to stew in this fug for twenty minutes or so and feel her fingers and toes coming back to life. She looked about her to see if she recognized anyone.

'Claudia.' An unemphatic voice from her left. She turned her head.

Johnny sat alone at a table for two. On the brown linen cloth stood a pot of coffee, a plate with the remains of a hearty breakfast.

He was pale and unshaven, but seemed otherwise prosperous in a heavy overcoat of herringbone tweed and thick-soled shoes. The dense, dull brown hair sprang from his hairline with its old vitality. A single lock hung down over his brow. His features resurged as if from a dream, vivid and intensely familiar, bony, foxy, the brown eyes amused.

It was like seeing a ghost. She approached his table. 'Are you real?'

He grasped her stiff, cold hand and held it in his warm fingers. 'Solid enough for you?' Then, with a smile, 'Won't you join me for breakfast?'

She sat down. 'How long have you been back?' It was no conventional enquiry. She was dazed.

'What difference does it make? Not long.' He gazed at her affectionately. 'Believe me, Claudi, it's good to see you. You're about the only thing I've missed . . . When I thought about Berlin it was your sharp little eyes I saw.'

The assertion filled her with craven gratitude. Quickly she changed the subject. 'You must tell me all about what you've been doing. The cards you sent were so runic.'

He shrugged, perverse as ever. 'I can't stand travellers' tales. Not listening *or* telling. It'll all come out by and by.'

Claudia ordered her breakfast from Georg, the waiter with the Nietzsche moustache who'd worked at the Tänzerin for years.

When he'd gone Johnny said, 'I hear you're with Sergei Rykov.'

A treacherous part of her wanted to disown him, to point to the expediency of their relationship. But she wouldn't sink that low. 'Yes, for nearly two years.'

'I hate couples,' Johnny said. 'They dilute one another.'

'I'd forgotten how loutish you were.'

He grinned as if at a compliment.

'What's it like to be back?' she asked, as Georg brought her coffee and a roll, soft scrambled eggs with chopped bacon in an earthenware bowl.

'I've been to some beautiful places but . . .' A twisted smile. 'In the end ugly people need their own familiar ugliness. Their own comfortable mediocrity.'

'What do you mean? You're not ugly. Berlin's not ugly.'

'Yes it is. But it's the ugliness I grew up with.' He glanced towards the window, at the pedestrians outside, heads ducked against a flurry of stinging snow. 'Look at those faces and tell me Berlin's not ugly. In the South you don't see faces like that.'

She laughed incredulously. 'Those faces are all twisted with the cold.'

'Berlin's ugly. Believe me.'

She sensed an irrational anger underlying his words and again changed the subject. 'What are you going to do? *Der Freibeuter*'s folded, so I hear.'

'I can do better than *Der Freibeuter*, I think.' He looked at her with cool conviction. 'I've gone beyond them.' He bent and patted a portfolio stashed beside his chair. 'I've been in Italy. I've got a set of drawings from there. Of the bastard fascists. At the risk of sounding conceited . . . They're good. They deserve better than *Der Freibeuter*.'

As he met up again with his former friends, Johnny's confident bearing conveyed the unspoken message that he was fine again, that he was well and truly over Amy. Perhaps he'd convinced himself. But the more she saw of him, the clearer it became to Claudia that, in his soul, he still carried a whole network of unhealed scars.

In April 1929 – a couple of months after his return to Berlin – Ingeborg, Johnny's quiet and patient mother, died of emphysema. He'd loved her and was plagued by guilt.

'I shouldn't have gone away,' he told Claudia dourly. 'I could've made the last year of her life a hell of a lot better.'

'I'm sure she never begrudged you your freedom.'

'She loved me more than anyone. I should have taken more care of her.'

At the funeral party he insulted his father as a hypocrite who'd terrorized Ingeborg all his life and now had the gall to parade his crocodile tears. He rushed at Stefan, fists raised, and had to be dragged away by neighbours.

Later he confided to Claudia, 'He's been a bully all his life and I've hated him for it. But at the funeral I felt as if I'd become him – the bully – attacking this sad little old man.'

Ingeborg's death absolved Johnny of any remnant of responsibility towards the female sex. He gave his misogyny free rein, seized on any opportunity for anti-woman jibes, spoke casually of tarts and bitches.

Yet, incredibly, there seemed no shortage of willing victims, seduced by his brutality. Smiling and joking, with his wolfish grin and narrowed eyes, his caustic humour, Johnny's presence was magnetic. He was able to pick and choose among the young, pretty, self-destructive women that haunted the fringes of bohemia, sleeping with each new candidate only a few times before becoming bored, while they continued to moon after him with anxious, love-sick eyes.

For the sake of her own sanity Claudia was grateful for the barrier Sergei represented. Without him there she could easily have been sucked once more into the soul-destroying vortex of her passion for Johnny. As it was, she offered him friendship – an ironic, self-protective affection. But at night, when she and Sergei made love, it was Johnny's lean body and taut features that Claudia conjured up.

She remembered him, years ago, describing the resentment that festered beneath everything his father, Stefan, said or did. A resentment which would come to a head like a boil, break out in violence and fury. Now Claudia saw the same tendency in the son. A simmering anger was never far from the surface. Like volcanic unrest it could remain latent or erupt at the slightest provocation. His friends became wary, though once she'd spotted the danger Claudia was prepared to give as good as she got.

But, as far as Johnny's career was concerned, this anger stood him in good stead. His drawings were phosphorescent with concentrated loathing. The sketches of fascist thugs he'd brought with him from Italy proved, as Johnny had foretold, to be highly saleable.

Several periodicals vied for the right to reproduce them. In the end they appeared in *AIZ*, the widely read workers' illustrated. As a rule *AIZ* confined itself to photography. Graphic work was featured only in exceptional cases, so this was a significant fillip for Johnny, bringing him to the notice of a far broader public.

The times were jumpy and volatile. The bubble prosperity of the mid-twenties was showing signs of bursting. Unemployment was rising alarmingly. The corrupt and stodgy democratic government inspired merely indifference and contempt. Politics were becoming increasingly polarized.

The people with conviction were the extremists – the communists on the one hand, the nationalists on the other. And, surprisingly, the nationalist movement was coalescing round that unlikely raggle-taggle bunch of Bavarians, the National Socialists. Violence was in the air and on the streets. The rival factions sabotaged one another's demonstrations, fought running battles in the working-class districts of Berlin. People were killed.

The violence answered a need in Johnny and his malevolent cartoons matched the mood of the times. He had his own personal *bêtes noires*. One of these was the president, 'Papa' Hindenburg, with his white moustache and *Pickelhaube*, the complacent Father-of-the-People image he projected. Johnny drew his venerable features monstrously bloated with a mixture of vanity and senility.

But the main object of his vitriol was the Nazi movement. And, more than Hitler himself, he detested the caressingly sinister Joseph Goebbels, the so-called Gauleiter of Berlin who, with his genius for publicity and organization, had turned the party from a provincial rabble into a national phenomenon.

Johnny depicted him as a spaniel-eyed Machiavelli, parading his culture while fostering the vilest instincts in his thuggish followers. To his glee the upstart cartoonist found himself regularly vilified in Goebbels's propaganda-sheet, *Der Angriff*.

Johnny frequented obscure brownshirt bars incognito, observing the young Nazi faithful by way of research for his lampoons. It was clear he was addicted to the tang of unpredictable brutality that pervaded these locales. At times be courted danger, arguing with the clientele, attracting their hostility.

'You're mad,' Claudia told him. 'There's plenty wouldn't think twice about kicking you to death.'

A dismissive shrug. 'What better cause.'

One night in *Der Seeräuber* he happened on Franz Edelmann, Rosa's brother, drinking with a couple of companions-in-arms. Franz was back in Berlin now, a big wheel in the movement. Johann Kröger was recognized at once as the local boy who'd gone on to become the cartoonist Johnny, debunker of the National Socialists.

He beat a discreet retreat, but was chased through dark streets and alleyways by the three toughs. Only his knowledge of the district saved him. In the maze of grimy courtyards that separated the tenements one from another Johnny managed to give his pursuers the slip. He was exhilarated by the episode and recounted it to acquaintances as a famous joke.

Friends urged him to take more care. He was contemptuous. 'If you let those bastards have it all their own way you might as well be dead.'

'There's a difference between that and cocking a snook at murderers like a cheeky kid.' Claudia condemned, yet was perversely impressed by Johnny's foolhardiness. Though less so by the self-congratulatory swagger that surrounded his exploits.

His researches in bars bore fruit, providing the blueprint for his most popular character. Franzl – named impishly for Franz Edelmann – was a thick-necked, broad-shouldered, wooden-headed young Nazi thug who wore outsize boots and spouted the racial and political obscenities of his mentors like a well-trained parrot. His adventures appeared regularly in the satirical review, *Eulenspiegel*, and were rapturously received. Franzl's low intelligence and general muddle-headedness were the point of the satire. With punchy eagerness he bungled everything he did. The droll little cartoon cut the brutes down to size, offering victims and opponents of the movement small moments of delicious revenge.

'Dare you. Come for a drink at the *Seeräuber* now.'

Standing in the doorway of Alberich's ground-floor flat, saying his goodbyes, Johnny tossed the flippant challenge to his friend.

'No thanks.' Alberich pulled down the corners of his mouth. Adding, rather pompously, 'I'm a family man. Political action's one thing. But I can't afford to chuck away life and limb on a dare.'

He had a child now, a three-year-old girl with stern black eyes like Anna, her mother. For the first time Johnny found himself almost envying Alberich's married state. He and Anna had their dramas, but their alliance had its own solidarity. And Elli, their daughter, was engaging with her funny, solemn observations on life seen through her infant eyes.

Johnny grinned crookedly. 'Life and limb? Let's not exaggerate.'

'I'm not.'

Striding along the Limburgerstrasse, Johnny felt savage and confused. He felt an outsider. Time was passing. He was nearing thirty. For all he rejected the conventions of his upbringing, the subconscious, atavistic ticking of his life-clock was not so easily ignored. By thirty a man should have a woman of his own.

Yet none of his lovers corresponded to Johnny's image of a wife. None was like Ingeborg, domestic, selfless. And anyway – though he no longer yearned after that heartless angel-whore, Amy – she'd made it hard for him to concentrate on anyone for long. Apart from Giovanna in Rome, with her wealth and her schemes. But she'd had her own agenda, and it wasn't his.

Fifty metres in front of him the illuminated sign of *Der Seeräuber* twinkled – a pirate in a three-cornered hat and cuffed top boots. The place had gradually become an out-and-out brownshirt bar. The locals stayed away, intimidated by the cliquishness, the hard, rowdy laughter.

Wiry, wrinkled little Falke, the resident compere, was the Nazis' jester with his wolfish grin, the fund of anti-Jew jokes he'd conveniently acquired. Falke had lived in the district all his life, knew everyone, and made use of his favoured position with the new clientele to settle old scores.

As he approached the sign Johnny knew that he would turn into the piss-smelling stairwell that led down to the cellar bar. It was late and he was thirsty and a couple of drinks would take care of his state of mind. He recalled the dubious look on Alberich's face but was in a mood to tempt fate. Fear, possible aggression, had healing qualities of their own, making all else seem unimportant.

There weren't more than twenty customers in the gloomy, red-lit bar. Johnny noticed Falke, slight and ruddy in his leather jacket, sitting with a couple of younger men and a dark-haired girl with the kind of over-soft white flesh that didn't attract him. Falke must be getting on for seventy but looked canny as ever. He said something that made the others laugh. Johnny recognized his nasal tones but couldn't catch the words.

Unobtrusively he took a seat on the other side of the room. A young waiter served him with a beer. Johnny downed it quickly and ordered another. He hadn't been noticed. Falke knew him from the old days, but the others were newcomers.

The second beer made him feel floaty and relaxed, dissolving the morbid thoughts he'd had earlier. The warmth of the bar, the din of voices gave him heart. Johnny surveyed the scene with detached interest. Obscurely the clientele put him in mind of Stefan, men disguising their inborn sense of grievance with forced joviality. Both at work and play, he mused, these Nazis were vehement. Even sharing a drink they had to prove something, talk louder, laugh longer than their companions.

A tall brownshirt got up from a nearby table, heading away from Johnny and towards where Falke was sitting. The man's light curly hair was cut very short. He was broad-shouldered, heavy-thighed, a touch flabby round the midriff, had a lumbering walk. Johnny saw that it was Franz Edelmann. His stomach lurched, yet a certain nonchalance remained.

Franz bent and greeted Falke, slapping him affectionately on the shoulder. They conversed for a while. Franz held a half-smoked cigarette between thumb and forefinger, the tip close to the palm of his hand. One of Falke's companions embarked on some story and Franz's interest lapsed. He glanced round the room, took a drag on his cigarette. Johnny held his breath. Franz's gaze scanned his features and moved on, then returned sharply towards him. At that moment the young waiter delivered Johnny's third beer.

'*Prost*.'

Affably Johnny raised the glass to his one-time friend, the man who used to bore him with his naïve plans for the socialist millennium. The gesture was stylish. Johnny could imagine himself on film, smilingly suave, positively Mephistophelean, Franz's Nemesis. Though simultaneously he acknowledged the fantasy as so much shit. It was he, on the contrary, who was now totally in Franz's hands.

The tall brownshirt started back across the room, walking slowly, wearing a quirkish, sarcastic smile. Johnny had the impression that Franz too was starring in his own mental film role, and with a great deal more conviction than himself.

Franz's round face used to have a sweetness to it, but Johnny could see little of that quality now. He must be thirty-five or so. His features had hardened and turned heavy, showed the early signs of an alcoholic bloating.

'*Johann, Grüss Gott.*' He greeted Johnny with sarcastic amiability and stood staring down at him. 'You must be mad to come here again.' His tone light and not unfriendly.

'Join me, Franz. I'll buy you a beer.'

Edelmann pulled out a chair and sat down opposite Johnny. The movements had a flamboyance about them that again savoured of acting. Head to one side, squinting as if through smoke, Franz drew on his cigarette again. Why was it, Johnny wondered, that holding it like that, between thumb and forefinger, made a man look hard.

Franz ignored the offer of a drink. 'Mad,' he repeated, tapping his own head briefly. Adding in a calmly informative tone, 'This time you won't get away.'

'Who knows? I did last time.' Johnny still had the sense of being alert and in control, viewing himself quite inappropriately as an angler playing his catch, deliberately blanking out all thought of the punishment that surely awaited him.

'This time you won't get as far as the door.'

For a second or so they faced one another in silence.

'When did we stop being friends, Franzl?' With provocative innocence Johnny used the diminutive, the name of his cartoon character.

The other man flushed. For a split second the look in his eyes was one of fear as if ridicule threatened to undermine the role he was playing. He replied with tight fury, 'When you used your filthy scrawlings to insult –'

'Your shitty Adolf, your slimy Goebbels.' Johnny relished the words and the calm manner in which he was rushing to embrace his own doom.

When the nurse, Gudrun, reluctantly showed him his face in a mirror he was shocked at first, then almost childishly pleased with how awful he looked – skin liver-coloured, mottled with an eerie yellow, eyes almost closed, the flesh around them like puffy rotting apples, lips grotesquely swollen and spotted with dry black scabs that disguised their disgusting, pus-filled cores. When he checked his teeth three were missing.

As he made his examination Gudrun watched him with soft, dismayed eyes. He'd already glimpsed the spectacular bruising on his body. Two ribs were broken, Gudrun said. Actually there would have been more damage. The two bouncers were all for it and Falke certainly was, but for some reason Franz had called a halt and they'd carried him out into the street, left him lying in the gutter.

Claudia, apparently, had had him moved from a public to a private ward. There was nothing to do here, nothing to look at. He just lay and rode with the pain and contemplated the images in his brain. That stuffy little back room he hadn't known existed. The two lard-faced young bouncers pounding their fists into his face while, over their shoulders, he kept catching sight of the dancing blue eyes of Falke, his sharp, wizened little face, a kind of frozen, ladylike stare on the face of the dark-haired girl, which he sensed was superimposed on a shivering excitement. Franz, surprisingly, had taken no active part, simply giving orders, as if exerting his authority were more important to him than the beating itself.

Then he'd been thrown on the floor and kicked. Falke joined in that. He encouraged the girl to and she'd done so in a giggly fashion, flaunting her feminine ineptitude at the men. All the same she caught him a shrewd blow in the Adam's apple with her scuffed high-heeled shoe.

After a bit Franz told them to stop. They grumbled and protested, but he repeated 'That's enough!' with a curtness that brooked no argument. Later, as Johnny lay in the gutter, one of the bouncers had opened his fly and pissed on him, but by then he couldn't have cared less.

His nurses varied from shift to shift, but he specially noticed Gudrun. She must be in her early twenties but made him think of a girl of fifteen, with her murmuring voice and pale, oval, unpainted face. Her features were pretty but unremarkable, apart from her eyebrows like two long, elegant dashes, straight, very even, very pronounced. She wore her hair in the old-fashioned style, long and drawn back into a low chignon. Gudrun was hardworking, quiet and deft, quick to blush – everything Johnny, in some primitive part of himself, thought a young woman should be. She seemed genuinely upset by his injuries.

One night, as she was tending him late in the darkened ward, he caught her by the hand. 'Kiss me goodnight, little Gudrun.'

Gently she pulled away. 'No, we're not supposed to . . .'

'Please.' Then, with an abrupt stroke of inspiration, 'I'm too ugly, aren't I?'

'It's not that.' Gudrun hesitated, then in a sudden rush she leaned forward to give him a quick peck on the forehead, her lips pursed like a child's. 'There . . . You mustn't think you're ugly, Herr Kröger.'

Entering the scrubbed ward, Claudia looked a million dollars, as they said in the American gangster films Johnny enjoyed. She wore a black, belted coat, a deep-brimmed matching hat, black patent leather shoes. Her lips were brightly painted, eyes dark shaded beneath the thick, coppery fringe. Next to her shiny jet bird of paradise, Gudrun resembled a small, unobtrusive wren.

'Claudi, you're a tonic.' His heart lifted at the sight of her. He grinned though it hurt him badly to do so. Through thick and thin, for so long, Claudia had been a friend.

She crossed to his bedside. 'They wouldn't let me come earlier . . .' Registering his appearance, her eyes widened abruptly.

'It was uncommonly good of you to arrange this ward for me, Claudi. I can't tell you how touched . . .' Johnny had bitten the bullet. He never made thank you speeches. But Claudia's kindness had warmed him unutterably. Yet it seemed his effort was wasted. She wasn't listening, simply gazing in horror at his face.

'You fool! You bloody fool.'

'Thanks.' Another painful grin. A wry grin. Actually he felt more at home with her insults. 'Just the encouragement I need in my fight for recovery.'

'Please, Johnny, spare me the rueful heroics. You walked into that bar with the express purpose of getting yourself beaten up. It was crass ... unbelievably stupid. You behaved like a complete ... It's not even as if you were rescuing some poor, benighted victim from the brownshirt hordes ...'

With surprise he saw that she was genuinely rattled. Hostile even. And the realization checked the surge of affection he'd experienced as she entered the ward.

'What I did doesn't have to affect you, Claudia. In any way.' His tone was cool and followed by some moments of silence.

Claudia stared at him, wearing a sort of incredulous frown. Then she spoke wonderingly. 'It doesn't ever seem to occur to you that what you do and say does affect others. You treat people like shit and you don't even know that you do.'

Johnny raised an eyebrow. 'Is that so?'

'I met that Dagmar kid the other day. One of the many you fucked twice and then ignored. You've probably forgotten the whole affair, but she's still devastated.'

'I can't be responsible for every ... I never pretended anything to her. Does it occur to you, Claudia, that you too have always been quite good at casual affairs?'

'It's not the same.' She shook her head. 'And *you're* not the same. You seem driven. You're not balanced. This thing at *Der Seeräuber* only goes to prove it.'

He had the impression that the sight of his injuries had given Claudia a jolt that cracked some layer of reserve, leading her to blurt thoughts long harboured, but kept hidden. The realization came as a disagreeable shock. Though a woman, Claudia was special. He trusted her. Her criticism hurt him badly.

Stung, he taunted her. 'Carry on. Tell me more about what a bastard I am.'

'Not a bastard but ...'

'What then?'

Claudia shrugged and sank down on the stark metal and canvas chair that stood beside his bed. She looked levelly at him. 'Not a bastard, but still bleeding.' A hesitation. 'It's Amy, I swear, made you this way. You're still frantically trying to prove you're free of her. And the more you try, the clearer it becomes that you're not free at all . . . She's somehow behind everything you do.'

'Bullshit.'

Sceptically she lowered her eyelids, but didn't contradict him.

Johnny found himself stunned. No one ever mentioned Amy to him. Claudia's accusation was a bolt from the blue.

He dismissed it. 'She's nothing to me now.'

'Liar.'

'A little English bourgeois out for a minor thrill.'

'You give yourself away when you reduce her like that. She's far from the dimwit you're trying to make her out.'

'It's none of your business.' He was angry. What right had Claudia to open a box he'd kept nailed down for years. 'Fuck your lectures.'

'If you say so.'

He made a half-hearted effort at conciliation. 'Look, I'm grateful for what you've arranged – the ward and all. And I'll pay you back the cost.'

'It doesn't matter.'

Stalemate. Silence. Claudia opened her bag and brought out some hothouse grapes. 'I brought you these.'

He smiled quizzically, sarcastically. Neither would say anything to soothe or appease.

Claudia stood up. 'I'd better go.'

Johnny felt chilled as he watched her chic, upright figure cross back towards the door, as if something had taken place that was far more final than a mere spat between friends.

In the following months Claudia thought back many times on that scene with Johnny and her reactions remained confused. At times she regretted not having been more tactful. Then again she would decide that, on the contrary, she been absolutely right to speak her mind. Some nights – in the discouraging small hours – she had the scared, hollow feeling that, between Johnny and herself, everything was changed for ever. Next morning her fears would seem ridiculous. True, they might sulk for a while, but one of these days they would run into one another quite casually and everything would carry on as before.

Johnny apart, the times were distracting. The collapse of the American economy had made waves all over the world. In Germany unemployment was reaching heights that seemed absurd, unreal. A half voluptuous atmosphere of doom pervaded. The sense – as during the time of inflation – that the extreme was normal, normality extreme. In this climate the Nazis were making massive gains.

The streets seemed, more than ever, to belong to them. Peter Eisler's studious, pretty young sister was roughed up by Nazi bullies, insulted as a Jewish whore. Peter's film was picketed. So, in late 1930, was a small exhibition of Sergei's most recent paintings.

'Where are the police?' people asked helplessly, until it became a cynical catch-phrase. But the forces of law and order seemed reluctant to meddle in the doings of these agitators.

Sergei began to talk about returning to the Soviet Union. He'd begun to miss Moscow, he said. He dreamed about birch woods and the huge empty spaces of his native land. During the revolution his family had fought on the wrong side. But Sergei had come to admire communism and the Russians claimed to have the greatest respect for artists of all kinds. Deploring the direction Germany seemed to be taking, he had a childlike trust that Moscow would welcome him with open arms.

They talked about the idea often, late into the night, in bed. Sergei urged Claudia to come with him.

In certain moods, warm and drowsy, she was half seduced. But on the whole Russia scared her, seemed alien, vast and amorphous. She would feel tiny, could imagine being swallowed up.

'I don't speak the language anyway,' she protested. 'How could I work?'

'You don't need to. We'll have babies. I'll earn the money.' He laid his rough, dark head on her shoulder. She could hear in his voice that he was smiling, picture his appealing, ugly face and broken nose. She was awfully fond of him but not fond enough to give up her own life. They bickered and prevaricated and came to no decision.

Time passed and she didn't see Johnny. Nobody did. But the

cartoons kept coming, more savage and prolific than ever, endlessly obsessed with Nazism. It wasn't just Franzl now and the grotesque anti-Hitler, anti-Goebbels lampoons. Johnny published drawings like the ones he'd done in fascist Italy. Sketches executed at Nazi rallies and demos, passionately observed, caricatures only by the narrowest of margins, studies of young and middle-aged Nazis, presenting them as limited, self-righteous, the bullied seizing their opportunity to bully.

Claudia bought copies of everything he did. And it seemed to her that, in some way, he was always depicting his father, that his relationship with Stefan was mysteriously bound up with his hatred of Nazism. Johnny's whereabouts remained unknown. She suspected he'd gone to ground. His was a dangerous stance.

One day, in the Potsdamerplatz, she glimpsed Alberich, Johnny's scraggy communist pal. They hardly knew one another but their eyes met and recognition dawned. Outside their mutual friendship with Johnny the two of them had nothing in common, so it was inevitable that he should be the subject of their brief conversation.

Alberich was full of a glee he assumed Claudia must share. 'Talk about a cliché. His nurse of all people! Anna and I didn't give that marriage two months, I can tell you. But there he is, on the way to becoming a dad and apparently thriving on it!'

He clearly took it for granted that Claudia was in the know and she didn't enlighten him, though she must have looked pretty vacant.

'And Gudrun's such a quiet little thing. Not his usual type at all . . .' He ventured a tentative leer in Claudia's direction.

'I've lost his address,' she said. 'You wouldn't happen to –'

'Top secret!' Alberich wore a self-important smile that revealed his none-too-attractive teeth. 'Our Johnny's a bit of a target, you can imagine. I could get him to write to you.'

She shrugged carelessly. 'Doesn't matter. Give him my love.'

On the corner of the Leipzigerstrasse Claudia narrowly missed being flattened by a tram. But the near-accident hardly registered. Home-going shop and office-workers sidestepped round her as she walked down the street, dazed. She felt nothing. Tired perhaps. As if she'd been carrying a heavy suitcase round with her for far too long and finally it could be jettisoned.

Part Three

Part Three

Chapter Thirty-two

'What idiots!' A bright flush spread under the transparent skin of Vicki's classmate Dora. Her blue eyes sparkled. It was bizarre how a perfectly intelligent girl could undergo such a transformation when there were boys in the vicinity.

Vicki Campion felt a tug on her long horse's tail of dark, coppery hair. Must be Percy Rhodes. Tony would never have the nerve. She ignored the provocation, wouldn't give them the satisfaction of a response.

'Vicki! Vicki!' Percy chanted *sotto voce* from his seat behind her on the bus.

Dora nudged her forcefully. 'Take no notice.' She must be clearly audible from behind. Her friend radiated a foolish air of excitement.

'I'm not,' Vicki replied distantly, irritated by Dora's tense participation in the undignified scene, amazed she could be so affected by the interest of these spotty nonentities.

In an undertone they continued to chant her name and she sensed that Dora envied her as the object of their interest. Vicki couldn't wait to be off the bus and gone. Only one more stop before her own.

'How's about a shag?' Percy varied his chorus with the muttered obscenity, then cleared his throat nervously, as if intimidated by his own effrontery.

'Come off it, Percy.' A mild remonstration from Tony Rowe, a tall, quiet boy who, so friends told Vicki excitedly, was mad about her. And she had noticed that, whenever their paths crossed, his face took on a sheepish, rigid look. But the knowledge left her cold.

Nearly her stop. Vicki got to her feet, swinging her schoolbag over one shoulder. 'See you Monday, Dora.'

' 'Bye, Vicki.' A sidelong, conspiratorial grin which Vicki did not acknowledge.

She didn't look at the boys seated behind her, but could imagine Percy's dancing eyes, Tony's fixed, panicked gaze. He was good-looking, she supposed, but seemed in a constant state of sweating turmoil.

'Snob,' Percy said conversationally as she passed.

Walking down the sunny street towards her home, fifteen-year-old Vicki reflected that the comment was not unjustified. She did look down on the two callow lads and their attempts to gain her attention, and despised Dora's feverish response.

Sometimes she worried about her own lack of interest in the silly boy-and-girl games that went on between the two sibling grammar schools. Perhaps she was odd. Some of her friends hung around the park, the library, the bus shelter, Marian's Café, in the hope of giggling encounters that struck Vicki as a total waste of time.

Last Christmas, when the two grammar schools had staged a joint dance, by way of an experiment she'd gone outside with seventeen-year-old Michael Fisher. People said he looked like the film-star Robert Taylor and Vicki guessed he thought so too. She'd let him kiss her and press his body against hers, watched his fumblings with a cool inner eye. Then afterwards she felt demeaned at having allowed the self-satisfied youth to paw her, seemed to see a complacent glint in his eyes as if he imagined he'd gained some advantage over her. So, yes, maybe she was a snob.

It was June. The tall, spacious houses of Belsize Park were looking their best in the late afternoon sunshine, front gardens blooming with roses and fragrant mock orange, poppies, Canterbury bells, frothy alchemilla. Vicki turned down Philadelphia Close. Her tall, white home rose up on the left.

She went through the side-gate to the kitchen entrance. On the step outside stood pots of parsley, basil, chervil, chives. As Vicki entered, her mother turned from the stove looking hot and flushed, her soft, fair hair dishevelled. She wore an apron over a blue house-dress.

With the back of one hand Amy pushed her curls away from her forehead. 'What a day to spend cooking for twenty.' She kissed Vicki on the cheek. 'Well, how was the maths paper?' It was exam time at the grammar schools.

'A breeze.'

'Pride cometh before a fall.'

'Not with me.' For years Vicki had been top of the class or thereabouts. It seemed the natural order of things. She grinned and reached for one of the fluted pastry cases cooling on the table, ready to be filled with strawberries.

Playfully Amy smacked her hand. 'They're for tomorrow ... There's loads more to do. I'll be at it till midnight.' The following day was Saturday and they'd be celebrating Amy's recent birthday. She'd invited the whole family.

'Why do you flog yourself? You could get Banquets Unlimited to do it.' Vicki mentioned a much-touted local firm of caterers.

Amy gave a wry smile. 'You know me. That's too easy. I'd rather suffer, then bask in the grim satisfaction of having done it all myself.'

'Day after tomorrow you'll have to think up a new project.' She and Noel teased Amy that her life was a series of schemes, that she always had some new plan on the go. Occasionally, vaguely Vicki wondered why. Was her mother's life so dull without them?

'Don't you worry. I'll find something.'

Amy had kept her fingers crossed and the weather had not let her down. It was an exquisite June afternoon – the kind of light heat you felt as a warm breeze on your arms and in your hair. It ruffled the leaves of the slender birches, the two thriving cherry trees that grew round the periphery of the Campions' pleasant town garden.

With the aid of Jane, the daily help, Amy had improvised a long table with boards and trestles kept in the shed. The whole thing was covered with the white damask tablecloths she'd inherited in profusion from Noel's family when his father died three years ago. There were white roses in earthenware jugs, napkins of terracotta linen. Amy was proud of the table, with the kind of pride you savoured inwardly, since the family gave such things only the most perfunctory attention.

Jane and a friend formed a serving team to keep the platters of food coming and going briskly, to stay abreast of the washing-up, but it was an informal, help-yourself meal that belied the thought and sheer hard work that had gone into its organization.

Perhaps the first of Amy's projects – on returning home from Germany and after she'd given birth to Grace – had been to learn to cook. The spell in cosmopolitan Berlin had opened her eyes to the possibilities. She took lessons, read cookery books, both home-grown and foreign, studied and experimented until she'd become skilful and inventive. Today's meal was simple and summery – roast chicken marinated in wine, olive oil, garlic and herbs, home-baked bread, a colourful variety of salads, strawberry tartlets, chilled white wine.

Amy sat at the head of the table, Noel at the foot. Between them the combined ranks of the Winters and the Campions. They were not a particularly close family – there were pockets of tension and there was indifference. Amy's siblings were scattered and pursued their own lives. Yet, on this summer day in 1936, summoned to celebrate Amy's thirty-fifth birthday, the guests tucked in eagerly and an animated conversational buzz rose from the table. Trees cast a flattering dappled shade on sun-warmed faces. You could almost, Amy reflected, imagine yourself in Italy or France, some mediter-ranean country where harmonious extended families gathered together to enjoy one another's company.

'It feels so cosy, Grandma, don't you think, to have the whole family sitting round one big, big table?'

Momentarily the clear voice of ten-year-old Grace rose above the rest, echoing Amy's thoughts. Her eyes were drawn to her daughter's bright face and the unsuitably fancy green lace dress she'd chosen for herself. Of all those present she was probably the one who treasured most keenly this gathering of the clan. Grace was gregarious and loved to have it demonstrated that a group of people existed who belonged to her by right.

She was so like Amy, everyone said, with her wide grey eyes and soft blonde hair, her full, curving mouth. But Grace's nature was far more buoyant than her own. More trusting too. She liked people, reached out to them, gave them her full attention.

Margaret's reply was lost in the babble, but Grace was probably the only person who could make her grandmother smile like that, without an undertow of constraint, even bitterness.

In her mid-fifties now, Margaret still cut an elegant figure, with her silver-streaked hair slickly drawn back, her simple dark dress, lithe body, slim ankles. Her features remained fine, her skin smooth, the reward for a sober and moderate life. She pulled an amused, quizzical face at some new remark of Grace's and Amy experienced a rare moment of tenderness for her mother.

Life had disappointed Margaret and she didn't hide the fact. More particularly, her husband had disappointed her. With his increasingly aggressive radicalism Edward had deprived her of her station in life.

Through the twenties the Vicar of Crofton had become less and less inclined to kowtow to the sensibilities of the local landowners. He'd preached egalitarianism from his pulpit Sunday after Sunday, practised almost a kind of reverse elitism in his own daily life, alienating not only the bigwigs of the village, but anyone who wanted or needed to keep in with them. By 1927 the feeling against him grew so strong that he was forced to resign.

'He *willed* his own ruin. And mine.' Amy had heard her mother dilate on the theme a thousand times. Cheated of her role as vicar's wife, Margaret felt aimless, had turned sour.

'Ma looks minimally perky,' Phillip, Amy's younger brother, remarked from his place on her right. 'It's a miracle. Only Grace has got the knack . . .'

'Grace is still young enough to be given the benefit of the doubt. Later on she'll go the way of Emily.' Amy was ruefully pessimistic. 'You mark my words.'

Emily, the youngest of the Winter children, was no longer the apple of her mother's eye. Nineteen now, and still living at home, she earned a decent wage as a typist, was vain and fast and selfish, according to Margaret, painted herself like a tart. Amy, the irreproachable wife and mother, had become the favoured daughter.

'Oh Emily.' Phillip grinned. 'She's always been one too many for Ma *and* Pa.'

The youngest of the Winter children sat halfway down the table. She seemed to be playing some kind of word game with her brother Andrew's eight-year-old boy, regarding the activity, Amy guessed, as she viewed the whole occasion, as a duty – but one which she would discharge to the best of her ability.

Amy was amused and rather boggled by her little sister's cool efficiency. She had noticed the well-stocked vanity case Emily had brought with her, the creams, powders and lipsticks graded according to colour, the travelling hangers to take care of any clothes she wasn't actually wearing.

The children were all mesmerized by her bandbox beauty. The hard, immaculate, thirty-year-old's hairstyle that framed her pretty, immature features, over which a smooth and perfect mask had been applied. The carefully ironed bias-cut floral dress with the floaty cap sleeves, the pale silk stockings, unmarked cream kid shoes.

Emily seemed perfectly pleased with herself. Unlike Amy she had never allowed herself to be terrorized by Margaret's snobbish certainties, her possessiveness. She'd always seen herself quite calmly as her mother's equal.

Margaret and Edward rented a terraced house now in Gloucester but, to all intents and purposes, they were separated. Most of the time Edward lived in a small, spartan room in Bethnal Green that fitted his prickly conscience like a glove. He worked with a local mission, ministering to drunkards and down-and-outs. And Amy sensed that never, since his early days in Africa, had her father been so at peace with himself.

He sat between Noel and Vicki at the far end of the table. Though Edward was seventy now, he still reminded her of John the Baptist – rather alarming with his emaciated frame, sunken cheeks, intense brown eyes, the wild, curling hair that had turned through grey to white. Amy had sympathy with her mother. It must be highly uncomfortable to be married to a saint. At the same time she respected her father's singularity and the non-judgemental attitude he had to the derelicts for whom he cared.

In colouring Vicki and Edward made a pair, dark-skinned among a group who tended to fair complexions, light hair. Both Amy and Noel had used Edward on occasion as a handy genetic explanation for Vicki's olive skin and dark hair. The deception as to the girl's birth continued, had become second nature, hardly rating a thought.

Vicki had Claudia's colouring and her cleanly etched brown eyes. But her mouth was quite different – not as wide, held with more gravity – and her chin was more pointed. Perhaps in these features she took after her father. Amy gazed fondly at her for a moment. She looked lovely in that wine-red dress. It was a colour that used to suit Claudia.

Vicki and Edward conversed companionably. Edward found Grace's eager *joie de vivre* difficult, but Vicki was quieter and more pensive. The two of them had always accepted one another.

'Andrew mentioned Noel's planning an American trip.' There was a look of keen interest in her brother Phillip's grey eyes. To the Winter siblings Noel had remained an object of fascinated respect.

'Yes. In August.' Amy shrugged, instinctively playing down the fact. 'It's logical for the board to send him. What with his American roots.'

'Don't be so blasé, sis.'

'Not blasé, just wildly jealous.'

In the mid-thirties *Witness* magazine was still thriving and Noel was prospering with it. A tentative expansion was planned into the American market. Noel was on the board now, one of the editorial big three. He'd written several more books for the righteous Atlas Press and his opinions on the latest developments in Germany were in constant demand.

Amy glanced down the table towards her husband. How many times in their more than sixteen years of marriage had she caught sight of him across gatherings of one sort or another, and always with pleasure and appreciation? Though their relationship was not the same as it had been once.

This was a homely setting. Noel sat between his elder daughter and his sister, Carrie. But even in this family atmosphere he exuded the familiar mixture of natural authority and respect for others that Amy admired and almost envied.

Distance always lent a kind of objectivity to her view of him, confirming that, at forty-five, the impression he created was an imposing one. He'd kept his figure, and his hair, though it was heavily streaked with grey. In middle age men's faces either sagged or clung sparely to the bone. Noel's features were becoming leaner and more lined. It suited him. He was a man, some would say, in the prime of life.

Phillip touched Amy's shoulder. 'Well, sister of mine, how does it feel to be thirty-five?' He was still in his twenties – just – a teacher and recently married.

'I'm not sure I can sum it up just like that. It's different things on different days.'

The truth was that she didn't think about it much. Who did? You just got on with things, feeling much the same inside as you always had. Everyone's life had high spots, like falling in love, having a new baby. But most of the time, if someone asked if you were happy, you'd have to give it some thought.

She was grown-up. Her life was busy and pleasant, virtually pain-less. She was regarded as a good wife and mother, had two daughters whom she loved passionately and who – barring the usual worries – gave her endless pleasure.

Amy looked at her brother and shrugged her shoulders. 'I'd like to say something illuminating and deep. But I don't feel any different really. I probably feel rather like you do.'

He gave a wry grin. 'Sometimes I feel ancient. The embodiment of discipline and order.'

But she *was* different. Outwardly at least. Imperceptibly you changed. Something slipped away.

'You're more beautiful than ever,' Noel told her sometimes, and quite sincerely.

Amy could see what he meant. She liked the way her face had got thinner and more interesting. Her hair was pretty and well-cut, her clothes expensive. She was slim. But an ingredient was missing. An animation. An excitement. Life was conducted along acceptable lines. Nothing untoward ever happened to her.

Amy used to deplore the way her youthful blonde prettiness led people to project their own illusions on her, see her as someone they wanted her to be, feeding their own fantasies, blind to reality. That didn't happen now and, perversely, she missed it. In those days there'd been a constant sense of possibility.

'Hush everyone! Hush.' Carrie was tapping a knife against a glass.

The conversational hubbub died away and Noel got to his feet. This summer afternoon the men were in shirtsleeves and the thin, smooth cambric showed Noel's still muscular torso to advantage. Almost subconsciously Amy approved the figure he cut.

'Has everyone got a drink?' he enquired. No need for him to raise his voice.

A small flurry ensued. Those who hadn't refilled their glasses. Briefly Amy noticed her mother teasing Grace, pouring her a tiny measure of orange juice, herself a big one, while Grace laughingly protested.

'I'd like to propose a toast to a supreme wife, mother, daughter, sister . . .'

An enthusiastic assenting buzz.

'Sister-in-law. Cook!' Carrie interposed.

'Hear, hear to that!' Andrew, the eldest of Amy's brothers.

'Hostess, horticulturalist, nurse, chauffeur . . . If we start enumerating Amy's multiple talents and perfections it'll never end . . . Let me just say that she's the very essence and bedrock of my own and our daughters' lives . . .'

He smiled at her down the length of the table, half tenderly sincere, half deprecating his own fulsomeness. Tersely Vicki nodded agreement, embarrassed by the public display of emotion. Grace grinned manically at her mother, leaning forward and raising her orange juice, defusing Noel's earnestness.

'Not yet, Titch,' Noel laughed. 'Hold on just a moment.' He picked his glass up off the table and held it high. 'Everyone, let's drink to Amy. Happy birthday, darling. May you have all the good things you deserve in the coming year.'

A swell of agreement.

'To Amy!'

'Amy.'

She smiled radiantly, thanked them prettily, blinked back a hint of tears. Melted by the warmth of the tribute. At the same time feeling trapped in a role that she would never shake off for long. That of obedient, obliging child, forever seeking, forever grateful for the world's approval.

Amy sat at her plain Bauhaus-style dressing table, peering into the glass, removing her make-up. A table-lamp threw a pool of amber light, leaving the rest of the room in twilight. Reflected in the mirror were the pleasingly sombre mauves and beiges of her new Evelyn Wild carpet, a recent extravagance. It was midnight. Amy felt peaceful. Over the years she'd come to love this house, its spaciousness allied to unpretentious domestic comfort.

Noel came in and crossed the room to kiss the back of her neck. 'Enjoy today?'

'I did.' Their eyes met in the mirror with affectionate familiarity.

'You must be tired. You worked so hard. No one cooks like you.'

'True.' She grinned at his reflection in the glass.

Casually they undressed, indifferent after all these years to one another's nakedness.

In bed Amy yawned. 'Don't set the alarm. I'll have a sabbath lie-in if the spirit moves me.'

He smiled in reply. 'Sleep well, Liebchen.' Since Berlin small Germanisms had entered their shared language.

'You too.'

They settled down, turning their backs to one another. It was rare nowadays, any kind of sexual contact between them. The understanding was mutual, unspoken, in no way dramatic.

Their relationship had changed. With the perspective of time Amy had come to see her affair with Johnny as the turning point, though at the time it hadn't been obvious. During her pregnancy Noel had been ardent – with a kind of jagged, self-hating passion – as if roused in spite of himself by the thought of another man possessing his wife, impregnating her.

But after Grace's birth that desire had never really returned. And, some years back, Noel had confessed to having a mistress in Berlin, where he still went often in the course of his work, a woman who took care of his sexual urges, was paid not to mind his impotence. Amy had received the information calmly as if he were talking about another couple. And she'd raised no objection. After her own defection it seemed only fair.

Her body had adapted to the void, succumbed to a kind of sexual torpor. If troubled by desire she relieved herself with masturbation, though she was ashamed of the act.

When Noel told her about Ursula – he'd used her name, his tone respectful – Amy had asked, 'What if I found someone? How would *you* feel?'

'I could hardly object. As long as you were discreet.'

But she'd never taken advantage of the dispensation.

Oddly, once passion was out of the way, everything else fell into place. They were partners, affectionate and mutually supportive. Noel earned their living in the world. Amy entertained his friends and professional contacts, took care of his home, cut an attractive figure on his arm, took pride in doing all these things well. And they were united, anyway, by the girls. No one else could ever love and understand them like she and Noel.

And then there were her projects, the schemes that Noel and the girls teased her about, the skills she acquired methodically, one by one. Cooking, driving, carpentry, upholstery, furniture restoring. Her welfare work with the unemployed. Noel approved these interests, admired her curiosity, and she never allowed them to interfere with her running of the home.

'Why?' Vicki sometimes asked, with a look on her face that suggested Amy was compensating for some lack.

But who wasn't, when it came down to it? Whose life was so perfect that distractions weren't necessary?

Beside her Noel was already breathing deeply and regularly. Amy shifted a little, pulled the pillow into a more comfortable position.

The day had gone well, better than she expected. Amy basked in a drowsy sense of satisfaction.

Her birthday always brought Claudia and Johnny to mind. Her twins, born the same year and month as herself, advancing through lives parallel to her own. Those days in Berlin seemed almost mythic, a story she'd invented about a younger and more reckless self.

But a new project was stirring in her mind, taking shape with quiet inevitability. Noel would be visiting America. There could be no better opportunity to fulfil the promise she'd made to Claudia, years ago, in another life, to return with the girls to Berlin.

Chapter Thirty-three

'Let's open the window, Gräfin, and let in the future!'

Horst Wedlin declaimed the line with a winning smile, a vibrant warmth, the *Schwung* praised by critics as his particular attribute.

Claudia crossed to the casement in a swish of floor-length taffeta, her wig a luxuriant silver-blonde onion. Horst caught her by the waist. Backs to the audience, heads triumphantly raised, they stood side by side artfully silhouetted against a dawning peach-coloured sunrise.

The curtain fell. The usual applause began to swell. Claudia and Horst grinned at one another. The last line of this dire naughty nineties romp had become a private catch phrase. Overdone, but irresistible. Claudia swore that at home in their flat Horst opened windows quite at random for the sheer joy of delivering, yet again, the thumping quote. On stage it was hard to keep a straight face.

'About turn, Gräfin.' Horst spun her round for the curtain call.

The red and gold curtain rose again to reveal the cast ranged along the front of the stage. In the centre Claudia and Horst stood hand in hand. The shared amusement made their smiles irrepressibly genuine. The audience warmed to such naturalness. There were stamps and cheers. They'd had a good time. *Countess Alexia* was undemanding entertainment, the theatre's most successful production in more than two years. And by chance Claudia – who normally played character parts, secondary roles – was the star.

The applause lasted for some five minutes before the curtain was lowered for the last time and the cast drifted offstage.

It was July. A heat wave. 'I'm going straight home tonight,' Claudia informed Horst. 'All I want is a cool bath and bed. It's fine by me if you want to stay and socialize.'

She never made any assumptions where Horst was concerned, made a point of demonstrating that he was free. He was nine years her junior, the company's juvenile lead.

'A cool bath and bed sounds good to me.' He smiled his sweet, uncomplicated smile.

'Meet you in five minutes.'

The auditorium of the Valentin Theater was tolerably plush. Backstage it was shabby and cramped. Star or no, Claudia shared a dressing room with all the other women of the company, jockeyed for her turn at one of the harshly lit mirrors.

On a night like this it was bliss to remove the tight, heavy wig, replace it on one of the row of egg-shaped stands, feel the coolness of the sweat evaporating from her scalp. Wigs were hell on the hair. Before a performance Claudia always clamped hers into rows of snail-like pin curls. Afterwards – in theory – you brushed out a riot of bouncy waves. In practice the effect was sad and flat.

She was blonde now. Three years ago she'd made the change, soon after the Nazis came to power. It had been a good career move, but sometimes she still got a shock encountering her own image unexpectedly in a mirror or shop window. Her colouring was wrong for the bright peroxide tones. Make-up was needed to smooth the effect. But, straight from the hairdresser, with her pearly powder in place, Claudia's shoulder-length platinum pageboy seemed to impress the new-style producers and casting directors.

Horst put his arm round her shoulder as they strolled alongside the dark water of the Spree in the dense warmth of the summer night. He was like a boy with his sweetheart rather than an actor with his mistress, a woman of a certain age.

Affectionately he ruffled the back of her hair. 'Tired are you, old lady?'

Without malice he teased her often about the difference in their ages. Claudia welcomed his joshing. It removed any possible anxiety from the situation. Horst was endlessly good-natured, lazy, sensual. Sometimes she felt like his mother, fond but impatient.

'I'm pooped,' she confirmed. 'It's the success. I'm not the type.'

'Not too tired for a tumble?'

She smiled at his homely choice of words. Truth to tell she *was* too tired. Horst was keen to make love every night, most mornings and sometimes all she wanted was to curl up and sleep. But he was persuasive and she liked his boyish insatiability.

'Never.' Claudia gave him an amused, ironic look, briefly squeezed his muscular waist.

Her lover was tall and long-legged, built like the side of a house. In the none-too-distant future he would run to fat – Horst wasn't the kind to worry about his figure. But, for now, his physique was impressive.

His features were rugged rather than fine, the mouth full and rather asymmetrical, nose bold and broad, eyes grey, wide-set. His hair was straight, thick and fair and he wore it rather long, doing away with the necessity for wigs.

On-stage he appeared the Aryan ideal, but in life his expression was too amiable for that. Horst was universally liked, but there were some in the company who shook their heads over his lack of ambition. He knew his acting range was limited and it didn't bother him. He got by on charm.

Temperamentally he reminded her of Sergei, who'd finally left and been reabsorbed into the amorphous, unimaginable vastness of the Soviet Union. Though, to be fair, Sergei had been intense about his art.

Wryly Claudia postulated a scenario for her future life. Envisaged a series of likeable, easy-going men. Men who, deep down, she didn't take seriously and who would cause her little suffering, even when they left. Men who were the opposite of Johnny.

They arrived back at their apartment block on the Bellevue Ufer, fifteen minutes' walk from the theatre.

'Post for you, Claudi.' Horst emptied the little letter box in the pleasant green vestibule. He handed her a couple of envelopes.

One was on thick, ochre-tinted paper with some kind of a crest. 'Bruno Berg,' she noted. He'd become very grand under the Nazis. The other bore an English stamp. 'And Amy . . . How nice.'

Their flat was on the third floor with evocative views over the river at night and in the early morning. It was modest but cosy and plenty big enough for two. They kept it simple and monochrome in the post-war style, apart from Claudia's collection of cushions and the plants she'd started to cultivate.

'They're your children, those plants of yours,' her friend Käthe used to say before she shook the dust of Hitler's Germany from her feet and went to live in Paris.

Horst thought Claudia's taste modern and chic. He was a small-town boy – from Darmstadt – and had never looked beyond the heavy, dark furniture of his parents and neighbours. 'Traditional' was making a comeback under the Nazis, but neither Horst nor Claudia was having any of that.

Claudia dropped to the floor in a nest of cushions. 'Better see what Bruno's got to say for himself.'

It was basically a fan letter. Bruno had at last found time to see her in *Countess Alexia*.

'You were charming, Claudia. And I'm seriously glad to see you becoming integrated into the new culture. I've always admired your style, but we must all learn to change with the times . . .'

Claudia pulled a face and passed the letter to Horst. He read it in silence.

'Pompous shithead,' he remarked mildly as he handed back the thick, smooth sheet of ochre vellum.

On one point Claudia was quite clear: the thing she liked above all else about Horst was his collusion with her in damning all things Nazi. Without the safety valve of their shared irreverence, she would suffocate, she would die.

At the theatre such frankness was simply not possible. You couldn't trust people nowadays. The regime punished all criticism and there were advantages to be gained from reporting a colleague who joked about Hitler or scoffed at the ham-fisted cultural policies of the Nazis. You even heard of family members denouncing one another to the police. So in public it paid to be extremely cagey.

But in private she and Horst could let off steam, jeer at Altenbach, the newly appointed theatre director who didn't know Goethe from a plate of Bratwurst, poke fun at Marianne, the juvenile lead, with her dirndl skirts and Gretchen coronet of plaits.

Both heartily despised the material they were called upon to perform. Any kind of experimentation in the arts was anathema now, anything that might baffle the average man in the street, or give him pause for thought. Crass comedy was king – a recent smash hit had starred a live sow – along with arch costume entertainment like *Countess Alexia* or portentous blood-and-soil peasant drama. Even the classics were not always considered quite 'safe'.

Most of Claudia's friends of the previous decade were *personae non gratae* now, and many were in exile. Claudia herself had thought long and hard about that option. She could have gone, with Sergei, to Russia, or to Paris with Käthe, or to England . . .

But Claudia considered her own talent small and idiosyncratic. She didn't think it would travel well. Her fame, such as it was, was of the cult variety. And to earn her living she needed the German language. She'd hummed and hawed and never taken the step, had stayed on to pursue an unsatisfying compromise of a career and to nurse a bad conscience at her own tacit acceptance of a regime she detested.

She was a misfit. No two ways about it. The fact that the regime accepted *her* was largely due to her association with the fabled Bruno Berg. He'd appointed himself her protector because of some sentimental, haphazard memory of Claudia's kindness to him in the past. Nowadays their paths rarely crossed but, when they did, he always greeted her like an old pal, and she thanked her stars for his patronage. In spite of Horst's disdain Claudia suspected that he was perversely impressed by her affable letter from this icon.

Under the Nazis Bruno's popularity had merely increased. The public had a seemingly insatiable hunger for the endless light comedy films he churned out, while claiming blandly in interviews that his heart lay in the theatre. He was on intimate terms with Joseph Goebbels, who visited him on set and publicly quoted his opinions.

Claudia had always respected his acting ability – on film he had a soft, sleazy charm she privately thought better suited to the good old debauched Weimar days. He was intelligent too, and she doubted he was as ecstatic about the straitjacket renewal of healthy German culture as he claimed. All the same he'd clearly been born for his role as attractive, literate ambassador for a regime that was by no means uncongenial to him. He'd ditched the louche Franziska and, in handmade brogues and paisley cravats – he dressed like an off-duty Edward of England – was now seen everywhere with a pretty, bright-eyed starlet called Magda Seydel.

'Bruno still loves you then.' Horst lay down beside her on the pile of cushions. Playfully he stroked her hair, nuzzled into her neck. 'You smell divine.'

'Of sweat you mean.'

'Sweat and that cream you use to take your make-up off. It's an aphrodisiac, I swear.'

With teasing ardour he undid the buttons of her blouse, one by one, each time pausing to kiss the skin beneath.

'I've got my other letter to read.' But the protest was for form's sake. Amy's letters were special and she would only read them when her mind was free and she had all the time in the world.

'Later.'

He flashed an inviting, heavy-lidded smile. She treasured that smile. It typified him. Consciously seductive on one level, sweet and self-mocking on another. She moved her hand to cup the bulge of his erection.

'How well you know me, Gräfin.' Horst parodied his role in *Countess Alexia*.

Making love with him was easy and pleasurable, carried no undertow of demons or darkness, none of the antagonism that used to excite and dismay her with Johnny. Horst liked people. He liked women, and overflowed with simple, sensual lust. After a year or more they knew exactly how to please each other and, as yet, no staleness had set in.

His large fair head moved down her body, came to rest between her thighs. His hands adjusted her underclothing. She smiled, tangling her fingers in his thick healthy hair, preparing to be pleasured.

It was nearly two before Claudia had the cool bath she had promised herself. Horst slept heavily in the bedroom next door. His capacity for sleep was prodigious, a trait she found both endearing and infuriating. If he had no rehearsal her lover was quite capable of spending half the day in bed. He was perfectly irresponsible, like a child, abandoning himself to sensuous slumber, trusting Claudia to wake him and see he got to his appointments on time.

She relished her time alone in the quiet small hours. After the bath Claudia rubbed in some of Horst's clove-scented talc. And then, in a silk kimono like the one Lotte used to wear, and by the light of her stylish opaline-shaded standard lamp, she settled down luxuriously to read her letter.

It pleased her enormously that, in spite of the distance between them, she and Amy had stayed in touch. Not just that, but their letters to one another remained chatty and alive, when their experiences were so different and so separate. For Claudia there was something liberating in the sense of an indulgent, unseen presence, someone who once upon a time she had known terribly well.

Amy always apologized because her news sounded so humdrum, but Claudia was fascinated by this first-hand insight into the kind of life she might easily have had, sometimes hankered after in fact – the continuity of a husband, the . . . selflessness of bringing up children. To her they were as exotic as Claudia's own precarious professional and emotional fortunes must seem to Amy.

Claudia could never stop herself from scanning her friend's letters – before she'd even started reading them properly – looking for references to Vicki. She felt sanguine now the girl was at a distance, content she'd done the right thing, no longer disturbed by sight and sound of the daughter she'd given away.

Vicki was bright, it seemed. Claudia glowed with muted pride at Amy's reports of exams passed and prizes won. Sometimes she sent photos and a couple were tucked into this particular letter, taken at her birthday junket the previous month in the Campions' leafy garden.

The child, Grace, was the image of Amy. Claudia stared long and hard, but could see no trace of Johnny in her lively, laughing face. Then, almost guiltily, she fell to studying the other picture, a three-quarter face snap of her own daughter, marvelling at the girl's serious, adult beauty. According to Amy both girls had new dresses for the occasion and Vicki had chosen the burgundy red Claudia used to wear a lot. The dress had fashionable wide shoulders and a neckline that revealed a V of smooth skin, youthful collarbones. In the black-and-white photo her hair looked dark, was caught in a ribbon at the nape of her neck, appeared to hang down almost to her waist. Her eyes were steady and beautifully shaped. She wasn't smiling, had a reserved, self-contained expression that pleased Claudia, as if she were her own person, not totally absorbed into her attractive and admirable English family.

'Do you feel old, Claudia?' Amy asked in her loopy blue handwriting. 'On my birthday people kept asking me that. Otherwise I'm not sure it would have occurred to me . . .'

Claudia smiled to herself. Sometimes she pondered whether having a lover in his mid-twenties made her feel older or younger. She could never quite decide.

After that her friend veered off on to the subject of some fancy new shelves she'd built, rubbed down and varnished. She was clearly proud of the achievement. Claudia was impressed. It was hard to imagine ethereal Amy tackling anything so practical.

Then came the bolt from the blue. Noel was planning a business trip to America in August. It happened that his absence would coincide with next month's Berlin Olympics. 'I promised you I'd come back with Vicki one day and I can't imagine a better opportunity. I'm bringing both girls, naturally, and a friend of Noel's has wangled us rooms at the Adlon. I've always had a decadent desire to stay there . . .'

Automatically Claudia read on as Amy discussed plans, arrangements, anticipations. As her eyes moved along the lines of writing she was surprised to discover that her prime response to this sudden bombshell was not joy, but apprehension.

She finished the letter, folded it and laid it down beside her. Then, for the second time, she picked up the photograph of her daughter, imagining that cool gaze she had so admired turned on herself. What would Vicki see?

Most of the time Claudia carried in her head the invigorating image of herself as a courageous woman in her mid-thirties with an enviable career, still attractive enough to hold the attention of a handsome and sexy leading man.

But there were days when this figure seemed self-delusion, and she saw a female whose looks were starting to fade, whose career had been marginal at best, enjoying a freak success in a play she despised. A woman whose relationships with men had always been short-term and basically unsatisfactory. A creature at odds with her degraded times, yet too weak-willed to do anything about it.

There were days when she compared herself to Johnny, who'd always seemed as frivolous as she. Yet how consistently he'd stood up against the Nazis. She used to get angry at his recklessness. But it was as if, at the time, she'd been blind to everything but the danger, while Johnny had seen into the future.

He was a legend now, living in Prague with his wife and young family, stripped of his German citizenship. His cartoons were a string of black, blistering, obscenely funny indictments of every aspect of National Socialism. They appeared in *Zum Totlachen*, an underground publication produced by German expatriates in Czechoslovakia, its emblem a laughing death's-head.

The magazine was a weedy thing, each issue a mere eight pages long, yet to be found reading it would entail automatic imprisonment, possibly far worse. Well printed on wretched paper, it was smuggled into the country – God knows how – and passed furtively from hand to hand. Eugen, the lighting man at the theatre, had access, and passed it on to Horst and Claudia. Accepting it from him, bringing it home and reading it, then handing it on to Alex, Horst's cousin – these actions, Claudia mused, represented their one puny defiance of the official regime.

And there had been that thing with Peter Eisler. So awful she'd trained herself to lock it away in one of the dark cupboards of her mind. Though she couldn't stop the memory seeping out and into her dreams from time to time. Then she would wake with an anguish that hung over her for days.

In the last disintegrating years of the Republic, Peter had finally achieved his breakthrough. He'd written a couple of successful screenplays and a novel. He had married. Jutta was a quick, fey creature – a gentile – who wrote poetry. They'd bought a house in the affluent Dahlem district.

Next door lived a man called Kiersch, the owner of a large plumbing firm, a pig-like figure straight out of a drawing by George Grosz. From the start Kiersch made it quite clear that the fact of having a Jewish neighbour was loathsome to him. When the Nazis came to power in early 1933 he became one of the thousands of March Violets – opportunists who suddenly discovered their National Socialist leanings.

From then on a campaign was launched against the Eislers. The house must have been watched because, after evenings out, they would come home to find a fresh crop of slogans painted on the walls. Jews out. Jewish blood. Jew death. Insults to Jutta as a Jew's whore. Indubitably Kiersch was behind it, though he didn't ply the red paint himself.

As he told her about it Peter had looked dazed and, illogically, ashamed. Whenever she remembered that shame, Claudia's throat constricted with hatred and passionate pity. Behind the wire-rimmed glasses Peter's eyes had once been so warm, so humorous.

'What about the police?' she asked at the time, but only because she didn't know what else to say.

His smile had been cynically reproving. 'You really think I haven't tried? You think they give a shit?'

The persecution continued. Peter and Jutta sat tight, refusing to be driven out. Then one night he'd heard a noise, went to investigate and surprised a youth with paint-pot and brush in hand. Provoked beyond endurance, Peter attacked. As he'd been meant to. From nowhere three accomplices materialized, punched and kicked him for what seemed to Jutta a long, long time. Later, in hospital, Peter died.

Jutta had recognized one of the young men. Both he and Kiersch were questioned. Blandly the police pleaded a lack of proof, mentioned a filthy anti-Führer joke Kiersch claimed Peter had repeated to him.

'He never even spoke to the bastard.' Jutta collapsed at the police station, watched coldly by an embarrassed young officer.

For weeks Claudia had been haunted by Peter's aloneness, his total lack of recourse to protection and justice. Then she got the job with the Valentin Theater and met Horst. The scab on her heart healed over. She made herself forget.

Tonight she was tired and morbid. Tomorrow things would feel better and she'd be glad at Amy's news. For now she needed to sleep in the warmth of Horst's big body.

Chapter Thirty-four

The scent of Balkan tobacco on the hot summer air was deeply familiar to Amy. Breathing it in after eleven years of absence, she had the momentary illusion of entering the skin of her younger self, recapturing the way she'd felt then.

The smell was the same but the main streets of Berlin had been smartened up almost beyond recognition. It was common knowledge that Hitler intended these 1936 Olympic Games as a grandiose advertisement for his proud new Germany. Massive renovation had taken place. She hardly knew Unter den Linden where the Hotel Adlon was situated. Hundreds of the big old trees had been sacrificed to make way for pretentious road-widening schemes. In their place were pompous Biedermeier-style lampposts and a forest of flagpoles from which fluttered the banners of all nations, liberally interspersed with the black and red swastikas of the Reich.

A contagious excitement bubbled in the air, the sense that this was an event. The well-dressed pedestrians were in a holiday mood and spoke a babble of different languages. Vicki and Grace were all eyes, clearly thrilled to be a part of this bustle, impressed by the size and the smooth, professional friendliness of the world-famous hotel.

'You'll be rubbing shoulders with all the crowned heads of Europe.' In the last days before he left Noel had jokingly fanned the girls' excitement. He'd pulled strings to secure a couple of rooms. The Adlon had been booked for months.

They ate dinner in a long dining room with swirly, heroic paintings on the ceiling, heavy white tablecloths, shiny silver and glassware. Rich odours of food tempted the appetite and an agreeable, well-fed buzz of conversation filled the air.

Grace stared about her avidly. Her pale hair curled wildly above a white dress with a sailor collar. Her cheeks were flushed, her eyes bright and over-excited.

'Looking for crowns?' Vicki teased.

Grace lowered her eyelids in an adult fashion that always amused Amy. 'I'm not as credulous as you seem to imagine.'

'Supercilious brat.'

As ever Vicki seemed as serene as Grace was curious. She looked lovely tonight, her skin smooth and tanned against a pale yellow dress, hair glossy with health and shining, under the ornate wall-lamps, with coppery glints. A young American at a neighbouring table glanced her way repeatedly.

Amy insisted the two girls had an early night. After kissing them both she went to her room. Claudia had promised to come to the hotel straight after her evening performance at the Valentin Theater.

Her room was pretty and fussy with brocaded rococo chairs, swagged curtains fastened with tasselled braids. She turned off the light. The streetlamps from outside made the room quite bright enough. Amy sat down near the window. It was still warm outside, a beautiful dark blue summer night. Sounds of traffic and carefree voices floated in at the window.

As she waited Amy's mind idled, drifted back to images from the past, culminating in that bleak last meeting with Claudia in the Café Josty. Her own half-facetious promise to return when they were both settled and staid. In those days she hadn't really believed that time would ever come.

Had it? Amy's fear was that, after all these years, Claudia would think her dull and dowdy, a housewife. To counteract the possibility she'd had her hair expensively cut, bought new clothes.

Shortly before midnight she heard a woman's voice in the corridor outside. 'Thank you ... You're so kind.' A light, breathy laugh. 'Thank you. *Auf wiedersehen!*'

Then a knock came at the door. Swift and resolute, like a swimmer broaching cold water, Amy crossed to open it. 'Hello, Claudia.'

'Amy!'

Apprehension vanished. They embraced in simple affection. Time changed nothing. How easy it was.

Claudia held her at arm's length. Her smile was as wide as ever. 'You don't look like a *Hausfrau*,' her tone amused and admiring. It was as if she'd read Amy's mind.

'You do look like an actress.'

Claudia laughed. 'The man in the lift recognized me, imagine that. That sort of thing's never happened to me before. And all on account of that piece of shit I'm appearing in . . . I've brought you tickets, by the way.'

'With a recommendation like that I can hardly wait.'

The old bantering tone between them returned. It was a shock, though, to see Claudia blonde, though Amy vaguely recalled her mentioning it once in a letter. Her hair was longer too. It made her look . . . more womanly, Amy supposed. She wore a silk blouse the colour of copper beech leaves, a well-cut cream skirt, carried the matching jacket over her arm. There was certainly less of the urchin about her. Was the change due to some difference in Claudia or merely down to fashion? The twenties were dead and gone. Their own and the century's.

'You must be exhausted, acting in this heat. I'll get us something to drink.'

'Something cold and white.' Claudia rolled her eyes blissfully heavenwards.

Amy ordered champagne to be brought to the room. 'It's a celebration.' She kissed Claudia's cheek, then briefly touched the smooth surface with her fingers. 'Flesh and blood. You're not imagination. I can't believe you're here after all these years.'

A crooked smile. 'I've never been away.'

The champagne was delivered on a gilded trolley with small caviare canapés. Both Amy and Claudia were amused by the baroque luxury of their reunion.

'The only thing that's wrong,' Claudia said, 'is these chairs. They're so upright, so flimsy.'

'There's the floor.'

They laid down pillows and cushions on the carpet and lounged with their glasses by the filtered glow of Hitler's fine new streetlamps. Amy felt the champagne beginning to suffuse her veins with a light and dizzy euphoria.

She smiled expectantly. 'Now tell me everything about yourself.'

'So, are you in love with this Horst?' Amy was asking.

'I don't think so . . . He's sweet. He's easy-going. He doesn't make me suffer.' Claudia gave a small, wry shrug. 'I can't believe it's love if I don't suffer.'

'How very *Sturm und Drang*.'

Amy hadn't lost her quick, delightful smile. Nor the gravity that somehow was always behind it – even when, as now, she was a little tipsy. Curled on the floor in a filmy black dress, pink-cheeked from the champagne, she seemed, to Claudia's eyes, as lovely as ever. Her hair still had its childish softness and curl, her legs their pale elegance. But she'd grown up. Her beauty was somehow more meaningful.

'It's the Nazis that keep me and Horst together,' she said with a flippancy which sounded false and overwrought. 'Our relationship is based on insulting them. He's as bad as me so neither of us is likely to go sneaking to the Gestapo.'

'I can't imagine what it's like to live . . . We saw the Ackermanns in London a while back.' Amy mentioned the landlord of Mailied and his family. They'd been friendly with the Campions, Claudia recalled. 'They've left. The way things are, Gustav couldn't earn a living any more. They're off to Palestine. They were forced to sell their property dirt cheap.'

'So I heard from Tante Agathe.' Claudia smiled with black humour. 'It's what she's been waiting for since 1917.'

'How is your aunt?'

'Older. Even more hidebound. She looks like one of those little old war widows with their grim felt hats and buniony shoes, the backbone of every church . . . She and Frau Kästner have a cleaning woman now . . .' Claudia had treated them to that luxury. 'A peppy little Nazi, always off on Strength-Through-Joy holidays and subsidized theatre trips. Forever yapping on about how good everything is. She's their political mentor.'

Actually Claudia suspected that Agathe had quiet misgivings about some of the darker rumours in circulation. But she chose not to acknowledge them. 'Whenever I see her she drones on about what a relief it is to feel safe on the streets once more.

'If you're not a Jew . . . How's Peter?'

At the casual question a prickly panic gripped Claudia. She was absolutely unprepared for the violence of her guilty reaction and knew she couldn't possibly tell Amy the true story, at least not now. There was too much shame involved – her country's and her own. A loved friend murdered in cold blood with the connivance of the system. And here she was, ebullient, prospering.

'Peter died. Didn't I write?' How insincere she sounded.

'No!' Shock and distress. 'How awful. What did he die of?'

'Meningitis,' Claudia improvised.

'When? I'm amazed. Tell me about it.'

'Amy, d'you mind if we don't talk about this tonight. It makes me feel so . . .' Straightaway Claudia read concern and understanding in her friend's eyes. 'Let's not be sad.'

She had an inspiration. 'Tell you what. I've got a little flask of schnapps in my bag. I brought it for us to celebrate, then you got the champagne. What do you say? Shall we make a night of it?'

'I'm game.'

With the schnapps burning soothingly in her gut Claudia began to talk, low and volubly, about her feelings of guilt and alienation in Berlin now, and about the near impossibility of defying such a ruthless regime, describing the self-disgust that crept up on her the moment she lowered her defences.

All the time Claudia was aware that her voice was cracking as if on the edge of hysteria. But it was impossible to resist the relief of pouring out all her bottled-up tension, of explaining herself to a new and sympathetic listener. Amy listened intently but said little, clearly didn't judge Claudia for keeping her head down well below the parapet.

'Yet I'm sure most of the tourists must think everything's hunky-dory. It all seems so bright and triumphant.' Amy shook her head. 'Not a sign of the anti-Jew notices, or that magazine Noel's told me about.'

'*Der Stürmer*.' Claudia gave a thin smile. 'With lovely, distressed Aryan maidens being lasciviously pawed by vile, hook-nosed Levantines . . . It sells in thousands. It'll be back.'

'Noel did a feature a few weeks ago. On Johnny. And his clandestine magazine . . . What a hero he's become.'

'Yes.' Claudia could hear the hollowness in her own voice. Mention of Johnny and his heroism hit home, reinforcing her sense of her own . . . flabbiness. And Amy spoke of him with such seeming insouciance, in blithe ignorance of the ugly jealousy that had once writhed and burrowed in Claudia's intestines.

'You know . . .' Amy hesitated. 'I think Noel's secretly impressed. Johnny's such an icon now.'

The statement died away into silence. Amy was clearly a touch embarrassed by Claudia's lack of response and took a sip of her drink. 'Do you ever come across that scrawny friend of his, that Alberich?'

'The communist . . . I imagine he's been done away with long ago in one or other of their round-ups. Either that or he's in Oranienburg concentration camp.'

Amy exclaimed in horror at an insight that, to Claudia, had become merely routine, a simple fact of life. Willy-nilly you became immune to the enormity, arranged your life to avoid and accommodate. They were interrupted by an altercation in the street outside, a blowing of horns, angry voices, rising abruptly from the warm night, then as quickly dying away. Suddenly Claudia grew impatient with her own endless, pointless preoccupation with a situation she could not alter. She looked across at the Englishwoman, half-reclining in one of the long rectangles of light that fell across the dark room.

'Just before you left, Amy – back then – I had a sort of dread of you.' The words slipped out quite simply. Words she'd never allowed herself to say. She was tight, Claudia realized. Her guard was down.

'A dread? What do you mean?'

'You never noticed anything. You were in your own little world then. Riding high, with Johnny and Noel as your slaves. And a

319

beautiful child.' She could have said 'my child', but that would have sounded too hostile. 'I felt like a smear of shit on your shoe.'

'Claudia!' Amy's voice held hurt and incomprehension. 'I don't understand. I'm amazed at what you're saying.'

'I'm drunk,' Claudia declared curtly. 'So I don't feel like being discreet. I just want you to know I was in love with Johnny.'

She saw Amy's eyes widen in bewilderment.

'I never told him, not him or anyone. He had lots of women.' Claudia gave a tough, theatrical smile. 'And I had plenty of men. I didn't want to look a fool. I behaved as if he meant as little to me as I did to him.'

'But he adored you.' Even before she'd assimilated the basic fact, Amy stepped in to soothe and reassure.

'He thought of me as a good mate. With sex thrown in. It wasn't like that for me. I was mad about him.'

'It never dawned on me . . .' Amy shook her head, addressing herself as much as Claudia. 'How could I have been so absolutely oblivious?'

'You asked me once if he was anyone special and I was perfectly cool and casual.' Claudia pulled a face. 'Knowing you, you'd probably never have started anything with him if I'd come clean. So I've only got myself to blame.' She was pleased with the dry neutrality of her tone.

She held up the bottle enquiringly. Amy shook her head. Claudia filled her own glass. 'Anyway, he fell for you and I was out of the picture.'

Treacherously her voice shook on the words and she felt tears in her eyes. She *was* drunk. She hadn't cried for Johnny in years.

Chapter Thirty-five

The sun's radiance edged the slate-blue clouds with margins of brilliant silver. In the huge new Olympiastadion all faces were turned upward. There was an awed, collective intake of breath as twenty thousand doves were released, ascending in a rush from the well of the stadium to the wideness and freedom of the sky. With the beating of their wings the light seemed to flicker. Their silhouettes were dark against the veiled brightness of the sun.

'Look at that,' Grace breathed, slipping her arm through Amy's.

Vicki was silent, but gazed skyward, her dark eyes entranced. The coup de théâtre was underscored by the full-bodied resonance of massed voices raised in the Olympic anthem. Amy felt the goose flesh break out on her arms. She'd never seen anything like it, and it only served to heighten the acute sense of unreality she'd been experiencing all day.

It was a platitude that in Berlin the air was so sharp and peppery that hangovers were an unnecessary indulgence, sleep an optional extra. And, in fact, after her session with Claudia, Amy was pleasantly surprised by how well she felt. At the same time she had the impression that, overnight, there'd been a shift in her perception. Everyone and everything she saw seemed larger and brighter than life, yet somehow twinned with a correspondingly black and sinister shadow.

She was haunted by Claudia's grimly negligent reply to her routine enquiry after Alberich. Amy considered herself well informed. She read the papers. Noel came here often and always kept her *au fait*. She was in no way starry-eyed about the German new order. And yet Claudia's casual acceptance that skinny, insignificant Alberich was either dead or in a KZ had hit her with more force – more genuine illumination – than any article she'd ever read.

His graceless figure had lurked in the back of her mind while the fanfares sounded and hundreds of banners unfurled in lazy, elegant, perfectly orchestrated unison, while the bronzed and magnificent German team in their gleaming white uniforms filed past, and the crowds in the stadium bayed wildly for Hitler. All this, she understood, was obtained at a deeply ignominious cost.

'Look, look.' Vicki nudged her. 'I think they're going to light the flame.'

She pointed to the eastern end of the arena where a slender athlete in white had appeared, holding the smoking, cone-shaped torch. This single human figure, running swift and silent, was dwarfed by the vastness of the stadium and the grandiosity of everything that had gone before. The contrast was enormously effective – another dramatic, calculated masterstroke.

'It's divine,' Grace sighed as the young runner bounded lightly up a flight of white steps to the brazier above. Her expression was as rapturous as any of the Hitler Youth lads in the arena below.

The athlete stood poised for some moments. The eyes of the crowd were riveted to his lean frame and to the torch held high above his head. Then, slowly, theatrically, the flambeau dipped to the level of the brazier and instantaneously the bright volatility of fire leaped from the bowl.

The oohs and aahs of the spectators swelled in a crescendo of sound that came in great crashing waves like the sea, and made Amy shiver with its power.

In the evening Claudia had invited them to dine at the Tänzerin Café in the Kurfürstendamm, where she and Amy used to meet often in the old days.

'You won't recognize the place,' she told Amy. 'It's gone all blood and soil.'

She was right. The long plate-glass frontage was the same, but the pared-down simplicity of the interior had given way to a folksy mock-Bavarian mode – rugged tables, chairs with heart-shapes removed from their back rests as if with a biscuit cutter. The waitresses wore bodices, aprons and dirndl skirts, the waiters waist-coats appliquéd with gentians and edelweiss.

'This is quaint.' Grace looked round approvingly. She would have preferred to stay on at the stadium for the evening's Pageant of Youth, but seemed mollified by the exoticism of the restaurant.

'Bit twee.' Vicki cocked a quizzical eyebrow.

Claudia hadn't arrived yet, so they sat down at a large table by the window and watched the summer evening strollers, the light suits and fluttering floral dresses punctuated with a liberal sprinkling of SA brown.

Amy looked forward to the evening ahead with interest. As well as Horst, her new lover, Claudia was bringing her brother, Rudi, who was keen to meet Amy, apparently.

'He's grown up hearing me talk about you and then there's, well, the money you and Noel provided for his schooling . . .' She'd spoken about him with a subtle glow of affection and pride. He was going on twenty-two and training to be an architect. 'I'd better warn you he belongs to a Nazi student thing, but only,' she added in a rush, 'because it's impossible to study unless you do . . . We don't have to watch our words with him.'

One of the waitresses crossed to their table. Her rustic costume was disconcertingly at odds with her flinty blue eyes and sharp, urban little face. Grace was vacillating between lemonade and apple juice when the heavy glass door to the restaurant opened and Claudia entered with two tall men.

She looked stunning and it wasn't just luck. Claudia had clearly taken trouble with her clothes and make-up, visited the hairdresser. Her platinum bob was light and shiny, fell gracefully across her forehead, waved softly to jaw level. She wore what appeared to be an extended tennis dress of some sinuous, body-skimming material. The paleness of her hair and clothes contrasted pleasingly with the muted tan on her face and limbs.

'You're here. I'm sorry. You haven't been waiting long?' Her smile was wide and vivacious, but Amy saw her eyes shift almost furtively to rest on Vicki.

'We haven't even had time to order a drink.' Amy embraced her,

then turned to the two girls. 'My friend, Claudia Farnholz . . . Claudia
– Vicki and Grace.'

As Claudia laid eyes on her daughter for the first time in eleven
years, everything else vanished into a peripheral haze – the kitsch
surroundings, Horst, Rudi, Amy herself.

Vicki had risen to her feet in polite welcome. She wore the wine-red
dress from the photograph Amy had sent and held out her hand to
Claudia with a smile that was pleasant but not effusive. The reserve
that had been visible in the photo was even more marked in the
flesh.

'I used to know you when you were a little girl,' Claudia said.
'You've certainly changed.' Banal words, but she tried to invest them
with a special friendliness. The girl's hand in her own was soft, but
her grip was firm.

'I think I remember . . . I have a sort of dreamy impression of you
and Mum talking, talking . . .' Her eyes lit up as she spoke. Her voice
was low and composed and, irrationally, Claudia was impressed by
her English accent.

She was pleased by the remark. 'If you'd been with us last night
you would have seen that nothing has changed.'

The girl was more beautiful than she had ever been, Claudia
thought with pride. Her style had the simplicity of the classic, her
long, healthy hair caught back and left to hang. She couldn't imagine
Vicki chopping it or dyeing it in an attempt to play with her image.
She was what she was.

With an instinctive desire to conceal the intensity of her curiosity,
Claudia turned to smile brightly at the younger child. 'Hello, Grace.
Now you I've never met . . .'

'But Mum is always going into raptures about the good old days.'
The kid's small face was both hoydenish and trusting. 'So I've heard
a lot about you.'

She was a vivid little figure in a white sailor dress, with hair that
curled more exuberantly than Amy's, and a wilful look in her eye.

'I hear you were at the opening ceremony today. You must tell me all about it.' Claudia pulled out the chair next to Grace's. It would be easier that way.

Vicki found herself impressed by her mother's friend and the two handsome men she'd brought with her. Glamour was not a quality she looked for in her parents' acquaintances, but these three had it in abundance.

Claudia, with her platinum angel-hair, made her think of a film star. In England they knew no one like that. She was witty too, had everyone laughing with her good-natured teasing. Though, Vicki noticed, she herself wasn't included in the ribbing. Claudia addressed her more soberly. It didn't surprise her. Vicki was used to people thinking her serious, even standoffish.

Rudi, Claudia's brother, was good-looking and sociable. Only there was a . . . mockery in his smile that made her wary.

But she warmed to Horst straightaway. Not just because he was big and blond and striking. There was something about him that . . . disarmed and relaxed her. He'd taken the lead in ordering the meal, quizzing the hatchet-faced waitress so amiably about the menu that she softened and smiled. But it hadn't seemed as if he were deliberately exercising his charm, rather as if his natural goodwill brought out the same quality in others.

With general agreement he'd ordered some hearty Bavarian meat-and-potato-dumpling dish, a speciality of the house, wine for the ladies, beer for the men, and a sweet red drink called Bella for Grace, which he claimed to drink all the time at the theatre.

'It gives you the energy of a . . . kangaroo,' he told her.

'She doesn't need it,' Amy had commented drily.

'Yes I do.' Grace was enchanted by his recommendation.

As it happened, Vicki and Horst were sitting side by side. At times he dropped out of the general conversation to address her in particular.

'First time in Berlin?' he asked.

She nodded. His English was staccato, impressionistic. Vicki had some schoolgirl German.

'You like it?'

'It's exciting . . . You know, we saw Hitler today at the stadium. I can hardly believe it.'

'Our dear Führer.' He raised an eyebrow. She liked the way he talked to her. Some men observed themselves humouring a young chit, but Horst treated her with as much respect as an adult. 'What was your opinion?'

'In England we act as if he's a figure of fun, with his moustache and the way he shouts. He's a joke. But I looked at him through my binoculars . . .' She demonstrated with her hands in case he hadn't understood. 'I thought he was dignified. Powerful. He didn't look like a joke to me.'

'He's not a joke. That's the last thing he is.' His eyes looked into hers with great earnestness and Vicki felt her temperature rise.

Amy thought Claudia's brother engaging, with his wide cheekbones and springy dark hair, his eyes that were brown and lively like his sister's. He had a would-be sophisticated smile that she found endearingly pretentious in one so young. There was still an adolescent angularity about him, though beneath the pepper-and-salt sports jacket his shoulders looked broad and muscular.

He teased Claudia about being a throwback, an old bohemian from a bygone age, who'd at last managed to find some decent material to act in. But it was clear he was being ironic and thought *Countess Alexia* as much of a dog as she did. He seemed very fond and enormously proud of his older sister.

'She's loaned me the money to study,' he confided aside to Amy. 'With money she saved from her film days. Once I'm earning a bit I'll pay her back for sure.'

He was envious of Amy's attendance at the opening ceremony. 'Claudia would have hated it. But I love a bit of Wagnerian spectacle. What was your reaction?'

'Admiration – no getting away from that. It was dramatic – and brilliantly organized.' She paused to think for a moment. 'But a show like that seems to demand something in return . . . You're supposed to surrender to a sort of collective intoxication. And I'd rather hang on to my own lukewarm . . . apathy.'

Straightaway it occurred to Amy that her reply had been too ponderous for such a casual question. But Rudi looked impressed. Everyone said Germans liked a bit of pedantry.

'You never lose yourself?'

Was she imagining the flirtatious glint in his eye? Surely she was . . .

'I'm not keen on having my emotions orchestrated, if that's what you mean.'

Claudia mused that she was temperamentally unsuited to peasant fare. She paused for a while and sipped her wine, surveying the chunky caraway-flavoured ragout on her plate. You'd have to toil for several hours in the fields or vineyards to be hungry enough for a solid chunk of nourishment like this.

Though it seemed she was in the minority. Even Grace was tucking in happily, washing down each mouthful with that bilious red liquid Horst had ordered for her.

Perhaps she herself was simply too distracted. By the pleasure of observing her daughter for this long, luxurious slice of time. It wasn't even necessary, really, to engage her in conversation. Just look and commit to memory each gesture and fleeting expression, to return to like a miser's hoard in the small hours when she lay awake and reflective, while beside her Horst was dead to the world. As the meal progressed and the conversation hummed, Claudia aped her own convivial personality, while a parallel self crouched, all eyes, a fervid Peeping Tom.

She marvelled at the apparent poise and harmony of her daughter's personality. Fancifully, Vicki made her think of a clear, unhurried stream bubbling over clean pebbles. Then from time to time the smoothness of her features would light up with a sudden playful, almost saucy smile – like Amy's.

It seemed to Claudia that, young as she was, the girl inspired respect. It amused her to see that, when he spoke to her, Horst wore

the serious, well-brought-up smile he used for women he considered
ladies.

'*Fechten.*' Horst twirled an imaginary rapier, parried and thrust with
as much bravado as he could manage within the confines of his place
at the dining table.

'Fencing!' Grace's intense little face was radiant with the fun of
it.

'*Speerwerfen.*' He leaned back in his chair, one hand statuesquely
poised at shoulder level, leaning judiciously to the right as if braced
to hurl some missile.

'Javelin throwing!'

'*Hochsprung.*' His fingers skittered along the table top, snapped
upward in a dramatic vertical lift, descended again perilously close
to Vicki's half-full wine glass. He flashed her a rueful, winning smile.
'*Entschuldigung.*'

'High jump.' Grace leaned forward eagerly, elbows on the table,
chin propped in her hands.

He made the same motion, but the fingers leaped horizontally,
scrabbling in the air as they flew. '*Weitsprung.*'

'Long jump.' She beamed.

Horst was at ease with children. They liked him. As he amused
Grace the others watched with indulgent encouragement, including
Vicki, who wore an adorable bemused grin.

Minutes earlier he'd backed away from his dialogue with her. It was
becoming too . . . heavy. Foolishly Horst found himself responding to
the girl's clear, earnest gaze with a racing pulse, a shortness of breath.
His eyes were too rapt.

When, in the normal way, he conversed with young girls, it was
they who blushed and became flustered. He'd look a fine prick if the
tables were turned by this well-mannered fifteen-year-old.

Throughout the meal a radio above the bar had been playing the
kind of optimistic, uncomplicated songs that – along with military

marches – were *de rigueur* nowadays. A new one struck up. Claudia knew she knew it.

'Oh-oh, it's Rosa's new hit.'

Softly Horst sang along for a few bars, wearing a breezy, resilient grin and moving his shoulders in the style of Rosa Edelmann. The child, Grace, giggled at the performance, though she had no idea who he was imitating.

'This is my sister's doppelgänger, Rosa Edelmann.' Rudi spoke in English, indicating the radio and glancing at Claudia with amiable malice. 'They sang together as poor working girls many years ago. Now both are big, big stars in the new Reich.'

'Sarcastic brat.' But Claudia was amused by his mockery.

He turned to Amy – Claudia was pleased, he seemed to have taken to her – and resumed in German, 'Rosa's gutsy, perky, not an intellectual bone in her body. She's adored by the new guard – really come into her own.'

Amy laughed. 'It's a catchy tune anyway.'

They were all too full for dessert, apart from Grace and Horst who devoured large, highly coloured ice-cream sundaes. Claudia was delighted by how swimmingly the evening had gone. The meeting was a gamble and could have turned out to be a stilted disaster. Instead of which they were all chatting happily as if they'd known one another for years.

She raised her glass. By now it held only half an inch of white wine. 'It's a bit late,' she said, 'but anyway, here's to friendship.'

They clinked merrily. Vicki's eyes were deep and animated, Claudia noticed. She'd been afraid the kid might be bored.

Rudi had borrowed a friend's car and he drove them all home. He dropped Claudia and Horst off at their flat, then headed in the direction of the Pariserplatz to deliver Amy and the girls.

'I've never set foot inside the Adlon.' He glanced sideways at Amy with a smile that made him look more of a boy, less the young man about town. 'I've always had the feeling they'd take one look at me and know I didn't belong.'

'Come in for a moment, if you like. Have a look round. Then it won't be such a mystery any more.'

He admired the sumptuous lobby with its massive, square marble pillars, the bar with its clubby worn leather upholstery. Then Grace urged him to come upstairs and see their rooms. Disarmed by her insistence he duly inspected the girls' room, then allowed himself to be dragged along the corridor towards Amy's. The warm night air from the half-open window mingled with the scent of fragrant polish.

'I see you look out on the ruin of Unter den Linden.' Rudi stared out at the harshly lit avenue with its pompous columns. 'I tell you, before Hitler this was a lovely, unpretentious avenue . . .' Then, like the sun coming out, he flashed a quick self-mocking grin. 'I sound like my old landlady.'

Amy found herself charmed and amused at the way in which his veneer of sophistication was undercut by moments of youthful self-doubt.

'I'm exhausted,' Vicki said. 'I think I'll turn in.' She kissed Amy, shook hands with Rudi, chivvied a reluctant Grace out of the door and off to bed.

And Amy was left alone with this young virtual stranger. In a sense it seemed quite natural, another facet of the kaleidoscopic sequence of the day. But the girls' absence left a void, requiring a change in approach.

'May I buy you a drink?' he asked abruptly.

She was taken aback. Perhaps Rudi had gathered – from books or films – that this was the correct thing to say under the circumstances. Perhaps it was. She knew no better than he. But Amy was tired, the lack of sleep beginning to catch up with her. 'It's rather late.'

'Please.' There seemed an obscure urgency in his tone, as if the request were important to him.

'All right. Why not? One for the road.' She had the impression that he felt a bit out of his depth, and had no desire to trample on his courtesy.

And he was appealing anyway, with that combination of callowness and genuine charm, his figure gangling but muscular, as he stood by the gilt-trimmed bedside table ordering brandies down the phone.

While they waited she asked conventional questions about his studies. He told her about his labour-service last summer on some new industrial housing estate north-east of Berlin. The homes weren't beautiful, Rudi said, but convenient and thoughtfully designed. He added almost defiantly, 'There's a lot done for working people under this regime.'

He was interrupted by the arrival of the brandies. When the waiter had left, they settled themselves one each side of the window in the ornate gold brocade chairs, a round gilded table between them.

He grinned. 'This is cosy.'

Amy raised her glass. 'Here's to your future. All the good, solid houses you're going to design.' The brandy revived her a little. 'I hear from Claudia that you've had to join some Nazi student organization.'

His brown eyes looked into hers with wary honesty. 'Claudia tells everyone it's been forced on me . . . In a way that's true, but . . . I'm not so dead against the Nazis as she'd like to believe.'

Their eyes locked. Rudi looked like a schoolboy owning up to some misdemeanour, resolved, come what may, to brave the resulting fuss.

'Oh?' Amy was at a loss. He seemed to be challenging her, to expect outrage, disbelief.

With mounting vehemence he began to explain himself. 'I'm not a fool. I'm as bored as anyone with their idiotic cultural rules and regulations. I'm happy to repeat Hitler jokes, Goering jokes with the best of them . . . All the same, after three years of the Nazis, I'm certain we're better off. People see a future for themselves, there's an optimism in the air . . .'

Rudi took a sip of his brandy. His hand, Amy noticed, shook a little. His face, with its broad, tartar-like cheekbones was pale and intense. She was touched by his passion, if not his views.

'I laugh at Claudia about being a superannuated bohemian. She had her heyday under the Weimar lot – freedom, fun – and the Nazis came along and spoiled it for her. But she forgets how bad things were for so many. All this talk of the wild, wonderful twenties makes me sick. People were hungry, terrified of the next market crash –'

Amy cut in. 'I can't deny it's terribly impressive. The big, pompous ceremonies and all that. The employment situation.' She sounded sarcastic. 'But there's the matter of the price. Thousands of women have been thrown out of work . . . and Claudia was talking about this little communist fellow we both used to know –'

'People are kids.' He was heated, contemptuous. 'They think you can have order and progress by just being nice . . . You can't.'

'And the Jews?' Her voice was sharp and cold.

Now he was defensive. 'I don't like . . . But that won't last. Already it's dying down. Public opinion won't allow . . .'

'That's pure wishful thinking.'

'No.'

A low hostility had blown up between them with the suddenness of a spring storm.

'I don't say everything's perfect,' he began.

'Let's leave it, Rudi. It's late.' She stood up. 'You should be getting on home.'

'I didn't mean for us to quarrel.' Rising to his feet. 'That's the last thing I wanted.' He looked stricken, his eyes large and black in the lamplight. She half pitied him. After all, he was just a kid.

She shrugged. 'I can't pretend to agree with you.'

They stood face to face. He made no move to go.

'Amy.' He lifted a hand to touch her cheek. 'Let's not part bad friends.'

The statement had a childish directness, the gesture a subtle sensuality. The combination moved her, caught her off guard.

Rudi looked down at her. His smile was regretful, bemused. He bent and kissed her on the lips, tentatively, as if expecting a rebuff.

'No.' She protested with whispered incredulity.

He kissed her again more slowly and at the warm touch of his lips she began to soften. Rudi moved closer. The feel of his body stirred old associations, old responses. She turned her face up towards him, raised one hand to his broad shoulder.

*   *   *

332

'It's a dream,' Rudi murmured.

He lay beside her, raised on one elbow, gazing down into her face. He dipped his head to kiss her, with simple tenderness, on the forehead, the eyelids, in the crook of her neck. 'I'm dreaming I'm in bed with Claudia's English friend, Amy.' His smile was playful. Dazed.

Lazily she laid one hand to his ruffled hair. 'That's right. It's a dream. Nothing happened.'

Amy lay on her back, her body languorous with sensations she'd almost forgotten, but which had come flooding back with an immediate voluptuous familiarity. It amazed her that such pleasure could lie dormant for so long, yet reawaken instantly at the touch of another body.

Though he was clearly no novice, Rudi was young enough, it seemed, to blur affection and sensuality and Amy found the confusion touchingly erotic. His kisses were warm as a child's, his body slim and hard. His skin had the same tawny colour as Claudia's. He'd caressed her at first with a sort of speculative shyness, a frown of concentration, as if a test was to be passed. But soon his desire gained its own momentum, the frown smoothed out to a glittering, fevered excitement that entered insidiously into Amy's blood, raising her to an altered state of passionate precision. She'd felt inspired, using mouth and fingers with a focused skill that half shocked her and made Rudi groan with anguished pleasure.

They were aware all the time of footsteps in the corridor outside, voices under the window, doors being opened and slammed shut, the vivid sense of other lives being lived only yards away. Against this counterpoint their lovemaking seemed recklessly intense, a sensuous and secret transaction.

'I hate to be . . .'

Gently he laid two fingers to her lips. 'I know, I know, I've got to go.'

She'd insisted he must leave in the small hours. There must be no risk of the girls discovering his presence.

He covered her body with his own so that, delectably, through her skin, she experienced all the smooth-rough textures of him, the resilience of muscle, his sheer solidity.

He made a growling sound of pleasure deep in his throat. 'I can't bear to leave you ... Will you let me come again? Tonight?'

She moved luxuriously beneath him. 'If you're good.'

Chapter Thirty-six

On stage Horst was conducting a sprightly flirtation with Claudia. His broad-shouldered, long-legged figure showed to advantage in narrow black trousers, a matching high-buttoned jacket, white wing collar, a spotted tie. His blond hair gleamed under the lights.

Vicki's German wasn't good enough to catch a twentieth of what they were saying, but she loved to watch Horst's amiable smile and the confident way he moved, and listen to the deep, full-blooded timbre of his voice.

She seemed to be missing a lot because the Germans all round her were in raptures, smiling with whole-hearted enjoyment at the scene being acted out in front of them, erupting into gales of laughter after every second line.

Claudia looked most unlike herself in frilled red taffeta and a silvery piled-up wig. Her cheeks were pinkly rouged, mouth held in a witty, lipsticked rictus of a smile that was probably right for the stylized character she was playing.

'It's a piece of shit.' Vicki grinned in the dark. Amy had mimicked Claudia's description of the piece, pronounced in formal Germanic English, with a small, supremely expressive upward movement of the eyes.

It seemed Claudia had to become someone else in order to play her part, whereas Horst casually used his native good nature and charm to breathe life into the stilted lines.

Next to her Grace looked glazed and bored. The early novelty of seeing people she knew up there on stage had long since palled, as they jabbered endlessly in an incomprehensible language. To her right Amy's profile was smooth, inscrutable.

Since they'd been in Berlin Vicki's perception of her mother was having to shift in order to accommodate this new side of her – a being who existed outside the realm of home and family, with friends of her own, an attractive woman whom men looked at as she walked down the street. It was disconcerting. Vicki wasn't sure she liked it.

But her attention returned to the stage. Horst and Claudia had been joined by a little old man like a spoof psychiatrist, with a beard and pince-nez, who talked in a wavery voice and kept interrupting Horst, to comic effect, so that the whole audience rocked with laughter.

'*Das ist ja merkwürdig!*' Horst exclaimed in a baffled fashion, when the laughter died away.

Vicki understood the line and it didn't seem that funny to her but, again, a gale of mirth shook the receptive onlookers as Horst screwed his face into a caricature of innocent puzzlement.

How sweet he was. She could happily have watched if he'd been acting in Chinese. Vicki admitted to herself that she had a sizeable crush on him. In her mind she appropriated the schoolgirl slang all her friends used. She was rather bucked at the realization. She'd thought herself unnatural, immune. But Horst was so much more worthy of homage than the spotty lads or the unattainable actors they favoured . . . After all, Horst *was* an actor, but he was real too.

With the success of *Countess Alexia* neither Claudia nor Horst was currently involved in daytime rehearsals. They'd all been out together quite a few times. Picnicking by the Wannsee. To the Olympics, where they all cheered for the triumphant black sprinter, Jesse Owens. And, on the theatre's evening off, to *Haus Vaterland*, a touristy café, or rather eight cafés under one roof – great fun – each with décor and music from a different part of the world.

Horst always made a great fuss of Grace. She loved him because he behaved like another kid, playing spit-the-plum-stones, drawing silly pictures on menus, getting her to repeat incomprehensible German tongue-twisters, imitating an obsequious waiter who kept bowing and calling Amy and Claudia '*gnädige Frau.*' Everything he did was invested with a kind of high-spirited glamour, everything was just right. Vicki was happy simply to watch and adore. She'd never been the clowning type like Grace.

Some people tried to make you feel stupid if you were serious at all. But Horst wasn't like that and neither was Claudia. Her mother's friend seemed to be really interested in all Vicki's doings and impressed that she did well at school. In fact she seemed to know all about her exams and things from Amy. It pleased Vicki to think that Amy wrote about her in that way.

After a swim in the Wannsee the other day, she and Claudia had sat in one of the striped basket chairs on the beach, sunning themselves in their swimsuits, and they'd had a really good conversation. Claudia said she'd been quite clever as a girl and would have taken her education further, only the war came and she lost both parents and she had to get out and start earning a living. Vicki asked how she'd managed and Claudia was so funny, talking about all the various jobs she'd had, including keeping house for Amy . . . It was fascinating and Vicki had the impression that Claudia really liked her.

'*Zum Befehl, Gräfin.*'

On stage the little old man had vanished, and Horst was kissing Claudia with flamboyant ardour, bending her backward, the way people only ever did in plays or films. Dreamily Vicki imagined herself in Claudia's place.

'I feel as if I'm living in a French novel,' Rudi said. '. . . Have you read *Le Diable au Corps*?'

Amy shook her head.

'It's about a boy who has an affair with a married woman, older than him . . . I forget what happens – maybe she dies or something – but it's the encounter that shapes his life.'

Amy smiled. 'I don't plan on dying in order to provide a memorable finale . . .'

'That's all right.' Across the table Rudi grinned, squinting a little from the sun. 'I prefer things not to be too hard and fast.'

He leaned forward, elbows on the table, a cigarette between his fingers, in front of him a small glass of kümmel. He wore his pepper-and-salt jacket, a white shirt, the tie casually loosened. There was a happy relaxation about his eyes and mouth, in the set of his body.

337

And in the bright daylight he looked quite dizzyingly young.

Horst and Claudia had taken the girls for a repeat excursion to the Wannsee. Amy had seen the free day as an opportunity to revisit some old haunts that would merely bore her daughters. But, in the event, Rudi had pressed her to come to lunch in Kreuzberg, the homely district where he lived currently, and she had allowed herself to be persuaded.

They sat now, over coffee and caraway liqueurs, on the terrace of a modest restaurant on the Chamissoplatz. The sun was shining and, for the moment, they had all the time in the world.

Indicating the square with a vague movement of the hand, Rudi remarked, 'People say it's like Paris here.'

'Is that good?'

He shrugged amiably. 'I suppose it gives the tawdriness a certain *je ne sais quoi*.'

She found the square congenial with its tall, rackety tenements, its willows and birch trees, the piece of park in the centre. Sitting here with Rudi, Amy felt wonderfully anonymous. She felt like someone else. Sipping the sweet, fiery kümmel, lazily living in the present. Strange how rarely one did that, consciously.

'Only two more days,' Rudi said, as if to prick her serenity.

'Two more nights,' Amy corrected. 'Do you realize I've never seen you by daylight before. Even that first evening at the Tänzerin those weird edelweiss lamps were on above all the tables.'

Their affair had been conducted in the twilight of her hotel room. Rudi came each time after midnight. There was no way to pretend, she thought wryly, that their relationship was other than sexual. Though afterwards, lying in the warmth of one another's bodies, they talked idly, intimately.

The end of their affair had always been present, even as they began. Both recognized the fact. When, in two days' time, Amy and her children left for England, it was unlikely that she and Rudi would ever meet again.

Last night, lying drowsily beside her, he'd said, 'When people talk about the Olympiad of '36, I'll see quite different pictures from everyone else.' He raised himself on one elbow to look at her. 'I'll

338

see this room with its fancy chairs and curtains, and our two bodies, and your blonde head going down on me.'

She laughed sleepily. 'Sounds a wonderful memory.'

It seemed to Amy that Rudi perceived his life, not as a horizontal line, but in bright, vertical segments, and in this instance she happily shared his view. Their relationship would be arbitrarily truncated. To Amy there was something healthy in the knowledge. There were times, after they'd made love, when she sensed in herself a melting infatuation, the potential for a self-destructive addiction to Rudi's youth and charm.

As it was, their affair was exhilarating – robustly opportunistic, yet with a vein of genuine tenderness that probably could never have survived the light of day, but which, in its shadowy place, was simple and sincere.

And Amy had renewed contact with a neglected part of herself, the parallel being that lurked in everyone – coexisting with the dutiful wife and perfect family man – feral and lawless, with a slit-eyed fixation on excitement and pleasure.

They lingered for a while longer in the sunshine, drinking more coffee and watching some children playing soldiers in the centre of the square, wiry little legs protruding from their shorts, marching and drilling ferociously.

'That'll be me next year,' Rudi commented glumly. He would have to do the now mandatory two years' military service.

'I'm not sure I'd like to see you in uniform.'

From nowhere Amy recalled something Noel had said the last time they dined with Robert Beadle and Hester. 'Anyone who talks as much about peace as Hitler has got to be planning war.' In a bleak flash of imagination she saw Rudi in field grey. Like it or not, a young enemy.

Oblivious, he turned to her. 'I wish you didn't have to go.'

'Horst, won't you go with Vicki and Grace to see the animals? Amy and I could wait for you under these trees. Then we'll all go to the restaurant for ice cream and coffee.'

339

'*Zum Befehl, Gräfin.*'

Claudia and Horst had agreed on the stratagem beforehand. They'd all had glorious times together, but Claudia hadn't seen half enough of Amy on her own.

There was a bench in the shade of some chestnut trees near the aquarium. In the middle distance the four chunky spires of the Kaiser Wilhelm Memorial Church cut into the blue of the sky.

They watched Horst's broad, retreating back. He had Grace by the hand, was bending his ear towards Vicki, who appeared to be recounting some complex anecdote.

'He's nice,' Amy said. 'Will it last, you and he?'

'I don't suppose so for a moment,' Claudia replied drily. 'But that's never been the point.'

'What a cynic . . . He's made a hit with the girls at any rate.'

Her skin dappled with the shifting shadows of the leaves, Amy looked pale. But there was another quality, a kind of low-burning, buried excitement. She wore a thin black dress patterned with scarlet poppies and the sharply contrasting colours underlined a fine-drawn tension in her features that had not existed, Claudia thought, when she first arrived. Or was it her imagination?

'I wish you didn't have to go,' she said impulsively.

'You've showed us such a wonderful time, both of you. It's beyond thanks . . . Vicki and Grace are in heaven. I'll never get them to settle back into ordinary life.'

'And you?'

'It's meant so much.' Amy's expression was rueful. 'You can lose yourself in family life, and perhaps you should . . . But it's easy to forget you're anything but a cog in the domestic wheel and getting away has reminded me . . .' She looked as if she were about to say more, but checked herself. 'I hate to leave. It'll be a wrench, more so than I can say. Still, there are things to be said for getting back to reality.'

'You're too philosophical for your own good.'

'Aren't I just?' Amy lifted her arms, resting them along the back of the bench, looking up at the sun with half-closed eyes. 'It's been haunting me the whole fortnight, you know. What you told me about Johnny. I can't forgive myself for not realizing.'

'I did everything I humanly could to hide it.' Today Claudia was dispassionate. Memories of Johnny couldn't reach her. 'So you can hardly blame yourself.' She turned her head towards Amy. 'There's one thing, though, I really regret.'

'What's that?'

'It's the way we parted. A meaningless little squabble. Not even a great big out-and-out screaming match . . . I still have the fantasy I'll meet him again one day and everything will come right.' She added, with dour emphasis, 'Though as long as the Nazis stay in power that's not hugely likely . . .'

They sat in silence for a moment. Then Claudia touched Amy's arm. 'Thank you for letting me see Vicki.'

'I think of it as your right.'

'And Noel?'

'He knows I'm adamant on some things.'

The slight evasion was revealing, Claudia thought.

Amy turned towards her with a movement that held a suppressed intensity. 'There's something I want to tell you. Something I've never ever told anyone before.'

Claudia was impressed by the urgency of her tone.

'It's about me and Noel.'

'Oh?' She was sharply curious.

'See, Noel had a pretty awful time in the war. In some way he's never recovered.' She hesitated, then seemed to take the plunge. 'Ever since I've known him he's been impotent, Claudia. He and I have never been able to make love fully.'

For a second or two Claudia was stunned. Then, as her brain began to assimilate the information, it made sense, explained certain things that had never quite added up. Amy faced her with a sort of defiance that precluded any well-meaning attempt at sympathy.

Chapter Thirty-seven

Gudrun Kröger lay beside her husband, contemplating the sloping ceiling of their room, her eyes accustomed to the near-darkness. Johnny was dead to the world, but most nights Gudrun lay awake for an hour, two hours, while her head spun with anxious thoughts, like a stale record someone played again and again and again.

Johnny slept peaceful and quiet. How did he manage to sleep so well? And the children too – once they'd stopped whispering and giggling – breathed light and sweet as angels. Gudrun felt clumsy, unworthy, because she slept so ill and woke with hollow eyes and, often as not, a headache that reverberated all day to every sound and shout that echoed up from the grey courtyard below.

Nearly all the time her head felt hollow, dizzy when she turned too quickly. She never used to feel like this. Gudrun understood that she'd never appreciated the freedom from tension, the sheer wellbeing of her life before they came to Prague five years ago in '33.

Here the slightest thing made her knot up – the sound of Eva, the neighbour, shouting at her kids, the way Johnny invariably pulled the tablecloth askew when he sat down to sketch, the fact that his drawing paraphernalia was always in the way at meal-times, the thundering vibration of the children's feet, up and down, up and down the walkway outside their window.

She felt a prisoner of the cramped tenement where they lived. Three storeys round a central courtyard, shared privies, and every drop of water had to be fetched from downstairs, lugged up in buckets from the communal standpipe. Not that she minded that particularly. Her family had done it all their lives in Berlin, and the barracks they lived in wasn't picturesque like the buildings here.

Only there she had been part of something, even if it was only to gossip about the Jews upstairs with their noisy children, or Lena Griff and the men who traipsed in and out of her apartment all day. Here she sometimes felt like a shadow as she queued with the Czech women, who had gossip of their own – in fact she was probably the subject of it as soon as her back was turned.

They weren't unfriendly exactly. They cooed over the children, pulled at her sleeve with emphatic dumb show to point out when it was her turn for the tap, spoke loudly to her in their own language, though she understood only the most basic words. But Gudrun felt alienated. Germans and Czechs had never got on, and no one cared whether they were Nazis or not.

'Little nurse, I wish you were happier,' Johnny said sometimes.

She used to like it when he called her that. Back in Berlin she was proud of who she was. Here she was nothing, just a wraith who walked up and down with buckets of water and cooked and cleaned. The two boys seemed to be thriving. Red-cheeked and boisterous, they didn't know any other world but this. Sometimes Gudrun felt like a pelican, as if she were feeding them with her lifeblood.

In the early days there'd been a magic, a whiff of adventure to their exile. They had planned ahead, managed to get most of their money out. And when they got to Prague there were lots of people in the same boat. Some of them were already friends of Johnny's. They all helped each other out, offering meals and beds, brothers and sisters in adversity. They used to sit up late, planning resistance. There was hope in the air. Gudrun felt special to be a small part of it.

There was a conviction that the Nazis couldn't last, could never hold out against all the ridicule and vituperation that was aimed at them. In those days Johnny seemed to glow with a sort of power – the drawings and ideas just flowed from him in a strong, vengeful stream that had her in awe. And there were ways of smuggling the subversive stuff into Germany, enough people willing to take the risk.

Johnny was happy because he was busy and because everyone said what a brilliant job he was doing, what a symbol he was to like-minded people back home. And the happiness made him sweet and tender. Hans was a toddler then and Gudrun soon fell for another baby.

Johnny even found it in his heart to forgive his father and name the child for him. Stefan. Back then he felt blessed and Gudrun felt loved. With their friends and the children they were self-sufficient. Their surroundings hardly impinged at all.

But the good days faded. So many of their fellow ex-patriates moved on, leaving for England, America, some of the Jews to Palestine. Neither she nor Johnny ever considered going that far afield. An umbilical cord tied both of them to Germany. She, Gudrun, had a longing like a sickness for her family, her parents and sisters, a superstitious dread of placing any further distance between them. And Johnny could not resign himself to the fact that his usefulness was coming to an end. Hardly anyone could be found any more ready to risk their lives distributing anti-Nazi propaganda. The enemy had become ever touchier, ever more ruthless.

The sloping ceiling of the room gleamed white in the darkness. Sometimes, as she lay staring upward, it seemed to sheer off at crazy angles. They lived and slept in this room. During the day their bed served as a sort of giant sofa. It was always in the way and the kids used it as a trampoline. There was a small cubbyhole next door where the boys slept and kept their few toys, a narrow galley of a kitchen.

They were on top of one another all the time. Johnny worked with the children playing round his feet, herself washing and cooking. Gudrun knew she irritated him with her pallor and the misery she couldn't shake off, no matter how she tried. But he never showed any impatience. He kept an iron grip because, if he didn't, they would turn and tear one another, savage in their frustration.

Going out was his escape. Sometimes he met one or other of the few friends they had left in a bar, numbed his sense of futility in drink and company. Most days he took the boys to one of the neighbouring parks, bringing them home fresh and glowing, and Gudrun loved them so much she could burst, but all she had to offer was her stale wretchedness.

Their closest comrades in Prague were Adam and Inge Raab. They hadn't known them before they came here, had only a nodding acquaintance for some time after that. They became friends more by a process of elimination than anything else.

344

Adam was a novelist. Johnny thought his books were rather good. They were short, for one thing – he hadn't the patience for weighty tomes. And the language they used was crude and direct. That appealed to him. Adam had never made much of a splash, but the Nazis burned his books anyway, along with the works of giants like Heine and Thomas Mann.

His wife, Inge, was a bit of a joke. Plump and frizzy-haired. Clever, people said, but a haphazard dresser who teamed awful floral blouses with corduroy trousers and ankle socks. The sort of woman Johnny considered beyond the sexual pale. He used to laugh at her as a frump and Gudrun was gratified. She often felt out of her depth among the arty people Johnny frequented, but at least she was pretty, and Johnny always said she was worth the lot of them put together.

But in adversity Inge shone. Adam was low in spirits. He'd written his best book ever, so he reckoned, but had no way of getting it published. Inge took over, retyping the manuscript several times, sending copies off to innumerable publishers in Switzerland, Denmark, even Russia, with a letter explaining her husband's situation. After months she triumphed. A radical firm in Berne was willing to take the novel on and give it publicity. The money was poor – they'd expected that – but the Raabs were jubilant, with a feeling that, in some small way, they'd outmanoeuvred Hitler.

Inge spoke several languages. She did the rounds of countless companies in Prague, on foot, begging for translation work, and wasn't afraid of appearing a pest. Her stubbornness paid off. The translations kept the wolf from the door and Adam was free to carry on with his writing. As a by-product of her persistence she obtained hack illustrating commissions to keep Johnny ticking over.

Now he spoke of her admiringly as a rock and Gudrun felt humiliated. She was failing where fat, dowdy Inge had succeeded.

He and Inge talked politics too. For some time they'd been exercised over a man called Konrad Henlein who'd been agitating for the Sudetenland to the north to become part of Germany. He and his party were financed by the fascists, Johnny said, and Inge agreed the whole thing was a ploy of Hitler's. Gudrun had never taken much notice. She was hurt when Johnny talked like that to Inge, as if he thought his own wife too stupid.

But two weeks ago the German army had marched into Austria, been welcomed with open arms, so the story went, and suddenly it was clear to Gudrun that the same thing could happen here. And the Sudetenland was only hours away . . .

Beside her Johnny stirred. Gudrun held her breath.

Clumsily he moved an arm towards her. 'You awake, darling?'

She snuggled into his warm flesh. It was the only thing that had the power to ease her tension. Moving her hand across his belly.

'More.' His voice was thick and sleepy.

Gudrun smiled. Finding his penis already engorged. Massaging it slowly with her slim, tapering fingers. He sighed luxuriously, halfway between sleeping and waking.

In the dark they could be free and equal. Two ghosts reaching blindly for comfort and forgiveness.

Chapter Thirty-eight

'Carefully, Grace!'

'Oh Dad!' A note of impatience.

What an old fart I sound, Noel thought, as he stared up into the branches of the cherry tree where his daughter climbed with the casual ease of a monkey. It was a tradition – dating back to when Grace was three or four and more hindrance than help – that each year the two of them together picked the cherries from the two spreading trees in the Belsize Park garden. They had baskets and a ladder, but a lot of the fruit remained inaccessible.

'One of us will have to go up,' Grace said. 'And I don't fancy your chances.'

Smiling at her irreverence: 'You think I'm past it?'

'I think I'm smaller and a lot more agile. Imagine you're a chimney-sweep sending up his climbing-boy.'

He looked on with amusement, and a tinge of anxiety, as her supple twelve-year-old figure shinned up and along the branches, flexing and stretching after the ripe cherries. She wore grey shorts, a white singlet. Her slim legs were tanned, her blonde hair a cloudy bob, her little face expressionless and intent. Noel felt a surge of love and pride.

'Here, catch.'

She leaned forward and down, letting fall a heavy handful of ripe fruit, her physical confidence easy and absolute.

'Grace, do hold on.'

Laughingly she provoked him, pretending to wobble. She was so like Amy. But Amy had been kept down as a child, could never have looked so carefree and full of herself. With her bubbling high spirits Grace altered the dynamic of the family. Constantly Noel prayed that nothing would ever happen to quench that inborn *joie de vivre*.

He'd arrived home yesterday from an investigative trip to Berlin. Once such interludes had been a pleasure. Nowadays he hated the atmosphere of the place, the more so since the city had once meant so much to him. It depressed him profoundly, the way the ludicrous Heil Hitler greeting had taken hold, pronounced at every turn without a flicker. There had always been violence on the streets, blowing up out of nowhere – demos, clashes between rival factions. Now brutality was legal. Just so long as it was Nazi brutality.

This summer of '38 the newspapers and the Propaganda Ministry handouts were full of sob stories about the oppression of the Sudetans by the Czechs, with pictures of helpless old men and pregnant women. Leader writers fulminated with righteous indignation. Clearly the stand-off in May had simply been an exploratory skirmish. Hitler was determined on a new Anschluss.

Picking cherries in a sunny garden on a Sunday afternoon. Such a quintessentially peaceful activity that his thoughts turned all the more insistently to war. Like his fellow journalists, like almost everyone who thought about such things at all, Noel was convinced it would come, sooner or later. In 1914 his fears and regrets had been all for himself. Having children changed all that. Now, increasingly, he was ambushed by a passionate awareness of his daughters' brightness and beauty, swept through by anguish at the way the world's upheavals sucked in the innocent and guilty alike.

'Bombs away!' Grace made as if to hurl a handful of cherries, then leaned down to release them with exaggerated carefulness. 'That's about the lot.'

Swiftly she descended to the fork of the tree, swung from one of the lower branches, then dropped to the ground, raising her arms with the triumphant air of an acrobat.

Noel grinned at her panache. 'And so another year's harvest was gathered in.'

'Boo hoo.' Grace was fiercely attached to their annual ritual. It was one thing she had over Vicki. She contemplated the two piled baskets. 'Mum'll have to get cracking with the pies and the jam.'

348

'We could stone some for her before she gets back.'

Amy had gone to one of Edward's anti-unemployment rallies. Noel admired his wife's dedication in giving up a glorious Sunday to something so earnest and unpleasurable. Futile too, he thought, though he wouldn't have said so out loud.

Grace pulled a face. 'In return for some lemonade I might . . .'

As they carried their baskets towards the house she hung clusters of cherries in her ears. Opening the refrigerator she took out the tall, stripy pitcher of iced lemonade. It was home-made and not to be drunk indiscriminately. Slices of lemon floated on the surface.

'Some for you, Pa?' She raised the jug enquiringly.

'Don't mind if I do.'

They drank the cold, tart liquid, sitting opposite one another at the bare, scrubbed kitchen table. Grace sighed with exaggerated bliss. Then Noel found a couple of knives and they began to stone one of the heaps of cherries.

'Ten days to the end of term.' Grace thought out loud as she split the juicy flesh. 'I can't wait . . . Can't wait to see Horst and Claudia again.'

Noel gave a non-committal smile. He could not suppress a small twinge of displeasure, could never decide whether his prejudice against Claudia was justified or not.

'Shame we can't go to Berlin again really. Still, a cottage in the country should be quaint.'

He'd been mildly put out, he couldn't deny it, when Amy and the girls came home from Berlin, two years ago it was now, on top of the world, and clearly having had a whale of a time. It wasn't that he didn't want them to enjoy themselves . . . Only perhaps, he thought wryly, not quite so much, not quite so obviously.

Noel had always had misgivings about Claudia's remaining in touch with Vicki, but that side of things seemed to have passed off perfectly happily. So really it was small-minded of him . . . Only Amy had looked so radiant, had clearly not missed him one bit. If he were honest perhaps his objection was that Claudia brought out his wife's independent side – an exhilaration, a wildness even, that deep down Noel feared.

'I wish you could come down to the cottage too, Dad. Couldn't you take a few days?'

Noel added another cherry stone to the cluster on the spread newspaper. 'I'm too busy, darling. I can't just up sticks whenever I feel like it . . .' Allowing a note of satire to enter his voice.

'You don't like Mum being friends with Claudia, do you?'

The shrewd honesty of the observation took him by surprise. But to reply with equal candour would be to open a can of worms that Noel was not prepared to broach.

He stalled. 'What makes you say that?'

Her expression was one he particularly loved. Lips drawn down, rueful, irresistible. She looked about six years old. 'Just something in the way you . . .'

'I've got a lot of respect for Claudia.' Which was true, but beside the point.

Vicki sat in the garden of the Pughs' old cottage in Crofton, pretending to read Aldous Huxley. But the print flowed past her vision, never connecting with her brain. All her senses were on the qui vive, straining, waiting. Amy had taken the Morris to fetch Claudia and Horst from Gloucester. With an emotion bordering on panic Vicki contemplated the incredible fact that, within minutes, Horst would flick the gate-latch, enter under the archway of purple clematis, walk up the cinder path, solid flesh and blood.

She was half convinced she would faint on the spot. Horst – or the idea of Horst – had become so significant to her. A secret she hugged to herself, along with two windswept photographs of him taken by the Wannsee. Vicki had stolen the negatives and had copies made so she could look at them whenever she liked.

He wasn't quite a secret. When they first came back from Berlin she'd told her friend Dora she had a crush on someone, talked about Horst and showed his photograph. Dora was pop-eyed and impressed. But, as the weeks went by, there was nothing new to report, and Vicki vaguely regretted having confided in anyone at all, was happy to let the memory peter out in Dora's mind.

This visit had been mooted a long time ago. Horst and Claudia had to plan ahead. They'd arranged a month when neither would be acting or rehearsing. August the first had been imprinted on Vicki's brain as a red-letter day for almost a year now. Once it had been established, Vicki was free to get on with her life. There were things she had to do before then, like pass her Higher School Certificate – she'd really worked hard at that.

There was even a boyfriend of sorts. Anthony Christie was studious like herself. He was tall and brown-haired, with long eyelashes and beautiful brown eyes. He was in love with her and sportingly respected the fact that she couldn't return his feelings. They lent each other books and she could talk to him.

Then again, Horst could quote Goethe and Schiller, even Shakespeare, but he was funny too, and sweet and warm, and his jokes never fell flat – nothing he said or did ever fell flat – and his looks made her catch her breath.

It wasn't that she expected anything from him, not realistically. He was ten years older and a lot more experienced, and Claudia's lover in any case. Vicki had repeated these facts to herself over and over in her head. She just wanted to recapture the pleasure of looking at him and being with him, being teased and smiled at by him. The magic *must* still work. Even stronger than her fear of seeing him was the fear of being disappointed.

'Nothing to report but a flock of sheep!' Grace was up in the branches of a willow keeping a look out for the Morris. She had ants in her pants recently, forever climbing and swinging and hanging upside down by the knees.

Vicki flaunted a calm she didn't feel. 'They'll come when they're supposed to come.'

'Well I never!' Grace mocked the truism. She climbed higher. 'A man on a bicycle . . . The suspense is unbearable.'

The Pughs' cottage was quaint – Grace's favourite word. It used to belong to an old village couple Amy remembered from her childhood – 'only in those days it always smelled of boiled cabbage.'

The inhabitants were beginning to realize that Crofton was

picturesque. Townspeople exclaimed over the storybook rows of houses, the golden Cotswold stone, the rambling roses. When the Pughs died their daughter decided to rent their cottage out to holiday-makers. At first the villagers looked askance, but others followed suit, sometimes even moving in with relatives during the summer months so they could let out their own homes.

This particular cottage, Vicki thought, with its gabled windows and half-timbering, the garden blooming with marigolds and snapdragons, could hardly be more rustic and English. Its very attractiveness she saw as a hopeful omen for the month ahead.

'It's them! It's them!' A screech from Grace, who began to scramble down from the willow in a fever of excitement.

Vicki felt her insides lurch. She took several deep, desperate breaths. Grace dropped lightly from the tree and ran out into the street, capering wildly in her plimsolls and shorts, as the Morris slowed and stopped outside the chest-high garden wall.

Her heart hammering, Vicki got up from the garden bench. She stood silent and still, watching, while Claudia alighted from the front passenger seat, kissed Grace with cries of pleasure, opened the rear door and said something to Horst, who was still inside. He passed out a couple of suitcases, then emerged from the car himself, bent double, easing his large frame through the doorway.

Grace launched herself at him. He seized her, lifting her at arm's length and holding her up for inspection. 'What happened to you? You're a giant now. Queen Kong.'

Instantly his bulky figure and smiling face, framed by the thick, straight fair hair, were as familiar and pleasing to Vicki as if she'd seen him only yesterday. Laughing and chattering, Amy, Grace and the two guests entered through the arched gateway.

'Vicki!'

In a green and black striped dress, her blonde hair bouncing, Claudia rushed to kiss her. The look on her face was glad and tender. Vicki caught the tang of some dry, spicy fragrance.

'You look so beautiful, Vicki! So grown-up.'

'It's lovely to see you, Claudia.'

The greeting sounded cool and formal by comparison with

Claudia's ecstatic embrace. Vicki was aware of Horst standing behind her, waiting his turn. She dared not meet his eye for fear of revealing the intensity of her anticipation.

'Look, Horst, what a young lady Vicki has become.' Claudia presented her with happy enthusiasm.

There was no avoiding it. Vicki lifted her gaze, as if towards something taboo, and looked directly at him. To her astonishment Horst's grey eyes showed the same tension, the same nakedness as her own.

'Hello again, Vicki,' he said.

Claudia thought it bliss to sleep late in the whitewashed bedroom with the patchwork quilt and roses nodding outside the window, to wake in her own good time, slip on a dressing gown, pad downstairs to the flagged kitchen and find breakfast ready and waiting. Restless Grace got up early, went out to buy milk, butter and warm, fresh bread for them all. There was real coffee, real butter, real bread. Such luxuries were becoming harder to find in Berlin. Everything was ersatz, substandard, thanks to Hitler's obsession with national self-sufficiency.

Sometimes she took her coffee out into the secluded garden and drank it sitting on one of the wooden benches, turning her face up to the sun and chatting companionably with Amy or Vicki or Grace – all of them took it negligently for granted that Horst would still be sleeping his fill. Claudia luxuriated in the leisurely pace of their days. She hadn't had a holiday in so long.

At the moment her real life was naggingly unsatisfactory. There were cracks in her relationship with Horst. Both had, on odd occasions, slept with other lovers. If they stayed together it was more from a kind of affectionate inertia than any pressing commitment. In a sense Claudia was sanguine. She had always known that they would end sooner or later. Only there was a staleness to her situation. She'd done it all before, and couldn't imagine summoning up the enthusiasm for a new affair ever again.

As for her career, Claudia was growing ever more jaundiced with the material she was obliged to perform. Her most recent role had been that of a feisty peasant mother. Some of her speeches – all wombs and bowels and male ploughs fertilizing the receptive female earth – made her cringe with embarrassment. She and Horst had been hysterical for weeks quoting those at one another. But, when it came down to it, there was something soul-deadening about earning a living you despised.

She'd worn a kerchief over her hair for the role and blacked out two of her teeth. Surveying herself in the harsh dressing-room mirror, Claudia had recognized that she would never play Countess Alexia again. The company had a new leading lady called Irmgard Klapp who monopolized those sort of roles. Her acting was excruciatingly affected but her Nazi credentials impeccable. The critics raved over her as the embodiment of German femininity.

All in all Claudia was none too optimistic about her future. She wasn't getting any younger and the Nazi ideology had no great use for older women, except as mothers or grandmothers of teeming, fecund families. But now she was here, all that was by the by. No point in poisoning her holiday by brooding.

Only there was something that went deeper than all this and she couldn't simply shut it off, not even in the Arcadian surroundings of this peaceful village. A suspicion that had shaken her whole system and continued to lurk like a cancer, sapping her cheerfulness, and ambushing her every now and again with a vicious jolt of insight.

One such moment occurred as she and Amy drank their morning coffee and watched some birds squabbling over crumbs Grace had thrown on to the grass. Beside her Amy's profile was smooth and untroubled.

'I'm scared for Sergei, you know,' Claudia announced abruptly.

Startled, Amy turned to look at her. 'Sergei?'

'I'm certain he's in some kind of a prison camp . . . labour camp.'

As Amy struggled to collect her thoughts, Claudia explained. She and Sergei had parted good friends and kept up a correspondence for years. But eighteen months ago the letters stopped coming. At first she thought nothing of it. To be honest she was surprised that wayward Sergei had written so faithfully for so long. He'd probably met a new woman and fallen in love. In time he might even think to tell her about it.

A little while later, at a party, she ran into a journalist she and Sergei used to know. Back in the Weimar days he worked for the Ullstein press, writing chatty, trivial stuff for photographic magazines. Like Claudia he had an uneasy relationship with the new regime, a troubled conscience. He'd been abroad recently, and met exiles, some of whom had spent time in Russia. They simmered with rumours, which were partly born out by experience.

'Compared to Stalin, Hitler's an amateur,' he told her cynically.

According to him the communist premier had established a vast network of labour camps where prisoners were worked into the ground, starved, beaten. To keep them filled there were mass arrests on the most flimsy of pretexts.

'Can't say I hold out much hope for Sergei.' Such was the man's gloomy verdict. 'His parents were White Russians after all, and he spent years in exile. That's plenty enough to damn him.'

'But Sergei was never political,' Claudia protested earnestly.

The journalist rolled up his eyes as if he'd never heard anything so naïve in his life.

It was impossible to find anything out. The Soviets were hardly going to publish lists of arbitrarily arrested victims. But Claudia was more and more convinced that this had been Sergei's fate, kept picturing him cowed and emaciated. Sergei – too easy-going to hurt a fly.

Amy listened in silence and had no reassurance to offer. It was clear she thought the journalist's scenario only too persuasive. 'We're so helpless, aren't we?' she said soberly. 'Ordinary people. Just swept along at the mercy of history. There's literally nothing you can do about Sergei . . .'

'So I give up and concentrate on my own little life?'

Amy watched as a couple of bully blackbirds routed a flock of indignant sparrows. 'Perhaps that's a strength rather than a weakness.' A dour smile. 'Or maybe not. I don't know.'

Chapter Thirty-nine

The hollow, with its rough dry grass, fell away to form the bank of a clear, slow-moving river. There were smoky-winged dragonflies, a bright clump of willowherb, its flowers shading from deep magenta through to the soft whitish-pink of the blooms that had faded. Behind them rolled straw-coloured meadows, edged with dry, dark hawthorn hedges. Clouds came and went, their shadows moving across the fields and alternating with bright patches of hot, mellow sunshine. Over the years, with parents and grandparents, Vicki had picnicked at this spot in the Slad Valley many times.

Glasses and plates from their meal lay next to a tartan picnic bag, along with her volume of Aldous Huxley, unopened. After they'd all eaten and lounged for a while Amy suggested a walk. Claudia and Grace were game.

'I'll stay here and be lazy with Vicki,' Horst announced.

She'd hoped he would. With each passing day Vicki was coming to understand that Horst had a special feeling for her, though it would be hard to put in words why she thought that. There was something in the way he smiled at her – it wasn't casual as it was with the others. And he found it hard to look at her, had to make himself do it. She only noticed because it was the same for her. Sometimes Vicki told herself she was imagining it. But she knew she wasn't. Now they were on their own the conversation between them was not significant. It was as if the mere fact of their *being* alone was momentous enough.

They lay in the grass, each propped on one elbow, facing each other, shy. Horst gestured vaguely at the undulating fields. 'I'm a town boy,' he told her. 'I'm out of place with trees and grass.'

'Don't you like this spot?'

'My parents took me to the country once –' the amusement in his eyes made Vicki smile too – 'and I was chased by a lot of cows.'

She grinned delightedly. 'What had you done to them?'

'Nothing, I swear. It was hot and there were flies. They felt . . . mean. And they saw at once I was the person to punish. No one else. They chose me.'

'People say they're more frightened of you than you are of them.'

'I didn't stand to find out.'

Horst was plucking idly at the grass they lay on. With a long, whippy stalk he tickled Vicki's chin. She'd seen people do that in films . . . lovers, courting couples. Vicki smiled, but brushed the grass away.

'I can't get used to being so lazy.' She was flustered.

'To me it's the most natural thing in the world.'

'I've just finished doing exams . . .' Vicki felt herself blush. What a kid she sounded.

'So now you can do nothing and be happy about it.'

'Not really. I should be reading more. I plan to try for university next term.'

He didn't reply, just gazed at her as if musing on what she'd said. Vicki felt rather at a loss. She wasn't used to such earnestness from him. Then, like the sun coming out, he grinned. 'You're so different from Grace.'

'I know, I know.' She'd been told so all her life. 'I'm the solemn one, the thoughtful one . . .'

'Don't be angry, Vicki. It's not a . . . *Kritik*. I like it. You're so young but sometimes you make me feel like a fool, shallow, hollow-headed.'

She mistrusted such humility. 'You've got a natural flair for making people happy, making them laugh. It's a gift. I'm sure you know that really.'

'I want everyone to love me. I give myself away. You don't do that. You're faithful to who you are.'

The look in his eyes was warm and insistent. Vicki was grati-fied by his view of her. But abashed, too, by his earnestness, their closeness. Perhaps Horst felt it too because he stood up and rummaged in the tartan bag for his camera.

'I'm going to take photographs of trees and grass. Perhaps I can even find a cow. It's not too late to learn to love them.'

He turned and smiled at her over his shoulder, an amiable blond giant. She was dizzy with his charm.

Knees drawn up, chin resting on her arms, Grace sat under the willow tree in the garden, half hidden by its dipping, trailing fronds. A storm was brewing, the sky a doomsday mix of deep slate blue and purple-grey. Yet from somewhere an unearthly light pierced, making the tiny blonde hairs on her arms and legs shine silver, flooding the leaves that surrounded her with a hard, intense yellow-green radiance.

Grace laid her forehead down on to her crossed arms and shut her eyes, shaking her hair forward to hide her face. She felt strange and detached, old and young at the same time. She felt she was finding things out. Behind her closed eyelids pictures came and went, thoughts drifted and dissolved.

Her images of those two weeks in Berlin were a hot, coloured blaze. She'd been so absolutely happy. In her mind Grace saw a swirl of holiday-makers, then Claudia and Amy – pretty in bright dresses, benevolent but slightly blurred. Horst, Vicki and herself were the central figures, walking through sunlit streets and parks, sitting in cafés, eating ice cream and drinking through straws, a laughing, conspiratorial threesome. She'd never met a grown-up like Horst who talked to her as if he understood her thoughts, and did all the wild, silly things children could only dream of. Berlin had been her Shangri-la.

Desperately she had wanted it to be the same this year, though the colours would be softer and more muted. There would not be the bright challenge of a foreign city. But they were the same people and under one roof this time. The fun need never stop. And yet, Grace reflected, it wasn't the same at all. She had been unable to recapture even for one minute the specialness of that time.

A sort of bewilderment had been with her even before she came here, from the moment she understood that Noel begrudged Amy her friendship with Claudia, had something against her and didn't want to meet her. Grace couldn't think why. Claudia seemed so generous and friendly, so genuinely fond of them all.

What was even more puzzling was that Amy knew Noel disapproved, but she was going ahead with her plans anyway, taking no notice of his opinion, when Grace had believed all her life that her parents thought with one mind, spoke with one voice, indivisible.

Her parents' hidden differences were unsettling. But there was one thing that really hurt, gnawing inside her, raw and tender as an open wound. In Berlin Grace had seen Horst as her special friend. She thought they were alike and that he saw it too. Vicki was always with them, of course, but she stood a bit aloof from their games. Now Grace knew she'd been living in a fool's paradise. It was Vicki that interested him. He was aware of her all the time and his eyes lit up with a defencelessness that made you want to look away whenever her sister so much as lifted her little finger.

He still laughed and joked with her, Grace, but she understood now what hadn't been clear when she was ten. Horst was just humouring her. She was a child to be entertained when he was in the mood. Yesterday, in the middle of demonstrating some spoof conjuring trick, his attention had snapped off like turning out a light, and he was watching Vicki again, and Grace saw how utterly unimportant she herself was to him.

This time Grace felt as if she and Vicki and Horst were living in a slow-moving dream-world that unrolled alongside real life. And in this dream Grace was a helpless witness to the fact that Horst was falling in love with Vicki. And Vicki saw it as well and signalled demurely that she knew. Grace was locked into the secret with them, but she was the odd one out. And all this was in dumb show, while the holiday proceeded as it should, and they picnicked and walked, went to the pictures and on sightseeing trips to Cheltenham and Oxford, as if nothing unusual were happening at all.

The rain began to fall in big, splattering drops. Grace turned her face upward, closing her eyes and opening her mouth, the way she used to when she was a kid. She felt a misfit here and couldn't wait for the month to be over and done with.

The pretty, creaky, white-washed bedroom was becoming nightmarish to Horst. The ceiling was too low for his height, the bed too short. The hand-sewn quilt, the eternal bobbing roses outside the window had a naïveté that grated like toothache. It all spoke of order and tame continuity, a dull 'like-father like-son' existence.

His nerves were stretched like thin rubber that might give way at any moment. For three nights now he had lain awake beside Claudia with a rage inside him against everyone and everything that wasn't Vicki. Come dawn he fell into a rancid, sweaty sleep and dozed fitfully through half the morning, got up to the teasing he'd attracted all his life with his limitless capacity for slumber. And Horst would smile and set the needle into the worn groove of his charming, easy-going personality.

Next to him Claudia had slept almost as soon as they finished making intense, silent love. She had been terrified of being overheard by Grace and Vicki in the room across the small, rickety landing. But she was aroused by her fear, lewd and passionate as she used to be in the old days. Horst, moving inside her, had the same breathless awareness of the two girls just metres away and, perversely, he wanted Vicki to hear him and know what he was doing.

But sex didn't bring its usual peace and lethargy. Horst lay awake in the small, too hot room, tense with longing for the girl, kaleidoscopic impressions of her swirling in his imagination, repeating themselves over and over. Details. Like the grey dress she'd worn yesterday in Oxford that made her look like a convent girl, the way the thin material rippled round her slim, tanned legs and across her breasts.

It had been wet and she had a little blue silk umbrella – child size – and in its shade her eyes were deep and shiny, skin soft with the freshness of the rain.

'Why don't you get a smaller one of those,' he teased.

'It's Grace's brolly. She likes me using it.'

She smiled, mischievous and knowing and just for him, as if she saw his obsession and was elated by it.

There was a photo Claudia kept, with some others, by her bed at home, a snap of Vicki at fifteen, by the Wannsee, in a black bathing suit. Her long hair was loose and wet and she was holding it out and away from her, confronting the camera with a grin that was open but coquettish too, and her young body was casually perfect, breasts small and hard, the curve of her legs elegantly precise. The memory of that picture kept returning to him here and now and, in conjunction with the flesh and blood Vicki, seemed the most erotic thing he'd ever seen. His body ached again at the thought of it.

Was his madness obvious to all? Certainly little Grace sensed something and had changed towards him. Horst missed the child's hero-worship, but felt incapable of the effort of resurrecting it. The kid had taught him a card game this evening, something called pontoon. She was a gambling demon, beat him hands down and crowed about it. But the ecstatic trust that used to shine from her eyes had been doused.

The whole social setup – family friends, schoolgirl daughter – was a nightmare. In his overwrought imagination Horst saw himself as a lecherous caricature – one of the obscenely leering Jewish bogeymen from the cover of *Der Stürmer*. Claudia must see something. But she'd never been the worrying type and probably thought his little aberration would die a natural death after the month was up. The thought was anathema. He was burning in hell, but dreaded escape.

In the stuffy bedroom Horst longed for some violent gesture that would still his fever, fantasized smashing his fists through the small rustic windows, lacerating his arms on the thorny branches of the smug pearl-pink rose outside.

The notion was pure self-indulgence. He would have to get up. There was an old pack of cigarettes in the pocket of his jacket downstairs. Perhaps a couple of those would soothe his nerves. If not he would go out and run across the nearby fields until he was exhausted. That shouldn't take long, Horst reflected wryly. He wasn't particularly fit.

Silently he pulled on trousers and a shirt, manoeuvred the bedroom

361

latch as carefully as he could. Claudia stirred but did not wake. The narrow stairs creaked beneath his bare feet. Horst's jacket hung on a peg in the hall. He felt for the crumpled pack of cigarettes and his lighter, then entered the low-ceilinged living room, ducking his head, switching on a small lamp that stood on the oaken table.

The leaded window stood ajar. Horst pushed it wider open and breathed in the cool air from outside. He lit a cigarette and began to smoke it, leaning his forearms on the windowsill. Almost immediately he felt calmer, but as though he'd come through some enervating struggle. An owl hooted some way off, and the sound pleased him like the cooing of a dove.

He thought he heard a sound upstairs. Perhaps Claudia had woken and missed him. This was a cottage full of creaks and rattles. He listened but heard no more. Horst took another drag on his cigarette. Tonight he craved the lulling effect of the drug, though under normal circumstances he could take tobacco or leave it alone.

'Horst.'

Sharply he looked round. Vicki stood framed in the doorway. She was barefoot and wore a girlish sprigged nightgown with a round collar and short sleeves. Her long hair hung loose on her shoulders, looking dense and dark in the dim lamplight.

He turned to face her. 'I couldn't sleep.'

'Neither could I. And I heard someone on the stairs.'

'Those little rooms are hot. It's cool outside.'

She crossed to the window and breathed in the night air with gratitude.

Horst touched the packet of cigarettes. 'You don't smoke?' Obscurely he guessed she would like his assumption of her adult status.

'Not really. I *have* with my friend.' It was clear Vicki didn't want to appear prim. 'But I don't enjoy it much.'

'You have nothing against . . . ?'

'Of course not. Go ahead.'

He did, though slightly self-conscious now. They stood side by side at the window and it seemed to him that this was only right and natural, and that both of them felt it. Was he imagining a sense of expectancy in the air? At that moment Horst would not have changed places with anyone in the world.

'I love being awake when everyone else is asleep,' Vicki said. 'You feel so peaceful and alone.'

'*We're* alone. You and I.'

'Yes.' She looked up at him with a mixture of boldness and evasion.

Horst found himself breathless, his whole body invaded by a tight excitement. With incredulity he saw and felt Vicki's fine-boned hand touch his arm, close over his wrist. He could sense the naked disbelief that must be showing in his eyes.

'I didn't know if it was you down here,' she said hesitantly. 'But I thought, if it was, I was going to say something . . . I'm not sure what. It's just that I feel as if there's something happening between us and we're both too . . . We're not free . . . brave enough to admit it . . .' Vicki's voice faded as if, at the end, her confidence failed her. But she recovered herself with a quick, rueful grimace that he found completely adorable. 'I'm making an idiot of myself . . .'

'I love you.' He heard himself say it – almost in reassurance – the words coming faster than thought. He could read nothing in her eyes. Horst lumbered on. 'I'm in love with you. Had you guessed that?'

'Sort of.' A child's unsure grin.

He felt her lips against his arm. The youthful ineptitude of the gesture filled him with emotion. He should stop it here by rights, save Vicki from an impulse that was not appropriate.

Inconveniently Horst still held the smoking cigarette in his right hand. With his left he tilted her chin, so that she looked up at him. Her face was blank, her lips smooth and expressionless. He kissed them softly, fervently.

Horst knew he was acting unforgivably. He was older. There was Claudia to consider, and Vicki's mother. It was his place to show restraint. But how could he pass up the most bewitching fantasy life had ever offered him? He would willingly be damned for it.

Chapter Forty

Noel was in New York for a week and Tuesday wasn't one of Jane's days to clean, so it was safe enough for Vicki and Horst to drop by the family home in Belsize Park, for Vicki to pick up her passport and throw a few clothes into a suitcase.

As the taxi from the station drew up outside the white, three-storey house, she was engulfed by a vivid awareness of its familiarity.

'So this has been your home.' Horst looked at her with the dazed intensity that was between them all the time.

'My habitat.'

She knew every stick and stone of the place – the odd yellowy slabs in the grey-pink crazy paving and, through the window, the splashy dark green of the downstairs curtains, the frosted green Lalique vase her parents had bought on holiday in France.

He paid the taxi. They would phone for another as soon as they were ready.

Trying to appear casual, in case the neighbours were at their windows, Vicki led the way through the side-gate, felt under the big, cracked pot of mauve sage for the back door key.

The kitchen smelled just as it always had, but concentrated, because in their absence all the windows were kept closed. Swiftly she steered Horst through to the hall where it was cool and dark.

He took her in his arms, holding her against his warm, massive body. 'I want to say it's not too late. I can only take you away from your family if you're quite, quite certain.' On the early morning train from Gloucester she had wept, imagining Amy's loving anxiety and bewilderment.

His voice was deep and rich, affecting her physically like chords played on a stringed instrument. She was mesmerized, enchanted,

Vicki shook her head. She could still feel the stiffness of dried tears on her cheeks. 'I promise you I'm not regretting it.'

But she was gripped by a kind of anguish as she led the way upstairs. This house was the background to her growing up, it was security. She had never realized how much. And she might never see it again, might not see her family for years. On the train she had written to Amy trying to explain. Horst had written to Claudia. Tomorrow morning the letters would arrive.

Her bedroom looked as it always had. The sun shining in at the window cast long rectangles of light across the lino and the woven black and red bedspread. There were her shelves with the line of red William books, her Jane Austen, Tolstoy, Agatha Christie, Virginia Woolf. There was her desk with a pile of the history books she'd been studying, and she felt a pang for the studious simplicity of her life up to now.

But to keep all this would be to lose Horst. What with her own school-girl status, the added complication of Horst's affair with Claudia, their relationship would never be allowed to bloom at its own pace, to glide through the conventional channels. Flight was their only option. And Vicki's world had changed so fast that the homeliness of this sunlit room had, in a flash, come to seem part of her past.

Horst paused in the doorway. 'A treasure-chamber. If there was time I could pass hours here, looking at everything and wondering about you.'

Vicki found her passport in the top right-hand drawer of her desk. Then she climbed on a chair and took a small suitcase down from the top of her wardrobe. Opening the wardrobe itself, she began to sort through the reduced stock of garments that hung inside. For the sake of authenticity neither had brought anything from the cottage. If surprised in their escape they could have claimed, however implausibly, to be going for an early-morning walk.

'This is beautiful.' Horst was examining a framed photograph of Amy when she was young, not much older than Vicki herself. Her hair was tied back in the same style Vicki now wore. 'But you don't look like her.'

'Grace is the image . . .' She looked up from her hasty packing. 'I take after my grandfather if anyone . . . Pass me that photo.' She added it to the clothes in the suitcase, found snaps of Noel and Grace in the desk and stuck them in.

Horst had moved on. With amusement he was eyeing two dolls propped on the windowsill. Geraldine and Moni.

Geraldine was made of peach-coloured china. She wore a baby's white layette knitted by Margaret in a complicated lacy stitch. Her face, so Grace always jeered, was like a big smacked bum. Moni – named for the maid who used to look after Vicki when she was a toddler – was a rag-doll with orange wool hair, a limp cotton dress and stripy stockings.

As a child Vicki liked to show Geraldine off to her friends but Moni was the one she took to bed. On an impulse she seized the rag-doll, stuffed it down the side of her suitcase, then snapped the clasps smartly shut.

'Right,' she told Horst. 'I'm ready.'

Claudia watched as, in the middle of the lawn, Grace performed a perfect handstand, holding the position for a moment or two before descending into a backbend, from which, in a single sinuous movement, she reassumed her original standing position. She used to do that as a child, Claudia recalled, glimpsing for a brief second how it had felt to be twelve and effortlessly supple.

'You're like a snake,' she called.

Grace wriggled exaggeratedly, as if to prove as much.

'Claudia.' In shirt and shorts she approached the slatted garden bench where Claudia was sitting.

'Yes?'

'D'you think they'll get married or live in sin?'

'To be married they would need your parents' permission.'

Grace arched her back, lowering her upper body into a second backbend. 'I guessed Horst was in love with Vicki – did you?'

'I thought he liked her. But I never dreamed this would happen.' Claudia spoke with a deliberate, cultivated composure, refusing to inhabit the role of a woman scorned.

She found the girl's unsentimental frankness a comfort. It did away with the necessity for hand-wringing, acknowledging the simple fact that the situation existed and had to be dealt with. For the second day running Amy was in Gloucester, at the police station, trying to do just that. She and Grace waited. The afternoon was sultry, the sky whitish and overcast.

'I wonder what Vicki's doing right now.' Grace had subsided into a sitting position. The child seemed elated by the lovers' flight, as if the event had supplied some much-needed drama to her days.

'Wondering what we are doing perhaps.' The reply was bland, cagey. All her energy and will were employed in suppressing the incredulity, the humiliation and pain that would rip and lacerate her if she let them.

Their room was on the fourth floor and had a balcony. From it you could see a pleasing cubist arrangement of tiled roofs – coral and grey-pink and coppery green. At the end of the street, in the ribbon of sky that showed between the close-set buildings, the white domes of the Sacré Coeur gleamed under watery sunshine.

Leaning over the wrought-iron railings, Vicki could just read the skewed sign *Hôtel de Genève – Confort Moderne*, suspended above the narrow, cobbled street. A stunted tree with a bulbous, peeling trunk survived somehow in the canyon below. Immediately beneath them was the faded striped awning of a greengrocer's and, opposite, a shop with *Tabac* in cracked brown letters over the window. Next to it an advertisement for Byrrh looked as if it lit up at night. She could see the tops of passing heads and feet and hear impatient voices, genial voices, calling in strident French. They had arrived in Paris at half-past eight this morning and everything looked just as it should.

Vicki stared down, feeling blank and shell-shocked. The previous night, on the boat, in the train, she'd had no sleep. She and Horst had travelled separately in case – somehow – the authorities were looking out for them. As the long night progressed, her conviction grew that she'd thrown in her lot with a random stranger, leaving her family, unforgivably, to cope with the consequences, and the misgiving lingered on.

Horst came out on to the balcony behind her. He seemed to read her mind. 'You can't live your parents' life, you know, and they can't live yours.'

She turned to look at him. His eyes were troubled as if a situation that had seemed clear-cut were proving to entail all manner of unexpected complications.

'You look like a piece of paper with burned black holes in it.' His hand was warm in the nape of her neck. 'You need to sleep.'

Last night, alone in the rustic bedroom, Claudia had tossed and turned, cocooned by the claustrophobic billows of the downy feather mattress, overwhelmed by a suffocating sense of guilt by association. She had introduced Horst into this pleasant, stable middle-class family and was – however unwittingly – answerable for the result.

In this context she forced her own sense of betrayal, her wounded vanity to take second place, though they gnawed like stealthy rats at the edge of her consciousness. Claudia told herself that she and Horst had together been living on borrowed time – both of them knew it. And both had been tempted at times to hasten an end that was inevitable. So however cruel her mortification, it was not without an insidious element of relief.

But her most pressing thoughts were for Vicki, so exquisite and young, on the threshold of her life. She'd thrown everything away – family, education, future. For Horst. An amiable man and seductive enough. But lazy and sensual, weak, without backbone. Her daughter, Claudia reflected, was bright and shiny as a new-minted silver coin. While Horst was base metal, tarnished, compromised. Unworthy of her in every way.

This morning she'd had a letter from him. He was affectionate and contrite but claimed to have been overwhelmed by feelings too sudden and strong to control. Claudia bet he had. She bet he couldn't believe his luck.

* * *

368

Foggily rising into consciousness, Vicki struggled to make sense of her surroundings. The room was beginning to get dark. She was possessed by a blissful torpor and moved her limbs languidly in the clean, flesh-warmed linen sheets.

Passive, she lay and stared at the shadowy room. An oval mirror gleamed dully from its gilt surround. She made out a radiator, the hard white of a hand-basin. As her eyes accustomed themselves to the dim light, she recalled the small round table, recognized the bulk of two green plush armchairs. Her grey dress lay draped across the back of one. The long window was still open on to the balcony. Lace curtains shifted in a slight breeze. Above the roof opposite a dull pinkish sky was just visible. A great calm had come upon her. She was here with Horst and didn't want to be anywhere else.

Next to her he lay sleeping, fully clothed, on top of the green and white printed coverlet. While she made ready for bed he'd gone out on to the balcony to smoke a cigarette. Vicki had been unaware of his lying down beside her.

Raising herself on one elbow, she stared down at him. Vicki had never seen him like this, oblivious, face smoothed of all expression. His fair hair fell raggedly across his forehead. She breathed in its healthy, acrid scent. Horst's large body suggested physical power, but there was an innocence about the sleeping man which was present too, Vicki realized, when he was awake. Obscurely she felt protective as if, in some way, she were stronger than he.

She watched him for a while, then bent to kiss the corner of his mouth. He stirred and opened his eyes, gazing at her uncom-prehendingly for a while before giving a sweet smile of recognition. She kissed him again and was moved by the naked gladness in his eyes.

Amy got back to the cottage around six in the evening, looking stricken, pale and tired. She poured herself a gin and tonic and one for Claudia. They sat down outside on the grass.

'All the ports have been notified, but I'm pretty certain they will have travelled yesterday, before we were sure they'd actually gone at all . . . And they may have travelled separately anyway. Someone at Gloucester remembered a tall blond foreigner buying a ticket to London, but didn't recall a young woman . . . They're not at Belsize Park, but Jane is certain someone's been in the house.'

'Have you spoken to Noel?'

'Yes, I managed to track him down and get through to him on the phone. He's flying straight home. He's taken it even harder than me. Where their daughters are concerned all men think of other men as dastardly seducers.' She tried to smile, but managed only a weary grimace.

'Horst is kind, you know. He won't treat her badly.'

'I hope you're right.'

Horst took her out to eat at a bistro called *La Fourmi* in one of the steep little streets that led off the Place du Tertre. Eight years ago, at the age of twenty, he had spent six formative months in Paris and remembered the time as one of the happiest of his life.

'I ate often at *La Fourmi*. It was friendly there and cheap and good.' The proprietor, Gaston, and his wife had made him feel part of the family of customers and friends, but he had no way of knowing whether they would still be there.

The interior was small and smoky, with three booths on either side, each containing a table flanked by two leatherette banquettes. At the far end, facing the door, was a brightly lit bar with a mirrored rear wall reflecting shelves of bottles and up-ended glasses. The counter was polished to a dark high gloss, beneath which the overlapping rings left by thousands of glasses combined with the grain of the wood to form a complicated and pleasing textural pattern.

Vicki and Horst sat down at one of the tables. The young waitress brought a savoury, chunky *soupe au poisson*, the dish of the day, and a basket of bread. Horst ordered a bottle of champagne.

As she ate and drank Vicki was invaded once again by a sense of unreality, but this time the feeling was warm and pleasurable. What luxury to be here alone with Horst. She felt quite unbelievably happy and, in a sudden flash of memory, pictured herself two years ago, a star-struck young schoolgirl in the dark of an auditorium, adoring the blond god who dominated the stage.

Sitting opposite her, in the flesh, so to speak, he seemed to Vicki every bit as splendid. And between them was a sense of exhilarated harmony, like a musical duet, each word, glance and gesture sparking a heightened response in the other. His face filled her world. They drank to their future and Vicki felt ready to fight for their happiness, whatever problems might lie ahead.

When they'd finished eating Horst approached the bar. Behind it stood a pale, slight Frenchman in his forties with a pompadour of thick, greying hair. Horst ordered a brandy. Vicki heard a sudden explosion of surprise and recognition and Gaston was leaning across the polished counter, clapping Horst on the shoulder.

'*Léonic, viens vite!*' she heard him call. From the direction of the kitchen appeared a hard-faced woman with dark, curly, centrally parted hair.

'*'Ors!*' she exclaimed and flew to embrace him, pressing her thin, heavily painted lips to both his cheeks.

There followed a torrent of animated French, too fast and furious, Vicki guessed, for Horst to keep up with, but he stood by with an amiable, slightly sheepish smile, clearly gratified by the enthusiasm of his welcome.

He made several attempts to indicate Vicki's presence and finally the message got through. Gaston and Léonie rushed over and she, too, was seized and embraced.

A trusted regular customer was installed behind the bar and the couple joined Vicki and Horst at their table, along with a young woman called Marcelle with short, brilliantined hair – their daughter, Vicki gathered. Horst marvelled at how much she had grown.

Léonie brought glasses and a bottle of Calvados – 'good' Calvados as she pointed out in her emphatic manner. Gaston poured five generous measures. Vicki's head was already swimming with the champagne so she didn't drink much and Léonie seemed to applaud her moderation.

They stayed for an hour or more, ebullient and voluble. Marcelle made unabashed sheep's eyes at Horst. Gaston called him '*mon vieux*'.

371

Both Léonie and Gaston seemed very taken with the idea of Horst and Vicki as a couple.

'*Quel beau garçon,*' Léonie enthused to Vicki several times, cupping Horst's chin in her small, practical hands.

'*Si jeune, si belle, si innocente . . .*' Gaston gazed at Vicki with sentimental, approving eyes.

Their interest was frank but somehow impersonal, and Vicki found it not at all offensive. Horst was genial and funny, and every so often his eyes would meet hers with a special enchanted complicity. She was pleasantly disorientated at finding herself in this company and it came to Vicki with sudden clarity that life with Horst would be quite different from anything she had ever known.

'Trouble is,' Amy said, 'I can too easily put myself in Vicki's place. At seventeen I was aching to escape from my family.'

It was nearly midnight. Grace had gone to bed. After the turmoil of the last two days the atmosphere in the cottage was flat and unsettled. Rain splattered against the leaded windowpanes. Amy had lit a fire in the empty grate in the living room. Tomorrow they would leave, Amy and Grace to return to London, Claudia to Berlin. There was no knowing when they would meet again.

'In her letter Vicki said we mustn't hate Horst – running away had been her suggestion . . . She just had to have the experience of being with him and knew we'd forbid it, Noel and I.' In the flickering firelight Amy looked exhausted, but had subsided into a kind of wan calm.

Claudia shook her head. 'It's hard for me to see Horst as worth such . . . But Vicki views him through quite different eyes and who's to say she's wrong?'

'I don't feel hate or anger . . . I do feel betrayed.' Amy was silent for a moment, then gave a wry and sober smile. 'Vicki was never much interested in any of the boys she knew. Noel and I used to joke, when she does see someone who catches her imagination, watch out . . .'

Sitting on the rug by the hearth Claudia experienced a pang of envy and sudden empathy for the impulsive passion of the runaway couple. Yet, pessimistically, she saw disillusionment as its inevitable sequel. But perhaps that said more about her than anything else.

Claudia stared at the embers of the fire, glowing orange and black. She had clamped the lid down hard on bitterness and hurt, would not allow these emotions so much as a toehold. Her head throbbed with the effort. She'd felt like this once before, a long time ago. Only then it had been Amy who'd captivated her man, and now it was her own beloved daughter.

It was rare for Horst to find himself awake while someone beside him slept. But he wanted to relish – consciously – the specialness, the magic of a night he knew he would never forget. Silently he noted all the elements that combined to produce this singular moment. The open French windows, the purple-red night sky. The neon light filtered through lace, casting a long luminous spear across the floor as far as the bed. Hollow-sounding footsteps on the cobbles below, shouts and laughter, quickly silenced. The downy warmth of the bed. His still, satisfied body. And this child sleeping beside him. She lay curled into him, breathing quietly, her long hair dark against the bolster, straggling across her bare shoulder. Beneath the coverlet her spare, soft flesh fusing with his own.

When they got back to the room he was determined to go slow and careful, not to rush her. But Vicki had decided she must lose her virginity. She explained this with an earnest candour that made him think of one of those erotic films of the late twenties – Louise Brooks with her credulous, calculated innocence. In the face of it Horst feared he'd be incapable, that the responsibility would chill him – he'd never wanted anyone so much. And of course he'd drunk a fair bit of Calvados.

But once they were in bed it was fine. He was randy as hell, but confident and in control, knowing just how to give her pleasure. Vicki had writhed in his arms, half-ashamed at the strength of her own response. His stomach knotted at the memory. And, insidiously, at the back of his mind was the thought that she was lucky to have him and not some fumbling schoolboy. Conscious at the same time that he himself had never experienced a desire so heightened and focused, so intense.

'I love you,' she told him, over and over, with a melting look in her eyes. And Horst felt strong and good.

Was what he felt love, or simply overflowing gratitude for a transcendental sexual experience? Was there a difference? Maybe he was serious for the first time in his life. The thought disturbed him. Seriousness was something Horst had always avoided like the plague.

Chapter Forty-one

Noel admitted to himself that Amy took Vicki's elopement far less histrionically than he did. Her feeling was that hysterics were beside the point. What was done was done. The thing now was to keep calm but seize any opportunity that presented itself to build bridges. His wife claimed that this actor his daughter had run off with was no monster, but a man like any other and more amiable than most. Amy pointed out that Vicki was as old as she herself had been when Noel first knew her, and the difference in their ages the same.

He found himself offended by her logic and had a sudden rueful insight into that great British caricature, the choleric ex-military man brandishing his horsewhip. Noel had the feeling that, if ever he ran into this Horst, he would be unable to stop himself from grabbing the fellow by the throat, shaking the living daylights out of him.

They had a couple of short letters, postmarked Lyon, assuring them that she was safe and happy, that she loved them all and they weren't to worry. But Vicki enclosed no contacting address and stressed that the notes had been posted by a third party in another town. The French police were issued with a description of the couple but gave the Campions to understand that this matter was in no way a priority. The girl was over sixteen and had, after all, left of her own accord.

Noel's missing of Vicki was like a sickness, ghostly images of the child – her smiles, her trust – superimposing themselves one upon another in his mind, culminating in the luminous young woman she had become. And this German lounge lizard had laid hands on his beloved, his unique daughter. Obscurely Noel blamed Claudia. If only Amy had broken with her as he had wished this could never have happened. But he kept his resentment to himself, knowing it to be irrational. After all, Claudia too was an injured party.

All through a breathlessly hot September a new and terrifying dimension was added to their anxiety – the growing fear of a war with Germany.

Hitler's demands for annexation of the Sudetenland became increasingly pressing. Panic-stricken negotiations were conducted by the British and French governments while at home trenches were dug, shelters erected, gas masks fitted. Hitler was no longer regarded as a Chaplinesque figure of fun. The man was dangerous. The French Army and the British fleet were mobilized.

In the main, the British public was chary of risking war to protect a country that was miles away, nothing to do with them at all. But there were authoritative voices declaring that a stand must be taken. The man was a bully, a menace, who would see any concession as a sign of fatal weakness.

Noel was torn. For months he'd proclaimed that Nazism must be confronted, Hitler's bluff called – if bluff it was. He'd consistently aligned himself with the anti-appeasement camp. Now, against his own principles, he prayed that an accommodation would be found. Purely and simply for Vicki's sake.

Nowadays Noel was increasingly concerned with *Witness* magazine's American venture. But Roland Delane, the review's ageing proprietor, was adamant that he should cover the German crisis. During the two critical weeks of negotiation he flew to Berchtesgaden, Godesberg and Munich. When Chamberlain signed the Agreement abandoning the Czechs to their fate, Noel felt weak with relief, and at the same time sickened and ashamed. Chamberlain, as the grim joke ran, had turned all four cheeks to Herr Hitler.

In the following weeks Noel found his nerves shredded by these twin concerns – grief over Vicki and the shameful peace. He understood too well the shaky relief of almost everyone at having so narrowly outflanked the slit-eyed wolf of war. But the short-sighted optimism, the craven joy repelled him.

Still, life went on, it had to. Noel locked his feelings inside him and went about his business, alienated, with anger ebbing and flowing constantly just below the surface.

One Saturday evening at the end of October Robert Beadle and his wife, Hester, came to dinner. The Campions had hardly seen anyone since Vicki's defection. Amy was animated and drank a lot, talked politics, goading Robert the way she used to, but sharper and more aggressive. Noel watched her with hostile eyes, thinking how pretty she looked and how overwrought. He could have warmed more easily to wretchedness and tears.

That night, as they got ready for bed, Amy remarked that it had been good to forget their troubles for a while. 'I think we should get out more. We really mustn't spend our lives brooding about Vicki.'

Noel perceived the comment as a reproach and didn't answer.

'Don't you think?' Amy persisted.

'Perhaps.' He shrugged his shoulders. 'Though I can't at this very moment summon up much enthusiasm.'

A silence. Amy hung her dress in the wardrobe. The white silk petticoat she was wearing shimmered with the warm amber reflections of her dressing-table lamp.

She turned back to face him. 'Please don't withdraw from me, Noel. This is something that's happened to both of us.'

He realized then that, in fact, he held Amy responsible. Surely she could have seen what was coming, kept a better eye on things. Noel had the feeling that, if he'd been there, none of this would have happened, but knew he had no proof for thinking so.

'I can't seem to be able to take the long view as you can.' The reply was evasive and – Amy was right – held her at bay.

'I'm not grief-stricken enough for you, am I?' she said accusingly. 'I can tell by the way you look at me, all the time.' Amy sat down at the mirror and, with repressed violence, began to brush her hair. 'Thing is, we both have to cope. I could weep and wail and give way. You'd probably like me better if I did. You'd think it was more "natural". But there's Grace to think of, apart from anything else. It seems preferable to remain in control.'

The potential skirmish petered out. Amy pulled on her nightdress, turned back the sheet ready to climb into bed. A confrontation had been avoided. Noel felt simultaneously relieved and frustrated.

While he wound the bedside clock Amy sat propped against the pillows. 'I had a letter from Claudia today.' Her tone was carefully amicable as if she had made a conscious decision to co-operate in the smoothing of ruffled feathers.

'Oh?' His voice sounded rusty and strained.

'She says she's resigned from the theatre. Horst's leaving gave her the jolt she needed. She's got a job selling books and magazines and says she feels happier being anonymous . . . No longer a cultural ambassador for the Third Reich . . .'

A hot, abrupt shaft of exasperation pierced his painfully cultivated detachment. 'Can't you see that, as things are, I'm not madly interested in Claudia's doings?'

Noel was taken aback by the aggrieved hostility of his tone. Surprise and hurt showed in Amy's eyes, but she rose to his aggression. 'You blame her, don't you? You've always expected something like this to happen. Wanted it even. So you can feel justified in your nonsensical prejudice against Claudia.'

Noel saw that a clash could no longer be postponed and he experienced a perverse rush of exhilaration. God knows, he'd held everything in for far too long. 'You're probably right. But it isn't her I blame. It's you!'

'So that's it.' Her smile expressed irony and a kind of triumph, as if, finally, she had manoeuvred him into the open.

'You talk about my prejudice. With you it's the opposite. You've put your damned friendship with Claudia before everything – my wishes, Vicki's best interests . . . The selfishness of it is bloody breathtaking.' Noel threw down the indictment like a gauntlet. He'd been longing to for weeks. For years.

'And you've always had this conviction that Claudia should be treated like a convenient chesspiece. Listen, it was *your* idea that we spend months cooped up in Yorkshire together, just the two of us. No wonder we became close. And I was there for the birth. And I saw how devastated she was at leaving Vicki and just going . . .' Amy's eyes were steady and righteous. 'And then you simply took it for granted that I'd sever all connection the moment Claudia had served her purpose.'

'She didn't do it for love! We had a bargain. I supported her aunt, educated her brother. Let's not forget that.' Noel was incensed at being cast as the villain of the piece. 'Whereas you, out of friendship –' he pronounced the word with vehement contempt – 'house Vicki under the same roof as her natural mother, her mother's lover, and she has no idea . . . Can't you see how grotesque that is?'

'And where did all the secrecy come from in the first place?' Amy was kneeling on the bed now in her pale satin nightdress, hands clasped. Her face blazed with an anger that matched his own, as if she too had long-nursed grievances to get off her chest. 'From your face-saving, your embarrassment, your bloody male vanity. If it weren't for all that we could have been frank with Vicki . . . I've gone along with it. I've kept quiet and kept faith. But deep down, let me tell you, I despise this whole pretence.'

'What a martyr,' he jeered, feigning indifference.

Amy had played the taboo card. His impotence. Noel felt his heart lurch with pain. He had to get out, walk, recover his equilibrium. He paused with his hand on the door-knob. Despair made him cold and savage. 'Anyway, darling, what all this stemmed from was your kind bulletin on Claudia's little ups and downs. Don't bother in future. Just remember I don't give a shit.'

The streets outside were dark, and a thin drizzle was falling. Noel walked blindly, stricken, vanquished. Not by argument but by the intransigence of his own body, the fatal flaw that poisoned his life and lay in wait, ready to drag him down however successfully he seemed to rise above it.

Early in November the Campions had another letter from Vicki. She was in Berlin now. She and Horst were renting a small flat. Vicki was taking German lessons – 'so I'm continuing my education, you'll be glad to know.' Horst had a middle-sized part in a UFA '*Prunkfilm*' – the usual harking back to the glories of Frederick the Great, so Vicki informed them airily. At last the two of them were embarking on their real life. Once again she assured them of her love, happiness, wellbeing.

In the immediate future she would remain incommunicado but, Vicki reminded them, she would be eighteen soon. Years of discretion, so she claimed. Perhaps some time soon it would be possible for them all to resume diplomatic relations.

In the interim even Noel had come to view his daughter's elopement as a *fait accompli*. He no longer harboured fantasies of storming her hideout with a posse of policemen and bringing his elder child back into the family fold. Young as Vicki was, she had taken her decision and showed no sign of regretting it. But his rancour against Horst continued to fester.

Two days after her letter arrived all the newspapers were agog with the Nazis' latest piece of mayhem. All over Germany – in a supposed 'spontaneous' display of public outrage over the killing of a German diplomat by a Jew – a cataclysmic pogrom was mounted. Synagogues were burned to the ground, the windows of Jewish shops smashed, their frontages defaced, their contents looted. Protesting proprietors were roughed up, insulted, kicked, beaten. Many died, and thousands of guiltless Jews were arrested.

Almost worse than the reports were the photographs that went with them – frozen moments of naked violence with gloating bullies, abject victims, firemen standing by, idle and grinning, while flames from a Berlin synagogue licked the night sky.

Kristallnacht they called it, after the broken glass that lay everywhere in sparkling heaps. The Jewish community was fined one billion marks for the damage inflicted. And Vicki was over there in that madhouse.

Her birthday passed, and Christmas, seeming empty and incomplete. She sent presents and a card with a coloured photograph of snow-covered fir trees in the Grunewald. Inside she wrote, 'Happy Christmas to my darling family from your prodigal daughter.'

In mid-January they had a letter from her, giving an address in Charlottenburg. She was pregnant, Vicki wrote, and wanted their permission to marry.

'If you don't feel you can give it, we'll simply have to continue to live in sin. There's no question of my leaving Horst. I love him, love him. So please, please say yes.'

The letter lay on Noel's desk for four or five days, ignored and unanswered. Each time, catching sight of the flimsy paper with Vicki's tidy handwriting, he was seized by a wave of helpless anger, profound sadness. It killed him to think of his lovely daughter, barely out of childhood, up the spout like some pathetic little teenaged tart. And glowing with love for the bastard who'd abused her youth and trust.

'It's time you replied.' Finally Amy chivvied him into action. 'She's in love. There's nothing to be done. We can play the heavy parents and lose Vicki for good. Or give in gracefully and salvage what we can . . . There's really no choice, is there?'

With bleak resignation Noel sat down and wrote, granting his child permission to wed her seducer.

Chapter Forty-two

The first letter had come in November of 1938, on yellow paper in big, sprawling capital letters, calling Johnny a pig-fucker, threatening to string him up by the back legs and slit his throat. By then he and Inge Raab were already working on plans to get all of them out and away from the menacing proximity of the Nazis. England was their objective. Inge was negotiating for sponsorship with an organization called the Lifeline Group. The two families were stateless and had no money beyond the minimum for food and rent.

Johnny burned the letter without showing it to Gudrun, but his bowels turned to water at the thought that some Nazi agent found him interesting enough, had taken the time and energy, to track him down. Two days later a second note came with a crude picture of two children with knives plunged into their eye sockets.

At once he and Gudrun and the kids decamped to a room on the other side of town, but made several subsequent forays to pick up their pots and pans, crockery and bedding. Presumably somebody tailed them after one of these trips because two days before Christmas a third letter came, with a drawing captioned 'Familie Kröger' and showing four pigs with their stomachs split open.

This time they journeyed by a devious route to Radlice on the outskirts of Prague, taking nothing but two suitcases of clothes, a few photographs and mementoes. They managed to rent a couple of damp rooms from an old woman who seemed half mad and terrified the boys.

Since then they had heard nothing from their tormentors and plans were laid for a complicated journey via Hungary, Italy and France. The Lifeline Group had guaranteed temporary accommodation for the Raab and Kröger families on their arrival in London.

Outside his tram window the sky was blue, the trees white and ethereal. A bright February morning. As he rumbled back towards Radlice, Johnny was warm in the thick overcoat of herringbone tweed he'd bought years ago in Paris. He'd stayed over at the Raabs' flat in Malá Strana last night, to talk about final arrangements. It wouldn't be long now. Johnny felt happier than he had in weeks.

But yesterday evening Adam Raab had seemed at the end of his tether. He'd looked awful, gaunt and pale, his eyes burning from deep brown sockets. His voice was hoarse and he kept clearing his throat. Johnny had never told Adam about the letters. He was far too close to the edge as it was. But he showed two of them to Inge. She was his *feste Burg* – his stronghold – like the hymn said.

Adam went to bed early, and Johnny and Inge sat up talking. She had a bottle of booze of some sort – Czech, colourless and fiery. One of her employers had given it her in payment for a rush translation job.

What with everything that had happened recently, Johnny was feeling worse than ever about the danger and uncertainty he was inflicting on Gudrun. The drink and the late-night intimacy brought everything to the surface. Johnny became maudlin.

'I should never have married Gudrun,' he told Inge over and over. 'All this has worn her down lower and lower, to a wraith. Sometimes she seems . . . transparent, hardly there at all. If only you'd known her before . . . so young and fragile and sweet. Gudrun's someone who deserves a peaceful life.'

'Under the Nazis?'

'She wouldn't have been touched by them. Gudrun's a nurse. She wouldn't have been compromised.'

'Everyone is.'

Inge was squiffy too and it made her dogmatic. Johnny knew that in his old life her simplification of the issues would have got on his wick. But, the way things were, he needed Inge's unshakeable conviction that, in leaving their homeland, they had all done the right thing.

In this situation he and Inge were a team. In the early days Johnny used to laugh at her messy hair and bad dress sense. How shallow he'd been. Her strength was like gold, transcending the frivolity of sexual flirtation.

Last night indeed, Johnny mused wryly, he'd almost found her beautiful, with her strong, dumpy body and wild black hair streaked with grey. Her olive skin had glowed against the dusky reds and pinks of the dressing gown she was wearing – Inge had a penchant for floral fabrics – and, as he talked, Johnny had speculated on the shape and feel of her heavy breasts. In fact, for a mad moment or two, he'd been hard put to it to stop himself from slipping an exploring hand between the mysterious overlapping edges of her kimono.

But the moment passed and this morning – after Johnny had snored drunkenly for four or five hours on the Raabs' hard sofa – the two of them were back to normal, comrades in arms, with the safety of their dependants uppermost in their minds.

As he sat somnolently on the trundling tram Johnny's mind drifted to his two young sons. They weren't used to him sleeping elsewhere and would leap at him no doubt when he walked in the door. They'd be boisterous, fresh and rosy-cheeked, their lips comically pursed for a kiss. He and Gudrun constantly rejoiced at how untouched they seemed by the odd circumstances of their upbringing. Every day he and his wife caught each other's eye, smiling over the children's sayings and doings. At the very least this bond between them was alive and well.

He stepped down from the tram by a ruined fortress wall that always made Johnny vaguely wish he painted landscapes. He could never resist running his hands across the rough-textured stone while admiring its subtle, mottled colouring, the splashes of lichen that shone piercing ochre in the bright morning sun.

The house lay beyond a patch of scrub ground, dotted with old rusty tin drums, the blackened remains of bonfires, a discarded, mud-streaked mattress. But this morning it all looked beautiful, silvered over with sparkling frost, cut through with strong blue shadows. In England, Johnny thought, they'd be safe. They could start from scratch. Gudrun spoke a little English. Maybe she could do some part-time nursing. The money would help and she'd feel useful again.

They would learn from the mistakes they'd made here. The euphoria of the early months had thrown everything out of kilter.

Lost in thought, Johnny had taken the way ahead for granted. But suddenly his vision was jolted by the unexpected. A hundred metres or so in front of him should be the grim little brown-painted one-storey house where his family lodged. Johnny frowned, his senses confused. He saw what looked like beams, joists dipping from roof to ground level. When he looked harder the house seemed a shell, as if two of its walls had been almost bodily ripped away. He began to run, and saw that debris lay scattered over a wide area – bricks and plaster and broken glass, a table on its side without a top. Men in blue overalls were desultorily picking over the rubble while a policeman stood by drinking coffee from a thick, white mug.

'What's happened?' Johnny addressed the policeman in his imperfect Czech.

The man shrugged. 'Gas.' He gestured with his hands, still holding the mug, an exploding motion, and blew out his lips. He was middle-aged, balding, his face ruddy with the cold. He didn't smile. There was an antipathy towards Germans and nowadays it was greater than ever.

Johnny still could not grasp the evidence of his eyes. 'And the people?' he asked haltingly. Maybe Gudrun and the boys were sheltering at the police station. He pictured them huddled in their night things.

The official turned down the corners of his mouth. 'Killed,' he stated stolidly. 'All killed.'

Stupidly Johnny repeated, 'Killed.' The word could not possibly mean what he thought it did.

'Four bodies. Two women, two children.' He held up fingers in grey mittens to demonstrate the tally. 'You live here?' he asked.

'When did this happen?' With an automatic part of his brain Johnny constructed the sentence.

'Three, half-past, this morning.'

'And the bodies. Where?'

The man said something he didn't understand. Johnny stood there vacantly, still unconvinced. This kind of thing happened to other people, always. Always.

From the pocket of his heavy greatcoat the man produced a note-book, a stub of pencil. He wrote an address. 'You come here . . . See . . .' Raising his hands to his eyes in explanatory mime. Then he repeated another word, with emphasis, four or five times. Johnny guessed he was talking about identifying . . . the corpses.

'Gas,' the policeman said again, as if to reinforce his verdict on the explosion.

But why now suddenly? Johnny thought, and momentously his brain made a connection. The explosion had something to do with the letters. It was meant for him. The scenario made perfect sense. He pushed the horror of the thought away from him and said nothing to the policeman. What difference did it make? The effect was the same.

Something brightly coloured lay among the debris. He bent to look closer. It was a framed picture, intact apart from a curved crack running diagonally across the glass. A small reproduction of a painting by Chagall, the first present he had ever given to Gudrun. It showed a pair of lovers in a naïve domestic setting. The man, kissing his sweetheart, was at the same time flying rapturously in the air above her head. Gudrun had been puzzled.

'It shows how I feel about you,' Johnny had said. 'Happy. Flying. Like the man.'

And in a flash of recollection he saw the look she had given him, pleased and tender but uncomprehending. It seemed to symbolize all of their life together.

'No!' He heard his own voice, abrupt, impassioned in the sharp, frosty air.

Gudrun. Hans. Stefan. How could they be gone from his life just like that? A wild anguish swept through him, a swirling, irresistible wave.

Part Four

Chapter Forty-three

The large woman next to Grace on the early morning bus flipped over to a fresh page of her *News Chronicle*. As she did so the face of Neville Chamberlain – former Prime Minister of Great Britain and eighteen months dead – flickered for a split second in front of Grace's eyes. His features were distinguished, yet somehow rabbity, and in this, the third year of war, they carried the inescapable connotation of weakness, credulity, shabby compromise. Peace in our time, he'd trumpeted, when his earnest appeasement of Hitler had seemed to succeed. But a year later he was forced to declare war.

In a flash of memory Grace recalled sitting by the radio with Amy in the kitchen at Belsize Park and listening to his solemn tones delivering the message that by now they all expected. Noel was away in town working. Edward was expected to Sunday lunch. There was a smell of roasting in the air and Chamberlain's voice, sounding old and tired, had competed with the sizzling sound of the joint in the oven.

'That's it then.' Afterwards, as she switched off the wireless, Amy had pulled a wry face. Then she started to mix batter for a Yorkshire pudding. Grace saw there were tears in her eyes and knew she was thinking of Vicki.

Now the bus carried Grace along Belsize Road towards her wartime job in a day-nursery in Kilburn. She was lulled by the warmth of the stout body beside her, but the jolting of the bus and the bright, harsh sunshine foiled her attempts to doze. As usual she'd not had half enough sleep. After the pictures last night Grace and her friend Ann had run into Raymond Perry from down the road, on leave from his base in Scotland, spruce in his uniform. He'd pestered them to come for a drink and it was late as ever by the time she got home.

'I'm sorry, duck.' Struggling to fold up the newspaper, her neighbour elbowed Grace's cheek.

'Don't worry.' Grace grinned. 'It's nearly my stop. I needed a prod.'

The woman laid the folded paper across her lap. On the front page was a photograph of Mr Churchill, making a new speech about the campaign in North Africa. Just as Chamberlain's features had come to symbolize failure, so Churchill's broad, blunt face conveyed reassurance and dogged determination.

The bus swung into the High Road. Grace excused herself, clambered past her neighbour and along the aisle. It was gone half-past six. She must get a move on. In this summer of '42 her life had its own rhythm, hectic but routine. By now people spoke of 'before the war' as an almost mythological era, and Grace wasn't sure she could envisage a time 'after'.

'What you up to tonight, Grace?' Betty Archer smiled expectantly. She knew the girl would be swanning off somewhere.

'There's a dance, Bet. Marble Arch way.'

The smile broadened. 'Ooh, the energy of the girl. After a day's work all I'm good for is cocoa and me knitting.'

Grace squatted down to tie little Terry Archer's plimsoll lace. 'Goodnight, Terry. See you on Monday.' The three-year-old planted a wet kiss on her cheek. She closed her eyes ecstatically. 'Mmm, what a lovely smacker.'

Betty Archer was a machinist at the factory down the road, which, under government contract, produced jackets, trousers and overcoats for the military. Her forewoman was a martinet who constantly kept her workers late, which put the nursery staff out too. Betty arrived most nights in a rush and a flurry of apologies. She took Terry's hand and started wearily for the exit. 'Have a good time, girl. Don't do anything I wouldn't do.'

'Don't you worry.' Grace closed the door behind her and called through to May, the supervisor. 'That's the lot. Anything else?'

'Just see to the floor, Grace.'

'Okay, May.'

Damn. It was gone seven already. No time to waste. Grace filled the galvanized iron bucket, squeezed out the mop. She could do the big linoleum floor in five minutes flat. May used to follow her round suspiciously, but had learned from experience that Grace was efficient as well as quick.

As she swabbed the large, empty ground-floor room, May came through from the kitchen with her shopping and her grey cardigan. Her short square-cut hair was combed, her going-home lipstick applied. The supervisor stood by, stern-eyed, waiting.

She wasn't bad, May. They'd got off on the wrong foot at first, instinctively disliking one another. Grace was posh, not from round here, a dilettante doing her war-time bit. May would be a bully if you let her.

But the kids liked Grace and she was good with them. After a bit May started to call her over specially to deal with the difficult ones, the ones who bawled when their mothers left, or threw things, spat or bit. Grace knew she could. She teased them, made them laugh unwillingly, they wanted to please her – Elaine from 'round here' hadn't the same knack. And the mothers liked to tease Grace about her hectic social life, her gallivanting.

'You'd charm the birds off the trees, you,' May told her once, with a mixture of disapproval and grudging admiration.

Grace finished the floor, rinsed the bucket and mop. The supervisor produced her keys and locked both doors behind them in her stolid, thorough fashion.

'Don't go mad over the weekend.' May allowed a glint of humour to pierce her deadpan mask.

'Can't promise.'

Grace said goodbye and set out at a fast lick down Kilburn High Road. It was still a lovely golden evening, bliss after the endless bleak months of winter blackout. Grace headed for the convenient public lavatory in Maida Vale that she used for her Superman act, transforming herself from sixteen-year-old nursery nurse to glamour girl on the razzle, twenty if she was a day.

In the cubicle she stripped off her old school blouse and knee socks, slipping into a low-necked blue voile top Betty Archer had run up for her, in return for Grace minding Terry one evening, while she went to bed with her soldier husband home on a twenty-four-hour pass – Betty had filched the material from bales left over from the factory's peace-time stock. Delving in her bag, Grace produced a pair of much-blanco'd high heels. You couldn't get stockings for love nor money nowadays, and suddenly it was patriotic to go bare-legged.

Outside was a washbasin and a square of steel mirror that made your face look all wavy like a fade-out in a film. Grace splashed her face with cold water, dried it off with her discarded blouse. Then she set about doing her blonde hair in a sophisticated style that she reckoned added years to her age. One side caught back with a dia-manté comb, the other brushed forward to dip over the right eye. Grace was lucky. Her hair curled naturally. She didn't have to go to the trouble of smelly lotions and perms.

Last came her precious Yardley lipstick. You had to hoard it like gold. Grace outlined her lips, spread the colour by rubbing them carefully together. Considering the final effect in the greyish, dis-torting mirror, she felt her spirits lift, with a ready-for-anything recklessness. She checked her tote bag for the packet of 'rubbers' some American had given her. It wasn't that she expected to use them, but better to be safe than sorry.

It was strange at home nowadays. For one thing the family lived on the ground floor only. Two of the bedrooms had been let to an elderly couple who'd been bombed out, another to a woman who worked for the Ministry of Home Security and wasn't allowed to talk about what she did. The fourth had been converted into a kitchen. The Campion household had been lucky during the Blitz, though early in '41 a nearby explosion had shattered most of the windows of the house. But at the time Grace had been in Shropshire, evacuated with the school, and Amy asleep in the shelter down the garden.

Like almost everyone, Amy was involved in war work now. Jointly she ran a canteen in Chalk Farm for civil defence and factory workers.

Grace and her mother left at the same time every morning, and Amy's hours were longer than her own.

Grace missed returning to a home made comfortable and welcoming by Amy's presence. Her mother, she realized, had been the vitalizing heart of the household and Grace had taken for granted that it would always be so. Now the big white house in Philadelphia Close seemed alien, dark and claustrophobic with the blackout curtains, simultaneously empty and full of strangers. On the other hand the new regime offered her undreamed of opportunities to come and go as she pleased.

Her father was absent for long periods in Washington and New York. Prior to Pearl Harbor, Noel had completed two gruelling cross-country lecture tours in an attempt to alert the American public to the perilous isolation of Britain's position. Nowadays, over and above his written journalism, he was dipping his toe in broadcasting. Sometimes, late at night, Grace and Amy caught him on the wireless, beset by atmospheric crackle, but sounding quite wonderfully himself.

Grace saw – with surprise – that when her mother and father did meet, there was strain between them. All her life she'd taken it as read that her parents' relationship was stable, harmonious, mature. Now and in perpetuity. But cracks showed, disconcertingly, in the goodwill they laboured to maintain. The moments of anger and impatience that had always existed between them were different now – like spyholes into an underground store of rancour. You could blame the war, the separation, the new and stressful pattern of their lives. But Grace knew that Vicki was the worm in the bud.

She and Horst had married. The Campions had flown to Berlin for the brief civil ceremony on a freezing cold day in February. Horst, in a white shirt and a suit that was just too tight, looked uncharacteristically sheepish. Noel hardly addressed a word to him. Vicki was pale, defensive, and wore an expensive camel coat they hadn't seen before. Amy tried to inject a little warmth into the occasion, but it fell on stony ground. Horst's father, a haggard, handsome man, seemed as disapproving as Noel. His plump, homely mother looked nice and Horst was protective of her, as if he felt she might be slighted. Grace was ecstatic at seeing Vicki again, but she seemed surrounded by a glass wall. You'd have to smash your way in or remain politely outside.

At the beginning of August '39 her sister gave birth to a girl baby, Christa. Amy planned a visit but war intervened. Now they had no means of knowing how Vicki was, or even whether she were alive or dead. And the anxiety was there between her parents like a ghost, dividing rather than uniting them, in a way that seemed senseless to Grace.

The spectral Vicki seemed to dominate the household until Grace began to feel that her sister's presence was more real than her own. The thought made her bolshy. She'd never been studious like Vicki, but had the impression that her parents expected her to fulfil her sister's neglected academic promise. Grace balked at the idea of becoming a second-rate Vicki clone.

To her parents' dismay she left school the summer after she was fifteen. The next week Grace saw an advert for crèche workers. She was interviewed by a clutch of upper-class ladies in aggressive hats who appeared to think she was nicely spoken and would set a genteel example to the babies and infants in her care. So they foisted her on May and Elaine.

Grace liked the work and she'd always enjoyed winning people over. There were plenty to work on – the kids, her colleagues, the mums . . . Now she was accepted, though May clearly thought she'd somehow been conned. The money was pathetic, of course. When she was eighteen Grace planned to join the forces. Meanwhile she was going to enjoy herself just as hard as she could.

In this third summer of war things were not going well for the Allies. You never seemed to hear anything but bad news. But London was full of soldiers from all over – Poles, French, Norwegians, Aussies and, best of all, the exotic Yanks. Everyone was out for a good time because tomorrow they might be dead.

Grace was later than she'd expected but Gene, the young American she'd met a few nights ago at the Lyceum, said he'd come out and look for her every twenty minutes or so. She needed him to get in.

They didn't allow just any lone female to sashay past the bouncers on the door. This was an Anglo-American friendship do, sponsored by someone-or-other, and the tone had to be maintained. Women from a local nurses' home had been invited, along with typists and secretaries from one of the ministries. The dance was held in the two big downstairs rooms of the Cheval Blanc restaurant.

Grace stood outside the sandbagged portico. Within five minutes she'd had several other offers, but a promise was a promise. She owed it to Gene to wait for a while.

It wasn't long before he put in an appearance.

'Grace!' He looked relieved and rather surprised. 'I wasn't sure you'd make it.'

She laughed. 'Come hell or high water.'

He was young, not more than nineteen, she guessed, with a smooth, guileless face, the olive skin and thick brilliantined hair she thought of as Italian. His eyes were beautiful, brown and long-lashed – his mother must have loved them, Grace mused, with the nursery still on her mind. The Americans were all so glossy and well grown, their uniforms fresh, pressed and properly fitting.

'You look . . .' He was sweet, shy, and seemed a little dazzled. Grace had a feeling he wouldn't last long inside. At dances like this there were always the pushy ones, just waiting to cut in and monopolize the women.

She took his arm. 'It's good to escape, I can tell you. I've been drying tears and wiping bottoms all day.'

He led her, past the leering bouncers, into a long, blacked-out, artificially-lit room, that exuded the festive, heightened atmosphere Grace craved. In one corner of the room a quintet of soldiers played swoony, sensuous music. There were uniformed men and young women looking lit-up and happy. There was dancing, a buzz of talk, eddies of laughter. Grace's blood quickened as she entered. This – currently – was what she lived for.

'Can I get you a drink, Grace?'

There was a politely leisured air to Gene's attention, as if he had the whole long evening ahead of him. Grace was an old hand and she doubted it.

'What's on offer?'

'There's beer – or coffee.'

'A beer would be heaven.'

She was parched, Grace realized. Hungry too. She'd eaten nothing since the brown soup May had heated up at lunchtime. But an empty belly was always part of the whole atmosphere. Later on there'd probably be ice cream and cake. The Americans were big on sweet luxuries that the British had almost forgotten.

Drinking their beer, standing among the noisy crowd, she and Gene made shouted small talk. Grace knew he came from Minnesota. Apparently he'd been training as an automobile mechanic before he was whisked into the military. The young private seemed to approve Grace's work, as if it tied in with his image of wholesome womanhood. Gene was sufficiently sensitive to pay lip service to Britain's privations and endurance. Some Yanks were arrogant, with the implication that at last they were here to step in and sort out Europe's mess.

Though neither attitude cut much ice with Grace. All that was by the way. What she was after was oblivion, glamour, unreality. The hedonism Noel and Amy had always teased her about.

The band began to play 'Memories of You'. The languorous tune filled her with shivery pleasure. 'Don't you just love this song, Gene? Why don't we dance?'

He smiled as though she'd been forward and he found it charming. When they stepped on to the floor he held her in a relaxed fashion, as if anticipating a long, easy dance. But, after less than a minute, a tall lieutenant cut in and, given his rank, Gene had no option but to relinquish Grace.

The man was older, in his twenties. His grasp was firm and he danced well. She was exhilarated by the sense of their bodies moving in unison, his veiled eyes and admiring grin. But soon she was approached by a third man. 'Hey, Blondie, my turn.'

This was how it went. There were never enough women at these hops. Her new partner, though, was muscular and something hard in his features told her he was unlikely to be challenged.

'You're the prettiest girl here,' he told her flatly, as if imparting a simple fact.

Grace raised a sceptical eyebrow.

'I mean it. I was watching you.'

As they moved he laid one hand heavily in the nape of her neck. With the other he drew her into his rock-like pectorals, guiding her mesmerically round the floor.

Then, without warning, the band swung into an upbeat number, 'Jazz Band Ball'. Grace's new partner – Mal, his name was – seemed to assume she would stay with him and her feet were already tapping. He was handsome in a loutish way that appealed to her on some instinctive level. Fleetingly she pictured poor, abandoned Gene, but already she and Mal were sucked in by the infectious rhythm.

Experimentally he took her hand, spinning her round, jitterbug-style. The new wild dancing craze had come over with the American troops, a scandal, an outrage, a scab the newspapers couldn't stop scratching. Grace was a novice, but agog to learn. Mal danced easily, not forcing the pace, and she picked the movements up from him.

He began to grin, as if this were the kind of communication that came naturally to him, and Grace smiled too, as their hands touched, her body twisted, feet moved in time to the beat. Other couples followed suit. Suddenly any other kind of dancing seemed staid. She was glimpsing something young and modern, something ecstatic.

'You're getting the hang of it.' His accent was aphrodisiac, echoing as it did all the films she'd drunk in blankly, avidly, since she was a kid.

She felt good, she felt exultant, alive with the resistance of muscle and sinew, dazzled by the strength of his arms as he drew her close, spun her round, lifted and supported her in the complicated but inevitable intricacies of the dance.

Now the band struck up the opening bars of 'In the Mood', a wartime myth of a tune, raising a buzz of recognition, anticipation all across the room.

'Ahh, Gracie . . .' The words emerged in a sort of growl that excited her. 'Let's go for this one.'

They were warmed up, already attuned. The melody had something insinuating – it rippled in her veins like forbidden pleasures as, eyes locked, they began to dance. With one part of her mind she

397

knew they made a striking couple – herself blonde, diminutive; Mal heavy-set, his looks dark and uningratiating.

There was something hypnotic in the way their movements reflected one another's, subdued at first, like an animal emerging slyly from its cage, but gaining rapidly in confidence and exuberance. Between them was a sixth sense, their bodies weaving in and out, smooth and sinuous, with something like rapture. The music gained in speed and insistence. Their movements kept pace. Grace was sweating, could feel her eyes deep and shining with the exhilaration of the dance, her hair whipping sensuously against her neck and shoulders.

Slowly she became aware that some of the other couples had stopped, were gathering where she and Mal were, watching, admiring. But the realization was somewhere on the outer edge of consciousness. The dance was the thing, the conviction, the complicity between Mal and herself, as the music rose to a climax and exploded in a burst of sound, leaving them hot and panting with feral excitement while the others stomped and cheered.

That had been the best moment, Grace thought, on the tube going home. After that she was sort of public property, plied with sandwiches and ice cream, and beer she didn't really want, and lost track of the men she'd danced with.

Mal had turned sulky as if she owed him something. Grace couldn't see that she did. They'd just danced together. What he made of it was his affair. He kept asking her to come outside and she guessed he thought she'd let him shag her in a shop doorway like the fourteen-year-old kids who waited for the Yanks on Rainbow Corner off Leicester Square. But she couldn't bear to be like them – despised, used. She wasn't a prude but her pride revolted ... It was a gut-feeling, though there'd been a few times when she got carried away.

Grace felt bad enough about lying to her mother – the evening class in childcare she had invented, the stories about sleeping over at Ann's house. And Amy trusted her. To get pregnant would be awful, a failure for everyone to see, an abject, pathetic cliché.

Three months ago, at a do not that far from where she lived, Grace had met a couple of Norwegians. They offered to walk her home. One of them had whisky in a silver hip flask and, not wanting to look like a kid, she'd downed her share. They were blond and outdoorsy like Norwegians ought to be, and all of them were joking as they walked along the dark, empty streets.

They passed a bombed-out building and, laughingly, one of them pulled Grace inside. Then they were holding her down and pulling at her knickers as if it were just horseplay, and then – in sudden, urgent silence – both of them raped her.

Afterwards they acted as if nothing had happened, as if it were all in a day's work for all of them. Grace had felt stunned, betrayed, her clothes and hair were gritty with brick-dust. She felt like crying, but wouldn't give them the satisfaction. Afterwards she wondered if she'd somehow been to blame. The memory was locked inside her. She would never tell anyone about it, ever.

Chapter Forty-four

Amy enjoyed early mornings at the canteen. There was something domestic about it, almost as if you were catering for family, and the steaminess of the kitchen was cheery, not oppressive, as it became later. Provisions were simple at this time of day, centring round the tea urn and the toaster, plus whatever else happened to be available – dried egg scramble or omelette, potato cakes or bubble-and-squeak from yesterday's leftovers. Just once in a while there'd be a bit of bacon and it would have everyone sniffing the air blissfully like a lot of superannuated Bisto kids.

Early on the customers came in ones and twos, not in great gangs like later. There were regulars – the two bus conductresses who dropped in after the pre-dawn workers' run, Derek off to his insurance job after a night's firewatching, Hetty and Jess who treated themselves to breakfast and a fag before clocking on at the furniture factory, lonely Tom, the warden, whose wife had been killed in a raid the previous year and who came in more for the company than anything else. There was time to chat and have a bit of breakfast yourself before starting on the feverish preparations for the two main sittings.

As the morning got under way it was time to set the huge soup pot on to boil and peel the everlasting mountain of potatoes. The aim of the British Restaurant scheme – government-sponsored, local-authority-funded – was to provide a nourishing three-course meal at round a shilling a head. Coupons were not required. So for war workers this was a convenient way of getting a decent hot lunch or supper while at the same time saving on fuel and eking out precious rations.

Amy ran her branch – in a vacated soft-furnishings shop – in tandem with a woman called Chris Carella. The two of them had met during the Blitz when both worked in a mobile WVS kitchen providing food, hot drinks and sympathy in bombed-out communities all over London. The inadequacy of contingency plans for the victims had been a national scandal and it was left to the ingenuity of individuals to cope with the situation.

The nightly air raids were, in any case, a situation for which there could be no rehearsal. Nothing like them had ever happened before and, day after day, well-intentioned novices struggled to cope, to provide warmth and shelter and food, a semblance of order amidst the chaos and confusion, for human beings abruptly dispossessed and bereaved, stupefied or aggressive with shock.

Amy had warmed to Chris's quiet imperturbability. The situation hadn't made her bossy or officious or over-hearty. She just did her job with compassion and to the very best of her ability. As a team the two of them had improvised wildly, making tea and soup and stew in a variety of unlikely containers, from washing boilers to empty dustbins. At times the raids were so relentless that they went without anything you could call sleep for days and nights at a stretch. The madness of the situation, the sheer gruelling hard work, had forged a tough, unsentimental bond between them.

When, by the summer of '41, the worst of the bombing was over, the country emerged to a future that was less dramatic, but grim and indeterminate. Germany, it seemed, was carrying all before her. Britain stood alone. It would be another six months before the Americans entered the fray. For civilians the essential now was dogged faith, long-term commitment to the grinding process of the wartime economy. On account of their chequered Blitz experience Amy and Chris were offered the managership of a newly opened British Restaurant.

They were delighted to carry on working in harness. Both had the same philosophy, a desire to make the canteen as good as it could possibly be. With shortages of many of the most basic foodstuffs it was a challenge to produce decent meals. 'There's a war on' was the excuse for all sorts of compromise and sloppiness but, within the limits imposed, both were determined that their menu would be as nutritious, varied and downright appetizing as they could make it.

They were bombarded with constant gung-ho directives from the Ministry of Food. The supply of meat, cheese, fish, fats, eggs might dwindle down, at times to vanishing point, but the bulletins retained an indomitable cheery optimism. 'Waste not, want not' was the ubiquitous maxim. Everything must be saved and used, from vitamin-rich vegetable water to the tough outer leaves of cabbages to simmer in the soup pot for the first course.

Only the main course was permitted to contain protein, though it might be in minuscule quantities. Variations on the stew were a standby, with the sparse presence of meat or fish distributed equitably throughout. From America came the novelties, corned beef and Spam. Hash and fritters made from these were among the most popular dishes on offer.

'Potatoes with everything' was another MOF slogan and vegetables were extolled as a universal panacea. In fact grated carrot attained the mystic status of an elixir of life, popping up everywhere – in salads, sandwich fillings, mixed in with mashed potato, converted into jam, appearing even in cakes and steamed puddings, a partial substitute for the failing fat and sugar.

Tom, the air-raid warden, cultivated the small backyard for them. In his bereaved state the gardening was therapeutic, the canteen staff a substitute family, and he was rewarded for his work with a free lunch or dinner. Amy and Chris insisted on plenty of home-grown herbs – parsley, chives, mint, savory, sage, Welsh onions – to add freshness and flavour, as well as a varied and intensive succession of salad vegetables to supplement their basic supplies.

Towards midday the lunch-time sitting began. The first to come were those who had the option of arriving while all choices on the menu were still available. Elderly couples, housewives out shopping with their young children – before half-past twelve there were special small, cheap portions for kids. Soon the numbers would swell, waves of office workers, factory hands, demolition and repair squads arriving pell-mell.

For a time it was madness, with Amy and Chris buzzing about like blue-tailed flies in the steam of the kitchen, the counter staff calling tersely through for top-ups of everything, and Rose, who did the washing-up, struggling to keep pace with a supply of clean plates and cutlery. Always they half-dreaded the daily rush but, almost to their surprise, muddled through somehow.

Then there was a breathing space, time to collect themselves, eat, and restore order, before they put on the soup, peeled the potatoes for the second sitting, though evenings were never quite as hectic. Then again they had fewer staff at night. By seven-thirty or so it was over, but the kitchen had to be scrubbed and everything put away, accounts checked, plans made for the following day. They were lucky to leave by half-past eight. But everyone was working dawn to dusk nowadays. That was just the way it was.

In the late twenties Chris Hugobuoni had been a dancer, earning a carefree living in touring musical shows, doing summer seasons in end-of-pier entertainments. Her father was a Southwark bricklayer of Italian ancestry. Chris was the third child of seven. She was light-hearted and pretty, with jet-black hair and pale, freckled skin, and dancing made her feel like someone special.

'In those days I didn't know I was born,' she told Amy once with a wry smile – some months ago it was now – as the two of them cleaned a daunting heap of undersized herrings. 'I lived in a sort of pink and blue cloud-land.'

Amy was fascinated. She could never remember feeling remotely like that as a young girl.

But one day, during a pierrot show in Southend, the stage collapsed and Chris was buried under a pile of bodies and rubble. Both legs were injured, but the left one was fractured in three places. The hospital did a creditable repair job, but she was left with a limp and her dancing days were over and done with.

'I felt as if my life had ended,' Chris said. She had a South London accent, an intriguing harsh timbre to her voice. 'I was twenty and all I wanted to do was hide like a dying animal.'

For a year she lived at home, in absolute despair, indulging her misery, flaunting it, lying about the house in a dressing gown all day, oblivious to sympathy and exasperation alike. Her mother became ill with worrying about her and the fact gave Chris a kind of savage satisfaction.

One day, on the wireless, she heard the song 'When the Red Red Robin'. It was a tune she'd never much cared for, oozing brassy bonhomie, but she'd danced to it in one of her seaside shows. Goose flesh broke out all over her body and Chris had a vivid flash of how it had felt to move to music, taking her strength and vitality rapturously for granted.

'I smashed the wireless, Amy. I couldn't bear it. Then I just cried. Actually I howled – I scared myself. But it was good in a way. I finally realized I couldn't go on like that.'

Chris had thought of herself as different and blessed because she could dance and didn't have to work in Woolworth's or R. White's bottle factory. Now she forced herself to come to terms with the fact that she was ordinary, repeating the word to herself over and over and, after a while, the idea didn't seem so terrible at all.

'I told myself my life was my life and if I didn't value it, no one would.' Confiding the words, Chris had a wary, self-mocking look in her slanting blue eyes, as if she thought Amy might laugh.

She got a job as a waitress, met and married a young waiter called John Carella, from an Anglo-Italian family like her own. They had two children, a boy and a girl, and saved hard to open a restaurant of their own.

But the war had intervened. John was with the army now in North Africa. Chris's father was dead and her mother had moved in with her in Camden Town to look after the children.

'We're still going to have it, that restaurant, when all this is over.' Chris set about coating each individual herring with oatmeal and flour.

It was still a lovely warm June evening when the two women left the canteen at twenty-five to nine. Their homeward journeys took them in opposite directions, Chris's to Camden High Street, Amy's towards Haverstock Hill.

Amy placed a quick kiss on Chris's cheek. 'Try not to worry. The chances are he'll be fine.' John Carella was currently in Libya and recent bulletins from there were not encouraging.

'There's no point in worrying. Not that that'll stop me.'

'Valerian juice, Chris.' All the newspapers that day had featured a round-faced, contented nonagenarian who swore by this particular remedy as an antidote to the stresses of war.

'It'll take more than that.'

'I could do tomorrow on my own . . .' Saturdays were quietish usually.

'No you won't. Anyway, working takes my mind off things.'

'True.' An image of Vicki loomed in Amy's brain.

Chalk Farm Road was still busy with people going home or out for the evening. There was a boisterous crowd of men and women in uniform outside the pub. In spite of everything the summer weather raised everyone's spirits. Amy didn't bother to hurry. Grace wouldn't be home until later. She had her childcare class, then she was popping to Ann's for a couple of hours.

Home seemed quite different nowadays, more like a hostel, with other people using her furniture, carpets, bathroom. Amy wasn't sure how she felt about it. She used to think she loved that house, had always enjoyed buying nice things for it, making cupboards and shelves with her own hands. Once upon a time, she knew, the thought of strangers making free there would have horrified her.

A healthy residue of that misgiving remained. At the same time, Amy reflected, there was a certain freedom, even a sort of relief in the idea of letting go. You lost one role – the nurturing heart of the household everyone thought they loved you for, though they took it for granted as well. The benefits were ambiguous – but there *were* benefits – when the house was just a place to sleep, a kind of spring-board from which you threw yourself into life. Only, without the exigencies of war, she would never have discovered that.

'Fuck off, Barry. Fuck off!'

'You prickface.'

A group of kids passed her, boys of eleven or twelve, scruffy and grinning, smoking cigarettes with quick, nervy movements. One of the bigger lads jostled a runtish companion, pushing him into Amy.

'Mind what you're doing!'

The boys turned to look at her, some blank, some insolent. One of the by-products of the times was children running wild, because their fathers were away, their mothers too bogged down with long hours of war work to keep track of them.

Amy worried about Grace. She and Noel had hoped their younger daughter would carry on with her studies, take her exams and go on to university. The school was evacuated to rural Shropshire. She would have been safe as well as properly supervised – 'kept out of mischief,' as Noel frankly termed it. But Grace wasn't having any. She felt buried alive down there and Amy could see that, with the future so risky and unpredictable, higher education must seem at best an irrelevance.

'I'm a free spirit. Got that? I loathe swotting!' she'd screamed at them. Amy could picture her halfway up the stairs, small face peaky with passion, while Elspeth, the lodger, hovered, embarrassed, on the landing above. Grace had stood dramatically aside to let her pass, in tense silence. As the front door slammed, she returned to the attack. 'Get it into your heads, now and for ever. I'm not Vicki!'

Grace had prevailed and everyone said what a good job she did at the nursery. Amy was proud of her daughter's vitality and practical good sense. But sometimes Grace had a look that scared her, sharp and wild. And she was so pretty. Amy insisted on being kept informed as to her daughter's whereabouts, made sure she was home without fail before midnight. She had to trust her. But, in the wakeful, discouraging early hours, her suspicion grew that Grace had secrets.

The small hours were the time when Amy felt at the lowest ebb, when she was ambushed by terror for Vicki. The fear was there all the time, dormant or active, living inside her, feeding on her blood like a malevolent foetus. She had no way of knowing how her child was faring, alone in enemy territory. Amy pictured her, cradling the unknown grandchild, surrounded by hostility. British bombing raids had started over Germany. To everyone else they were a source of savage satisfaction, a righteous revenge for the carnage of the Blitz.

But, after each triumphant bulletin, Amy was transfixed by a pain that never grew less.

The only person who could feel as she did was Noel. She could enter into his mind. With each successive raid he would be reeling, as she was, with an anguish as great. But, somehow, their dread for Vicki had not brought them together in mutual support, but dredged to the surface all the rancours and angers they had never really dared to address.

She'd not seen her husband for nearly a year now. That was nothing. Half the women in the land could say the same. And, on his last visit, they'd played their parts, co-operating, never rocking the boat, so that almost they were lulled into a belief that everything was as it should be. Only Amy knew, and so did he, that they were spanning the thinnest of bridges over a deep and boiling chasm.

'That you, Amy?' a voice called from upstairs as she opened the front door to her house.

'Yes, it's me, Florence!'

Florence Barker and her retired husband, Leonard, occupied Vicki's and Grace's erstwhile bedrooms, sharing the upstairs kitchen with Elspeth. Eighteen months ago, an incendiary bomb had left the couple homeless.

'I'm just making a cuppa, duck. Can I interest you?'

'You certainly can.' Wearily Amy began to mount the stairs. She'd allow herself a ten-minute sit-down. After that there was the washing to rinse.

Chapter Forty-five

William Tilly was some sort of writer who worked at the Ministry of Information in Malet Street. He had a strangely nervous manner, florid skin with the texture of orange peel, luxuriant greying hair. Johnny would have put his age at around forty, but Bill claimed to be twenty-nine. He'd taken to Johnny for some reason and, every so often, they spent lugubrious evenings drinking watery beer in the cavernous Swiss Tavern in Old Compton Street. Bill always seemed happy to buy the drinks and Johnny let him. Anything he could screw out of this tight-arsed country was fine by him.

'Wotcha, Bill.' A pudgy man skirted their beer-splashed table carrying a couple of tankards. Frizzy hair thrust from his side parting in an aggressive wedge-shape. 'Still shuffling the old papers?' The activities of the MOI had a reputation for muddle and futility.

'Got it down to a fine art, Jules.' Bill smiled, but he rarely met anyone's eye.

Jules nodded, just perceptibly, to acknowledge Johnny's presence, but clearly wished no closer contact. The feeling was mutual. Johnny recognized him as one of the self-conscious bohemians for whom this pub was a local.

Bill was amused by the wide berth Johnny was accorded in this company. 'It's like walking in the door with a panther on a chain.'

Johnny had no time for the so-called artists, posturing like a lot of spoiled kids, with their safe, soft jobs writing propaganda booklets or documentary film-scripts. There'd been an evening, so Bill informed him – Johnny could hardly remember, things seemed to pass him by these days – when gin was on offer and Johnny was knocking it back like water and ended up insulting everyone, Jules included.

Apparently Johnny had been sounding off about the sentimental picture the British had of themselves as an island race, standing alone, 'taking it' during the Blitz, all that self-congratulatory mumbo jumbo.

'You'd no choice but to take it,' he shouted. 'You just had to be there and let the bombs rain down. You couldn't do anything else. It doesn't make you heroes!'

That was Bill's story and Johnny had to believe him, though the opinions expressed sounded rather beyond his skill in English. He'd got into a fight with someone who took umbrage and ended up with a bloody nose. The injury was there, large as life, in the morning, bearing witness to an alcoholic fracas Johnny could barely recall.

'Anything on the work front, old man?' Bill asked. He always sat with his head on one side, eyes on his beer, only occasionally lifting them to Johnny's face.

'Some column-breakers for *Courier*. Otherwise . . .' Johnny shrugged. '*London Opinion* takes a Hitler cartoon . . .' He pulled a face. There was little satisfaction to be had from lampooning the Führer when such an attitude was the cosy norm. And he was in too precarious a position to tackle the British establishment. Johnny almost preferred the meaningless, poorly paid column-breakers. 'I don't make the bank happy.'

'Have you tried *Witness*? They pay better than most.'

'*Witness*?'

'Come back to my place later. I'll give you a couple of copies to look at . . . I've done reviews for them.' Bill had raised his eyes, momentarily. Now he lowered them again. 'Feel free to mention my name.'

He had a room in Riding House Street to which they would adjourn later on in the evening. Bill would probably cook sausages, so stuffed with bread that they would burst in the pan. Usually he served them with more bread – several thick, stale doorsteps, sliced off a grey national loaf, the meal only made palatable by a dollop of bright yellow, eye-watering mustard.

Somehow the writer always had a bottle of whisky – though the price for such a treasure was astronomical – and they would get plastered together, two lonely men bemoaning their lives.

Johnny was fond of Bill in an exasperated sort of way. The writer saw him as representing the fabulous, licentious culture of twenties Berlin. Bill felt able to confide in this rootless exile the momentous, raw secret of his homosexuality, his sense of terrifying isolation and moments of despair, swallowing great nervous gulps of alcohol as he spoke while, from the mantelpiece, the framed photograph of a tousle-haired young man, bare-torsoed in khaki shorts, laughed flirtatiously down at them. The Adonis Bill had loved and lost. One evening he'd made a half-hearted pass at Johnny, but his very lack of conviction anticipated the inevitable rebuff.

Bill listened with equanimity, even a kind of masochistic pleasure, as Johnny inveighed against the English as smug, arrogant and small-minded, and sympathized when he complained about the stifling sterility of his life. But his eyes glazed over if Johnny brought up the subject of Gudrun and the children, his grief and self-lacerating remorse. Bill hated families and, anyway, was not emotionally equipped to deal with such naked pain.

Bill's room was the kind of fusty bachelor hideaway Johnny had always tried to avoid, fetid-smelling, the bed unmade, the blackout curtains never drawn. Teetering piles of books and magazines lined the walls.

'I know I've got some back copies of *Witness* somewhere.' Bill looked about him vaguely, helplessly.

'Doesn't matter.' Johnny couldn't face the upheaval that would be involved in finding them.

'You'll thank me, Johnny, you'll see. I should think they'd welcome you with open arms. An exile like you, just dripping integrity.'

'I expect they see every day twenty or so.'

But Bill would not be discouraged. He began to run his fingers down the piles of periodicals, extracting anything promising with breathless care in a usually unsuccessful attempt not to topple the rest of the precarious edifice. After some minutes' huffing and puffing he managed to locate three copies of the review, limp affairs printed on the dismal wartime economy paper.

Johnny flipped through the top one with polite disinterest, the print racing past his eyes. Suddenly it seemed to him that one of the

410

flickering names had been familiar to him. He flipped more attentively. There it was. Noel Campion. The by-line heading a piece on
political in-fighting in Washington.

'Noel Campion,' he said out loud, and the provocative image of
Amy that had never left him shimmered into his mind.

'You know him?'

'He was in Berlin. I met his wife. Not him.'

'Nice chap. I've met him a few times at *Witness* dos. And at the
house of some mutual acquaintances. Amy too.'

'She's in America?'

Bill shook his head. 'I seem to remember she's doing some patriotic
war work or other. A canteen or some such.'

Johnny was dubious. He couldn't imagine Amy doing anything so
earthbound. Bill had probably got it wrong. 'Could you find where?
I'd like to look her up.' He was pleased with the casual colloquialism,
though his heart was racing with an absurd sort of hope.

'Probably. You might as well use all the contacts you can get.'

For nine months of the war, from the summer of 1940 until spring
'41, Johnny had been interned in a camp on the Isle of Man. Adam
and Inge Raab were imprisoned elsewhere on the island. The black
irony of the fact still had the power to induce in him an abrupt and
boiling rage.

He, Johnny Kröger, had from the first risked everything to expose
and vilify Nazism. His wife and children had paid the final price for
his stubborn integrity, his criminal recklessness – whatever. Yet he'd
been locked away as a danger to democracy by these people who'd
crawled on their bellies to Hitler, appeasing and appeasing him like
a bellicose child, rushing to give him whatever he wanted, in an
attempt to cling abjectly to their blind, callous peace. The betrayal
had left him with a bitterness against this country that rankled,
throbbed and flared like a toothache.

He'd shared an unheated shed with three other men – one of
scores of similar sheds, erected on a bare compound surrounded by
barbed wire. The hut had a stone floor and contained four bunks,

four lockers, and one stinking bucket into which all of them shat and pissed.

All four men had reason to hate and fear the Nazis. They'd seen Britain as their sanctuary.

Johnny's particular companion had been Egon, a Jewish schoolteacher from Vienna, whose brother had been beaten to death by SA men in the immediate aftermath of the Anschluss.

'What are we being punished for?' Egon asked often with eager indignation. As if the question had an answer. As though, given access to the right authorities, he could personally sort out the whole sorry muddle.

'Shut up, Egon.'

None of the rest of them now harboured any such illusions. Experience had proved conclusively that – whatever the regime – individuals were meaningless pawns, the right to justice mere misty self-delusion.

As winter progressed Johnny developed acute bronchitis. He couldn't get warm and felt as if he were coughing his lungs up, bit by bit. He was nearly forty, had always taken health for granted. But the cough was like a bird of ill omen, its claws buried deep in his hunched shoulders. It had taken him over, he couldn't shake it off.

By spring the worst of the internment panic had dissipated. Prisoners were being released in dribs and drabs and Johnny was given a dispensation on health grounds.

Soon afterwards Adam and Inge Raab from Prague were released. But the vicissitudes of the last years had finally derailed Adam. He was sunk in a hollow-eyed, impenetrable depression and was admitted to a mental ward.

'You and I, Johnny, should make the best of things and take a flat together,' Inge declared matter-of-factly. 'For the companionship – not to mention the economic advantages.'

But, after the months of internment, Johnny had had quite enough of life at close quarters and, fond as he was of Inge, he'd no desire to be domestically organized by her.

Some days, though, the two of them escaped and took a bus or train out to the country. Inge, in a flower-splashed blouse, hiking boots, a pair of Adam's shorts, cut an outlandish figure. Johnny knew that in younger, shallower days he'd have been mortified to appear in public with such a creature. Now he was amused, even proud of her sturdy contempt for appearances. Inge borrowed maps and looked out long, circular route marches. And together they would walk and walk until exhaustion put them beyond the reach of their respective demons for a while.

Johnny took a room on his own in West Hampstead. Alone he could deal better with his rage, guilt and pain. It was as if these emotions were contained in a vast reservoir and, lying by himself on his bed in the evening, he would tap a little of the harrowing cocktail. Rationing himself a measured amount. Allowing it full rein for a while, torturing his mind with self-reproach, memory and loss, then blotting out the turmoil with alcohol and sedative pills he got from a friend of Bill's in Soho. By this slow means, Johnny reckoned, he would gradually use up the whole reservoir of grief, though it would take him years.

From the time of his marriage Johnny had retained two articles – the cracked painting he'd found in the ruins of the house in Prague, and one photograph of his wife and two boys. Everything else had been lost in transit or in the blast.

The photograph showed the three of them in the courtyard flat where they'd lived longest, all sitting on the big bed which was covered with a plaid blanket. The boys smiled, so sweet and mischievous, seemingly without a care in the world. Gudrun smiled too, but her eyes had a lost look. Already out-of-date by the time of their deaths, the picture had been safe in his wallet, in the breast pocket of his herringbone overcoat. And behind it he kept a dog-eared snap of Amy.

One summer evening, back in '39, before the war, when he'd not long arrived in London – confused, grieved, dazed – Johnny had followed a slim young woman in Hampstead High Street. She wore a soft cream dress that skimmed her graceful body, and her hair was pale and light like Amy's. He knew it wasn't her, but tailed the girl up a side road until she turned off into a luxuriant front garden. Her image plucked a chord in his heart, reminding him of past happiness and pleasure, so that for a time he forgot who and where he was.

In those days he was living in the spare room of a history professor and his stern-looking wife, members of the group that had sponsored him and the Raabs. He slept on a canvas camp bed among rows of olive-green filing cabinets, and all his worldly belongings were contained in a cheap cardboard suitcase on the floor.

The room had no curtains and at night the streetlamps cast the chequered shadows of the window frames across the floor and walls. Johnny's strongest memory from that time was of lying awake in the small hours of the morning, gazing at the rectangles of light – slightly cloudy from the imperfections in the glass – his whole being frozen with a numb despair.

But that night he fell to thinking about Amy, wondering why he'd condemned her so violently back then. He saw suddenly how young she'd been – they both had – a wife and mother, with old-fashioned ideas of loyalty and duty, which at the time Johnny himself had jettisoned. The wonder was, not that she'd left him, but that she'd entertained the idea of an affair at all. In that alien, makeshift room he'd felt reconciled to the lover of his youth and fell asleep for once in a state of fragile peace.

'Could you tell Mrs Campion that a friend would like to speak with her?' He'd rehearsed the sentence in his head, so he'd be sure to come straight out with it.

'Pardon?' The tall redhead on the counter stared blankly at him.

'Could you tell Mrs Campion that a friend would like to speak with her.' Johnny was acutely aware of his German accent. He was shabby too, but so – after nearly three years of war – were most people.

Her eyes were cold and insolent. He met them with hostility. In his own country Johnny would have had a sharp witticism ready on the tip of his tongue.

'You want to talk to Amy?'

'Exact.'

'You'll have to wait. I can't leave this counter.'

With the spatula-like instrument in her hand, she levered a portion of some kind of vegetable pie on to one waiting plate, then another. Reaching for a large spoon, she added two helpings of salad. A plump girl served potatoes speckled with parsley.

'Could you move. You're in the way.'

Johnny went and stood by the wall. He looked about him. The place was functional but bright and quite pleasant. There were flowers on the tables. The restaurant seemed popular. The queue was continuous. The red-haired woman called through a hatch and, a while later, a dark, pretty woman in her thirties delivered a long aluminium tray that held more of the pie, marked out into squares.

The counter assistant shouted something at her, nodding towards Johnny. The dark woman approached him. She walked with a limp.

'Amy's not free just now. This is our busy time. If you'd like to sit and wait . . . Ask Rose for a cup of tea.' She was friendly, but harassed.

'Thank you.'

No tables were free but he managed to find an empty chair which he carried to an unobtrusive corner. For more than half an hour he sat and watched the comings and goings of the diners with impatient disinterest. His misgivings grew. The idea of a reunion struck him increasingly as misconceived. Amy's life was clearly busy, not empty like his own. He dreaded the idea that her heart might sink on seeing him, as an unwelcome revenant from a past that was over and done with. He'd viewed the young Amy through an erotic haze, and maybe that was all there had been. They were both middle-aged by now, both changed. Would they have anything at all to say to one another?

Eventually the customers began to thin out. Johnny sat waiting, hands in pockets, one leg crossed high over the other, his posture by now hostile, defensive. Then the canteen was almost empty.

Two figures emerged from a back room, the kitchen presumably. One was the dark woman he'd seen earlier. She pointed him out.

Her companion began to cross the room towards him. A slight

woman wearing a striped blouse, sleeves rolled, belted over black trousers. Her fair hair shoulder-length, curling, beaded with moisture, touched by the coral of the evening sun which shone through the plate-glass window behind him. She was frowning slightly with puzzled enquiry.

Johnny stood up to face her. His heart thumped with the foolish expectancy he'd been trying to suppress ever since William Tilly first mentioned her name. The small woman advancing towards him had been in some ways the most potent figure in his life.

'Amy.' The greeting emerged in a hoarse, over-dramatic rasp.

Back-lit by a long ray of sunshine, his face must be in shadow. Amy wore a look of confusion, mystification.

'You don't recognize me . . .' His voice was steadier this time.

Up close he could see she was hot and tired from her activity in the kitchen. Johnny attempted to superimpose his recollected mental image on the face in front of him. He recalled the wide grey eyes and sweet, sensuous mouth. Her features had become more deeply etched, tightly drawn, but her aura remained as he remembered it. Amy had always gazed out at the world with a quite personal mixture of eagerness and reserve. He used to love that look, until she left him. After that he devalued it in his mind as insincere. Johnny saw now that it was not.

Amy stared at him in silence. Then, finally, incredulously, recognition dawned and she found her voice.

'Johnny . . .' Speaking with a rising inflexion, like a question mark.

He grinned crookedly. 'Yes, it's Johnny . . . Returned from the grave.' A sudden bleak stab at humour.

'I'm . . .' She was dazed. 'I can't believe it . . . This is the most . . .' With a bemused and wondering smile she raised her hands to her head.

For all her confusion Amy's voice held gladness and goodwill. Johnny was moved by her obvious emotion. How sincere she was and how kind. How had he ever allowed himself to see her as shallow and treacherous? He made no move to touch or embrace her. It was as if such a gesture would have been merely conventional, when the air around them seemed to vibrate with the specialness of their reunion. With his eyes Johnny drank in the features he had once loved. She was the first happy thing to have come his way in years.

On Sunday morning two young Americans called to take Grace and Ann walking on the Heath. They seemed polite country boys, addressing Amy as ma'am and bringing a packet of real coffee from stores as a goodwill gift.

Before they all left Grace came to find Amy in the kitchen and gave her the packet. 'Here. Take it to your friend from me.'

She was intrigued by the dramatic surfacing of this unknown political refugee, a former friend of Claudia's.

Amy demurred. 'No. This is yours.'

'Go on. I'd like him to have it.' Before her mother could protest further she bounced out of the room to join her companions. Amy heard her say, 'Right! Let's go promenading.' And she was left to ponder a little dubiously on the irony of her younger child sending a gift – in blithe ignorance – to the man who had fathered her.

Amy had been unable to have more than a few minutes' conversation with Johnny the other night. Margaret was visiting that week from Gloucester. She resented Amy's work as demeaning and unnecessary, taking her away from her rightful place at home. The boys were all in uniform, Emily in the Wrens – Margaret regarded the war rather in the light of a personal inconvenience, designed to deprive her of the company of her children, and in particular her daughters. She expected Amy to rush home and do what she could to make good the neglect.

Margaret had left yesterday. Today, her one day off, Amy had arranged to call on Johnny at his address in West Hampstead. She was still reeling from his startling resurgence, had been ever since in a strange, altered state of disorientation, expectation, unreality. Faint images had licked at her memory all week, like tiny cool flames flickering from the seemingly dead ashes of their relationship. Now Grace's impulsive gesture brought to mind that Johnny used to pride himself on making excellent coffee . . .

It had been a shock to encounter his ageing, as it must have been

417

for him to register hers. He'd looked strained, thin, and something else . . . There'd been a sort of confusion in his eyes, which were heavy and dull – they used to have that cocky, subversive gleam. The change touched her in some raw spot. Yet, in spite of everything, wearing a dark polo–neck and slacks, Johnny still radiated a defiant chic.

Then came the bombshell. Amy had asked after his family.

'My wife and children are dead,' he stated baldly, looking her in the eye, as if he'd discovered from experience that brutal directness was the best way for him to speak the news – some skulduggery of the Nazis, so he said. She could not begin to imagine how he coped with such pain.

Later, taking leave, she asked, 'Are you all right?'

Her aim was simply to voice concern, but how crass and ineffectual the question sounded to her ears.

A droll, black glint of irony was visible behind his eyes. 'Fine. Just fine.'

He lived on the second floor of a tall, terraced building in grey-brown brick. Each door, Amy noticed, bore a different name. The stairs and landing had the run–down look you saw everywhere nowadays. Scarce resources could not be wasted on maintaining private homes.

She found Johnny's door and knocked. He opened at once, looking brighter than the other evening, in a loose short-sleeved white shirt. There seemed more warmth to his complexion. His face was taut but lined, giving Amy the fleeting impression of a wrinkled adolescent. The thick, dull brown hair was shorter, rising from his forehead like a crest, silver threads shining in the sun that poured in through the open sash windows.

'Amy.' He kissed her decorously, then held her wonderingly at arm's length. 'Unbelievable. It's quite, quite unbelievable.' Today he spoke German, the way they used to.

'Since Tuesday I've been shell-shocked.' She smiled at him as if they were two old friends, as if separation had not prevented their affection from ripening. As if time had done its work, with or without them.

'Sit down.' Johnny indicated a cracked leatherette suite of stolid design. He pulled a face. 'These chairs aren't my choice, you understand.'

She recalled his apartment in Berlin, clean and spare and stylish when she'd arrogantly expected male squalor. He hadn't the scope here to impose his own preferences, but the room was pleasant-smelling and tidy, with touches that reflected his stark, simple taste.

He'd distempered the walls plain white, retained only the outer blackout curtains which moved in the slight breeze from windows open above a square of unkempt garden with its half-buried shelter. A black and white plaid rug on the bed echoed this austere colour scheme, and on the walls Johnny had tacked striking pen-and-ink portraits of persons unknown to her. The carpet, though – beige and pink, rose-splattered – quarrelled with the atmosphere of almost monastic plainness.

'I've brought something for you. From Grace, my younger daughter . . . Look. Real coffee!' She flourished the packet triumphantly.

'From your daughter?' He cocked his head, amused. 'Such kindness to a poor exile. We'll have some right away, shall we, Amy?'

Today there was a playfulness about him that had been markedly absent the other evening. Amy sensed her visit had a significance for him that she could not know, ignorant as she was of the twists and turns that had led to this stage in his life.

There was a gas-ring by the fireplace and Johnny set about the ritual of making coffee. Watching him was companionable. In the old days their times together were spiced less with friendship than sheer focused sex.

'Such a perfectionist.' She smiled at his concentration.

'I like to do some things right.' Amy was charmed by the wry way he said it.

The coffee was strong, black and fragrant. How pleasurable it was to sit one each side of the empty fireplace, while the afternoon sun streamed in.

Amy sipped hers. 'I'd forgotten how good it tasted. And, Johnny, you haven't lost your knack.'

'The taste brings back good times.' He lit a cigarette and leaned back luxuriously. 'You know, Amy, I was astonished to see you working in that place – my picture of you was so shiny and ethereal, your feet hardly touching the ground ...'

'Sorry to disappoint you.'

He shook his head. 'This is better. I couldn't have dealt with that person, not now ... How do you like it there?'

'I'm not sure I can explain ... I'm proud of the work I do, proud of myself ... I try to do it the best I can.'

'I understand that.'

A silence, calm and amiable. Johnny topped up her cup.

Amy said, 'Tell me about your wife ... if you want to.'

Johnny shrugged. 'About Gudrun I have nothing coherent, just a whole muddle of emotions that come and go and shift about. Mainly guilt – terrible guilt – that eats into me any moment I'm not on my guard ...'

'Surely guilt's the wrong –'

'She was killed because of what I did – my cartoons, my poking fun. And I didn't even start it in full seriousness. Make no mistake, I was against the bastard Nazis from the start but, if I'm honest, in the beginning it was just me showing off, indulging a quite trivial desire for irreverence, and it ended in the death of my wife and children ...' A puzzled, haunted look. 'How can that have happened?'

'What was she like, your Gudrun?'

'Sweet, too good for me ... I'll tell you quite honestly that I made a mistake in marrying her. We both made a mistake. Yet I loved her, I was moved by her ... I married an idea – my theory, back then, of what a young woman should be. I brought her unhappiness. And I brought us both loneliness.'

'Loneliness?'

'I was here.' He held one arm out sideways, then flung the other one wide. 'And Gudrun was over here ... We loved our children, though. There was that.'

'Yes,' shades of her own family filling Amy's mind.

*　　*　　*

Later they took a bus to Regent's Park and walked in the sun. It was sunny and breezy and the crowds were out. Everywhere they saw men and women in uniform – British, French, Czech, American – but, that aside, it seemed a perfect peacetime Sunday.

They sat side by side on a bench facing the lake. Johnny had shaken off his melancholy and seemed keen to reminisce about Berlin. 'I can't tell you what a luxury it is to be with someone who's got some of the same memories as I have.'

'If only Claudia could be here. I often wonder how she's surviving. I miss her letters. I miss her.'

'You wrote all those years?'

'Of course. Some people are friends for life . . . Touch wood.'

'We stopped seeing one another. Quite suddenly and stupidly.'

'She thought so too. She was sad about it.'

'Really?' He looked cheered by the thought, with a quick, quirkish smile. Amy found he still had a powerful attraction for her.

As they sauntered back towards the bus stop, Johnny said with feeling, 'This has been the best day since I came to this country.'

Amy was touched, but in some way saddened. The old Johnny had been far too cavalier to say anything so . . . humble was the word that sprang to mind.

Kissing her goodbye he said almost casually, 'I shan't need to drink myself to sleep tonight.'

A suppressed savagery in his manner kept her at bay – she felt unable to probe the remark. All the same, arriving back at Philadelphia Close, Amy was elated at their reunion. She was greeted by Grace, who told her Chris Carella's mother had rung to break the news that Chris's husband had been killed in the fighting for Tobruk.

Chapter Forty-six

'Cheese, Amy?'

His wife patted her flat stomach and shook her head. 'Thanks, no. I'm full to bursting.' She looked up at the elderly waiter. 'Those raspberries were marvellous.'

The man beamed. Amy still had that effect on people, Noel reflected.

'Just two coffees then.'

This November he was home on a week's leave. Tonight's meal at the Savoy was intended as the climax, when he wined and dined his wife, offering her a taste of forgotten luxury. Amy had taken a couple of hours off work, had had her hair done, changed into a cobwebby dress she hadn't worn for literally years. Yet it had proved impossible for her to metamorphose into a frivolous butterfly. She had too much on her mind. Over the oysters, the rich casseroled chicken, Amy seemed to want to discuss work worries, Chris Carella's state of mind, Grace's future, as if the unaccustomed champagne had loosened her tongue.

He'd discouraged her at first, tried to keep the conversation light, but finally became mired in Amy's concerns. Perhaps it was for the best. They'd not seen one another for so long, and time was so short.

Noel too had a matter he needed to broach. He hadn't intended mentioning it tonight but since, willy-nilly, issues were being raised . . . The coffee came, a tray with a silver pot, small silver spoons, tiny white bone china cups.

'There's something I've been meaning to talk to you about.'

'Oh?' Amy was in a receptive mood, Noel apprehensive.

'I'm not sure how to begin.'

'Sounds mysterious.' She was intrigued, unworried.

'Laura Krell contacted me a few months ago.' The Krells had been their dearest friends in Berlin but, over the years, the families had lost touch.

'Why didn't you tell me?' Amy's face lit up. 'How are they?'

'She and Art are divorced.'

'No! Why?'

'Art fell for someone else, apparently.'

'Poor Laura! How's she taken it?'

'Badly at first. But she's better now. She's got a small flat in Washington, near her daughter and son-in-law.'

'Some months ago, you said. I can't believe you didn't –' Amy stopped short, puzzled suspicion dawning in her eyes.

Noel took the plunge. 'We've become . . . close.'

'You mean you're having an affair?'

He nodded. There was silence between them, wary, suspended.

Amy bit her lip. 'I'm . . . I mean that's . . .' The sentence trailed away. She sounded dazed. Silence again, then she asked guardedly, 'Where does that leave us?'

Steadily he met her gaze. She'd changed over this last year – no, since before then, but he'd noticed it particularly coming home this time. He'd been shocked by how thin she'd gone, how drawn she looked. And he noticed a sort of toughness that was new. She was overworked, he thought, and felt regret for her bonny looks, but also a half-reluctant respect for the life she was living without him.

'I'd say it left us very much where we are now.'

She made no reply, sat waiting for him to expand on the statement.

'We both know there's been strain between us – distance – since Vicki left. We don't fight necessarily – there's no one big, overriding issue – but there's a feeling of grievance.'

'Yes.'

In some perverse way Noel would have preferred her to deny it, assure him she loved him as much as ever, beg him to finish with Laura. But Amy had always been disconcertingly honest.

'I suppose,' Amy said, 'it's not that surprising, given the way things are between us.' She looked him wanly in the eye. 'It hurts, though. I feel betrayed by Laura too . . .'

'She feels badly about you.'

Amy pulled a sceptical face.

Noel felt tenderly protective of Laura. To him she was a friend, a good woman, her cosily appointed flat like a home from home. He loved to go there at the end of the day and talk and have her cook for him. Her war work was social and undemanding – committees, charities. She looked rested and vital, well-dressed, seductive when she let down her long red hair. He could talk to her about his fears for Vicki. One night he'd confessed to her the secret of his impotence. He'd done it quite deliberately in an attempt to exorcize the obsessive secretiveness Amy complained of. Laura had been discreet and kind. Their affair had started that night. Her body was comforting rather than exciting. He gave her satisfaction she said. They were happy with their loving companionship.

'She's sincerely fond of you . . . But I can hardly expect you to feel charitably disposed towards her . . .'

He would never think of telling Amy, but they had talked about her a lot, and about their respective marriages. One evening Laura accused Noel of always having been jealous of anything or anyone that deflected Amy's attention from himself. With her new insight Laura put it down to his impotence, his fear of losing his wife. Since then Noel had reflected on her words, reluctantly seen truth in them.

'Are you leading up to asking for a divorce?'

He shook his head. 'I've never for one moment considered it.'

The elderly waiter came to remove their tray of coffee. Noel asked him for the bill.

When he'd gone Amy said, 'You know Johnny Kröger's in London. I've met up with him once or twice.'

In spite of everything – almost as if to bear out Laura's words – his guts stirred immediately with the old familiar fear and pain. 'Are you sleeping with him?'

'No.' She shook her head with a mixture of sorrow and exasperation, as if she'd known that this would be his first thought. 'He's in a bad way. He's lost everything. I'm just a lifeline, an old friend.'

'I'm jealous, I can't help it. Though I've got no right to be.' Across the table he grasped her hand.

She looked at him, in her eyes a kind of bruised affection. 'You think I'm not?'

Tonight everyone kept saying she looked like Lana Turner, but inside herself Grace was Marlene Dietrich, legs crossed to show the slinky silk stockings a boy called Bradley had given her last week, a cigarette held casually between two fingers, an enigmatic smile on her lips.

A Frenchman named André had lifted her onto the bar. Everyone was flirting with her tonight. Grace felt a bubbly excitement in the pit of her stomach. Her head was woozy, but pleasantly so. She was only drinking cider. Perhaps somebody had sneaked something stronger into her glass.

Across the public bar of Iron Mary's in Panton Street she could see her friend Ann conversing earnestly with a fair-haired soldier. Sometimes she got awfully serious. It was out of place in the whirligig of their evenings out. Grace thought of these nights as just a series of moments, all strung together, and tried to enjoy each separate one.

André, a Parisian, had ginger hair and a pasty sort of face, but his eyes glittered with manic amusement – he was the life and soul of the party. He stuck obstinately close to Grace, stretched a possessive arm out behind her along the bar where she was sitting and, every so often, under guise of a laughing fit, laid his head exuberantly in her lap.

For André's benefit a Canadian called Glenn started singing 'The Last Time I Saw Paris', but he ran out of words, and he and someone called Jimmy tried to piece the song together bit by bit. Grace became animatedly involved in the process, suggesting possible lines. Gradually everyone's suggestions became sillier and sillier, more and more suggestive. Then the lines had to be explained to André, which made them seem that much more hilarious, and all the time the three men were watching Grace and watching each other, all vying for her attention.

In his fractured accent André began to sing 'We'll Meet Again', flashing a satirical Maurice Chevalier leer. Grace joined in with her hoarse, sexy Marlene Dietrich drawl. Glenn and Jimmy took up the refrain, along with a group of British airmen standing behind them.

After that Glenn started to warble 'It's Only a Paper Moon', shaking his shoulders and rolling his eyes.

Grace reached out, cupped his face in her hands. 'I've loved that song since I was little . . . But you have to do it properly.'

She began to sing along. The tune seemed beautiful to her, the lyrics wise and perspicacious.

'Golly, I think I'm drunk,' she giggled.

Glenn hoisted her up so she was standing on the bar, crooning the familiar number and people were listening. Grace had total faith in the song and in her own ability to put it across. In any case they'd give her the benefit of the doubt. She felt reckless tonight and irresistible, hair curling just right, in her new stockings and the tight ribbed sweater Elaine from the nursery had knitted her out of unravelled wool. All around masculine faces were turned towards her, grinning, admiring. Grace could picture herself, small, brave and jaunty. It was like a scene from a film.

But, as she reached the end of the song and her audience erupted into cheers and whistles, Grace became aware that her head was spinning perilously.

'Sorry, got to go to the little girls' room,' she said to anyone who could hear her.

It was an expression she despised but it seemed to fit in with the person she was being. With the help of several strong arms she managed to descend from the bar without toppling, then – via iron self-control – to cross the room with a show of unconcern, smiling sassily at the flirtatious remarks that punctuated her progress. She avoided stumbling at the foot of the stairs, retreating thankfully to the cool, brown-panelled silence of the lavatory, where she was cataclysmically sick.

When she'd recovered sufficiently Grace went to the basin to wash her face and hands. Her image peered at her from the mirror, dead white, eyes glittery and moist. She couldn't face re-entering the bar just now, with its noise and boisterousness, the air thick with beer fumes and cigarette smoke.

At the bottom of the stairs was a side door. Furtively she slipped behind the long black curtain that covered it, flicked the latch, emerged into an alley that smelled of piss and housed the pub's dustbins. In spite of this the damp November air seemed astringent, revivifying. Leaning against the pub wall, weak and drained, Grace breathed in great draughts of it, staring up at the sliver of cold, white moon. Savouring the dark and the solitude.

'Hello.'

With the blackout visibility was almost nil. Grace sensed rather than saw a figure uncoil from a crouched position. The lighted tip of a cigarette glowed in the dark.

'Hello. Whoever you are.'

'You're the kid who sang the song, aren't you? I recognize your voice.'

'Kid!' She was indignant.

'Let me guess. Sixteen? Too young to be drinking in a bar.' To Grace's ears the accent was indeterminate-American. Not one of the regions she could place.

'I'm nineteen.'

'Yeah?' The voice sounded amused.

'Not that it's any of your business.'

'Right.'

A silence.

'Oh God.' A further dizzying wave of sickness churned her stomach. Grace bent over the gutter, retched, vomited again, though less copiously this time.

Her unknown companion laid a hand across her back. 'You okay? Anything I can do?'

'Just leave me alone to die.' She was humiliated. Sixteen. Unable to take her liquor. Her earlier vivacity seeming mere foolish, drunken over-excitement.

'I seem to recall there's a building across the way with steps. You could sit down.'

He lit a match and peered into the darkness. In the sudden flare Grace caught a brief glimpse of long, narrow eyes, a mouth that drooped humorously.

'Over there.' He led her across and down the alley to a flight of four steps. 'Sit down . . . What's your name?'

'Grace.' She shivered.

'Larry.' Taking off his uniform jacket and placing it round her shoulders.

'Thank you. Hello, Larry.' Grace closed her eyes. 'God, I feel awful.'

'Lean on me if it helps. I won't take it as encouragement.'

Like a rag-doll she flopped against his shoulder. Larry put one arm around her. There was relief in letting go. She had no sense of time passing. Perhaps for a while she dozed off.

Some time, later on, Grace drifted back into a state of consciousness. She opened her eyes. 'Gosh, what time is it?'

'Quarter after ten.'

'Goodness, I must find my friend. She'll be going spare.' His jacket still hung from her shoulders. She tugged at it. 'You must be frozen. You've been so kind. And I've been rather like a sack of potatoes.' Grace summoned up a desperate vestige of liveliness. 'Young man, how can I ever repay you?'

'You could come out with me tomorrow. Just me. Just you.'

'Can't. I've got something on.'

'After that I'm not free until Wednesday.' He sounded discouraged, as if he could not imagine her attention span enduring for so long.

Grace decided to surprise him. 'Meet you on the steps of the National Gallery. Half-past seven.' She was in a rush to be gone.

In between times she regretted her airy impulse. Generally speaking Grace preferred crowds, mass amusement, flirting, changing partners. That way there was no need for boredom. And here she'd agreed to spend a whole evening with a man she didn't know. Larry had been kind, of course, but that didn't guarantee he'd be lively company.

She couldn't even remember, really, what he looked like, probably wouldn't recognize him. Though he'd had a good view of her, of course, larking about on the bar at Iron Mary's – the memory and its aftermath now made her hot with mortification. Suppose he didn't turn up. She'd look a famous wallflower hanging about on the National Gallery steps on a cold November night.

All in all Grace saw the evening as ill-starred.

As it happened May kept her and Elaine late at the nursery to plan a Christmas entertainment they were supposed to be putting on. The discussion took for ever, and May ignored their fidgety impatience.

'I've got to meet someone,' Grace finally protested.

May was imperturbable. 'If he likes you enough he'll wait.'

There wasn't even time for Grace to do her quick change routine in the ladies' lav. Arriving at the National Gallery at ten to eight, breathless and sweating, she still had on the trousers and baggy sweater she'd worn all day for work.

It was a popular meeting place. At any time of day groups, couples, lone men and women could be seen sitting or standing, idling, waiting on the broad, commanding sweep of steps. Grace glanced about her, but no face seemed familiar. Perhaps Larry had been and gone. She had the glum apprehension that all her bustling had been in vain.

'Grace!' A tall young man in lieutenant's uniform bounded up to her. 'I'd about given you up.'

She stared at him. The timbre of his voice struck a chord and so, on closer inspection, did the long eyes she'd seen the other night by the flare of a match.

'A million apologies. I was kept late.' She gestured towards her workaday outfit. 'I haven't even had time to change.'

'You look fine. You look terrific!' He was clearly relieved and elated by her arrival. 'Are you hungry?'

'Famished. Only with me dressed like this we can't go anywhere posh.'

They went to the nearest Lyons Corner House. It was cosy, a carpeted, amber-lit womb, excluding the cold and dark of the night. They ordered rissoles and scalloped potatoes, two glasses of beer.

Grace studied her escort. He certainly wasn't handsome. His face was too thin, his nose too big. But some quality he exuded pleased her. It was hard to pinpoint. A sort of amiable disdain that showed in the hooded eyes, the full lips that drooped quirkishly. A clever face? Maybe, but that wasn't quite it. An *aware* face. Grace had the unnerving impression that he saw through her, was several jumps ahead of her.

'You were awfully gallant the other night. I felt an utter nincompoop. I'd like to thank you.'

'This *is* your thanks, isn't it? Spending an evening with me. Alone.'

Grace grinned. 'It's not such an ordeal.'

'I guess it's up to me to see it's not.' She liked the way he said that, flashing a smile that was amused and mock nervous at the same time.

He was twenty-two, she learned, and from Vermont, one of five children, his father a country doctor. Larry had been studying law when his call-up came. He was frustrated hanging around London doing nothing very much and yearned for the Second Front, a chance to do something and get the war over and done with. Since Alamein the tide of the war had, after all, turned decisively in favour of the Allies.

'I'd rather be bored than killed,' Grace said. 'And I don't like being bored.'

'I never think of getting killed. Being a soldier just isn't real to me. I feel like an actor in a movie.'

'In any case you won't get your Second Front for ages. Not while the Russians are fighting our battles for us.' Grace aired the current cynical credo.

She told her own story. Larry appeared fascinated by her account of a sister in Germany, father in Washington, mother out at work for the first time in her life, Grace's own job in the nursery.

'So what do you do for fun?'

'Go out. Have a good time. As often as I can.'

'Doesn't that get repetitive?'

'Not yet.' She declined to be squashed by the implication that her joys were shallow ones. 'To be honest this war is the best time of my life.'

'Do you often wind up singing on the bar?'

'Never before.' Grace smiled perversely. 'But I might again – who knows?'

'I'm not mocking you, Grace, or criticizing.' He seemed to sense she was provoked in some way, and hastened to reassure, his eyes intent suddenly, naked. 'Quite the opposite. You looked . . . To me you were the embodiment of everything vivid, vibrant . . . the life-force.' Attempting to defuse his earnestness with a teasing tone. 'I sat there like a fool, mad in love with you.'

For all its apparent light-heartedness, she was taken aback by the confession. Impressed and flattered too, admittedly, since Larry had uttered it with such . . . sang-froid. Some men looked foolish when they turned serious, but Larry appeared quite confident that sincerity was strength.

Oddly it was she who felt wrong-footed. But Grace took refuge in a playful smile, an ironic cliché. 'I suspect you say that to all the girls.'

Chapter Forty-seven

❦❦❦❦❦

Witness turned out to be only indirectly a source of work for Johnny. Roland Delane informed him regretfully that the magazine had nothing specific to offer. Such graphic work as they required was already spoken for. But the proprietor knew Johnny's name and reputation, wanted to help. He put him in touch with a publishing firm in the early stages of collating a project called *London Forty-Three*, an anthology of poems inspired by the war-time capital, illustrated by atmospheric drawings of destroyed buildings.

'I'll put in a word for you,' Delane promised.

The illustration work was very much to Johnny's taste. In the disturbed and sombre state of mind in which he found himself, the drawings of doom-laden buildings under angry skies were his indulgence, his savage pleasure, with desolate echoes of his own personal tragedy. During the winter of '42 Johnny worked on the project with greedy passion.

The only other focus of his life was Amy. For him her sudden reappearance was a wonder he could hardly credit. The mere knowledge that she was there, accessible, was a pleasure that illuminated his dour existence.

He was consoled by the fact that she was no longer the fantasy figure he remembered, with the seemingly charmed life. Amy had her own demons – in particular her gnawing terror for the daughter in Germany. His Sunday afternoons with her were a landmark in the featureless desert of his weeks. Their time together soothed him like cool hands laid on his forehead. For days afterwards Johnny felt human, less like a howling soul in torment.

Since Gudrun's death he'd had no heart for sexual initiative. But, as autumn shaded into winter he began to look at Amy with a kind of quickening, a reawakening. Like everyone she was shabbily dressed. She often looked strained. With the fuel shortages her body was shrouded in layers of sweaters. Frequently she wore her hair tied up in a scarf, turban-style – soap and shampoo were increasingly scarce.

Perversely all this caused him to imagine all the more vividly the warm, tender flesh hidden inside the graceless clothing. One day, kneeling to set a match to the gas-ring, Amy revealed a flash of white thigh above the heavy stockings she wore, and Johnny was electrified by a stab of lust more potent than anything he had experienced for years.

He began to dream about her vulnerable nakedness, like a delicate fruit inside its rough, fibrous husk. He would wake with a desolate ache, an overwhelming longing for the intoxication of flesh on flesh. Yet he hesitated to approach her. In his private mythology Amy had been elevated to a good woman – like Ingeborg, his mother – the kind it was right to respect. Some primitive taboo forbade him to equate such a being with the grossness of sex. He dreaded driving her away with an overture she might find repellent.

One December afternoon of heavy rain, when the sky grew dark around three o'clock, he and Amy sat in his room chatting by the fire. Johnny always managed to save some coal for days when they were to meet. Amy occupied one of the worn leatherette fireside chairs. Johnny was cross-legged on the floor, stretching out his hands towards the blaze.

Amy was laughing about the complexities of running a restaurant when there was almost nothing of anything to be had. Currently the Ministry of Food were attempting to foist a newly discovered fish on the public with the bare-faced assurance that, though it might not look much, the flesh was succulently reminiscent of chicken.

'It's an absolute lie, of course, though they're right about the way it looks. We had some in last week and I tell you, Johnny, they were the spitting image of Werner Krauss . . .' Amy mentioned a film actor from the old Weimar days.

It was so good to talk to someone who'd seen the same films, read some of the same books as himself. He laughed, reaching out with

433

impulsive affection to touch her leg. At once it occurred to him that she might be offended but Amy made no move to pull away. The shared laughter gradually died, he left his hand where it was, looking into her eyes for a response. She gazed down at him for a moment, serious, then bent swiftly to kiss him on the lips. Their embrace was like a home-coming, had at first less to do with sensuality than sheer mutual need, the desire for comfort, an irresistible outpouring of damned-up emotion. But later, with the black curtains closed, with rain gusting against the window and flames licking lazily in the hearth, they made love.

Back in Berlin, all those years ago, at the time of their affair, Amy had been in a sense his own creation, her perfect body and youthful face a blank canvas on to which Johnny projected his own fantasies. Since then time had changed them. Their bodies were no longer arrogantly young. Now he saw Amy as a fellow human being, flawed like himself. She was thin, with jutting hipbones, her breasts smaller and less buoyant, her flesh no longer so taut and luminous. But he rediscovered the particular texture and flavour of her skin, the moves and gestures she used back then, her smiling sensuality, a poignant mix of memory and desire.

What they needed now was different. Tenderness. Consolation. That was understood. But not just that. They needed a baptism of fire. A passion urgent enough to bring oblivion, with the power to obliterate for a while all the pains and anxieties of their respective lives. In the firelight their bodies were pale, fleeced, animal, mortal. He was wildly aroused by their blind pull towards one another. In a shift of perception he saw them as lost souls from some vision of hell by Hieronymus Bosch. Puny figures, frenziedly copulating. God, how he'd missed this chaos.

Johnny spent Christmas with Inge and Adam Raab in the four-bedroomed house in Hampstead they were currently minding for a writer who'd opted to sit out the remainder of the war in America. Though handsome and well-proportioned the place was bleak and cold. With fuel restrictions it was only possible to heat the kitchen.

They had their festive meal on Christmas Eve, sitting like servants round the trestle table, which they'd pulled up close to the boiler. Red cabbage with chestnuts, and some special spicy sausages Inge had managed to acquire on the black market, two bottles of metallic-tasting red wine.

Adam was out of hospital but on some medication that made him distant and strange. Alcohol was forbidden but he defied the ban, summoning up an unnerving, febrile, short-lived gaiety, his gaunt face growing flushed and heavy.

Johnny knew Inge found it difficult to cope with her husband's alienation. In a valiant attempt to keep her spirits up she was turning into a parody of herself, relentlessly loud and feisty. Much as he loved her Johnny found this bluster hard to take. And Inge seemed to envy and half resent his relationship with Amy, as if Johnny were somehow deserting them, playing to new rules. A couple of times during the meal she referred to his English friend with ill-natured sarcasm. For old times' sake he bit back the sharp riposte that trembled on the tip of his tongue.

After the meal Adam collapsed into snoring inertia. Johnny and Inge manoeuvred him to bed, then cracked open the half-bottle of whisky – courtesy of William Tilly – which was Johnny's contribution to the feast. This seemed to be the pattern of their meetings now. Adam drugged and comatose, Inge and Johnny drinking themselves into a sort of numbed detachment.

With the whisky glowing in his veins he felt the need to talk about Amy, not caring if, by so doing, he hurt Inge's feelings – her ungraciousness still rankled.

'She's tender and loving, but she won't promise more than she can give . . .' he confided. 'I trust her. Because of Amy I feel more kindly towards this country.'

Inge gazed at him sardonically across the cluttered table-top. 'You're going soft in your old age.'

'Making love with her now isn't like anything I've ever known. It's honest, no game-playing, but absolute, intense . . . For the first time in all these years there's something powerful enough to drag me into the present. I'm not living a totally leftover life.'

435

'Good for you . . .' Her voice had a hollow ring.

Inge sat across from him, chin in hand, one elbow resting on the trestle table, a large tumbler of whisky in front of her. She had on her good silk dress, splashed with cornflowers. For a decade he'd seen her wear it on high days and holidays. Over it she'd pulled on a grey cardigan of Adam's, felted and darned. Inge was in her mid-forties now, her exuberant hair more grey than dark, her face – when she wasn't emoting – set in downward lines of defeat. The last difficult years had aged her.

She looked sombrely reflective. 'Good for you, Johnny. Only nothing like that's going to happen to me . . . I'm not going to be redeemed by sex. I don't envisage a brave new future,' picking up her glass and downing a sizeable slurp of the booze. 'The way things are, it looks as if Hitler will probably lose in the end. But what's for us, for Adam and me, after that?'

Tears shone on her cheeks. Clearly she was pissed. All the same, Johnny was shocked. Inge was the one that kept them going. She never admitted to weakness or pessimism. He pushed back his chair, crossed to where she was sitting, kneeled down and put his arms round her dumpy body. She leaned her head wearily against his shoulder.

Outside the hospital window the fresh spring leaves of a chestnut tree fluttered against a blue April sky. Next to the bed stood a tall vase of pale narcissi, each with its delicate orange central frill. Amy sat on a tubular canvas chair and watched her father as he slept. The curtain was drawn round his bed. From the corridor she could hear the comings and goings of the nurses. The general bustle did not concern her. Here, in Edward's small cubicle, all was peace.

Her father lay comatose, seeming barely to breathe, his head sharply outlined by the starched white pillow-slip. His face was immobile, bloodless, the beard freshly clipped, thick white hair sweeping away from his forehead. How patriarchal, how . . . biblical he looked. She saw in his appearance a sculptural dignity.

Throughout the winter there had been a number of health alerts.

Edward had been in and out of hospital with congestion of the lungs that, apparently, was heart-related. A week ago, he had contracted pneumonia. Amy had been informed that he could not now last longer than a few hours – a day at the most. Edward knew and accepted the fact.

'Don't bother your mother,' he'd instructed hoarsely a couple of days earlier. 'There's no point in her coming all this way.'

On the telephone Margaret requested, 'Just keep me up to date, Amy.' She sounded more business-like than emotional.

Amy was disconcerted by their sober acceptance of the fact that, even *in extremis*, they had nothing to say to one another. She might have expected Margaret to come to her husband's deathbed, Edward to desire her presence, for form's sake, if for nothing else. But it seemed that their marriage had been too bitter to them even for that. The thought seemed bleak to Amy, but Edward might not have agreed. He'd always rather pooh-poohed happiness as a luxury for the idle.

The curtain was pulled aside and a pretty young nurse entered the quiet cubicle, a brisk, plumply nubile little figure, her red-gold curls gleaming richly in a shaft of sunlight. Expressionless, she bent to take Edward's pulse, then shook her head, pulling down the corners of her mouth.

'Faint.' Raising her eyes to Amy's. 'Very faint.'

She sponged his face and straightened his bedding. Edward lay passive. The juxtaposition of the dying man, the young woman in the warm bloom of her youth, struck Amy as achingly poignant.

Turning to go, the nurse touched her arm. 'You're all right here on your own . . . ? I don't think it will be long.' A hushed, respectful tone.

'I'll be fine. Thank you.'

Amy laid one hand on the cool, dry wrist lying inert on the white coverlet. Out of nowhere she recalled herself and Edward taking part in an anti-unemployment rally he'd helped organize, some time in the mid-thirties. After it was over he'd walked her to Bethnal Green tube station. It was a hot day and his swarthy skin had glowed with the sun and with a kind of radiant energy. Her father bent to kiss

437

her goodbye, abstractedly, perfunctorily. He'd another meeting to go to that evening.

'Don't meet yourself coming back,' she said, mildly stung.

By then Edward had started off back down the street. She guessed he'd already forgotten her existence, but he stopped short and turned to face her with a grin.

'Purposeful activity.' He swung his arms with an uncharacteristic touch of satire. 'It's the only real pleasure.'

Considered one way, his life was admirable. Edward's sole passion had lain in helping the disadvantaged. Even religion meant little to him towards the end. Her father's face on the pillow was austere, the cheekbones sharply prominent. For a second she saw him as a stern philanthropist from a much earlier age, an exotic anachronism.

'All he wants is to be worshipped as a saint by those down-and-outs of his!'

Margaret had screamed the damning verdict at Amy once, when she'd ventured to defend her father's way of living. To her, on the contrary, he was a selfish obsessive who'd deprived her of the home in which she'd invested over twenty-five years of her life.

And it seemed quite clear to Amy that his family had never been as real to Edward as the underdogs he championed. It had always been Margaret who saw to the children's day-to-day needs. Edward was Olympian, his eyes directed towards wider horizons.

Of his five children Amy was probably the closest to him. Yet, far from feeling chosen, she had the impression that a mere accident of geography had singled her out – in latter years she had simply been the nearest to hand – that and the fact that she had inherited some shadow of Edward's social conscience.

But his preoccupation was not the whole story. With a flicker of surprise Amy remembered how he used to lend her books, how eager he was to know what she thought of them, his almost humble tenderness towards Margaret when she was pregnant with Emily. That side of him only showed itself in flashes and she would never know why. Amy felt the tears spring to her eyes.

'Father.' She heard her own voice rustle into the silence. Standing up, she gazed down at the spare features on the pillow, and it seemed to her that the fragile breathing had stilled. His face was suddenly lifeless. Edward had slipped away. She bent and placed a kiss on his dead lips.

To her enormous relief Johnny was at home when she arrived around six in the evening. The windows of his room were open and he sat with a pad propped in his lap, idly sketching the rooftop view. In his left hand a cigarette drifted blue smoke. Next to him on the floor stood an empty glass.

'Amy!' His expression was one of pure pleasure. She never came other than at an arranged time. Her life did not leave her that free.

'I've come from the hospital.'

'Your father?'

'He's died . . . I haven't told anyone yet.'

He stood up, came and gathered her to him, laying her head against his shoulder, cradling it with his hand. 'How do you feel?'

'Dazed. Empty.'

'I've got some whisky.'

'Yes, please.'

He poured her a drink and another one for himself. They stood side by side at the window. The sinking sun glared whitely through a haze. In the garden below bluebells and bright mauve honesty mingled with the encroaching weeds. The whisky spread a robust warmth through Amy's veins, though she could still feel the tears in her throat.

'It's such a waste,' she said, 'the way you take people for granted until they're gone . . . There was so much I didn't know about him and never took the trouble to find out . . .'

'Amy, everyone thinks that. I even thought it about my old bastard of a father. Something must have made him like he was. But I'll never understand now.'

'I can't stay. I'll have to go soon and start phoning everybody.'

'Not right away.'

He turned and kissed her on the lips, then nuzzled into her neck and breasts. Amy breathed in the acrid tobacco scent of his thick

439

hair, treasuring the sheer earthbound imperfection of him. Inconsequentially an image rose in her mind of the buxom young nurse ministering to her dying father. She put her arms round Johnny, holding his head to her breasts.

'Death makes you think of everything human. Birth, youth, ageing, all that . . .'

'Fucking.' The old subversive gleam. He placed a hand between her legs, raising her skirt, caressing her.

'That too.'

Instantly she felt herself becoming wet. She'd come here for this, needing sex to balance her experience of death – though they seemed not polarized, just two aspects of the same thing. Her mind raced. As Johnny roused her she saw Edward's lifeless face, she pictured Noel and red-haired Laura, her features twisted in orgasm. All fragile mortals, all prey to the same compulsions. Death would get them all soon enough. Johnny pulled her down on to the floor, eased down her knickers. In no time at all she had come. He unbuttoned his fly and entered her unceremoniously. As he thrust into her she experienced each separate stroke with absolute involvement as if his gathering climax were her own.

Chapter Forty-eight

'You look like a Hollywood divorcée,' Ann said.

'Do I?' Grace drew on her cigarette with an air of infinite languor, contemplating the black dress of Amy's – laughably twenties – she had found in a trunk, the black rayon stockings her grandmother had lent her for the funeral.

If she were honest Grace had been more distracted by her own fancy dress appearance than by grief for Edward. For as long as she could remember he'd seemed to back away from her. Though she had always admired his style. The image of Abraham Lincoln Larry had said when she showed him a photo.

Ann had come round straight from work and the two of them reclined in deck chairs under the flowing magnolia, with their sneaky cigarettes. It was unseasonably warm for April and the late afternoon sun cast long leafy shadows across the lawn.

'What was it like, the service?'

'Full of do-gooders and respectful drunkards. And family – me, Mum and Grandma. Uncle Phillip. Everyone else was too busy winning the war . . . One of the drunkards kept shouting out rude words and had to be led away.'

'Honest?' Ann grinned delightedly at the thought. Sometimes she looked like a little girl with her hairband and pretty, plump face. Almost immediately her mind moved on. 'You coming to the Inter-Allied dance tomorrow?'

'No, I'm seeing Larry.'

'Bring him.'

'We're going to the flicks.'

'Change your minds.'

'I don't think so.'

'You'll turn into Joy Fisher if you're not careful.' Ann mentioned a girl from their class who'd been walking out with her lanky, large-eared boyfriend from the age of fourteen, gazing into furniture shop windows like a soulful sheep.

'No I won't.' With demure insouciance Grace blew a small flurry of smoke-rings.

But inwardly she had to admit to a radical change in outlook. Time was she had gloried in a non-stop frenzy of activity, going out night after night to dance and drink and flirt, lying shamelessly to her mother so as not to miss a single evening's fun. Now she anticipated like secret treasure the prospect of time alone with Larry.

Grace had struggled against the transformation – Larry's jibe about repetitive pleasures had rankled. All through the cold, black winter nights she'd forced herself to dress up and behave as she always had, flaunting her right to her own freedom.

He'd never for one moment stood in her way but, from the beginning, Larry had made his own stance quite clear. His attraction to Grace was absolute, his aim to make her feel the same way. He stated the position with perfect candour, never stooping to prevarication or game-playing. She was curiously impressed by his honesty.

'"Leila's just a one-man girl . . ."' Provocatively Ann sang a snatch from a current song, a teasing-meaningful look in her opaque brown eyes.

Grace held up two fingers in a rude gesture. The truth was that, reluctant as she was to abandon the freewheeling image that had buoyed her up through the dreary years of the war, its first fine careless rapture had already faded. Grace was beginning to compare the men she met to Larry, to find them flat, their drunken boisterousness jangling and mechanical.

Larry had grown on her almost imperceptibly, almost in spite of herself. His looks weren't straightforward handsome, but their uniqueness was that much more addictive. His nose might be too big, his cheekbones too prominent, but his eyes fascinated her, grey, bemused, with something ironic in their depths. He was slow to smile – his lips were full and drooped perversely when he teased her or told some tall story. When he did smile wholeheartedly, it was like a gift. Grace never tired of watching how his expressions reflected the flicker of his thoughts. Yet always he seemed to retain a core of self-possession, amusement, reserve. That quality of his stayed with her, more compelling than easy, drunken flirtation.

'What you going to see?'

'*The Grapes of Wrath*.'

The information clearly justified Ann's gloomy misgivings. 'Sounds damned heavy.'

'I reckon I'm up to it.'

The fascination was a two-way process. Larry saw qualities in Grace that she didn't know she had. He said something radiated from her – an optimism, a natural exuberance, the ability to cheer and encourage the people around her.

'I'm almost jealous of the kids in your kindergarten,' he told her, 'with you shining your light on them all day long.'

Larry saw these traits as evidence of a deeper strength and resilience. Life-force was the expression he had used on their first date.

'You make me sound like a heroine,' Grace mocked.

He looked at her with his long, slow-burning eyes. 'You're my heroine.'

He was laughing, but he meant it too, and Grace was exhilarated by the enhanced self-image that Larry offered.

She leaned back blissfully in her deck chair. 'Isn't it a beautiful day? Isn't life just wonderful?'

'You've just been to a funeral, Grace,' Ann reproved.

'I'm sure Grandpa would have agreed with me . . . Whoops, watch out.'

Amy and Margaret appeared at the top of the garden. They had been to Edward's lodgings to sort through his meagre belongings. Hastily the girls stubbed out what remained of their cigarettes, dropping them into a clump of bluebells growing in the rough grass at the foot of the magnolia.

'Grandma!' Grace called. 'Come and sit down. Let me mix you a huge gin and tonic!'

Margaret smiled broadly. She never touched alcohol but loved

Grace to tease her this way. No one else would have dared. No one else would have got away with it.

As 1943 advanced into high summer, Grace gradually admitted to herself that she was in love. The *fait accompli* had crept up on her. Larry had declared himself promptly and with absolute conviction – his feelings had never been in doubt. It seemed almost too tidy, too pat that she should find herself responding in kind.

But, each time, the sight of his gangling, graceful figure in the inevitable uniform, his familiar half-smile, the secret dazzlement in his eyes lifted her instantly into a higher gear. His presence had a physical effect. Grace experienced a sharpening of the senses, a quickening of the blood, her spirits soared, her voice was more harmonious, her conversation more sparkling. Between them there existed a complicity both easy and electric. When he bent to kiss her the impetus was almost involuntary – two magnets tugging towards one another – whether on the steps of the National Gallery, in the Rainbow Club, or on the doorstep of her home in prosaic Philadelphia Close.

'Okay, you win,' Grace declared to Ann one day in July. 'I *am* iike Joy Fisher. Last night Larry even came to supper with my mother and the lodgers . . .'

Though not for a moment did Grace believe what she said. Joy Fisher and her young man were dull and dutiful and always would be. She and Larry were all lit up inside.

Grace was half disappointed that she did not even have the satisfaction of braving opposition. Amy liked Larry immediately. Mr and Mrs Barker from upstairs pronounced him a straight kind of a lad. With Elspeth Larry discussed the differences between the English and American legal systems, and their intellectual lodger was clearly surprised to find that flighty Grace had settled on a young man with something between his ears. The only fly in the ointment was Ann, who quoted back to her friend all the scornful statements she'd ever made about bright-eyed, bushy-tailed 'inseparable' couples who basked in the wholesome approval of their elders.

When Amy was out, though, Grace and Larry would lock the door of the piano-room – where Grace now slept – pull the curtains and make love in her single bed beneath the patchwork quilt Margaret had made her when she was just a little girl.

It felt unreal to Grace. The room contained so many childhood memorabilia – old picture books, the framed snap of herself and Vicki as kids in knitted swimsuits with bows in their hair, the suave signed photo of Clark Gable, her scuffed teddy-bear watching them from his single glassy eye as they twined, naked and panting, sobbing, rapt.

Their privacy was intensely precarious. Florence Barker was apt to call down the stairs for her, the doorbell might ring. Then she and Larry would lie tense and silent in one another's arms, hearts beating wildly, until the danger had passed.

But the stuffy twilight room, with their clothes draped across the piano stool, was a small secret world. This tenderness, this exploration was so different from the quick couplings with virtual strangers that had been Grace's experience up to now. With his slim, hard body next to hers, his lips, his hands, the dizzy sensitivity of skin and nerve-endings, Grace felt ready to burst, with rapture, with sheer love. They talked about getting married when the war was over, throwing away the condoms Larry hated so, having babies, being a family, and the prospect seemed too delightful for words.

All through that summer there was public agitation for the definitive European invasion to be launched. After all, North Africa was safe, the Allies had landed in Sicily, the way seemed open. Grace lived from day to day, dreading the announcement that would take Larry away from her. She simply could not bear to contemplate the annihilating thought of losing what she had found. Autumn came and – to the disappointment of the population at large – no decision had been taken. Come Christmas Larry was still ensconced in his makeshift barracks in Willesden.

Noel came home for a few days over the holiday and Larry was invited to a festive evening meal. They ate in the kitchen – the dining room was now Noel and Amy's bedroom. Grace hung home-made paper-chains and put candles on the table. Amy eked out the meagre

Christmas ration of imported frozen beef with glazed potatoes and a delicious savoury stuffing.

To Grace the evening was magical. For her sake parental tensions were pushed into the background. Larry was welcomed wholeheartedly into the small family circle. He and Noel talked American politics and their liberal views meshed. It was clear they took to one another. For all her past waywardness Grace understood the warm pleasure of being approved, being good. Her eyes met Larry's across the table, glowing in the candlelight.

In February his unit moved to the South Coast on hush-hush manoeuvres. It seemed that plans for the big invasion were at last under way. Larry managed to see Grace only one weekend in four, though they each wrote every day.

When he did come to London the couple were nervy, with a jumpy awareness of impending danger and separation. They careened from laughter and horseplay to sudden squabbles, tearful reconciliations. So rare were Larry's visits that they became, in a sense, public property and it was hard for him and Grace to find the privacy to make love. Once they slipped away to Hampstead Heath, copulated on the damp ground in a thicket of spiky bushes. Used condoms strewn on the scrubby earth around them revealed that others had had the same idea.

Afterwards they were grouchy and quarrelled. Then, at the station, they clung together as if to the one life raft in the swirling waters of a threatening world. On the bus home Grace sobbed uncontrollably.

In April Larry gave her a ring. Not a tasteful diamond like the other engaged girls she knew, but one he'd found in an antique shop – heavy silver, enamelled with a bold sunburst in orange and black.

'The sun should be your emblem,' he explained almost shyly. 'All that radiance and energy . . .'

The colours seemed baleful to Grace and, in a brief, bright flash of imagination, she saw Larry dead, the winking eye of the sun still on her finger, taunting her grief.

She shook her head, dismissing the vision, and turned to him with a brilliant smile. 'It's beautiful. I love it.'

That was the last time she saw him before the Allied landings in early June. His May leave was cancelled. A pre-arranged password in one of his letters warned Grace that the invasion was imminent. She read it looking out on the soft green glory of the late spring garden, and it came to her with terrifying clarity that Larry would be facing a real enemy, real guns, real bullets and explosives, and there was nothing in the world she could do about it.

'I'm going for a walk, Mum.'

'Bit late, isn't it?' Amy objected. It was half-past nine in the evening.

'If I don't I'll go mad.'

Since Larry had finally left for Europe, Grace was like a cat on hot bricks, anxious, restless, edgy. She'd lost weight and her face was drawn beneath the unruly cloud of pale hair. There were smudges of mauve beneath her eyes, which were unnaturally bright, almost feverish.

Amy longed to throw her arms round the girl as if, in so doing, she could protect her from all the suffering and uncertainty of the world. But she was powerless. And Grace would not be comforted by the unsolicited emotion.

'I'll come. I could do with some fresh air myself.'

'No.' Grace shook her head with a crooked smile. 'I'd rather be on my own.'

'I'm not too keen ... For God's sake keep your ears peeled for doodlebugs.'

After years of relative safety London was being terrorized by a new weapon. The harsh, grating roar of the V1 pilotless bombers came at all hours of the day and night. Since it was impossible to be on the alert all the time, Londoners took cover simply on a last-minute basis.

'You're just as likely to be bombed in your own kitchen,' Grace countered, justifiably.

She let herself out, a slight, upright figure in a faded gingham dress, and Amy's heart ached for her. Vividly her mind conjured up a memory of Grace and Larry in the garden a few weeks earlier, laughing and pelting each other with grass-cuttings like a couple of kids.

From the perspective of her forty-three years Amy saw Larry as little more than a youth, far too young for the responsibility of defending freedom and democracy. And yet, it occurred to her with a drift of tenderness, Noel must have been Larry's age – younger in fact – when he first went to war.

Amy found her daughter's youthful love affair touching, endearing, but couldn't deny regrets that wilful Grace had not lived longer, done more before . . . surrendering was the word that sprang to mind. Grace would marry young, it seemed, as she herself had. Only Amy had learned lessons in the last few years and after the war she wasn't going to lose the ground she had gained.

Afterwards, though, was still unreal, almost unimaginable. And it receded all the time. The newspapers had spoken grandly of the Second Front as a simple mopping-up operation, but it was proving to be a great deal more complex than that. The Allied landings had been concluded successfully enough, but the Germans were not going quietly. Through July they continued vigorously to dispute each and every advance claimed by the US-Anglo-Canadian 'Army of Liberation'.

Grace had hidden the sunburst ring Larry bought her in its box at the back of a cupboard full of old bedding. She would not even look at it until the fighting was over and Larry was safe. Amy struggled to set aside her terrors for Vicki in the same decisive way.

Chapter Forty-nine

There had been no shooting in the immediate vicinity for a couple of hours now. With trepidation Claudia emerged from the cellar and began to walk up the stairs of her apartment block. They were strewn with brick dust and fallen plaster. She tested each step with her foot, put her weight on it only with extreme caution, peered up the stairwell for the possibility of falling slates, bricks, whatever. Though, at that moment, death by falling masonry seemed almost preferable to one more minute in the crowded, stinking cellar with the whining Fischer children and Frau Braun's mad old father babbling his litany of obscenities.

'Stay, Fräulein Claudia,' Frau Braun had wavered. 'It's just not worth the risk.'

'I'll be careful. I'll come hurtling back, don't you worry, if I hear gunfire.'

In April of '45 the endless, relentless bombing had stopped quite suddenly, giving way to a new nightmare. The Red Army was about to be loosed among them and, for Berliners, the prospect held a horror that was more personal, like a child's terror of the bogeyman or the devil. Miraculously the months of raids had left this pleasant, grey-gold building near the Schlossgarten pretty well intact. But Russian shells had put paid to their charmed immunity. Yesterday they'd felt the house shudder under two direct hits but, with the mayhem audible in the streets, no one yet had ventured out to examine the damage.

Claudia had reached the first-floor landing and, as yet, no disaster had befallen. Gingerly she started up the flight of stairs that led to her own two rooms on the second floor. Looking up she saw daylight filtered through shattered crossbeams in the roof, a number of tiles precariously balanced which would topple with the slightest vibration. The second-floor landing crunched with fallen rubble. Claudia pushed the door of her flat and peered anxiously round.

Her rooms were still there. She still had a home, though jagged shards of glass gleamed from the floor, and debris from the roof and flat above lay piled on and around the table beneath a portion of ceiling that had buckled and given way. A gritty dust covered everything and the stink of sewage seeped in from outside, overlaid with the acrid, abrasive aura of smoke. For months the back window had looked out on a row of partially destroyed buildings, discoloured and uneven as huge rotting teeth. Now flames licked from one end, vivid and vibrant against the inert ruins. Claudia registered with amazement that the sky, behind the swift, dense smoke, was azure blue. It was a lovely day. The dark cellar had been her world ever since the Red Army had begun its triumphant push into the German capital.

A group of men staggered past the line of buildings. Russians. The first she had actually seen. Though in the distance, towards the centre of the city, the boom of big guns was continuous, these men were laughing and clearly drunk, passing a couple of bottles from one to the other, rifles slung carelessly from their shoulders. Claudia gazed at them with awe and dread as if at a group of mythical beasts.

Horrified rumour depicted the Russian Army as a rabble of ruthless brutes and, God knows, they had reason enough for revenge. Claudia stood well back from the window, her whole body tensed, heart bounding like a wild animal in a cage, until the men straggled off at a tangent along the forlorn, rubble-strewn avenue that led to the Schlossgarten.

As the figures receded she recalled that her mouth was parched and that her main aim in leaving the cellar had been to fetch a bucket of water that still stood by her stove, left behind in the confusion. Its lid was spattered with the grit that covered everything, but the water had been protected. Claudia found a cup and drank with tremulous relief. The water tasted stale and brackish, but the luxury of fastidiousness had been jettisoned way back. She downed a second cup, refreshment flooding her body. In the cellar the shared basins of water were strictly rationed and well-nigh exhausted.

Before she took the bucket down, Claudia decided to check on Frau Braun's flat. Crossing the landing, she felt for the secret spare key her neighbour kept hidden in a recess above the doorjamb.

'I tell you, Fräulein Claudia, because you've been a good friend to me and Papi,' Frau Braun had assured her earnestly. 'But I wouldn't trust the rest of this riffraff.'

The neighbour's living-room was in the same state of disarray as Claudia's own but, passing through to the kitchen, she stopped short. Claudia could see street and sky. The window and half the end wall had vanished, leaving a jagged, gaping wound. She felt dizzy and disorientated. It was like standing on a parapet. The cramped bathroom next door was in a similar state, the lavatory perched with surreal tranquillity above an abrupt void.

Claudia decided to investigate the third floor, to try to get a clearer picture of the overall damage. There was danger, of course, but there was danger everywhere. She was in no particular hurry to return underground. The stairs were hard to negotiate, made treacherous by a scree of plaster and slate. The roof was open to the sky, the landing buried in rubble. The two doors that led off it were blocked by fallen debris. It might be possible to clear . . .

From downstairs Claudia heard a sudden shouting, and froze. The male voices were rowdy, echoing in the stairwell, and immediately she understood that they weren't speaking German. The intruders were on the ground floor. She heard them kicking at the doors, then ramming them with something. The vibration loosened small eddies of grit which fell on to the landing where she crouched. Claudia guessed they were exploring the ground-floor rooms, for loot perhaps. They called to one another and laughed.

Then there was another bout of hammering, cursing, ramming, the rumpus of a door caving in. Screams as it crashed down the cellar steps. Then silence for a while. A confusion of voices. Claudia strained her ears but could not guess what was happening.

'Leave me!' A sudden shocking shriek. 'Leave me alone!'

Emmi Hermann from the ground floor, a pretty, precocious kid, thirteen or so, her usual demeanour cool, slyly smiling.

'Don't touch her!' The harsh yelp of her mother Brigitte slicing

451

through the general commotion. Then a sharp cry of pain. Screaming. Shouts from the Russians like threats.

A fresh hubbub, muffled. Shouting, another scream, a shot. Claudia closed her eyes, curled into a ball, covering her head with her arms, every nerve and muscle tensed.

For a while all Claudia could hear were the voices of the Russians, again on the ground floor. There must be six or seven of them, joking, laughing. Suddenly the thin wail of a female voice, silenced abruptly, by what means Claudia could not tell.

Some time later the sounds changed. She could hear a faint sobbing, the men seemingly discussing something. Then the inevitable. Feet mounting the stairs. Claudia shrank, curled tighter into herself. A sudden massive blow to the balustrade shook it from top to bottom, dislodging a great portion of ceiling plaster, a shower of slates that crashed past her and hurtled down the stairs. Cries of surprise and consternation, the low rumble of voices, footsteps receding.

A hush followed that seemed to Claudia wary, exploratory, as if the very air of the house were on guard, no one quite daring to believe that the Russians had gone for good. A muffled sobbing sidled into the silence and rose in passion. Still Claudia hesitated. But finally, painfully, she descended the debris-strewn staircase to the main entrance hall below.

The door of Brigitte Hermann's flat hung obliquely from a single hinge. The weeping came from in there. Claudia stepped up to the open doorway. The child Emmi sat on the floor, huddled in her mother's arms. Brigitte's brown hair hung forward over the girl. Emmi was naked, her body stark as a skinned rabbit in the gloom of the curtained room, all the bones of her ribs and spine visible through the pale, childish skin. Her thin frame shuddered with anguished sobbing.

'Brigitte.' Claudia stepped inside. The room had been ransacked. Clothes and bedding lay strewn, pots and pans, broken crockery.

Brigitte Hermann lifted her head and with horror Claudia saw that one eye was closed, the socket and the whole left side of her face grotesquely swollen, lips split and bleeding.

'They raped her,' Brigitte said, her voice made thick by the puffed lips. 'Four of them. A child.'

452

'And you?'

She nodded. 'That doesn't matter . . . They've killed Frau Braun's father.'

'God's sake!'

In the fetid cellar there was an air of total shock. The stink of excrement hit Claudia, blunt and brutal as a cosh-blow, after her foray into the upper reaches of the house. In the gloom she made out the emaciated husk of Frau Braun's father sprawled at the foot of the stairs, his upper body resting on the heavy door that lay where it had landed. A jacket had been laid across his face. It was clotted with thick blackish blood.

'They shot him like a mad dog, Fräulein Claudia.' Frau Braun's voice was overloud, uninflected, like a deaf person's, as Claudia descended the steps. 'What sense in it? What a way for a life to end!'

Claudia embraced her neighbour but the gesture was almost perfunctory. The situation was way beyond conventional comfort.

'It was when they got hold of Emmi,' Klemens, the elderly caretaker, explained. 'The old boy began to cry – in his own little world as usual. He stood up and the tears were running down his old cheeks. He'd already pooped himself again. He stank . . . and he was coming out with those sounds he makes . . .'

Klemens was dour. Frau Braun's father was not popular in the building. His daughter spent her life on the defensive and Claudia often supported her against the hostility of the tenants.

'It was the quietest of the bunch. A runtish little rat. He just got out a pistol and put it to the old fellow's head and pulled the trigger . . . Casual as swatting a fly . . . Bastards took our watches too.'

After that the cellar – which had been their refuge through the months of bombing, the early days of the invasion – no longer seemed safe. It became clear that, for many of the Russian troops, active service alternated with periods of drunken entertainment in the form of looting and rape, along with arbitrary killing if they were crossed in these activities.

Since at present there was no shelling in the immediate vicinity, it seemed wiser to retreat to the upper storeys of the house, block off the lower flight of stairs with rubble carried down from the third floor landing. The ruse might convince future intruders that the building was deserted and dangerous. Claudia's flat was habitable, along with part of Frau Braun's, as well as some of the rooms on the third floor.

The change was for the better. Upstairs there was space and light, not to mention fresh air, given the shattered walls and broken windows. A further relief – it had to be acknowledged – was the sudden absence of Frau Braun's father, with his cursing, his smell, his scary, inexplicable vehemence. As Claudia toiled with Klemens and Martha from the top floor, constructing the barricade of rubble, there was no denying a fragile and temporary sense of something like gaiety, the feeling that they were taking active steps to ensure their own eventual survival.

It was the rare opportunities for activity that kept Claudia from going mad. Even now she would rather risk exploding shells, sniper-fire, marauding Russians, to queue at the standpipe for water, than spend twenty-four hours out of the twenty-four cooped up with the fractious fear, the empty, rumbling stomachs and stale, repetitious complaints of her fellow tenants. Martha from upstairs felt the same. Coincidentally she was also strong as an ox.

Klemens used to come with them. But a man in the water-queue was an anomaly now. Sixty-year-old Klemens was in the *Volkssturm*, was supposed to be fighting and dying in a last-ditch stand for Hitler, but knew the effort to be futile. Comparatively speaking he was well-equipped. He'd a rifle, though no ammunition. Klemens was staying close, lying low, fearing to be arrested as a deserter and summarily shot just as the whole shebang was drawing to a close.

As May approached the tenants sat and waited in the shelled upstairs rooms, scared, bored, without food, pissing and shitting in a bucket on the second-floor landing.

The decomposing body of Frau Braun's father lay outside in the yard, swaddled in a torn sheet until such time as it could be buried. Frau Braun fidgeted, tidied her battered apartment, her movements seeming sprightlier now she was relieved of the burden of her disgraceful parent. Martha paced like a lion in a zoo. The Fischer children squabbled and grizzled for food. Claudia tried to forget the clawing emptiness of her own stomach in a book. Klemens snored in the one armchair that hadn't been broken up for firewood. Emmi Hermann lay silent and withdrawn under Claudia's feather quilt, wincing with pain, hands clenched between her thighs.

A motley community they formed, united only by circumstances. The time passed, oppressive, open-ended. When the wind was right the scent of lilac drifted in through the broken windows from what had once been a garden.

Chapter Fifty

❧━━━◆━◆━◆━━━❧

On the second day of May the guns fell silent all over the city. The battle for Berlin was conclusively lost.

That night, from a big ruined courtyard three streets away, they heard a troupe of their conquerors playing the accordion, laughing and singing. They saw flames leaping up into the red-black sky and smelled the achingly desirable odour of roasting meat. It pervaded the building, tantalizing their hunger.

'God knows, I'd eat a barbecued rat if I could find one,' Klemens growled.

Since the previous week they had not been bothered by Russians, though twice, briefly, they'd heard footsteps and voices down on the ground floor.

'They're peasants,' was the sage verdict of the water-queue. 'Not keen on high buildings, or even stairs . . .'

In the early hours, after Emmi and Brigitte Hermann had lain down under the shared quilt, Claudia remained sitting at the window of her room. The fighting was over. She felt merely empty and flat. Lit by flames from bonfires and burning buildings all over Berlin, the scene outside had a savage, desolate beauty, the jagged shapes of the ruins silhouetted against the vibrating smoky red of the sky.

From the nearby victory celebrations a male voice rose in a sad song she seemed to recognize. A female voice joined him, backed by the mournful wheeze of the accordion. The sound had a powerful beauty. For a suspended moment Claudia forgot everything and just listened.

*　　*　　*

Queuing for water a couple of days later, Claudia met an old acquaintance. Julius Fürstenau had been a character-actor with the Valentin Theater, a nice old fellow, thin and dapper, a bit of a dandy, with a look on his face of benevolent cynicism. No lover of the Nazis, he'd kept his nose clean enough to hang on to his job.

Julius had lived only a few streets away from Claudia. She'd run into him at intervals throughout the war and always felt better for a chance encounter with the old actor's foxy fatalism. But the block he lived in had been bombed out back in December and, since then, Claudia hadn't known whether he was alive or dead. The two of them fell into one another's arms.

She was shocked, though, by his appearance. Fürstenau must be seventy or so, but throughout the war years he'd managed to retain a certain bounce, even a youthfulness, though the good clothes he wore had become steadily shabbier and more threadbare. Today he was filthy, skeletal, hollow-eyed, his cheeks and chin covered with a patchy white stubble, shrunken lips clinging grotesquely to his false teeth, giving him a distressingly simian look.

'How are you managing?' Claudia asked. 'I thought maybe you'd left – or been buried under several metres of rubble.'

'Still here, for my sins.' A wry grin. 'But I doubt I'll ever play Graf Rothfels again.' Referring to his role in *Countess Alexia* as a foppish bon viveur.

Claudia laughed grimly. 'Be grateful for small mercies . . . Where are you living?'

'In hell.'

'A shelter?'

He nodded. 'Near the Seeling Bridge . . . At my age a few metres of rubble sounds almost the more congenial option.'

Claudia reached the front of the queue. She filled her two buckets. Fürstenau stood and waited, holding his litre bottle carefully between two hands.

'Incidentally,' he said, 'I'm sharing quarters with an old friend of yours.'

'Who's that?'

'Horst Wedlin.'

457

'Horst? Never!'

'The lad's in a bad way. Advanced tuberculosis, so it seems. A couple of Russian winters didn't help.'

'Poor devil . . .' But she could think about Horst later. 'Is his wife with him?'

'Yes. And a child.'

Lugging buckets along the familiar, devastated route was becoming more and more of an exertion, although that morning Claudia had breakfasted off a couple of stale, semi-sweet rusks. Klemens had acquired a packet from somewhere and sold her two on the quiet. The sugar had sung in her veins. But, on the return journey, her knees felt weak, her heart beat uncomfortably, as if the emotional jolt she had received were more debilitating than the physical effort. Yet, beneath the turmoil of her feelings, lay a slowly pulsating relief – from a fear she had refused to let herself acknowledge. Vicki was safe.

Claudia had never allowed herself to examine too closely her deep-down reaction to the elopement of her lover with her daughter. At the time she'd forced herself to put a brave face on it, telling herself – quite truthfully – that the affair with Horst was petering out in any case, that she'd never taken the young actor altogether seriously. Claudia had channelled her moral energy into concern for Vicki, deploring the idea of a young and clever girl saddling herself with someone so lightweight, however charming he might be.

With hindsight she had come to realize that the event had been a massive body blow, shaking her up to the extent of dislocating her whole way of life, top to bottom.

It had been like waking from a dream, understanding that her life was an illusion, a butterfly thing without substance or usefulness. She'd seen herself as some kind of artist, but she wasn't, and now she no longer even had youth on her side.

She was ordinary, and she would become ordinary, earn her living unpretentiously, keep her head down like any man or woman in the street. Claudia applied to run a newspaper and tobacco kiosk near the Schlossgarten, found a small flat in the vicinity, embraced the day-to-day routine of her existence like a new-found faith.

She was proud of her decision. And her days, though essentially repetitive, were not without their pleasures. To Claudia there was something romantic about opening up her kiosk in the mist of early morning, sitting yawning with her flask of ersatz coffee, chatting to her regulars, grumbling about the latest shortages. She enjoyed the cautious freemasonry of the anti-Hitler renegades, men who would surreptitiously whisper the latest joke about the Führer, once they'd tumbled that she was one of them. There was something simple and satisfying, too, in walking home through the darkened streets, like any worker, to cook herself supper. At times this life she had chosen appeared to Claudia her ultimate role. She had not been unhappy.

Imperceptibly, over the years, the pain inflicted by Vicki and by Horst had healed. She could let herself think about them now and admit, belatedly, just how great the hurt had been. As Claudia trudged past the pinched women and whey-faced children, the defeated old men, with her heavy buckets, an impulse stirred her heart, like a ray of spring sun striking the corner of a shaded courtyard. With all of her being she yearned to see Vicki again, to see the child and, yes, Horst.

The low door, in a concrete wall, was open. The entrance was down a long, dark, narrow corridor, a ramp that led underground. Claudia walked straight in, unchallenged, to be met by an almost tangible wall of heat, human heat, filled with fetid, unwashed human smells.

After the daylight outside, it seemed pitch-black, though candles burned under glass high up on the walls. But Claudia could see the huge room was full of figures, featureless and shadowy, sitting on long rows of benches, standing, squatting, a few prone on the bare concrete floor.

The murmur of voices sounded somehow damped and subdued in the crowded, airless space. The overwhelming impression was one of apathy and utter hopelessness. Hell, Julius had said and Claudia would have chosen the same word. Even now the bombing, shelling, fighting were over, these people had nowhere to go. There was nothing they could do. Her own small cellar, the inhabitants at least known to her, seemed almost cosy by contrast.

She gazed about her, feeling helpless.

'Are you looking for someone?' A sharp, officious voice. It came from a man around Klemens's age and build.

Claudia had no idea what the position was. Could you just barge in as she had done, or was there some kind of a procedure that she had managed to side-step.

'I'm looking for my brother, Horst Wedlin.'

A woman standing close by overheard and approached diffidently. 'I know Herr Wedlin,' she told the man who might or might not be an official. Then, to Claudia. 'I think you'll most likely find him in the next room.'

'Thank you.' Claudia moved away and the man did not try to stop her.

It was no easy matter making her way across the massive room. Every inch of floor-space was occupied. Claudia trod gingerly, excusing herself with every step. Beyond the doorway lay a second room exactly like the first.

How would it be possible to track anyone down among this huge, shadowy mass of humanity? Her eyes were becoming used to the darkness, but still the people all round her were featureless silhouettes, like figures from some black engraving by Daumier.

Claudia began to push her way through the shelter, questioning every second person. Some shrugged, some simply ignored her. She felt idiotic, wanted to scream, was close to tears. Perhaps, after all, Julius had been mistaken. If Horst *were* here it ought to be easy – a strapping fellow in the prime of life, when most of the males were either kids or old men.

'The soldier? With the English wife?' The miraculous words came from a scabby boy of fourteen or so wearing a shapeless check jacket made from a blanket.

'Yes.'

Claudia had hesitated to mention Vicki's nationality in case she and Horst had kept it secret. But since it was known . . .

'Follow me.' In a cavalier fashion the child began to elbow his way through the crowd. She kept up with him as best she could.

'There.' The lad pointed to a figure lying in the angle between two wooden benches, cushioned from the concrete floor by a single thin blanket.

Claudia was puzzled and it crossed her mind that the boy was playing a trick on her or not quite right in the head. The person on the blanket was shrunken, emaciated. He was old.

She stared at the ravaged figure who wore a filthy field grey uniform. He was tall and large-framed, but a bag of bones, the sparse, sallow flesh of his face clinging to the skull beneath, hair lank and receding, the nose a jutting beak. The man's eyes were closed but now they flicked open as if he'd become aware of being watched.

For a long, blank moment they gazed at one another. Claudia had not thought of her appearance for . . . months, it seemed. Today her hair was tied up in a scarf and she wore a pair of baggy trousers that had once belonged to Brigitte Hermann's husband. Trousers were reputed to dampen the ardour of rampant Russians.

A look came into the invalid's eyes that didn't belong – animation, pleased incredulity – and a familiar voice said wonderingly, 'Claudia? Am I dreaming?'

'It *is* you.' She couldn't disguise her distress.

'Right.' A smile, bleakly humorous, revealing missing teeth. 'This carcass is Horst Wedlin. *Zum Befehl.*'

'Julius Fürstenau told me you were here. How long . . . ?'

'Three weeks, a month. It feels like eternity.' His voice rasped painfully.

'You've got no home?'

'We've had two collapse about our ears. Looked at one way we're lucky to be here.'

'Where's Vicki?'

'She's taken Christa – she's our daughter – to the toilet. In here that can take an hour or more.'

'And they're all right?'

'Vicki's my guardian angel.' Horst pulled a face. 'I'm no good for anything. As for Christa . . . she's in a bad state, mentally.'

461

Claudia kneeled down beside him, touched his cheek.

'It's good to see you, Claudia,' Horst said. 'Like meeting a friendly face in purgatory.'

A young woman picked her way through the throng, holding a thin, solemn child by the hand. Claudia got to her feet and watched her daughter approach.

Vicki's face was painfully pale and gaunt, the cheekbones standing out sharply. Her glorious hair was dirty and lank, and caught severely back from her forehead and cheeks. Like herself – and no doubt for the same reason – she wore trousers. They were large and shapeless, the bottoms clumsily rolled.

Yet, to Claudia, the young woman had a quiet, unassailable dignity as she threaded a path through the sea of strangers. With a polite, self-contained smile, she excused herself to an old woman, then manoeuvred her daughter by the hand past a crowd of listless youngsters huddled together on the floor.

Vicki was twenty-four now. It was hard to glimpse in her the blooming, romantic schoolgirl Claudia had last seen, back in the summer of '38. She felt nervous, unsure of her welcome. To Vicki she was no one – just a middle-aged friend of her mother's, whose boyfriend she had captivated and married, and from whom she probably hoped never to hear again.

'Vicki.'

Claudia thought for a second she might faint, from emotion and apprehension, exacerbated by sheer physical weakness.

Startled, puzzled, Vicki looked at her, and Claudia saw that her face had taken on a fierceness it never used to possess. Vicki frowned, and then recognition dawned. Without hesitation she stepped forward, laid a hand on each of Claudia's shoulders and kissed her as simply as a child.

The greeting was absolutely unexpected, absolutely uncharacteristic as she perceived Vicki's reticent nature. The touch of her daughter's cool lips on her cheek – even in this hellish, hopeless bunker – overwhelmed Claudia with a rush of pure happiness.

462

'This is amazing – you're not living here too?' Her German, Claudia noticed, was well-nigh accentless.

She shook her head. 'I can see how lucky I am. I've still got two rooms. A bit battered but perfectly serviceable.'

The child, Christa, had taken refuge behind her mother. She would be five, going on six, Claudia calculated. A thin, rather beautiful girl with Horst's grey eyes, Vicki's hair, though it hung in rats' tails on her shoulders.

'Hello, Christa.' Claudia smiled, attempting to exude calm friendliness but the child looked scared and hid her face in Vicki's sweater.

Vicki caressed her daughter's hair and did not reproach her. 'It's not the ideal place for children.' A crooked smile which Claudia recalled from years back.

'Come with me,' she heard herself saying. 'I've got room for all of you – it's no palace but it's a thousand times better than this . . . For Christa's sake, for Horst's, I really think you should.'

The caretaker, Klemens, was none too pleased when Claudia turned up with three extra bodies in tow, but she wasn't taking orders from him. During the worst of the emergency the tenants had all made common cause, but Klemens was and remained a sneaking, overbearing pig of a Nazi.

'You can bully some people.' Claudia smiled at him thinly, sweetly. 'But you know very well you can't bully me.'

In any case Klemens's stout allegiance to the Party, once a source of authority and petty power, had abruptly become old hat.

'You always did like to please yourself, Fräulein Claudia,' he replied with a sourly impotent grin.

Horst was in terrible shape. It had taken Claudia and Vicki more than two and a half hours – with frequent stops for him to sit, ashen and wheezing, among the rubble and recover his strength – to manoeuvre him the mile or so from the shelter to Claudia's flat.

But Claudia was as anxious for Vicki. A couple of lorries full of exuberant Russian troops had slowed right down, the occupants whooping lustfully at her. In Berlin now such signs of appreciation had terrifying implications. But the incident had ended there. Christa was clinging to Vicki's trousers, and street wisdom had it that the Russians would never molest a woman with a young child . . .

All the same Claudia was vastly relieved when she'd got them all upstairs and the rubble that camouflaged their presence in the house was back in place.

The residents eyed the newcomers with blank mistrust. But, miraculously, Vicki had in her bundle two stale, bulky loaves of rye-bread, a tin of meat. She divided them between the tenants with scrupulous exactitude and their hostility diminished a little.

The Wedlin family had their own bedding, though little else, and soon they settled down to sleep in Claudia's back room. The Hermanns lay down beneath the feather quilt and Claudia was left on her own.

She slept little nowadays, felt too prickly and restless. Tonight, as she sat at her shattered window, the image of Vicki, Horst and their child lying together under the dirty grey blanket warmed her like a fire. Claudia could find in herself no rancour for the past. The situation they were living through was so extreme that it swamped the everyday jealousies and disappointments that normally loomed so large. What remained was the memory of friendship and the need for friendship now. Defending Vicki and Horst against Klemens's truculence she'd had the exhilarating illusion of protecting her own family. The thought filled her with a terrifying joy.

Chapter Fifty-one

Under the blazing summer sun Vicki and her partner Vera sorted bricks from a rough heap which, during the last few days, they had extracted painfully, by hand, from the ruins of the block where Julius Fürstenau used to live. After they had chipped the crusted remnants of mortar from each with their rusty hammers, the perfect bricks were stacked neatly in one pile, the imperfect but usable in another, rubbish in a third.

Across the wide, dusty arena other women were engaged in the same laborious task. Across Berlin, across Germany and the whole of Europe, a similar herculean effort was under way.

'It's like a kid's game of bricks,' Vera said. 'First you build them up, then you knock them all down, then you pick them up again.'

She was a peaceful person to work with. Vera accepted Vicki's Englishness without hostility or ingratiation. A widow from the previous war, she'd lost her son at Stalingrad, her daughter to allied bombers over Hamburg. Vicki had seen a photograph of her in '39, a rosy-cheeked matron with crisp grey hair, flanked by two good-looking children. Now Vera appeared twenty years older and was alone in the world. Every day Vicki met people who were a lot worse off than she was.

The dust that rose from the debris clung to the sweat on her face and arms, caking them with a layer of grey-white grit, cut through with channels of perspiration, like the parched delta of a river. But when she got home Claudia would have fetched water, enough for her to have a decent wash. Vicki blessed the day they'd met her.

Toiling as a *Trümmerfrau* conferred on Vicki a higher grade of ration card. Both Horst and Claudia rated only the lowest, the so-called death card, representing slow starvation. Horst was too weak to work, but Claudia remained jobless by choice. Time was at a premium when, to survive, you had to queue for water, forage and bargain for even the basic ration, let alone the scarce extras that meant the difference between life and death.

Claudia's determination and *savoir-faire* were worth infinitely more to them than the little bit of extra cash, the few additional rations she might have brought in. Berlin was her element and, where a less resourceful person might be defeated by the effort it took simply to stay alive, Claudia was energized, ready to follow up the smallest lead that might result in some meagre food find, a new black market contact, a fresh angle on the everlasting search for nourishment.

'We three are your cross, Claudia, your ball and chain,' Vicki joked one evening when Claudia was shattered, having chased about all day to track down the wherewithal to mend Christa's broken-down shoes. And there was the silent ghost, the guilt for her own and Horst's past treachery, rising up to haunt her in the face of Claudia's hospitality and protection.

Almost angrily Claudia dismissed her fears. 'Don't talk nonsense! If I didn't have you lot to think about, I'd simply lie down and give up the struggle.'

Vicki was warmed by her reassurance, but knew Claudia would never dream of throwing in the sponge, any more than would Vera. Both had bounced back after one devastating war and, if their health held out, they would survive this one.

Vera lived in a kind of cave in the basement of her ruined home, along with a neighbour and her two frail, bronchial children. She did not possess even a bed – the Russians had seized all the furniture she had left for their own use.

'It's only a hole in the ground, but it's my hole in the ground.' Vera flaunted a black humour but, sometimes, as they sat side by side chipping away at their respective bricks, Vicki would see that tears were rolling down her partner's cheeks. She'd learned not to try and comfort her. At such times Vera preferred to be left alone.

And Vicki could understand that. Sympathy could be disruptive, cutting in on whatever method you had devised for coping. Over the last years she'd developed a hardness that wasn't a shell because it went right through her like seaside rock. Her strategy for survival was to take things in small doses, live in the present, never look around her, or ahead into the terrifying void.

In this way she had handled the loneliness of the war years, her fears for Horst and for Christa, dealt now with hunger and monotonous, often backbreaking work, the stinking, decomposing bodies they uncovered often in the ruins. While she laboured among the rubble, Vicki would not allow herself to think of time, just do what she had to at that very moment, just plod away, dumb and stupid as an animal.

'Christ, I brought you to this. I can't live with it. It's all my doing . . .'

Horst used to go insane when she got home, filthy and drained, her face grey with exhaustion and hunger. Vicki could not bear his ravings. They jarred her composure, made her as agitated as he was.

'That's fucking nonsense . . . But if it's what you feel, for God's sake keep it to yourself,' she had snarled. 'Don't burden me with your conscience.'

Vicki accepted that she must work and Horst was beyond it. That was simply the way things were. Way back, years back, before he became a soldier, she had experienced flashes of impatience at his fecklessness, his limitless capacity for sleep. Now he was disabled and there was no blame attached. God knows he'd suffered and suffered still. No matter how bad things were, Vicki could be gentle and kind, just as long as nothing ruffled her trance-like equilibrium. Claudia saw this and buoyed her up with practical help and unsentimental optimism.

'Here's Freda,' Vera said.

Unconcernedly Vicki continued to sort the bricks from her corroded bucket on to their respective piles. Then she straightened up. 'Not before time.'

Freda came by every afternoon carrying a kind of yoke across her shoulders from which hung two large cans containing herbal brews she cooked up from whatever she could lay hands on.

Vera sniffed the air. 'Mint.'

'Where did you find mint growing?' someone asked.

'That would be telling.' Freda grinned showing broken teeth, a tall, raw-boned woman in threadbare black, looking fifty, though she claimed to be thirty-five.

The women clustered round her. Young and old, all were caked in the vile chalky, gritty dust. A workforce merely – so many pairs of hands – beyond vanity or pretension.

Freda charged a couple of pfennigs for her wares and you brought your own cup or took a chance sharing one of the four cracked vessels she carried with her.

'By the time Berlin's rebuilt you'll be a millionaire,' the women joshed.

'Coffee and a Turkish cigarette.' A woman called Nelle basked with her cup on a chunk of masonry, eyes closed, a twig protruding from the corner of her mouth.

'Silly tart,' her partner jeered.

Sitting on the ground, back against a pile of salvaged bricks, Vicki sipped her brew. The tang of mint was refreshing. In these reduced circumstances the drink gave her as much pleasure as she would once have derived from a cup of Amy's rich, aromatic Brazilian coffee. Too soon, though, the break was over and the women returned to their drudgery. Doggedly, the sun burning into her shoulders, Vicki began to fill her bucket with bricks.

This was all there was. In a corner of her brain the vision lingered of the white house and pleasant green garden of her childhood, the cherry trees in blossom, kind voices, smiling faces, the indulgent love of her family, appetizing food, order, plenty. It all seemed a distant, Arcadian dream. What she had now was real life. Vicki could not imagine another and, perversely, did not want another, only that this one would improve. She had thrown in her lot with Horst and with Germany for better or for worse.

'Don't you regret it? Running away, coming here?' Claudia had asked her one night, as they sat by the window in the dark apartment, while Horst and Christa slept.

Vicki shrugged, looking up at the white moon above the jagged black buildings. 'Regret it? What would be the point?'

She'd left for an infatuated illusion, out of a wild, childish eagerness to plunge into living and feeling. At the time she'd looked no further than that. No one could have foreseen the chaos that would descend on the world. Time and circumstances had brought them low, ravaged their lives in every conceivable way. But she loved Horst's sweetness still, she belonged with him and their child.

'I'd do the same again,' she said.

But it wasn't only love that kept her here. There were other, less definable reasons. Vicki experienced a stubborn desire to align herself with the underdogs, stay with the sinking ship, though it contained bullies and brutes, unimaginable evil. They knew now about the death camps, monstrous as some barbaric myth, only the myth was true.

'There were plenty of hints.' Claudia refused to cry innocence, flaunt her shock and horror. 'We knew what the Nazis were like and we stayed and closed our eyes . . . It's only a question of degree.'

Vicki respected her attitude. Even at seventeen she herself had harboured no illusions about the regime. But she'd put love before ideology and wasn't going back on it, not even now.

Each evening Horst dreaded the moment when Vicki came home, his young wife appearing in the doorway, half-dead with fatigue, head swathed in a filthy kerchief, her whole body greyed over with dust, like an animated statue to human drudgery.

Tonight her overall was dark with sweat, face and arms burned black by the sun beneath their grimy coating. Her arms were sinewy now, and stick-thin. Once he had marvelled at their spare, elegant curve and apricot smoothness.

'It's Mutti!'

Christa's gaunt little face was radiant. She accepted her mother's appearance, knew she mustn't try to kiss her until she had washed and changed into the dress she wore in the house. The child waited, smiling and eager. It was a game. She accepted this nightmarish world.

Claudia spread out a torn sheet and on it she placed two buckets of water. Vicki stripped off her working clothes and dropped them on the floor. There seemed not a centimetre of flesh on her anywhere, collar- and hipbones jutting against the tender skin, her thighs narrow as a child's. As always Horst was shocked by the contrast between the white of Vicki's body and her limbs, face and neck, burned dark as a navvy's. Finding himself, at the same time, obscurely aroused, as if his wife stood naked in stockings and long gloves. Vicki's hair had become so caked with brick-dust that she'd hacked it off to chin-level. It lay close to her skull, flattened by the kerchief she had worn, the ends uneven and jagged. Inwardly he raged against the mutilation.

'Aaah.' Vicki used the first clean water for her face and hair, plunging her whole head into the bucket. There was no soap to be had anywhere.

Christa stood by, handed her a threadbare towel. Vicki dried her face and rubbed at her hair, closing her eyes in a kind of ecstasy. She smiled at her daughter. 'Thank you, Mausi, I feel almost human.'

Setting one foot at a time in the bucket, she splashed one leg and then the other, sluicing off the dust as best she could. Claudia rubbed her back with a square torn from the sheet. Then, kneeling by the second bucket, Vicki washed herself all over, slowly and thoroughly, drying herself with a second towel.

'Here you are.'

Proud, wreathed in smiles, Christa held out Vicki's worn blue house-dress. Watching, Horst experienced a piercing tenderness. Christa was gradually starting to lose the terror and sadness that had gripped her during the months of bombing and shelter-life. Small rituals like these lent a shape and security to her days. Since Claudia had taken them in she was getting slowly better.

He himself was sinking, hawked and spat endlessly, could not cross the room without gasping for breath and sweating like a feverish pig. He had his uses, of course, was invaluable as a child minder, so Vicki and Claudia assured him constantly, in what he recognized as a conspiracy to boost his morale. Horst didn't doubt the importance of his contribution. And he loved to look after Christa, especially since – in flashes of cold realism – he knew he would not see her grow up. His health was broken and, in the absence of drugs and decent food, could never mend.

None the less, he found the role reversal galling. All his life Horst had traded on glamour and panache. Now he was the housewife, Vicki the gallant figure who fought for them in the outside world. Contemplating his own abjection, Horst felt himself tossed like a worthless piece of detritus on great swirling waves of despair. Only he'd come to understand that the best gift he could offer his wife and child was to keep his misery to himself.

Vicki pulled on her dress and combed her hair in Claudia's mirror. With the careful side-parting and square-cut bob she looked a school-girl. She turned again to her daughter. 'There, Mausi. Now it's time for our cuddle.'

Taking Christa by the hand, she led her across to where Horst lay on the floor, on Claudia's mattress, the old grey blanket rolled beneath his head.

Expansively he spread his arms, plastering a great jaunty grin on his death's-head of a face, saying the words that made Christa giggle, as if she'd never had a care in the world.

'Time for a lovely great armful of my two favourite ladies.' He gathered them to him, a stone in his heart.

Claudia watered the plants that stood on her windowsill. It was her favourite chore, the first she performed after Vicki had left in the morning, before she got Christa up, scratched around for some break-fast for all of them.

The dark red geraniums were years old. She'd bought the original plant in a shop in Grunewald before the war. They'd come through the war, through all the bombing. The thought amazed her. But there were other things, useful things. She'd learned to pick up plants where she found them, collect earth from the devastated garden over the way. Luckily she possessed a good collection of pots.

She had mint and sorrel, some dill, a clump of salad onions. Her best find had been a couple of tomato plants she'd noticed pushing their way through the rubble a couple of streets away. Now they stood proudly poised above the devastated street, sporting fruits that were slowly turning yellowy-orange. In terms of filling their bellies none of this added up to much, but it all offered flavouring, a little variety, to the basic bread and potatoes that kept them alive.

In the other room stood six fine tobacco plants she'd raised from seed. The most reliable unit of currency in Berlin nowadays was proving to be the cigarette, and people were raising their own, in allotments and window boxes – even a few cigarettes might make a difference, buying a little butter or bacon on the black market. Claudia picked off a couple of withered leaves.

She turned to find Horst watching her. Christa still slept, fragile, angelic. Horst looked better than when she'd first come across him in the shelter three months ago, but he was terribly weak and Claudia could not see him lasting through the winter.

Eyes semi-focused, he smiled. He murmured groggily, 'Let's open the window, Gräfin, and let in the future.'

She laughed, remembering their catch-phrase from way back in the days of *Countess Alexia*. In another life. Most of the time it slipped her mind that the two of them had once been lovers. The idea of Horst-Vicki-Christa as a unit had definitively superseded that image of him.

Claudia felt blessed, a woman with her family around her, though they were ignorant of the fact. Sometimes Christa talked about 'our family' – quite naturally including Claudia – and a shaft of pure pleasure would pierce her heart, warm and golden as sunlight. Agathe had died of cancer in the early years of the war. Rudi . . . she hadn't had word in almost a year. Claudia presumed he was a prisoner of war.

Horst sniffed the air. 'Do I smell scrambled eggs and coffee?'

Claudia laughed again, more to encourage him than anything else. So much of the time Horst faked a cheerfulness he didn't feel. While respecting his effort it made her sad. Good humour used to be as natural to him as breathing.

'Bacon on the side?'

'All the trimmings.'

He looked old and unshaven lying there, his skin the unhealthy colour of candle wax. There was a little bread, a few blackberries stewed without sugar. What use were those to him? A decent breakfast, a full stomach could have lifted his spirits at a stroke.

Christa opened her eyes, saw Claudia and leaped from beneath the blanket. Her skinny figure had surprising vigour. Claudia lifted her so the child's bony legs straddled her waist. Christa was happy. To her the crow's nest they lived in was paradise.

'Is there some bread?' she asked. In Christa's experience the question did not imply deprivation. It was all she could remember.

'Let's go and see.'

Claudia had been promised some butter today in return for the last two pairs of silk stockings from a parcel Rudi had sent her from Paris in the early euphoric days of the war. She had to meet her contact at midday in a street off the Ku'damm. She'd told no one for fear of disappointment, but her mind dwelled on the rendezvous as if on an assignation with a lover.

Claudia cooked the usual potatoes on the communal fire, alongside Brigitte, Frau Braun, Martha, Magda Fischer. Neither gas, electricity nor running water had yet been restored to the building. All of them contributed whatever wood they had been able to find. Vicki brought a fair bit home from the site. Some of it they kept for the winter. The rest Claudia put towards the cooking-fire.

She had bread too, and cut four pieces, spreading each one generously with butter, slicing a couple of the half-ripe tomatoes really thin and laying them on top. After Vicki had finished washing Claudia put the potatoes in a dish, laid a dab of butter on each, cut some dill and salad onion over the top.

Always she made them drink the hot potato-water first. It had half the vitamins in it and it filled them up a bit. When they'd got that down she brought in the buttered potatoes and the bread, with a triumphant flourish. The meal looked almost festive.

'Is that . . . ?'

'Yes.' A crooked grin. 'Who needs stockings anyway?'

Seated one each side of her small table, they ate ravenously. The rare addition of fat to their meal made it filling and satisfying. The mild, fresh butter contrasted with the strong, sour rye bread, the earthy potatoes and the tang of the herbs. Each mouthful was perfect, delicious.

A blissful satiation glowed in Claudia's belly, suffusing all her limbs, and she experienced the satisfaction of the others as keenly as her own. Particularly she noticed Christa tucking in with appetite and relish, her peaky face and dark-ringed eyes absorbed and intent. Hungry as she often was, the child could be finicky, worrying them all.

'Good is it, Christa?'

'Yes.' She looked up briefly, surprised at the question. To her food was food, hunger run-of-the-mill.

'That was heaven, Claudia.' Vicki laid calloused hands on her narrow belly. She moved her chair closer to Horst's and lolled on his shoulder in a parody of repletion.

'And there's more for tomorrow.' As she said it Claudia was ambushed by the sudden sharp awareness of Vicki's privileged upbringing, her Englishness, the glossy perfection of her as a girl. It was easy to forget. Sharing their day-to-day privations, speaking their language, she seemed so much one of them – the abject defeated.

Charlottenburg, where they lived, formed part of the sector administered by the British. They treated the Germans under their control with all the icy arrogance due to a degraded and brutal race.

'I can't think of them as my people,' Vicki had marvelled a couple of days previously. She smiled dourly. 'In some ways I feel almost closer to Klemens and Brigitte, die-hard Nazis that they are . . . It's as if I belong in the cellar with the rats.'

A few days ago, on the Kurfürstendamm, Vicki had seen an overweight sergeant, his face red with fury, chasing a group of emaciated kids away from the rich pickings of the garbage bins outside the officers' club. Thousands of orphaned children were living wild in the ruins of Berlin.

'I'd have killed the bastard.' Her daughter's anger had startled Claudia, scared her almost. 'Is he too stupid to understand that their trash – the stuff they don't need – could keep those kids from starving? Or does he actually want them to die?'

The colour had flooded from Vicki's face and her eyes were like an avenging angel's, dark, deep and glittering. It was clear she superimposed the ghost of Christa on the scavenging children. With hunger, stress, whatever, her moods could fluctuate like those of the sea.

The sense of identification she nursed for the disgraced survivors went further. Vicki could not face an encounter with her own family. She knew, via UN channels that they were safe and well, and she had sent a message to the same effect. But – while stressing her love for them – Vicki had begged them not to track her down.

Claudia protested. 'That's too cruel. They must have gone through hell all these years . . .'

But Vicki would not budge. 'I won't let them see me like this. They'll go mad, they'll rant and rave and try to make me leave . . . They won't understand that I can't . . .'

Chapter Fifty-two

Amy always looked happy when Johnny called to pick her up from the snack bar she ran with Chris Carella in Chalk Farm Road. In a row of shabby buildings even the exterior had an optimistic air, the cracked frontage white-washed over, the name 'Lunch-Box' picked out in some red oil paint Johnny had hoarded through the war and let them have. Pots of red geraniums in the window echoed the colour.

Sometimes he thought this was the only cheerful place in London. VE Day, sixteen months ago, had been euphoric, the supposed dawn of a brave new era. But no magic wand had been waved. Life was pinched and drab, the food, fuel and housing situation worse than during the war. Even bread was rationed now. All the same, no one would starve.

Johnny found himself reading everything he could find about Germany, about Berlin, obsessed with the desperate scenario depicted. There must be, he reflected, a certain . . . clarity in the sheer fight for survival. Frequently in the last months an image of Claudia shimmered in his brain – the sceptical eyes and golden body once so familiar to him. While recognizing the notion as romantic, Johnny half-envied the back-to-the-wall priorities that must govern her life.

He had to admire the way Amy and Chris rose above the dreariness, the lack of everything. The place they ran was unpretentious, catering to a lunch-time workers' trade. But there was a flair and a light-heartedness about it. They certainly made the most of the things you could get – mainly vegetables – and used them in imaginative ways. Alongside the basic sandwiches they made wonderful soups and baked their own herb breads. A pensioner called Tom, who used to tend the garden behind their war-time restaurant, had become a sort of partner, with two allotments dedicated to their needs. Their range was necessarily limited, but what they did they did well. Customers were intrigued.

A notice hanging in the window stated, 'Sorry no Welsh rarebit today due to shortages.' It was printed in bright, splashy letters and decorated with their emblem, a red geranium.

Johnny knocked and peered through the glass panel in the street door. Chris came and let him in. He liked her black hair and pale, freckled skin. She interested him, an attractive widow making her own way in the world.

'Hello,' she said. 'We need a dustbin. Have you got room for the last knockings of the carrot and caraway soup?'

'Always . . . There's not a piece of your onion bread?'

'Sorry. Sold out.' She grinned maliciously. 'Look at your face! Don't worry, we kept a bit back for you.'

'You're a gent.' The expression amused him. He'd picked it up from William Tilly.

'Come on through to the galley. Or people will think we're still open.'

In the sunny, cluttered kitchen Amy was on her knees packing supplies into the new refrigerator, their pride and joy. She turned to him with a bemused smile. 'This is like a three-dimensional puzzle.'

Experimentally she tried to shut the door, opened it again, rearranging the contents. This time it closed.

In a lithe movement she got to her feet and crossed the room to kiss him. Her fair hair bounced as she walked. Amy claimed to be going grey. Johnny could not see it. To him she looked on top of the world. During the war she'd seemed so tired.

She poured soup for him from a saucepan, unwrapped a hunk of onion bread. 'Here. Get that down you.'

He cleared a corner of the table and sat down to eat.

Superficially, coming here always raised Johnny's spirits. By the time he arrived the snack bar had closed, the two women were clearing up, making preparations for the next day, pleased with themselves, with time to welcome him and flirt a little. Sometimes Chris's younger sister was there helping, a bold, pretty girl, very Italian-looking. An atmosphere prevailed of good humour and slightly dazed success.

But later he was left with a gloomy consciousness of the contrast between Amy's life and his own. Hers was full of purpose and plans for expansion. He was marking time. Johnny had work, but nothing he cared about, little line drawings for magazines like *Courier*, frontispiece illustrations, the odd advertisement. He could take no interest in British politics. The new Labour government struck him as worthy, dull. He lost track of its squabbles.

'I feel half asleep,' he'd told Amy last time they met. 'Perhaps I need tyranny to bring me to life. Danger. *Was weiss ich . . . ?*

She had shrugged with a perplexed smile, not knowing what to say.

It was a glorious September day. Johnny and Amy decided to walk in Regent's Park for a while before taking the bus back to his place. The sun had a particular late-afternoon, autumnal mellowness. Amy turned her face up to it with a look of lazy pleasure. Johnny felt vaguely rattled by her palpable wellbeing.

Churlishly he needled her. 'You're so carefree. Who would think you had a daughter camped in the ruins of Berlin . . . And one about to disappear with her American soldier to the other side of the world.'

She turned, startled by his flash of ill will. Stung. 'Vicki's alive. That's the main thing. She knows she could come home. I'd give my right arm if she would . . . If I could just see her . . . But she's made her choice and we have to respect that.' Amy stopped short with a cool, elegant shrug. 'I really don't know why I'm justifying myself to you . . .'

He experienced a private, unworthy satisfaction at having got under her skin. Amy seemed abruptly to have forgotten the sun, the bright autumn leaves fluttering against the cornflower sky. She had a preoccupied air as if, in spite of her disclaimer, Johnny's jibe preyed on her mind.

As they approached the lake, festive with its little rowing boats, Amy said, 'If I went around in sackcloth and ashes it wouldn't do her any good . . .'

'Absolutely.'

'I've come to understand that my children have to lead their own lives. And I have to let go and lead mine. In the end you can't live through them or for them . . . It's a cliché, I know, but everyone has to find out that it's true.'

A searing image of his own two sons flared in Johnny's brain and he felt ashamed of his desire to puncture Amy's pleasure simply because he couldn't share it. He loved her. She'd been his lifeline over the last years. But always the resentment rankled that he'd never, ever been central to her life.

'I had a letter today from America.'

'Oh?' Her interest was lukewarm as if to punish him for his hostility.

'Some publisher from Potsdam – an exile. He wrote via *Courier* . . . He's putting a book together of anti-Nazi humour. He wants to use some of my Franzl strips . . .' A shard of sunshine pierced Johnny's numbness, a pleasure he hadn't yet allowed himself to feel. 'He's got *all* of them, can you imagine.'

'Honestly?' Her face lit up. 'That's wonderful! That's the best bit of news I've heard in a donkey's age.'

Amy was genuinely delighted at the development, Johnny reflected. His own despondency had made him grudging to others.

'Let's not exaggerate,' he growled.

For all the brightness outside there was an autumnal chill in the air. Waiting under the high, vaulted roof of the station, Grace shivered. Her eyes focused on the distant, dark aperture of the tunnel where the twin lines of track converged. Larry was coming. In just a few minutes the train would emerge from that tunnel and stop by the platform, a carriage door would open and Larry would step out. In the flesh. The thought made her feel faint, with a sudden giddy sense of something like destiny.

For so long she'd lived on letters. Phone calls too, more recently, since he'd been back in America. But they cost so much, had to be planned and booked. Each time the mere sound of his voice resonated through her body, her nerve-endings. But always there was that longing to say something thrillingly significant, and her mind went blank, their talk seemed inconsequential, and she was left feeling disappointed and let down.

Her senses felt sharp this morning. Grace breathed in the cold, acrid smell of the station. Smoke drifted lazily below the struts of the roof. She relished the soft warmth of her clothes against her skin. But the skirt and sweater were old and worn. Arriving from America, Larry would be unused to threadbare women. She would have liked to wear something new to greet the man she was to marry. As it was, only her nylon stockings, bought from a spiv in Camden Market, offered a hint of glamour.

It was almost exactly a year since she'd last seen Larry, in September '45. He'd been stationed in the South of Germany, was on the point of being demobilized finally, and shipped home with his unit. He'd had to crawl and lick ass, so he told her, to get these few days' leave in London.

It had been a funny time, sort of nervy. It was as if a stranger – thin, tanned, toughened by experience – had been superimposed on the unassuming boy who loved her. His sexuality was urgent and close to the surface and, again, there'd been the problem of privacy. In desperation, one afternoon, Larry had rented a hotel room for a few hours. In her mind's eye Grace could still see the shiny pink eiderdown, damp-mottled walls, the sheets worn thin as cobwebs.

Larry was relentless, insatiable – they made love on and on. It seemed to Grace as if, all the time he'd been away at war, Larry had been thinking up new things to do with her. At first his focused lust had aroused her wildly. But, as the afternoon passed, the whole thing began to feel like a marathon. Grace was bruised and sore, and still he wanted more.

'I can't . . .' Finally she'd rolled up into a ball, like a hedgehog, prickly and resistant.

'Grace, baby . . .' He curled up behind her, cradling her body against his, enfolding her with his arms, tender and solicitous, penitent, as if he knew he had driven her too hard. He murmured, 'It's scary . . . How can anyone love anyone as much as I love you . . . ?'

Drowsily it occurred to her to wonder if he'd slept with anyone else while he was away but, lulled as she was by his protective warmth, the thought seemed unimportant.

In any case Grace had a secret of her own. One evening at a party she'd necked with Raymond Perry, almost gone the whole way. All her life he'd lived down the road to her. But the war had given him a kind of arrogance that had its own repellent attraction. Later she'd felt sad, lonely for Larry and his sweetness, his honest love.

But, after Larry was gone again, back to the States, Grace did sleep with Raymond. He had a heavy, muscular body and there was a sort of . . . bullying quality to his wooing that was like a challenge she just had to take up. After that, though, she refused to go out with him again. Grace knew if she did she'd end up in bed with him once more.

Ironically, Amy was always pressing her to go out more, have a little fun, live in the present. But all this year – while Larry wrestled with the red tape his end, the visas and authorizations needed to wed his English sweetheart – Grace had stubbornly shut out the here and now, looking towards the future. In some ways their marriage would be a leap of faith, she and Larry had spent so long apart. She must trust in the memory of their courtship when the prospect of a life together had seemed so easy and right, so delightful.

Suddenly the train appeared in the mouth of the tunnel, small at that distance, but growing larger as it drew closer, gliding to an eventual halt alongside the stretch of the platform. In a moment doors began to open, figures to alight, footsteps echoing hollowly in the station void. Grace was invaded by a muffled panic. What if she saw him and felt disappointment, or mere indifference.

'Don't look for a uniform . . .' Larry had written. Grace had never seen him in anything else.

She stood and stared. Passengers were walking up the platform now, singly and in pairs, with bags and suitcases. Then, abruptly, from a way off, she spotted the figure of a young man, a gangling figure in the kind of light-coloured jacket that only Americans wore. Grace took a step forward, picturing herself for a second as standing in the current of a stream, the travellers flowing past her like water . . . her heart beating, legs ready to buckle with the tension inside.

He'd seen her. Their eyes met. He was close enough for Grace to recollect that expression of his she used to love, the amused half-smile, the long eyes with their mixture of shrewdness and sincerity.

'Grace!' His voice, vibrant with pleasure, lifted her heart.

In love stories the presence of the hero was signalled by metaphorical fireworks, hearts, raptures. Reality was different, less showy, more complex and profound. Grace couldn't have analysed the emotion she felt at seeing Larry walk towards her, or put it into words, only she knew everything was going to be all right.

'Hi, stranger.' She greeted him, elated but serene. She beamed. 'You're not a figment of my imagination, are you? You *are* real?'

'Yeah.' He drew close. 'I'm your mail-order bridegroom, Gracie.' Larry gazed at her with a wide, irrepressible smile.

Grace was married at Hampstead Registry Office on a blustery day in October. She looked adorable, Noel thought, though slightly chilly, in a two-piece run up for her by one of the nursery mothers from some thin, pink pre-war woollen stuff Margaret had managed to find.

'Too milkmaidy.' Grace wasn't keen on the colour but Noel thought she looked sweet in pink. Heartbreakingly sweet. In her bright, eager smile he saw twenty years of baby photos, school photos, holiday snaps. She had always been so radiantly open to life. His heart bled inside him.

Yet he approved wholeheartedly of Larry, a sensible, amusing boy, almost painfully in love. To his relief Grace seemed to have made a thoroughly good choice. Given her headstrong nature, he and Amy had often anticipated the worst.

But, however suitable, the lad was a stranger who would be taking his daughter far away. Noel knew that marriage was a long journey involving compromises and clashes of will that were never resolved. He yearned to protect Grace from the attrition.

'Come on now.' Amy laughed at his fears. 'It's a wedding, not a funeral. Grace'll cope. Your little girl is tough as old boots.'

* * *

The previous year Roland Delane, editor of *Witness*, had retired due to age and poor health. It was well known that he saw Noel as his successor. Noel had duly been offered the post, and was on the point of accepting it, when it occurred to him that he wasn't at all sure he wanted the job.

For America hostilities had ended later than in Europe, with the bombing of Hiroshima and Nagasaki. In the euphoric aftermath most of Noel's acquaintances seemed to view the new atomic bomb as a righteous instrument in the hands of God's chosen people, the annihilation as a fitting, climactic finale to the war.

On VJ Night Laura Krell had given a party in her congenial flat. Though he liked everyone there Noel had felt alienated among the whooping high spirits. He'd got into a debate with Laura's son-in-law. Noel argued that, in using the bomb, America had released something terrible that could never be put back in the bottle, and would alter the face of world politics for years to come, possibly for ever. The son-in-law, more than a little drunk, a flick of blond hair hanging in his eyes, was feeling jingoistic. He began to get heated and abusive and, out of consideration for Laura, Noel shut up.

At half-past five in the morning, when everyone had gone, and Laura and Noel had stacked glasses and plates in the kitchen for the maid to wash, they sat out on the balcony, above the parched, land-scaped garden, and watched the sun come up.

'Highly symbolic,' Laura said. She'd changed into a flowered housecoat and her red hair hung on her shoulders, the roots beginning to show grey. 'It feels like the dawning of a new era.'

'A time for taking stock if ever there was one.' Noel squinted at the harsh brightness, watching the lazy silhouette of a plane circling distantly above the airport. The air was warm and already humid. He would refuse the editor's job. He had no heart for it.

For Laura the new dawn signified something quite different – an ultimatum. Either Noel would get a divorce and marry her or they must part.

'What's it to be?' She leaned back against the balcony's guardrail, her eyes challenging, her robed figure dark against the sun. She was a good woman. They'd been kind to one another. But he could not imagine himself married to her.

'If it has to come down to a choice, then I suppose we'll part.'

Noel answered bluntly, responding to Laura's provocation. Later he regretted it and tried to make clear how he valued and respected her. Laura seemed to have second thoughts about her edict. But the sense of reawakening in the air had kindled in Noel a longing for his own home, his own wife.

He resigned as American correspondent to *Witness*. A successor had already been lined up in anticipation of his accepting the editorship. The changeover was swift and painless and, in January 1946, Noel had returned to England.

In the weeks before his arrival Amy had been wary. She had her life in order, she was pleased with it. The newspapers were full of dire warnings for couples re-adjusting to togetherness after the dislocation of war. Amy was apprehensive that Noel would expect their life together to be a continuation of their pre-war domesticity. She was all foreboding, prepared to fight her corner.

She was unprepared for the soaring of her spirits at the sight of him in the flesh, walking towards her in a black and white tweed overcoat she had never seen, his thick grey-blonde hair ruffled by an icy wind, his lined face pale with the cold, the fatigue of the flight, but set in the amiably quizzical grin that had become natural to him. He exuded something, Amy saw, that he hadn't when young – a sort of good-natured acceptance of self. Noel had mellowed, she realized, and knew that her worst fears of his trying to force her back into some outgrown mould would prove to be unjustified.

'Hello you.' Her smile held years of shared intimacy.

'God, it's good to be home.' They hugged joyfully, two travellers coming together after their own separate journeys.

As they began to live together again, Amy understood with a kind of dazed surprise, how she had missed going to sleep and waking next to another body, chatting companionably in the warmth and dark of their bed. She experienced a constant surprised pleasure at the sight of Noel back at his desk. It was delightful to have someone to come home to, good to share an early-evening drink, welcome together the first signs of spring in the garden. They made love and that, too, seemed suddenly natural, as if absence and even their respective affairs, had exorcized a tension that once kept them apart. During his absence Amy had relished her freedom but belittled the warmth of intimacy and shared habit, of belonging.

Amy felt a wondering contentment. Wellbeing made her loving and lovable. Her business venture with Chris was going well – financed by a loan they would not have received without Noel's backing. She was busy and creative without the numbing exhaustion of the war years. She had vaguely feared that Noel would resent the time and energy she gave to her work, but his attitude was encouraging. Amy came to suspect Laura's influence here – he mentioned once in passing that she had criticized his too-proprietorial attitude to his wife . . .

Even small, mundane matters fell into place. Amy had worried that Noel would become impatient with the presence of the lodgers. She'd broached the matter early on.

'I'd hate to tell them to go. You can't find flats now for love nor money.'

He'd merely shrugged. 'When Grace is gone we'll fit into the ground floor like square pegs in square holes.'

Flo and Len Barker rather hero-worshipped Noel. They considered him 'in the know', adopted his opinions on world affairs as their own. Elspeth, Amy suspected, had something of a crush on him. All in all harmony reigned.

Which wasn't to say that there weren't anxieties, even bones of contention, beneath the limpid surface of their parallel lives.

After Washington, Noel found it hard to adjust to the puritanical bleakness of Britain post-victory. The everlasting semi-hunger and semi-cold, the absence of any heartening frivolity, exacerbated his feeling of not quite knowing where he was going. It was as if, having jumped agilely off one train, there was no other waiting to whisk him on his way. He was bridging the hiatus by working on a book on war-time Washington, based on the diaries he always kept on foreign assignments. Given his standing as a journalist, it would be well-received and sell acceptably. But it was hardly a change of direction.

'Make it a novel,' Amy laughed. 'A *roman-à-clef* set in the corridors of power . . . Now that'd be something new.'

'I think you should stop seeing Johnny Kröger.'

He'd made the declaration in bed one night a month or so after his return. She couldn't see his face, but his voice was low and purposeful, as if he were obeying some abrupt inner resolution to risk himself in choppy waters.

Beside him Amy stiffened. There was silence. Then she said softly, 'No, I can't do that.'

Noel didn't reply. The hush between them was electric with a potential conflict neither wanted. Their new-found peace and pleasure was too good to spoil.

She tried to explain. 'We've been good friends while you were away. I've kept him sane and he's buoyed me up. God knows, I give him little enough of myself and my time . . . I won't just abandon him.'

Still Noel said nothing. Her words rustled into the sightless bedroom as if into a black void.

'After all, you and Laura –'

'That's over.' He spoke at last. Terse.

'But it was your decision. I didn't force your hand. It died its own death and so will this in the end.'

Restlessly Amy raised herself on one elbow. 'Look, I can't pretend not to . . . You and I haven't exactly been . . .' Impatient with her own prevarication, she blurted, 'He means a lot to me, damn it.' But even *in extremis* she was careful not to mention love.

This time the pregnant silence went on and on. Amy perceived it as judgemental.

'Another Claudia.' When Noel finally spoke, his voice shook with bitter passion. 'Only this one can fuck you.'

She was shocked by his angry despair, had no answer for it. Amy could not tell how long she lay, heart thumping, staring up into nothing. Much later, she turned and laid an arm across Noel's body. She could tell by his breathing that he was still awake, but he gave no answering sign.

The next day they resumed diplomatic – even amiable – relations and Johnny wasn't mentioned again. But the issue, along with the Claudia-Vicki grievance, would linger on, like a monster inhabiting the cold, black depths beneath the shimmering surface of a loch.

As Amy had predicted back in February, her affair with Johnny died its death, but not until nearly Christmas. It was already dark when he picked her up from the snack bar. On the way home to his place they stopped off at the pub on the corner of his street.

Germans, however righteous, had a tough time in Britain, but Johnny was a regular here and much liked. Above the bar hung framed cartoons he'd done of Ray, the landlord, and his wife, Belle. Early in the evening, while the bar was still empty, Ray would pour each of them a double from his small secret store of Scotch.

Amy and Johnny had their own secluded corner, protected by a high-backed bench upholstered in the same toffee-coloured leatherette as Johnny's chairs at home. The place was comfortable enough in its gloomy brown fashion, though, with the fuel situation, hardly warm. The first sip of whisky spread a small, welcome glow in Amy's veins.

Johnny lit a cigarette, inhaled, crossed one leg over the other. He seemed jumpy somehow. 'Any news of Grace?' he asked.

'Yes. She sounds on top of the world. Got a job in a petrol station. Larry's studying hard. His grant's come through . . .' She took another sip of her drink, enjoying the warmth that flared in the pit of her stomach. 'I miss her though, dreadfully.'

'She's in Vermont, isn't she? Is that near New York?'

'Relatively.' The factual query didn't sound like him. 'Why?'

'Reasons.'

He looked thoughtfully at her. After all these years she was still addicted to his odd, bony face, ravaged, but animated as always with a secret gleam of youthful subversion. Johnny's war-worn clothes sat on his spare frame with easy grace like a second skin. He had a native elegance she thought of as peculiarly European.

'You're very enigmatic.'

'I've taken a decision.' He drew on his cigarette, exhaled, narrowing his eyes against the drift of blue smoke. A self-mocking grin. 'The first in years.'

Amy raised an eyebrow. 'Good for you.'

'I'm leaving.' His expression was wary. 'For New York.'

It took a moment or two for her to absorb the meaning of his words, so far was she from expecting them. Her first reaction was astonishment, nothing more emotional. 'Since when?'

'Remember the fellow who contacted me about my cartoons? Name's Braff, Ernst Braff. We've been corresponding. He's been urging me to come. He can get me work, a visa . . . He can get me sponsored.'

'You've been doing all this in secret!'

'If I'd told you, I would have been committed.' Amy detected a flash of malice at her dismay. Since for ever – since all those years ago in Berlin – he'd been at *her* beck and call, and felt it keenly. 'All along I've hung on to the knowledge that I could back out and no one would be any the wiser . . . Only now I've made up my mind.'

She was still struggling to encompass the thought that this person – whose presence she experienced with her nerves and skin, heart and soul, who was part of her – was about to vanish from her life. A sense of panic invaded her, a passionate adumbration of loss. Yet immediately she saw that the prospect of radical change must be more heartening to him than his half-life here.

'I'm pleased for you.' She hardly knew what she said.

'I don't want you to be pleased, I want you to be broken-hearted.'

Amy had always known this moment would come. She'd talked about it, so cool and glib. Now she was overwhelmed by a surge of something like terror, understood that she'd taken too much for granted the role he played in her life. Yes, she was stimulated by her work, and by the mere fact of working. Yes, she was warmed by the new harmony of her relationship with Noel. But it was Johnny's presence that raised her world above the mundane. He was the secret ingredient, the magic, a cocktail of lawlessness, bohemian chic, raw sex, unsentimental friendship. Once upon a time he'd given her his whole heart. She had rationed her response, diluted it with her sense of duty. But even as Amy condemned herself she knew it could not have been otherwise.

'I'm numb. But rest assured, I'll be broken-hearted. I may even go crazy when you've gone.'

'Come with me.' A cynical challenge. Once he would have meant it, but it was too late. She would always put family first. Out of decency or cowardice.

'Don't, Johnny.' She pushed her empty glass towards him across the shiny, cracked table-top. 'D'you think Ray could spare another of these?'

He glanced towards the bar. 'It's Belle . . . Perhaps if I offer her my body . . .'

'When do you go?'

'Next month, or February.' He smiled crookedly. 'I'm terrified.'

Chapter Fifty-three

In the autumn of '46 Claudia saw her brother, Rudi, for the last time. She'd barely heard from him since summer '42, when he'd been on leave from Paris, lithe and handsome in Waffen-SS uniform. At that time he'd been pleased with life, enjoying his Paris posting to the full, in love with a young French woman. He had a photograph of her, a southern type, with thick dark hair, vamping the camera with an eloquently mysterious smile.

Rudi had brought presents for Claudia. Perfume, a bottle of Armagnac. They'd spent an evening together, got drunk, talked a blue streak, more frankly than ever before. She'd told him the truth about Vicki, he confessed to having had a fling with Amy at the time of the Olympic Games. Plastered as they were, the mutual confidences had a quality of unreality, like stories they'd invented about themselves.

He'd been in his late twenties then, strikingly attractive – she could see that – harder and more worldly than she, with a callousness she'd never noticed before. In the cold light of the following day, Claudia felt she was a disappointment to him, his stylish actress sister turned magazine-seller, living an obscure and humdrum life.

Every so often, from Paris, she would receive parcels of good things – stockings, dress materials, a couple of pairs of teetering shoes in soft leather, for which she had no use, but which she'd traded on the black market. After the German evacuation of France Rudi was sent to Poland. He'd written once from there, a curt, uninformative note. Since then she'd heard nothing. Neither had the clerks from the *Suchdienst* been able to come up with any information about him, not even that he was dead.

One Friday evening in late September Claudia was plodding home alongside the canal. For the past three months she had been working part time in a shop that sold newspapers and tobacco. The job left her space to get Christa off to school first thing in the morning, then queue for their bread. It paid a pittance but each week she received four packets of twenty cigarettes, with which to trade on the black market. Claudia had a couple of regular suppliers who were good for the odd can of meat, packet of flour, tinned fruit or soap purloined from Allied supplies. Recently she'd managed to get hold of a decent pair of second-hand boys' shoes for Christa, which would see her through the winter.

The evenings were beginning to draw in and Claudia wasn't looking forward to the cold months ahead. There was no coal to be had anywhere. Water and electricity supplies had been restored but the latter was severely rationed. Still, it was good to be able to cook indoors, in privacy. The enforced communal spirit that prevailed among the tenants during the time of emergency had fragmented into the shifting alliances and petty rivalries that came more naturally to them.

Claudia turned into the street that led home, flanked on both sides by the hollow shells of buildings. The ruins had been tidied, by women like Vicki, but were ruins still. Ahead of her the lone figure of a man lingered by the garden across the street. He turned now and walked towards her. Lost in thought, she registered only that he was tall, dark, a German she assumed from his raw-boned look, his dirty clothes.

'Claudia.' A few paces away from her he called her name.

She looked up sharply, gazed at him mystified.

'It's me. It's Rudi.'

'Good God.'

As he bent and kissed her, the dark features were newly, profoundly familiar to her, but wasted, hardened and set, with that look everyone wore – whether abjectly or aggressively – of shame and defeat. She clung to him, as if protectively, though he hadn't needed her protection for years, and she had none to offer. Rudi smelled rankly of sweat and damp clothing. He'd always been so well-groomed.

'Where have you been? I've tried to find out. I thought you must be a prisoner.'

'I've been near Wittstock – not so far away – mending roads . . . My name is Karl Haus,' he added, a note of warning in his voice.

'Oh.' For a second she was puzzled. But a change of identity was far from rare in this time of flux. 'Come home with me. We can talk more easily . . . Some friends are living with me now.'

He shook his head. 'Then I won't come up . . . There's not a café or something?'

She smiled wryly. 'You're asking a lot . . . There's some sort of a place a few blocks away, though I've never been inside.'

The Café Wilhelm occupied two ground-floor rooms beneath a scarred, but comparatively sound, block of flats. The frontage was decorated with a pair of stylized lilies in semi-eroded bas-relief. Inside the place was bare but clean, contained a motley assortment of tables and chairs. Along the end wall of the first room stood a bar built from bricks salvaged from the rubble.

The proprietor – Wilhelm, presumably – was tall, pale, lugubriously handsome, rather likeable. His wife served as waitress, a beautiful, tired-looking woman in grey with braided hair. Only one other table was occupied, by two depressed-looking elderly men. There was a choice of beer or ersatz coffee. They chose beer. It was weak, warmish, sweetish, but not unpleasant.

When they were settled with their drinks, Rudi said, 'I've come to say goodbye.' He spoke diffidently, as if to downplay the drama of his words.

'Where are you going?'

'It's more what I'm becoming.'

'Don't be so runic.'

Arms crossed on the table-top, mostly ignoring his beer, Rudi talked fast and furtively as if, even in this bare, barn-like room, he was scared of being overheard by someone who could do him harm. He'd been in Poland when the Russians arrived and had deserted before he could be taken prisoner and sent to a labour camp. Rudi had made his way back to Germany with the thousands of ethnic Germans expelled from Polish soil. He'd sorted himself out a passport of sorts, purchased from a woman whose husband had been beaten to death by avenging Poles. He'd been up north for some months, found work, but his Karl Haus persona had become precarious.

'Give yourself up to the British,' Claudia advised. 'Nothing much can happen to you.'

'You're wrong.' Deliberately he met her gaze. His eyes were hard. Opaque. 'In Poland, I tell you, I did things that would put me behind bars . . . I'm no hero. I did what I was told without protesting. I obeyed orders, as the saying goes.'

Claudia stared at him. How reduced he was, her charming little brother. Tanned by his outdoor work, but half-starved, filthy, hair lank and thinning, cheekbones almost grotesquely prominent. Perversely his confession induced in her a rush of raw and passionate pity. At another time in history Rudi would have lived a blameless life. Studied, worked, married, had kids. His worst transgression a little adultery perhaps, or financial sharp practice . . .

'So I'm disappearing now. You'll never see me again. I've got a foolproof new passport, curriculum vitae, a *Persilschein* . . .' He mentioned the whiter-than-white certificate exonerating the holder from Nazi involvement. 'Tomorrow a corruptible American will drive me to Frankfurt.'

He shrugged. They gazed at one another, soberly, silently.

'Anyway, Claudi, how are you?'

'I'm fine.'

There seemed no point in launching into a description of her life. It was irrelevant. And, in any case, Rudi was too strung up to listen.

'Hold out your hand.'

Bemusedly she did as he asked. He closed it round a pair of hard, metallic objects.

'Put them in your pocket, quick. They're all that's left of my Parisian gewgaws after buying myself a brand new identity. Maybe they'll get you a packet of decent coffee.'

In the days that followed Claudia was haunted by her encounter with Rudi, which in her mind took on an unbelievable, almost a hallucinatory quality. She was beset by mental images of him as a child and a young man. But reality drifted back. She had been without him for so long. And the strategies involved in living day-to-day absorbed all her energies once more.

Life remained a struggle and, as was becoming increasingly clear, an unfair struggle. The Allies' grand denazification plan – whereby it was projected that the guilty would be punished, the virtuous rewarded – was proving unworkable in practice. The procedure was slow, cumbersome, riddled with anomalies, liable to be snatched off-course by red herrings and grudge denunciations. It was all too easy for officials to target the small fry, people like postmen, forced to join the party in order to keep their jobs. But it was noticed that bigger fish, who could be useful to the occupiers, were finding their way back into positions of responsibility. The ineptitude and hypocrisy of the process led to sour simmerings of mistrust and resentment against the new masters.

In Claudia's own small circle, Klemens had always been the most enthusiastic Hitlerite, the one you had to watch, an informer, ears flapping all over the place. Yet the opportunistic caretaker had landed a cushy sideline as boilerman to a block of flats a few streets away, occupied by the British. His burgeoning belly and growing wardrobe bore witness to the fringe-benefits of the job. It seemed that, after all, Klemens had never actually signed on the dotted line with the Party. His employers saw him as an obliging, respectful fellow, with a ready smile, someone who met them halfway and laughed at their jokes.

Emmi Hermann, who lived across the hall from Klemens and his wife, discovered her own way to raise her standard of living. She was fifteen now, a pretty blonde. Each night she went out on the town, found herself an allied soldier and brought him back to her room, while her mother made herself scarce.

'She won't go with Russians, though,' Brigitte confided to Claudia.

But her British and American boyfriends paid her with chocolate and cigarettes, cans of meat and fruit juice, coffee, stockings. Sometimes Claudia purchased items from Emmi's surplus stock.

'*Unverschämt.*' Frau Braun shook her head at the girl's lifestyle.

'Come on, Frau Braun, if we were twenty years younger . . .'

Claudia coaxed away her neighbour's disapproval. Frau Braun's lips twitched in a reluctant smile. Claudia recalled all too clearly the aftermath of the previous war when she'd been of an age to offer her own family the fruits of sin.

'You can't tell the good girls from the bad nowadays . . .' Klemens was pruriently fascinated by Emmi's trade. He hinted to Claudia once that Vicki could do well for them if she'd only primp and preen more – bit of lipstick, a little swing of the hips – he smiled libidinously. Claudia didn't repeat his suggestion to Vicki. She didn't think it would be appreciated.

The present from Rudi turned out to be a pair of gold earrings. Claudia told Vicki that her boss at the tobacconist's knew a woman who worked in the records office at the local hospital. Apparently, given the right inducement, she was willing to nudge prospective patients higher up the waiting list. Claudia proposed to use the earrings as a bribe.

Horst had been on the list for a bed for fourteen months but, suddenly, in early November, he was notified of his imminent admission. In hospital he would have access to medical treatment and three decent meals a day.

Vicki visited him every night and each time he looked stronger and talked about food he hadn't seen in years. He managed to slip her a couple of apples for Christa, who thought them so pretty, round and red she didn't want to eat them.

Privately Vicki hoped he would be kept in for longer than the three weeks guaranteed. But the competition for beds was fierce. Tuberculosis was endemic, along with typhus, hunger-oedema, infections of all sorts due to the lowered resistance of the whole population. Horst responded to treatment and was promptly discharged to take his chances back in the real world.

'God, but it's good to be back with my harem.' With anguished tenderness Vicki recalled the fake heartiness he used to bolster everyone's spirits.

'We're going to have a lovely Christmas,' Christa told him.

'The best ever,' Horst confirmed.

To Vicki his voice sounded rougher, hoarser than it had been before he entered hospital, but that must be her imagination. A superficial flush of health overlaid the irreversible degeneration of his large frame. Her heart went out to him, huddled inside his ancient uniform jacket and grey scarf. Horst's hair, still worn long as in his prime, clung limply to his ravaged cheeks and temples. His eyes were less sunken, but their brightness had something feverish about it. Deep down Vicki recognized that the three weeks of rest and decent food could only have the most temporary effect.

One day in early December Vicki saw a clutch of small Christmas trees for sale, ready planted into pots. She was enchanted by the blue-green bloom, the healthy bushiness of the plants. They seemed so utterly unaffected by the upheavals of the human world. She bought one and it stood in one of their paneless windows, decorated with cardboard stars Christa cut from cigarette cartons. For all of them the sturdy little tree seemed symbolic of a joy still to be found in the dislocated environment they inhabited.

But halfway through December it began to freeze and a cutting wind drove snow in at the windows. The old blankets they'd pinned up against the elements all last winter became useless and saturated in no time. They managed to rig up planks across the window in one of the rooms and all slept in together. Recklessly they burned the sticks of firewood collected all year and prayed for the cold snap to pass.

But, for Christa's sake, for everyone's sake, they celebrated on Christmas Eve with a meal to which Frau Braun, and Martha from upstairs, were invited. Beforehand they lit candles and Martha played her guitar, and they sang 'Stille Nacht' and 'O Tannenbaum', which Christa had learned at school. Emmi Hermann came upstairs with a couple of bars of chocolate for Christa. In a red dress, her blonde hair curled, she looked so pretty it did your heart good. Emmi stayed and sang along in a sweet, true voice that reminded Vicki how young she was.

Afterwards she kissed them all. 'Happy Christmas, everyone. I'm off now, got a party to go to.'

And for once Frau Braun spared them her strictures on modern youth.

They gathered round the table for a meal of tinned ham, which Claudia had been saving since September, and potatoes cooked in goose fat, courtesy of Martha. Frau Braun contributed a dish of sauerkraut, and a packet of *Lebkuchen* she'd paid the earth for in the Christmas market. There was orange juice purchased from Emmi, and Vicki had traded some of Claudia's cigarettes for a quarter-bottle of schnapps decanted into a medicine bottle.

Horst was quite his old self, expansive and amusing. He and Claudia got to telling preposterous stories of their days at the Valentin Theater and had everyone in fits. Vicki knew he would suffer for the exertion but it was delightful to see him in such genuinely high spirits. Christa hung on his every word, her grey eyes – so like his – brilliant and enchanted in her white little face.

Later, as they sat talking round the table over schnapps and *Lebkuchen*, Horst stood up and, with a casual excuse, disappeared into the next room. Vicki let him go, making no comment. But afterwards, as Claudi and the two other women cleared the table and Christa played with a rag-doll Frau Braun had made her, she went to find him.

The other room was icy and, by now, semi-dark. Horst sat on the mattress on the floor, chin in hand. Vicki sat down beside him and took his arm but he gave no sign.

'Christ, I make myself want to puke,' he rasped. His tone was flat and tired. 'Forever acting the part of this brave stinking saint. I want to be me, like I was. I want to be weak and cowardly and selfish. I want to be whole.'

All over Europe the freezing weather continued, with temperatures falling to thirty below zero. It was the worst winter in living memory. Day after day blizzards swept in from the Arctic and snow lay in the streets until March. A drastic shortfall of coal led to constant cuts in the power supply. Schools and firms closed down. Public transport ground to a halt. In windowless, unheated houses frostbite was a constant threat. Wolves were seen in the woods round Berlin. Food became scarcer still, an increasing proportion of the population coming to rely on meagre welfare handouts. In the doom-laden atmosphere there were even rumours of cannibalism, a market in human flesh.

For Vicki, Claudia, Christa, Horst – as for most others – life became simply a matter of enduring until the winter finally drew to an end. They huddled in a single room, wearing all their clothes all of the time. Each day was a search for something to eat, something to burn, all too often unsuccessful.

With the New Year Horst's condition deteriorated rapidly. The congestion in his lungs was like molten tar, oozing and thick. The smallest exertion wiped him out. He lay, silent and still, not even complaining of the cold – resigned, so it seemed, to total passivity, unable to control his bladder and bowels. There was nothing to be done. The hospitals were bursting at the seams. He'd had his chance there.

Finally he stopped eating. His limbs were skeletal. Vicki tried to feed him potato-water on a spoon, but after a couple of swallows he turned away, with a weariness that suggested the process was futile.

One morning, when she woke, Vicki found him dead alongside her. She lay for a while on her side, contemplating his inert, sunken face. He seemed a stranger. She felt nothing, her emotions as frozen as her body. Vicki got up and asked Claudia to take Christa upstairs to Martha. Then she went out and informed the authorities, had Horst's body removed to the morgue. The earth was too hard for graves to be dug.

Chapter Fifty-four

She'd seen photographs of course. Yet, in the summer of '49, as their plane circled above Gatow Airport in the British Sector of Berlin, Amy stared mesmerized, awe-struck by the vision of chaos below.

Block after block, mile after mile of blackened, windowless ruins. And this landscape of annihilation, shining in the summer sun, vivid with fireweed, was Vicki's home. That she had survived at all seemed suddenly a miracle.

There was devastation aplenty in London, but not on this scale. And people went on living here, working, hoping. Tears filled her throat. Not just because of Vicki, but at thoughts she could not begin to encompass. The self-destructiveness of humans. And their resilience. Her eyes met Noel's but neither spoke. The sight below dwarfed any possible words.

Two weeks ago, out of the blue, they'd had a note from Vicki. Amy had not dared believe her eyes when she saw the writing on the envelope, the German stamp. They had heard nothing from Vicki since, soon after the war, she'd sent a message via the UN Relief Agency informing them baldly that she was alive, but begging them not to seek her out.

The edict had been obeyed, though the sheer relief Amy had felt on learning the bare fact of Vicki's survival, had spiralled into a sick longing to know more, to set eyes on her daughter and granddaughter, find out how they lived. But Amy had forced herself to concentrate on her own life and trust to fate that Vicki would contact them when she was ready. She'd accomplished the emotional feat with determination and some success. But sometimes, in the night, she saw her anxieties as captive tigers that would reveal their true ferocity if the cage were allowed to open even the tiniest bit.

As Amy slit the envelope it was as if all the strength she owned were draining down and away. She was helpless, at the mercy of her singing hope, the despair that would engulf her if the hope was dashed. Pulling out the single sheet of flimsy squared paper, she scanned it wildly for proof. There it was. The name, Vicki. A row of childish kisses . . .

The note was short and factual. Horst had died. Vicki and Christa, Amy learned, had joined forces with Claudia, they'd set up home together. It was like reading a story that made no sense. Amy felt unable to imagine a reality behind the words. Vicki sounded hesitant and unsure of their reaction to her sudden overture, but she asked whether – some time, when they were ready – all of them might meet.

The letter had the force of an electric charge, galvanizing them into activity. They'd booked a flight and somewhere to stay – Noel had pulled strings with a couple of men he knew in the Control Commission. Amy had arranged cover for the time she would be away from work.

Yet, boarding the plane in the early morning sunshine, she had not allowed herself to imagine what lay ahead, to hope or to fear. It was ten years since she and Noel had seen their elder daughter. The whirlpool of conflicting feelings stirred up by the prospective meeting was better left unexamined.

Amy lifted her eyes from the scene below. Outside the windows the sky gleamed, an innocent azure blue.

Vicki peered at herself in the ebony-framed mirror Claudia had somehow never traded for food or soap, whatever. She rarely looked in it except to tidy her hair or check that her face was clean. Now she attempted to see herself as if through someone else's eyes.

'You look so fierce now, Vicki.'

She remembered Horst saying that to her once and it had been a shock. At the time she knew she was thinner, her hair short and never really clean. But did the basic expression on your face really change? Naturally the mirror couldn't answer that question. Faces went blank at such times, people sucked in their cheeks and lifted their chins, lied to themselves basically. That wasn't how they appeared in real life.

She could see a severity in her mouth and in her eyes. She looked pared-down, no softness, no frills or illusions. Her hair was long again and she wore it pulled back for sheer convenience. Vicki accepted her appearance. Once she must have been more like Emmi, who had a sort of bloom on her and hair whose texture enhanced the softness of her skin, a wonderment in her gaze, in spite of everything she'd lived through.

What Vicki dreaded almost more than anything was to read sorrow in her parents' eyes at the change in her, a shock too quick and spontaneous for them to hide.

Over the past twelve months her desire to be reconciled with her family had intensified into a raw and almost physical longing. The most powerful catalyst had been the air-lift. In its aftermath there was a new spirit in the air, a solidarity and pride, but also an outward-looking optimism that had entered everyone's veins like a revivifying drug. They'd beaten the Russian bullies at their own game. And the Americans and the British had helped them do it. The change signified a complete turnaround in the 'us' and 'them' dynamic.

The scheme had been grandiose, crazy. The aim to fly in all the food, fuel and medicine, all the basics of life needed to keep the western sectors going, to cock a decisive snook at the cynical Russian blockade. It had been hard going, another winter of frozen discontent, with power supplies down to four hours a day, two of them at night, so women got up at two in the morning to cook and wash and iron. They'd survived – on powdered potatoes mostly – but they'd survived. The Russians had thrown in the towel. And their former enemies – the Amis and the Tommies – had turned protectors, human beings who dropped chocolate for the children and seemed to care whether they lived or died.

One day, on the radio, Vicki had chanced on an interview with a British pilot. He spoke German the way Noel did, he sounded just like her father. She'd sat and listened, on her own in Claudia's flat, the tears running down her cheeks, and she didn't want the interview to end.

Noel's friend arranged an army driver for them and he dropped them on the corner of the particular devastated street that housed their daughter. Amy prayed that Vicki had got their letter. There was no way of knowing. They stood and stared about them as if they'd landed on the moon.

Noel pointed. 'That looks like some sort of garden. And there's the lilac bush.' Vicki had mentioned it as the only landmark.

They gazed up at the building opposite. Solid, burgherly blocks of grey flats these must have been once. There was a hole high up in the brickwork like a chest wound, from which a sheet of tarpaulin flapped. The roof was patched up with some lengths of planking. Only a single pair of ground-floor windows was glazed.

They knocked on the street door. An elderly man answered it, in braces, his trousers hitched chest-high. His hair fell in a yellow-grey wedge across his forehead, and the skin beneath his eyes was the colour of earth. His pat smile seemed superimposed on remote and empty acres of indifference. But apparently he was briefed.

'Herr Doktor Campion. Frau Doktor. Please go up. Second floor. Your daughter is expecting you.' He added, in halting English, 'She is a beautiful girl.'

They murmured vague acknowledgements. The staircase seemed sound, though the stairwell was mottled with a grey-green, damp-smelling fungus. A creeping melancholy invaded Amy at the thought of Vicki living like this.

Two anonymous brown doors led off the second-floor landing. Next to one of them a small square of cardboard read 'Farnholz, Wedlin'.

'Oh God.' Amy felt her legs might buckle beneath her. She looked at Noel, saw how tense and serious he was.

He knocked and it was as if the world stopped turning. The door opened. In the embrasure stood their daughter, a still, pale, austere figure. For a suspended moment they gazed at one another.

Vicki spoke. 'Are you real?'

She stepped forward. Wonderingly she kissed first Amy, then Noel, her lips smooth and cool.

They followed her inside, glazed, entranced. Amy realized she had pictured a tearful embrace, an ecstatic, emotional reunion. But this young woman in a felted grey sweater and shabby skirt, hair pulled tightly back, face thin and watchful, seemed a stranger. Someone separate and formidable, a survivor.

'Let me look at you.' Vicki sounded foreign, her English intonation stilted with lack of use. She took both their hands and stood back, smiling, ill-at-ease. 'I'm frightened you're just going to melt away again, into thin air.'

Amy talked, and Vicki was grateful. She felt strangely shy, aware of the ten years of living that separated them, as if they were sitting on opposite sides of a broad ravine. How much older her parents looked than she remembered, but how familiar and how dear. Yet some barrier of stiffness and reserve prevented her from saying what was in her heart. So she listened to her mother, nodded and asked questions that, to her own ears, had a bland and conventional ring.

Her father appeared more vulnerable than Vicki remembered, greyer, more earth-bound, perhaps more accessible. Her mental picture was of a tall, commanding figure who would take effortless charge of the situation, but he seemed as overwhelmed as she was.

She recalled her mother as a smiling woman in an apron, physically warm, meltingly pretty. The surface image had faded – her skin was matt, her smile less ready. Yet some quality came through that it was hard to name. It was as if, for better or worse, Amy was more herself, less dependent on the approval of others.

It seemed she had assigned herself the task of bridging the gap between them, by whatever plodding, painstaking steps were necessary. The first priority was to fill Vicki in on family news. She listened agog. Berlin, her own small sphere, was so much with her that Amy's words were like a window on a wide, unbelievable world.

Vicki had somehow imagined that they would all remain the same, her family, preserved in amber, until she brought them back to life. But they'd been changing and developing in ways she could not credit. Hoydenish little Grace in America now, married, with a child. Noel writing novels and doing rather well, no longer the international traveller but a man relishing the ordinariness of his own home. And Amy in partnership, running an expanding restaurant, focused, involved.

In contrast Vicki felt that she had been treading water, scrabbling wildly, simply to survive.

To Amy's relief Vicki was opening up. She'd begun to talk back.

'I'm giving English lessons now. I have been for a year – I have the flat to myself during the day and suddenly everyone wants to learn . . . Things are getting better, more stable . . . Looking back, the past years are like a nightmare. Only at the time you're too busy to think about it . . .'

To Amy the room seemed appalling and she could sense the same horror in Noel. Clean and orderly, admittedly, with plants ranged along the windowsills, but like a bird's nest perched up here, open to the elements, patches of damp and mould on the wall, the plaster cracked, discoloured, peeling. A mattress on the floor, its dilapidated state disguised by a folded blanket. A table. Three upright chairs on which they perched. Today the sky outside was blue, the clouds shone white and silver, but in winter, starving, freezing . . . Yet she kept her thoughts to herself. Clearly Vicki found her surroundings acceptable, even desirable.

'Without Claudia,' she was saying, 'I'd have given up, I think. We've been like a family. I owe her everything.' Her daughter's voice strangely lilting with the unaccustomed English. 'She rescued us. The shelter was indescribable, a stinking black hole. Christa was in an awful state. And Horst just lying there on a filthy blanket in the middle of everything . . . Claudia gave us a home and stability. We pulled together.'

Vicki paused, her eyes clouding. 'Christa misses Horst, though.

504

he adored him, and he her . . . It's such a waste . . .' Her voice roke on the words and she turned away, covering her eyes.

s she spoke Vicki was ambushed by a big, bright vision of Horst Amy must remember him. Blond, broad-shouldered, sexy, flamoyant, on stage a magnet for the young girls in the audience. A rger-than-life figure, but in private a simple man, genuinely, effortssly good-natured and kind. He should have metamorphosed over he years into the corpulent father of a clutch of children, as indulgent ith them as with himself, teased, loved.

But instead his life had been hijacked and perverted. Along with housands of others he'd been packed off on a fool's errand into the oundless Soviet void. He had been forced to force others – ordinary eople like himself with no redress – to dig their own graves, then e'd shot their brains out, had their gore plastered across his coat, is skin.

And her memory of him had been similarly perverted, the man he had loved replaced by the abject image of a broken invalid, a seless mouth to feed, horrified at himself and his helplessness, but ping the genial giant he used to be . . . And she, Vicki, had colluded ith him in sweeping his misery under the carpet because it was too nuch for her to bear.

A great sob erupted from her for his humiliation and his courage. he'd never mourned for him, just plodded on doggedly with her fe. Now the dam broke and she tasted the relief of scalding, sensuous ears. Amy reached for her and she laid her head against her mother's ody.

Chapter Fifty-five

On Saturday Noel would take Vicki and Christa to the zoo, and Amy would spend the day with Claudia. Joe Tasker of the Control Commission, with whom they were staying, lent Amy his Ford. She and Claudia decided to drive out to the lakes for a picnic and take the opportunity to see what had become of Mailied, the house that held such potent memories for them both.

They parked the car and walked the final half-mile or so, down residential streets. Grunewald was in the American Sector now and almost all of the comfortable, spacious villas were occupied by administrators, servicemen, their wives and families. There was a neighbourhood feeling. The houses were all in a decent state of repair. Women with prams gossiped and there were children everywhere, well-fleshed and healthy, very much at home. The only Germans on the streets were domestic servants.

In these surroundings, Amy reflected, Claudia stood out, initially for the shabbiness of her appearance but also, paradoxically, for an air of natural distinction. Her carriage was upright, her face, though sallow and lined, wore an expression of sharp, self-reliant intelligence. She'd been a blonde when Amy last saw her. Now her hair was dark again, grey-streaked, the forward locks held back by two side-combs. Clearly no hairdresser had touched it for years. Claudia wore a black blouse and skirt, stark and without ornament. Their very plainness lent her something heroic. Amy could imagine her the leading figure in some Grecian tragedy. Antigone. Electra. She half expected the two of them to be challenged as intruders, noticed a couple of women eyeing Claudia with suspicion, but nothing was said.

'Soon as we round this corner we'll see it,' Claudia said.

And sure enough, as they skirted the bend, the house came into view. Approaching it, Amy was rapt. Once you'd lived in a house its outline and texture were imprinted deep in your soul, secret and personal, the stuff of dreams. Even after years its particular atmosphere rose up to greet you, a distillation of experiences and impressions barely remembered. She gazed upward. There was the steeply pitched roof, with the old fretwork horses' heads nodding east and west, the chalet-like shutters ranged alongside windows which were meaningful to her, each marking a room she had known. The surrounding lawn was smooth, mowed and edged.

'It's like dreaming.' Claudia's expression was ambiguous, mingling wonder and some darker emotion.

A ladder leaned up against the house and a young German – his blond forelock flopping in his eyes – was painting one of the first-floor window frames.

In a sudden babble of urgent young voices five children came round the side of the house nearest to the two women. Under their arms they carried rolled towels. The brightness of their clothes was striking to Amy.

'Car's open, kids!' A woman followed, attractive, red-haired, her shoulders fleshy in a flowered sundress.

The children tussled and squabbled their way into a dark red limousine parked at the kerb outside the house.

'Where's your swimsuit, Richie?' a dark woman called from an upstairs window. Something was waved through the slit of the door.

'Okay.' Moments later she emerged from the house, closing and locking the front door, small and tanned, wearing a white shirt and blue trousers to mid-calf. She hailed the boy on the ladder. 'We won't be but a couple of hours, Christoph!'

He nodded curtly, his expression unreadable. When they were gone Claudia called to him and explained that she'd lived here once and wondered whether he'd be good enough to let them have a quick look round the back. Her manner was courteous, confidential, German to German. He seemed only too pleased to comply and spat on the ground in a gesture Amy interpreted as contemptuous to his American employers.

The lake sparkled in the sun as it always had, but the willows, jetty and boathouse were gone.

'Firewood,' Claudia commented tersely.

Yet when they stood at the water's edge and looked back towards the house, nothing had changed. The white house stood, spacious yet homely and inviting, seeming to nestle into the long, sloping lawn – scattered now with children's toys. Clematis and roses tumbled over the verandah rail as they used to.

To Amy the vision harked back to a time she saw as leisured and golden. It came to her suddenly how much she'd had in common with the occupying families they'd briefly glimpsed. And Claudia, conversely, with the boy, Christoph.

'My mother's yellow rose,' Claudia marvelled. 'It's smothered in bloom. It must be *years* old . . .'

'You know, Claudia, Johnny was in London during the war.' Amy turned to look at her. Not searchingly. That was too strong a word. With curiosity.

Claudia felt surprise, interest, no stronger emotion. 'Naturally he'd have had to quit Prague . . . How was he?' It was like asking after an old schoolfriend.

'He was in a bad way.'

His wife and children had been killed by the Nazis, Amy explained, and Johnny was tormented by grief and guilt. It was frightening how she, Claudia, accepted the story as almost commonplace. She knew of so many tragedies. 'What's he doing now?'

'He's in New York. He never felt at home in London. I've heard from him a couple of times. He seems much happier . . . No shortage of women, reading between the lines.'

Amy had parked the car on a small headland looking out towards the Pfaueninsel. She'd brought sandwiches – cheese, ham – a flask of real coffee. The unaccustomed luxuries filled Claudia with a sense of wellbeing, an agreeable detachment.

'We had an affair for a time during the war. We both really needed each other.' Amy smiled crookedly. 'But it sort of outstayed its welcome. Noel was home and that felt good ... Johnny was at a loose end. I missed him a lot, though, at first.' A silence. Then Amy said, 'He always regretted that you and he had parted bad friends ...'

'Did he?' A face shimmered into her mind – young, foxy, amused – a face she'd been wild about. The proverbial love of her life. But so long ago.

Ahead of them the River Havel – blue-green, hazed a little towards the horizon – snaked round the curvy, leafy contours of the Pfaueninsel and far off the white sails of a pair of yachts wheeled lazily.

It was gratifying how comfortable she felt with Amy. After all the turbulent years of separation they could still sit and talk, desultory, companionable, as if the depth of their shared history did away with the need for sound and fury. It was warming, Claudia thought, to see your own ageing mirrored in another, and to find that person enhanced. Amy pleased her. A woman who'd learned – the hard way perhaps – to take pleasure in life as it was. No longer a dazzling beauty, she radiated a kind of harmony.

Amy held up the flask. 'More coffee?'

Claudia offered her cup. As she sipped the dark liquid a thought occurred. 'You know, I made a stage appearance last month.'

'Tell me.'

'A do to celebrate the end of the blockade. I'd met this man ... this boy, really ... in the shop.' A sardonic smile. 'The only person in Berlin to remember me as anything but Countess Alexia. His father worked at UFA and he had reels of old film ... I sang a couple of songs. It felt strange, but good.'

'Will you do any more?'

'Who knows? Probably not ... The thing I remember most about the evening was being introduced to Günter Neumann.' She mentioned a Berlin wit – a legend – whose anarchic radio programme had cheered everyone through the months of the air-lift.

Amy cleared away the detritus of the picnic, opening the car doors and scattering the crumbs. Then she got out, arching her body and stretching her arms above her head, silhouetted against the hazy sky.

She turned to Claudia. 'Want to stretch your legs?'

They strolled on the shiny, springy grass. The sun was just warm enough. A breeze ruffled Claudia's hair. It was a day to make you think life could be good again, wide and spacious, with scope for pleasure.

'Christa is enchanting,' Amy said. 'There's something so sharp about her, something wise, as if she sees all and doesn't judge . . .'

'A great deal of experience has been packed into her little life.'

'You've been such a rock, to her and to Vicki.' Impulsively Amy took and held her arm. 'If I lived another hundred years I could never pay you back.'

Claudia shrugged. 'You're wrong. They've been *my* reason for keeping going.'

Amy stopped short, turned and faced her. 'Noel and I . . . We think Vicki should be told the truth. That you're her mother . . . If you're in agreement, that is.'

It was a moment before Claudia could react. She stood, blank, the implications of Amy's suggestion licking at her mind like small, tentative flames. There was a low exhilaration, but also fear, superstitious reluctance. They'd all reached a balance and it seemed to work, why not let sleeping dogs lie . . .

She shrugged again. 'I don't know.'

Vicki strolled arm-in-arm with Amy between the neatly stacked banks of rubble. At each moment she tasted the wonder of having her mother beside her – the elemental presence she'd once taken so casually for granted.

'There's a bit of a clearing just along here,' she said. 'A sort of square – they've rigged up some benches. We can sit in the sun and have our "serious talk".' Vicki gave the words a mischievous emphasis. Suggesting a walk, a tête-à-tête, Amy had looked terribly intense. But they'd already exchanged all news. Vicki couldn't imagine there could be anything that world-shattering left to say. She put an arm round her mother's shoulder. 'I'd forgotten how little you are . . .'

She sensed a tension, almost a nervousness in Amy as they sat down on the improvised benches. Two elderly ladies in black, occupying a neighbouring seat, eyed them with half-disapproving curiosity. They were a type, a sign of the times – women whom the war had robbed of their families, sustained by cantankerous friendships with fellow survivors.

'Well, what's all this about?' Vicki turned back towards her mother.

'Something you should know ... Dad's in complete agreement with my telling you ...'

The solemnity of the pronouncement was impressive, producing a small frisson of foreboding. In self-defence Vicki pulled a droll, satirical face. 'I'm agog.'

Amy reached out and laid a hand over Vicki's. 'Listen, love ... This is going to come as a shock. Please try to stay calm ...' She seemed to take a figurative deep breath. 'You see, Vicki, you're ... Your father and I adopted you ... as a baby ... in fact as soon as you were born.'

She looked warily into her daughter's face for a reaction, but Vicki was struggling to make sense of Amy's bizarre words ...

Her mother continued speaking, fast and nervous, apologizing for the bombshell, wondering whether it would have been better for Vicki if she had been brought up in full knowledge ...

Vicki listened, dazed and bemused, believing yet unable to grasp ... Almost automatically she murmured a reassurance. 'I'm quite certain you and Dad did what you thought best at the time ...'

'There's more,' Amy said.

'More?' Vicki gave a look of wry panic.

Her mother was silent for a moment, her expression unreadable. Then she gazed at Vicki with steady eyes, announcing quietly, 'Claudia is your real mother.'

Again there was silence. Amy's words triggered a response that was overwhelming but confused. On the one hand a blinding incredulity, yet alongside that a sense, equally strong, of illumination, mysteries made plain. So much was explained by this stark and simple fact – the special kindness Claudia had always had for her, the offer of a home ... the forgiveness for her filching of Horst ... Vicki floundered in a swell of disordered emotions.

Amy was urging how desperate things had been after the last war, how Claudia had become pregnant by a married man who'd thrown her over, she'd been penniless, with dependants to support ... It was as if Amy felt she must defend her friend against any charge of indifference. Vicki didn't need telling. She knew what it was like when times were hard.

As Amy spoke Vicki wrestled with the extraordinary idea that she was someone else, not the person she'd always believed herself to be. It was going to take some time to absorb that thought. Amy's words echoed and vibrated in her head. And yet – for all her agitation – there was no suffering. She was an adult after all, with a child of her own. Finally, essentially, how much real difference would this new knowledge make to her life?

Here and now Vicki's most immediate concern was for Amy, who looked troubled and unsure of herself, even scared. 'I love you,' she said. 'I love you, Mum. I always have. I always will.'

The air-line steward brought Noel the gin and tonic he'd ordered, along with a couple of sheets of notepaper. He nodded his thanks, took a swig of the drink and placed it on the tray in front of him. Then he lit a cigarette, reached for the pen in his inside pocket.

'Sure you won't have a drink?' he asked Amy.

'Maybe later.' She settled back into her George Eliot. For as long as he could remember she'd had a taste for fat nineteenth-century tomes, in which she became lost, bog-eyed. He watched her for a moment with tenderness.

Then he settled to make notes on a new idea that had come to him for a novel – after a conversation he'd had one night with Joe Tasker – set against the background of the denazification process. The anomalies and double-think of the whole ritual would provide a fascinating, topical starting-point ... And a good excuse, Noel reflected, to make one or two research-trips to Berlin and visit his daughter. Claudia's daughter, he mentally corrected himself, and the thought brought no pain.

As he wrote Noel experienced a sense of unruffled contentment. At this precise moment all the strands of his life were in harmony.

Work, marriage, family. He drew on his cigarette and pondered a little, looking out at the light blue sky. It had been cloudy when they left Gatow. He recalled an incident Joe Tasker had recounted and began to note it down.

The move he'd made to fiction-writing was pure pleasure and, with his years of journalistic experience, he was able to enrich his plots with a wealth of convincing background detail. His first Washington novel had been well-reviewed and sold reasonably. Another American-based work was in the pipeline. He wrote under the name of Neville Casey, but his publishers were suggesting that his real identity might profitably be leaked, highlighting the authenticity of his settings.

Noel drained his glass. The visit, he thought, could hardly have gone better. He'd been oddly moved by the three generations of women, Claudia, Vicki and the child – so independent, so interdependent. He was charmed by Christa, lanky as a Bisto kid, but serious and sensitive, making him think of Vicki when young. Claudia had impressed him and he admitted to himself that, in the past, he'd been too blinded by prejudice to get to know her properly.

He and Amy had been horrified by their cave-dwellers' existence. Before flying out to Berlin they'd envisaged bringing their daughter home, could not imagine anything would bind her to the place now Horst was dead. But they'd been forced to realize that Vicki valued her way of living, and had long ago decided that her future lay in Germany.

She said things were getting better all the time. She felt she had a stake in the future of Berlin, its regeneration and regrowth. After all she'd grubbed bricks from the rubble with her own bare hands. He was in awe of her sheer guts. He and Amy, Noel mused, could offer her a better standard of living, but not, perhaps, an equal sense of purpose.

Claudia had earned the right a thousand times over to be acknowledged as Vicki's mother. Noel astonished himself by how keenly he felt the step to be right. It was Claudia who had hesitated, as if somehow it might bring them all bad luck. At the same time she'd burned with a low, luminous pleasure at the thought.

He glanced at Amy. He'd always loved to watch her when she was unaware of him. He laid a hand in the nape of her neck.

'You were right. And I'm sorry.'

She looked up from her book, surprised, amused. 'Accepted, I'm sure. What for?'

'The way you stuck by Claudia.' He'd always viewed her as wild, a bad influence on his wife. A threat, so Laura used to say. He recanted entirely. 'I was wrong. I apologize.'

'Better late than never.' The look she gave him was slow-burning, ironic. It held depths of grievance, but also of understanding. She closed her book. 'I could fancy that drink now.'

Chapter Fifty-six

Shortly after Johnny left for New York he'd heard that Adam Raab had hanged himself following a fresh episode of the crippling depression that had haunted him for years. In February 1950 he paid a visit to his homeland. Inge was back in Germany now, in Bonn, the unassuming capital of the new Federal Republic. She was working as a translator in one of the many new government departments, and had a small flat in the pleasant Venusberg area. She was the first person Johnny looked up.

She appeared quite different now, less individual, less *farouche*. The exuberant hair, now wholly grey, had been delivered into the iron grip of a permanent wave. In place of the splashy florals she used to love, Inge wore what he imagined to be her work-clothes – a white blouse beneath a navy jacket and skirt. She looked dumpy, anonymous, a woman he'd never have noticed if it hadn't been for their mutual adversity.

'Darling Inge.' He enclosed her in a warm bear hug. From his overcoat pocket he produced a bottle of schnapps. 'Well, are we going to get drunk together like old times? Or are you too respectable now?'

'It's so good to see you, Johnny.' A broad, irrepressible grin contrasted with the staidness of her appearance. 'It's true, I don't do that sort of thing nowadays, but for you I might make an exception.'

The flat was newly built – pleasant, plain and modern, with furniture to match in smooth, blonde wood. Everything seemed to fold away to maximize space. She cooked him supper, pork and potatoes, a tankard of beer. Afterwards, with a challenging smile, she placed the schnapps and two glasses on the table between them.

Inge poured two measures of the spirit. 'So, Johnny, tell me all about New York.'

'I don't know where to start. I liked the feel of it right away.'

He'd felt rock-bottom when he set sail, convinced his life, always, would be a mixture of aimlessness and regret, dogged by the impasse that marked both stages of his affair with Amy. He landed in a snow-storm and immediately fell in love with the tough vitality, the cosmopolitanism of the city. It was as if, by moving, he'd physically left his grief and frustration behind.

'There were food and clothes and drink in the shops. Ernst Braff, my publisher, had rented me a room in Greenwich Village. There was a German deli down the block, a Greek one over the road. It felt like a neighbourhood. I fitted in. I'm there still.'

'I hear it's better to be an old Nazi in America than an old communist.' Clearly Inge felt the need to bring him down to earth, the way she used to.

'Luckily I was neither.' She caught him on the raw. The anti-communist hysteria of the USA scared and repelled him. But how deep did the new German democracy go? 'They say the Germans don't regret that Hitler started the war, only that he lost it . . .'

'Touché.' She shrugged. 'What the hell, Johnny? We're on the same side . . . How are you surviving, anyway? Have you got work? You look prosperous enough.'

'I keep busy.'

'And women?'

'I've had a few affairs. No one special.'

Johnny had found, rather to his surprise that – with his accent? His past? – he could attract bohemian young women the way he used to. For a time he'd been intoxicated with the availability of young female flesh, as if he could become once again the man he'd been during the Weimar years.

But, finally, you couldn't go back. Too much had happened since then. Sex was one thing, but Johnny found himself impatient with the opinionated young females he fucked. They talked so much pretentious rubbish. What did they know? They hadn't suffered.

'You're becoming an old fart,' Inge told him.

'I don't want to be. I'm not proud of my intolerance. Maybe I'm just becoming old.'

So far Johnny had steered clear of the subject of Adam for fear of distressing her. But round about midnight, with the half-empty bottle and an ashtray full of dog-ends between them on the table, he felt it was safe to ask.

'How are you doing, Inge, without Adam?'

She sat slumped across the table, arms folded, shook her head with a sour grimace. 'More than anything I'm still angry. I know that sounds hard, but it's how I feel. I squandered so much of my life and energy on him . . . If he was going to . . . he could have given up years ago and saved me the struggle . . . I feel he sucked my blood . . .' Inge sat, pondering, tracing the words on the bottle-label with a finger. 'Or maybe I sucked his blood. I don't know . . .' Belligerence spiralling abruptly into self-doubt.

'Darling Inge.' Johnny took her hand. He was maudlin, he knew. How fond he was of her. Sometimes she exasperated him. But he loved her all the same.

'I have quiet pleasures now.' She grinned at him, tipsily self-mocking. 'Concerts. Music is so wonderful. And flowers . . . trees . . . These things are so vivid to me. I have good neighbours. And a man friend. Nothing romantic. He's a widower. Fought in Russia. We go for long walks on Sundays. Like me, he just wants peace and quiet . . .'

Inge fell silent. Now she traced the veins on the back of his hand with drunken absorption. She looked up. 'You're off to Berlin?'

'Just curiosity. And there's an old friend I want to see.'

In the last months Claudia felt as if, quite slowly and steadily, she was coming to the end of a long, dark tunnel. That was a cliché, of course, but clichés arose on account of the truths they encapsulated. The light ahead of her was not blindingly bright and demanding, but a mellow glow that asked no more of her than she was willing to give.

Already day-to-day life was far less of an effort than it had been.

This winter had been positively luxurious, with glass in the windows of the flat at last, rations not plentiful, but reliable, new coats for all three of them and stout shoes.

Claudia had a new haircut. One day in a magazine she'd seen a picture of a French dancer called Zizi Jeanmaire, who wore her hair short as a boy's with a flick of fringe – simple, sharp and modern. And Claudia knew that was the style she needed to feel special again, her own person, someone living her life rather than simply enduring everything that was thrown at her.

Emmi from downstairs had opted for hairdressing. She'd taken evening classes and was close to qualifying. Claudia showed her the photograph and asked if she could copy it. Emmi was always game for a bit of practice. She ran her fingers through Claudia's hair and made snipping motions with her fingers, screwing up her smoothly powdered little face in a speculative fashion.

'I reckon I can do it. If you trust me.'

'With my life, Emmi.'

Her heart in her mouth Claudia watched in the glass as eighteen-year-old Emmi cut great confident swathes through her hair. The dark locks lay around her feet, irrecoverable. When finally she'd done, Emmi took up her comb and swirled back the sides, flicked the fringe deftly into a comma above Claudia's eyebrows.

She stood back to admire her handiwork. '*Schick! Reizend!*'

And Claudia had the pleasing illusion that the woman who stared back at her from the mirror had been resurrected from an earlier, frivolous and more stylish incarnation of herself.

Vicki loved it. 'It's the way you are inside.'

On the surface little had changed between the two of them since Vicki had learned the truth about her birth. To both Vicki and Christa she was still Claudia. Amy and Noel remained Mother and Father, Grandma and Grandpa. Claudia and her daughter shared and co-operated as they had for years, affectionate and matter-of-fact. There was even a half-superstitious reserve between them, neither quite wishing to disturb the status quo. But sometimes, playfully, Vicki addressed her as Mutti, and Claudia was pleased and amused, as if at some occasional treat. Yet below the surface, like an underground spring, the knowledge of their connection welled, nourishing them on their journey towards a better life.

The boy, Karl-Heinz, who'd got Claudia the singing engagement, stopped by at the tobacconist's at least once a week to chat. He had a fresh, round, impudent face and a studied image – lumberjacket, sunglasses, a snap-brimmed hat worn casually on the back of the head.

In January he came up with another offer. A friend of his was throwing a birthday party in a club called *Höllenfeuer*, and Karl-Heinz had been asked to put a cabaret together.

'A twenty-first party,' she mocked. 'Be realistic.'

'He wants you,' the lad protested. 'He asked specially.'

Claudia didn't believe him for a moment. Karl-Heinz was a sharp little character who told people what he thought they wanted to hear. But then again, why not? She'd enjoyed herself last time, and it was only for fun.

The club was in the American Sector and made the *Seeräuber* look up-market, the venue a cellar beneath a bombed warehouse, cold and stinking of wet rubble. In the pock-marked plaster of the corridor entrance Claudia saw a pair of sleek rats looking very much at home. But she was touched by the young guests in their American cast-offs, consciously avant-garde, intoxicated with life, the first generation of post-war students.

Karl-Heinz must have puffed her shamelessly because a ripple of interest ran round the dark, smoky cellar when she appeared in the makeshift spotlight. As far as clothes were concerned Claudia had few options, but her new streamlined hairstyle somehow lifted the plain black blouse and skirt she wore. Claudia was on first and she was glad. She felt, if not precisely confident, at least sanguine. After all, she was moonlighting. This was no longer what she did.

She sang a song of Peter Eisler's called '*Ungelogen*', and a Brecht–Weill tango ballad. The choices had been dictated by necessity. She'd had almost no chance to practise with the musicians, and these were two numbers they all knew. Unrehearsed though they all were, the performance worked, and Claudia was moved by the warmth of her reception. Only it was just an interlude, an amusing diversion. Nothing at all to do with her real life.

But Karl-Heinz, it seemed, had unplumbed depths, and he hadn't finished with her. The irrepressible kid had written a film-script and submitted it to an outfit in Stuttgart dedicated to fostering the arts in the new Germany. He'd written one of the parts with Claudia in mind. She read the script and thought it fresh, but terribly naïve, couldn't imagine anyone financing it.

'You've become old and timid,' he told her, taking off his sunglasses for once and fixing her with his naked pale blue eyes. 'Anyone can do anything if they hustle hard enough.'

One cold, wet night towards the end of February Claudia climbed the stairs towards her flat. The stairwell seemed particularly dispiriting that night with the nauseating patina of green-black mould that covered the walls. But it was always a pleasure to get home to the newly glazed flat, the familiarity of Christa slumped over her homework, plaits dangling, and Vicki just finishing with her final pupil.

But tonight, as she opened the door, Claudia was waylaid by Christa, pop-eyed and bursting with news.

'There's a man here. He's talking to Mutti in the other room. He wants to see you.'

'Old or young?' Christa, surely, would recognize anyone who was likely to call.

'Sort of old. Your sort of old.'

Claudia hung up her damp coat. She could hear muffled voices from the room next door. Some official perhaps. Though why she couldn't imagine.

She pushed the door and entered the neighbouring room. The man with Vicki got to his feet. He had on an overcoat, a check scarf. They looked thick and new. He wore his hair *en brosse*.

'Claudia.' He stepped forward with a grin that touched raw nerves in her memory. 'I came to ask if you could come out to play.'

For a moment she stared, her perceptions confused. She knew the face, the voice from long ago.

Then realization dawned. 'Johnny!'

The Tänzerin was still there on the Kurfürstendamm, a section of the city that had sustained less punishment than some. In Hitler's time the café had flaunted a rustic Tyrolean style. Now the chairs and tables were simple and functional, post-war vintage. The walls were white-washed, but on one someone had daubed a mural – stock Italian with grapes and Chianti bottles – done in a scribbly, inept 'modern' style. Over the bar Claudia noticed two of the old hanging edelweiss lamps still going strong.

To Claudia it seemed both incredible and entirely natural to be sitting here with Johnny, eating sausage and caraway potatoes, drinking beer – like a habit temporarily suspended and now resumed. They'd been so close once that, even after all this time, a bond remained, a sense of connection, real and resilient enough to be revived.

His face, though ravaged, was deeply familiar to her. His movements were still rangy and restless. His smile had the same irreverence, shining through in his brown eyes, giving Claudia the unsettling impression that the youth she had known stared out at her from the mask of a middle-aged man.

'I've been walking round the ruins,' he told her, 'looking for places I used to know. It's awesome, isn't it? A *Götterdämmerung*. I've had this fantasy all day that it was my doing . . . like a kid whose father dies, and he thinks it's he who's killed him with the power of his own murderous thoughts . . .'

'A bizarrely arrogant delusion . . .'

'Bizarre circumstances.'

'I hardly notice the destruction. It's become normality.'

'I've been trying to find Alberich – you remember Alberich? – or at least find out something about him, but I've drawn a blank.'

'A little fish, caught and pan-fried, I imagine. A little communist . . .'

'The other day, out of the blue, I thought of Rosa Edelmann . . . Whatever happened to her?'

Claudia shrugged. 'No idea. She was big in the thirties. But I haven't heard of her for years. Or her brother.'

'Franz . . . Bastard had me beaten up once . . .' Johnny mused briefly. Then another thought occurred. 'What about that film-star bloke? Bruno Berg. He was really thick with the Nazis.'

'I don't think he went to prison or anything. I think he qualified to sweep streets.' She pushed her plate away. 'He stood by me in the Hitler days, got me work. I wrote a letter to the authorities telling them that.' Pulling a face. 'I'm not sure whether it helped him or compromised me.'

Johnny drained his glass and replaced it on the table, the gesture expansive and relaxed. 'I can't tell you, Claudi, how good it feels to be with someone who can put a face to all these names . . . In New York I'm a man without a past.'

He summoned a waiter, ordered another beer for himself, a coffee for Claudia. 'When Amy wrote me about her visit I had a sudden sick longing to see Berlin.' Johnny hesitated, gave her a searching look. 'And I've wanted for years to patch things up with you.'

'There's nothing to patch up.' She meant it. They were old friends, both – at this stage in their lives – appreciating the value of old friends. 'We never really quarrelled.'

He leaned back in his chair, linking his hands behind his head and smiling at her. 'That haircut of yours is ace. Only the really avant-garde girls in New York have the nerve for it.' A sassy grin that hit her hard.

Hastily she changed the subject. 'So what are you doing now?'

'Caricatures. They're my bread and butter. I've got a magazine contract. I do cartoons of actors to go with the reviews . . . Apart from that, whatever illustrating work I can get.'

'Nothing political? Don't you miss that?'

He shook his head with a frown. 'There's no point. In the States I'm in no position to start criticizing the system. They'd just kick me out.' He shrugged. 'I've made the decision simply to enjoy what I do.'

A young waitress brought their drinks. Johnny paid, sipped his beer, then returned to the subject. Claudia had the impression it was something that had preyed on his mind. 'I made my mark with political stuff for how long? Eight years? It felt good. I felt useful. Righteous. But I'm not going to spend my life harking back to what used to be ... What about you, Claudi? D'you do any acting, singing ... ?'

Laughingly she told him about Karl-Heinz, the two engagements he'd offered her. 'You know me. I've always aspired to the kind of career where I'm appreciated by about eight really discerning people ...' She smiled. 'Actually, there's a potential film in the offing. I'd be playing a wise, debauched old demi-mondaine.'

'Sounds about right for you.'

She shook her head. 'Sadly I haven't been debauched for years.'

That night Claudia couldn't sleep, and all next day at work she felt dazed and disorientated by the unforeseen pleasure of her reunion with Johnny. She found herself replaying their conversations in her head again and again, recalling the exact tone of his voice, the look on his face. Their estrangement had been one of the regrets of her life and now, miraculously, friendship and harmony had been restored.

She had to admit to herself that the quite genuine detachment she'd experienced, when Amy mentioned his name, had vanished at a stroke. She was stirred up by his presence. And it wasn't simply that a precious friendship had been returned to her. She still found his lean, quirky face and sardonic personality disturbingly attractive. When he went away again it would take some time for her feelings to subside.

The following evening Claudia invited him to supper. Johnny found himself intrigued by her present life, the ad hoc family, the space they occupied – a safe cave, a refuge from the mouldering gloom of the building outside and the desolation beyond.

Last night Claudia had told him the strange, true tale of Vicki's birth and upbringing, confided her joy at having the truth finally out in the open. Johnny had to admit he was wary of Vicki, whom he'd met the previous evening. She struck him as self-contained and rather aloof. But Christa was adorable, with those big serious grey eyes in her pale, pure face. She thought for herself, had an original little mind and was talkative with it.

Vicki had cooked them a sort of goulash. It was homely sitting round the table in the lamplight. With the life he led it was rare for Johnny to dine *en famille*. He began to ask them about the years immediately after the war. He'd read so much about that time in papers and magazines, but found it hard to visualize. In no time the three women were reminiscing freely. Even Vicki opened up, became chatty and friendly. She had a stern beauty he found rather imposing, and some of her gestures made him think of Amy. The stories they told quite casually of life back then made his hair stand on end. Johnny listened spellbound.

He was finding the evening quite magical. A sense of warmth and intimacy had sprung up between them all out of nowhere. Johnny felt accepted and the sensation was quietly gratifying. It seemed quite natural to talk about Prague, Gudrun and the boys, and they listened with a sympathy that was sober and unsentimental. He was moved when, on her way to bed, Christa touched her young lips to his cheek.

At the end of the evening Claudia showed him down the mildewed stairs to the main door of the house.

'I like your family,' he told her. 'You live a good life.'

She looked almost surprised to hear him say it. No doubt she still thought of him as a cynic, incapable of admitting to tender feelings, from whom it was advisable to hide all sincerity. But then she gave him that wide grin he recalled from when they were both kids after the last war, would-be bohemians, living on their wits.

She shrugged. 'I'm lucky.'

'No.' He laid his hand against her cheek. 'You've got no more than you deserve.'

*   *   *

524

On the tram out to Grunewald Johnny had the sudden brief illusion that he and Claudia were man and wife. There was a moment when she turned to him to point out where some former theatre was being rebuilt and he felt as if he'd known her for ever. The notion persisted, poignantly, as she turned back to take a second look, her cropped head boyish above a swathed black scarf, lips smiling, relaxed, eyes bright with character and humour. He was proud of her, proud to be with her.

It was Claudia's day off and the two of them had decided to go for a walk, leave the everlasting ruins behind for a few hours. An acid late-winter sunshine filtered through the slender trunks of the birch trees, which shone bone-white, blue-tinged. Underfoot the leaf-mould was damp and yielding, coppery, smelling richly of earth. They breathed great gulps of the cold, bright air.

'Blood and soil.' She glanced at him. 'Doesn't it make you feel patriotic?'

'In town I do. The umbilical cord still holds.' Johnny had been surprised by the poignancy of his response to the ghost town that had been his birthplace. Yet the thought of burning his boats, returning for good filled him with a sort of superstitious shiver.

Claudia was distracted by a new thought. 'I had a letter today. Karl-Heinz has got an offer of finance for his film.' She gave a wry, mischievous smile. 'Shows you never can tell. I'd obviously be a fool to underestimate the lad . . . You should meet him some time, Johnny – he yearns to go to America.'

'I wish you'd come. You'd love New York.' The idea of introducing Claudia to his adopted city seemed suddenly delightful.

'Maybe one day. The world is opening up.'

'It's a wonderful place. Half the people there are from somewhere else.'

She looked at him. 'You're not lonely?'

He wondered what had made her ask that suddenly.

'Yes, in a way I am lonely. I see people. But no one's mine.' An impression filled his head of a woman he'd been dating, as they said over there. He could picture her breasts, pale and buoyant with nipples the colour of light coral, but her face remained cloudy. 'My own fault. I don't care enough for people to care for me . . . I envied you the other night with Vicki and Christa.'

'They'll move on one of these days, get their own place when things are better . . .'

'But you won't lose them.'

'I hope not.'

In a clearing beeches had been felled and lay smoothly stacked, their branches removed and piled into a jumbled heap close by.

Claudia stooped to examine the tangled boughs, pulling at likely pieces with her gloved hands. She smiled up at him. 'When I see free wood, I itch to take some home.'

'No, Claudi,' Johnny pleaded. 'For God's sake, let's not lumber ourselves . . . I promise to buy you some briquettes when we get back, to make up for it.'

'I'll hold you to that.' She laughed. 'If I ever come out to see you I'll be stealing fenceposts from Central Park for firewood.'

He felt absurdly pleased by her reference – however flippant and insubstantial – to a visit to New York. When they walked on he linked his arm through hers. Until now he hadn't dared. She glanced at him briefly, but matched her step to his. It felt entirely natural.

'Do you miss Amy?' she asked quite suddenly, as if voicing a question that preyed on her mind.

'Not now.' Amy's face rose up in his imagination, smiling but preoccupied. 'In the war she was my good angel, and I couldn't let go of that for some time. When I went to America I did . . . We've always been somehow at cross-purposes.'

They walked in silence for a while and Johnny thought about what he'd said. He added to it. 'When I was young I didn't really see her. She was a fantasy . . .' His tone was dry. 'A mixture of sex and purity. It was the same with Gudrun. She wasn't so much a real human being, more an idea I had.'

He turned to Claudia. Her hair was tousled. Her cheeks glowed with the cold air. She was robust and down-to-earth. 'You never were. You were always a person.'

She looked sideways at him, amused and sceptical. 'That's where I missed out.'

'I was a fool in those days.'

His hotel was near the zoo. From his window Johnny could see, a way off, the semi-ruin of the Gedächtniskirche, a building whose florid ugliness had always appealed to him. The room was clean and strictly functional, the powdery whiteness of the walls broken only by a small yellow notice stating tariffs and meal-times. There was a bed covered by a pale green blanket, a bedside table with a white ashtray, on which lay propped a half-smoked Lucky Strike. Johnny's overcoat was draped over the back of an upright slatted chair. In one corner the arms of a navy sweater protruded from his half-open suitcase. Johnny lay on the bed with a glass of bourbon waiting for Claudia to arrive. They were off to a smart bar tonight to meet this Karl-Heinz character.

Claudia filled his thoughts, a breathtaking discovery, a magical shift in perception. She was so absolutely and perfectly right for him. And had been all along, no doubt, if only he'd seen it. But if he had, there would not have been this new and miraculous sense of a jigsaw piece slotting, with quiet inevitability, into place. He wanted her for himself. He wanted to live with her – with her tolerant intelligence, her ironic flashes of humour, her instinctive, unemphatic sexuality. Over the years, it seemed to him, she had gained in stature and self-sufficiency. And he wondered if the same could be said of him. She didn't need him. What had he got to offer, apart from the fact that he now valued and loved her as he never had before?

A knock came at the door. He stood up to let her in, his heart lifting at the exhilarating familiarity of her.

She looked about her, at the rumpled blanket, the half-empty glass, the acridly smoking cigarette. 'That's what they do in moody American films – lie on their beds drinking, smoking and musing. You've gone native, Johnny.'

'Join me.'

'No to the cigarette and the bed. But I'll have a small whisky . . . You drink too much.'

'Part of my image, I'm afraid.'

Claudia took off her coat. She was elegant in a black skirt, a red silky sweater, her hair shining, gamine. She looked terrific. He kissed his fingers. 'Positively Parisian.'

'Borrowed, sadly, from the girl downstairs.'

He poured her a drink. She carried it across to the window, gazed out at the night streets. 'What a view. It's good to see the lights on again.'

Johnny stood alongside her, laid an arm across her shoulder. Mischievously he provoked her. 'If you want to see lights come to New York.'

'Shut up about your New York.' Claudia turned to him, her expression enigmatic. 'I'm going to miss you.' Clearly she'd aimed at a lightness of tone, but her words had a dying fall.

He was moved. 'I love you.'

'Don't say that.'

'I love you.'

Chapter Fifty-seven

Little Jake, eighteen months – the younger of Grace's two boys – shrieked with joy as Christa pushed him round the garden in the old wooden wheelbarrow, weaving in and out of the trees and shrubs. His small round face glowed with a sort of unfocused merriment. Eleven-year-old Christa had grown tall and rangy since Amy last saw her. Her long hair bounced as she ran, legs protruding, pale and coltish, from her tennis shorts.

'*Vorsicht, Christa!*' Vicki called, in warning yet indulgent tones.

She lay on the pumped-up Lilo, lazily propped on cushions, wearing the old black school swimsuit discovered in a box in the loft. She'd been doing some reading ready for the teaching course she was about to embark on, but a languorous idleness had prevailed, and now she simply lounged, soaking up the September sun.

Under the cherry tree Noel sat at his typewriter, wearing shorts and sandals, a black and white Hawaiian shirt Grace had brought over for him. He had the ability to work in pleasant, convivial surroundings while ignoring distractions. He wrote steadily, stopping every so often to reflect. There was a relaxation in his eyes and at the corners of his mouth. His new lifestyle sat easily and pleasurably on him, bringing the bonus – he was almost sixty – of a new kind of success. His first two books were still selling steadily, boosted by the leaking of his identity. And the Berlin novel, to be published early in the new year, looked set to consolidate his reputation.

Close by, Larry, Grace's husband, in jeans and sneakers, lay sprawled on his back on the grass. He was reading the second of Noel's novels, holding it up against the sun, his ugly-intelligent features blank and glazed as his eyes moved along the lines. He must be enjoying it because he'd taken his eyes off Jake for a while, trusting him to the others. Larry was the most attentive of fathers.

Grace had taken three-year-old Robert to visit her friend Ann. She'd discovered Amy's old bike in the shed, with the child's seat fixed behind the saddle, and cycled everywhere, wild pale hair bobbing above her strong little body.

To Amy it was a miracle to have the girls back under one roof, if only for a couple of weeks. In bed, at the end of each day, she and Noel rhapsodized on the joy of it, on the cleverness and beauty of their grandchildren. And they knew that, whatever compromises and tensions had marked the course of their married life, this was one thing they shared with each other, and with no one else.

They shared, too, the secret of Grace's parentage. In this respect Amy had never been tempted to come clean. Ignorance was bliss – Johnny had a life elsewhere. Noel deserved the white lie. Unreservedly Amy conceded him the comforting deception.

She closed her eyes and, like Vicki, luxuriated in the rich, mellow heat of this Indian summer. Amy had no idea how long she'd basked before the snap of Larry closing his book brought her back to consciousness. He unfolded his lanky body from the grass and stretched, throwing back his head against the hot blue September sky.

'Great stuff, Noel.' He turned to his father-in-law. 'A real page-turner.'

Noel looked up from his work, pleased. Raising an eyebrow: 'Can I quote you?'

'Be my guest. If you think the name Larry Lucas carries the slightest weight.'

'A law man. Who better?' Noel grinned and returned to his typewriter. The two men were fond of each other in a laconic, undemonstrative fashion.

'I'm going to stretch my legs a little,' Larry announced. 'I'll take Jake . . . You coming, String-bean?' He addressed Christa, who had been charmed by the nickname once it was translated for her. She was bemused and delighted by the discovery of these American relatives.

'That okay, Vicki?' Larry seemed a little in awe of his sister-in-law, regarding her as foreign and exotic, where Amy and Noel were not.

'*Bitteschön.*' Vicki smiled, playing up to his image of her. Amy saw that she liked Larry, but it would take some time for the two of them to feel at ease.

He led Jake, waddling unsteadily, towards the side-passage that gave on to Philadelphia Close. Amy watched them go, touched as ever by the juxtaposition – tall, protective father, small child learning about the world in the shadow of that protection. Christa held Jake's other hand and Amy felt a warm pleasure at the sight of these two grandchildren from different continents coming to accept one another.

'Aah, don't they look sweet?' Vicki echoed her mother's thoughts.

It was understood that by 'stretching his legs' Larry meant he was going to meet his wife. After four years of marriage his love for her was as raw and naked as ever. When the couple returned home Larry would be joining a small legal practice in Hanover, New Hampshire. They were keen for their children to have a small-town upbringing.

'This is heaven,' Vicki murmured from her prone position. Her voice had a blank, torpid sound. 'I'm storing it up, all this sun and leisure. In a week's time life gets serious again.'

Vicki looked healthier, Amy thought, than when they'd visited her last year. She had more colour, a little more flesh on her bones. Her hair, cut to shoulder-length, had regained some of its gloss. Amy and Noel were gratified by how much more relaxed she seemed, her native earnestness melting often into the playful smile they recalled from her childhood.

She was about to start on a course that would qualify her to teach English in German schools. And she was becoming active in a group that campaigned against nuclear weapons. Berlin was on the front line in the new Cold War, her inhabitants more sharply aware than most of the potential threat.

The girls were affectionately happy to be together again. And yet all was not sweetness and light between them. Their temperaments had always been at opposite ends of the scale and the divergence of their lives had intensified this. Vicki regarded the US as a shallow, conformist country and clearly thought Grace blinkered by the

American Dream. They'd had one or two acid exchanges on the subject, soothed by Amy and Larry.

Laughter rippled from the front garden, a jumble of voices, approaching round the side of the house. Grace appeared carrying Jake, Larry behind her, and Christa now holding Robert by the hand.

If Vicki's appearance still reflected the privation of her post-war life, Grace was a radiant tribute to the plenty of America. She was twenty-four now, in full bloom, her limbs palely tanned, cheeks smudged soft pink like the skin of an apricot, face framed by exuberant blonde hair. She wore a striped fisherman's top and three-quarter-length trousers, the clothes loosely skimming her slight, taut body. To see her was to be dazzled by her vitality, her air of happiness.

'How was Ann?' Amy called.

'Good, fine.'

Her mother detected a reserve. With the seemingly eternal climate of austerity at home, some English people found Grace's 'yankee' health and high spirits hard to take. Amy suspected that Ann might be one of these.

Grace set Jake down like a little doll. 'Christa says you've been so-o good.' She kissed him and the child's face lit up, his small world filled with rapture at her return. Amy saw the flash on her finger of the bold sunburst ring Larry had bought her before he left for France, and which she'd refused to wear until she knew he was safe. Grace sniffed Jake's rompers. 'But he needs a clean diaper.'

As they entered the house Larry caressed her bottom and Grace nudged him with her hip. Their attraction for one another was ever-present, close to the surface. They slept in the piano-room – 'It's got such raunchy memories.' Grace was blithely frank now about their courting days.

Amy thought Vicki was too hasty in her judgement of her sister. For all her seeming frivolity she saw in Grace a kind of blood wisdom. Amy might privately wish the girl had done more before settling to marriage, but Grace valued what she had, deeply, consciously. She earned and defended her own and her family's happiness.

'You think I just float through life – that's all you see,' she'd retorted to Vicki one day. 'You never look below the surface.' For once she looked serious, almost angry, but soon the two sisters were laughing together, reminiscing about some eccentric teacher they'd both had in primary school.

'Hey, Mum!' Grace stuck her head round the French windows.

'What is it?' Amy turned smiling.

'I forgot to say . . . Ann says she went to your restaurant the other night . . . She raved about it.'

'Good.'

She and Chris Carella were always bucked by compliments. They had a pact, though, not to be lulled by them but spurred on. They opened evenings now and were negotiating to rent some larger premises further up the street. But that would be it. Their ambition centred round quality rather than quantity. Their aspirations were still restricted by rationing, shortages, but things were getting better.

On the ground by Amy's deck chair lay a magazine. Vicki had bought it at the airport to read on the plane. Amy picked it up, flicked it open.

'You must have read that thing from cover to cover. It seemed pretty dull to me.' Vicki spoke with a lazy lack of emphasis, her mind on the sun.

'Each to his own.'

Amy turned to a page she'd read before. Several times. It contained a short interview with a writer called Kurt Schröder. A humanist, the magazine stated portentously. Apparently, Schröder had written an allegory on love and war. Short, brilliant and brutal, so Amy read. The book was called *Verflucht und Zugenäht*. The writer was good copy, rapping out a series of pithy one-liners. Above the piece was an undistinguished photograph. She studied it for the umpteenth time. The man had a good face, broad cheekbones, lively eyes. He was balding slightly. And Amy was almost sure it was Claudia's brother, Rudi.

She'd turned to the photo again and again, obsessively, as if she might surprise the truth in a fleeting impression. But – whether it was he or not – the image conjured up an atmosphere to her. Hot,

brightly coloured days in Berlin, spiced with the hard triumph of
the new Nazi regime. And the contrast of her nights there with Rudi,
dark, secretive, intense. A wildness that seemed to belong to someone
else.

She and Claudia wrote often now and Vicki had brought fresh
reports. Life was opening up again for her friend. She seemed to be
acquiring a certain cachet – among young people mainly, intrigued
by the supposed racy glamour of twenties Berlin. She'd done some
more singing, acted in a film that would be coming out this winter.
Claudia took it all with a pinch of salt – 'a nine days' wonder' – but
admitted to being tickled by her new allure.

She'd visited Johnny in New York and loved it. The two of them
had sent Amy a postcard – a flyer for the diner in Greenwich Village
where they ate most evenings. And the thought of them writing it
together, elated, expansive, had made her feel lonely for a while.
They planned to marry next month in Berlin, maintain a base there
and in New York, commute between the two.

Amy was glad for them. God knows they deserved their happiness
a hundred times over. The impending marriage struck her as absolutely . . . 'right' was the word that sprang to mind. Yet she couldn't
deny a sadness at the thought that Johnny was finally, definitively
lost to her, a pang of envy at the fresh exhilaration of Claudia's life.
She recalled Claudia telling her once how jealous she'd been, way
back, at seeing Amy in possession of the two beings who mattered
most to her – Johnny and Vicki. And now it seemed that the tables
had finally been turned.

Vicki sighed, yawned and got to her feet. 'I'm going inside to get
a bit of reading done before supper.' She bent and kissed the top of
her mother's head. 'Anything you want done?'

Amy touched her hand, a brief, affectionate gesture. 'I'm fine,
love, organized as ever. Got all the time in the world this week.'

She watched Vicki go, upright and angular in her schoolgirl swimsuit. She was prickly, independent, strangely awe-inspiring. And Amy
had not lost her. There was room in Vicki's heart for both her adopted
and her real mother. Amy felt the moment of discouragement melting
away. Probably one of the side-effects of getting old was thinking

how your life might have been different. But regrets were so much wasted time. When it came down to it, her life was what it was because she'd chosen it. Her happiness was one of consolation. She had work, children, grandchildren, a marriage that had survived against the odds. She wouldn't swap all that for anything.

'That'll do for today.' Briskly Noel rolled the page out of his typewriter, adding it to the pile beside him. He leaned back in his chair, hands linked behind his head, contemplating the autumnal garden, the mauve blaze of the Michaelmas daisies, the piebald yellow-green of leaves beginning to turn.

'I think I'm for a gin and tonic.' Looking across at Amy, his expression quizzical, affectionate. 'Can I tempt you, missis?'

How arbitrary it was, Amy thought, the process by which your life became linked to certain people and not to others. Why Claudia? Why Johnny? Why had these two, out of all the world, become and remained so important to her?

Standing before the registrar in the big, light, official room with its long table and shiny rubber plant, they exuded a sort of weathered vitality. Johnny oddly formal in a dark suit, the effect subverted by a rainbow-speckled Jackson Pollock tie. Claudia's urchin head rising from the high collar of a dress in the dark red Amy had always associated with her. She watched them with love and pride, no trace remaining, on the day, of her earlier qualms. Mentally she gave them her blessing.

Outside the registry office the October sun was high, fine and sparkling, gilding the ruins and the strong, bright weeds that grew from them, making the devastation look positively photogenic. Karl-Heinz took pictures of them all with his splendid new camera, hamming it up, crouching, even lying on the ground to get the angles he wanted. Christa giggled at his contortions. Vicki photographed him photographing them. A group of workmen from a neighbouring site watched, grinning, with their mugs and sandwiches. Behind them a brand new block of offices was rising from the rubble.